AND THE BIRDS KEPT ON SINGING

And the birds kept on singing

By Simon Bourke

First published 2017.

ISBN 978-1539634126

Printed in the UK by CreateSpace

Cover design by Design for Writers

Edited by Elaine P. Kennedy

Visit www.simonbourke.net to learn more about this author.

Manchester, 1984

1

"THIS IS NOT THE KIND of thing you should face alone, love. Is there someone you could ring? A friend?"

The nurse scanned the patient's face in search of an answer, but was met with the same blank expression the girl had worn since admission.

"No one?"

A slight shake of the head, a mumbled response, and then back to staring out the window.

"Very well," the nurse muttered, scurrying off to find someone more worthy of her attention.

The patient watched her go, glad of the respite. All she wanted was some peace and quiet, just a few moments alone before it began. No friends, no family, no-one. No more interfering, no words of wisdom, just her and a room full of clinical instruments. A procedure, that's all it was. The same as having a kidney stone removed, or an appendix. The joy of life, the wonder of creation: it meant nothing. This was a routine medical procedure which would rid her of her burden. Once it was over, she just wanted to go home and forget about the whole thing, and she would – just so long as she didn't have to see *it*.

Right now her primary concern centred on the procurement of drugs. She'd heard about the pain, been told all about it, and had no intention of suffering any more of it than necessary. She wanted to be dosed up to the eyeballs with everything they had; pills, needles, suppositories, she wanted them all. This thing had already caused her enough heartache, she wasn't about to let it administer one final beating before it departed. The nurse

1

had prepped her, done a few routine tests and got her changed into a gown. But there hadn't been any drugs, none that she could remember anyway. It was too late to call her back; she was away helping pleasant ladies and their pleasant husbands. She wouldn't be returning to the sullen cow in Room Nine if she could help it. Who would give her the drugs? She'd need them soon.

She looked around the room. There were a couple of promising-looking cabinets on the wall opposite. Perhaps there was something in there that would knock her out cold, comatose, so that by the time she awoke it would all be over and she wouldn't remember a thing. Wouldn't that be fine? But no, she couldn't go rummaging around in cabinets. Once Doctor Morgan arrived, everything would be all right. He would take command of the situation and give her all the drugs she needed.

She lay back on the bed, suddenly tearful, wishing the nurse would come back and hold her hand. She was right; it wasn't the kind of thing you should face alone. She only had herself to blame, though. It was her own fault; she'd been a silly girl who had succumbed to her desires, and now she'd have to reap what she'd sown, or at least reap what *he* had sown. And sown he had, with not a care in the world. Came, conquered and disappeared, never to be seen again. What was he doing now, she wondered? Probably going about his business, like any other day. Would he be thinking of her? Of course not. His blissful ignorance made her feel better. A simple misadventure between two wholly unprepared organisms was about to come to a satisfactory end. There was reason to be thankful for that at least.

*

"Just relax, Sinéad; this kind of pain is perfectly natural."
How the fuck would you know?
"Just breathe, that's the girl."
Oh do fuck off, you condescending prick.
"Pretty soon it'll all be over."
Yeah cos I've only been here seven hours so far, a walk in the park really.
Doctor Morgan had at one point been a source of great comfort, a rock to cling to during some rough times, but now ...

Now he was a man in a woman's world. A man coaxing her through an experience which he'd never have to endure. There had been a man at the beginning of this ordeal; she wasn't about to end it in the company of another.

"Dr. Morgan?"

"Yes, dear, what is it?"

"Is there any possibility you could leave me with the nurses until this is over?"

"But, Sinéad, I'm your obstetrician. I *have* to be here."

"Says who?"

Her tone had changed, only slightly, but enough to signal danger.

"Says everyone, Sinéad. Now stop fretting and let's get this little tyke out, eh?"

"I want *you* out, now!"

The atmosphere in the room changed, becoming thick and muggy. Outside, birds stopped singing, children stopped playing, traffic came to a halt.

"I'm sorry, Sinéad, but that's simply not possible."

Eruption.

"GET THE FUCK OUT!! GET OUT, GET OUT, GET OUT, GET OUT, GET OUUUTTTTT!!"

Various medical paraphernalia flew into the air as Doctor Morgan scrambled for safety; for a man of his years he moved quite swiftly and managed to avoid her clutches. Sinéad sat with her fists balled, eyes ablaze, froth dripping from her mouth. She had tried to scratch his eyes out, but would have been content to draw blood. Dr. Morgan watched from the safe environs of the door well, a look of confused terror on his pale face. And they had been getting along so well.

Now, with just a couple of grim-faced nurses for company, she could finally get down to business. No more cloying words of comfort from that fucking *man*. One of the nurses, a stout lady who looked like she'd spent the majority of her years pulling calves from the dark recesses of their mothers, locked eyes with Sinéad.

"Now listen to me, little missy, you keep that temper of yours in check and do as I tell you, and everything will be fine. Okay?"

Sinéad's eyes watered. Unable to speak, she nodded acquiescence.

"Good girl. Now, deep breaths and push when I tell you."

She nodded again, her face crumpled in misery.

Someone dabbed her head with a towel. A hand grabbed hers and she gripped it tightly, gratefully.

She pushed and pushed with all her might, tears rolling down her cheeks. Maybe if she pushed hard enough, she could get rid of it all; purge herself completely. She could pretend it had never happened – meeting him, their sordid alliance, becoming pregnant at seventeen. Begging him to stay with her, to support her, and being told that it just wasn't possible; he had his own life to live. The shame she'd felt, the fear and finally the realisation that she couldn't keep it, that she had to leave before it was too late. Creeping away in the wee hours, like a thief in the night, not knowing when or if she'd be back. Only knowing that she had to get away. Arriving in England, burden in tow, to her cousin; the one she'd always promised to visit. Then becoming a burden herself, her shame growing in tandem with her stomach. The looks she got, looks that told her: *We know. We know exactly why you are here and what you have done.*

If she pushed hard enough she could start anew. A clean slate. Be back home, this whole thing just a detour on an otherwise happy ascension to adulthood. So she pushed and she pushed and she pushed, fighting as she'd never fought before; fighting for her freedom, for her future.

And then it was over. There had been screaming, her own, but it had stopped; all was quiet. Her eyes swam as they adjusted to the brilliant colours surrounding her. The world seemed peaceful, serene, not the place she remembered. All around her were smiling, reassuring faces. What was this? Why was everyone so happy? Had she done something right, for once? As the swaddled bundle was gently placed into her arms, she remembered. She looked into its eyes, his eyes. She *had* done something right; she had created something. Created life. She stared at this beautiful, marvellous thing she had made, and vowed to never let it go.

2

"I'LL BE HONEST WITH YOU, Mrs. Philliskirk: at this point, I think we have explored every possible avenue. All that's left to consider ..."

Margaret stopped him short. "Please, don't say it. I understand. Please."

She raised her hand to signify that not only was this the end of the conversation, it was the end, full stop. They were finished; they had tried their best, but it was over. Malcolm thanked the doctor for his time and assisted his wife from her chair. She came willingly, too willingly; all the fight had left her. She had nothing left to give. As he led his defeated wife to the car, Malcolm couldn't help but wonder if things would ever be the same again. The frustrating thing was they could be the same again. In fact, they could be better, if she could bring herself to agree.

He'd been relieved that it wasn't his fault, relieved that his swimmers were as determined as they were plentiful. Although he knew no one was really to blame, he secretly felt that he'd done his part. But his heart ached to see her suffer. She blamed herself, asked for his forgiveness, told him she would understand if he chose to seek solace elsewhere. He told her not to be so silly, vowed never to leave her side, but it shook him, made him fearful for their future. Maybe this was a sign that they weren't supposed to be together. He wanted kids, always had done. What kind of life would they have, just the two of them? Growing old together, childless, their nest permanently empty? But they could have the life they'd always dreamed of, if only she would agree. He was willing to take the fruit of someone else's loins and love it as if it were his own; why couldn't she do the same?

Every time he broached the subject he met with steely resistance. It wouldn't be ours, she told him. It wouldn't be the same. No, it simply wasn't an option. They would keep on trying and hope that God was on their side. Neither of them had been particularly religious, but disappointment and despair had made believers of them both. Suddenly they couldn't get enough of the Almighty; Margaret had the whole street praying for them. But unless God himself were to come down from the heavens and impregnate her with his holy phallus it would all be for nothing. No amount of praying could counteract the cold hard facts: they couldn't conceive, medical science said so.

They left the doctor's office, the latest disappointment ringing in their ears, and drove home in silence; Malcolm frustrated and embittered, Margaret a broken woman, her last hope extinguished. He wanted to say it, to air that well-worn line just one more time. Surely she could have no valid objection at this point? But he relented out of love for her. She was already hurting; why heap more misery upon her? So they both sat there, unable, or unwilling to offer words of consolation. They knew words meant nothing now; there was nothing more to be said. Maybe his wife would become a mute. A silent, vacant shell, shuffling through life on auto-pilot. At least there'd be no more arguments about what to watch on telly.

Then something magical happened. The silence was broken. And broken in a most unexpected way.

"Malcolm?"

"Yes, dear?"

"Who do we see about applying for adoption?"

3

"It's eight months old, Marge; it's not going to care how you look."

Malcolm sat on the edge of their marital bed, fastening his tie in the mirror. A mirror to which he had intermittent access due to the movements of his increasingly agitated wife.

"Come on, love, calm down a bit – this is supposed to be a happy day!"

But she barely heard him, so intent was she on putting the final touches to an ensemble she hoped was befitting for a mum-to-be. There would no maternity wear for her, no unsightly bump or lactating breasts. Her outfit fit snugly over her trim figure, a figure which would never be subjected to the horrors of stretchmarks or post-pregnancy scars; but rarely could an expectant mother have been so thoroughly worked up. Labour was nothing compared to the emotional wringer Margaret Philliskirk was putting herself through.

Having watched his wife do upwards of forty-five laps of their modest master bedroom, Malcolm intervened. He rose from the bed, tie still unfastened, and stood in front of the mirror.

"Malc, get out of the way; can't you see I'm busy?"

"Yes, I can see; I've been watching you run about like a headless chicken for the last half-hour."

He took her by the shoulders and looked her square in the eye. She squirmed under his grasp, eager to resume her pursuit of matronly beauty.

"Let me go, for crying out loud. We've got to be there in an hour."

"Yes, an hour. And how long does it take to get there?"

She resisted his gaze, refusing to answer. He was right. She knew he was right, but under no circumstances was she about to concede defeat. She wriggled free, and headed towards the en-suite bathroom to check her make-up for the umpteenth time.

"How long?" Malcolm called after her.

Silence.

"How long, Marge?"

Still nothing.

"Margey, how long does it take to get to the adoption centre?" he sang, imagining her surly expression turning into a smile.

The door was flung open.

"Twenty fucking minutes, now fuck off!"

The door closed as quickly as it had opened. Shocked at this rare display of profanity, Malcolm could do nothing but shake his head amiably as he finally fastened his tie in the now-accessible mirror.

Denise, their social worker, was waiting for them outside the adoption agency.

"Hi, guys, how are we all feeling today?"

"This one is a tad nervous," smiled Malcolm, giving Margaret a reassuring squeeze.

"Oh not to worry, Margaret, this is only the first meeting, you don't have to bring him home today or anything."

"I know, I know," replied Margaret. "I just want to make a good first impression, that's all."

"Well, he's only eight months old, so you shouldn't be overly concerned."

"That's exactly what I said," responded Malcolm, relieved to be in the company of another sane person.

But still Margaret fretted. What if she took him in her arms and he screamed his head off? What if she turned out to be one of those people babies hate? Everyone would 'ooh' and 'aah' at the baby as he gurgled in delight, but once he was placed in her arms all hell would break loose. He hated her, and all the other babies would too. Word would spread about this nasty little woman coming to steal all the lovely babies, and before she knew it the whole building would shake with their cries any time she came near. *Oh, Christ.*

"How many forms do we have to fill out today, then?" joked Malcolm, as they passed through the reception area into the new, unexplored environs of the nursery.

"Ha, none whatsoever, my love," grinned Denise. "But we do need you to sign a few things; mere formalities, nothing to worry about."

Malcolm signed with a flourish and then watched in bemusement as Margaret's pen slithered across the page, leaving an illegible scrawl in its wake.

"Sorry Denise, I ..."

"It's fine, Marge. Let's get the introductions underway, eh?"

She consulted her clipboard.

"He's just through here, Room 7B."

Denise entered the room ahead of the Philliskirks, who stood by the door, unsure how to proceed. Decorated in a neutral beige with a colourful trim depicting the adventures of some cartoon character they didn't recognise, the room housed four infants, all under the age of twelve months. Which one was theirs? *Oh, God, I hope it's not the one crying in the corner,* thought Margaret, checking herself lest her thoughts spiral out of control once more. She looked up at Malcolm; he grinned down at her, an expectant father eager to meet his first-born. How could she be nervous with him by her side?

"Come on in," Denise said, beckoning them over to the crib in the far corner of the room; not the one housing the caterwauling child, thankfully.

"Here he is, the handsome little devil. He'll be a heartbreaker, this one."

She lifted the child from the cot and ushered the new parents into the strategically-placed chairs. Margaret yearned to scream, '*Give him to me, he's my baby!*' But she primly sat in her chair as she'd been told, never once taking her eyes off the carefully-swaddled infant in Denise's arms.

"Now, here we all are," said Denise. "Seán, I'd like you to meet Margaret and Malcolm: they're going to be your new mummy and daddy."

And with that she handed them the blue-eyed bundle of hope and innocence. He didn't cry. He didn't scream out in protest. He went to his new mother without complaint. Margaret took him in her arms, cradling him as she'd been taught, and gazed into those sparkling blue eyes. He stared back at her for what seemed an age, then broke into a beaming smile.

1986

Seán

1

THE YOUNG WOMAN WRESTLED THE pram onto the gangway. A couple of her fellow travellers offered assistance but she steadfastly refused; accepting help would draw attention, and she wanted to remain as nondescript as possible. Red-faced and dripping with perspiration, she approached the smiling crew member with an air of steely determination.

"Nearly there, Seán. Won't be long now."

The outstretched figure in the pram made no response. His ability to sleep through the bumpiest of rides never ceased to amaze her. She had practically thrown the buggy onto the ferry and yet still he slept, with not a care in the world. He would wake later, urgently demand sustenance and then resume his attempt to break the world record for most hours slept in a lifetime. Such a simple, enviable existence.

"Good evening, Madam. May I see your boarding pass, please?"

He was slightly camp, but weren't they all? Or was that just the on-board entertainers? She couldn't remember. Sinéad suddenly realised she had no idea where she'd put her boarding pass. *For fuck's sake.*

"Sorry, just bear with me a moment."

Where was it? She rifled through her pockets, trying to ignore the lengthening queue behind her. The one thing she had wanted was to complete this journey with as little human contact as possible; that seemed unlikely now that she had become 'the silly bitch who couldn't find her boarding pass and held everyone up for ages.'

"I'm really sorry. I know it's in here somewhere. I had it just a few minutes ago."

"That's perfectly fine Madam; take your time."

But the look in his eyes betrayed him. It said: *Oh, look at you: too busy getting pregnant to care about such trivial things as your boarding pass, you dopey cow.*

"Found it, found it!"

She triumphantly whipped the pass from her handbag, half-expecting a jubilant cheer from the waiting crowd. No applause, just a quick tear in half by Mr. Judgemental and she was on her way.

She trundled the pram on board and immediately set about finding a quiet corner for them to sit. The large lounge area, although inviting, was a big no-no. It was already filling up with thirsty customers eager to take advantage of the cross-channel licensing laws. Indeed, some of the patrons looked like they had paid their fare with the sole purpose of indulging in some early hours drinking. They hovered around the bar, keeping a watchful eye on any member of staff who strayed within a square mile of the taps. Let them enjoy their jolly-up, as long as they didn't disturb her. She hurried through the lounge towards the dining area, taking care not to trap the wheels of the buggy in the spongy carpet. His Lordship would awake from his slumber soon enough, and there would be trouble if there wasn't a tasty meal to greet him. She checked her watch: 6.05 a.m. Any minute now.

Unlike the lounge, and its promises of alcohol, the restaurant was relatively quiet. There was no shortage of chefs, waitresses and dogsbodies willing to pander to their guests' requirements, but the needs of the man in Sinéad's life currently outweighed her own. She found the quiet corner she was looking for and set about preparing her son's morning meal. A gloopy combination of puréed vegetables was hardly what you'd call the breakfast of champions, but she knew that her own little champ would positively lap it up. With the food ready to be administered and a suitable beverage on hand to wash it down, she waited for Seán to emerge from his coma. He was late. Having a little lie-in, apparently. She sat back in her chair and allowed herself to relax. In a few hours she would be on home soil for the first time in over two years.

Home. She had never stopped calling it that. It may have only been a small town in the southeast of Ireland, but to her it was everything. She had never wanted to live elsewhere. Her friends had vowed to 'get the fuck out of this shithole' as soon as they could, but not she; Sinéad had been content just where she was. Her plan had been to meet a nice fella, set up house in one of those fancy new estates and rear a family of picture-book children; a simple life but a happy one. The irony was that she'd been the first to go. She was the one who left her friends behind, headed for pastures new. Her friends had festered in the 'shit-hole' while she'd left them behind, living it up in the bright lights of the big city. Well, not exactly; she had left in a fit of panic, terrified to tell her father what had happened. She had fled, but now she was returning. Furtive phone calls to Adele, her younger sister, had indicated that the time might be right, that the storm clouds were finally clearing. The coast wasn't quite clear, but it was as calm as it was going to get. How would they react? She knew she'd let them down, running off like that; but she'd been young and scared and, as corny as it sounded, she had done it partly for them. Another mouth to feed was the last thing they'd needed, not to mention the shame of having a bastard child in the house. No, she had done the right thing then, and now, despite her growing unease, she was doing the right thing again. Leaving behind her cousin Colleen and her family had been almost as difficult as leaving home, but she was convinced they'd be glad to be rid of her. From now on, it would be different; she was striking out on her own and wouldn't need anyone's help from here on in.

It sounded so easy when she put it like that: striking out on her own. But she had nothing to her name. No savings. No qualifications. No skills. What exactly would she do once she got back to Ireland? Moving back in with her parents was out of the question. They wouldn't want her for a start, not with a two-year-old in tow. Oh, they'd be happy to see him all right; he was their first grandchild, after all. But would they be so happy when he woke them up at six in the morning asking for his potty? No, she'd stay with a friend for the first couple of nights and then see about getting a flat, somewhere small, until she'd sorted herself out. And then ...

"Hello, Mr. Sleepyhead. I was wondering when you'd wake up."

He smiled back at her and yawned contentedly. Any second now, wait for it:

"Bobba, bobba!"

The smile disappeared and his little face screwed up in annoyance. Tears brimmed around his eyes as he began to realise just how hungry he was. For Sinéad, this was a road oft-travelled. Barely had the words left his mouth before his 'bobba' – his bottle of tepid milk – was produced and planted firmly in his appreciative gob. Crisis over. He glugged merrily, his eyes fixed on her, those baby blues that everyone commented on. *He'll be a heartbreaker, that one.* He already was – he broke his mother's heart every time she looked at him.

The ferry jolted into action, taking her by surprise. Finally, they were on their way. Having dispensed with his milk and the vegetables which followed, Seán was now eager to explore his new surroundings, the ferry's gentle cadence the least of his concerns. Sinéad began to wish she'd put a little stiffener in his 'bobba' as he wrestled free from his restraints and set about acquainting himself with the other travellers.

"Seán, come back! Come back for fuck's sake," she hissed, as he gambolled towards an elderly couple a few tables away. A sudden surge sent him sprawling across the floor but, undeterred, he picked himself up and continued on his merry way. People laughed at the sight of this jaunty little seafarer as he weaved his way uncertainly through the restaurant, but his mother wasn't laughing. She was in hot pursuit, eager to bring his adventure to an end before he did himself, or someone else, a mischief. She gathered him up in her arms, ignoring his protests and apologising profusely to the couple he'd been intent on disturbing. The lady smiled kindly at her.

"I bet he's a handful."

"Ha, sometimes," Sinéad replied, making her way back to her seat.

But Seán had taken a liking to this woman. No sooner had he been placed back in his buggy than he was on his feet and making a beeline for her once more.

"Seán, come back here! I'm sorry about this; he's usually so well-behaved."

"Not at all, my dear, in fact why don't you join us? Might be easier that way."

For the first time Sinéad sized up the object of Seán's desire: mid-sixties, greying hair cut in a fashionable style and well-dressed. The husband seemed a jolly sort, well-fed by the look of him; his paunchy midriff clearly visible even from his seated position on the inside of the booth. He had clearly been one of the thirsty folk waiting for the bar to open, as he had two frothy pints in front of him and another in his hand. It was like something her father would do: stock up on drink as soon as they opened the bar, just in case they ran out.

"Thanks," she said, taking a seat.

2

NORMAN AND JEAN WERE FROM Dublin, and had just spent a week visiting relatives in Cardiff. It took Sinéad a second to figure out why their names seemed familiar, but when it clicked they took her teasing in good humour. Norma Jean. Neither was a Marilyn Monroe fan, but they had heard all the jokes on numerous occasions.

"So how old is this little mite, then?" asked Jean, as Seán munched on the bag of jelly babies she had insisted on buying him.

"Two in May," Sinéad replied, happy to have another adult to speak to and happier still to find security with such nice people. She had worried about some drunken weirdo accosting her and her child, but she felt safer now.

"Have you kids of your own?"

"Yes, two," Jean replied, "a boy and a girl. Or should I say a man and a woman, they're both in their thirties now!"

"Do you see much of them?"

"Oh, yes, they live quite close. Myself and Granddad here are full-time babysitters for our grandchildren," she replied, patting Norman on the knee.

"Wouldn't change 'em for the world," he said wistfully, draining the last of his pints and automatically looking towards the bar.

"And how many grandchildren have you got?" asked Sinéad. "Sorry if I'm asking too many questions," she added, anxious not to pry too much in case they did likewise.

"Three. They're the light of our lives."

"One of them's about the same age as this little chap here," Norman said, tousling Seán's hair.

"Howya, buddy," he said, grinning at Seán as he glanced in his direction.

He might as well have been talking to the fish in the sea. Seán only had eyes for Jean. He was besotted by her, his first love. He sat snugly in her lap, toying with her necklace, occasionally gazing up into her eyes long enough to receive a smile and then looking away again. I wonder would they take him off my hands? thought Sinéad to herself, half-joking. Perhaps this was a sign. She could return home and tell everyone that she'd been on an extended holiday, apologise for not phoning and move back into her old room. They wouldn't suspect a thing. Norma and Jean clearly loved kids, so why not give them one to keep? He'd be happier with them. They looked well-off; they could give him the kind of life she'd never be able to. She could visit at weekends. They'd call her Auntie Sinéad, and no one would be any the wiser – until he grew up and began asking questions.

"How old were you when I was born?" he'd ask his seventy-four-year-old mother.

"Sixty-two," she'd reply. "A medical marvel, that's what you are, my love."

"Ah, I see," he'd say, going off to consult his science books; then, armed with new info, he'd return with more questions.

"Why is my hair dark when Daddy is ginger and you're... grey?"

And so it would continue until the truth was revealed: Auntie Sinéad is actually your mother. She gave you to us on the ferry one morning.

No, despite her son's attachment to this kindly lady, he would be returning to Sinéad once they docked in Dublin. Anyway, Jean was starting to struggle now, unable to deal with the sugar-high that had kicked in shortly after his second bag of jelly babies. Seán clambered all over her like a young chimp testing out its play area; feet connected painfully with Jean's face, breasts were unintentionally mauled, and at one point he seemed about to climb inside her cardigan and come out somewhere south of her midriff.

"Come on, you," Sinéad said, deciding to take him out on deck – perhaps to throw him off, she wasn't sure yet.

The waters had calmed down sufficiently for them to stand and take in their surroundings. The sky was pale blue with hardly a cloud in sight. The sea, by contrast, was inky dark, almost black. Despite it being a relatively short crossing it still seemed like the middle of nowhere, as if they and they alone existed in this barren, forbidding seascape.

Careful not to stray too close to the edge, Sinéad lifted Seán on to her shoulders.

"Look, Seány! The sea."

"Sea," he replied.

"Isn't it beautiful?"

15

"Sea, sea, sea, sea, SEA," he chorused, another word added to his ever-growing vocabulary.

"Yes, the sea, that's right. As far you can see, nothing but sea."

They climbed the steps to the upper deck, and then she saw it. It may have been just an outcrop of earth but it was home, and the sight of it lifted her heart: Ireland. Sensing that this was a moment of great significance, she approached a fellow passenger and asked if he would take a picture of her child's first contact with his motherland. She cared little that the man in question looked as if he'd rather jump overboard than take a picture of her and her little snot-nose.

"Just press it here."

"There?"

"Yes, hold it down and wait for the flash. Thanks. Come on, Seány, pose for the camera!"

She had taken him down from her shoulders and held him in her arms.

"Smile for the man, now, Seán; that's the boy."

The reluctant photographer lined up the shot as best he could.

"Erm cheese, or something."

Mother and son beamed back at him, Sinéad hoping that for once her eyes wouldn't be closed when the picture was developed.

"Thank you," she said as the man returned her camera and went to peer over the edge of the deck. He looked as if he wanted to end it all, gazing as he did, into the water's murky depths. Sinéad didn't notice. She was heading home, and she couldn't wait.

3

HAVING GRATEFULLY ACCEPTED NORMAN'S OFFER of a lift into town, Sinéad said her goodbyes, clutching a piece of paper in her hand. Imagine them giving me their phone number, she thought. Promise you'll call us any time you're in Dublin, they'd said. She knew they meant it, too, but she hoped she'd never have to take them up on their offer. Her travelling days were over; once she got home, she wasn't going anywhere else ever again. But she had to get there first, which wouldn't be easy. Dooncurra was situated at the southern tip of County Kilkenny, flanked on both sides by towns from neighbouring counties, Waterford and Tipperary. Because of its peculiar geographical location, there was no direct access to Dooncurra from the capital. She would first have to go to Kilkenny city and then take another bus to her hometown. According to the timetable, there was a two-hour waiting time in between, which would bring her total journey time to almost five hours: longer than it had taken to cross the Irish Sea. It was an absolute nonsense. There was nothing else for it; she was getting the train. She didn't care if it cost more; it would get her there faster, and offered the kind of comfort she and her boy deserved. They'd slummed it up to now, but they would do the last leg of their journey in style.

As soon as they got on the train, she knew she'd made the right decision. The carriage was practically deserted and they had their choice of seats.

"Look, Seán, we've got a table and everything," she declared to her uninterested son.

He was flagging now, with any luck he'd sleep through the last stage of their journey. Sinéad propped him up in his buggy by the window, taking the aisle seat herself. The crossword book she'd bought at the station would keep her occupied while he slept. She was growing nervous now. They were almost there, and her parents had no idea she was coming. She hadn't spoken to them in over two years. How would they react? Adele had assured her that the time was right, but what if she was wrong? What if they'd already disowned her, wanted nothing to do with her? Worse still, what if they reacted angrily? She didn't want Seán's first meeting with his grandparents to be coloured by violence. She pushed these thoughts out of her mind, and instead tried to imagine the scene in the house this very minute. Her mother would be busying herself in the kitchen, cleaning up the lunch things left by her mob of hungry hippos. That's what she called them, her 'hungry hippos'. An ad for a new children's game had come on the telly one night and her mother had cried out, "That's ye! A crowd of feckin' hungry hippos, gobbling up everything in your path." They'd all laughed. It was true, they were hungry hippos. Their dinner table wasn't the place for small talk. They went there to eat, and eat was what they did. Her brother Patrick, the only boy, was the quickest. He'd once eaten an entire plate of stew in a little under two minutes. Her mother had timed him. He hadn't even noticed her standing in the door-well, eyes on the clock, wondering what kind of an animal she'd reared.

"Would you ever take your time, Patrick," she said. "You'll make yourself sick."

But he was already out the door, fork in mid-air, returning to whatever mischief his dinner had interrupted. Of all those whom Sinéad had left behind, it was Patrick she missed the most; the baby of the family, the golden child, the long-awaited boy. He could have been the devil incarnate and they would still have doted on him. The fact that he was the sweetest creature to walk the face of the earth just made it easier. Sinéad and her sisters practically fought to be in his company. He was torn this way and that, forced to join in with their girly games and mollycoddled to the point where his father would intervene and take him fishing, to remind him that he was a boy. Patrick wasn't just his parents' child, he was the family's child. Each and every one of them considered him their baby, even Valerie, who was usually far too caught up in her own existence to bother with the rest of them. For Sinéad to be apart from him, without explanation, for this long, had been torturous. He'd be twelve years old now, no longer the spry, angelic child she remembered. He probably fancied girls already, went to discos; she smiled at the thought. Whatever about her parents, she hoped Patrick would welcome her back with open arms. She imagined him ambling in the door, schoolbag slung lazily over his arm, calling out a greeting to those within earshot, and then sticking his head in the sitting-room to see who was home. His features would slowly change as he caught sight of her: first a look of incomprehension, then a flicker of fear, before finally his eyes would light up and he'd run to her. She'd hold him tight and mumble apologies through her tears until they broke free, at which point she'd ask: "Want to meet your nephew?"

The train left them off in one of the neighbouring towns, about four miles outside Dooncurra. It was only a short walk to the bus stop, and there would almost certainly be a bus going that way within the next hour. However, they had grown accustomed to a life of luxury by now and so Sinéad hailed a taxi, asking the driver to drop them at the bottom of the hill leading up to the estate. Her parents lived in the outskirts of Dooncurra, almost in the countryside. It was quiet there, and the sight of a taxi arriving at the McLoughlin household on a Tuesday afternoon would be sure to get the neighbour's curtains twitching.

"Oh, here she is, that little Jezebel; I was wondering when she'd come back.

And look what she has with her? A little baby without a daddy. Wait till Mrs. O'Leary hears about this."

She paid the driver and waved him goodbye. In front of her lay the hill which she'd walked, run and skipped up and down more times than she cared to remember. Now she faced it with trepidation, anxious about what lay in store at the top. As she began her ascent the memories came flooding back: setting off for school each morning come rain, wind or shine; Patrick lagging behind, moaning, begging to go on the dag. Having to forcibly carry him inside the school gate, before continuing on to the secondary school with Adele and Valerie. The walk back home, debating what might be for dinner, praying it wouldn't be bacon and cabbage. The summer holidays, sprinting down to Bartley's for 'Mr. Freezes'. Sitting on the wall, waiting for them to melt before slurping them down, the chill going straight to their heads. Playing hide 'n' seek in the nearby woods. Gravitating to kiss-chase, running slow so that Gary Whelan would catch her. Then no more school; instead her first job, waiting tables in one of the town's two restaurants. That was where she had met *him*. He worked in the adjoining bar, but seemed to spend most of his time loitering around the restaurant. It took her a while to figure out that he was coming to see her. She was flattered. All the girls fancied him. He wasn't really her type, but when someone like him asked you out you didn't say no. So she went out with him, started dating him, and it was fun; he was fun. He was reckless, a bit wild; her complete opposite. But when that recklessness caught up with him, caught up with *them*, he didn't want to know. It was her problem; nothing to do with him. As she walked home from work that night, up that hill for the last time in a long time, she knew what she had to do. She would pack her bags, empty her savings account, and seek pastures new. It had seemed the only way. According to Adele, he'd left Dooncurra a few months after she had, up the country somewhere; probably to escape another unwanted pregnancy, knowing him. It was better that he wasn't around though.; less complicated. Her boy didn't need him in his life, not yet anyway. But he did need a strong male presence, that was something Sinéad felt strongly about. Perhaps her own father could fulfil that role? She could only hope so.

She'd walked up this hill a thousand times or more, but never with a buggy in tow and her entire belongings on her back. It was hard work and she had to stop every few minutes to catch her breath. She wasn't bothered about being conspicuous anymore; a lift up the hill would have been great or, failing that, a strong man to push the buggy would have sufficed. There were a few houses dotted along the hillside, brightly-coloured bungalows with well-tended gardens, but they appeared completely devoid of life. Even the cows in the fields opposite were keeping to themselves, too busy flicking away bothersome flies to even look in her direction. Completing the scene on her left lay the woods, dark and ominous even in the bright afternoon sun. She wasn't used to such stillness after two years living in an industrialised town in the northwest of England. While Sinéad was having trouble readjusting to her surroundings, however, Seán was having a whale of a time. He cooed and trilled in delight as they inched up the hill, pointing this way and that, bouncing up and down in his seat and babbling away in his own indecipherable language. He'd been to almost every park in the Greater Manchester area, but this was different. This wasn't manufactured, man-made greenery, this was God's earth in its natural state; the smell of horse manure wafting in the air was testament to that.

They finally reached the top of the hill, and there before them lay Ard Aulinn. It looked the same as it had the day she'd left. A couple of the houses had received new paint jobs, but for the most part nothing had changed. The Brunnock's dog was still barking his head off. Jim Hegarty's car was still blocking Paul Hanlon's driveway. And her house, her mother's house, the place where she'd grown up, was still tucked away at the back of the estate in the corner, peering out at the woods. It looked so unassuming from here, just a collection of bricks and mortar; you'd never imagine that it could stir the emotions in the way it did. The sight of it made her heart sing and her stomach drop, filled her with joy, and laden her with dread. But there was nothing for it, she had to march onwards. The sooner this was over, the better.

She wheeled Seán through the estate, feeling like a cowboy in the wild west as she made her way through the deserted cul-de-sac. At any moment she expected a door to spring open and a gap-toothed local to cry out, 'What you doin' round these here parts, young lady?' But no one did, and she made it to Number Sixteen unmolested. She paused in front of the house. A two-storey semi-detached, which at the time of its construction had been considered quite upmarket; now it looked a bit shabby. She couldn't really describe its colour, her best guess was grey but it might have been white once, she couldn't recall. It didn't look much from the outside but would be spotlessly clean inside – Patricia McLoughlin wouldn't have it any other way. Sinéad opened the rusting gate, wincing as it squeaked, and made her way up the garden path. Again she paused, considering. No one ever used the front door unless they were visitors, proper visitors who couldn't make do with the back door like everyone else. Which category did she fall into now? She didn't feel entitled to go around the back of the house and let herself in as people usually did. She'd lost that privilege; right now she was just a visitor. So she took a deep breath, composed herself, and knocked primly on the door.

4

PATRICIA MCLOUGHLIN HAD JUST SAT down with a cup of tea. She'd been flat out all morning, and all afternoon for that matter. It was already four o'clock, and this was the first minute she'd had to herself. Where had the day gone to at all? The dinner would have to be put on soon. But first she was going to have a cup of tea and watch a bit of television. She'd barely settled in her seat when she heard a knock at the front door. Her brain immediately spun into overdrive. Who could it be? All the bills were paid. The coalman wasn't due until Thursday. It wasn't anyone canvassing; there'd only just been an election. What if it was the Guards? What if one of her children had been hurt? It was probably someone selling something. Well, whatever they were selling, she wasn't interested.

"Who could this be?" she muttered, as she fluffed up her hair and rubbed the creases out of her clothes. She went to the door and peered out the little window beside it. All she could make out was a buggy with a little child in it. Another knock.

"Just a sec," she called out, rattling the security chain free and unbolting the safety lock at the bottom of the door. She carefully opened the door and peered out at the visitors.

"Hello, Mammy."

Patricia stared at her eldest, shifted her eyes to the pram, and then looked once more at the daughter she hadn't seen for more than two years.

"You'd better come in," she said.

*

Sinéad sat tentatively on the edge of the armchair, ready to take flight at the first sign of danger. Her mother was in the kitchen making the tea. There had been no dialogue, no recognition of her grandson. She had simply sat them down and disappeared into the kitchen, taking some time to assess the situation, no doubt; planning her next move. All Sinéad could do was wait.

"Is it still two sugars, Sinéad, yes?"

"Yes, Mam."

Bizarre, but so typical. The elephant in the room would be ignored until the last very minute. As if sensing the gravity of the situation Seán, the elephant, had lapsed into a contemplative silence. Usually, upon entering new environs, he would be off and running the first chance he got. Here in his granny's house, he remained still and silent. The only sound was that of the kettle coming to the boil and the clinking of mugs and spoons.

"Do you reckon we'll get any fancy biccies, Seány?" she whispered to her son.

Seán looked up at her, smiling hesitantly. He didn't understand the joke, but he knew his mother was trying to be funny. She could be very funny at times.

"Maybe she'll bring out the cake seeing as we're visitors and all, eh?"

"Cake," Seán replied, nodding.

Patricia came bustling in from the kitchen, two mugs of tea in her hands, but not a biscuit in sight.

She plonked the mugs down on the coffee table and returned to the kitchen, reappearing a moment later with a glass of orange, presumably for her grandson. Beverages doled out, she eased herself into her chair and gazed out the window into the front yard.

"Lovely weather out there. Did ye get a taxi? I didn't hear a car."

"He dropped us off at the end of the hill. I felt like a walk."

Patricia nodded guardedly. It was a nice day for walking.

"He's the head off Patrick when he was that age," she said.

It took Sinéad a moment to figure out that she was referring to Seán, her son. The little boy sat in the buggy beside her. Her mother had acknowledged him. This was a good sign.

"Oh does he, yeah?" she replied casually.

"Course he does, look," Patricia took a photo of her beloved boy from the mantelpiece. "The head off him."

She handed the picture to Sinéad, who went through the process of pretending to compare and contrast these two little boys. But all the while she was waiting for the bombshell, wondering when the questions would begin.

"Mammy, I –"

Her mother's glare stopped Sinéad in her tracks.

"I don't want to hear it, Sinéad. What's done is done; you're here now, so let's leave the heartfelt confessions for another day, okay?"

The younger McLoughlin nodded meekly and quietly sipped her tea. It could have been worse. At least there hadn't been any shouting. There was still her father to come, though, and his slipper was probably still warm from the last time one of the children had stepped out of line.

"What do you think Daddy will say?"

"Ha, you know your father as well as I do. He'll most likely shrug his shoulders, grunt a hello, and hide behind his paper for the night."

"Is he mad at me, though?"

"Sinéad, we're all feckin' mad at you! But you're our daughter and he's our grandchild and – well, despite everything, we still love you. You *and* him," she said, jabbing her thumb in Seán's direction.

"Would you not like to hold him at all, Mammy?"

Patricia hesitated, her maternal instincts duelling with the desire to show her daughter she was still upset with her. As if on cue, Seán began to pull at the straps on his buggy, finally feeling comfortable enough to run amok. Unable to undo his restraints, he became frustrated. And with all sense of decorum lost, he wasted no time in voicing his concerns.

"Mum!"

Patricia's mouth opened in mock surprise. "What's that I hear? Is that an English accent? On a McLoughlin boy? You'd better get him out of here before your father comes back, that's all I can say!"

"I'm sure he'll lose it within a couple of months. He only has a handful of words, anyway," Sinéad replied, almost apologetically.

"So you're sticking around, then? This isn't just a flying visit?"

Sinéad looked at her mother as if she was crazy; of course she was staying. Then she thought of how it must look; the long-lost daughter returning without a word of warning, and certainly nothing constituting a plan of action. It was natural enough to assume she'd just come back for a holiday.

"Well, yeah, that was the general idea."

"I see. Have you thought about where you're going to live at all?"

Sinéad knew this was a loaded question, her mother's way of laying a trap for her. She wanted her daughter to ask if she could stay with them. And then the lecture would begin: *you can't just come swanning back in here and expect us to drop everything. Where will you sleep? We're overcrowded as it is. And the baby; will he be crying every night? Your father doesn't like to be disturbed once he's in bed, you know that.*

But Sinéad had planned ahead. She'd rung Lily, one of her oldest and best friends, and asked if they could stay with her for a few nights.

"Ah you're grand thanks, Mam. I'm going to stay with Lily, Lily Dolan."

She could see the disappointment in her mother's face. Was she disappointed because they weren't staying, or because Sinéad hadn't fallen into her trap? It was hard to tell.

"So yeah, I'll be staying at hers tonight. But I just wondered if it would be okay to see the lads before I go?"

She was playing it extra safe, very much the contrite daughter.

"You can, of course. You can even stay for your tea if you like," replied her mother, not missing a beat.

"Oh, Mammy, that'd be lovely," Sinéad replied sweetly, finally taking off her jacket.

They both knew she wouldn't be going anywhere that night, or indeed for the next few nights, but neither would admit as much; neither would back down. The things they really wanted to say to one another would remain unsaid, and they would adapt to their new circumstances as best they could; mother and daughter in perfect disharmony.

5

By the time Patrick came idling up the garden path, the trap had been set. Seán sat in his nanny's lap, chewing on a rusk and littering her dress with crumbs, while she gently rocked him and sang songs about Irish druids and faeries. Sinéad, barely able to contain her excitement, was out in the hallway sitting on the stairs, patiently waiting for the signal.

"Mam?"

"Yes, dear, I'm in here."

"Can I get a biscuit before me dinner? I'm starvin.'"

"No, you can not. Your dinner will be ready at half five, just like it always is, so you may wait till then like the rest of us."

Patrick's shoulders slumped in dismay. Half five? That was an hour away!

"Ah, Mammy, come on. I'm a growing boy."

"That may well be the case, but we want you growing up, not out."

He strode into the sitting-room, lifting his shirt to show her his protruding ribs.

"There's not a pick on me, Mam, look …"

Patrick stopped in his tracks. "Who's he?"

"This is our new baby. Say hello to Seán."

With perfect timing Seán swallowed the last of his rusk and beamed cheerily up at his uncle. "Allo."

"Our new baby? No, he's not."

"Obviously I didn't have him, Patrick; I'm a bit too old for that. A lady came round today selling babies, and I bought one."

"You BOUGHT him?"

Patrick's eyes bulged out of his head. Was this possible? Could you buy babies now? He'd seen the news reports about the poor little orphans in Chernobyl; maybe this fellah was one of those? But it could just be another one of his mother's tricks. As the youngest of four he was used to being the butt of their jokes, and this had all the hallmarks of another carefully-crafted ruse.

"Right so, if you bought him where's the receipt?" he offered, pleased with himself.

"They're going to post it to us," replied his mother smartly.

Could it be, he thought, could it really be? He liked things the way they were; there was no need for another baby. On the other hand, he'd always wanted a brother; but he wanted an older brother, not one that still wore nappies. This lad was too young. He'd be no use whatsoever.

Patrick flopped down on the couch, sizing up the new arrival. There he was, smiling away, delighted with himself, as if he belonged here; not stopping to think about him and how he might be affected.

"Can you really buy babies, Mammy? How much was he? I thought 'twas only African babies from the telly you could buy."

"Oh, no, you can get little English ones too. Can't you, Seány?" she replied, cuddling her grandson.

"He's *English!*" cried Patrick, incredulous. This was going from bad to worse.

"Yes, he's our little English baby; they were selling him cheap because most Irish families won't take a Brit."

"And we would?"

"Why not? You have to admit he's pretty cute."

"What will Daddy say? There's no way he'll allow an English baby in the house, Mammy, surely?"

"He has no choice now. I'm after paying for him, and there's no returns allowed."

"Oh, Jesus, Mammy," cried Patrick, beside himself, "the lads will give me some slagging when they find out I have an English brother. Oh, Jesus."

He began pacing up and down the floor, wringing his hands as he went, his hunger long since forgotten.

Sinéad sat on the stairs, listening to every word. As soon as Patrick had arrived she'd starting laughing and now she rocked back and forth, silently chuckling away, tears rolling down her eyes. She couldn't take it anymore. If it didn't stop, she was either going to piss herself or let out such a roar of laughter that the game would surely be up. But she had to wait for the signal. The plan was to send Patrick next door for some sugar, at which point Sinéad would take the place of her mother and await his return.

"Look, Patrick, you're just going to have to get used to having a little brother, I'm afraid. And he's going to be sleeping with you, too."

"Wha ..."

He could barely utter a response at this stage; his world was falling down around him and there was nothing he could do to stop it.

"I need to make his bottle now, but he likes a spoon of sugar with it. Could you go in next door and ask Mrs. Kiely for a cup?"

Facing up to his new, horrific reality, Patrick mumbled compliance and slouched out the back door. This was the signal Sinéad had been waiting for. She quickly entered and took her mother's place in the chair. Neither of them spoke, they just giggled at one another as they swapped places. Even Seán laughed at the madness of it all.

Within a couple of minutes the Brit-fearing boy returned, complete with sugar for his new brother.

"There ya go, Mammy," he said, putting the cup on the table.

"I asked Mrs. Kiely about this whole baby-buying yoke and she said she's buying one next week! Is it me, or has the world gone mad?"

The look of earnest concern on his face was enough to send Patricia over the edge. She broke into hysterics, hooting and squealing with laughter, using the worktop to steady herself lest she fall to the ground in a heap.

"What? What is it? What are ya laughing at, Mammy?"

Unable to respond, Patricia pointed in the general direction of the sitting-room as she bent over double, gasping for air.

Patrick, presuming that the English fellah had done something funny, obediently went to see what his new 'brother' was up to. He popped his head round the door, expecting to see Seán doing some hilarious British dance or suchlike.

"Hiya, Pat," whispered Sinéad.

"Shinnie?"

"It's me, Pat."

He collapsed into his sister's arms, almost crushing Seán in the process. Pulling away for a moment, he checked to make sure it was really her and then resumed his death-grip.

"I can't believe it. I can't believe it," he repeated, his voice barely audible beneath her arms.

"It's me, Pat. It's me, honestly."

It was only when Seán began to complain about being suffocated that Patrick remembered he was there.

"Who's this fellah, then? Is he with you, Shins?"

"Yes, Pat. He's not your brother, he's your nephew."

"Aw, thank God!"

An uncle at twelve: his friends would be so jealous.

"Howya, nephew," he said, jabbing a friendly fist at Seán's cheek.

"Nevoo," replied Seán, smiling up at his uncle Patrick.

*

Next to arrive was Adele. She'd known her sister would be there but managed to act surprised. What she hadn't known was how her mother would react to the return of the prodigal child. Adele had encouraged Sinéad to return and told her everything would be all right, but really she'd just wanted her back and had no idea how the family would react. Thankfully, it seemed her mother was just as happy to see her as the rest of them.

"Look at you! You're flippin' gorgeous, a proper little sexpot." Sinéad scanned her sixteen-year-old sister up and down, barely able to comprehend the transformation she'd undergone.

"Sinéad, don't talk like that to your sister; she's still a child," scolded Patricia.

"Ah, Mammy, she needs to be told. She's an absolute fox. I bet she has all the lads driven mental."

"Stop it, Sinéad," warned her mother.

Adele stood there, red-faced, while her sister appraised her figure. She was embarrassed but it was okay; Sinéad was back, and the house rang with laughter again. Even her mother appeared to be happy, at least by her own miserable standards. Sinéad's departure had had a chilling effect on them all, but it was her parents who'd been hit hardest. They never discussed it with the children, of course, that would have been far too logical. Instead Adele and Valerie had had to deal with Patrick's plaintive questions. *Where's Shinnie? When will she be back? Why can't I go visit her?*

Their parents carried on in stoical fashion until their father had a few pints in him; then the arguments would start. The children would listen from upstairs, catching snippets here and there:

"It's your fuckin' fault."

"You should have been stricter."

"What's his name? I'll fuckin' kill him."

"Wake me up early in the morning. I'm headin' to England."

This would go on until the shouting died down, to be replaced by sobbing.

"I miss her, Tricia."

"I just want my little Nades back."

"I don't care how many fuckin' kids she has."

Sinéad had always been her father's favourite. He would never admit as much, but they all knew it. They shared a bond that none of them could breach, a deep understanding which set them apart from the rest of the family. He said she reminded him of his mother, with her penchant for devilment and her sarky little mouth. And she was a daddy's girl, tailing him wherever he went, accompanying him on his long walks in the woods when no one else would. Surprisingly, their relationship didn't change as she grew into adulthood; if anything, it strengthened. The dynamic changed, no longer consisting of playful conversations and fawning favouritism. Now they were just two brooding figures locked in deep discussion, setting the world to rights, passing judgement on those they deemed their inferiors. When she left with not a hint of warning, he blamed himself. Told himself he should have seen it coming. Had he been too attached to her? Was that why she'd left? But no matter how many times he read the note he could never understand why his little Nades had left him.

Adele still remembered that morning. Sinéad had confided in her days previously; she'd told her what had happened and what she intended to do. She was leaving the country, getting rid of the baby, and would be back in a couple of weeks. 'They abort them in England,' she'd said, 'I'll only be gone a couple of days'. Her bags were packed and left at a friend's. She'd go to work as normal, but when her shift finished, instead of returning home, she'd get on a bus. The bus would bring her to the dock, and from there she would board the ferry and be gone. Adele was under strict instructions: *Get up in the middle of the night and leave this note on the table; make it look like I left it there.* She had to have enough time to make her escape or else her father would come after her.

So, like the dutiful sister she was, Adele had crept downstairs at the break of dawn and left the note on the kitchen table. She'd retreated to her bed and waited for all hell to break loose. She'd prayed it would be her mother that would find it but knew, just knew, that it would be her father.

And sure enough, a couple of hours later the pandemonium had begun. He'd come bounding up the stairs, taking them two at a time. "What do ye know about this?" he'd cried, waving the note in his hand. "About what?" Valerie had replied, as Adele aped her nonplussed expression. He'd then turned his rage on their mother, accusing her of being in on the whole thing. The raised voices and the blue air had brought Patrick from his bed. And, like most children, the sight of his parents screaming and shouting had brought tears to his own eyes.

"Your sister has gone away for a while, she'll be back soon," Patricia had told him.

"Where's she gone, Mammy?" he'd asked. "She was supposed to help me with my homework tonight."

Thanks, Sinéad, Adele had thought. *Thanks a lot.*

The contents of that note had never been discussed, but their effect was there for all to see. Their father had changed overnight. Never the most communicative of men, he'd become habitually silent, sitting alone on the porch step after his dinner, staring into the distance as if awaiting her return. His forty-a-day smoking habit, vanquished the previous year, had returned with a vengeance. Never a heavy drinker, he'd taken to visiting the pub almost every night. He had disengaged from his family, done everything he could to get away from them. As a result, they had all drifted apart. Patricia had tried her best, but her children needed their father and she needed her husband. Valerie, always the most difficult child, had turned the upheaval to her advantage. With no one to discipline her she did as she pleased, came and went as she pleased. Her parents hadn't the heart to challenge her. The concerted appeal to leave school early, once vociferously opposed, had been granted with barely a whisper of protest. *Let her do what she wants,* her mother had sighed wearily, the fight well and truly knocked out of her. And that's what Valerie had done; she'd left school at sixteen with barely a qualification to her name. Her father had still had the wherewithal to insist she get a job at least. The irony of her finding work as a housekeeper when her own home was so badly in need of repair had seemed lost on them all.

The two youngest, Adele and Patrick, had become inseparable; bound by circumstance. He would come scurrying into his sister's room whenever the fighting started, huddling up beside her, listening to the raised voices coming from downstairs; wondering if his father was going to kill his mother or vice versa. The arguments had become a regular occurrence, both parents fighting with their own demons as well as each other. Their love for one another had been forgotten, ignored and neglected, as they'd watched their family fall apart. Where they'd once met the challenges of parenthood together, they'd become too immersed in their own individual problems to tend to their children. The arguments had always taken the same form, Noel pleading with his wife: "Can we not go and get her, bring them both back?" But Patricia wouldn't budge. "No, she left us. If she wants to come back, she can." She always had the final say in the McLoughlin household and it had been no different this time. She had wanted her daughter back just as much as the rest of them, but believed that what she had done was wrong. If Patricia had done something similar at that age it would have been away to the nunnery with her, banished, never to be seen again. "Things are different now," her husband had argued, "it isn't the dark ages we're in any more, girl." But she'd remained resolute. Her daughter's decision had to have a price. "And anyway," she said, "how do we know she wants to come back? Maybe she's happy where she is." But they'd both known that wasn't true. Sinéad had always been the most home-loving of their children, the one least likely to fly the coop. She had left because she'd been afraid of their reaction. They would have insisted she marry the child's father, whoever he was. Pregnant at seventeen, without as much as an engagement ring on her hand? That just wouldn't do. No, she would marry this man, and that would be the end of it.

But maybe that was why she had fled. She didn't want anything to do with the father. Or he didn't want anything to do with her. So where was he now, then? Who was he? Who had done this to their little girl? They'd listened out for news of any young men disappearing unexpectedly. Dooncurra was a small place; it wouldn't be hard to find out, but no word came. All the young, eligible bachelors remained *in situ*. The culprit could have been among them, but there was no way of knowing; perhaps he didn't know himself. The poor sap could have been wandering the streets calling out her name, wondering why the love of his life had deserted him when he'd needed her most. But he didn't call to the house. No one called. So the die had been cast – they would carry on as normal, as though nothing had happened. Talk of Sinéad had become taboo; it was as if she had never existed. They'd hoped for her return, but that was all they'd had: hope.

6

VALERIE ALLOWED HERSELF A SLIGHT smile. She hadn't been privy to the secret communications and was taken aback by her sister's reappearance. Her response may only have amounted to a small gasp and a hug lasting all of a microsecond, but she was happy to see her; she really was. Everyone was happy. Everyone was here. Everyone except their father. As the clock ticked toward six, the atmosphere changed. They became nervous, watchful, unwilling to get too caught up in the excitement. But it was only Sinéad who was fearful; Patricia, Adele, Patrick and Valerie were mere spectators, afforded front-row seats at one of the biggest events of the year.

"Homecoming or not, your father will still be hungry when he gets in," chanted Patricia, busying herself with the dinner. "Set the table, Patrick, there's a good boy."

"Anything I can do to help?" asked Sinéad, eager to flaunt the culinary abilities she'd gained during her exile.

"No, thank you, Sinéad," came the reply from a mother not ready to give up her domain just yet.

Sinéad knew better than to argue, and they convened in the sitting-room to await her father. Seán, who had been playing up to the crowd all afternoon, was now flagging. He'd met enough new people for one day.

"Can I put Seán to bed, Mammy? Anywhere at all will do him."

"Put him up in our bed," came the reply from the kitchen.

Sinéad thought this odd, but didn't complain.

"You're getting the master bedroom, Seány," she said, as she cajoled, then dragged her son up the stairs.

In her parent's room, she pulled back endless layers of covers. It looked incredibly cosy, and reminded her how tired she was herself. But she could last a few hours yet; her son couldn't. Tired as he was, though, he wasn't getting into any bed without his pyjamas.

"Jim-jams," he whined, rubbing his eyes.

She didn't want to go back downstairs and start tearing at her luggage. Her father would be home any minute and she wanted Seán in bed before he came. A thought popped into her head. She quickly crossed the hallway and entered the room where she had spent the first seventeen years of her life. Not much had changed. Her bed was now in the possession of Adele and the posters of Bono had been replaced by ones of Bros, but that was about it. Valerie's side of the room was the same as it had always been: organised chaos. She went to the wardrobe and braced herself for the mayhem inside. True to form it was like a car boot sale, minus the car boot. Sifting through her sisters' clothes, she found what she was looking for: a black sack containing her baby clothes, the ones that hadn't been handed down to her sisters.

Opening the bag brought memories flooding back; old T-shirts worn at the beach, runners held together with masking tape, the jumper knitted by her grandmother that she'd hated. But the stroll down memory lane would have to wait for another day. There was a sleepy child in the next room looking for his jim-jams. She rooted down to the bottom of the bag, through shorts, socks, scarves and hats, pushing her way past until she alighted on her own childhood pyjamas. They were well worn by this stage but the little boy in the master bedroom would just have to make do. She pulled the fraying pyjamas from the end of the bag, gave them a quick rub and decided they would suffice.

"Seány, look what Mummy has for you! Some lovely jim-jams that she used to wear."

Seán sat on the side of the bed, a look of sullen determination on his face. But the sight of the night-time attire seemed to lighten his mood.

"Jim-jams?" he enquired, as Sinéad laid the items on the bed.

"Yes, jim-jams. Aren't they lovely?"

He picked up the flowery pyjamas and examined them for a second, then he gazed up at his mother, his face masked with doubt. It was a look that said, *These? Are you sure?* But he was too tired to complain any further. He dutifully raised his arms when told, placed his legs where they were supposed to go, and a few moments later the ensemble was complete.

"There ya go, now. Aren't ya lovely?" Sinéad said, tucking him under the covers.

He looked tiny in her parent's bed, his minute frame submerged by a myriad of blankets. If it weren't for the mop of brown hair just visible above them, you wouldn't have known he was there at all.

"Are you okay there, Seány?"

The only response was the soft sigh of her son's sleep. She kissed him on the cheek, leaving him to his dreams, making sure the door was slightly ajar so that the light from the landing illuminated the gloom.

The sounds and smells coming from the kitchen told her that dinner was now served. Her stomach growled in anticipation. She'd almost forgotten how good her mother's cooking tasted. Such was her eagerness to get back downstairs, she completely forgot about the one member of her family she had yet to meet.

"Mmm, that smells like good oul' Tricia McLoughin stew," she proclaimed, re-entering the living room. "Where's me feckin pl-"

Her father was at the sink, washing his hands. Sinéad's cheeks flushed and her words tailed off, hanging in the air like a bad smell. She swallowed deeply, waiting for her father to acknowledge her presence. But Noel continued washing his hands, his back still to her and no apparent change in his demeanour.

"Hello, Daddy," she ventured at last.

He buckled slightly at the knees, his shoulders slackening as if absorbing a heavy blow; then he slowly turned to face her.

"You're back."

Sinéad couldn't tell whether this was a question or a statement.

"I am, Daddy. Did you miss me?"

He shook his head ruefully, dried his hands on a tea-towel and looked at his wife.

"What did you know about this?"

"Nothing!" Patricia retorted, hurt by the allegation.

"And you?" he asked, looking at Adele.

"Nothing, Daddy," she replied, aping her mother's indignation.

"Jaysus, ye're an awful shower, do ye know that?" he said, taking his seat at the head of the table.

Sinéad stood at the entrance to the kitchen, wondering if it was safe to come in. Her father looked up at her, a familiar twinkle in his eye.

"You gonna sit down or what, girl?"

Sheepishly she pulled up a seat, her old seat right beside her father, and joined the rest of her family. She dared not look at him but he was right there, filling his mug with milk, buttering his bread, waiting for his dinner: carrying on as normal.

"Could you pass the salt, please, Daddy?" Sinéad asked primly.

He handed her the salt shaker, their eyes locking.

"Thanks, Daddy."

"You're welcome, Nades," he said with a smirk.

Sinéad stared at the ground, a smile spreading across her lips. She didn't want to get ahead of herself, but it looked like he was going to forgive her.

*

Dinner was a raucous affair; everyone fighting to be heard, but no one saying anything worth hearing. Patricia surveyed the scene, marvelling at the wonder of it all. Usually even her best efforts were devoured without as much as a 'thank you', but now it was as if they were feasting upon a royal banquet. Smiling faces beamed out from every corner of the table; appreciative grunts filled the gaps in the conversation. At one point she thought she heard a compliment thrown her way. Her youngest, the hungriest hippo of them all, appeared to be chewing on his food rather than swallowing it whole. It was quite something; her family were civilised for once, like something you'd see on the front of a Christmas card.

"That was delicious, Mammy. What's for dessert?" asked Sinéad, licking her plate clean.

"Hmm, there might be some Swiss Roll in the press."

"Swiss Roll, Mammy? Swiss Roll?" Patrick said, outraged. "Surely we should get something fancy for the day that's in it."

"Sure what day is in it?" Noel asked. "'Tis only a Tuesday as far as I know."

He raised a sly eyebrow in Sinéad's direction.

"But Sinéad is back," Patrick continued. "We'll have to get something nice."

"Oh, I'd say you're very worried about your sister," Patricia replied haughtily.

"Mammy, an occasion like this calls for *Viennetta* at the very least."

Noel fished in his pockets for some change. "Here, son, go down and get whatever you can with that," he said, giving the boy a handful of coins.

Patrick studied his haul, saw that it was mostly pound coins and fifty-pence pieces and declared himself happy.

"Right, I'll be back in five minutes," he said, skipping out the door.

"Get wafers too, Patrick!" his mother shouted after him.

"G'way, Mammy, no one likes them yokes," he called back. And before Patricia could protest he was gone.

"Need a hand with the washing-up, Mammy?" Sinéad asked, rising from the table.

"What are you asking me for? Sure I'm not doing any washing-up," Patricia replied, going into the sitting-room to join her husband. "Tis your sisters you should be asking."

"Well, girls?" Sinéad asked, turning to her younger siblings.

"You're on drying, Nades," said Adele, flinging a tea-towel at her.

"Drying? That's the worst job; leave me do the washing."

"I'm afraid not, sis. I'm the resident washer-upper nowadays. That's what you get for feckin' off to England for yourself."

"Well, fuck the pair of ye so," Sinéad said, as she squeezed in between her giggling sisters and took a soapy plate from Adele's hands.

"LANGUAGE, SINÉAD!" shouted their mother. "No swearing in this house; nothing's changed there."

"Yeah, Sinéad, language," mimicked Valerie, flicking her with suds.

"Yeah, Sinéad," Adele said, "fuckin' language."

They all creased up with laughter, desperately trying to stay quiet lest more words of warning come their way.

Noel listened to his daughters from his chair in the sitting-room. Ordinarily he wouldn't put up with anyone talking during the evening news bulletin, and certainly not in that manner. But it felt so good to have her back, they could have been shrieking at the top of their lungs and he wouldn't have batted an eyelid. The headlines were over, anyway. They'd progressed to regional news now, stuff that wasn't of any interest to him. He stared distractedly at the television as the ads came on. There was one for kitchen cleaner; a hot and bothered woman having her work cut in half by this miraculous new product. Then one for beer, which reminded him; he fancied a pint later. Next was one for nappies: a child frolicked around on the screen before tumbling over and laughing: *ah isn't that cute.* But it reminded him of something too. He wasn't sure what though. It niggled away at him, stuck in the back of his brain. Something he'd been thinking about earlier. What the hell was it? Then he heard Sinéad's voice filtering in from the kitchen and he remembered.

"Tricia," he whispered.

"What?"

"Is there a baby?"

"Where?"

"With Sinéad; does she have a child?"

His wife smiled with pleasure. She had one over him this time.

"Oh, yeah," she said.

"She does have a child? Well, where is it?"

Patricia peered into the kitchen and then back at her husband.

"Come on," she said, nodding her head upstairs.

Noel duly followed, hoping this wasn't one of his wife's stupid jokes.

She led him up the stairs, pressing her finger to her lips as she went. They came to the landing, and Patricia instructed her husband to keep quiet while she went into their room for a moment. *She's setting me up, I know she is*, he thought, but he stood there in silence nonetheless. His wife returned and beckoned him inside.

"Quiet now," she said as they tiptoed into the bedroom.

"Is there a feckin' child in this house or not, Tricia?" Noel muttered harshly, feeling foolish for getting his hopes up.

"Shush," she replied irritably.

At first he couldn't see anything. The curtains were drawn, and the thin sliver of light coming from the landing only made things shadowy and ghostly. What was he supposed to be looking at? He scanned the room for signs of life, but he couldn't see anything. Then, as if determined to make his presence known, Seán emitted a faint sound from the bed. Noel's head spun around in search of its source. He had already looked at the bed and seen nothing there, but now he looked more closely. There at its head lay a tiny little figure, whether a boy or a girl he couldn't tell. The only thing visible was a mop of hair sticking out from beneath the covers.

Noel looked to his wife. "Can I?" he asked.

"Yes, but be quiet."

He padded over to the bed and fell down to his haunches. Yes, there she was, a little girl in her granddad's bed, and wearing her mammy's pyjamas by the looks of things. He gently raised his hand to Seán's head and stroked his hair.

"What's her name?"

"Seán," his wife replied.

"Seán?"

"Yes."

"Shawna?"

"No. Just Seán."

Noel looked at the child again. This was a girl, surely? What kind of a boy wore his mother's pyjamas and had hair like this?

"It's a boy, Noel, I assure you."

Again he wasn't sure if it was one of his wife's pranks. If this was indeed a boy then he had some work to do, but nothing that a few fishing trips wouldn't fix.

"A boy it is," he said, continuing to stroke Seán's hair. "A boy it is."

JONATHAN

1

Margaret Philliskirk had never been happier. That gnawing void had been filled, the lack of fulfilment addressed; she felt whole, complete, and the reason for it all lay sprawled in his cot a few feet away. Her little boy: her life. Most mothers cherished these quiet moments, but she hated them. Any time spent away from her child was to be endured, not enjoyed. Over time she'd learned to let him sleep, but it hadn't been easy. For the first year she'd kept a continuous bedside vigil, counting down the minutes until he awoke and she could be a mother again. And when he was awake she made sure he was never out of her sight, never out of her arms if she could help it. Malcolm had told her it wasn't healthy, that the child didn't need round-the-clock attention. But what did he know? He spent half the day away at work. How could he possibly understand their child's needs? No, she would look after her baby her own way.

Eventually she began to relax, allowed herself some sleep of her own., but even then she was on guard; one eye half-open, an ear cocked, just in case. If he cried out, she was there by his side before the cry had left his mouth. She would pick him up, feel his warmth against her chest, his soft breath on her neck, and soothe him back to sleep. Her little boy. Her little Jonathan. No one could placate him like she could. Her touch instantly calmed him, drove away his fears, made him feel safe. That was her job, and she did it well. She could admit that to herself now: she was a good mother. There was no denying it. Everyone said so. She'd come a long way since that first meeting when she'd sat there consumed with terror, convinced the baby would hate her, that all babies hated her. That she would take him in her arms and he would cry and cry and cry. He would cry so much they thought his little vocal chords were going to sever. And she would have hand to him back, apologise for being so inept, and return to her miserable, childless life.

That hadn't been her worst fear, though; what really chilled her was the notion that she might hate the baby. This poor, defenceless mite would crave her attention, yearn to be mothered and she would respond with disdain. She would look at this bastard child, the progeny of another woman, and ask herself why she, Margaret Philliskirk, should care for it. It was nothing to do with her; it wasn't her problem. If it cried, what did she care? She was nothing more than a cold, heartless bitch with nary a maternal bone in her body. She would send the baby back, explain that it had all been a terrible mistake and forget it ever happened. She could blame Malcolm; he'd forced her into it against her will. It would probably break them up; they'd divorce, and he would marry a woman capable of bearing his offspring. All for the best, really. But none of that happened. The baby cooed and gurgled when she took it in her arms, and almost immediately her heart melted. Almost immediately, she vowed to die for this child. It sounded crazy but she meant it.

When they were finally allowed to bring him home, one of the first things they had to decide upon was a name. They had bought every baby-name book they could find and sat up in bed till the small hours going through the lists: Aaron, Abraham, Antonio, Axel – Zacchaeus, Zack, Zerxes, Zeus. But nothing had stuck, nothing had felt right. It was because he wasn't here with them. They needed to see him to decide what name would fit. Once he arrived, they would just know. He had been Seán for the first six months of his life, but they agreed without argument that they would change it. Neither of them had any objection to the name Seán; but a primal desire to claim their prize drove their decision. They narrowed it down to five – Andrew, Jonathan, Elijah, Nathan, and Toby – and decided to choose one once he'd been with them for a few days. After the first day, Margaret knew which she wanted. He was a Jonathan; everything about him was a Jonathan. His darting, dancing blue eyes, the tuft of light-brown hair which swirled atop his perfect little head, and the puckered little mouth which seemed constantly ready to break into a smile: he was a Jonathan, from top to bottom: Jonathan. Thankfully, her husband agreed. She had broached the subject first.

"Any thoughts on his name?" she'd asked as they stared into the cot.

"Well – " he replied.

But she'd known he had thoughts, strong thoughts too by the look of it. He could never hide his feelings from her.

"Come on," she'd demanded. "Out with it."

"I don't want to say, in case you've already set your heart on something else."

"I won't be disappointed, I promise," she had lied.

"How about writing our choices down on a piece of paper and handing them to each other? That way I'll know you're not agreeing with me just for the sake of it."

"Okay," she'd replied, running off to find some paper, laughing at the idea of her agreeing with her husband's choice of name *just for the sake of it*.

When she'd returned they'd hurriedly scribbled down their preferences, folded up each paper and handed it to the other.

"Will we open them now?" he had asked.

"Sure," she'd replied, readying herself for battle. No way was her Jonathan being called Elijah; no bloody way.

But when she'd opened the piece of paper, she'd seen her son's name in her husband's writing. It was meant to be, written in the stars. They had their Jonathan.

2

BUT HER LIFE WASN'T COMPLETE; not yet.

"Would you like a little sister, Jonathan?" she'd ask as she changed his nappy. "Someone to play with? You'd love that, wouldn't you?"

She knew he couldn't answer yet, but it felt right to run it by him. Anyway, she was sure he'd agree. Of course he'd love someone to play with; any child would. He would be so happy. And why stop there? She could get him a sister, and a brother too; as many as he wanted. She was a dab hand at this parenting lark, and there were thousands of babies out there just waiting for someone like her to come along. Maybe she could become a foster parent, have a house full of little babies? But then Jonathan might feel neglected, and she didn't want that. No, a little sister would suffice for the time being. All she had to do now was tell her husband; he was still a part of this household, after all.

She was sure Malcolm would be open to the idea. She saw how he was with Jonathan, how his tired eyes lit up whenever his son was in the room. He was a great father, as she'd always known he would be. He loved parenthood just as much as she did, and he'd always wanted a little girl. But there was the financial side of it to consider. The costs involved in Jonathan's adoption had taken her by surprise, but the money needed to feed, clothe and rear him had been another matter entirely. She had given up her part-time job at the flower shop and become a stay-at-home mum, which meant that they had to survive on Malcolm's salary. To ease the strain, he'd taken on more hours at the office: staying late, working Saturdays, doing his utmost to provide for his family. He burned the candle at both ends. Often he'd return home from a twelve-hour day, and within minutes of finishing his tea he'd be off to bed. 'We'll do something nice at the weekend', he'd say as he kissed her goodnight and held his son for the first time since the night before.

To be honest, though, she didn't miss her husband all that much. Her love for him hadn't waned, but it had been supplanted by something else. The love she felt for Jonathan went beyond mere affection and care; it was primal. She knew her husband was tired, and she knew that spending so much time apart wasn't good for their marriage; but Jonathan was her main concern. So what if Daddy was away all day, and sometimes all night; that just meant more time with Mummy, didn't it? Everything else in her life was secondary to Jonathan, and unfortunately that included her husband. She listened to him sighing deeply in his sleep at night, wondering if she was betraying him by feeling this way. Should she return to work and lessen his load? She'd consider all this before lapsing into her own fitful sleep, which would inevitably be broken by the anguished cries of her beloved. And when Malcolm arose for another day of boardroom meetings, number crunching, and whatever else he did in that alien world of his, she'd smile to herself; soon he would be gone, and then it would just be Mummy and Jonathan again.

3

MALCOLM HAD ARRIVED HOME EARLY, catching her by surprise. He hadn't called ahead to forewarn her so there'd been no dinner ready for him, but he'd said he wasn't hungry. When she lifted up their son to kiss him, he'd simply brushed her away.

"I'm going outside," he'd said flatly.

That's where he was now, sitting in the back garden on the rocking bench. He sometimes went out there after his tea, but only when the evenings were nice. Right now, in mid-March, the evenings were far from nice; grey skies and misty squalls prevailed, the kind of weather best witnessed from inside. But there he was on the rocking bench, which was probably damp from the drizzling rain, and there he had remained for what seemed like an eternity.

Why would he waste this rare opportunity to spend some time with his son? she wondered as she debated whether or not to join him. Something was clearly up, and whatever it was she probably didn't want to hear it. She could always play dumb, pretend that Jonathan was getting narky and she couldn't leave him alone. But that was the coward's way out. Her husband was clearly in need and it was her duty to go to him. She took a deep breath, checked on her son one last time and headed for the back door.

"Honey?"

A brief flicker of the eyes suggested acknowledgement, but he seemed miles away, staring out at the dreary March evening like a man condemned.

She sat down beside him, the bench rocking gently from the added weight, and studied him closely. He was still as handsome as ever: deep brown eyes, that strong jawline she so admired, and the thick black hair which showed no sign of greying or receding as he entered his thirties. But he looked different; she could see it now. This was probably the first time in months she'd looked at him, really looked at him. He looked tired, but it was more than that; it was as if the life was being sucked out of him, his essence draining away, leaving nothing behind but the shell of a man. How had she not noticed this before now?

"Is everything okay, Malc?"

Again her words barely registered. A shiver ran down her spine; she was really worried now.

"Why don't you come inside, Malcolm? Spend some time with Jonathan?" She took his hands in hers, looking him up and down, hoping for clues, a sign, anything to help her understand what was happening.

"I – " he began.

"Yes, love, what it is? You can tell me anything, you know that."

He paused, overwhelmed by the enormity of his feelings. He turned to look at her.

"I ... I ... I can't take it anymore, Margie. I just can't bloody take it."

Tears welled in his eyes. As his face seemed about to collapse he buried his head in her chest, directing his sobs there instead. Margaret's maternal instincts, by now well-sharpened, kicked in. She took him in her arms, gently stroking his hair as she tried to pacify him.

"Whatever it is, we'll get through it, don't you worry about that," she said reassuringly over his muffled cries.

But what the hell was it? *What* couldn't he take anymore? It was her fault. She should have seen this coming, noticed the changes in his behaviour, but she couldn't remember the last time they had talked – really talked. Yes, they spoke to one another, but only casually, and as for sex: she vaguely recalled a drunken coupling on New Year's Eve, but nothing since. She had neglected her husband and now here he was, like a child in her arms. This was what happened when men were left to their own devices.

She brought, almost carried, him inside and laid him down on the couch. He was deathly pale and trembling all over. Margaret covered him with a blanket and put the kettle on before returning to his side.

"Malcolm, dear, you must try and talk to me. I'm getting worried now. What is it?"

He lay there, curled up in the foetal position, his teeth chattering as he shivered.

"Will I call the doctor?" she asked.

"NO! No doctor," he shouted, suddenly becoming animated.

"Well, what can I do, then?" She touched his brow; it was thick with sweat.

"I'm not well, Margie. I'm not well," he said with an effort.

"You're ill? What is it?" Her concern heightened as she imagined cancer and other fearsome, terminal illnesses.

Malcolm gritted his teeth and gathered himself before he spoke again. "Yes, I'm ill. I'm so fucking ill I can't even provide for my own family, that's how ill I am."

Margaret was shocked to hear him speak this way. She rarely swore, but she was a potty-mouthed heathen compared to her husband.

44

"You're not making any sense, Malcolm."

He looked at her sadly, with pity, then with great effort he pulled himself up to a seated position. He drew his knees in front of him, wrapped his arms around them and perched his head atop them so that he peeped out at her like a child.

Margaret squeezed in beside him and began gently rubbing his shoulders. She would wait for as long as it took. After a time he seemed to come round, the worst apparently past.

"A drink of water," he croaked and she rushed to the kitchen to get one. It was only then she realised she hadn't thought about Jonathan once during this entire episode. That must have been how Malcolm felt every day: of secondary concern, a mere distraction while the more important family member was tended to.

When she returned, he had squatted down beside his son's playpen.

"Here's your water, dear."

He thirstily gulped down the entire glass before going to the kitchen to fill another. Then he took Margaret by the arm and sat her down on the couch.

"Margie, we need to talk."

*

It all came tumbling out. It was work, just work; nothing else. She was relieved, imagined it had been something worse, something much worse, but it was bad enough.

He had worked for the same company for the past twelve years: Betanide, one of the region's largest providers of pharmaceutical goods. Starting out as a warehouse hand, he had worked his way through the ranks. He had taken extra training courses, availing of whatever was on offer, and eventually elevated himself upstairs with the suits. His progression continued, moving through customer services to sales, and even getting his own office. That had been the end of the line as far as he was concerned; he had no desire to move further up the chain. The money he earned was excellent, and with what Margaret earned from her job in the florists they brought in more than enough to live a life of relative luxury. That had all changed when Jonathan arrived. Margaret gave up her job to become a stay at home mum and suddenly he was the sole breadwinner. He still earned enough for them all to live off comfortably but things were different now; he wasn't working so they could afford a holiday to the Maldives, he was doing it to sustain a new life, to ensure this little person they'd brought into their lives was cared for.

Suddenly there was all this pressure, all these responsibilities. He thought he'd been ready, had presumed he'd just adapt to fatherhood and that he'd thrive in his new role. But it was just the opposite; he felt trapped, cornered into something he wasn't prepared for. His job, which he'd once enjoyed, now became a grind. He toiled his way through the days, getting through them with grim determination and not much else. He was used to clocking off at five in the evening and forgetting all about work until the following morning, but he was providing for a family now and couldn't afford to be so lax. He had to be on the ball, make sure his standards didn't slip – one mistake, one cock-up, and it would all go pear-shaped. How would they survive if he got sacked? On the dole?

His mind was constantly on his work. He arrived home each evening to his wife and son, to the perfect family he'd always dreamed of having, but all he could think of was meeting his targets and getting that next big bonus. And he couldn't switch off. Even at night, while he slept, he thought about work. He had nightmares: disastrous scenarios where he was sacked for losing an important client; no severance pay, no references, just get out and don't come back. He didn't realise that the reality was completely different. He had become so dedicated to his work, so determined to improve his sales figures, that his superiors had taken note. They summoned him to their offices, congratulated him on his stellar work, and asked whether he would be interested in a new role: Chief Operations Officer. It sounded terrifying. He didn't want it; all that extra responsibility, more hours. No, thank you, he was quite happy where he was. But then he thought of his family, his new son and his wife. Wouldn't they like it if Daddy made more money? They could get a new car. Jonathan could go to the very best schools, have piano lessons, whatever he wanted.

He took the job. It wasn't even up for debate. He told his wife about it over dinner that night; told her rather than asked her. He knew it was a decision he had to make by himself. Naturally she was thrilled, but it wasn't the joyous occasion it would have been a couple of years previously.

Already he could feel the pressure intensifying, the walls closing in around him. He'd hoped it would be a cushy number, that he could be one of those middle-management types who spent half their time dining out, enjoying liquid lunches. But those hopes were dashed from day one; the hours were long and the work demanding. Not only was he worrying about his own targets and his own goals, he was now worrying about everyone else's too. He had become a company man; someone who checked the stock exchange to see how the business was faring, someone who lived or died by this institution into which he had become embedded. No longer was he a cog driving a small part of the wheel onwards; now he was a large rivet upon which the whole wheel depended, and without his input it would grind to a halt. This had never been what he'd wanted.

That wasn't even the worst of it. He now had to make decisions which affected members of staff, those who had once been his colleagues but were now mere underlings, dispensable components of the wheel. He was a suit now, no longer one of the lads. His friends avoided him at lunch, found excuses to sit elsewhere, leaving him with the other executives. He had nothing in common with those people, though, cringed when they used phrases like 'touch base' and 'close of play'. He had no desire ever to touch base or close any play; he just wanted to be back at his old desk at the nine-to-five. A drone, that's what he was by nature. That was all he'd ever been cut out for.

But there was a child to think about now. He was building a future for them all, and he couldn't deny that the money was great. Only the best for our Jonathan, he'd remind himself as he drove to work on the brink of tears. He couldn't tell anyone how he was feeling, least of all his wife. She was the happiest he'd ever seen her, and how could he spoil that for her? So he struggled on, growing more miserable by the day. His sleep suffered, and so did his work. He began to suffer from chest pains, palpitations and dizziness. Was he on the verge of a heart attack? Maybe that would be for the best; at least then he wouldn't have to endure this hell for a moment longer. He should have gone to a doctor, but he couldn't afford to take the time off. It was a busy time of the year, they needed him. Instead he decided to self-medicate. He'd only ever been a social drinker, but alcohol seemed a viable solution at this point. Bottles of vodka were spirited into his office and carefully poured into the hip flask he kept hidden in his breast-pocket.

It helped, a bit. Allowed him to relax. The targets, the goals and the pressure were all still there; he just didn't worry about them like he used to.

But his bosses weren't stupid. They noticed the change in the bright go-getter in whom they had placed so much faith. Where once he'd been assiduous and alert, he was now lackadaisical and slovenly. His performance suffered, and in turn the company suffered. A few careful chats seemed to clear the air. *Come to us*, they said, *if there's anything troubling you then we need to know about it*. But he could never tell them. What would they think? He'd barely been in the job a month and already he was falling apart. They'd demote him, maybe even fire him, and what would happen then? His child would starve to death, that's what. So he muddled on as best he could. He tried to control his drinking, aiming at relaxed merriment, but sometimes he went too far; it became obvious to all but the most myopic of observers that he was drunk at work.

The tone of the chats changed. The friendly one-to-ones were replaced by stern reprimands and written warnings. He promised to improve, told them he was just going through a rough patch, but it was all just words; what he really wanted was to be put out of his misery. He would gladly have accepted a public flogging, a beheading, whatever dastardly method of punishment they could come up with. Instead they put him on gardening leave, told him to get some help and that his job would be there if and when he was ready to return. That had been three weeks ago, and Malcolm hadn't told his wife. He'd just carried on as normal.

Every morning he'd gone through his usual routine; reading the paper over breakfast, spending a few precious minutes with his son, before pecking his wife on the cheek and cheerily heading off to work: a promising young executive with a bright future ahead of him. Then he would drive to the park, find a nice bench and take the hip flask from his pocket. As soon as the acrid warmth hit his stomach, he felt better; his head would begin to clear and his thoughts form more readily. He found ways to rationalise his behaviour, told himself that this was just a temporary state of affairs and that he'd go back. By the time the pubs would open at noon he'd be already drunk. He'd found a watering-hole suitable for his needs: a quiet spot in a quiet part of town, where the barman didn't ask questions and the clientele kept to themselves. All the regulars knew him by now; they would nod a greeting as he arrived at five past the hour, and then leave him to his own devices. They understood; it was that kind of place. He would take his seat – he had his own – and nod to the barman. *Fill her up and keep them coming until I say otherwise.* And when the time would come to leave he'd swap double vodkas for strong black coffees in a desperate, futile attempt to sober up. He'd drive home way over the limit, almost asking to be caught, and carefully turn the key in the door, hoping to disappear up the stairs without being seen. He'd crawl into bed and fall into a fitful, fevered sleep, not waking until his wife joined him hours later. Then he'd creep downstairs, search out the lovingly-cooked dinner prepared for him some hours earlier and eat it, alone and ashamed. Still, it was another day done and his wife was none the wiser.

But he couldn't hide the truth forever and on this day he had finally succumbed. Sitting in the pub surrounded by fag smoke and broken dreams, he had risen silently from his seat, paid the barman and walked out the door. As he'd driven the short distance to their three-bedroom suburban paradise, he'd felt a strange sense of liberation. Whatever lay ahead could not be any worse than this; the deceit, the shame, the waking nightmare his life had become. Like a man preparing to meet his maker, he'd been ready. On the drive home he'd carefully planned his speech; he would spare her the worst of it, tell her there'd been some trouble at work and he was taking some time off. He'd be intentionally vague; there was no need to worry her. But when he'd seen her coming to greet him, ready to tell him about their son's latest miraculous feat, he'd folded. He hadn't been able to do it. He'd retreated to the back garden, hoping she would come to him, that she would somehow save him. And when she had come to him out of love, concern for his well-being, he had crumbled. It had been so long since she or anyone had shown him affection, he had been powerless to resist. Her mere touch had sent him over the edge, all the pent-up emotion rolling out, the floodgates opened.

His initial plan to 'spare her the worst' had been quickly forgotten. Now he told her things he had never even admitted to himself: how he sometimes felt jealous of Jonathan and yearned for those summer days when it was just the two of them, how he'd considered ending it all one morning as he drove to a job he hated. He opened up his soul, exposing his darkest, deepest secrets. Through it all she remained silent, staring at him intently and lovingly. Not once did her face betray any sign of disgust, although she must surely have felt some. He had gone beyond caring; let her be disgusted, he deserved it after all. Malcolm purged himself until there was nothing left and he had bled himself dry. *Do what you will with me, I am at your mercy.*

"God, look at the time," said Margaret. "You must be starving!"

He looked at his watch: half past ten. Was this still the same day? Had he really begun it on a park bench? He couldn't remember when he'd last eaten, but he wasn't particularly hungry.

"How about a fish supper with mushy peas and the works?" she asked, holding the phone, waiting for the go-ahead.

"I can't think of anything I'd like better," he answered. It was true; the words 'fish' and 'supper' resonated in his brain and his stomach rumbled in response.

He listened as she called in the order, hoping she would collect it. He wasn't ready to face another living soul just yet.

She returned from the hallway and stood over him. *Here it comes,* he thought, *eat your fish supper and get the fuck out of here, you pathetic excuse for a human being.* But she cupped his face in her hands, bringing it close to hers.

"We'll get through this, Malcolm, I promise you."

"But ..."

"No 'buts', we're in this together. Starting tomorrow, we'll look into getting you some help and go from there. Okay?"

He didn't get a chance to respond. She was gone again, out to the kitchen, rattling knives and forks, cursing the vinegar for being so far back in the cupboard.

"Let's have it in here, shall we? It'll make a nice change." She set down the cutlery on the coffee table, briefly looking in on Jonathan as she went.

"I can't go back there, Margie; you know that."

She paused and returned to his side.

"You don't have to go back there, Malcolm. A man of your skills shouldn't be wasting away inside an office compartment. See this as a beginning, not an end."

His collapse had reinvigorated her. She still wanted nothing more than to climb into Jonathan's playpen and settle down for the night, but now she understood that there were two men in her life. It wasn't enough to be a mother, she had to be a wife too.

They stuffed themselves on crispy haddock, soggy chips and mushy peas and then went to bed, exhausted from the evening's events. For the first time in months, Malcolm slept; not the febrile, disturbed sleep of recent times, but a deep slumber full of vivid, dramatic dreams. When he awoke the next morning she wasn't there, and for a brief second he thought she had left him; drugged him and crept away in the night, never to return. But as he shuffled down the stairs he heard the sounds of mother and son at play. His family was still intact, at least for today.

"Oh, hello, sleepyhead. You finally decided to join us, did you?" His wife smiled up at him from her position on the floor with Jonathan.

"Can't remember the last time I slept like that," he said, as much to himself as to her.

"Will you take over here while I get your breakfast?" she asked, going to the kitchen to cook a full English.

Malcolm surveyed the mass of brightly-coloured bricks spread out all over the floor. "What are we doing here then, Jonathan?"

Jonathan looked at him warily, as if querying his presence. *What are you doing here?* the look said. *This is my time with Mummy; why don't you just go back to the pub?* Then he smiled, happy to have a new playmate. "Bwicks," he declared, bashing two of the bigger pieces together to underline his point.

"I see. And what are we building?"

"Bwicks," came the reply.

Malcolm couldn't help but laugh, and Jonathan, seeing his father laughing, decided to join in – bricks were pretty funny, he had to admit. Each fed off the other's laughter, and before long they were both curled up on the floor giggling hysterically.

"What's going on here, then?" cried Margaret in mock annoyance. "I go out to cook for you two lazybones and all hell breaks loose!"

They looked up at her then back at one another, and once more broke into fits of hysterics. Margaret returned to the frying pan with a big grin on her face. Everything was going to work out just fine.

1991

Seán

1.

SEÁN MCLOUGHLIN LOVED SATURDAYS. THEY were by far his favourite day of the week. He'd wake up early – usually around nine – and head straight for the sitting-room to watch the cartoons. But he always made sure to keep the volume down, because his mammy would still be in bed. She didn't get up until eleven on Saturday, sometimes even noon. She worked late on a Friday night and often didn't get home until after midnight, so she was very, very tired. When she did eventually get up she'd make Seán runny boiled eggs with soldiers to dip into them, and while he ate they would discuss their plans for the day. They always spent Saturdays together. He loved Saturdays.

Usually they went to his nanny's house, which was only a twenty-minute walk away, though sometimes Seán's mammy insisted on getting the bus. He preferred it when they walked, though. They passed three sweetshops on the way to his nanny's house, so there was always a chance he'd get something nice if they walked there. But even if his mother didn't buy him anything on the way, he knew his nanny would fuss over him as soon as they arrived. She'd make him a lovely sugary cup of tea with some biscuits to dunk in it, usually chocolate digestives. They never had chocolate biscuits in his own house. When he was sure there were no more nice things to be had, he'd go into the living-room and tell his granddad about his week. He'd tell him about the test he took in school and how he got ten out of ten, even though he'd only got nine. He'd tell him about the game of football they'd had at lunchtime and all the goals he'd scored. And he'd tell him that yes, he would be a good boy for his mammy no matter what. Seán loved his granddad; he was probably his favourite man in the whole world, apart from his uncle Patrick. He wasn't sure if Patrick was a man or not, though. He had asked his mammy and she'd said: "He's eighteen, which makes him a man in the eyes of the law." "Why does the law have eyes?" Seán had asked, but his mammy couldn't answer that one. He would have to ask Patrick instead.

Patrick wasn't always there on a Saturday, but when he was they had a brilliant time together. If the weather was nice they'd go out the back for a game of football. Patrick was really tall and could kick the ball so high in the sky that Seán couldn't even see it. He knew how to do lots of cool tricks, too. He could flick the ball over his head, do bicycle kicks, and he'd once done 50 keepie-uppies. Seán knew this because he'd been there and kept count, his eyes growing wider with each passing milestone. Patrick would play for Man. United someday, Seán knew that for a fact. He already had a car, so if he had to go to Manchester it wouldn't be a problem. Sometimes they went for a spin in Patrick's car, and Seán was allowed to sit in the front seat. "Don't tell your mammy," Patrick would say as the speedometer inched past fifty miles per hour. He needn't have worried; Seán would never tell his mammy. He would never betray his uncle like that.

Yes, he absolutely loved Saturdays, and his favourite part of the day was waking up and realising there was a whole Saturday stretching out before him. That was what he was doing now, just lying in bed enjoying the fact it was Saturday. There was no hurry on him, it was only half eight and the best cartoons didn't start till nine, but having savoured the moment for all of thirty seconds he decided it was time to get up. He swung out of bed, hopped into his slippers and made for the sitting-room. They had moved into this house over three years ago; it was in a new council estate called St Mary's Terrace. He couldn't really remember the day they'd moved in, but according to his mammy Seán had chosen the bathroom when she'd asked him which room he'd like for his own. He must have been really thick then; only an idiot would choose the bathroom. But he'd been just four at the time, so in a way it was understandable. In the end he got the back bedroom, which faced out onto the modest garden. At the time he'd had hardly any stuff: just a few boxes of toys and two pairs of football boots. Since then, though, he had accumulated much more stuff, and his room now resembled that of a normal seven-year-old boy – complete and utter carnage from one end to the other. On several occasions Sinéad had earmarked a Saturday as the day they would finally tackle the mess, but time and time again Seán had wriggled out of it. She'd said the same yesterday and Seán had just nodded along, all the while knowing there wasn't a snowflake's chance in hell he'd be lifting one Action Man from the floor.

Poor Mammy, he thought to himself as he crept past her room, *sure she's only trying her best*. That's what all the oul' wans said when they stopped in the street to talk. They'd come out with the usual things about how he'd grown and how lovely he was, before turning their attention to his mammy and waffling away for what seemed like hours. Occasionally he'd get some money out of them, maybe as much as 50p, and on those occasions he was happy for them to talk for as long as they liked; they'd paid their way and were entitled to have a good chat. They'd say stuff to her like, 'sure aren't ya great, working and all,' or 'it must be an awful strain on ya, love,' and Seán would wonder what was such a strain on her. It was probably just one of those things that adults talked about, and he had learned not to ask about those. He had also learned never to disturb his mammy when she was sleeping late. So, after a moment's consideration he bypassed her room and headed to the sitting-room for some Saturday morning cartoons.

A noise from the sitting-room made him stop in his tracks. It sounded like there was someone in there. Who could it be at this hour on a Saturday morning? If it was a burglar, then Seán was ready for him. He had a hurley up in his room, and he was well able to swing it. Any burglar would have to deal with him if they thought they could just come into 22 St. Mary's Terrace and take all their stuff. He stood in the hallway listening intently, his little heart thumping in his chest. There was someone in there all right, two of them by the sound of things. Two men, in his house! He bunched up his fists in preparation for a fight; there wasn't time to get the hurley now. But then he heard laughter and the sound of a can being popped open. That was strange. As far as he knew burglars didn't laugh, they were usually too busy robbing. And they definitely didn't drink cans; sure how would they get one past their balaclavas? It had to be Patrick. He was the only man Seán knew that laughed. He'd probably called round with one of his mates to watch the cartoons with him; typical Patrick. But when Seán opened the door to greet his uncle, his face dropped in disappointment. It wasn't Patrick; it was two big eejits he didn't recognise, drinking beer and smoking fags. Great; the one time of the week he got the telly to himself, and it was going to be ruined by drinking, smoking adults.

"Howya, buddy," said one of the men, beckoning him in.

He had long blond hair and big wild eyes that seemed to bulge out of his skull. He looked like a madman, really scary. Seán didn't like him.

"Come in, sit down for yerself," the man said. "Have a chat with us."

He was clearly pissed out of his brain. Seán had learned that phrase two weeks ago when his granddad had come home early from the pub one night while he was staying over. He and his nanny had been watching *The Late Late Show* when his granddad came in with chips. Seán had been thrilled; he loved chips. But his nanny had got very cross and told his granddad they'd already had their tea and he shouldn't be coming in 'pissed out of his brain while the child is here'. This had instantly become Seán's favourite saying. He used it a lot, but only when he was sure no-one was listening. That got boring, though, so one day he decided to try it out in school. It was brilliant: all his friends loved the phrase too, and by morning break everyone was saying it. But it had all backfired on Seán when he'd used it during class. Ursula Conway was the thickest girl in their class, probably the thickest girl in Dooncurra, and when she couldn't remember the longest river in Ireland Seán couldn't resist.

"Ah, Ursula, you must be pissed out of your brain if you don't know that!"

Everyone laughed, and for a second or two Seán felt great; then he saw the teacher's face and knew he was in big trouble. He'd been summoned to the headmaster's office and Mr. Bowe had made him cry. After that, he went back to only using his favourite phrase when he was sure no one was listening.

But this scary man was definitely pissed out of his brain, there was no doubt about it. He had a can in his hand for a start, and there were loads of empty ones on the table – on *their* table. He was still beckoning Seán in, inviting him to sit down beside him. Seán had been taught to be well-mannered around adults so he did as he was told, taking a seat on the couch beside him. The other man, sitting in the armchair in the corner, still hadn't spoken; he just sat there with a stupid grin on his face, seemingly mesmerised by this simple exchange.

"You must be Seán," said the first man, offering his hand to him. Seán solemnly shook it but remained silent. Who were these feckers, and what were they doing in his house on a Saturday morning?

"Nice to meet ya, Seán. My name is Daryl and this here is Chezz. We're friends of your mother's."

"Hello," replied Seán meekly, as the idiot in the corner waved a greeting.

"I hope we're not disturbing you or anything, are we?" asked Daryl.

Seán couldn't tell if he was serious or not but thought it best to answer honestly.

"Well, yeah actually, ye are."

"We are?" cried Daryl, and this time Seán knew he was mocking him. "What are we keeping you from, buddy?"

"You're not my buddy," answered Seán quietly. He could feel himself getting angry at these men. He wished they would go away and never come back.

"Ah, come on now, little man; I'm only trying to be friendly with ya," said Daryl, sounding hurt.

Seán weighed up his options. He still wanted to watch his cartoons. It wouldn't be as good with these two fools here, but if they stayed quiet he might get to see the *Gummi Bears* and *Teenage Mutant Ninja Turtles*. His best bet was to humour them and hope they had the decency to stay quiet while he watched TV.

"I want to watch the cartoons," he said firmly.

"Well, we're not stopping ya, buddy. Go right ahead," declared Daryl, popping open another can.

"I will," said Seán, switching on the TV. "And ye're not to talk while they're on."

"We won't say a word," promised Daryl, but Seán found it hard to believe him.

The other idiot, this Chezz fellah, was still giggling away to himself in the corner. Seán wondered if he was like Richie Hegarty, who had to go to a special school thirty miles away. Richie was always laughing, too, but he was dangerous. One time he'd punched Rebecca Hahessy's cat in the face and nearly killed it. Another time he'd taken out his willy in the middle of Mass. He'd walked up to get his communion, willy hanging out, and no one had said a thing, not even the priest. That's how dangerous Richie was. If this Chezz was anything like Richie Hegarty, then Seán would have to be very careful.

The TV flickered to life and Seán was disappointed to find that the *Gummi Bears* had already begun their weekly adventure. If it hadn't been for these two eejits he wouldn't have missed the start.

"Haha! Look at them mad little fuckers, what are they?" exclaimed Daryl. "Mad lookin' yokes, haha."

Seán didn't answer him. How could you explain what a Gummi Bear was to someone like this?

They both continued to guffaw and hoot with derision as Gruffi and Sunni engaged in an epic struggle with the Carpies. Seán did his best to ignore them but eventually he could take no more. He rose from the couch and turned the volume up a notch or two, glaring at the unwelcome guests.

"Turn that down, for fuck's sake," hissed Daryl. "I can't hear meself think with it."

"Why should I? This is my house!"

"I don't give a fuck whose house it is, I'm not listening to that shite at this hour of the morning," replied Daryl, rising from his seat. He went to switch it off, but Seán was two steps ahead of him and blocked his path.

"You're not turning it off," he said fiercely.

Daryl sized up his pint-sized opponent and decided that it wasn't worth it.

"Fine, boy, watch your fuckin' cartoons," he muttered, backing away and returning to the couch.

That wasn't enough for Seán. He wanted these stupid men out of his house and he wanted them out now.

"Ye have to go now," he said quietly.

"We're not going anywhere," replied Daryl, resembling a sulking child as he sat with his arms folded and his face screwed up in scorn.

"My mammy will kill ye when she gets up."

"Haha! I doubt that very much; your mammy and me are becoming pretty good friends if you must know."

Something in the way he said this stung Seán; there was an unspoken meaning that made him feel bad. Tears welled in his eyes as he struggled to remain calm. He stared at Daryl.

"Get out," he repeated, but the words came out in a squeak. Chezz laughed hysterically in the corner. All of this was just a big joke to him, to both of them. They thought they could just swan in here and wreck his Saturday morning as if it was nothing. But they were wrong; this was his house and he wanted to watch his cartoons. He felt things go fuzzy, his cheeks flushed and his teeth clenched. Suddenly he was upon Daryl, his fury unleashed in all its glory.

"Get out, get out, get out, get out!" he screeched, as Daryl fought to fend him off. Seán flailed wildly at his tormentor, weeping uncontrollably, overcome by his emotions. His frustration deepened when he realised that his spirited attack was making no impression on this big strong man. He wanted to punch his face in and scratch his eyeballs out, but instead his little hands flapped harmlessly on Daryl's arms and torso.

"Calm down, kid, for fuck's sake," croaked Daryl as he dodged another blow intended for his face. "I was only having a laugh with ya."

He managed to peel Seán off him and held up his hands in peace.

"Look, boy, we were only pulling yer leg; no need to go off on one! Friends?"

He held out his hand again to Seán.

Seán, red-faced and puffing, regarded Daryl with utter hatred.

"Fuck you," he whispered.

Daryl Cassidy had seen a lot and done a lot in his twenty-six years, but he was still slightly unnerved by this little boy's show of defiance.

"Come on now, Seán, there's no need to be like that."

But there was every need to be like this, and he wasn't finished yet. He shot his opponent another malevolent look and picked up the ashtray from the table, full to overflowing with their filthy fag butts. He stood in front of Daryl and repeated the words.

"Fuck you!"

Then slowly but surely he tipped the entire contents of the ashtray over Daryl's head. Too stunned to respond, Daryl let the ash and fag butts cascade over his face as Seán shook the last of it onto his straggly mane of blond hair. Satisfied he'd made his statement, he turned to leave, then he heard Chezz chortling away to himself in the corner. Did he ever stop laughing? Seán stopped in his tracks and spun round to face them once more. Fearing another assault, Daryl shifted uneasily in his seat. But he'd already been dealt with. Instead Seán turned his attentions towards the other interloper, who had grown mysteriously silent.

"Fuck you too!" Seán seethed, picking up a half-full can from the table and flinging it at Chezz in one swift movement. It missed by inches, whizzing past his ear and exploding against the wall, sending Smithwicks spraying all over his stupid, gormless face.

As Seán walked away to stunned silence he noted sadly that the *Turtles* had just started. He never missed the *Turtles*; never.

Back in his room, the tears started. He couldn't help it. He wasn't really a tough guy, he'd only pretended he was to get rid of those men. All he wanted was for them to go so he could watch his cartoons and wait for his mammy to get up. But they were still here; he could hear them. They'd probably never leave. What had Daryl said? *Your mammy and me are becoming pretty good friends, if you must know.* Yeah, that was it. The words themselves seemed harmless enough but it was the leering, knowing way in which they'd been delivered that upset him. It made him feel sick and afraid. What was Daryl doing to his mammy? Seán didn't want to share his mammy with anyone else, least of all that horrible bad man. All he wanted to do right now was to go to her room and snuggle up beside her, just the two of them, just like always. He checked the time: 9.35. Maybe it would be okay. He peeked out into the hallway; there was no one there. Maybe they were gone. Maybe he'd scared them off after all. This Saturday could be saved yet! He'd just check in on his mammy and then go back to the sitting-room. He'd have his Frosties, watch the rest of the cartoons and then they'd go to his nanny's. He tiptoed towards his mother's room, but stopped at the door; he could hear voices coming from inside. His stomach turned. It was Daryl, in there with his mammy. He'd woken her on a Saturday morning. Seán listened for his mother's voice. She would surely be giving out to Daryl for waking her up at this hour.

" – he's just a little protective – don't worry about it – I'll speak to him later."

That was his mammy's voice. Seán couldn't believe it; she didn't even sound cross. Daryl had gone in there and told on him and now she was taking *his* side. Seán was going to get into trouble, even though he'd done nothing wrong. Well, feck them; feck the whole lot of them.

He ran back to his bedroom and quickly pulled on his clothes. He didn't know where he was going but he was getting out of here, away from *them*. He emptied his piggy bank onto the bed and swept up the array of coppers and loose change. *I'll show them! I can manage well and good on my own, just you wait and see.* With that he eased open the window, clambered through it and headed out into the early autumn morning.

2

HE'D NEVER RUN AWAY BEFORE, so he wasn't sure where to go. His first instinct had been to go to his nanny's, but that would be no good; they'd just ring his mother and before he knew it, he'd be back home again. He might ask Patrick if he could live in his car for a while. But although Patrick would probably agree, and allow him to live there for as long as he liked, it would only be a matter of time before his mother found out, so that idea was ruled out too. He couldn't rely on anyone else. He had to do this alone. And, now that he was alone, he was his own boss. That meant he could go anywhere he liked. So, Dooncurra Woods it was.

The woods had long been a source of fascination for Seán. They loomed over Dooncurra on three sides, stretching into the nearby mountains and beyond – he called them mountains, but really they were little more than hills. Sometimes when he couldn't sleep Seán would gaze out his bedroom window at the dark, forbidding woods and wonder what happened there when night fell. He imagined great beasts emerging from their dens in search of food, snarling ferociously as they began their hunt. They were huge, unlike anything else in the wild; taller than horses, more vicious than wolves and stronger than the biggest of bears. Covered in long black hair, they were almost invisible at night, their bright red eyes the only thing giving them away. All the smaller animals hated them and scurried to the safety of their homes as soon as the sun dipped below the horizon. But you were never safe when the beasts were around. The foxes, deer, hedgehogs and all the other friendly animals peered out in terror as the beasts sprang into life, bounding across the forest floor, sending firs tumbling from their branches and the few remaining animals back to their hideouts. But there was always one unfortunate mite who hadn't noticed the evening light beginning to fade, who hadn't realised that it was time to take refuge, and by the time they did it was too late. The poor little rabbit or squirrel stood frozen in the middle of the forest, an acorn in their tiny little hands, as the monsters descended upon them. The other animals covered their eyes as the beasts enveloped the defenceless creature, tearing it to shreds, showing no mercy; and when they'd finished it started all over again. It carried on right through the night, the forest's inhabitants hiding in their little houses, willing the sun to come up so that the beasts would disappear back to their murky lairs. But the nights were long, and these great beasts never seemed to get full. They hunted, and hunted, killing and maiming until finally, mercifully, the sun peeped through the trees and they lumbered back to whence they had come. The inhabitants of the forest breathed a collective sigh of relief; they had survived another night, and for that they were grateful.

Seán loved the woods but he'd decided that he never wanted to be there at night. He was very brave when it came to tackling burglars and unwanted house-guests, but great beasts with fiery red eyes were another matter entirely. So he contented himself with walks with his grandfather in the safety of daylight. Sometimes as they walked he would peer into the forest's dark recesses and wonder if the beasts were in there, sleeping, sparing themselves for the night ahead. The thought sent a shudder down his spine. He never told his granddad about the beasts, though; he had enough to be worrying about. Instead Seán pestered him with question after question about other things that interested him. "How many squirrels do you think live here, Granddad? How high is the tallest tree in the forest, Granddad? Could you beat a deer in a fight, Granddad?" This would go on and on until his granddad, exasperated, sent him off on a wild goose chase in the hope of getting a minute's peace and quiet. These missions included, among others, locating the pot of gold at the end of a rainbow, finding the unicorn that lived in the trees behind the picnic area, and staying silent long enough for a friendly fox called Charlie to come out and talk to them. None of these challenges kept Seán occupied for very long, so after a brief hiatus Noel was back fielding a barrage of unanswerable questions from his beloved grandson. There would be no granddad to answer his queries today, though; if Seán had any more questions they would have to wait until he'd finished running away.

Having decided on his destination, all that was left to do was purchase some provisions. He couldn't hope to survive life on the road without some food in his belly. It was just as well he'd remembered to bring some money, then. Seán dug into his pockets and carefully extracted his life savings: a couple of twenties, a few tens, and ooh, a big fifty! A grand total of £1.29. He was loaded. Bartley's newsagents was nearby; he'd stock up there and then set off for the woods. He regularly went to the shop on his own, getting fags and milk for his mammy, so they wouldn't suspect a thing when they saw he wasn't accompanied by an adult. He marched confidently into the small, musky shop, the jingle of the bell signalling his arrival. The hope had been that Mrs. Bartley would be working today. She was lovely, and didn't seem to mind when he took ages to decide which colour Bonbons he wanted. But she wasn't there. Instead of her welcoming smile he was greeted by her husband, Bulldog Bartley, the grumpiest man in all Ireland.

"Hello, Mr. Bartley. How are you today?" he enquired cheerily.

"Hmmph," came the response from behind the counter. Mr. Bartley was propped up on a high stool with the morning papers laid out in front of him. He was wearing his glasses and had a little pen in his hand. Seán knew what he was doing; he'd seen this before.

"Any tips for me, Mr. Bartley?"

Mr. Bartley glared at him from over the top of his glasses, his jaw jutting out, jowls hanging limply beneath; just like a bulldog.

"What tips do you want, boy?"

"For the horses."

Bulldog stared at him intently for a couple of moments, and then wordlessly returned to his paper. That was that, then; he didn't have any tips.

Seán returned to the matter at hand: getting provisions. What was it to be: a first-aid kit? Some bottled water? Or those cheap noodles his mother got when they were broke? These were all fine suggestions but boring ones. He never got to spend this amount of money in one go, so he wasn't going to waste it on noodles and bottles of water. He scanned the wall behind Bulldog which housed the jars of sweets. There was so much to choose from: Pear Drops, Strawberry Sherbets, Bullseyes, Chocolate Mice, and then the Bonbons, which came in pink, white, yellow and green. This was going to take some time.

"Hey, young fella, if you're not buying anything get the fuck outa here."

"I've got money, Mr. Bartley. See?" He held out his hand, displaying his riches. That seemed to satisfy the shopkeeper. He returned to his paper, keeping a watchful on his young customer.

Seán continued his ruminations: Jelly Babies, Flogs, Milk Teeth, Kola Cubes, Clove Rock – ugh, not Clove Rock, that was disgusting – Watermelon Twist Kisses, Fried Eggs, Dolly Mixture. He knew all their names off by heart. But that didn't make it any easier to decide what to get. Finally, though, after ten more minutes of perusing and increasingly complex mental calculations, he came to a decision.

"Mr. Bartley?"

Bulldog shifted the paper ever so slightly to the right and fixed Seán with a glare. Seán took this as a response and forged ahead.

"Could I have 129 penny sweets, please?"

Bulldog's expression didn't change one iota. He simply shifted the paper back and continued reading. Was that a 'yes'? Seán stood there a second, waiting for Bulldog to get his fat arse off the stool, but he didn't budge. Maybe he hadn't heard.

"Mr. Bartley?"

No response. He didn't even move.

"Could I ..."

Still no response. How was he going to get provisions if this fecker wouldn't even serve him?

But then Bulldog came to life, slamming down his pen and leaning out over the counter.

"C'mere," he said gruffly, motioning for Seán to come close.

Seán obliged and walked expectantly towards Bulldog. At last, a bit of service!

He stood in front of the stout, bald man with the pudgy nose and the jowly face, and waited for the sweets to be dished out. But instead of filling up a bag with Black Jacks, Jelly Babies and Fizzy Cola Bottles, Bulldog remained where he was; hung over the counter with a big red head on him. At this rate, Seán would have to go elsewhere for his provisions. Bulldog jabbed his stubby finger into Seán's chest.

"What kind of a fuckin' eejit do ya think I am?"

Seán pondered this for a second. Was he expected to answer? What would he say – an awful eejit, a big, fuckin' eejit or just a regular, normal eejit? None of these sounded right so he played it safe.

"I dunno, Mr. Bartley. What kind of an eejit are ya?"

This seemed to anger him. His face grew even redder as he repeatedly jabbed his thick, sausage-like finger into Seán's chest.

"You think you're so clever, you and your little mates, comin' in here robbin' my sweets and upsetting Vera. Well, no more. No fuckin' more!"

These last few words were delivered with an extra hard jab to his chest and Seán recoiled in pain.

"But I've never robbed sweets from you, Mr. Bartley; honest." And this was true, mostly. There had been that one time after Mass when he'd stolen a Bounty after being dared by Mattie O'Halloran. But even then he'd thrown it away. Not because of guilt, but because he didn't like Bounties; he didn't like anything with coconuts in them.

"Go in and ask Mrs. Bartley; go on, she'll tell ya," he continued, indignant now.

"Oh, yeah, you'd love that, ya little bollix. I go inside and by the time I come back there's not a sweet left in the fuckin' shop. Ya must think I'm an awful eejit."

Again with the eejit questions, thought Sean, this fella is obsessed with being an eejit. Enough of this messing around. He had some running away to do and he couldn't waste any more time here talking to this, well, eejit.

"Lookit, Mr. Bartley, I have £1.29 here. All I want is 129 penny sweets and I'll be on me way." He plonked the money down on the counter and stepped away from his tormentor.

Bulldog looked at him once more before scooping up the money and popping it in the till. For a second, Seán thought he was going to sit back down with his paper. Instead he ripped a little plastic bag from the wall and went over to the penny sweets.

Seán followed him over, ready to count along as every sweet went into the bag. He needn't have bothered. Bulldog put one of his big, fat paws into the Milk Teeth box and threw a few dozen into the bag, repeating this with several of the other sweets before tossing the bag on the counter.

"Now," he growled, "fuck off."

Seán didn't need to be told twice. He was out the door and halfway up the road before Bulldog was back in his seat. Once he'd reached a safe distance, Seán took a look inside the bag. He could scarcely believe his luck; there had to be at least three hundred sweets inside. *Aboy, Bulldog, ya big feckin' eejit!* And with that he skipped merrily up the hill towards Dooncurra Woods.

3

THE ROAD LEADING TO THE woods would be busy on a Saturday. Every weekend cars weaved up and down its narrow, potholed expanse before depositing picnicking families, mobs of feral children and outdoor enthusiasts into the parking area. From there the crowds made their way into the woods, sticking to the approved paths and trails, the hubbub dying down as they gradually dispersed into smaller groups. Seán wanted to avoid these crowds. The last thing he needed was some nosy parker asking him where his mam and dad were. His plan was to take a different route, one which involved several short cuts and a couple of detours through muddy fields; once he'd reached his destination he'd be far away from the masses, from interfering adults and their stupid questions. Stuffing the bag of sweets into his pocket, he took a quick look around. No one was watching and there were no cars in sight. He vaulted over a wall, landing in a field populated by a few dozy cows. The grass was sopping wet and almost up to his knees. If only he'd brought his wellies, but instead he had his brand-new runners on, the ones his mother had told him were for good wear only. She'd kill him if she knew, but she would never know because he was on the run now and she'd never find him.

He carried on across the field, his feet squelching beneath him as he made his way past the inquisitive glances of the grazing cattle. *Hello, cows, don't mind me; just out for a stroll is all. Enjoy your grass.* On reaching the edge of the field, he looked for a way into the adjoining one. There should have been a gate, but if there was he couldn't see it, so he had to navigate his way through a cluster of briars and large thorny bushes. By the time he'd squeezed through to the other side he was sporting several cuts and grazes on his face, and his jacket had been torn in several places. It didn't matter, though; he only had himself to answer to now. He carried on through another couple of fields, hiding from a tractor on one occasion, until he reached the one which would take him to the edge of the woods. He'd learned about this route while out rambling with Patrick. It had been an amazing day. They'd taken Hughie, Patrick's Irish Setter, and spent the day roaming through the fields, the woods and loads of other cool places Seán had never seen before. They'd even found a quarry. He would have loved to have gone back there but he couldn't remember where it was. He wasn't even sure if he was going the same way as they had that day. But the woods were there in the distance, so he must be on the right track.

Finally, after more fields and more scrambling through ditches and undergrowth, he made it to the outskirts of the forest. A few thin, bare trees signalled the beginning of Dooncurra Woods. He was there. He had made it. He hurried on until he reached a point where all he could see were trees. Now he was free, in the middle of the woods, far away from everyone; out on his own. This was great. His instinct was to run around a bit, climb some trees and just revel in his freedom. But first he had to do something about his clothes. His jeans were stuck to his skin and his runners were completely soaked. If Huckleberry Finn were in this kind of pickle, he would simply have stripped off and hung out his clothes to dry in the hot Missouri sun. But Seán wasn't in Missouri, he was in Ireland, and it was the middle of October.

Even now, at its highest point, the sun offered little warmth and very few beams of light penetrated the forest's canopy. It wasn't great drying weather; even Seán could see that. Anyway, what was he supposed to do? Amble around the woods in his underpants while his jeans dried on a branch? No, thanks. Instead, he compromised. He took off his runners and socks, pulled his jeans up to his knees and continued on his way. The damp, cloying earth was cold on his exposed feet, but he'd get used to it. Things like this were just part of life on the road. His next task was finding somewhere to sit so he could eat his sweets. He found the perfect spot beneath a large oak. Its thick, gnarled roots stretched out across the forest floor, providing him with a suitable nook in which to sit. He even had armrests on both sides.

"Ah, this is the life," he said, a shaft of light warming his bare feet. He was hungry; starving, in fact. That whole thing with Daryl had completely ruined his routine. He'd had no breakfast; no bowl of Frosties. And no lunch, no soldiers or eggs to dip them into. He should have had two meals under his belt by now but he'd had none. Just as well he'd come prepared. Pulling the bag of sweets out of his pocket, he marvelled again at the sheer volume of delights within and settled down for his first meal of the day. This was definitely the best thing about life on the road: he could have sweets for breakfast, lunch and dinner, and there was no one around to tell him he couldn't.

He munched away on the sweets, tackling them with gusto, sometimes putting three or four into his mouth at the same time. This was great, this was the life: out on his own, doing whatever he wanted, and no stupid adults bossing him around. After a few minutes of sitting and eating, however, he began to feel lonely. It was no fun being free if you had no one to share it with. Why hadn't he brought Millie, his own dog, a black Labrador cross? She was his best friend in the entire world – well, her or Mikey Nolan who lived in number 25. Either of them would have done him. But he hadn't had time to plan any of this. If he had he would have brought wellies, and Millie, and Mikey Nolan. Mikey was probably still watching cartoons, and Millie was most likely asleep in the shed. He worried about her now that he was gone. Who would feed her? And who would rub her belly, making her hind legs jerk in excitement? Certainly not Daryl. He probably didn't even like dogs. Maybe Millie would come looking for Seán. She would notice his absence and, worried out of her mind, hurdle the five-foot wall that surrounded their back garden. Then she would press her nose to the ground and seek out her master, following the exact same path he had taken until they were back together and Seán had someone to accompany him on the road. He really missed Millie, and Mikey.

If Mikey were here now, they'd be having the best time ever. Mikey was a year older than Seán and really strong and brave. When they climbed trees together, Mikey would always go higher than Seán. He'd nimbly traverse the uppermost branches until he found himself at the very top, at which point he would yell out loud: "Mikey Nolan, the best tree-climber in the whole world." Seán would nod his agreement from further down the tree; Mikey was a brilliant tree-climber. If he were here, he'd have loads of ideas about how to survive in the wilderness. He'd try to take charge but that would be okay – he was a year older, after all. Mikey could be the leader and Seán his trusted companion. Together they'd build a camp deep in the woods with a treehouse to sleep in at night. Then they'd hunt rabbits, collect berries and build a huge fire to warm them while they ate. The beasts were afraid of fire so they wouldn't have to worry about being attacked while they stuffed themselves. But Seán wasn't sure how long Mikey would stick it out. He had loads of brilliant toys and his father drove a car, so chances were he'd get homesick after a couple of days. He'd start whinging and Seán would have no choice but to banish him from the camp and continue on alone. He didn't need that kind of drama. This was serious business. He was running away, and he had no intention of ever returning home.

4

It had been after two by the time Sinéad had ushered out the last of the drinkers. She'd practically had to shove them out the door. Thankfully Nigel had offered to close up, allowing her to head home at something approaching a godly hour. Usually she'd get a taxi, but Daryl Cassidy had offered her a lift. He was probably over the limit, but it wasn't far. I guess you could say Daryl was her boyfriend now. They had been seeing each other for the past three months and things were going well. She hadn't allowed him to sleep over yet, though. She didn't want to expose Seán to this new coupling until it was unavoidable. But last night she'd been too tired to argue when he asked if he and his brother could come in for a nightcap. She'd stayed up with them for a while, but after a couple of glasses of wine she could barely keep her eyes open and had retired to bed. Daryl had wanted to come with her but she'd flatly refused. They could stay and finish whatever drink they had, but they were to be gone by morning. That was the last thing she remembered until she found herself being rudely awakened some hours later.

"Sinéad, wake up! Wake up, Sinéad, will ya!"

She resisted with all her might, trying her utmost to cling on to sleep's warm embrace, but whoever was trying to wake her wasn't about to give up easily. Reluctantly she opened her eyes, resigned to her fate. How many times had she told Seán never to wake her on a Saturday? But it wasn't Seán; it was Daryl.

"Wake up, Sinéad. That child of yours has gone mad!"

She propped herself up on one elbow and surveyed the scene. It was daylight. What the hell was Daryl still doing here? What was he saying about Seán? And why did he have a dirty fag butt in his hair?

"What are you doing still here? I told you to be gone by the morning."

Daryl opened his mouth to speak but was interrupted by Sinéad, now wide awake and ready for battle.

"And what are you saying about Seán? He's not ready to meet you yet. I told you that!"

"Meself and Chezz fell asleep in the living-room. We'd had a skinful."

Sinéad looked at him doubtfully. "Then what?"

"Yer young fella came down and told us to get out 'cos he wanted to watch his cartoons."

Sinéad smiled as she imagined her indignant son tackling the two Cassidy boys.

"So why didn't ye go?" she asked.

"We were going to but then he just went nuts, started firing drink all around the place and tipped the fuckin' ashtray over me head."

Sinéad giggled as she plucked the fag butt from Daryl's hair. "He can be fiery all right; gets that from his mother."

"Well I know it," said Daryl, smiling.

"Look, ye'd better go," she continued. "I'll deal with him; he's just a little protective, that's all. I'll speak to him later and maybe we can arrange a proper meeting for ye two, eh?"

"All right. I'll call you later, okay?"

She kissed him on the cheek and shooed him out of the bedroom. Moments later she heard the front door close. They could at least have tidied up a bit before leaving. The thought of the mess awaiting her sent her crawling back to bed. She'd get up in a few minutes, clear away the cans and bottles and the empty pizza boxes, and go talk to her son. But first she'd just close her eyes for a second; it was early yet.

*

Sinéad awoke with a start, feeling guilty but not sure why. She checked the clock on the bedside locker: 12.45. *Fuck's sake.* Why hadn't he woken her up? Probably too engrossed in his cartoons; but no, they would be over by now. He always woke her at eleven on a Saturday; as soon as the credits rolled on *He-man*, he was up like a rocket. With a growing sense of unease, she slid out of bed and wrapped a dressing-gown around her. In the living-room she called, "Seán? Seány? What are you up to?"

No answer. He must be in his room, sulking probably. Nothing that a few runny eggs and toasted soldiers wouldn't solve. But before she could even think about making Seán's lunch, she had to tackle the mess left by her guests. Daryl had actually made an effort to clean up. A token effort. The living-room wasn't too bad – save for the cigarette butts littered on the couch and a couple of errant bottles lying on the floor. But they'd just moved everything into the kitchen and left it there. Empty beer cans lined the worktop, the sink was full of dirty glasses and the two pizza boxes were attracting attention from a handful of meandering flies. It wasn't the biggest mess she'd ever seen, but she hated seeing her little house like this. It was supposed to be a home for her and her boy, not a den of iniquity. She resolved to spend the day on her hands and knees scrubbing the smell of alcohol out of the house. Maybe Seán could tidy his room while she did it. She opened the back door to let in some air and noticed that the shed door was still locked. Why hadn't Millie been let out? Seán always let her out first thing on a Saturday morning.

She tiptoed across the wet concrete and released the latch on the shed door. Millie came bolting out, almost knocking her over. Once she'd relieved herself the dog returned to Sinéad and looked at her questioningly. *Where was Seán? And why had she been left in the shed till this hour?* But Sinéad was too busy filling up the bin to deal with the dog's queries. She returned to the kitchen, closing the door behind her. Already the place looked better. Putting the kettle on to boil, she went to check on Seán. Perhaps this would be a good time to explain about herself and Daryl. She tapped quietly on his door before entering.

"Seán?"

He wasn't there. The bed was unmade and the room was a mess. That was normal, but a few anomalies set the alarm bells ringing. His runners were gone, the ones she'd got him for 'good wear', only to be worn on Sundays. And the clothes he'd had on yesterday weren't lying on the floor like they should have been; they were nowhere to be seen. Strangest of all, the window was open. He never opened the window, he was always complaining about the cold. For reasons unknown to herself she stuck her head out of it, as if he might be sitting beneath looking up at her. All she saw was Millie running around the backyard like a lunatic. Where the fuck had he got to?

She tried to remain calm. He'd probably just gone to the shop, or over to Mikey Nolan's house. At a stretch, he might have set out for his grandmother's without her; punishment for inviting those strange men into their house. But he never went anywhere without asking her. He wouldn't even go out to the ice cream van without permission. He could be a cheeky little scamp when he wanted to be, but there were certain rules he never broke. The more she thought about it, the more she feared his disappearance was related to the incident with Daryl. If only she hadn't gone back to sleep; if only she'd checked on him straight away. Cursing herself, she dressed and went out the front door. With any luck, he'd be over at the Nolan's' house. She'd knock on the door and there he'd be, bold as brass, wondering what all the fuss was about. As she walked up the drive she scanned their house for signs of life, signs of Seán; screams coming from inside, injured children, fleeing parents, emergency services outside: all the things you'd expect from a house containing Seán McLoughlin. But it was eerily quiet. As she stood at the porch waiting for someone to answer her knock, she already knew he wasn't there. It was Mikey who came to the door.

"Howya, Mrs. McLoughlin."

"Mikey, is Seán here with you?"

"No, I haven't seen him since yesterday, Mrs. McLoughlin. I was gonna call over for him, actually, but – "

But Sinéad was already gone, hurrying back down the drive towards her own house. Now she was getting worried.

5

THERE WERE ONLY A COUPLE of houses in the entire estate that had phones, and Sinéad's wasn't one of them. The Glovers a few doors down had one, but they were weird and a bit creepy. She'd had to go over there once to take a call from Patrick, who'd been pissed drunk and stranded in some faraway location. As she'd tentatively followed Mrs. Glover into their house, she'd thought of all the horror films she'd seen and how gullible most of the victims were. This was how killers enticed strangers into their homes, with stuff like this. A phantom phone call. Something so simple. And once she was inside, that'd be the end of her; she'd be down into the cellar with the rest of the Glovers' victims. Despite her paranoia, she had got out unscathed. The conversation with her younger brother had been a brief one (ring Mammy and stop being such a baby) and she was back home safe and sound within minutes. The Glovers hadn't murdered her that time, but who was to say they wouldn't the second time around? The thought of making an outgoing call from their home terrified her. Would Mr. Glover have her on the clock? That'll be two pounds fifty, please, Sinéad – or maybe you'd like to pay me another way?

There was a young couple who had only moved into the estate the previous summer; they also had a phone. But she barely knew them, and she only knew they had a phone because Maeve Nolan had told her. How Maeve knew such things was beyond her, but she was a reliable source and if she said they had a phone then it was true. It would be just as quick to walk the couple of miles to her mother's house and see if Seán had turned up there, but she didn't want to involve her parents if she could avoid it. She didn't want them to see how she'd failed. How she'd managed to lose the one child she had. Classic Sinéad. Another vintage piece of parenting from the worst mother ever to breathe air.

There was a phone box just down the road, but she'd have to ring and then get her mother to call back; read out the number to her, get Patricia to jot it down, and then wait an interminable length of time for her to dial it. No, she'd just go there; all this pissing about with phones would only slow things down. Trying to ignore the calamitous scenarios playing out in her head, she wrote a little note for Seán, stuck it on the fridge and began the walk to her parents' house.

Gone to Nanny's. Come up when you read this.

She'd never had to leave out a note for him before – he was only seven, after all. This was probably the first time since he'd been born that she didn't know his exact location and what he was doing; but he was almost certainly at her parent's house. He had to be.

As she hurried up the road she scanned her surroundings, looking for something, anything, which might point to his presence. There were a couple of old ladies at the bus stop near their house, but they hadn't seen him. Neither had Mr. Talbot, who seemed a bit put out when she carried on before he could tell her how his fuchsias were coming along. She ducked into the local newsagent's, Bartley's, to see if anyone in there had seen him. Mr. Bartley was serving, or 'Bulldog' Bartley as they'd called him when they were young.

"Hello, Mr. Bartley. You haven't seen my Seán at all today, have you?"

As usual he barely registered her presence, never mind answered her question. Unabashed, she continued. "About this high, dirty blond hair, cheeky little smile? Ring any bells?"

Bulldog shuffled his paper, cleared his throat and continued to ignore her. What was wrong with him, seriously? Losing patience, she approached the counter and stood directly in front of the seated shopkeeper.

"HELLO, MR. BARTLEY. I'M TALKING TO YOU."

This seemed to do the trick. He slowly lowered his newspaper and looked at her for the first time.

"No need to shout; I can hear you well enough," he said calmly.

"Well, why didn't you answer me then?"

If he wanted an argument he'd bloody well get one.

Bulldog got up from his seat and walked over to a section of the shop which apparently needed urgent attention.

"We get lots of little boys in here. How can you expect me to remember all of them?" he muttered, straightening out some magazines.

"I'm not asking you to remember them all, just mine. Come on, you must know him by now; he's always in here."

"Is he one of those bold boys, the ones that give my wife guff every time they're in here?"

"No, he is not. He's seven years old and he loves sweets, especially penny sweets."

"Ah," replied Bulldog. "The 'penny sweet' boy."

"So you do know him," said Sinéad, relieved to be getting somewhere. "Was he in here today?"

"Oh, he was, the little shite; gave me an awful time, so he did," moaned Bulldog.

"How long ago? Which way did he go?"

"Wanted me to hand-pick sweets for him, and me with my back so bad," he continued, warming to his theme.

He shuffled back behind the counter, ignoring the distressed woman who was now affixing him with a deadly stare. As he took his seat, he noticed the deranged look in her eyes and decided to be forthright while he still could.

"It was a couple of hours ago. I think he went up the hill."

Sinéad turned on her heels and left without a word.

Bulldog winced as the door slammed shut. He rubbed his back and returned to his paper with a dismissive grunt.

Sinéad carried on up the hill as Bulldog had suggested. At least the trail was getting warm now. He must have gone to her parent's house; he had no other business coming up this way. She jogged the final few metres past the turn-off to the woods and into the estate she'd lived in for most of her life. Their house was at the very end of the avenue, right where the cul-de-sac bottomed out into a wide, circular space where her father usually parked his car. His red Nissan was the first thing she looked for whenever she walked into the estate, but today it was nowhere to be seen. He rarely drove anywhere on his own, so if he was out then her mother was gone with him. Seán must have called here and they'd gone off somewhere together. That was it. Panic over. But they wouldn't have gone anywhere without telling her, they knew better – didn't they?

She carried on to the house and around to the back garden, half hoping to find him kicking a ball against the side of the house, or hidden beneath some bushes firing shots at an unseen foe, but it was deserted. Sinéad tried the back door, it opened; there was someone here at least.

"Seán?"

A used cereal bowl sat on the kitchen table, a carton of milk beside it.

"Seán?"

She opened the living-room door. Patrick lay on the couch, he appeared to be nursing a hangover.

"Is Seán here?"

"Huh?"

"Is Seán here?"

"No."

"Where are Mam and Dad?"

"Dunno."

"Did they bring him somewhere?"

"Who?"

"Seán!"

"What are you on about, Nades?"

Sinéad pulled the cushion from beneath her brother's head, causing his head to bump against the arm-rest.

"Ow, fuck's sake, Sinéad!"

"I don't know where Seán is, Patrick. I can't find him."

Her younger brother sat up straight, "Seán's missing?"

Sinéad nodded, tears welling in her eyes.

"When did you last see him?"

"Not since last night. I was just in the shop and Bulldog said he came up this way."

Patrick stared at her a moment, rubbing the spot where his head had hit the arm-rest.

"Why did you leave him out on his own, he's only seven for fuck's sake!"

"I didn't leave him, he ran off," Sinéad protested.

"Ran off?"

"Yeah. I'll explain later," she said, picking up Patrick's runners and dropping them at his feet.

He put them on without complaint, already guessing where they were going. It was obvious. Bulldog had told he'd carried on up the hill. He wasn't here, and he fuckin' loved those woods, so that was where he'd gone. Simple; elementary, my dear McLoughlin. Knowing he was in the woods and actually finding him, however, were two different things entirely.

6

SEÁN DUG HIS HAND INTO the bag of sweets. Nothing. Empty. They couldn't be all gone already, he'd only been getting going. He peered into the bag; all gone. Feck. His entire rations depleted within the first hour. This wasn't good. And he was thirsty now, too. He really wanted a cup of tea, a cup of his nanny's tea. Her house wasn't far from here; if he wanted, he could just trek back through the fields and be there drinking tea in less than an hour. But no, he was running away from home. He didn't need them, or their tea. There was probably a pond or a lake nearby that he could drink from. That was what you did when you were in the wild; you improvised. He'd find a watering-hole, drink his fill and then set out some traps. The traps were for the rabbits. He didn't really want to kill the rabbits. He liked rabbits. But he had no choice, really; he had to eat something. So he would capture some rabbits, maybe a hare or two, skin them and then cook them over the fire he planned to light later. Once he'd eaten, he'd retire to the hammock he'd have built from leaves and branches and settle in for a good night's kip. The fire would have to be tended to a couple of times overnight, though, to keep the beasts away. But all that could wait; he wanted to do some exploring first. He made a mental note of his location, and set off into the woods, barefoot and full of sugar.

7

JUST LIKE HER SON, SINÉAD had been fascinated by the woods as a child. For as long as she could remember her father had taken long, solitary walks there every evening. One day, after years of begging, she was finally allowed to go with him. Then, of course, because she was going, they had suddenly all wanted to go. Noel had shaken his head bitterly and told them to get their coats, the one bit of peace and quiet he got now ruined, potentially forever. But he had a plan; he would walk the legs off his children, walk so fast and so far that none of them would ever ask to come again. It had almost worked. Patrick was the first to succumb; ten minutes in and he was asking to go home. Valerie was next to pull up, abruptly sitting down in the middle of the path and declaring herself bored; then Adele, an imaginary stone in her shoe the cause of her malaise. But, try as he might, he couldn't shake Sinéad. He really put the pedal down, getting out of breath himself, but she carried on, grinning at him affectionately, having a great time. In the end he'd been the one to admit defeat, tersely suggesting they head for home when he felt the sweat begin to roll down his forehead.

From that day forth they had become a twosome, a pair of hiking enthusiasts; father and daughter roaming in the wild. It became their thing. Some parents played football with their children, others did arts and crafts, but Noel and his daughter walked. It wasn't just the walking, though. It was being outdoors, at one with nature. Breathing in the fresh air, listening to the birds, marvelling at sunsets, half-moons and full moons. Sinéad had found her childhood obsession. While her sisters received dolls and dresses for birthdays and Christmas, she got books about trees and bird-watching, binoculars and hiking boots. Her parents were happy to indulge her; any hobby which allowed them to keep such a close eye on their daughter was to be actively encouraged. The only problem was containing her enthusiasm; she wanted to be out walking all the time. The small public walkways she and her father used to circle were now considered childish. There was a whole world out there to explore; how could they expect her to walk around the family-approved paths for the rest of her life? So Noel took her round the rarely-used hiker's trail, the one which stretched around the entire circumference of the woods – all eight miles of it. It nearly killed him in the process, but his little Nades was happy and that was all that mattered. They got her a camera, a second-hand Nikon, and she began documenting her adventures: taking pictures of trees, sky-lines, flowers, anything which caught her eye.

But then, almost as soon as it began, it was over. Adolescence came hurtling into her life and suddenly Sinéad was interested in wildlife of a different kind. Their walks became less frequent; Noel always had to ask her now. And when she did go she was distant and uninterested, her mind full of mystery and strangeness. Then one morning he'd woken up to find his little Nades gone, having flown the nest without any warning. There would be no more walks together now. He was back to going alone.

But when she'd come back, when she'd unexpectedly, amazingly, re-turned, they'd resumed their pastime; not every evening as before, but at least a couple of times a week and always after dinner on a Sunday. Seán had come too, at first in his buggy but recently on his own two feet. They'd stuck to the shorter walkways during these excursions, the ones which delved in and out of the forest's more picturesque areas and were dotted with small picnic areas and public amenities. As far as Sinéad was aware her son had never been beyond these small paths, so it was there she planned to begin her search. Even though it was a damp, dismal October afternoon, there would still be plenty of people milling around the woods; surely one of them would have seen her boy.

There was a dozen or so cars parked loosely in the lay-by, and some of the early morning walkers were returning to their vehicles for the drive home. Sinéad and Patrick approached one couple, ruddy-cheeked and radiant from their walk, but they hadn't seen Seán. Neither had the family squeezing into their car, nor the middle-aged man walking his dog or the boisterous gang of kids. Undeterred, they started up the walkway, calling out Seán's name as they went. They hurried along the path, continuing to call Seán's name and asking passers-by if they'd seen him. With each negative response Sinéad's heart sank a little further.

Patrick did his best to keep her spirits up,

"Any second now, Shinners, you just wait."

"He'll surely be along here."

"There's only so far he could have went, Sinéad, don't panic."

But after an hour of fruitless searching those reassurances began to ring hollow. She looked at her brother and saw the despondency in his eyes, knew that he no longer believed the things he was saying, and that the situation was growing out of their control.

The anxiety which she'd been holding at bay spewed forth. Her cries grew ever louder; she was now screeching her son's name at the top of her lungs. A concerned onlooker offered his assistance; taken aback, Sinéad could only whisper her thanks, leaving Patrick to direct the helpful citizen to another part of the woods. Another person joined them, then two more. They spread out; some going up ahead, others deviating off the beaten track. Their numbers swelled, more and more people alerted to the cause; the continual shouting of Seán's name drawing them to the crowd like moths to a flame. By the time Sinéad and Patrick completed a circuit and arrived back at the car-park there was upwards of twenty people gathered there, and more were joining the ranks with each passing minute. Sinéad didn't recognise many of them, did they know who she was? Did they know it was her son they were out looking for? One well-to-do gentleman had appointed himself party leader, he approached Sinéad, holding out his hand to greet her. "Sinéad, right?"

"Yes."

"I'm David. I hear your boy's gone missing."

"Yes. I think he's in the woods somewhere."

"Well, we won't be long about finding him, there's plenty of us here. Best to get moving before dark, though."

He was right, it was four in the afternoon and the sun was beginning to slouch low in the sky. In a couple of hours the woods would be completely dark. She imagined Seán alone and afraid somewhere in the forest, and her heart sundered in two. Worse still, he might not even be in the woods; Bulldog could have got it wrong. Someone might have snatched him, he could be miles away by now in the back of a van, tied up and gagged. *Jesus Christ.*

The man, this David fellah, was talking to her; something about torches and blankets and flasks of tea. She nodded her agreement, feeling numb now, wanting someone to hold her. Patrick had moved into the crowd, issuing orders of his own. Sinéad spun round, resisting the urge to fall to her knees and begin screaming her son's name at the top of her lungs.

"There's a phone in the ranger's cabin; I've used it before," David said.

A phone, thought Sinéad, *but who will we call?*

"Come on," he said, taking her by the arm.

She found herself walking beside him, struggling to keep us as he strode towards the cabin.

"Thanks for helping, David," she mumbled, remembering her manners despite the gravity of the situation.

"Don't be silly, Sinéad. Once I speak with the sergeant we'll get a proper search going, have Seán back in no time."

Sinéad stifled a sob and allowed herself to be led into the cabin.

8

MUCH TO SEÁN'S DISAPPOINTMENT, THIS new unexplored part of the woodland was much the same as the bits he'd already seen. There had been some incredible trees, trees which even Mikey Nolan would have struggled to scale, and a creek with a thick green surface, which he'd pierced with rocks and sticks. That was about it, though. There hadn't been a stream or lake for him to drink from (he'd considered drinking from the creek but judged it unfit for human consumption), nor had there been a secret network of underground tunnels like he'd hoped. And now, after just a couple of hours on the run, he was bored. He sat dejectedly on a stump, picking the dirt from between his toes. His feet were filthy and his jeans, which had been rolled up to his knees, now flopped limply against his ankles, still wet through. Unsurprisingly, he was getting cold now too. He decided he'd had enough. It had been good while it lasted and he might do it again sometime, but he was fed up with running away. He was going home. His mammy would be delighted to see him. They'd laugh about his little excursion and all would be well again. He'd have to explain why he'd tipped the ashtray over Daryl's head and thrown the beer can at that other fool, but she'd understand; he'd been protecting her in his duty as the man of the house. He hadn't known those fellas, and he'd had to resort to desperate measures to combat them. They'd threatened him and he'd acted in self-defence. With any luck his mammy would be proud of him and buy him an ice cream by way of reward. Sometimes violence paid off; not often, but sometimes.

He heard rustling to his left; movement, something fast. He didn't want to look, afraid of what he might see. It could be a beast. It wasn't dark yet, but for all he knew they came out early at the weekends. Perhaps they'd been following him the whole time, waiting for their moment. And that moment was now. Here he was sitting on a stump, not a stick, a rock, nor a weapon of any description to his name. Defenceless. He really wanted his mammy now. There was that noise again. It sounded like something small. He hoped it was something small. A little otter that wanted to be his friend. That would be nice. Ollie the otter. They would hang out together and he would stroke Ollie's soft fur. Ollie would find him nuts to eat and they would munch on them together, smiling away at how lovely the nuts were. Did otters eat nuts? He couldn't remember. His brain was tired and he couldn't think straight; the comedown from his sugar high was affecting his thought processes. The noise came again, but this time he saw what had made it: a little squirrel. What a relief! It wasn't a beast after all, just a little squirrel. Not a red one, though, it was grey; they were the baddies, according to his granddad. They spread disease among the reds and stole all their food. He didn't like grey squirrels, and he certainly didn't like this one.

The squirrel stood on its hind legs staring at him. Seán stared back balefully. This Mexican stand-off lasted for all of thirty seconds before the squirrel, curiosity sated, darted off in another direction. Buoyed by his victory, Seán shouted after it. "Get out of here, and stop killing all the reds!" That was him told. But this fleeting contact with another life form had a detrimental effect on his spirits. Now he felt lonely. Why couldn't the squirrel have stayed a while? He shouldn't have shouted at it like that; now it would never come back. It was probably going home to bed, because it was bedtime in the woods now. They were all snuggling up in their dens and hideouts, all the little animals; cosy and warm, their bellies full of nuts. And here he was miles from home, sitting on a tree stump, without any shoes or socks. It was time to go. It was definitely time to go.

The question now was 'which way?' Which way was home? He stood on the stump and looked around, to his left and to his right, in front of him and behind him. But the forest had grown dim and gloomy, and he could barely see more than a few yards in any direction. Even then, all he could see were trees. If he could only find the creek: once he'd found that, he'd be able to find the tree he'd climbed and before he knew it he'd be back at the start where he'd left his runners. He got down from the stump and squinted his eyes into the distance. That looked like the creek up there. He hopped down from the stump and trotted in the direction of what he hoped was the creek. Already he was imagining his return home; a hero's welcome. How happy they'd all be to see him! After what seemed like an age, though, he still hadn't found the creek. Maybe it wasn't over here after all. What if he should have gone the other way? Should he turn back or continue on? He was really thirsty now, thirstier than he'd ever been in his whole life. If he did find the creek he was going to drink from it, green ooze or no green ooze. Where was it, though? He spun around helplessly. A bird fluttered violently in the trees, frightening him. The sun was rapidly disappearing now, its fading light completely enveloped by the darkness of the woods. With a growing sense of panic, Seán realised that he had no idea where he was or how to get out of the forest.

Now he was really scared. He began to mewl softly. "Mammy, Mammy, Mammy, MAMMY! MAAMMMEEEEE!!"

His shrill cries reverberated around the forest, but they didn't reach their intended target. There were no friendly beings within earshot, only beasts and grey squirrels. He dropped to the ground, curling up into the foetal position. There was no escape now. Before long the beasts would be out hunting for food, and it wasn't very often they found little boys lying around just waiting to be eaten. Oh, how happy they'd be to find him, a tasty little morsel, a rare treat. He wouldn't even fight them. *Take me away, beasts, go on. It's me own fault for running away and thinking I could survive life on the road on me own.*

9

IN AN IDEAL WORLD, THIS whole sorry affair would have been wrapped up before her parents had even found out about it, but the sight of her mother coming swiftly up the hill told Sinéad that that was wishful thinking. Her father followed, head down, betraying no emotion.

"What have you done?" her mother screamed, grabbing Sinéad by the shoulders. "What did you do to make that poor child run away?"

"It's not my fault," Sinéad protested. Deep down, though, she knew it was true; it was all her fault, and the criticism was entirely justified.

"I knew this would happen. I knew it," continued her mother, wringing her hands in despair. They were standing in the car park where a group of about forty people had assembled, all there to search for Seán.

Noel caught up with them and took Sinéad in his arms, ignoring his wife's dramatics. "It'll be all right, Nades, it'll be all right. We'll find him, don't you worry."

Sinéad allowed herself to be coddled, glad to be someone's child for a moment.

"Will we, Daddy? Will we?"

"Of course we will, Nades; don't you worry. Your old dad is here now and everything is going to be all right."

The guards had arrived, three of them; Sergeant Barrett and two younger men. They'd set up a 'base of operations' in the car-park and brought proper order to what had been a dysfunctional affair. The sergeant took command; everyone was assigned a task, organised into groups. A plan of action began to emerge, high-visibility jackets were issued, along with flashlights and whistles. And still more people arrived. They came in their droves, as if some mysterious force had compelled every car in town to gather at the entrance to the woods. They spilled out of their vehicles brandishing torches, blankets and flasks. A couple of them even had walkie-talkies. Walkie-talkies, for fuck's sake! Sinéad watched this procession in a daze. All these people for her little boy: what if he wasn't even in the woods? She would be so embarrassed. Because yes, in spite of everything, she was still concerned about 'putting people out'.

They'd all gathered around the sergeant, waiting for instructions. Patricia had been escorted to the cabin, and was to remain inside until further notice. This was no time for hysterics, one of the guards had advised.

"Thank God for that," muttered Noel, watching her go. "I love your mother, but she's not the kind of person you want in a crisis."

Sinéad watched and felt a pang of shame. After all she had put that women through. And now, just when things had seemed to be improving, she had done it again.

"She's right, though," she said. "It's all my fault."

"Why do you think that, Sinéad? Kids run away all the time; these things happen."

Sinéad shook her head sadly. These things only happened when there was a reason.

"I had Daryl round last night and he and Seán had an argument, and now he's run away and it's all my fault."

Noel mulled this over for a moment. He wasn't sure what to make of Sinéad's new boyfriend. He was an improvement on the last couple of chancers, but was he good enough for his daughter? More to the point, was he good enough for his grandson? If they were already arguing, it didn't bode well for the future.

"Introducing him to boyfriends was always going to be difficult," he said flatly.

"They weren't even supposed to meet. Daryl and Chezz should have been gone ..."

"Look, we can worry about that later. See all these people?" Noel gestured to the crowd. "They're here for Seán. He'll be back home in no time."

"I hope so," Sinéad sniffed.

They stood watching the congregation. A curious *joie de vivre* filled the air. Sinéad may have been at her wit's end, but these people were here, as one, to help avert a tragedy.

"Remember the time I ran away, Daddy?" Sinéad asked suddenly.

Noel's face went blank as he struggled to recall his favourite daughter ever giving him a moment's trouble.

"No," he said, puzzled.

"You don't remember at all?"

"No. When was it?"

"I was about seventeen at the time."

"What, seventeen?"

"I went to England, remember?"

"Ah, that doesn't count, Sinéad. Don't be so silly."

He took her hand and they walked over to where the sergeant was holding court. Everyone was equipped with a torch and instructed to fan out at regular intervals, thirty feet wide. The plan was to walk in unison, each person carefully scanning their area as they went. If the first search didn't turn up anything, they would move to another part of the woods and carry out the same procedure. The sergeant had carefully plotted their routes, and appeared confident that they could cover every inch of the forest in just a couple of sweeps. He positioned Sinéad somewhere in the middle of the line, himself to her left and her father to her right.

"Right," he said loudly. "We'll start walking from here. Stay in line and proceed slowly."

This message was relayed across the line like Chinese whispers, and the search began. Sinéad shuffled forward, and promptly tripped over a log or a stone, she didn't know which. Scrambling to her feet, she picked up her torch and went on, but within seconds she was spread-eagled on the forest floor once more. It was hopeless; the forest was too dark. Even with the other lights bobbing along beside her, she couldn't make out where she was going. How on earth could she search for her child when she could barely stay upright? The whole thing seemed impossible: this vast expanse of wood and grass, and her little boy somewhere in the middle of it all. She dutifully marched on, however, casting her eyes downward as she picked her way carefully through the terrain, and as she went, she called out her son's name over and over. Everyone was calling out his name; it was weird to hear this late-night cacophony in honour of her errant son, all those voices uttering that one syllable again and again: "Seán! Seán! Seán! Seán!"

Most of them had never even met her boy, yet here they were echoing his name like druids in a pagan ceremony. If Seán was in the woods, the sound of his name being chanted over and over again by a group of strangers would terrify him.

For the first time since her ordeal had begun, she realised, she wasn't in a state of blind panic. She couldn't afford to be panicked now; the sergeant had said she must walk slowly and be part of the team. Up to this point she hadn't been sure exactly what she was doing; her desire to be reunited with Seán had caused her to act with little or no thought. God, what must people have thought of her during the past few hours? She hadn't even looked in a mirror before leaving the house. What was she wearing? She had no idea and it was too dark to see. It was beyond her how Bulldog Bartley had stayed calm when confronted by this wild-eyed madwoman. But there were deeper issues at play here than her bedraggled appearance. She knew why Seán had run away. She had brought a strange man into the house, into their house, and it had scared him. He wasn't ready for that yet. His whole life had consisted of just him and his mammy, but now that was changing and she was the one responsible. This was all her fault. She just hoped she wouldn't spend the rest of her life regretting it.

10

BEFORE SHE'D MET DARYL THERE had been a couple of other men, but nothing serious; one or two dates, a drunken kiss at the local nightclub, but that was it. Her son was the only man in her life, and she was devoted to him and his happiness. As time passed, however, she began to feel lonely. She hadn't had a real boyfriend in over six years. There was a void in her life, one that couldn't be filled by her son, no matter how lovable he was. But what man would want her with all her baggage? Because, like it or not, when it came to the dating game that's what Seán was, baggage. Some people had a drink problem, others intimacy issues; she had a seven-year-old boy. Working in a bar meant several suitors on a nightly basis; drunkards offering her the world, despite not being able to afford another pint. She smiled at them and told them to go home to their wives. Occasionally someone promising did enter the pub, and her eyes would light up. Hello, she'd think as the handsome man walked in, alone and unattached. Only for him to go straight to the table occupied by a trio of young, footloose and fancy-free ladies, girls the complete opposite of her. She was twenty-five, and already in danger of being left on the shelf. Then she met Daryl Cassidy.

He wasn't like the other men who propositioned her on a nightly basis; he had a full head of hair, for a start. He and his friends had been passing through Dooncurra on a stag do. They'd come in early on a Saturday evening, a whole busload of them piling into the little pub, noisy and high-spirited but mostly harmless. Unprepared for this influx of thirsty customers, Sinéad had done her best, but she couldn't keep up. She'd hurried this way and that, pulling three pints at once, getting orders mixed up, giving out the wrong change and generally being run off her feet.

Although they seemed like a good-natured bunch, she'd felt a little threatened by them. She'd been the only woman in the bar and there had been about twenty of them, jeering and leering as only a group of drunken men can. Each lascivious comment had been laughed off, the culprit reprimanded and called a cheeky sod, but deep down she'd been scared and wondered whether she should ring Brian, the landlord. A man was needed to take control of the situation.

But she resisted. They were on a stag do, a mystery tour, so surely they wouldn't be here for long. One round of drinks and they'd be on to the next place, wasn't that how it worked? Alas, no. They'd stayed for a second round, and then a third. And, as the drinks flowed, she had watched the number of empty glasses on their tables grow and grow, and the ones on her side of the bar dwindle until hardly any remained. If they stayed for another round or if anyone else came in, she wouldn't have enough pint glasses to serve them. She couldn't put it off any longer, she would have to go out and clear their tables. As soon as she'd approached, the catcalls began; sleazy remarks, hilarious wisecracks, a proper bunch of comedians. If it had stopped at that she could have suffered it; what she couldn't abide was someone taking liberties, laying their hands on her. As she'd collected the last of the glasses and made to return to the bar, one of the men had grabbed her by the arm.

"Hey, love, I'm the best man; don't I get preferential treatment?"

"You're not the best man in here," she'd replied, much to the delight of the rest of the group.

They'd hooted and brayed with glee, chastising her suitor for his lack of tact. He hadn't seen the funny side. Red-faced from being ridiculed in front of his mates, he'd grabbed her firmly and tried to pull her onto his lap.

"Come on, now, don't struggle, just sit up on me, that's the girl."

She'd tried to wrestle free but he'd held her even more tightly.

"What's wrong with you, for fuck's sake? I only want a kiss and a cuddle."

He'd redoubled his efforts and succeeded in toppling her into his lap. A great cheer went up from his friends. His honour had been restored; surely he would let her go now.

"Now, there's the girl. See, wasn't so bad, was it?"

"Let me go, you eejit," she'd growled, continuing to struggle. Why hadn't she called Brian when she'd had the chance? The 'best man', buoyed by the cheers from his friends, had put his arms around her and tried to force her head towards his.

"Come on, one little kiss is all I want."

Sinéad had looked to his entourage for assistance but none was forthcoming. They'd seemed to be enjoying the show and were eager to see it to its conclusion. She'd been about to call over old Frankie at the bar when her assailant suddenly relinquished his grip.

"WHAT THE FUCK ARE YOU DOING TO THIS POOR YOUNG WAN, YA LITTLE CUNT?"

She'd spun around and seen a tall, lean man lifting the 'best man' from his stool. He'd grabbed him by the scruff of the neck and frogmarched him out the door, returning moments later with a face like thunder. His expression had changed when he saw Sinéad.

"I'm really sorry about that, love. Did he hurt you? Fuckin' gobshite thinks he can do whatever he wants."

Sinéad had dusted herself down, aware that a button in her blouse had popped open during the skirmish.

"I'm okay, thanks. We deal with idiots like that all the time."

The man had studied her for a second.

"Well, he won't be coming back in here again, so you don't need to worry about that."

"Thank you," she'd replied. "It's nice to see at least one of ye has some manners." The rest of the party had looked away sheepishly.

After that the tall man had sat at the bar, apologising again for his pal's behaviour. They'd got chatting and she'd liked what she heard. His name was Daryl; he was from Stoneyford, not far from Dooncurra, and worked in a factory with the rest of the stags. He was 27, lived alone and was single. His last relationship had recently ended and he was 'taking some time for himself'. *Aren't we all*, Sinéad had thought. The factory job was only temporary; one day he hoped to start his own business. So far so good; she liked ambition in a man. He had one brother, one sister and a niece that he doted on. Good with kids too, it got better and better. All he had needed to do was ask. And, after a couple more pints, just as the party were leaving, he did.

"Fancy meeting up sometime?"

"Okay," she'd replied, as casually as she dared.

"Here, next Friday? Without all these gobshites?"

"It's a date," she'd confirmed.

And then he'd gone, waving a shy goodbye as he'd ushered his friends outside. She had watched him go and felt her heart skip a beat. There he went, her knight in shining armour. She was already smitten.

As much as she liked Daryl, and she liked him a lot, she had still been reluctant to introduce him to Seán. She and Daryl had been getting on great, meeting up a couple of times a week for the past three months, but still she worried. When she'd told him she had a son, he'd taken it in his stride. 'I love kids,' he'd told her. 'When can I meet him?' 'You might love kids', she'd replied, 'but have you ever dated any of their mothers?' He didn't understand the complexity of the situation. To him it was just a matter of buying Seán an Action Man and kicking a ball about with him in the back garden. Yes, at first Seán would be thrilled by someone buying him presents and playing football with him, but once he realised that Daryl wasn't just his friend but his mother's too, then they'd have a problem. He'd never had to share his mammy with anyone and now this strange man was here, sitting on their couch and sleeping in their house, becoming a part of his life. She knew she had to try to make him understand, but how could you explain such a thing to a seven-year-old? How could you tell him that his mother didn't want to stay on her own forever, that she would like to meet a man of her own? That this idyllic childhood of his may be about to change forever? The truth was he would never understand, and no matter how good Daryl was with kids it would still be difficult.

She made tentative plans to introduce them. A trip to the park, perhaps? Neutral territory, so Seán wouldn't feel threatened. Daryl took the idea and ran with it. 'I'll bring a ball, or maybe even a kite.' Her heart melted at his enthusiasm; surely nothing could go wrong. They arranged a date; a Sunday a few weeks from now. She'd explain to Seán that Daryl was her friend, a close friend who was very important to her. She would let them spend some time together, see if Seán took to him. After a fun-filled day they'd say their goodbyes and she would press her son for an opinion: *Did you like him? Would you mind if he came round sometime?* If he answered in the negative, then they would have to rethink. But surely Seán would love him; how could he not? Daryl would play football with him, maybe get him an ice cream. She'd probably have to prise them apart at the end of the day. That had been the plan. But, of course, that plan had since been laid to waste.

Daryl had brought his brother, Chezz, to the pub with him on that fateful night. And as her shift came to an end, they'd suggested going back to hers for a nightcap; stupidly, she'd agreed. They'd got some cans to take away, stopped at a chipper for some food and returned to her house to eat, drink, and be merry. After a couple of glasses of wine, though, Sinéad had had enough. She'd been knackered and just wanted her bed. Daryl, of course, had been keen to accompany her but that was never going to happen, at least not until he'd met Seán. She'd bade them goodnight, her parting words: 'I don't want to see ye here in the morning.'

Now, almost twenty-four hours later, she was out looking for her son, who was presumed missing. This was what happened when you brought strange men back from the pub. Daryl's explanation had seemed plausible enough at the time, but maybe there was more to it. Seán could be a temperamental little so-and-so, but tipping an ashtray over a stranger? *Firing drink all over the place?* She had taught him better than that. Then again they had been drinking, maybe their words had been misconstrued by her sleepy-headed boy? Perhaps he'd felt threatened, lashed out? All of this ran through her mind as she stumbled through the woods, but none of it would matter if they didn't find him. The who, what and where would lose all relevance if her boy was lost. If they did somehow find him, all would be forgiven. She would never scold him for anything ever again. He could eat chocolate ice cream for breakfast, dinner and tea, watch cartoons from morning till night, never have to tidy his room until the day he moved out. Most importantly, she would happily die a spinster if it meant laying eyes on her child again. She would promise never to have another boyfriend – well, at least not until he was eighteen. It would just be the two of them from here on in. That was a promise.

They'd been walking for almost two hours when a shrill whistle from Sinéad's left brought everyone to a halt. Apparently the sounding of this whistle meant they all had to convene in the centre for a briefing from Sergeant Barrett. This was the first she'd heard of it; that's what she got for not paying attention at the start. She followed the crowds regardless, making a mental note to send them all 'thank you' cards when this was over. Her father appeared by her side and walked with her in silence. When they reached the gathering, flasks were being handed around and she found herself accepting a mug that was thrust into her hands. She listlessly sipped at the hot broth, realising it was the first thing she'd eaten all day. Why were they stopping? This was hardly the time for soup and idle chat. Once everyone was present, the sergeant addressed the crowd.

"Judging by my instruments, we're about halfway through the forest," he began.

Instruments? What instruments? She really should have listened at the start. The items in question were a compass, a map and a few other things she didn't recognise. Sergeant Barrett went on speaking.

"We'll take a break here for ten minutes and then resume the search. He can't be far now."

With that, he stepped down from his pedestal and made a beeline for her. During the sergeant's speech her father had moved off somewhere, so she found herself alone with the man tasked with finding her son.

"How are you, Sinéad?" he asked.

"I'm fine; anxious to get going again, to be honest."

"Don't worry, we'll start searching again in no time. He surely can't be far now. My guess is that he entered the forest from the far side and got lost somewhere between there and here."

"I hope you're right, Sergeant, I really do."

He touched her gently on the arm. "We'll find him," he said, with a little less certainty than before.

She downed the last of the hot soup and looked for someone to return the cup to. A thin man wearing glasses approached. "I'll take that, thanks."

She handed him the cup and stood there awkwardly, waiting for the inevitable questions.

"How are you holding up?" he asked.

"I'm fine, thanks. I just want to get going again."

"Of course," replied the man. "I'll go tell the others."

"Thank you so much for your help," she blurted out as he turned to walk away.

"Don't mention it, Sinéad," the stranger replied. "I'm sure you'd be out here searching if it were my boy who had gone missing."

I wouldn't bet on it, she thought guiltily as he hurried off to get everyone organised.

11

SEÁN HAD BEEN DRIFTING IN and out of sleep for hours. He awoke, startled, from vivid nightmares where beasts pulled at him with razor-sharp claws, dragging him down into lairs of unspeakable horror. Momentarily, he relaxed; he was safe. It had only been a dream; he was back home in his bed, warm, cosy and safe. Then reality closed in on him: the cold night sky and tall dark trees told him that he wasn't safe, that he would never be safe again. He was out here all alone with no one to protect him. He covered himself in leaves and burrowed a little hole in the ground to hide in, but he was still an easy target. Soon they would come. The night was still young. He sobbed himself back to sleep. With any luck he wouldn't wake again.

12

IT HAD BEEN AT LEAST two hours since they'd stopped for a break, maybe more. There couldn't be much more of the woods to search; soon they would have combed its entirety. What would they do then – go back and start all over again? She couldn't expect all these people to stay out here any longer. They would make their excuses and leave, until it was just her, Patrick and her parents.

Soon the search would be called off for the night. *There's no point in carrying on at this hour*, they'd say, *we'll resume in the morning. Resume all ye like, I'm not stopping till I find my boy.* She would roam these woods night and day for the rest of eternity until she found him. There was one problem, though: the batteries on her torch were starting to run out. There wasn't much chance of her finding Seán, or making her way through the forest, without some light to guide her. She had first noticed it half-an-hour ago, but rather than slow things down she had dimmed the light and carried on. Now it was flickering on and off continuously. It was only a matter of time before it failed completely. Without a torch, she might as well be back in the cabin with her mother. She could walk right past Seán and not even notice.

The light from the sergeant's torch beamed brightly on her left, just as it had done since the start. He'd probably had some spare batteries, kept them with his *instruments*. If she'd been listening at the start, she might have heard him tell them how to bring the search to a halt. No doubt they were supposed to shout some nautical term or relay their thoughts through Morse code, but she'd been too busy worrying about her only child and whether he was still alive. *Excuse me for being so ignorant.*

"Sergeant!" she called, thinking how strange it was to call someone else's name after hours of 'Seán' intoned over and over again. There was no reply, so she called again, louder. Still nothing. Perhaps she should address him by his real name? His real name was Hugh, but people called him Hughie. She went with Hugh, just to be on the safe side.

"HUGH!"

His head was turned away from her. She opened her mouth to shout again, but before she did something magical occurred. There was a flurry of activity to her left. No longer could she hear her son's name repeated over and over again; the mantra had ceased, and in its stead were unfamiliar words: words she had feared she would never hear.

"We've found him!"

"He's here!"

She ran, staggered and stumbled, to the source of these words. Her torch was now all but dead, but what light did she need? She was being guided by an altogether more powerful force: her love for her child. Tears streaked down her face as she fell, got up again, ran a few yards and fell once more. She couldn't hear their words anymore, the sound of her beating heart drowning everything out. Her eyes now followed the light which had sprung up somewhere in the distance. It was the light of a dozen, fully-operational, torches. It gave off an eerie, preternatural glow amid the intense darkness of the forest; as if a group of solemn angels had been sent down from the heavens to protect her baby, to guide him to safety.

"He's here!" the voices repeated. "We have him."

She was almost there when another fall, a heavier one this time, took her breath away, but she was up within seconds, bolting forward like a racehorse who'd unseated its rider. Finally she reached them, the beautiful angels and their glorious shimmering light. She broke through them, instinctively knowing where to go. One of the angels, a fat one in a woolly hat, held her child in their arms. She pounced, grasping both child and angel. The angel allowed her to gently prise Seán from their arms, and he came willingly.

"Mammy?" he said.

"Yes, Seány, it's me. Everything's okay now."

"I hope this isn't a dream, Mammy."

"It's not, Seán, I swear."

*

He was rewarded for his endeavours with burgers, chips and as much fizzy orange as he could drink. His nanny and granddad, his aunts and Patrick all came round, and everyone made a huge fuss of him. He'd thought he might get into trouble, but they appeared to be having a party to celebrate his running away. Seán vowed privately to run away more often. He was having a great time, and would happily have stayed up all night telling Patrick about the beasts he'd killed. His mother had other plans, however; she bundled him up in her arms and announced that her little adventurer was going to bed.

"Ah, could you not leave him stay up for a while?" objected Patricia.

Her mother had been doing her utmost to undermine Sinéad's authority since they'd found Seán. They'd had to bring him to the hospital for a check-up and Patricia had insisted on accompanying them despite her daughter's protestations. In the examination room she'd made certain the doctor knew exactly why Seán was there, explaining in great detail what had happened; that this little boy had run away because his mother had invited some strange men into her home. It had continued back at the house. Cutting remarks were casually inserted into the conversation; Patricia questioning Sinéad's ability to rear a child, her living arrangements, her line of work, her morals, and whatever else came to mind. But it was done subtly, with the skill and nous of a tactician. Sinéad had refused to respond, knowing that a confrontation was inevitable but trying to delay it as best she could.

"Say goodnight to everyone, Seán," she instructed, ignoring her mother's protestations.

Seán waved them a sad goodbye and after a cursory brush of his teeth and a rapid change into his pyjamas he was tucked up in bed. No sooner had his head hit the pillow than he was out for the count, safe and sound and back where he belonged. When she returned, Adele and Patrick were getting ready to leave. Sinéad made eyes at them, pleading with them to stay. If they left, her mother would have a free run at her, and she'd been itching all evening to give one of her sermons. They were going, however, and when Valerie saw they were off she jumped ship too. Sinéad hugged them goodbye, thanked them for their help and promised to update them on Seán's condition in the morning. She closed the door behind them, and turned hopefully to her parents with a look that said 'shouldn't ye be going too?' They weren't going anywhere, though. This was what her mother had been waiting for.

"Sit down, Sinéad," she said, as her daughter lingered by the door.

She did as she was told; it was easier that way. She stole a glance at her father, hoping for salvation, but he just shrugged and returned to his whiskey. This was his wife's territory, he had no business getting involved.

Her mother looked at her earnestly. "How did this happen, Sinéad? *Why* did this happen?"

"Can we not leave this till tomorrow, Mam? It's been quite the day if you hadn't noticed?"

"But sure we're all here now, love, and you know how I worry about him."

Oh, poor you. It must be awful having to worry about him so much. What can I do to help?

"I hear you've been seeing a new man?" Patricia began.

"Yes; what about it?"

"It's a very delicate situation, you know, Sinéad. You can't just bring in man after man and expect your boy to accept it."

Sinéad simmered; one man had suddenly turned into several.

"I've never brought a man into this house, never," she replied, surprised at how easily the lie came.

"Well, as long as you know what you're doing, Sinéad. You have to put his needs first, you know."

Once more Sinéad bristled, but she held her tongue. Engaging in an argument with Patricia McLoughlin was an exercise in futility. Her mother was a true master, a black belt in the art of verbal jousting. She had a way of infuriating others while remaining completely calm herself. Pithy put-downs and thinly-veiled insults were delivered through smiling lips, with eyes warm and friendly. Her tone never changed, her emotions never betrayed her. Meanwhile, the victim slowly reached boiling point, frustration rising with each passing moment until, despite the best of intentions, they eventually lost it; firing a volley of expletives, a salvo of insults they didn't mean, and storming out in a huff, leaving the estimable Mrs. McLoughlin stunned and highly insulted.

Over time Sinéad had learned that the best course of action was just to agree with her, or at least pretend to. So she sat there, silently fuming, nodding tersely every couple of minutes as her mother preached about the vagaries of being a single parent. If she was lucky, Patricia would grow tired of tackling such a passive opponent and call a halt to proceedings before sunrise; but she showed no sign of tiring. This was her idea of heaven. She revelled in these altercations, brightening up at the prospect of a good squabble. If she had been a man, she would have spent her evenings roaming the streets picking fights with unassuming strangers.

Sinéad watched her as she spoke, her mother – this woman whom she had admired for as long as she could remember – and thought how old she looked. Her face wasn't beset with wrinkles or significantly aged; on the contrary, she could easily have passed for a woman ten years younger. Her spark, however, had gone. She looked tired. Defeated. Even now, in full flow, she seemed dull and lifeless, her eyes misted over as if in a trance, no sparkle or animation behind them. She was lethargic, just going through the motions, like a presidential candidate who knows he's beat but continues to state his case because that was just what you did. Her mother rarely spoke of her own parents, but Sinéad knew that her relationship with them had not been good. They were both long since gone, dying within a couple of years of each other when Sinéad had still been a child; she remembered the funerals: strained, tense affairs where no one said much and everyone seemed happy when it was all over. Then that was it; they were never mentioned again. There were no pictures of them in their house, their grave was never visited and their anniversaries passed without comment.

Occasionally she would ask about them; gentle, probing queries designed to shed some light upon these enigmatic figures. The answer was always the same: 'I don't want to talk about them.' So she turned to her father, hoping he could enlighten her. But Noel knew better than to break rank. If his wife wasn't going to tell the children about their grandparents, neither was he. Sinéad persevered, though, her curiosity piqued by the wall of silence, and eventually one night, after he'd had a few, she caught him off guard.

"Your mother had a terrible childhood, Nades; terrible," he had said, looking into the distance as he spoke, as if envisaging terrors he had only heard about.

"In what way, Daddy? What happened?"

He'd made to speak and then stopped. Sinéad had remained silent, afraid of spooking him. Just when she'd given up, her father spoke.

"He was a bastard, your mother's father; an absolute bastard."

"What did he do, Daddy?" she'd whispered, almost afraid of the answer.

"A lighting bastard," Noel had said quietly. "And she wasn't much better, the mother. How your own poor mother turned out so well, I'll never know."

Sinéad had thought of contesting that statement but decided against it.

"They used to beat her, you know; both of them."

"Why?"

But he hadn't been listening.

"Nothing more than a skivvy, that's all she was to them."

Her father's hand had shaken as he lifted the glass to his mouth, but the drink seemed to steady his nerves. He'd turned to face his daughter, a solemn look on his face.

"Now you listen to me, Sinéad; your mother loves you and the lads with all her heart, but she's had a hard fuckin' life and it's affected her in ways none of us could ever understand. I know she's not the easiest person to be around at times, but we all have to try our best for her, don't we?"

"We do, Daddy," Sinéad had replied.

"That's the girl," he'd said, putting his hand on the nape of her neck as if to pull her in for a hug.

Sinéad had shifted in her seat in anticipation of their embrace, but then Noel had removed his hand and stared into the distance once more. This time the conversation had finished, never to be continued.

*

It was after midnight when they finally left, her father all hugs and drunken kisses, Patricia still proffering advice as Sinéad bustled them out the door. She shut it behind them and breathed in deeply. "Thank God for that," she said to the empty room. She picked up the latest array of empty cans and bottles and brought them out to the kitchen. The whole house stank of booze, fags and takeaway food. Was this really the kind of environment in which to bring up a child? She didn't want her son getting used to waking up to this kind of scene. So, tired as she was, she set about tidying up. She began gathering the remaining rubbish, clearing off the table and washing it down with kitchen cleaner. The carpet would need hoovering, but that could wait till morning. She'd almost finished and was standing in the middle of the room, stretching her back, when she saw the stain on the wall behind one of the armchairs.

"What the fuck is that?" she said aloud, walking over for a closer look.

Running her fingers over the stain, she noticed that it was still damp. It ran all the way to the floor, where a gloopy, viscous liquid had congealed beneath the skirting-board. The pungent, unmistakable odour told her all she needed to know: Smithwicks. Of course: Seán's riposte to the two intruders in his house. She felt a surge of pride as she imagined her pint-sized guardian hurling projectiles at his tormentors, but that was wrong; she couldn't encourage that kind of behaviour. He'd receive a stern talking-to in the morning, and then she'd make him clean it up. Up to now he had been treated like a king for running away, but it was time for a reality check; as soon as he awoke, he would be donning a pair of rubber gloves and getting down to business. She laughed at the thought of it: the protestations, the grumbling as he half-heartedly rubbed at the stain. Chances were she would eventually buckle and do it herself, but not before he'd at least made an attempt at it.

With the rest of the room tidy, she switched off the light and went to bed, first checking on her son – just in case.

"Night, Seán," she called into the darkness. The sound of his steady breathing told her he was fast asleep, but still she lingered. Standing in the doorway, she listened to the gentle rising of his chest for a few moments more, and then, satisfied that he wasn't going to jump out the window once her back was turned, she at last sought the comfort of her own bed.

13

WHEN SHE AWOKE THE FOLLOWING morning she knew what she had to do. It was time to sit her son down for a chat, a serious chat. Neither of them were likely to enjoy the chat – tears were not only possible, they were likely – but it would benefit them both in the long run. Once she explained to Seán that Daryl was her boyfriend and that he was an important part of her life everything would be so much easier. They could start over, maybe arrange that long-awaited play-date. The memory of Seán and Daryl's first tumultuous meeting would soon be forgotten, and a new relationship would be forged under her watchful eye. But it was vital she did it today, that she didn't allow the yesterday's events to go unmentioned. The longer she left it, the harder it would it get. This was her opportunity and a better one was unlikely to present itself.

Before any heartfelt one-to-ones could be conducted however, there was some cleaning to be done

"Right, mister, I think it's time you tackled this big stain you made on the wall, don't you?"

Seán looked at her, aghast. An episode of *Dogtanian and the Four Muskahounds* had just started, one he'd only seen four times previously. But his mammy had that look in her eye, that dangerous look. He knew that look well and knew he'd be a fool to disobey her right now. Sometimes when she asked him to do something he'd grumble and complain, have a right good moan and hope she'd take pity on him. He wasn't going to do that today, though; she wasn't in a pitying mood.

To his surprise, cleaning the stain was kind of fun. He was given a basin full of hot, soapy water, a cloth and a towel, and told to scrub the stain until it disappeared. Seán got really in to it, furiously rubbing the mark on the wall, creating more and more suds as he tackled the job with gusto. He began to hum to himself, a song he'd learned in school, one about a horse that ran all day and never got tired. He was like that horse, except instead of running he was cleaning. This lasted for all of thirty seconds.

"Mam, my arms are killing me," he said, rubbing his tiny biceps for effect.

"Keep going," Sinéad instructed.

Seán muttered under his breath, huffing and hawing as frustration set in.

"I can't do it Mam, it's too hard."

"Seán..."

He knew that tone, it invariably accompanied that look in her eye; together they spelled shouting and a potential smack on the bum. Seán continued scrubbing, this time without complaint.

After a couple of minutes of genuine, concerted effort, Sinéad relented.

"Come up out of it," she said, relieving him of his duties. Seán came willingly, his spirits immediately lifted.

"I didn't do a bad job on it, Mammy, so I didn't?" he said, cloth slung over his shoulder as he admired his work.

"Amazing, Seán," said Sinéad, sourly.

Pleased with himself, Seán returned to the couch. Hopefully that would be the end of 'cross mammy' for the day. He'd done what she'd asked of him and now they could go back to being friends again. He hated it when she was cross, it scared him. Sometimes, when she was like this, she told him he was the boldest child in all of Dooncurra. Other times she sent him to his room, or shouted at him; he never knew what to expect with 'cross mammy', she was capable of anything.

"Are you still cross, Mammy?" he asked.

"Who said I was cross, Seán?" she replied.

"You seem cross, Mammy."

This was as far as he was willing to push it, he'd let her do the rest of the talking.

Sinéad looked up from her position on the floor; the stain was proving to be more stubborn than she'd expected and her exertions had caused her to sweat.

"I am cross, Seán, you're right."

"Why Mammy? Why are you cross?" Sean pleaded, desperate for things to go back to normal.

"Because of what happened yesterday, Seán, you can't just run away like that."

Ah, so it was the running away thing she was cross about; he'd almost forgotten about that.

"But I'm back now, Mammy," he said, smiling.

"That's not the point, Seán," said Sinéad, getting to her feet and joining him on the couch. This was her moment: she would explain who Daryl was and what he meant to her. She would ask how Seán felt about this and maybe suggest they do something together, just the three of them.

"What is the point then, Mammy?" he asked, sincerely.

Sinéad studied her son, gazed upon this picture of innocence and felt her resolve weaken. She knew it had to be done, that she had to prepare him for what lay ahead, but it was so much easier to do nothing, to say nothing. Besides, it wouldn't be right to upset him again, not after what he'd went through the day before.

"Oh, I don't know, Seán," she said sadly, taking him in her arms.

I don't know either, thought Seán, as he reciprocated her hug, *but it doesn't matter now 'cos we're friends again.*

14

SEÁN EYED DARYL WARILY AS he ate. He couldn't believe it, he really couldn't. There he was, stuffing his face as if he'd lived here his whole life and this was his own kitchen table. Well, it wasn't, it was his. His and his mammy's.

"Come on, Seán, eat up," urged his mother.

He scowled in response.

Ordinarily he'd be wolfing this down. It was one of his favourites; shepherd's pie and beans with loads of gravy. Some people just liked the shepherd's pie on its own; Seán could never understand those people. He liked his shepherd's pie with beans and gravy. The beans were vital, a few healthy spoonfuls added to the mix right from the off. But it was the gravy that sealed the deal. His mother always told him to say 'when' as she slowly drizzled it on top of his food, but he never said 'when'. *Just keep pouring till it's all gone, Mammy, good woman yourself.* Once he had his gravy and his beans, he set about turning the whole thing into one big beautiful mush of spuds, meat, carrots and beans (and gravy). Then and only then was he ready to eat. He had that today; loads of gravy on top of a lovely big mush of shepherd's pie and beans, but he couldn't eat it. Not just yet, anyway, because there was a distraction sitting at the other end of the table: a big, ugly distraction that he couldn't take his eyes off.

Daryl, for his part, barely seemed to notice the daggers being thrown in his direction. He rarely got fed like this; mostly he lived on takeaways and pre-cooked microwave meals from the supermarket.

"Is it nice?" asked Sinéad as he continued to demolish the contents of his plate.

"Fuckin' lovely," he replied.

"Don't speak with your mouth full," barked Seán from his seat at the other end of the table. He looked to his mother for assent. "Isn't that right, mammy?"

"Yes, Daryl; don't speak with your mouth full," she repeated, a grin on her face.

"Okay, sorry," he replied, returning her grin.

Seán looked at them angrily. She'd hardly even given out to him! If that had been him spewing bits of spud all over the table, he would've been fucked out of it.

He waited until Daryl had finished his dinner before beginning his own, never once taking his eyes off him. Once they went to the living-room for a fag he got stuck in, thankful it was still warm. And with new boundaries seemingly in place, he took it upon himself to make as much of a mess as he possibly could. If Daryl could eat with his mouth full, then so could he, and not only that, he could also use his fingers and his hands. He could dribble food from his mouth, flick bits of it at the wall and dip his entire face into his plate. Sure why not? Anything went these days.

By the time he'd finished he had more than made his point. He didn't usually like to waste any of his favourite dinner, but this was a special occasion. It was everywhere; on the table, on the floor, on the chairs, on the walls, on his face, in his ears and even inside his jumper. Forming a little hat made entirely out of potatoes and carefully placing it on his head was maybe going a step too far, but his mother could be the judge of that.

"Finished!" he shouted out. "Is there any dessert, Mammy?"

Sinéad came in to the kitchen to collect his plate. "Why don't you go down to Bart – Seán! What the hell are you doing?"

"What's wrong, Mammy?" he replied, looking up at her.

"This mess, that's what wrong! How many times have I told you to mind your manners at the kitchen table?"

"But Daryl was allowed speak with his mouth full!"

"That was different, Seán, and you know it."

"No, I don't," Seán replied. "I don't know anything."

He pushed out his chair and stomped sullenly to his room, his spud-hat crumbling to pieces and falling to the floor as he went.

Sinéad shook her head and set about tidying up. Lately it felt like all she was doing was cleaning up messes.

"What's up?" asked Daryl, coming into the kitchen.

"Oh, nothing, just some dinner-time dramatics."

"Fuckin' state of the place," he said, picking up a cloth. "Shouldn't let him get away with that, y'know."

Taken aback by the sight of a man cleaning up her kitchen, Sinéad chose to overlook his criticism of her parental skills.

"It's difficult for him, you have to understand."

"I do, but I didn't think it'd be this hard."

Sinéad flinched at his words. "You're not having second thoughts, are you? I mean, if this is too much for you I'd rather you told me now and saved us all a lot of heartache."

Daryl put down the cloth and placed his hands on her hips. "Of course not, Sinéad. I love you more than anything in the world. I'm willing to be a father to that boy, too, but he's not making it easy for me."

Sinéad rested her head on his chest. "Maybe one day we'll all look back at this and laugh. You never know."

She looked up at him for an answer but he just smiled down at her. The truth was that he didn't know how things were going to work out. There was a barrier between him and the boy, one that he didn't know how to penetrate. He'd thought it would be easy; he'd just stroll in the door, crack a few jokes and before you knew it, they'd be sitting by the TV watching football together. That Seán was a strange one, though; the way he glared at him was unsettling. He didn't seem like other children of that age, how he questioned everything and trusted nothing. A hard nut to crack, that's what he was, but Daryl was willing to work on their relationship. He truly loved Sinéad, and if that meant taking on a child that wasn't his then so be it. Hopefully one day they would have children of their own, and maybe then things between Seán and himself would get a little easier. For the moment, though, it was just the three of them, and if they were going to get along he had to be the one to make it happen.

"Will I give him his present now?" he asked.

"I don't know, Daryl. He ran away the other week and we treated him like a lord; he wrecks the kitchen tonight and gets a present for his trouble. Not exactly sending out the right message, is it?"

"I just thought it might make a good peace offering, seeing as he clearly hates me."

"Oh, he doesn't hate you, Daryl, he's just protective of his mammy. It's quite sweet, really."

"Well, I'm here to protect ye both now," Daryl said, fishing Seán's present from the shopping bag. "Will you call him down? He won't answer if I do it."

"Seán, Seán, come down a minute!"

Silence. A sickening thought struck Sinéad.

"Jesus, if he's after running away again I'll fuckin' kill him," she said, hurrying to his room.

But he was there safe and sound, lying on his bed reading a comic.

"Why didn't you answer me when I called you?" she asked.

Seán ignored her.

She walked over to the bed. "Seán, answer me now or you'll be sorry."

He flashed her a venomous look. "I won't be sorry. I won't!"

With the aggressive approach not working, Sinéad decided to change tack. She sat on the edge of the bed and began to tickle Seán's stockinged feet. "Stop," he giggled as she went to work on his little toes. "Mammy, stop it!"

But it was no use. She had him. Try as he might he couldn't resist, and before long he had succumbed, breaking into peals of laughter as she tickled his feet, ribcage and armpits.

"Mammy, stop, stop," he wheezed as the onslaught continued, his stomach sore from the laughter.

She eventually relented and stood up from the bed. "Now come on down to the sitting-room, young sir; we have a surprise for you."

The smile vanished from Seán's face. "What kind of surprise? Ye're not getting married, are ye?"

"No, no, nothing like that. Come on and I'll show you," she said, taking his hand.

"Okay," he said, allowing himself to be escorted to the sitting-room.

"What was all the laughing about? Sounded like great fun," Daryl said when they entered.

Seán squeezed his mother's hand. He didn't want Daryl knowing about their game. He didn't want Daryl knowing anything about them.

"It was just a joke Mammy told me," he said.

"Ah, a joke. I love jokes; go on, tell me it."

"You wouldn't get it," Seán said dismissively, as he went to the kitchen in search of something to replace the dessert he'd missed.

Daryl looked at Sinéad beseechingly. "I can't win," he whispered, raising his eyes to heaven.

"Seán, come in here," she said. "I told you we've something to show you."

"We've no biscuits, Mammy, none at all."

"Forget about the biscuits and just come in here, will you!"

Sensing that this was his final warning, Seán skulked back to the sitting-room.

"What is it?" he asked impatiently.

Sinéad nudged Daryl, and he reached behind the couch for the shopping bag.

In spite of himself, Seán felt a tremor of excitement. *A present. Nice one!* Maybe this whole Daryl thing would have its benefits after all.

"You're a big soccer fan, aren't you, Seán?" Daryl asked hesitantly.

"Yes."

"You follow the boys in green, yeah?"

"Yes."

"Italia '90 and all that?" he continued, pulling a package from the bag.

"Yeah. David O'Leary," said Seán, following Daryl's hands as the mysterious item made its way towards him.

"Well, this is for you," Daryl said. He handed the carefully-wrapped present to the little boy. "Hope you like it."

Seán looked to his mother for affirmation. She nodded and he took the present.

"What do you say?" Sinéad asked.

"Thank you," Seán murmured.

"Thank you, what?" she pressed.

"Thank you, Daryl."

Seán took the present, laid it down on the floor and took a seat beside the television.

Sinéad and Daryl looked at each other, incredulous.

"Well, aren't you going to open it?" she asked.

Seán gazed over at her with sad eyes. He beckoned her over and she rose from her seat, crouching down beside him.

"What is it?" she asked in a low voice.

Seán pressed his mouth to her ear, "Can I open it later, when he's gone?"

"No, you'll open it now. He went to a lot of trouble to get you that and it means a lot to him."

"Okay," Seán sighed. "But you stay here while I open it, okay?"

She nodded in agreement and moved to the side so that Daryl could watch him open the gift.

Seán already knew what it was anyway, he wasn't stupid. It was a Jackie Charlton T-shirt or, at best, a pair of pyjamas with Paul McGrath on them. Either was good, though, he didn't mind. He carefully undid the wrapping, trying to savour the moment – he loved presents. As the contents were slowly revealed, he let out an involuntary gasp. It wasn't a T-shirt or pyjamas, it was a feckin' jersey, the Ireland jersey, the one they'd worn during Italia '90. *Feckin' hell. Gwan, Daryl, ya fecker!* If this had come from anyone else he would already have been running around the house, jersey on, recreating David O'Leary's penalty against Romania. But instead he plucked the shirt from its packaging, looked it up and down a couple of times, and went back to watching the telly.

"Well, Seány, what do you think?" his mother asked.

Seán couldn't lie. It was amazing; maybe the best present he'd ever got.

"It's brilliant," he said. And then, looking at Daryl: "Thanks, Daryl. It's a great present, it really is."

Taken aback by this sudden sincerity, Daryl was unsure how to respond; but the boy had finally afforded him some respect, and it was only right to respond in kind.

"No bother," he replied.

Jonathan

1

MALCOLM'S NEW BUSINESS WAS FLOURISHING. Since its inception five years ago his small web-hosting firm had gone from strength to strength, growing from a tiny one-room operation to a company employing over fifty staff. He and his partner, Dennis, an old friend from Uni, had invested their entire savings in it, risking everything they had. But thanks to Malcolm's astute marketing skills and Dennis' expertise in designing and developing websites, they were soon running a profit. Within a year they'd moved to new premises and had a young and ambitious workforce doing the majority of the hard work on their behalf. Two years later there was another move, further expansion necessary if they wished to compete with their rivals. And now there was talk of additional upgrades; they needed more staff, better computers, the latest in technology and, most importantly, more clients. Philliskirk & Barnes was the fourth biggest web-hosting business in the northwest, and Malcolm was its Chief Executive. The final months in his previous job had long been consigned to history, a dark period in his life which he could now see as a turning-point. He was an entrepreneur now, a businessman, with a salary to match.

"I'm the CEO, Marge; I can pay myself whatever I want," he'd joke as she stared in amazement at his pay-slip.

All those zeros sent her head into a spin. Of course she was proud of him, inordinately so, but for her it had never been about money. All she wanted was enough to be comfortable; enough for a holiday in the summer, enough to buy Jonathan presents from Father Christmas. She had no need for anything more. But now her husband was a high-flier who drove a brand-new car and wore expensive suits to work every day, and if he was a high-flier, what did that make her? She still hoped to return to her old job at the florist's, but was that now unbecoming for a lady in her position? Should she spend her days golfing, playing tennis and lunching with the ladies, shopping in classy department stores? No, thank you. She would devote herself to motherhood and keeping her house in order. And if she had any spare time she would tend to her garden, maybe watch some television when she really wanted to indulge herself.

Being financially secure, however, had set her mind to work in another way. She had refused Malcolm's offer of a newly-fitted kitchen, pooh-poohed his suggestion of a holiday in the Seychelles, and positively bristled when he'd mentioned moving to a bigger house. There was something she wanted, though, just one little thing – and it wouldn't even cost very much.

"Malc?" she began nervously as they returned home from the park one Sunday afternoon.

Jonathan was asleep in the back seat, having run around in circles for four hours with two kids he'd befriended in the sandpit.

"Yes, love?"

"Would you say that we're stable, financially I mean?"

"Oh, yes, definitely," Malcolm replied, wrapping his hands tightly round the wheel of his BMW.

"Good."

"Why do you ask, love? Having second thoughts about that kitchen?"

"No, nothing like that."

"Uh-oh, what is it, then?" he teased. "I knew you'd think of a way to bankrupt us!"

Margaret turned to look at her sleeping son, then back to Malcolm.

"I want another child," she said, twisting in her seat to face him. "A little girl."

Malcolm took the news in his stride because, in truth, he'd thought about it too – in a more wistful way than with any seriousness, but why not? What was there to stop them? If it made his Margie happy, it was a good idea.

"Yes, okay," he said with a grin. "A girl, you think?"

"Really, Malc?" she cried, grabbing his arm, nearly causing them to crash.

"Flipping hell, Marge, take it easy!" he said, laughing as he righted the car and hastily returned her kiss. "Do you want me to collect the forms from the agency?"

"No need," she said. "I got them last week."

He threw her a sideways glance, which she replicated mischievously. She had been one step ahead of him all along.

Before any decision could be made, however, they would have to consult the other member of the Philliskirk household. Jonathan would surely be thrilled by the prospect of a sister, but they couldn't just magically produce a baby and not expect him to ask questions. Even at his tender age, he understood where babies came from. When his Aunt Ellie had been pregnant he'd spent hours listening to her tummy, refusing to believe there was a baby inside. Even when it kicked, he argued that Ellie had a special tummy which could kick nosy little boys. But a few months later, when they went to greet the new arrival at the hospital, there could be no doubting the truth: it was there for all to see, swaddled in Ellie's arms. Jonathan stared at his new cousin and then at Ellie; so it was true, babies did grow inside tummies. After that he had taken great delight in pointing out pregnant women in the street, at the supermarket, and even on the TV. This posed problems of its own. Explaining that not all fat women were necessarily with child was a challenge in itself. More than once they'd had to offer apologies to random plump women who'd been accosted and asked: 'When is your baby due?'

Unless Margaret went on a high-carbohydrate diet or stuffed her clothes with padding for a few months, Jonathan would suspect foul play. He knew that babies came from fat women, and his mum was a slim size eight. The only other option was to tell him the truth; that his sister would be adopted, just as he had been. He was only seven, but it would make sense to tell him now before he started figuring out things for himself. Ever since he'd started playschool Margaret had worried that he'd pick up on some remark from the other children or their parents. He understood that Asian kids had Asian mothers and that black kids had black mothers; how long would it be before he started comparing his appearance with that of his parents? As a toddler his hair had been golden blond; now it was starting to darken, and his eyes, a deep blue, were of a different shade to those of his parents. How confused would he become if a sister arrived who didn't look like him, his mum or his dad? It was decided that they would tell him without going into too much detail. They would explain that he hadn't been in Margaret's tummy but someone else's, and that when he was very young he had come to live with them. They were his mummy and daddy, his real mummy and daddy, but one day he might meet the lady in whose tummy he had grown. For now though, all he needed to know was that they loved him very much and wouldn't change him for the world. Once the initial bombshell had been delivered, they would soften the blow with news of a potential addition to the family.

They chose a Saturday evening and planned it in advance. Jonathan had just had his bath and was cross-legged in front of the telly, a large bowl of ice cream at his feet. They'd been working towards this all day, manoeuvring him into position so that they could deliver the news when he was at his most receptive. Now everything was in place; Margaret had just emptied the washing machine, Malcolm had come in from the garage, and their little boy was sitting still for the first time all day.

The A-Team had just finished and the moment was ripe.

"Jonathan, we want to talk to you about something," Margaret said gently.

He swivelled around on the floor to face his parents. His ice cream had long since melted but he'd been loath to give it up and had spent the last ten minutes creating funny patterns on its surface.

Sensing that they would have his attention for only a matter of minutes, Margaret cut straight to the chase.

"How would you feel about getting a little sister, Jonathan?"

He stopped trailing his spoon through the ice cream and stared at his mother in amazement.

"Really, Mum?"

"Yes," she said, looking at Malcolm, who nodded agreement.

"A sister," Jonathan said thoughtfully.

He pondered for a second before arriving at a conclusion.

"I think I'd prefer a brother, Mum."

They both smiled, his reaction coming as no surprise to them. Jonathan had already developed a deep mistrust of girls, and more than once had stated that he'd never be friends with one as long as he lived.

"I'm sure you would, Jonathan," Malcolm said. "But your mother and I would like a girl."

Jonathan screwed up his face in frustration. He was outnumbered here.

"Okay," he conceded. "I suppose a sister could be all right."

"That's great, Jonathan. We're glad you agree," Malcolm said with a touch of sarcasm.

Decision made, Jonathan began to warm to the idea.

"When will she be here, Mum? You're not even fat yet! Is she in there now?"

He got up from the floor and made for Margaret's stomach in anticipation of a right good listen. But she stopped him in his tracks.

"She won't be coming from my tummy, Jonathan."

He stared at her, crestfallen, then looked at his father. Was it possible?

"Is she going to come from Dad's tummy? I saw a really fat man the other day; he *definitely* had a few babies in his tummy."

Malcolm patted his own modest midriff. "Do you think there are any babies in here, Jonathan?"

"Stop that, Malcolm, you'll confuse him."

Jonathan was already confused. If his sister wasn't going to come from his mum's tummy, then where would she come from?

"Jonathan, sometimes mums can't grow babies in their own tummies so they get them from the hospital instead," Margaret said. "This is called *adopting* a baby."

"Adopting?" Jonathan repeated.

"Yes, adopting," Malcolm said. "Your mum can't grow a baby, so we'll go to the hospital for one instead."

"Where does the hospital get the babies?"

"They come from mums who couldn't look after them, Jonathan," Margaret said, her heart pounding. She was acutely aware that what she was telling him now could scar him for life if it wasn't handled correctly.

"Why couldn't they, Mum?"

"Lots of different reasons, Jonathan."

"What kind of reasons?"

Margaret stared at her husband, desperate for assistance. To his credit, Malcolm did the best he could.

"Jonathan, sometimes these mums couldn't afford to care for their babies. They might not have had money for nappies or food."

"But why did they have a baby if they didn't have money for nappies?"

This was a question too far, even for Malcolm. How could you explain the concept of an unwanted pregnancy to a seven-year-old?

"I don't know, Jonathan. Maybe they lost their job or something like that."

He seemed satisfied with this explanation. Grown-ups could be really stupid at times though. Imagine deciding to have a baby and then, when it came, having to sell it to the hospital so you could buy food! Such silliness. He would never understand their ways. Then something else occurred to him; if his mum couldn't grow a baby, where had he come from?

"Mum?" he asked, softly.

"Yes, my love?"

"Am I adopted, then?"

"Yes, dear," Margaret confirmed, stifling a sob.

"So you bought me from the hospital?"

"No, Jonathan," she laughed. "We didn't buy you!"

"Why not? Did you *steal* me, Mum?" he asked, excited by the notion of being a kidnapped child.

"No, Jonathan. We didn't steal you and we didn't buy you."

"So I was free, then?"

"Well, not exactly, but we didn't have to pay the hospital for you."

"So you just gave the money to the lady whose tummy I was in, so she could buy food?"

"No, not that either, Jonathan. Adopted babies aren't bought; they are given to mums and dads who can't grow their own."

"I see," he said, finally seeming to grasp it. "So when you couldn't grow one, you went to the hospital to pick one out?"

Margaret opened her mouth to correct him again, but Malcolm interjected before she could speak.

"That's right, Jonathan. We went in to where they keep all the babies and looked to see which one we liked best."

Jonathan's eyes lit up. "Was it me, Dad?"

"It was, Jonathan."

"How many babies were there, Dad?"

"Oh, loads; hundreds, I would say."

"And you chose me?" he asked, pointing to his chest.

"Yes."

"Wow," he said, awestruck. "What made you choose me, Dad?"

"Simple, you were the cutest."

"Was I, Dad? Really?"

"Yes, the cutest by miles."

"By miles?"

"Yes."

"Out of hundreds of babies?"

"Yes, Jonathan."

Jonathan decided that being adopted was the coolest thing ever. He felt special, knowing that out of all those babies, they'd selected him. He'd seen pictures of himself when he was small and he had to admit that he'd been pretty cute. But *that* cute?! He'd had no idea. Wait until his friends heard about this! They'd be so jealous.

So caught up was he in his voyage of self-discovery that he'd almost forgotten about this sister, but now, having remembered, and finally understanding what adoption was all about, he had one final question.

"Dad?"

"Yes, son?"

"When you're going to pick out my sister, can I come?"

"We'll have to see what the hospital says, Jonathan."

2

SADLY, JONATHAN WASN'T ALLOWED TO help choose his new sister. On the day of her arrival he was left at home with his Nana Grimes, while his parents went to collect his sibling-in-waiting. Jonathan liked Nana Grimes. She was very old; seventy-one, which made her the oldest person he knew. She was his mum's mum and had grown his mum inside her tummy. His mum wasn't adopted like he was. Nana Grimes was very small, with white hair, and wore thick blue cardigans. She always had sweets too, loads of them, hidden in her handbag. Jonathan had long wanted to look inside her handbag, to see if it was filled with sweets and sweets alone, but she never let it out of her sight. So he had to be content with being given sweets from the bag whenever she saw fit. He loved that bag.

Because of Nana Grimes' age, he was always on his best behaviour when she babysat him. His dad had told him to be very careful with his nana, and Jonathan followed those instructions to the letter. There would be no games of football, no building of forts and certainly no jumping on beds, while Nana Grimes was looking after him. He didn't want to end up killing her. He'd play whatever games she wanted and hope that by doing so he would receive the entire contents of her lovely, sweet-filled bag.

As soon as his parents' car left the driveway, Jonathan looked expectantly at Nana Grimes. She was in charge now, so what would they do? She stared back at him from her position on the armchair, suppressing a smile. That was one of the thing he liked best about his nana, she was always up for a laugh. Sometimes it felt like she was his age, instead of seventy-one. They remained like that for a few moments, grinning at one another.

"Board games, Nana?"

"Oh, I thought you'd never ask."

He darted off to the playroom to get the board games. He had lots of them but *Connect Four* was his favourite. He was the current champion and had never lost a game. His mum had beaten him once, but the result was overturned after it emerged that she'd been cheating. He didn't like playing his mum; she was too good. He preferred playing his dad, or ideally Nana Grimes. She was hopeless at *Connect Four*, really bad, which made her the perfect opponent. Sometimes he felt guilty as he beat her time and time again and occasionally he even offered to let her win one, but she always refused and promised to try her best in the next game. Her best was never good enough, though; she was up against the *Connect Four* champion, after all.

"Red or yellow, Nan?" he asked as he set up the game.

"Oh, I think I'll be red, Jonathan."

"Aw, I wanted to be red, Nana!"

"Okay then, Jonathan, I'll be yellow."

"Cool," he said, emptying out the coloured counters and dividing them up.

One of the yellows had gone missing a few weeks ago, but he decided not to tell Nana Grimes about that. She might be rubbish at the game, but he couldn't take any risks. A couple of minutes later he had secured his first victory of the day, a straightforward win: four reds right down the middle. Poor Nana, her eyesight wasn't the best. But after a string of victories, each one easier than the last, he began to grow tired of *Connect Four*.

"How long till my sister gets here, Nana?"

"Not for a while yet, Jonathan. They've only been gone half an hour."

"She's going to be adopted; did you know that, Nana?"

"Yes, Jonathan, I did."

"I'm adopted too, Nana."

"I know that, Jonathan."

"Did you know that Mum and Dad picked me out from a hundred babies, Nana? I bet you didn't know that!"

Nana Grimes pursed her mouth in surprise. "A hundred babies!"

"Yes," Jonathan said proudly. "I was the cutest."

"I'm sure you were."

"I'm bored, Nana. What'll we play next?"

"What do you want to play, Jonathan?"

"Can we bake some gingerbread men like we did last time?"

"Oh, no, Jonathan, I'm sorry. I haven't got the ingredients."

"What are ingredients, Nana?"

"They're the things you use to make the gingerbread men; flour and baking soda, things like that."

"Can't we go to the supermarket and buy some baking soda?"

"But how would we get there, Jonathan?"

Jonathan paused for thought. Nana Grimes didn't have a car; she was too old to have one. They could get the bus, but the stop was very far away and he didn't think Nana Grimes could walk that far. What he really felt like doing was going upstairs and jumping up and down on his bed. That was one of his favourite things to do, especially when his mother wasn't around. But something told him that Nana Grimes wouldn't enjoy that game as much as he did. He could pretend he was going to the toilet and then sneak into his room for a quick jump around, but it was never as much fun on your own. The best part about it was looking at the other person as they tried to jump higher than you.

"How about having a bath?" said Nana Grimes, breaking his reverie.

Bath? Jonathan's heart sank. No one had told him he'd have to have a bath. This was supposed to have been a fun day with Nana Grimes.

"But I had one last Saturday," he whined in protest.

"Well, you have to have another today. I'm under strict orders; can't have you dirty when your little sister arrives."

Jonathan was starting to go off the idea of having a sister. If it involved having baths all the time, then he'd rather not have one.

"But why Nana? She won't notice."

"You have to be clean for the party later."

Party? Now she was talking.

"What party, Nana?"

"Your sister's homecoming party."

Jonathan had changed his mind; getting a sister was great if it meant parties, because parties were brilliant.

"All your cousins are going to be here, and your aunts and uncles."

"Really? Even Uncle Tony?"

"Yes, even Uncle Tony."

Tony was his absolute favourite uncle. This was going to be some party.

"When does the party start, Nana?" he asked, looking around for signs, anything that would point to the party's beginning.

"Oh, not for a while yet Jonathan. Your sister has to get here first; but the party can't start until you have your bath."

"Okay then, Nana," he declared, hopping up from his seat. "Let's go!"

He bounded up the stairs two at a time, having discovered a new enthusiasm for bath-time. His grandmother followed him wearily, agreeing to the inclusion of *Action Man* and several other toys, if only to shut him up.

By the time she'd found a temperature to his liking, the bath was full to overflowing. First it had been too hot, then too cold, then a tiny bit too hot, then way too cold and so on until she was fit to chuck him in, clothes and all. But finally he'd been happy with it, and after the prolonged drama of washing his hair and giving him a thorough scrubbing, she was happy to leave him alone with his boats and submarines.

"Let me know when you're ready to get out," she said, drying herself with a towel.

"I will, Nana," he replied as another monumental splash undid her work.

She sighed and left him to it. At least he was relatively quiet, which would allow her to regroup until her next challenge: getting him out. It was nothing that a few threats wouldn't solve, though; one mention of the party being called off and he'd be as good as gold. Eleanor Grimes had brought up four children of her own in far humbler surroundings. She knew exactly what buttons to press and when to press them. So, although

Jonathan might have believed he was playing her for a fool, it was entirely the opposite. He could splish and splash, cover himself in suds and sing to his heart's content, but in less than an hour's time he would be sitting in that living-room like a brand new pin, his hair perfectly combed, his shirt tucked into his trousers and his ears squeaky clean, inside and out.

3

JONATHAN FELT ITCHY AND UNCOMFORTABLE. His shirt collar was too tight and his stupid new shoes were hurting his toes. His hair looked silly too; he longed to mess it up, but one look at his nana was enough to tell him that this would be a bad idea. She'd been very mean to him since bath-time. He wasn't sure he liked her anymore. The friendly nana who was useless at Connect 4 and baked him gingerbread men had been replaced by an angry one. Even crying hadn't affected her; she'd ignored his tears and warned him that if he didn't stop he wouldn't be allowed to attend the party. He tried asking for his mum, just to see how that would go, but that didn't work either. Nana scolded him for being so selfish and told him he had to be a big boy now that he had a sister to mind. He was starting to think that this sister business was just about the worst thing that had ever happened. When he had been told about it he'd imagined a new playmate: endless games of Connect 4, someone to watch cartoons with and, most importantly, someone to jump on beds with. He'd been quite mistaken. Everything was changing; now he was being told he had to be a big boy. He didn't want to be a big boy. He liked being a little boy.

But he kept reminding himself that there was a party in the offing. He'd seen it with his own eyes. His nana had laid out the table with all kinds of lovely stuff; iced buns, cheesecake, fancy chocolate biscuits, Rocky Road, Swiss Roll, sausage rolls and lots of other things he didn't recognise. Then she'd covered it all up with tinfoil and warned him not to touch anything. This was very unfair; he'd been a good boy like she'd asked, and he wasn't getting a thing in reward. He'd sat there in his silly green jumper, left his hair alone and been as quiet as a mouse and still he was being treated like an animal, having to look at all that delicious food while his belly rumbled in complaint. Flipping Nana Grimes; he was going to ask for a new babysitter as soon as his mum got home.

"Here they are! Here they are!" shrieked Nana as the car pulled into the drive.

Jonathan, still sulking, feigned indifference but followed her to the door nonetheless. Some of his mates were outside playing football, so he hung by the doorway in case they saw him in his ridiculous green jumper.

"Come and see your sister, Jonathan," said his mum, getting out of the car.

"I'm all right here," he mumbled sadly, listening to the thwack of the ball as another goal was scored.

He could see her from where he was, anyway. She was in the back seat in a pink baby chair, a girl's one, not like the red one he'd had. Even from here she looked tiny. Malcolm opened the car door, carefully lifted out the chair and there was his sister: a bald little baby with drool spilling out of her mouth. Jonathan doubted she'd seen a cartoon in her entire life. He watched solemnly from the door while the three adults made a tremendous fuss over the baby, feeling terribly alone and neglected. They didn't care about him anymore. From now on he would have to be a big boy; there would be no more cuddles and kisses for him. Malcolm carried her into the house and they all followed him, Jonathan trailing at the rear.

They placed her on the sofa, still in her baby seat, so that everyone could get a proper look.

"Come on, Jonathan, meet your sister," his mother urged.

Reluctantly he stepped forward. As he sized her up he felt a sudden desire to knock the seat over and topple his sister out, so that she'd fall to the floor and hurt herself. They would have to bring her back and that would be the end of that. It would be just him and his parents again; no sisters and no big boys.

Instead he approached the little baby and peered at her inquisitively. "She's very small."

"Yes, Jonathan. She's just a baby, only eight months old."

"She won't be able to play football with me, will she?"

"Not for a while, I'm afraid Jonathan."

"Hide and seek?" he ventured.

"Maybe hiding, but not seeking."

"War?"

"I'm not sure that even *you* should be playing *War*, Jonathan."

"Okay, Mum," he said, studying the baby.

Gently he moved his hand to her face. It looked so soft. Before he could touch her, she grabbed his index finger with her little fist and began to squeeze it.

Jonathan's mouth opened, astonished. He turned to his mother to make sure she was seeing this, and then to his father and his nana too.

"Look," he whispered, afraid he might break the spell and the moment would pass. "She's grabbing me."

"I see, Jonathan; isn't she clever?" Malcolm whispered, leaning in beside him.

"She's really strong," he said as the infant continued to squeeze.

Jonathan stared at his sister in admiration, watching her as she moved his finger towards her mouth. He looked at his mother for reassurance. How was this going to end? Exactly what was this child capable of? Then she popped his finger inside her mouth and began to suck on it.

"Ooh, that feels funny," he giggled.

"She's teething," said Margaret by way of explanation.

Jonathan had no idea what this meant but it felt funny, in a nice way.

"Can I have my finger back now, please?" he asked.

The child continued sucking, her eyes locked on her big brother.

"Please?" he asked, before gently extricating his finger from her mouth and examining it to make sure it was still intact.

"Ah, isn't that nice," said his grandmother, barging her way to the front, anxious to bond with her newest grandchild.

Jonathan moved to one side and stood beside his father while the two women henpecked the baby. He looked up at Malcolm and smiled knowingly, and then back at the baby, who, despite being fawned over by her mother and grandmother, still stared out at him.

They'd barely had time to settle her in before the guests started arriving – some wanted, some not. Mrs. Clegg from next door hadn't been invited to the party; Jonathan knew that for a fact. Here she was, though, as bold as brass, tickling his sister and telling her she was 'the loveliest thing she'd ever seen.' She obviously hadn't been here when they'd brought *him* home. At least she hadn't brought her kids with her. Jonathan played with the

Cleggs when he had no one else to play with, but he didn't really like them. They always wanted to borrow his toys and never offered to give him any of theirs. If they'd been here now they'd be eating all the party food, the food he'd been watching all day: *his* food. There was no way he was letting the Cleggs eat the Rocky Road, no way. But they were in their back garden, playing; Jonathan could hear them. There they were, playing away, totally oblivious to what was going on next door. Pretty soon his cousins would arrive and then the party would start in earnest. They'd stuff their faces with cake and head out into his back garden to play games of their own. Philip Clegg would stick his big, stupid face over the fence and ask, "Hey, Jonathan, what's going on? Can we come in to play with you lot?"

And he'd simply smirk, and reply: "Nah, Philip, we're having our own game. See ya later." That'd serve him right for borrowing his A-Team van and not giving it back.

But right now he was still the only child here, apart from his sister, of course. His other nana had arrived, Nana Philliskirk, with his granddad, his only one. Jonathan didn't like his granddad. One time he had grabbed his ear and twisted it so hard Jonathan had cried out in pain, and from then on he had a deep mistrust of him. He couldn't remember why his granddad had twisted his ear, but it had hurt and he'd been scared. His granddad was a bad man, and Jonathan did his best to avoid him whenever he visited. On the other hand, Nana Philliskirk was nice; not as nice as his Nana Grimes, but still nice. She gave him pound coins sometimes, silently slipping them into his hand, winking slyly at him and then walking away. After the first time she'd done it, he made a point of standing near her whenever they visited in case there were more pound coins to be had. This presented a problem, because he was simultaneously trying to avoid his granddad. They were always together; if one was here so was the other and once they arrived they stood, or sat, side by side, with barely a couple of feet between them until they left. Over time, though, he'd learned that the pound coins usually came out when they were leaving, so he kept his distance until he saw his granddad looking at his watch. This meant they were going soon, so from that point on he stood near Nana Philliskirk, making sure his hands were free to receive whatever came their way.

No one would be leaving this party for a long time yet, so he was content to give them both a wide berth for the time being. He was more interested in showing everyone the new tricks he and his sister had learned: the finger-grabbing one and the finger-sucking one. But any time he tried to get near her she was escorted off into someone else's arms, and he was left helplessly moving from one group to another, no one giving him the slightest bit of attention. It was incredibly unfair. She was his sister after all, and he'd only had five minutes with her.

"Mum, I want to show them the tricks," he whined, but as soon as he complained he had aunties chastising him for being naughty and telling him to be a good boy for his new sister. He was getting sick of this 'good boy', 'big boy' nonsense now. When he'd woken up this morning he'd just been Jonathan Philliskirk, aged seven likes cartoons and having fun. Now all of a sudden he was Mr. Big Brother, Mr. Good Boy. You couldn't change that fast, and he wasn't going to change; no way. He didn't care what they said. He was going to stay the same, no matter how often they told him to be a good boy and a big brother.

He was starting to get fed up of this party too. But then, with perfect timing, the first two cousins arrived: Paul and Susie. Paul was eleven and loved dinosaurs. Jonathan had visited his house once and Paul had showed him his dinosaur collection. It was very impressive, but Paul was a bit boring; he talked funny and never listened to what Jonathan had to say. Jonathan preferred Susie to Paul. She was eight and really, really naughty; naughtier than Jonathan at his very worst. He loved playing with Susie. She came up with brilliant ideas for games and didn't care if she got into trouble. And because she didn't care, Jonathan didn't either. It was never as bad getting into trouble when there were two of you. The last time Susie had been here, they'd got into massive trouble for making mud pies and flinging them at one another in the house. Even when his mum was yelling at them and promising to take all his toys away forever he didn't mind, because Susie was there and she was taking half the blame. And it was really all her fault, anyway, because it had been her idea to make the mud pies, to throw them at one another and then to take the battle into the kitchen.

"Hi, Paul. Hi, Susie," he said to his cousins when they came in. "I got a new sister; she's over there."

"She's cute," said Susie without a hint of sincerity. "What's her name?"

"I don't know. I don't think she has one," replied Jonathan.

"That's stupid," said Paul. "Everyone has a name, even a baby."

"I don't think babies this new have names," Jonathan ventured hopefully.

He actually had no idea why the baby hadn't a name. Maybe if he'd been given time to talk to his mum, he could have asked her about it.

"They do," continued Paul. "And anyway, that's not a new baby."

Paul was already being a pain.

"She is so," Jonathan replied defensively.

"No, she's not. She's nearly a year old."

"That's cos she's *adopted*, Paul," Jonathan said.

He couldn't believe that someone aged eleven didn't know about adoption.

"I know," chimed Paul. "And you're adopted too."

"So?" Jonathan countered.

"So that means your mum and dad aren't your real mum and dad."

"They are too my real mum and dad."

"No, they're not. You were abandoned as a baby and they got you 'cos your real mum didn't want you."

Paul smiled contentedly as Jonathan struggled for a response. Paul's version differed from the one his parents had told him. Where was the bit about being chosen from hundreds of other babies? Worse than that was his tone. He was mocking Jonathan and his new sister. He seemed to think being adopted was something to be ashamed of.

"Shut up, Paul," he said crossly and stormed off.

Susie hurried after him, leaving her brother to find someone else to upset.

"Wait, Jonathan," she shouted, weaving her way through the chattering adults. "Wait for me!"

Jonathan ignored her, running out into the back garden away from his cousins, away from them all. He wanted to be alone for a few minutes. But she had seen him, and she knew where Jonathan's hiding-place was; he had shown it to her last summer. She crept quietly out onto the freshly-cut lawn. Aunt Margaret's garden was much bigger than hers. It had a pond, and lots of trees and bushes perfect for hiding in; but only one of them contained her cousin. It was a tall, fluffy one which looked perfectly innocent from the outside but turned into a mystical hideout once you pushed away a few branches and stepped inside. She and Jonathan had spent hours hiding in there during that long hot summer, and no one had known where they were. Then, when they were sure no one was looking, they'd sneaked out and walked into the house as if nothing had happened.

Jonathan's mum had been shocked. "Where have you two been?" she'd asked.

They'd said nothing, just giggled impishly and headed inside to watch *Thundercats*.

"Jonathan," she whispered. "Are you in there?"

"No! Go away."

"Can I come in, Jonathan, please?"

"No."

"Come on, Jonathan. We can hide again. They won't know where we are."

There was no response. She was about to go back inside when Jonathan spoke again.

"Come in, then," he said rapidly. "But don't let Paul see you."

No sooner had the words left his mouth when she was inside beside him. It wasn't the same as last time, though. She'd got wet forcing herself past the leaves, and the hideout was damp and uninviting. Jonathan had found a dry spot and he sat there glumly, not even bothering to look at her.

"Jonathan, there's nowhere to sit; the ground is all wet."

"Sit here," he said dispassionately, brushing away some of the dirt to reveal a drier patch beneath.

"Oh, thanks. You're so clever, Jonathan."

"Well, it is my hideout."

They sat in silence for a while. It wasn't as much fun as last time. Susie wished she'd brought some crisps.

"I hate your brother," Jonathan said after a spell, and, just to confirm who he meant: "Paul. I hate him."

"'Cos of what he said?"

"Yeah."

"I hate him too," Susie conceded.

"Why?" Jonathan asked, glad to have someone who shared his grievances.

"He's always mean to me."

"He is mean," Jonathan agreed. "I don't like him."

"There's nothing wrong with being adopted," said Susie.

"Isn't there?" Jonathan asked.

"No. My mum said that you and your sister are an absolute blessing to Auntie Margaret."

"Really?"

"Yeah."

Jonathan mused on this for a minute.

"Your mum knows much more about it than Paul, doesn't she?"

"Yes, loads more," said Susie.

"Paul is a fool, isn't he?"

"A big fool," she nodded in firm agreement.

Jonathan brightened up. Susie's mum was right: he was a blessing, and so was his sister.

"Let's go in and steal some food and bring it out here," he said, getting to his feet. Susie smiled. That was more like it.

But when they got inside people were already eating. Half the plates had been brought into the living-room and everyone was tucking in with reckless abandon. Jonathan panicked; if the Rocky Road was all gone, there'd be trouble. He scanned the room. No one was eating the sandwiches – hardly surprising, they were rubbish – but the buns had taken a sizeable hit. The biscuits, the cake, the sausage rolls, all that other good stuff was being decimated, but he couldn't see the Rocky Road anywhere. They couldn't have eaten it all, not this fast. He spotted his mother, for once not surrounded by interfering adults.

"Mum!" he said, running up to her and lowering his voice. "The Rocky Road?"

Margaret smiled at him and raised a finger to her lips.

"Where are they?" he whispered. "Are they all gone?"

She shook her head. "They're in the fridge," she mouthed. "I was keeping them for you."

Jonathan grinned; good old Mum. "Can I get them?"

Margaret nodded and took him by the hand. Away from prying eyes they went to the fridge, and from deep inside she extracted a plate full of Jonathan's most favourite thing in the world.

"Why don't you and Susie go upstairs and eat these between you?"

"Really, Mum?" he said.

"Yes. Quickly now before someone sees you and wants some."

He didn't need to be told twice. Waving frantically at his cousin, he scampered up the stairs and went straight to his room. Seconds later Susie came in, eyes wild with curiosity.

"Look what I've got," Jonathan said, revealing the plate full of thick slices of Rocky Road.

"Oh, my God," said Susie, clasping her hands to her chest.

They sat on the floor, took a piece each and began to eat.

"Mmm," said Jonathan.

"Mmm," replied Susie.

They grinned at each other, teeth thick with chocolate, and took another piece. Jonathan had already done the maths; there were thirteen pieces, which meant that one of them would get seven and the other six. He intended to be the one who got seven. By the end of his third piece, however, he was already starting to feel full. The rich chocolate and marshmallow combination sat heavily in his stomach. He felt a little queasy, but it tasted so good. He couldn't stop eating. Susie was suffering too; after her fourth piece she declared herself full, lying flat on the floor, panting like a dog. Jonathan really wanted to stop too, but every time he decided he'd had enough he went back for another bite, just one more little bite. Eventually he had to admit defeat and joined his cousin on the floor to recuperate.

"So yummy," said Susie dreamily.

"I know," Jonathan replied in a daze.

A sudden cramp in his stomach caused him to flinch. He felt like farting but was afraid of what might come out.

"Ooh," he moaned as the pain increased. "I'm really full; I think I've had too many."

"Can never have too many," whispered Susie reverentially.

"Maybe if I have some more the pain will go away."

"Get me one if you're having one," Susie mumbled.

Jonathan sat up and immediately wished he hadn't. His guts were rumbling ominously.

"Just going to the toilet," he croaked as he crept to the bathroom.

Inside, he perched himself on the toilet and relaxed. A cacophony of squeaks, rasps, toots and parps rang around the Philliskirk bathroom. To anyone listening outside it would have sounded as if a brass band was being put through its paces by a frantic conductor. Jonathan groaned and moaned as half his body weight passed through his system. He paused for breath. Was it over? His stomach certainly felt better. But then another deluge, and even more this time. He winced as his bowels continued to empty, the splish-splash of the water causing him to giggle despite the pain. By the time it finally came to a halt he was crumpled in pain, rocking back and forth, his hands pressed to his aching stomach. He waited a few minutes in case there was more, but that seemed to be it. He'd probably never have to poo again.

"Flippin 'eck," he muttered as he cleaned himself up and flushed the foul load far, far away.

As he washed his hands, he wondered if he should have some more Rocky Road. He didn't feel sick anymore, so why not pick up where he'd left off?

"Susie, I hope you haven't ..."

He stopped in his tracks. Paul was sitting there on his bed, bold as brass, and on his lap was the plate of Rocky Roads – what was left of them.

"What are *you* doing here?" Jonathan asked angrily.

"Having some Rocky Road. Auntie Margaret said I could."

"No, she didn't," Jonathan said, sure that his mother would never betray him like that.

"She did," said Paul, reaching for another helping. There were only three pieces left now.

"Get your hands off! They're mine; mine and Susie's."

"I don't want anymore," sighed Susie from the floor.

"She doesn't want them, Jonathan. Which means more for me," Paul smiled.

This was too much. First Paul had come into his house and told Jonathan his mum wasn't his real mum; now he'd gate-crashed his room and started eating his Rocky Roads. Who did this guy think he was? The worst cousin in the entire world, that's who.

"Get your hands off them or you'll be in trouble," Jonathan warned.

"Yeah right, what will you do?"

This was a good question. Jonathan had only ever been in two fights; one with a boy the same age as himself and one with a girl two years older. He'd won both fights easily, but that was neither here nor there. Paul was eleven and represented a much greater challenge. He was skinny, though, and quite puny for his age, plus he wore glasses. All kids who wore glasses were weak. He was eleven, though. In the end, the decision was made for Jonathan. Sensing trouble, Paul chose to wave a white flag and give up the Rocky Roads.

"Here, take them," he said haughtily. "They're not that nice anyway."

Jonathan snatched the plate from his hands. Not that nice? How come he'd eaten two pieces, then?

"Get out," he said as Paul rose to leave.

"I'm going, I'm going, *Jonathan*," he jeered.

Jonathan watched him go, waiting for him to leave before resuming his assault on the Rocky Roads. As Paul left the room he stuck his head back inside, a wicked smile playing on his lips.

"Oh, Jonathan?"

"What?"

"Your mum isn't your real mum."

Jonathan carefully placed the plate on the floor, calmly, like a waiter presenting an expensive main-course, and then went for his cousin. But Paul was a step ahead; he'd been expecting this. He raced down the stairs away from Jonathan's clutches.

"Mum, Mum!" he shouted as the younger boy tore after him. "Jonathan's trying to kill me!"

Paul rushed to his mother and hid behind her. Seconds later Jonathan came tumbling into the room, teeth gritted, eyes ablaze.

"JONATHAN!" his mother said as her son darted after his prey. "Stop that right now, do you hear!"

But he wasn't listening. He stood in front of his Aunt Cath with his fists clenched, waiting for Paul to come out of hiding.

"Now what's all this about?" Margaret asked, moving to his side.

Her sister-in-law, Cath, wholly unperturbed by the commotion, remained locked in conversation with one of the other guests while her son hid in her skirts.

"He said you're not my real mum, and my real mum didn't want me," Jonathan said, jabbing his finger at Paul.

A few people had been drawn to the kerfuffle, among them Jonathan's favourite uncle, Tony.

"He said what, Jonathan?"

The sound of Tony's voice momentarily shook Jonathan from his fury. He looked up at him and, buoyed by his presence, made a grab at Paul. But the older boy skilfully evaded his clutches, sneaking to the other side of his mother while Jonathan clawed at thin air.

"He – he –" Jonathan started, so angry he'd begun to hyperventilate. His breath came in ragged, short bursts as he struggled to contain his emotions. Realising he was about to cry, and not wanting to act like a baby in front of his uncle Tony, he ran out of the room, but not before delivering one final message to his cowardly cousin.

"SHE IS MY REAL MUM, AND YOU'RE JUST A STUPID IDIOT!"

He was out the back door and in his hiding-place before anyone could catch him. And there he sat, knees pulled to his chest, crying his heart out, until his uncle Tony stuck his head in through the foliage.

"Room for one more, pal?"

Jonathan looked at him curiously. Adults weren't really supposed to be in here, but then Tony wasn't like the other adults. He was cool. He always played games with him while everyone else sat inside drinking beer and talking rubbish.

"Okay," he said softly.

Tony huddled up beside him; he was a bit too big to sit down properly so he crouched, leaning his back on the tree's trunk for support.

"Nice little place you've got here, Jonathan."

"Thanks, Uncle Tony."

"Not as good as the place me and your dad had when we were your age."

"No?"

"We had a tree house, a proper one with a ladder and everything."

"A tree house?"

"Yep, it was ace. Maybe we could build one for you some day."

"I would *love* that."

"We'll have to see if you've got any trees big enough first, though."

"Oh, yeah," Jonathan said. "I hadn't thought of that. Will we check now? We could start building one!"

"Later, okay, mate?"

"Okay, Uncle Tony."

The two of them sat in silence for a while. It was getting dark outside, and darker still in their little hideout. They could hear the sounds of the party from the house, muffled voices and the occasional laugh, a fine time being had by all.

"Some party, eh?" Tony said.

"Mmm," replied Jonathan sadly.

"Jack and Chloe are inside, if you want to play with them."

"Maybe later." Jonathan had had enough of cousins for one day.

"And Paul," Tony said with what Jonathan presumed was a smirk.

"I'm never playing with him again," Jonathan said firmly.

"Don't blame you, mate. He's a little shit, isn't he?"

"He is," Jonathan laughed. Uncle Tony really was the best.

"What were you two fighting about?"

Jonathan didn't reply. He just wanted to forget about the whole thing. He wanted this party to be over, he wanted his sister to go back to the hospital and he wanted everyone to stop telling him he was a big boy.

"He's lying, Jonathan. You know that, don't you?"

Jonathan sighed deeply. He didn't know what to think. His head felt funny. He didn't like being adopted anymore, not if people were going to make fun of him for it.

"She is my real mum," he whispered, as much to himself as Tony.

"Of course she is, Jonathan, and she loves you very much."

"Why am I adopted?" he asked, turning to face his uncle.

"Because you're special, Jonathan. Your mum and dad couldn't have a baby so God gave them you."

This was the third explanation Jonathan had been given: first he'd been chosen, then he'd been given away and now he was being handed down from the heavens. They couldn't all be telling the truth, could they?

"And the new baby?" he asked.

"The same," Tony replied.

"Is she really my sister, then?"

"Yes, she is. She's part of your family now: your mum, your dad, you and your sister."

"Our family," Jonathan said. He liked the sound of that.

"Yes," Tony said.

"My real mum, my real dad and my real sister."

"Exactly."

"And you, my real uncle."

Tony laughed and put his arm around the boy. "You bet, pal, my favourite nephew and all."

Jonathan snuggled up beside him, delighted with his new accolade. They stayed like that for some time, listening to the party but feeling no urge to join it until eventually Tony's knees started cramping up and he suggested they go inside.

"Where have you two been?" asked Malcolm as they came in the back door. "We're just about to toast the new arrival."

Toast? At night-time? Jonathan didn't see why not, although he would have preferred the rest of the Rocky Road.

But when they went into the living-room there was no sign of any toast; just the same stupid grown-ups with glasses in their hands. His parents stood at the head of the room, waiting to address their nearest and dearest.

"We'd just like to thank everyone for coming," began Malcolm. "It's been a big day for us, and we're grateful you're all here to share it. Unfortunately, the little one has had to retire for the night, but she sends her best wishes too."

Everyone laughed.

"If she provides us with half the happiness that Jonathan ... Where is he? Jonathan? Come up here, son."

Jonathan obliged, his face reddening as all the women went *aww* and said how handsome he was.

"Here he is," said Malcolm. "My little man, my best little man. How do you feel about having a sister, Jonathan?" he asked, playing to the crowd.

"I didn't even get to show anyone our trick," Jonathan replied glumly.

"What trick? You have a trick already?"

"Yes."

"Maybe you'll show me tomorrow, eh?"

"Okay."

"Where was I?" Malcolm faltered, the extra couple of lagers and the excitement of the day catching up with him. Margaret whispered something into his ear and he nodded enthusiastically, before continuing.

"We want to toast the latest addition to the Philliskirk family, but before we do we should tell you what we've decided to call her."

Excited murmurs spread throughout the twenty people crammed into the living-room. Every time someone had asked the new parents about a name, they'd been met with stony silence.

"To Sophie," cried Margaret abruptly – she'd never liked standing on ceremony.

"Bloody hell, Marge, talk about stealing my thunder!" Malcolm complained.

But then, seeing that everyone had raised their glasses, he did likewise.

"To Sophie," they repeated in unison.

Jonathan looked around the room at the drunken adults, all smiling and clinking their glasses. Why did they look so happy? Sophie was a rubbish name.

4

JONATHAN WATCHED HIS MUM CHANGE his sister's nappy. It was by far the most horrific thing he had ever seen.

"Mum, that's disgusting! She's disgusting!"

Margaret looked at him in amusement. "Yours was worse, you know."

He shook his head dismissively.

"Yeah, right, Mum! She's minging; I was never like that."

"You were, though," Margaret continued.

He refused to believe this; nothing could stink as badly as Sophie's arse. It was worse than the time Nana Grimes had fallen asleep after Christmas dinner and spent the entire evening farting. Jonathan had guffawed in delight until the smell hit him and made him feel sick; he'd had to stop eating his selection box after just three bars. It was that bad. He loved Nana Grimes, though. He didn't love Sophie's arse, or Sophie for that matter. He knew he should have pressed for a brother when he'd had the chance.

"Explain it to me again, Mum. How can she be my *real* sister?"

"Jonathan, we've been over this," Margaret replied, exasperated.

"I know, but I've forgotten."

She looked down at him; he was just seeking reassurance, she knew that, but it was growing tiresome. All morning she'd been explaining to him how she was his real mum, how Malcolm was his real dad and how Sophie was now his real sister. She could have killed Paul, and had told Cath not to bring him over again. But there would be other Pauls; this was only the beginning. Kids could be cruel and Jonathan would have to deal with a lot in the coming years. His sister would too. They hadn't asked to be different but here they were, already being singled out by their peers.

She finished changing Sophie and set her down in her walker. The toddler immediately set off on another aimless adventure, charging forward, not a hint of concern for her wellbeing. Jonathan whooped with glee and began following her, the two of them laughing as they went. Real sister or not, she was a decent playmate.

Margaret sat down for the first time that day and watched her two children run around in circles. Usually her days were spent devising ways to entertain Jonathan, ways to tire him out and keep him quiet; but now Sophie was taking care of that for her. If only she'd known, she would have got a second child much earlier. The next step would be training her to make the tea while she rested her weary bones. She could certainly have done with a cuppa right now. She had a hangover. A bad one. It had been after two when they'd got to bed, and the few hours' sleep she'd got were broken up by the cries of her new daughter. Sophie Philliskirk, it appeared, didn't do sleep. She'd been on the go all morning, and her poor mother was well and truly knackered. Margaret allowed herself to rest her eyes a moment. She would just close them for a bit, it helped with the headache ...

She awoke with a start, cursing herself for nodding off. The children were nowhere to be seen. Sophie's walker lay empty in the middle of the room. The house was eerily quiet. Panic set in. What had she done?

"JONATHAN!" she shouted and waited for a response.

But the house remained silent. She rushed upstairs into his bedroom. It was completely empty. She checked under the beds, in the wardrobes, all his usual hiding-places: nothing. Sophie's room was pristine, as it had been when she'd left it. Their own room, the master bedroom, showed some signs of disturbance however. Some of Malcolm's clothes had been thrown on the floor, mainly his shirts, though nothing appeared to be missing. Her underwear drawer had also been tampered with; various bits of lingerie lay scattered around the room. She felt sick. Had some weirdo been in here? Had he gone through all her stuff before taking her children? An image flashed through her mind of herself and Malcolm facing the media, tearful and guilt-ridden.

"MOTHER WHO FELL ASLEEP BEGS FOR HELP IN LO-CATING HER CHILDREN."

"SUSPECT, A CROSS-DRESSING CHILD-SNATCHER, CON-SIDERED HIGHLY DANGEROUS."

She stifled a sob and looked around in dismay. Everything she had dreamed of, everything she valued, lost because of a hangover.

As she glanced around something in the garden caught in her eye. A huge bay window overlooked their back garden and on bright, sunny mornings like this you couldn't help but be taken by its grassy magnificence. It wasn't that which caught her attention, though, but the sight of two little, she struggled for the word ... *soldiers?* Out there in the garden, shuffling through the grass, was a boy dressed head to toe in the camouflage fatigues she'd bought him for Christmas, and a little girl, much smaller, dressed in what appeared to be a man's shirt and a bra. The bra was draped over her head, presumably in lieu of a helmet and matched both the colour of the grass and the shirt, which covered her entire body. Margaret choked back her tears and moved closer to the window. If she hadn't just seen her whole life flash before her she might have found the scene amusing, but as it was she just wanted to make sure these were her children and not a pair of pint-sized terrorists on a highly sensitive mission. Yes, it was them alright: General Philliskirk and his willing accomplice, Sergeant Sophie the Brave.

She hurried down the stairs to the back door.

"JONATHAN!"

Jonathan looked up at the source of the voice, shook his head irritably and held a finger to his lips, motioning her to be silent. Margaret was in no mood to be silent; she ran towards them and picked up the smaller of the two assassins from the wet grass. Malcolm's olive green shirt hung limply from Sophie's body, the shape of her legs barely visible beneath. The matching bra had been drawn across the front of her face so that one cup covered her head and the other her chin. Jonathan looked up accusingly at his mother as his game was brought to an abrupt halt.

"MUM! We were nearly there!"

"Where, Jonathan? Where?" she asked in spite of herself.

"The house, Mum! We were planning an assault."

She dragged him up by his arm. He was soaking wet; they both were.

"Get in," she said quietly, pointing to the house.

Jonathan obeyed her command with no little haste. On the way in he thought about crying; but soldiers didn't cry, they took their punishment, and they took it with dignity.

Sometime later, after they'd been bathed and changed into dry clothes, Margaret sat Jonathan down for a one-to-one talk.

"Jonathan," she began, "what did I tell you about playing games with Sophie?"

"Play lots of games?" he replied hopefully.

"No, you know I didn't say that. Now, what did I say?" She remained calm, but what she dearly wanted to do was to grab him by the shoulders and shake him till he understood.

"No football and no war," he mumbled sadly.

"That's correct, Jonathan. And why did I say that?"

He shrugged his shoulders.

"Why did I say that, Jonathan?"

"'Cos she's too small."

"Well done. One last question, what were you doing out in the back garden just now?"

"Planning an assault." He was on the verge of tears now.

"But what was the name of the game you were playing?"

"*War*," he whispered, ashen-faced and full of remorse.

"That's right. You were playing a game I told you not to play."

"I'm sorry, Mum. I really am."

"It's not good enough, Jonathan; you can't do things like this. You almost gave me a heart attack."

Jonathan's eyes widened. "Are you okay now, Mum?"

He didn't want her to have a heart attack. His Granddad Grimes had had a heart attack and died shortly after.

"Yes, I'm fine, Jonathan," she replied wearily. It was always difficult to stay angry at him, which made his aberrations all the more infuriating. But she had to make him understand.

"Now, as punishment for being so naughty, you're not allowed to have any chocolate for the next two days."

His bottom lip began to quiver as he remembered that there was a second plate of Rocky Road in the fridge.

"But, Mum ..." he began.

"But nothing, Jonathan. Mummy is very cross. I'm only doing this so you'll learn."

"Okay, Mum," he said and got up from his seat.

Margaret hadn't decided whether she was finished with him or not, but as she watched him amble up the stairs she thought it best to let him be. He wouldn't forget this in a hurry. There would certainly be no more games of *War* for the foreseeable future.

She hated falling out with him, though, hated it. Life would be so much easier if he could just do what he wanted all the time. If she never had to tell him off and he was always happy. She'd feed him Coco Pops for his dinner, congratulate him when he told the neighbours to fuck off and increase his pocket money when he misbehaved in school. He'd be so happy, the happiest child alive, but completely without morals; a feckless, horrible brat with an enormous sense of entitlement. He'd reach eighteen morbidly obese, with no friends and little formal education and head out into the real world, only to scurry home days later asking her to bake him a cake. No, this short-term pain would lead to long-term gain. Every little upset would help to mould him into a fully-functioning, responsible adult. It had better.

But knowing that didn't make it any easier. As soon as she'd told him off she yearned for the moment when all would be well again, when his time in the doghouse would be at an end and things could return to normal. Bizarrely, this only happened once she'd apologised to him. Even though he'd misbehaved, she'd feel so bad about telling him off that she'd come begging for forgiveness a few hours later. All that effort scolding him and setting him straight, undone by an apology born out of guilt. She couldn't help it, though; she never wanted to see him sad and certainly never wanted to be the cause of his sadness, but she had another one to worry about now and life could no longer revolve around Jonathan Philliskirk and his flights of fancy. His apology would have to wait; at least until after lunch.

When lunchtime came she went to the kitchen to see what she might make for him. It'd have to be something nice, one of his favourites: a peace offering. His favourites changed so often though, 'the best thing in the world, ever' could become 'horrible, I'm never eating that again' in a matter of days, so she decided to wait until he came downstairs and then ask him what he'd like. Strangely, though, he hadn't yet emerged from his room. She'd never known him to miss a meal; you could usually set your clock by his stomach. She waited until a quarter past and then went upstairs to see what was wrong. Sophie was asleep in her cot, worn out from her morning adventure, and the door to Jonathan's room was firmly shut; he was really taking this one to heart, which wasn't necessarily a bad thing. It killed her to think of him in there all sad and contrite, though, his poor little belly rumbling.

"Jonathan?" she said, gently tapping on his bedroom door. "Can I come in?"

"Yes," a voice replied from inside the room.

He lay flat on the bed on his stomach, reading a comic.

"You haven't come down for your lunch," she said, sitting on the end of the bed.

"No," he said, not taking his eyes from his *Beano*.

"Weren't you hungry?"

He shrugged his shoulders and sighed.

Here came the apology. She couldn't help it.

"I'm sorry, Jonathan for being cross at you."

"It's okay, Mum. I deserve it."

This was new; usually her apology was met with a loving embrace and the ending of hostilities.

"You weren't really to know, Jonathan."

Now she was really back-tracking. At this rate she'd be joining them for war, football and who knew what else.

"No, Mum, you were right," Jonathan said, turning to face her. "But don't send me back. I'll be good from now on, I promise."

She looked at him, puzzled. "Send you back where, Jonathan?"

"To the hospital."

"Why would we send you back to the hospital?"

"Because I'm bad."

"Jonathan," she said, moving up beside him, "you're our son!"

She took him in her arms and plonked him on her lap. Of late he'd begun complaining when she'd tried to sit him on her lap, but he came willingly now.

"But you might be able to get a better one in the hospital," he said, casting his eyes downward. "One that doesn't play *War*."

Her thoughts immediately turned to Paul: what had that little brat told her son?

"Jonathan," she said, tilting his head so that he was forced to look at her. "You're our son, our only son, and no matter what happens or what you do you'll always be our son. We're not taking you back to the hospital or sending you anywhere. Okay?"

"Are you sure, Mum?"

"I'm sure. I promise."

"But how do you know?"

"Because we love you with all our heart and we couldn't imagine life without you."

"But my other mother gave me away. Maybe you will too."

She pulled him to her chest and held him tight. He seemed so matter-of-fact about it all, as if he'd given it serious thought and accepted his fate.

"I promise you, Jonathan. I promise, promise, promise we will never give you away, ever."

"Okay, Mum," he mumbled through a face full of cardigan and blouse. She eased her grip, realising she was in danger of smothering him.

"Do you know how much we love you, Jonathan?"

"Lots?" he asked uncertainly.

"Yes, lots."

"How much, Mum?"

She spread her arms as wide as they could go. "This much."

"That's a lot," he said, pleased.

"Even more than that," she said, standing up. "From here," she said, pointing to the wall behind Jonathan's bed, "to here," pointing to his door.

"Really?" he asked, raising an eyebrow. "That's loads, Mum."

"I know, Jonathan. My arms aren't long enough to show you much we love you."

He liked that. "I love you from here to here as well, Mum," he said, pointing from the wall to the door. "But if my arms could spread from here to Nana Grimes' house, I'd love you that much."

She took him by the hand and gave him one last tight squeeze.

"Do you want some Rocky Road, my love?" she asked.

5

His mother's words had reassured him, but Jonathan decided to be on his best behaviour for a while, just in case. She'd said her arms weren't long enough to show much she loved him, but all that could change if he didn't start being a good boy. So that meant no more War with his little sister. From now on he would only play the games his parents had approved. This was very boring, though. He quickly learned that nine-month-old babies were limited in the games they could play. Sophie had been a brilliant soldier because all it had involved was crawling through the grass and staying low; unfortunately, she had little else in her skill-set. He brought down all his Star Wars figures and his Millennium Falcon and lined them up in his playroom – it was their playroom now, but he still referred to it as his. Then, thrusting a few Stormtroopers into her hands, he told her that she was the dark side and her job was to stop the rebel invasion. This didn't go well. No sooner had he turned his back to jettison his troops when she was off crawling down the hallway, Stormtroopers still in her hands, enemy base vacated and vulnerable to attack.

"Sophie! Come back!" he yelled, the carefully-constructed game crumbling before his eyes.

But it was no use; she just wasn't interested. Maybe if he let her be the rebels it'd be different, but there were no guarantees. In one last desperate attempt to involve her in his greatest passion, he took out his beloved light-sabre from its case. He never let anyone use his lightsabre, and only used it himself when he was feeling particularly strong in The Force. But she was his sister, so if she broke it his mum would have to buy him a new one. They sat in the playroom, cross-legged, facing one another.

"Here, Soph," he said, handing her the plastic weapon. "You hold it like this."

He grabbed the handle and swung the Jedi sword gently through the air.

"Now you try," he instructed, forcing it into her hands.

She gamely held on, and for one magical moment it looked like she was going to cut a swathe through Vader himself, downing the terrible Sith Lord in one foul swoop; then the lightsabre dropped limply from her grasp, flopping down in front of her where she gazed at it accusingly.

"Ah, Sophie, you're useless! Do you know that? Useless!"

He picked up the device and put it back in his toy box. That was it; no more Star Wars. No more wars of any kind.

However, over time he accepted her limitations, loved her for them even. He no longer cared that she couldn't play Star Wars with him. They made up their own games, silly little things only they understood, or, in truth, only Jonathan understood. The majority of these games just involved throwing things at one another and rolling around on the floor, but every now and again they got creative. They built forts and spent hours in there giggling and laughing. They sang songs; Jonathan making up the words, Sophie humming and shouting along. They had crawling races, the route never predetermined, but usually taking in three or four rooms and a lap of the garden.

When she began to learn to walk, it extended their fun. They played hide-and-seek around the house, and sometimes Margaret and Malcolm joined in. Sophie was a terrible hider, though. Her sole trick was to shuffle off to the kitchen and sit beneath the table, chuckling at her own cunning as she concealed herself behind the legs of the chairs. The rest of them dragged the game out for as long as they could, with the usual cries of "Where's Sophie? I can't imagine where she could be." Until finally, when it looked as if she might explode, they checked under the table, exclaiming in surprise: "I've found her!" And it never lost its appeal. Even after the hundredth time.

When the weather improved they took their games outside. Malcolm had constructed a swing set and a seesaw, and, under the watchful eye of their mother, they put the new apparatus through its paces.

"Careful, Jonathan," Margaret warned as Jonathan arched his back for more purchase.

He was already swinging dangerously high, so high that the nuts and bolts, fastidiously tightened by his father, were creaking in protest.

"I want to see if I can go all the way around, Mum!"

"You are not going all the way around, Jonathan."

While Jonathan attempted to defy gravity, kill himself or both, Sophie was content to be gently pushed back and forth by her mother. This was nice. Her stomach did a little turn every time she swept forward, and for a second or two it got really scary. But then she returned to where she'd started and it was all okay again.

"Whee," Margaret sang as Sophie soared all of two feet into the air.

Her cries spurred Sophie on; she began bucking backwards and forwards like her brother. She wanted to go higher, as high as the sky.

"Higher, Soph?"

"Eee," she replied assertively.

Margaret did as instructed, pushing her daughter with slightly more force, propelling her a little bit further into the stratosphere.

She was really moving now; at this rate she'd catch her brother up in no time. She could feel the wind against her face, soft and warm, refreshing. Her little strands of curly hair had been brushed into neat pigtails by her mother a few hours previously; now they flapped in the breeze, free and loose, like herself.

"Eee," she commanded, when Margaret took a momentary break.

"EEE!"

"Coming, coming," Margaret replied, assuming her position at the rear of the smaller swing.

Momentum restored, Sophie concentrated on her brother. He was going very high, but with a little hard work she could not only match his swing but surpass it. She bucked in her seat, her face set determinedly as she cast her gaze towards the skies. The sun burned brightly from above, causing her to squint as she propelled herself forward; then it disappeared and she was thrown into darkness. It was Jonathan: he was blocking it out. Her brother was so big and so strong, he could obscure the entire sun. Forward and back he went into the sky like a shadowy demon, eclipsing the light with each swing. Sophie kept watching, her face a picture of concern as she watched him climb higher and higher, relief washing over her each time he came hurtling back down to earth. He began to call out her name, the word starting way above and ending somewhere in the depths of the surrounding countryside.

"SOOPPHHHHIEEEEEEEE ... "

It was a mesmerising spectacle. She stopped thinking about her own progress and instead focused on Jonathan. This boy, her best friend, her big brother, could fly; he could touch the sky. She was seeing it with her own eyes. Then something inexplicable happened, so shocking she could barely comprehend it. He swung into the air once more, calling her name, obscuring the sun – but this time he didn't come back. He simply vanished. She looked up, panicked. Jonathan was nowhere to be seen, and the sun had resumed its fiery place in the middle of the pale blue sky. Sophie's lower lip trembled. Where had he got to? What had happened to her brother? She looked sideways, twisted around in her seat but saw nothing, only the smiling face of her mother as she continued to push her. "Whee." Sophie didn't want to *whee* any more, though. She wanted to know what had happened to her brother.

Suddenly, as quickly as he'd disappeared, he returned. There he was, walking towards her as if nothing had happened; as if he hadn't just vanished into the sky and worried her half to death.

"Mum, mum, did you see me jump?"

"I did, Jonathan."

"Was it good?"

"Very impressive, love."

He got back on the swing beside her, idling half-heartedly. Sophie was swinging higher than he now. But she had grown tired of this game and tired of being deceived. She wrestled with the buckles around her waist, twisting impatiently, making it clear she wished to play something else. Her mother released her. "Seesaw?" she asked. Now Sophie was in another seat, one which moved up and down rather than backwards and forwards. This was fun, too. Jonathan sat on the other side and her mother helped her to go up and down, up and down. The best thing about this game was being able to see Jonathan all the time, right there directly across from her. When she went up he went down, and vice versa. She laughed incessantly as Jonathan went from being all the way down on the ground, to being way up high in the sky. She made sure to keep a close eye on him this time, lest he disappear once more; then without warning he hopped off his seat, bringing the game to a premature end.

"Playin' football," he announced, running off to the garage.

Sophie watched him go, sad that the game was over.

She sat on the grass for a while, watching Jonathan kick the ball, until Margaret went to get some ice-pops from the freezer. All three of them sat slurping their lollies on the decking, Sophie insisting she hold her own despite dropping it on the ground every few seconds.

"Mum, can I tell you something?" Jonathan asked presently.

"Of course, Jonathan."

"It's about Sophie."

"What about her?"

"I think I love her now, Mum."

Margaret's first instinct was to cry. His words jabbed at her heart like a pitchfork, prodding it until it almost bled.

"Do you, pet?"

"Yes, Mum."

"Do you know how I know I love her?" he continued.

"How?"

"Cos when I think of her it makes me feel nice, the same way I feel when I think of you and Daddy."

That finished Margaret. She tried to hold back the tears, but it was no use.

"What's wrong, Mum? Don't be sad!"

She sniffed away her tears. "I'm not sad, Jon. Sometimes you cry when you're happy, too."

"Is this one of those times?"

"Yes, Jonathan. You've made me very happy. You're a very good boy."

Jonathan was delighted with this. He liked it when he was a good boy; it usually meant sweets, and sometimes even a present.

As they spoke Sophie watched, melting ice-pop in her hand. What were they saying? Why was her mum crying? Then they both smiled and she smiled too. She liked it when they smiled; it meant they were happy. And if they were happy, she was happy too.

6

THE PHILLISKIRKS SEEMED TO HAVE successfully negotiated this potentially difficult time in their lives. Sophie had settled in without too many problems, and after some initial misgivings Jonathan was now comfortable with being adopted. The issue of what to tell him had come up sooner than they'd anticipated, but he had dealt with it remarkably well and would surely benefit in the long run. True, they couldn't shield him from everything, from the Pauls of this world, but as long as they answered his queries honestly and quelled his fears, they wouldn't have anything to worry about. There had been some slight behavioural changes in the immediate aftermath of his enlightenment; a slight neediness, the constant seeking of reassurance. The books said that was natural, a phase, and just his way of processing the information. In time he would grow out of it. He did indeed grow out of it. He accepted that he was different, that he had come from someone else's tummy, but understood that he was as beloved and cherished as any little boy could possibly be.

Then came the Family Tree project.

Jonathan was in Year Two now and, according to his teachers, was a studious and attentive pupil. This thrilled Margaret: her boy was an academic. She didn't want to become one of those pushy parents who put their kids under pressure to succeed, but if he were gifted then it would do no harm to offer a little encouragement. She took a greater interest in his studies, sitting down every evening with him and going over his home-work. It didn't matter that he was only seven years old and that his teachers had merely suggested that he was a good little boy; this was the time to capitalise on his talents. While all the other kids sat in front of the TV watching cartoons, her Jonathan would be brushing up on his arithmetic and his spelling. His spellings were something to behold; he never got one wrong, never. One time he had spelled the word *immediately* correctly, with little or no prompting from herself. It was remarkable. There couldn't have been too many seven-year-olds in the country, never mind in his year, who could spell such a difficult word with flawless regularity. His adding and subtracting were exemplary, too; he didn't even need to use his fingers and thumbs when calculating the more difficult sums. Margaret could hardly wait for Malcolm to get home each evening so she could perch Jonathan up on a chair and have him perform his latest tricks like a circus animal.

Occasionally, when he wasn't spelling difficult words or naming the ten longest rivers in the world, Jonathan had to do art projects. Margaret wasn't so keen to help with these. She understood that it couldn't be all about books and learning, and that he needed to have fun sometimes too, she accepted all of that, and it wasn't a problem. The problem was that these art projects invariably involved glue and paint and scissors and sticking bits of paper to things. The project itself took a few hours to complete, but the clean-up operation lasted for weeks. It had reached the stage where it was easier for her to do the projects all by herself; it was quicker and far less messy. When Miss Jones asked her Year Twos to complete a family tree,

Margaret was eager to assume control; but this particular project posed larger problems than how to get paint out of one's hair.

"Jonathan's got to do a family tree for school," she mentioned to Malcolm one night, when the children were in bed.

"Has he?"

"Yes. What do you think we should do?"

Malcolm pondered this for a moment. "Well, I know he doesn't like my dad, so maybe he could leave him out."

"Malcolm, I'm serious," she replied. "This is bound to raise some questions."

Her husband reluctantly moved his eyes from the TV. His selfish side told him that he worked long hours to provide for his family and that someone else should deal with stuff like this. He knew that was wrong, though, and how hard it was for his wife. Besides, he wanted to have as much input as possible in his children's lives.

"*Everything* raises questions, Marge," he replied.

"You know what I mean, Malcolm. What if he asks about *her*, and wants to put her on his family tree?"

The idea terrified Margaret. What would they call her: the *other* mother? His birth-mother? And more to the point, where would they put her? In the middle of the tree, with Margaret relegated to a lesser spot on one of the outer branches? What would the other kids say when they saw Jonathan's tree? It'd be like Paul all over again, except that this time there would be an entire playground of baying children instead of just one.

But the thing she feared most was giving this *other* mother a life. At the moment she was alive only in their imaginations, but if she were to be immortalised in a family tree, she would become very real. They knew little about her, only that she'd been young when she'd had him – in her teens – and that she wasn't from the area. Her details were on file for Jonathan when he was older, but for now they were happy to remain ignorant.

"I don't think he will," Malcolm said decisively.

"Why not?"

"He's seven years old, Marge. Kids that age don't think about stuff like that."

"But what if he does?" she persisted.

"Well, if he does and he wants to put her on the tree, then we'll have to let him put her on the tree."

This wasn't what she wanted to hear. She wanted her husband to take her side, to see how damaging this could be for their child's development, but she also wanted him to understand how much it would hurt her.

"What if he wants to put his birth-*father* on there too?" she asked spitefully.

Malcolm shrugged his shoulders, but she could see he didn't like the idea, didn't like it one bit.

"Look," he said, holding his hands up to signal a truce. "This is just the beginning. The older he gets, the more questions there are going to be. Our job is to answer those questions, and make sure he understands why he was adopted and what it means for him. Unfortunately, our own feelings don't come into it."

He was right, of course. Now that they'd opened the floodgates, there was no turning back. They had to answer every question and be as honest and as forthright as they possibly could. She didn't want her son to have issues when he grew up or to harbour grudges against them, to become one of those problematic teens whose troubles stemmed from a difficult childhood.

"Okay, Malcolm, you're probably right," she conceded. "I'll have a chat to him about it when we're doing the chart tomorrow."

"Great," Malcolm said, turning back to the TV.

Newsnight was just about to start. Perfect timing.

*

"Mum, where's the Pritt Stick?"

Margaret looked at Sophie in desperation. Sophie stared back casually. *Don't ask me, my job is to just sit here and be cute.* There was no avoiding it any longer. Her daughter had been fed, changed, sang to, played with and burped. If only she'd been one of those cranky babies that cried at the drop of a hat. Not Sophie though; she was as good as gold. Little Miss Perfect.

"Wait a minute, Jon," she shouted. "I'll get the stuff ready now."

Jonathan had grown tired of waiting. She'd been putting him off for an hour and he was fed up, so he'd started by himself. He'd collected all his crayons and paints, and found some sheets of paper in his dad's study. But that wasn't enough. He needed more stuff. So he'd tipped out the contents of his big toy-box, and discovered that he could still fit inside it despite being two years older now. For a while he stayed in there, hidden, laughing away to himself, hoping his mum would come looking for him. Then he remembered why he'd emptied the box in the first place, and set about sifting through the pile of old toys and various junk he'd left in the middle of the floor. He found some great stuff: Skeletor's head, which he'd presumed lost; one of his favourite toy cars, which he'd blamed Phillip Clegg for taking; and loads of old toys that he'd completely forgotten about. He found an old colouring book which had only been half-finished, so he fetched his crayons from the kitchen and busied himself with that for a while. It was only when he'd finished colouring in some trees that he remembered his project, realising with fevered excitement that he could take the page containing the trees and stick it to another, larger page.

He stood in the kitchen holding his colouring book, spying the scissors and wondering if he could use them unchaperoned. His mum was rummaging through the cupboards, she wouldn't notice. He inched toward the scissors, keeping an eye on his mum all the while. But then she pulled out a bright red shopping bag. He hadn't seen that before. It looked new, as if she'd bought it this morning.

"What's in there, Mum?" he asked, hoping that the answer was sweets.

Lifting the bag onto the kitchen table, she said, "This is the stuff for your project."

"But I've nearly finished the project, Mum. Look!"

He held up the colouring book and the sheet he'd been working on for her perusal.

"Hmm," Margaret said, surveying his work. "This is all very good, Jonathan, but I think we can do a better job."

"Are you sure, Mum? I coloured it in really well," he said, pushing the sheet closer to her face in case she hadn't seen it properly the first time.

Margaret made a big show of examining the green and brown blobs on the paper, before shaking her head and leaving the sheet to one side.

"Come on, Jonathan, let's start again."

"Okay, Mum. Is Sophie going to help us?"

"I don't think so," Margaret said hurriedly, envisioning a paint-streaked baby with her hands glued to her face. "She's fine where she is."

"Okay then, Mum, let's get started," said Jonathan, peering inside the bag to see what he had to work with.

Margaret knew that the biggest obstacle to the project's completion would be Jonathan himself. His projects usually went something like this: She would come up with an idea, a general plan for how the project would take shape. Jonathan would say that this was a fine plan, and offer up his services in whatever way they might be needed. She would assemble all the things needed for the project: scissors, sticky tape, empty toilet rolls, pens, markers and so on, and Jonathan would immediately begin working on something else, his own mini-project. Happy to work without interference, she would get to work on the project and, despite herself, actually start to enjoy it. Jonathan, seeing that her project was better than his, would then butt in and start suggesting she do things differently. She would accede to some of his more reasonable requests, but flatly refuse a complete overhaul. Jonathan would then act as a willing helper for all of five minutes before declaring himself bored, leaving Margaret to complete the project by herself.

Once, just to see what would happen, she had let him dictate things and run the project by himself. The project in question had involved the solar system and the alignment of the various planets. It started off quite well; the sun was placed in the middle of the chart, Earth nearby and the moon at a reasonable distance from both. Then things went slightly awry. The moon began to grow, becoming bigger than the sun, so that he could draw a little face on it. Then several spaceships were sent out into the Milky Way for signs of life; a great battle ensued between mankind and an un-named alien species. These aliens had technology superior to that of their human counterparts and before long Earth was under attack, the future of humanity in serious doubt. By the time Jonathan declared himself bored Earth had been completely destroyed, and none of the other planets had seen the light of day. From that day forth, Margaret had decided that all projects would be tackled as a team. In other words, she would complete them while he watched.

"Okay, Jonathan, what do you know about family trees?" she asked, laying out an A2 sheet in the middle of the table.

Jonathan thought hard. He'd been told about this in school, but he was too excited to remember it right now. He loved doing projects with his mum, but he didn't like having to remember things from school.

"It's something to do with Nana and Granddad," he said finally. "They're at the top of the tree and I'm at the bottom."

"Very good, Jonathan, that's exactly it."

"Is it?" he asked, surprised.

"Yes. Your family tree is all the people in your family, from you to me and your dad, right up to your grandparents or even farther back."

Jonathan fell into silence while his mother began cracking open packets of crayons and stickers. She'd had a stroke of luck that morning when she'd come across a sticker-book asking her to *Create your own magical forest full of birds and other wildlife*. Oh she'd be creating a magical forest all right, one so magical, so full of birds and other wildlife, that her son would receive an array of gold stars from the blissfully unaware Miss Jones.

"Mum, I really don't get this."

"How do you mean?"

"The whole tree thing; what does it mean?"

He looked at her earnestly, awaiting the answer that would explain everything. Margaret had never considered the concept of a family tree before and was at a loss; Jonathan's questions often left her considering things she'd never really thought about before. And this particular question was the most difficult kind to answer, because it dealt with the abstract; there was no actual tree involved, but it was still called a family tree. In scenarios like this, she found it best to improvise.

"Our family tree is the one in your nana and granddad's back yard."

"The big yellow one?"

"Yes," Margaret replied.

He stared into space, lost in thought. He'd been in that back yard lots of times; there wasn't much to do at Nana and Granddad Philliskirk's, so he often spent hours out there making his own amusement. He'd tried to climb that yellow tree on numerous occasions, but he couldn't even reach its lowest branch

"So we've got to draw a picture of the tree in Nana and Granddad Philliskirk's back yard, Mum?"

"That's right, Jonathan."

"And that's it?"

"No, then we have to put all our family into the tree."

"Like monkeys, Mum?"

This was hopeless. She could spend hours trying to explain it to him this way, and he still wouldn't get it. She decided to change tack.

"It works like this, Jonathan – imagine all your family: me, your dad, your sister, all your cousins ..."

"Uncle Tony?"

"Yes, even Uncle Tony. We're all one big family, and the only way for us to keep track of one another is to draw a big tree with all our names on it. Then when you want to remember whose mum is who, or whose brother is who, you just look at the picture of the tree."

He nodded, seeming to understand.

"Am I on the tree, Mum?"

"Yes; it's your tree, so you're in the very middle of it."

"Wow! Can I put a tree-house in it?"

"Of course. We just have to draw it first."

"Great. Me and Tony will be in the tree-house, anyway," he said primly, picking up a crayon and pulling the sheet towards him.

She began to protest, indicating the sticker-book with all the lovely pictures of trees, the oaks, sycamores and horse-chestnuts, but it was too late; he'd already begun drawing what she presumed was himself and his uncle sitting in a tree, but could just as easily have been a continuation of the assault on Earth by the alien forces who had blighted their last project.

Margaret discreetly pulled out another sheet and got to work by herself. None of the stickers was big enough to use, but inside the book was a picture of a tree that fitted her purpose perfectly. She placed the sheet over the book and traced the tree onto it. It looked good, too good to fill in with a marker or a crayon. What she needed was something that would stand out, something that would put all those other seven-year-olds to shame. She rummaged through the bag, but nothing there helped. Then an idea struck her, something that would have Miss Jones gasping in awe and Jonathan placed at the very top of the class. She would go into their back garden and collect some leaves from the trees, then stick them to the page with glue. Then she would get a knife, strip some bark from the branches and use that for the tree-trunk. It would be incredible.

But she looked at the mess they'd already made, and then outside, at the drizzly April afternoon, and decided it wasn't worth the effort. Instead she would get all Malcolm's old *National Geographic* magazines and cut pictures of trees out of those. It would end up as a collage of sorts. Most of Jonathan's classmates probably didn't even know how to spell collage.

By the time she'd finished, the notion of explaining how family trees worked had become secondary. She'd been so engrossed in her work that she'd hardly even noticed Jonathan slip out of the room. Stepping back to take a look at her work, she cooed in admiration; it was quite something. If only she'd been this dedicated during her own schooldays.

"JONATHAN, what are you doing?" she called. "Come and take a look at this."

He padded in from the sitting-room and re-joined her at the table.

"Look at mine first, Mum," he instructed, pushing his work towards her.

She peered over for a look. True to his word he had drawn a tree-house, and it looked like he and Tony were inside. They appeared to be playing football, and there were no other family members in sight; just a great big tree with two people sitting inside it. There was no sign of herself or Malcolm, unless it was they who were lying on the ground outside the tree-house with blood pouring from their heads.

"Who are those people, Jonathan?"

"Oh, that's the Cleggs. They tried to get into the tree-house, but me and Tony kicked 'em out."

"Please don't ever do that to the Cleggs, Jonathan."

"If they try to get into my tree-house I'll have to, Mum."

"Why don't you take a look at mine for a minute, Jonathan?" she suggested, shifting her work towards him. "What do you think?"

"It's very good, Mum," he said solemnly, but she could tell he wasn't impressed. In fact, his interest in the project had begun to wane considerably.

"Will we start putting the family into it now?" she enquired hopefully.

"Okay," he smiled, his enthusiasm returning.

"Great," she said. "Who will we put in first?"

"Tony," he replied, not missing a beat.

She had already left spaces for him to draw in each family member so, indicating where to draw, she invited him to do his best representation of his uncle Tony.

They continued in this manner with more family members being added (she was pleased to come in at number four, two places ahead of her husband), until just one place remained. She had purposely left a vacant spot on the far reaches of the tree's outermost branch. Jonathan could add his birth-mother here if he so desired.

"Who will we put here, Jonathan? There's just one space left."

He studied the chart, reciting the names as he went through them and repeating the action just to be sure.

"I think we've got everyone, Mum," he concluded.

"Are you sure, Jonathan? There's no one else you'd like to add?"

"I'm not putting Paul in, Mum; no chance."

"That's fine, Jonathan. I didn't want you to put him in."

"Well, who then?" he enquired.

Margaret hesitated. It would be so simple to take the easy way out. She could just tell him to put in her father, who'd died when he was still in nappies, or she could suggest putting in his pet goldfish, Hannibal. Either would seem plausible to him and would bring the project to a satisfactory end. But she could hear Malcolm's voice, his mild indifference cloaking a profound disappointment. She would have failed him, and in the process failed her son too.

"How about the lady whose tummy you came out of?" she asked, as brightly as she dared.

Jonathan smiled uncertainly. Was this a joke, another one of those silly games adults played? It didn't look like it; his mum appeared to be deadly serious. She'd gone completely mad.

"But she's not in our family, Mum! We don't even know her!"

"We might know her someday, Jonathan."

"When, Mum?"

"When you're older."

"Well, we can put her in the family tree then, can't we?" he declared, getting down from his stool. Taking one last look at the project, he said, "Why don't we put Hannibal in that space, Mum? He's part of the family."

Hand shaking, Margaret picked up an orange crayon and drew what she hoped resembled a goldfish.

1999

Seán

1.

SEÁN MCLOUGHLIN HATED SCHOOL. HE was much the same as any other fifteen-year-old boy in that regard. But as much as Seán hated school – and he really hated it – he hardly ever missed a day. Even when he was sick he went. His grades might have been mediocre, but his attendance record was unrivalled. In fact, it was so good, that he had received a special commendation from the headmaster. He'd been called to the office one day, with no prior warning. On the way he'd racked his brains for any recent misdemeanours. He couldn't think of any. Was it possible that the principal had found out about the time he'd called Laura Griffin a 'dirty fuckin' slut' in front of the whole class last year? He'd fretted about that for months after, thoroughly expecting to be summoned to the office any time the intercom system crackled into life. But that had been a whole year ago, an entire summer had passed since then.

When he got to the office he nervously took his seat, eyeing Mr. Aylesbury warily as he did so. But there was no dredging up of the past, no threats of suspension and no calling of his parents. Instead, he was praised for something. Praised. In school. It might have only been for turning up. But still, it was praise.

"You've only missed two days in your entire time here. Did you know that, Seán?"

"Yeah, I had an idea all right, sir."

"That's one of the best attendance records I can ever remember, Seán."

He shrugged indifferently.

"You might not be the most gifted student, or the most hard-working, but your commitment to the cause cannot be questioned."

"I'm not sick very often," Seán offered meekly.

"Well, nevertheless, it's quite an achievement."

They carried on like this for a few minutes more; Mr. Aylesbury showering his student with platitudes, Seán batting away the acclaim like an Oscar-winning actress. Eventually he was permitted to leave, after promising to keep up the good work.

He walked away from the office feeling better than he'd done in months. Maybe he wasn't such a good-for-nothing after all. His commitment to the cause could not be questioned, that's what the headmaster had said, and if anyone knew, he did. What he didn't know was that Seán only came to school every day because it was preferable to being at home. He would have rather have been anywhere than at home, because *he* was there: Daryl, his stepfather. He was there, skulking from room to room, simmering, just waiting for Seán to say the wrong thing. He was there in that house, in his home. Seán would have stayed in school all day and night if they'd let him.

But that wasn't possible. At 3.45 every afternoon the bell rang to signal the end of another day. The sound was greeted with joy by most of the students; it meant freedom, the end of a day of drudgery. For Seán, though, it meant the resumption of hostilities. It meant returning to that house to face his nemesis. His mother would arrive home at six, but until then he was on his own. As soon as he walked in the door, it would begin.

"Don't leave your shoes there, Seán, that's not where they go. How many times have I told you about that before?"

He moved the shoes, wordlessly and without complaint. He couldn't remember ever being told about it before, but he knew better than to argue. Hoping to avoid any more confrontation, he retreated to his room; but Daryl was right behind him, always right behind him.

"Have you got homework to do?"

"Yeah."

"Well, get to it then; that last report card was a disgrace. And you're not to leave this room until it's done."

Seán took out his books and stared at them for a while. He couldn't remember the last time he'd actually done his homework; usually he just copied it from one of his friends in school the following morning. If Daryl asked to see what he'd done, he would just show him yesterday's work. Not that it mattered; his stepfather's education had been curtailed before he'd even reached his teens. That didn't stop him criticising Seán's academic performance, however. He reacted to each report card as if it were a personal insult. How dare Seán get an E in Maths? There Daryl was, busting his arse in work every day, providing for the family, ensuring they all had a roof over their heads – and Seán had the nerve to underperform in school? Maybe he was just a thick bastard, was that it? Seán assured him that he wasn't, that he was in fact more intelligent that Daryl could ever hope to be. But that just led to threats of physical violence and more name-calling; he was a waster, a good-for-nothing, a fucking leech. After a while, Seán began to believe his stepfather. He was a waster. He was a good-for-nothing. He was a fucking leech. So why even bother trying? Why do his homework or pay attention in class? He was never going to amount to anything anyway, so what was the point? He'd just do enough to get by and hope he passed his exams in a few years' time.

So instead of doing his homework he just pottered about, counting down the minutes until his mother returned and he could finally relax. He got a drink of water from the kitchen, creeping in and out so as not to alert Daryl, but no sooner had he returned from his sortie when Daryl appeared at his door once more.

"What have I told you about leaving the lights on? Do you pay the electricity bill?"

They both knew he didn't. He had no viable income, what with being fifteen and all.

"Well, do you?" Daryl repeated as Seán stared at the floor, determined not to answer.

Eventually Daryl was forced to answer his own question.

"No, you don't. I do," he said, jabbing a thumb into his chest, "which is why I turn off lights when I leave a room."

Sometimes, during these entirely pointless sermons, Seán would stare into Daryl's eyes in the hope of gaining a better understanding of the man; but it was like staring into an abyss. There was nothing there; plenty of animation, yes, eyes that danced back and forth, a mouth that spat out words with venom and disgust. But no real feeling. Did he know or care what he was doing? What could he possibly be getting from it? It seemed to Seán a rather pitiful existence.

These daily showdowns were wearisome in the extreme, but he could deal with them. They rarely escalated to anything beyond a good dressing-down, or ritual humiliation on a bad day. The real fun and games started at the weekend.

Sober, Daryl was easy enough to handle; you just kept quiet and waited for him to get bored. Drunk, Daryl was a more difficult proposition, and from Friday evening until Sunday afternoon this was the version Seán had to deal with. He countered this by spending the majority of his weekends with his friends, either at their houses or just hanging around in the local park. He couldn't stay away forever though, and if he stayed out too late even his mother would ask questions. In one way it wasn't so bad; Daryl was in the pub a lot, which meant Seán sometimes had the house to himself for a few hours. But even during these times of blissful solitude he had to be on his guard at all times, because as soon as he heard the scuff of Daryl's work-boots in the porch and the jerky scratching of his key that followed, he knew trouble lay ahead.

His stepfather always seemed to return home from the pub with one grievance or another: an unsettled argument with a fellow drinker, a three-legged horse that had let him down for a couple of hundred or, most commonly, someone leering at his wife as she pulled pints behind the bar. Of course, Seán could just have gone to bed and avoided it all. But he never had the place to himself, and weekend nights were the best for telly. Anyway, there was no telling what time Daryl would get home or whether his mother would come back with him. Those were the best nights, when she was with him. He'd hear their voices as they came in, and know that there wouldn't be any arguments that night. Sinéad would put her husband to bed and then it'd just be the two of them, mother and son. They'd talk for a while about school, about work, about their plans for the weekend and then she'd go to bed too, leaving Seán to watch telly for as long as he wanted.

Usually, though, Daryl came home alone and when he did, Seán was there in the living-room in *his* armchair, remote control in hand, living the high life. Kevin, Seán's younger brother, was in bed, which meant it was just the two of them. Even at this late juncture he had the chance to avoid confrontation; all he had to do was slip quietly to his room before Daryl got settled. But something inside him made him stay put. Even though he dreaded what was coming, he refused to run away from it. He would take whatever came his way like a man.

In came Daryl, muttering away to himself, already vexed by some perceived slight. Seán braced himself, listening to his stepfather rattle around the kitchen. He heard the ping of the microwave, the clink of cutlery. Any second now, he'd have company. He could have moved over to the couch, made things easier on himself. But why should he? No, he'd stay right where he was and watch the end of the film.

"Up," Daryl commanded as he came in with his plate.

Seán looked at him for a moment, hesitated and then moved to the sofa, bringing the remote with him.

"What's this shite?" Daryl asked, glancing at the television.

"A film," Seán said quietly.

"I hope it's nearly over."

"It's not."

"Well, if you think I'm sitting here looking at that for the night, you can think again."

Seán said nothing, he knew what was coming next. From the corner of his eye he could see Daryl scanning the room for the remote. It wasn't on his arm-rest where it was supposed to be. It wasn't on the table in front of him; where was it?

"Where's the remote?" he asked testily.

Silence. Seán's heart thudded in his chest, but his eyes remained fixed on the television. The film was ruined now, that much was obvious, but he wasn't going down without a fight.

"You must know," Daryl persisted. "Where is it?"

A shrug of the shoulders, barely perceptible.

Daryl laid down his plate and got to his feet, spotting the object of his desire as he did so.

"You have it there; give it to me."

"I'm watching this."

"Gimme the remote."

"No."

"No? Who the fuck do you think you are, boy, eh?"

More rhetorical questions. He didn't *think* he was anyone, he was just a teenage boy who wanted to watch the late film on a Friday night.

"Give me the remote, Seán," Daryl repeated flatly.

Again he chose neither to answer nor oblige. He often wondered what would happen if he dragged it out a bit longer, continued to deny his master. Could he drive him to physical violence? Was that what Daryl really wanted? Probably not; he was too cute for that. A physical fight might leave marks, things that would be hard to explain; so the abuse remained psychological, emotional and verbal. The worst he could do would be to switch off the television completely, so that they both sat there in silence; Seán staring at the blank screen and Daryl, the victor, scoffing his food.

On this occasion Seán relented; by doing so he could make a statement, one last gesture as his ship sank.

"Here's the remote," he said sweetly, handing the valuable piece of plastic to the king of the castle. "How could you live without it?"

As the transaction was made he fixed his stepfather with a look; a look of utter contempt and loathing.

"Don't you fuckin' look at me like that, you little cunt!"

Seán held his gaze, a smirk playing across his lips.

"Think you're fuckin smart, don't you?" Daryl spat. "All you are is a little bastard. We don't even want you here; you're not part of this family. The sooner you finish school, get a job and get the fuck out of here, the better."

His words meant nothing to Seán, he'd heard it all before. Daryl, Kevin and his mother, one big happy family; and Seán, the outsider, the unwanted baggage. So what? Who on earth would want to be related to Daryl Cassidy?

This would have been the perfect time to say his goodbyes for the evening, to walk away with one last withering glance and retire for the night. But he stayed right where he was, stood in front of Daryl, ready to receive his lecture.

"Fuckin' looking at me like that," his stepfather snarled. "Who the fuck do you think you are? You little cunt. Who do you think you are? I'm talking to you, Seán."

"I'm a little cunt," Seán replied. "Or is it a bastard? I can never remember."

"Fuck you," Daryl growled. He didn't like his weapons being taken away from him.

He changed tack.

"We don't want you here, you know. This is *our* house; you're just a lodger, a sponger. When I was your age I was contributing, working since

I was thirteen. But I don't think you'll ever get a job. Who'd hire you, a thick cunt? You'll probably fail all your exams and we'll be fuckin' stuck with you for life."

This was a relatively new theme, the subject of work. Since Seán had turned fifteen it had become commonplace. *Get a weekend job. Contribute to the running of the house. Pay your way. You're just a sponger.* This was what he had to look forward to for the next few years. While most kids his age were preparing for exams and planning for the future, he was being told to get a job and pay his way. Of course he could have got a job, had actually considered it a few times, but what would be the point? Rather than be congratulated for showing some initiative, it would simply open up a fresh can of worms. *How much are you earning? You can pay for your upkeep now. What are you spending that money on?* And so on and so on. So he stuck resolutely to his guns, for what they were worth. He'd endure this for a few more years, until he'd finished school and could get out of here, away from this shit, away from this pathetic excuse for a man. He'd go somewhere safe, somewhere he could call his own, have his own home.

For now, though, all he had was his room. Once there, safe and snug under the bedcovers, he fantasised about the day his revenge would come. He imagined a Friday night with an altogether different outcome. On this night Daryl would return from the pub and begin his usual routine, stamping around the house like a caveman, effing and blinding under his breath, before eventually coming into the living-room to start on his stepson. As usual, Seán would take it on the chin, sitting there in silence, listening to the insults and the abuse until the storm died down. This time, however, he wouldn't go to bed. He would wait until Daryl had finished his food and eased himself into his armchair. He would wait until he fell asleep, the remote still firmly gripped in his calloused hand. Then he would strike.

His first task would be to check on Kevin; there could be no witnesses to this crime. His little brother would be dead to the world; he slept like his father that one. Next he would go to the knife rack in the kitchen, where he would pull out the thickest, longest blade available. He'd stand there a moment admiring the blade, caressing it, allowing it to catch the light so that it glimmered menacingly. He wanted to savour this moment, to remember it. But there was no time to waste, his mother would be home soon. So he would return to the living-room, the blade gripped firmly in his hand, and once there he would take a final look at Daryl, standing over his quarry, knowing that in a matter of seconds he would take everything away from him. A small part of him might feel sorry for his stepfather, a hard-working man only trying to provide for his family. Those thoughts would quickly be banished; there would be no pity, no mercy shown this night. He'd take one final look at his tormentor before raising the knife high above his head and plunging it into his chest. Daryl's eyes would shoot open in horror, his mouth gasping for air; *too late now Daryl, far too late.* Seán would pull the knife free and watch the blood spurt from Daryl's chest like a sprung dam all over his mother's new carpet. Someone would have to clean up that mess later. But he wasn't finished yet. He'd bring the knife down again and again in a delirious frenzy. Daryl would raise his arms in protest, pawing the air in a last, desperate fight for his life, and then it would be all over. There'd be lots of blood, the living-room now a crime scene. He'd leave the room, stripping off his sodden clothes as he went. A quick shower would wash away the rest of the blood, and as he stood under the water he'd feel a weight lift from his shoulders. He was free, free from it all. Soon enough they would come to take him away. But let them come. He'd done what he'd set out to do. He was happy now.

2.

HE MIGHT HAVE SPENT HIS nights fantasising about killing his stepfather in cold blood, but when it came to his education Seán was under no illusions. The Junior Cert was just months away, and he was going to fail it, and fail it miserably. But it didn't bother him in the slightest. His enthusiasm for school and his studies had begun to wane at the first signs of puberty. The hairier his balls grew, the lower his grades went; he was no mathematician, but that was one equation he could fully understand. It wasn't that he was too busy chasing girls to bother with school. He did have the occasional fumble here and there. It ran deeper than that. He became self-aware, looked inwards and didn't like what he saw: someone shameful, an embarrassment to others. He didn't have a father, didn't even know the man. Seán had never questioned his mother on his origins, but he'd picked up bits here and there from other members of the family. He'd been an accident, a mishap; she'd had to leave the country because of him. His father hadn't been interested and had bailed as soon as he'd found out. Instead Seán got Daryl; a man who reminded him every day that he wasn't wanted, that he'd never been wanted and that he was doing him a favour by allowing him to live with them.

He looked around the room at his classmates; they all seemed different to him. They spoke of Mam and Dad and cars and family nights out. They had money to spend at lunchtime and got nice sandwiches packed neatly in proper lunchboxes, with an apple wrapped in cellophane or sometimes an orange, and a mini-treat. He got a couple of hastily-arranged cheese singles, or some luncheon meat, on the cheapest bread available. Was he poor? In comparison to his classmates, he seemed to be. Daryl worked on and off at the same factory he'd been employed in for years, an injury sustained on the job preventing him from working full-time. Seán never asked questions, but to his mind the injury was fabricated and Daryl was simply skiving; not that it mattered to Seán, since any money that his stepfather made had nothing to do with him, as he'd been told often enough. His mother worked at the pub, but any money she made probably found its way back behind the bar between the two of them. They weren't alcoholics, or he didn't think they were, but they were out three or four nights a week. There wasn't enough money for him to go to the chipper at lunch-time, but enough to spend on booze.

There were other kids worse off than him at his school, the really poor kids who reeked of poverty. Most of these were in the lower strands, however, and hadn't yet progressed beyond long division and the twelve-times tables. By virtue of a strong entrance exam, Seán had found himself in the top echelon of his year, alongside more privileged children from well-to-do families. At the start he was just like them, a bright and intelligent young scholar, blissfully unaware of how different he really was; however, that changed sometime in the summer between his first and second year. He began to doubt himself and retreated into his shell, fearful of making mistakes. Teachers would ask him questions in class and eagerly await an insightful response from one of their best pupils, but what they got was sullen silence. These excruciating interludes were usually broken by one of Seán's friends coming to the rescue with an answer. *Cheers, man*, he'd whisper as the disappointed teacher moved on to their next victim. It wasn't that he didn't know the answer – he often did, even without studying the subject or doing any homework – it was that he was terrified of making a fool of himself by saying the wrong thing. What if he got it completely wrong? The whole room would erupt into laughter, including the teacher, and they'd all point and stare at the stupid McLoughlin boy and his shitty cheese sandwiches. So he chose silence as the safest option. And that was how he intended to see out his schooldays. He wouldn't be any trouble; he'd sit at the back of the class minding his own business, and hope to see it through to the end with as little embarrassment as possible. A couple of his teachers tried to encourage him. "Come on, Seán," they'd say, "you're better than this." *Nah, I'm really not*, he'd think as he sat there in silence. *Just leave me be.* In time, they did leave him be, recognising him for what he was: a lost cause. He was just another student who had threatened to fulfil his promise but in the end chose not to. They'd seen it before, and they knew better than to waste their time on him when other, more willing pupils needed their attention.

And he *would* have seen out his years in the back of the class, not bothering anyone, were it not for his report cards. He could hide from his teachers all he liked, but once those exam results came through the letterbox there was nowhere to run. From the moment they broke off for the holidays at the end of each term, he waited for his results to arrive. He listened out for the postman every morning, dreading the sound of his hurrying footsteps as he approached their door and deposited his foul load. Seán had learned to recognise how it sounded when it came through the letterbox; running to check, still in his underwear, he leafed through the bills and junk until he found the offending object. It came in a grey envelope, always a grey envelope, and had the school's crest emblazoned on the top-left hand corner: Mrs. S. Cassidy, 20 Grange Manor, Dooncurra. That was it. He was dressed and out the door within minutes. Let them digest the news for a few hours, maybe they'll cool down a bit. That was his only hope.

But eventually, driven back by hunger, he'd return to face the music. His mother would reason with him. "Seán, what's going on?" she'd ask. "These are terrible marks, and you used to be so good." *What's going on? Look around you. Look at the man you married, how he treats your son.*

But he just looked at her sadly, mumbled something about trying harder next year and waited for her to stop talking. Then it was Daryl's turn. "This is fuckin' disgraceful," he'd rage, waving the papers in his hand. "He's changing schools." Seán thought this rich coming from a man who hadn't even attended secondary school. How could he rant and rave about Seán's shortcomings when his own education had barely progressed beyond learning his ABC? And why did he suddenly care so much about Seán's future? The truth was, he didn't; he just saw the arrival of those papers as another stick to beat him with, a way of putting him down. He was probably secretly thrilled by his demise. He'd dragged him down to his level. Maybe one day they could learn the ABC together, get drunk and fight afterwards. He'd like that.

Seán was performing poorly in almost every subject, but he reserved special levels of ineptitude for maths. Failing it in both his Christmas and summer exams in second year, he'd taken it up a notch in third year. An 'NG' – No Grade. That's what had stood glumly beside the word 'Mathematics' in his Christmas report card. He knew he had to knuckle down if he were ever to pass the subject in his Junior Cert, but that would require effort, hard work and dedication, and he didn't like the sound of that. It was far easier to sit at the rear of the class and stare at the back of Rosie Power's head. That's what he was doing now, all the while praying that Mr. Sheehan had forgotten about last night's homework. In truth this would be unprecedented, Mr. Sheehan had never forgotten about the homework before. But there was a first time for everything.

Seán had briefly considered actually doing his homework. He'd flipped open his maths book with serious intent; this would be the night he would finally crack trigonometry. How hard could it be? A few equations and the like. Surely anyone could do it, even him? Then he'd taken one look at the assorted diagrams, numbers and letters and decided to leave it for another night. Sure 'twas only the Junior Cert; everyone knew it didn't really matter.

But as he sat in class, sweating it out, he wished he'd at least made a token effort. He hadn't even had time to copy from the lads when he'd got in that morning, so he had nothing, just a blank page. Soon Mr. Sheehan would go around collecting the homework and Seán would be in deep shit. Until then, though, he was content to stare at Rosie's head. He didn't fancy Rosie or anything like that, her head just happened to be in front of him so he chose to look at it for a while. He'd give her one, no doubt about that, but she was too much of a culchie for him; she had big rosy red cheeks and hair the colour and texture of straw. She was tall and rather stout, a bit burly perhaps, but with an innate femininity; in other words, she had massive tits. Tits that she kept under wraps for most of the school year, but when the weather got warm in late spring, the girls would take off their jumpers to reveal crisp white blouses; under these lay bras and in some cases breasts. Rosie's were the biggest in the class, at least a DD by Seán's reckoning – he didn't know how cup-size was measured but a DD seemed about right. They tried to make Rosie run so they could see her breasts jiggle up and down, and sometimes the braver lads pinged her bra strap and then sprang out of her reach, cackling manically. Seán never pinged Rosie's bra strap, or any bra-strap, for that matter. He just checked them out. All of them, not just Rosie's. He wondered what they'd be like, these breasts, if they were freed from their constraints, bare and naked, at his mercy. He daydreamed in class, concocting complex scenarios where he stripped them all down to their knickers, sucked each and every one of their tits, before flipping them round and wanking off onto their arses. Today, though, he wasn't dreaming of Rosie's tits or any arse-wanking scenarios. He was simply looking at her hair and the way it scrunched up at the top before falling down about her shoulders. How did she get it like that? Why did young wans go to such lengths to style their hair, when it was much nicer long and flowing? That was what he preferred: a natural beauty with long, silky hair cascading down her bare neck and naked shoulders.

That set him off. He began constructing a plot where he was looking for summer work out in the countryside. It was a blazing hot day, and he'd walked for miles. He was well outside Dooncurra, in a part of the countryside he'd never seen before. He hadn't seen a car in ages, and he'd passed the last house at least an hour ago. It was the middle of nowhere and he was stranded. He was just about to turn back and begin the long walk home, when he came to a quaint little two-storey building with a small red tractor in the yard. He'd try this place, and if there were no jobs to be had he'd forget about it. Knocking on the door, he was surprised to see it was Rosie, his classmate, with the big tits, who answered. "Seán," she said, "what are you doing here?"

She wore a light summer dress with a plunging neckline and short hem, and her hair was suitably long and flowing.

If this situation had occurred in real life, Seán would most likely have flushed bright red, stammered, "Any jobs going?" and then cursed himself for being such a loser as Rosie went off to find her father. This was make-believe, though, and he was in charge of what happened.

"Oh, hi, Rosie," he said, with his most winning smile – that famous McLoughlin smile, *have that Rosie, ya big-titted bitch.* "I was just wondering if there's any work going on the farm for the summer? I'm hoping to go to the Reading festival in August and I'm looking to make some cash." The Reading festival – as if. He'd be lucky to get to the circus, which rolled into town for two weeks every summer.

"Oh, Reading, wow!" Rosie cooed, clearly impressed. "My dad's not in right now, but I've been doing some work in the hay-barn which you're welcome to help me with."

He followed her through the house and out into the yard. There wasn't a soul in sight, the only sound the distant hum of machinery as crops were harvested by faraway farmers. She showed him into the cavernous barn, leading him to its lower end, away from prying eyes.

"Just here," she said, taking him by the hand. She shot him a meaningful stare, before lying down on the straw, her hair merging with the golden hay until it looked like her head was just floating in the air. Then she slowly parted her legs, revealing her bare crotch and more straw-like hair. Savouring the moment, Seán stood over her and said – "McLOUGHLIN, ARE YOU EVEN LISTENING TO ME?"

He was dragged unceremoniously from the barn and Rosie's crotch right back into maths class. All he had now was a raging erection and an irate middle-aged man standing over him.

"Sir," he replied weakly.

"Sir, what? 'Sir, I am listening' or 'Sir, what the hell are you talking about?'"

Seán considered his options, and quickly came to the conclusion that he had none.

"Um, what are you talking about, sir?"

Mr. Sheehan slammed his fist down onto Seán's desk. The whole class took a collective intake of breath and settled in for the show.

"I ask the questions around here, McLoughlin!" Mr. Sheehan bellowed. Like all the teachers, he had a habit of dragging out these public floggings. *Just cut to the chase and be done with it*, thought Seán as he stared directly ahead, painfully aware that every set of eyes in the room was trained on him. *Enjoying yourselves, are ye, lads? Yeah, lap it up while you can. Wankers!*

All he could do now was try to limit the damage. He'd been caught on the hop though, with no time to prepare an excuse. Perhaps honesty would work; he'd never tried it before, but it was worth a shot.

"I'm sorry, sir. I wasn't listening to you for a minute there."

"A minute? A MINUTE?" shrieked Sheehan, who was laughing now; but it wasn't a good-natured laugh, it was the laugh of a man with bad intentions.

"I've been watching you since the start of class, sitting there gazing at the back of Rosie's head with a big dopey look on your face."

This set off a few guffaws from the gallery. Now he was going to be slagged about fancying Rosie Power too.

Sheehan was warming to his theme, playing up to the audience.

"Just what is it about Rosie's head that so fascinates you, McLoughlin? Is it her lovely blonde hair? Is that it?"

Seán looked up at him. *Smirking little prick; fat, middle-aged balding wanker. So smug, so self-satisfied, enjoying his little power-trip, showing off in front of the rest of the class. Just another pathetic excuse for a man, someone who has to pick on a kid to make himself feel big.*

"Oh do fuck off," he replied witheringly.

The guffaws were replaced by gasps; eyebrows were raised, mouths gaped open, one of the more delicate girls appeared on the verge of tears.

Sheehan recoiled in horror, the wind taken out of his sails.

"What did you say, McLoughlin? What did you say?" he asked querulously.

Christ, what a soft little shite.

"You heard me," he replied firmly. "Fuck off."

He stood up to face his oppressor. There was nothing threatening in his movement; he didn't even know why he had stood up. But the teacher instantly backed off, his body tensed as if expecting to be struck at any moment.

"FUCK OFF," Seán said one last time, enunciating each word clearly in case there was any doubt as to the message he was trying to convey.

He grabbed his jacket from the back of his chair and his bag from under the table and slung them both over his shoulder. Not stopping, for fear of changing his mind, he brushed past him, exited the room and disappeared down the hallway. Mr. Sheehan watched him go, dabbing at his forehead with a hankie. A couple of the other students, infused with rebellious spirit, considered following Seán, but quickly came to their senses. After all, the headmaster would be here soon.

3

WHY HAD HE DONE THAT? He really had no idea; it had just happened. He hadn't been in a bad mood. There was nothing playing on his mind. It had just been an ordinary day and an ordinary encounter with one of his most ordinary teachers, but something inside him had snapped. Maybe this was to be the start of something, a one-man uprising. He would become someone not to be trifled with. A dangerous individual. He didn't really want that though, to be that disaffected kid sticking two fingers up at society, railing against injustices and fighting the powers-that-be. He just wanted to be left in peace. Mr. Sheehan was probably nice enough away from school; a father with a modest house, good kids, and maybe a little dog, a garden.; a simple life, made possible by teaching maths to ungrateful shits like Seán. But he had come at Seán in a way that had left him with no other choice. He had set out to embarrass him, to make a fool of him. It wasn't enough to just deliver a simple reprimand and be done with it; he'd had to push it. And now look what had happened. There was no coming back from this one. Seán didn't even want to think of the consequences.

As soon as he'd left the classroom his brain went into survival mode; he had to get off the school grounds, and quickly. Once Sheehan raised the alarm they'd be after him in a shot. If he didn't move fast he'd be dragged back within minutes, kicking and screaming.

There were two main entrances used by the students: the front door, flanked by the headmaster's office, and a smaller side entrance which led to the bike-shed. He wasn't going to use either of those. To do so would be to risk immediate capture. Instead he headed toward the back of the building, beyond the area permitted for student use and down a dark corridor towards the maintenance and utility rooms. He wasn't supposed to be down here, but he couldn't get into much more trouble anyway. The object of his desire lay at the end of the corridor, an emergency exit which would put him onto the edge of the school's playing fields; from there he could run fifty yards to the wall which separated the school from the railway track. It was a high wall, and one which he'd never scaled unaided, but he'd have to trust his athletic abilities and hope for the best. Once on the track he would be home free. There was no near access to it by foot, and Mr. Sheehan would never be able to climb the wall – nor would any of the teachers for that matter.

Seán reached the end of the corridor and the emergency exit. It was one of those ones with a horizontal bar across the middle which opened when you pushed down on the bar. When he did, though, nothing happened. The door didn't yield as he'd expected; instead the bar braced against his weight before popping back into place. He pushed harder, really putting his back into it, to no avail. Stupid fuckin' door! Why did it have to be so awkward? He tried to think. It was too late to turn around and go back the way he'd come. He'd surely be spotted; the element of surprise was lost. And Sheehan probably had sentries positioned at all the major exits by now anyway. He could hide in the utility room, but that would only delay the inevitable. They'd hunt him down like a pack of wolves, tearing him to shreds when they found him cowering beneath some old hurleys. He pushed down on the bar frantically, pumping it up and down, but the door didn't budge. Maybe he was missing something? A lock somewhere? A button that had to be pressed? He scanned the surrounding walls but all he saw was grey; grey uniformity. The colour of a prison. Which was where he was headed if he didn't get this fucking door open. In one last desperate effort he grabbed hold of the bar, leant back and pushed downwards, using his entire body weight. Lo and behold, the door opened; swinging out politely, revealing the lush green grass of the playing fields and potential freedom. He hurried out, making sure to close the door behind him with a solid shove. Now he faced his next challenge, the wall. It stood before him, imposing, intimidating, a Goliath to his David. He wasn't ready to scale it yet; he was only a third year. This was a challenge for sixth years. He had no business even trying to reach its summit, but these were special circumstances and his need was great. He'd only have one shot at it; if he failed, there was no chance of backing up for another go. One of the classrooms on the second floor overlooked this part of the playing fields, and he'd probably already been seen by some daydreaming students. They wouldn't take much notice if they thought he was just an errant third-year traipsing through the green. But if they saw him hurtle towards the wall at great speed and land flat on his arse they'd nudge their mates, who'd nudge their mates, and before long the whole class would be staring out at him. Then the teacher would be alerted to his presence and would ring down for the headmaster, and before long the posse would have encircled their quarry. So it was all or nothing: make it to the top and his escape was complete. Come tumbling back down and it was straight to the headmaster's office for the bollocking of his life.

He took a deep breath and sized up the barrier. The key was getting his hands over the top; if he could do that, it'd be easy enough to drag himself up the rest of the way. But there weren't any footholds on the wall-face with which to propel yourself upwards; the speed of his run-up would determine whether he reached the top, and then he would have to rely on his upper-body strength. He was quite a fast runner, usually at the front when fleeing from neighbour's doors during games of 'Tap the Rap', but he wasn't particularly strong. He wasn't feeble either, but his arms were spindly and ill-equipped for the job in hand. However, there was another element at play here, something that could tip the balance in his favour: adrenaline. It had already helped him open the emergency door; that feat of Herculean strength had to have come from somewhere. Now, with his heart still racing and his limbs twitching in anticipation, he fancied that he had just enough of it left for this final task.

Taking one last deep breath he burst into action, dipping his head down slightly like he'd seen sprinters do in the Olympics. The grass was soft and squidgy, the victim of one too many spring showers, but he ploughed through it unhindered. He powered on, head down, until he was within a few feet of the wall then, without hesitation, he leapt outwards and upwards, reaching for the top of the wall with his outstretched arms. He thudded against it about two-thirds of the way up, the impact knocking the air out of his chest. But there was no pain, he hadn't time for pain. His fingers scrabbled for traction, clawing and tearing at the wall, desperately searching for that grip which would elevate him to the top. For a split second it appeared as if he were magically suspended in mid-air, going neither up nor down, defying the laws of gravity. Then his legs began to give way; he was being pulled towards the ground. It was over. It had been a valiant effort though, right? He'd definitely be able to climb the wall next year.

Then, just when he'd given up hope, his right hand dug into something, a groove, a fissure, it didn't matter. He swung his other hand round to join it and clamped his toes into the bulk of the wall. He could make it from here if his arms could take the strain. Slowly he began to pull himself up, his entire body trembling from the exertion, but his grip wasn't strong enough; he was stuck in the middle of the wall like a stricken insect caught in a spider's web. He composed himself and tried to clear his thoughts. The top of the wall was curved, arching in a semi-circle before beginning its drop to the other side. This allowed those who reached the summit a comfy seating position from which to mock those below. If he could just get a hand over the top to the back of the wall, it would give him enough leverage to complete the job. But could he swing his arm all the way over the top? Was he near enough? There was only one way to find out. Holding one hand firmly in position he clawed with the other, looking for the back of the wall. His remaining hand began to falter, unable to bear his entire body weight. It was now or never. Bending both of his elbows for extra trajectory he pushed off from his handhold, kicking upwards with his feet in the same motion. His fingers gripped something solid and held forth, which allowed his forearms to follow, then his shoulders and finally his torso. He was like a baby exiting the womb, entering a brave new world. Finally, after much grunting and groaning, he found himself atop the mighty beast. Lying on top of the wall, drenched in sweat, his arms aching from his exertions, he grinned widely. He'd only gone and done it. A third year climbing to the top of the wall: was there no end to his brilliance?

Celebration would have to wait. Once the buzz of his escape had worn off, he faced reality: he'd told a teacher to fuck off and then ran out of school. Those were the bare facts. A suspension was on the cards, but that would be nothing compared to the punishment he'd receive at home. His mother always tried her best to see his side, to view things objectively before delivering her final judgement. However, in this instance there were no mitigating circumstances, no case for the defence. He'd been a twat and deserved everything coming his way. And then there was Daryl. He was going to love this; it would make his day. It'd be off to the borstal with Seán and no delay. He'd think about that later; right now he just wanted to sit somewhere quiet and reflect upon what he'd done.

4.

ONCE HE REACHED THE OUTSKIRTS of the woods, his spirits lifted. This was the one place he felt at ease, the one place he could gather his thoughts in perfect solitude. He broke off from the main walkway and headed into the thickest part of the forest – hopefully he'd get lost, as he had all those years ago. As he walked, he listened to the forest's familiar, comforting sounds. Birds sang and chirped merrily. They didn't care that he was in more trouble than he'd ever been before; winter had turned and they had reason to rejoice. Trees swayed amiably in the breeze, the whisper of their leaves growing to a roar before dying out and beginning the process once more. Beneath them, the woodland animals went about their business, the sound of their movements masked by the cadence of the great oaks and yews, alders and ashes. All around him the woods teemed with activity, a sense of life and living permeating the cool, mid-morning air. But to Seán, the future had never looked so bleak.

Walking alone in the woods had cleared his head and allowed him to calm down, but he now felt an immense sadness. Before today his life had been miserable yet tolerable. He hated school and he hated being at home, but at least he had a routine, a fair idea of what lay before him on any given day. Right now he didn't know what the future held, but it threatened to be a lot worse than what had come before. He sighed deeply, his heart heavy, his spirit crushed. What he wanted to do now was to lie down and try to forget about it all. Finding a gnarled old tree whose branches had grown in every direction, he hoisted himself up and lay in the crook of a bough. This would be his hideout until it was safe to re-join the human race.

5.

THE ONE THING SINÉAD HAD wanted when they'd moved into their new house, was a phone. She was a woman of modest ambitions, and having her very own phone to ring her friends whenever she wanted was something she dreamt of. It had remained a dream, however. Daryl had said they couldn't afford it. They earned enough between them to cover the bill, she argued, but he wouldn't budge. Who did they think they were? Only posh people had phones. She relented, accepted defeat; one of many compromises required to maintain harmony in their young marriage. Without a phone of her own, though, she was back to scoping out the neighbours, looking for clues to work out which of them had a landline. Once that had been established, she'd have to go over, cap in hand, and ask if she could use their phone. And, further down the line, give out her neighbour's number as her own contact number should anyone ever need to reach her. It was so shameful; she would gladly have paid her entire weekly wage to avoid the indignity of it all. Thankfully, she had since forged a solid, if lukewarm friendship with her next-door neighbour, Sheila Corcoran. Sheila had a phone which she was 'more than welcome to use any time, free of charge'. Thanks, Sheila, I'm just going to ring my long-lost auntie in Australia. Oh, did I mention she likes nothing more than a two-hour chinwag with the charges reversed?

But as Sinéad crossed her front lawn, badly in need of its first cut of the year, she knew it wasn't an aunt from Australia waiting on the line. Sheila had said it was the school, Seán's school. Was there any chance that it was good news? Had her boy done something remarkable in class, so amazing that they had to call her immediately? If previous form was anything to go by it seemed unlikely, so she steadied herself before taking the handset from her neighbour.

"Hello? Sinéad Cassidy speaking."

"Oh, hello, Mrs. Cassidy, yes. This is Mr. Aylesbury from Dooncurra Vocational School, yes."

"Hi, Mr. Aylesbury," she said, trying to sound surprised and calm at the same time.

"Mrs. Cassidy, yes, yes."

Mr. Aylesbury had a strange habit of peppering his conversation with the word 'yes' at various intervals, as if to underline what an agreeable fellow he was, despite generally being the bearer of bad news. Sinéad had first come into contact with him at a specially-arranged meeting to discuss Seán's sudden academic freefall, and found herself stifling laughter as he took her through her son's litany of underachievement. It was all 'yes, yes' this and 'yes, yes' that; for a moment, she'd wondered whether he had someone secretly servicing him under the desk as they spoke.

"It's about Seán," the headmaster continued. "He's got into a spot of bother, I'm afraid, yes, yes."

She waited for him to continue; on the other end of the line, Mr. Aylesbury was evidently waiting for her to enquire about the nature of this 'spot of bother'. When it became clear she wasn't going to break the silence, he resumed, with some reluctance.

"Well, Mrs. Cassidy, yes. He – how can I put this? He entered into an altercation with one of the teachers and told him where to go. Yes, yes."

It was worse than she'd expected. This went beyond the normal blackguarding and skitting; she now had a 'problem child' on her hands.

"Oh, my God, Mr. Aylesbury, I'm so sorry," she said plaintively.

"Yes, indeed; yes, a terrible state of affairs. He will of course be suspended indefinitely, yes."

Oh, he'll love that; a holiday right in the middle of term.

"I understand, Mr. Aylesbury. Will I come for him now?"

She'd have to get a taxi to the school.

"You're more than welcome to come to the school, Mrs. Cassidy, yes; but Seán isn't here."

"No?"

"Yes, it appears that he left the school in the aftermath of the event, yes, and he hasn't been seen since."

Sinéad sighed; not only did she have a potty-mouthed miscreant on her hands, she also had a runaway to look for – and not for the first time. She thought back to that misty autumn Saturday when she'd had the entire population of Dooncurra looking for her little boy. She thought of how scared she'd been and the help she'd received from all those strangers. But most of all she thought of the relief, the pure, unbridled relief when they'd found him. How she'd grabbed him and vowed never to let him go.

At the time she'd put it down to childish impudence on Seán's part. But when his behaviour continued to deteriorate, when he changed from an angelic, butter-wouldn't-melt little boy to a sour-faced, insolent young man, she knew it wasn't just a phase. She knew the cause of his discontent, of course she did, but had hoped that it would resolve itself in time. Even when he countered her pleas for him to never run away again with one of his own; to get rid of Daryl, she ignored it. Instead she tried to explain to him, about how she deserved some happiness too, how a woman needed a man beside her and how he might benefit from having a strong male presence around. But he had wanted no part of it.

She'd hoped the move to a new house would change things, give them a new start, but it got even worse. Sinéad tried to bridge the gap between them, to get them to communicate with each other, but her son didn't want to know. When it was just the two of them, mother and child, he was once more the good-natured, sweet little boy she adored, but as soon as Daryl appeared he withdrew into his shell, and then back to his room. The battle lines had been drawn and there was nothing Sinéad could do. Perhaps the arrival of a sibling would bring them all together. She yearned for a daughter, prayed for one, but when a boy arrived she consoled herself with the belief that he would at least be good for Seán. He, however, looked at the new arrival with barely-concealed disgust; during one family photo-shoot, it took several threats of violence to make him pose with his baby brother. She tried to understand his hostility but it exhausted her. All she wanted was to be happy, to build a family unit. It wasn't perfect, but surely it wasn't that bad?

She knew there was no point in going to her own parents for advice. Although neither of them came out and said it, it was clear that they both disapproved of Daryl and the situation in general; her mother through some perverse Catholic doctrine and her father through plain enmity. They cosseted Seán at every available opportunity, 'that poor child, look what he has to go through,' and it wasn't uncommon for him to spend entire weekends there when the mood took him. If they had their way, he would stay there all the time; but she wasn't going to let her family disintegrate like that.

After reassuring Mr. Aylesbury that Seán would be fine and that she'd notify him of his suspension once he'd been located, she thanked Sheila and crossed the lawn back to her own house. She knew where he was;

he was up there in the woods, moping around like some latter-day poet, ruminating on the injustice of it all. She sympathised with his plight, but she had a dinner to put on and hadn't all day to go traipsing through the undergrowth looking for Dooncurra's answer to Oscar Wilde. If he was big enough to tell his teachers to fuck off, then he was big enough to come home and face the music. He could stay there for as long as he wanted, but eventually he'd have to answer for his crimes. She filled the pot with water, put it on the hob and set about peeling the spuds. Seán or no Seán, they still needed their dinner.

6

SEÁN WEIGHED UP HIS OPTIONS. He could stay here and live off the land as he'd planned to do all those years ago, or return home and listen to his stepfather lecture him on how young men should behave in the classroom. Or, option three, the curveball: he could go to his grandparent's house. He'd face no lectures there. They'd just be glad to see him; he never called on Tuesdays. He'd be using them, in a way, taking advantage of their love for him, but he didn't know what else to do. If he could get them on his side, he stood a chance; otherwise it would be just him against Daryl, his mother a floating voter in the background. He didn't really give a shit what his stepfather said but he worried about the confrontation, the tension which would envelop the house in the aftermath. He couldn't face that. Daryl would know about it all by now and be relishing Seán's return, ready and waiting with all kinds of directives: "Four hours' study a night. Nine o'clock bedtime. No going out at weekends." Proper sergeant-major stuff, laughable, really.

The funniest thing of all was that whatever he said didn't matter. It would be Seán's mother who had the final say. Because what she said, went. If she wanted Seán to go to a boarding school where they fed you nothing but porridge and muddy water, then that was where he would go. And if she thought he needed a two-week break in the Caribbean to clear his head, he'd be on the first flight out of Dublin in the morning. The trouble was that there was no telling which way she'd lean; she was as likely to offer him a total reprieve as to be there on the side-lines, cheering on the hangman as he was led to his death.

With his grandparents on board he'd feel safer. She'd hate him for that, call him conniving and sneaky, but he wasn't facing this alone. They always ganged up on him anyway, them fuckin' Cassidys; he was going to need a few McLoughlins to even things up. Decision made, he hopped from the tree and headed for Ard Aulinn. He didn't know what time it was, but if he hurried he might make it there for dinner.

7.

PATRICIA McLOUGHLIN HEARD THE GATE clang and looked at the clock; he was early today. The dinner wasn't ready yet though, so he'd have to wait. She listened out for her husband's steady steps as he walked around the back of the house. But it wasn't him, it was someone else; someone lighter on their feet, not so world-weary. She stood in the kitchen waiting for the door to open, expecting one of her daughters, hoping it would be Adele. It wasn't one of her daughters or even her son, but someone even better. It was Seán, her grandson. Her favourite grandson.

"Seán, my dear, what brings you here tonight?"

She ushered him inside, sat him down at the table and began setting a place for him.

"Just thought I'd come for a visit, Nan. You needn't make me any dinner, I'm grand."

"Don't be silly. You'll sit down there now and eat your stew with your granddad when he comes in."

Stew? Not bad. He'd been hoping for shepherd's pie but it would do.

"You're looking very thin, Seán. Are they feeding you at all?"

Patricia always referred to Sinéad and Daryl as 'they', like a pair of kidnappers holding her grandson against his will.

"Ah, yeah, Nanny, they're feeding me grand. I just have a fast metabolism, that's all."

She had her back to him as she tended to the pot, but he knew the face she was making; it said: *Yeah right kiddo, you're not fooling me. Wait till you see what I put on your plate.*

"How's school?" she asked.

This was his opportunity. He had to be careful with his response; the wording was crucial. If done correctly, he could rely on both his nanny and his granddad to fight his corner. If he fucked it up, his last remaining allies would be lost forever.

"I've been having problems with one of my teachers, Nan."

"Oh?"

"Yeah. It's my maths teacher; he makes fun of me."

That got her attention. She spun round, ready to fight this fun-making teacher right there and then.

"What's he been saying to you, Seán?"

Mission accomplished. Seán paused for effect before pouring out his poor troubled heart.

"He knows I'm not great at maths and that sometimes I can't follow what's going on, and then today he asked me something and I didn't know the answer and he started mocking me, in front of the whole class and everything."

A shadow crossed over his grandmother's face. He'd seen it before, but only on the odd occasion. Like when his grandfather had broken one of her good plates. It spelled danger.

"He WHAT?"

"Started mocking me, Nanny."

"In what way?"

"He said I fancied a girl in the class 'cos I was looking at the back of her head."

"What girl?"

"Ah, you wouldn't know her, Nanny."

"What girl, Seán?"

"Rosie Power."

"And do you fancy her?"

"No, Nanny."

Patricia stared at him, biting her bottom lip as she considered her next move. She rubbed her hands on her apron and made for the hallway.

"Where ya going, Nan?"

"Where do you think I'm going? I'm going into that school and I'm going to have a word with this *teacher*. How dare he! How dare he!"

"Whoa, hold on, Nanny," Seán said with genuine alarm. "What about the dinner?"

"Ah, don't mind the dinner. Your grandfather can fend for himself for once."

She had her coat off the hanger and was rummaging around in the pocket for her keys. This was way too much. Yes, he wanted her on his side, and yes, he was delighted to see her fight his corner with such gusto. But there was a time and place for everything. Right now he needed food, comfort and reassurance; he needed someone to tell him it was going to be all right and that they had his back no matter what. Maybe tomorrow, or the day after, she could go to the school and take Sheehan to task. But there was his mother to deal with first, and Daryl.

"Nanny, you can go to the school tomorrow, okay?" he said, taking her by the shoulders and gently removing her coat. Patricia's eyes had glazed over but now they softened. She stopped in her tracks, allowed him to take off her coat, and to then lead her back to the kitchen.

"You're right, Seán, you're right. Your granddad will be here any minute now."

"He will, Nanny," Seán replied, grateful he wouldn't have to watch Noel McLoughlin attempt to serve up a dinner for the first time in his life.

While they ate Seán revealed as much of the story as he dared. His grandmother listened attentively, at times gasping, grimacing and muttering under her breath. Noel remained completely silent throughout, solemnly chewing on his food, ignoring his wife's increasing agitation. That was his way; he'd take everything in, mull it over for a while and then suggest what he thought was the best course of action. Seán thought his granddad flinched a little when he got to the part about telling Mr. Sheehan to fuck off, but he couldn't be sure; he was too busy focusing on his grandmother and her reaction. She responded to this part of the tale in exactly the way he'd hoped; the look of stricken anxiety momentarily left her face, to be replaced by a victorious smile and a nod of assent. He had played it to perfection. She was now his staunchest supporter. Surely it would only be a matter of time before his granddad followed suit.

They retired to the sitting-room, Noel to watch the news and Seán to drink tea and eat as many biscuits as his grandmother would give him. Patricia plotted out her course of action. She was going to the school first thing in the morning, and she meant *first thing*. She would arrive before the caretaker, before everyone, and stand outside the doors until someone let her in. Once inside she would take a seat in the headmaster's office and wait for him to come in. He'd probably try to fob her off, tell her she needed an appointment, but she wouldn't be having any of that. She would demand the resignation of *that teacher* and advise him that her grandson would require a public apology, both in word and print, before he would even consider returning to continue his studies.

Seán appreciated his grandmother's vigour but he wasn't really listening now. His focus had switched solely to his grandfather. Which way would he go? It was still too early to tell. He was hard to read, that lad. The sports news came and went, then the news for the deaf and the weather, but still not a word out of him; he just sat there in silence, completely inscrutable. Seán needed to know his stance soon; his mother could arrive any minute, full of her own prejudices and notions. He had seen clashes between the two McLoughlin women and knew that, for all her forcefulness, Patricia couldn't win round her daughter single-handedly. It would need the wise, salient words of her father to make her see sense. As the first of the soaps began, Seán glanced expectantly at Noel. This was usually his cue to speak, but he rose from his chair, picked up his empty cup and went out to the kitchen.

"Bejaysus, that was a lovely cup of tea," he said as he left the room.

Seán couldn't take it anymore; the suspense was killing him. He followed his grandfather into the kitchen, quietly closing the door behind him. He didn't want his nanny getting involved in this discussion. Calm heads were needed here.

"Oh, hiya Seán," he said. "Thought you'd have gone by now, off chasing girls or something."

What was he playing at? Did he genuinely not know what was happening, or was he just being a cute whore? It was hard to know with him. Seán suspected that he tuned out most of what his wife said nowadays, so it was entirely possible that he hadn't heard a single word of what they'd been discussing. He joined him at the sink and began drying the dishes Noel had been washing. They worked in silence for a couple of minutes, Seán anxiously looking at the pile of dishes and wishing there were more of them. His grandfather might be headed off to the pub after this. He had to broach the subject before then.

"Granddad?"

"Yes, Seán?"

There was a lengthy pause, punctuated by the slosh of the water as Noel scrubbed at a particularly stubborn stain.

"Granddad?" he repeated.

"Yes, Seán?"

"What do you think?"

"About what, Seán?"

Jesus Christ.

"About what happened in school."

"Ah sure look, Seány, that's none of my business; it's between you and your mother, really."

That was it; he had spoken. He might as well not have. A lifetime of jousting with his wife had most likely knocked all the fight out of him, and now he took cover at the first sign of trouble. That was no good to Seán; he needed warriors, not pacifists. Leaving him to the washing-up, he went back into the sitting-room and joined his nanny on the couch. They shared a little smile; it was just the two of them now.

8

DINNER WAS OVER IN THE Cassidy household too. After fending off several enquiries as to the whereabouts of the other family member, Sinéad sent her husband and son into the living-room so she could be alone. Sitting at the kitchen table, she chain-smoked for a while, gnawing at her nails between cigarettes. It would be dark soon and she had no idea where he was. But he was fifteen now and often stayed out late, made a habit of it, in fact. He came and went as he pleased most of the time. He never missed his dinner, though. It took something out of the ordinary to keep him away from his food; something like impending doom, perhaps. He knew what was waiting for him when he did come home, so he'd drag it out as long as possible. Well, no matter how long he left it or what time he came in, she would be sitting here waiting for him.

He was most likely off getting pissed somewhere. She knew he drank or, to be more accurate, she knew he had drunk – whether it was a regular thing or not was still to be figured out. He was probably out with his friends, laughing it up, acting the hard man in front of the lads. That's what he thought he was now, a man; but, like it or not, he was still her little boy and he couldn't stay out all night without telling her where he was. Sinéad stubbed out the last of her cigarettes and got up from her chair. She'd have to go and buy a fresh packet if she intended to sit here all night, and it wouldn't do any harm to ring her mother while she was out.

It was never the easiest of tasks, ringing her; she made it so. Sinéad had to do it, though; she had to rule out the possibility of him being there before she started worrying in earnest. It'd almost be worth hearing the condescension in her mother's voice if she knew he was there, safe and sound.

She stuck her head in the living-room on her way out.

"Just going for some fags, back in a sec."

She was gone before Daryl could reply.

Sinéad hurried through the estate onto Pearse Street; this phone call wasn't for the Corcorans' ears. There was a phone box a little way up the street. She hated using it though. It was situated outside a couple of pubs which usually housed the most desperate and destitute drinkers of Dooncurra. Unlike the refurbished drinking establishments in the centre of town, these pubs hadn't really moved with the times, which explained their popularity with the miscreants. Usually she wouldn't walk around this area after nightfall – there was no telling who you'd meet –but this was an emergency. She squinted into the distance, trying to see if the phone was occupied. It wasn't uncommon to find drunken ne'er-do-wells bedding down for the night inside the booth, often in a pool of their own vomit, urine, or both.

Thankfully on this occasion it was empty. She rummaged in her purse for a few twenty-pence pieces and hurriedly dialled the number. As she waited for the connection, she imagined the goings-on at the other end; her mother sat there with her knitting, singing quietly away to herself, her father – if he wasn't in the pub – watching whatever god awful shite was on the telly and complaining about the price of the license-fee. Once the phone rang, Patricia would look at him accusingly and ask, "Who could that be?" Her father, tired of this familiar routine, would casually say, "Only one way to find out, girl," and leave her to it. Her mother always answered the phone in the McLoughlin house.

It took five rings for someone to pick up. And it was her mother. Sinéad listened to her fumbling with the handset; moving it from the cradle to her ear seemed to take an eternity. Then the customary clearing of the throat and no doubt the fixing of the hair before a voice shakily answered.

"Hello?"

"Hi, Mam, it's me."

A pause. A mind working overtime as it considered its response.

"Oh, hello, pet. We have your Seány here."

Sinéad's shoulders fell in relief, the knot in her stomach instantly floated away. She could have kissed her mother, or, at the very least, given her a brief hug.

"Did he tell you what he did, Mammy?" she asked, hoping for her mother's support on the issue. It wasn't forthcoming.

"He did, Sinéad. Them animals in that school have him tormented."

Sinéad shook her head in exasperation. Seán had gone there for support, and support was what he had got. He could assassinate the Taoiseach and she'd still take his side.

Her instinct was to lambast her mother for being so foolish, falling for his lies. But there was no point in creating further conflict, so she held her tongue and tried to be as diplomatic as possible.

"He's not entirely blameless himself, Mammy, y'know," she managed with a grimace.

"Oh, come on, Sinéad; he'd never react like that without provocation. It's simply not in him."

"Look, Mammy, I didn't call to argue about whether he was right or wrong, I just wanted to see if he was there."

"Well, he's here all right and he's settled now."

That was her way of saying that she thought he should stay the night, as if walking the mile to his own house would be too traumatic for him at this late hour.

"You don't mind him staying, then?"

"Not at all. I aired the bed in the spare room just in case."

"Good, he may stay there so."

"Grand. We'll have a lovely time."

"He's not on holidays, Mam; he's been suspended from school."

"Oh, don't mind that, Sinéad. I'll go down there tomorrow and sort that all out."

"Please don't, Mammy."

But it was pointless arguing. She'd go down there and cause blue murder, while Seán slept till midday and had steak for his lunch. How was he ever supposed to take responsibility for his actions if his nanny fought all his battles for him?

"You have enough to be worrying about, Sinéad, my pet. Let me handle this one."

The woman's delusion knew no bounds. *Let her do what she wants,* thought Sinéad; *she couldn't possibly make things any worse.*

"Fair enough, Mammy. I'd better go now."

"Okay, my dear. What'll I tell Seán?"

"Don't tell him anything, Mammy."

"All right, pet. Bye bye, now."

"Bye, Mam."

Patricia put down the receiver, composed herself and went back into the sitting-room.

"Would you like to stay with us tonight, Seány?"

9

SEÁN WAS AWOKEN BY THE dulcet tones of his grandmother's singing voice. She hadn't a note in her body, but that had never stopped her. He recognised the song but couldn't put a name to it; most likely some evangelical number with an Irish twist. He stretched out in what had once been Patrick's bed. They hadn't changed his room much since he'd left, the walls still bore posters of Harley Davidsons with scantily-clad models draped around them. His uncle had loved motorbikes when he was Seán's age. He had started out with a little Honda 50, a 'nifty-fifty', and progressed all the way to a Yamaha YL1 before getting his girlfriend pregnant. They'd married shortly after, and that had been the end of the bikes. The Yamaha was traded in for something sensible, a car befitting an expectant father, a Citroen or suchlike. Patrick still spoke of getting a Harley but he and everyone else knew that he would never be allowed to; his wife would see to that. Seán would never end up like his uncle: settling for a life of mediocrity before he'd even hit thirty. What a wasted existence.

Right now, though, his existence centred round filling his stomach and finding out if his nanny had been to the school. He looked at his watch; it was after eleven. She'd probably been and gone, had strung them all up by their ears and then returned home to bake bread and scrub floors, singing as she went. He hauled himself out of bed, dressed quickly and went downstairs.

"Good morning, young sir!" she chirped. "What would his lordship like for breakfast?"

Seán smiled at his grandmother. He never got this kind of greeting at home.

"I don't mind, Nan; whatever's going."

"Well, let me see. A full Irish with all the works: how does that sound?"

"Brilliant, Nan," he said, taking his place at the table.

As his grandmother fetched the rashers and sausages from the fridge, she told Seán her news; the news she'd been dying to share with him since half past nine that morning.

"So," she said, her voice faltering, "I went to your school this morning."

"Did you, Nan?"

"Yes. We've to go back there this afternoon, me and you."

"For what?"

"Do you want beans?"

"Yes, please, Nan. What do we have to go to the school for?"

She stood there with a carton of eggs in one hand and a tin of beans in the other, looking at him as if he were mad. "For a meeting, of course!"

The pan sizzled as she added the oil and slid three fat, juicy sausages into it.

A meeting, with Sheehan and Mr. Aylesbury, no doubt; but at least he'd have his nan with him. Chances were she'd do most of the talking, and he'd get away with mumbling a few sullen promises and half-hearted apologies.

"What time is it at, Nan?"

"Half four, when everyone is finished. I told you I'd get all this sorted out, Seány, didn't I?"

"You did, Nan."

"How many slices of toast? Four?"

The bread was in the toaster before he had the chance to reply.

"We'll have you back in that school in no time, Seány," she said, cracking the eggs into the close to overflowing pan. Soldiers going into battle wouldn't have been fed as well.

*

"Come in, come in, Mrs. McLoughlin, yes. And you too, Seán; yes, yes."

The headmaster of Dooncurra Vocational School ushered his two guests into the classroom which, at first glance had appeared empty, but there in the corner behind a desk sat the lonely, forlorn figure of Seán's maths teacher, Mr. Sheehan.

"As you can see Mr. Sheehan is here, ready and waiting. He's just as eager to get this resolved as you are, yes, yes."

Mr. Aylesbury's tone was entirely conciliatory, his ardour most likely dampened by the earlier meeting with Patricia McLoughlin. He wasn't a very imposing headmaster to begin with; small and slight, with his hair slicked into a side parting, he could have been mistaken for an overgrown first year were it not for his immaculately-pressed suits and well-polished shoes. What he lacked in stature, however, he more than made up for in spirit. He possessed a dogged determination to make every one of his student's lives a misery, or at least that's how they saw it. If you were to ask Mr. Aylesbury, he would you tell he was working towards the betterment of Dooncurra Vocational School and nothing more. He would tell you he was entirely justified in dragging students into his office for not having their shirts tucked into their trousers, using profanities on the school grounds, or chewing gum inside the building; running in the corridors, littering, slouching or loitering. He was moulding these young people into mature, responsible adults, and he took his responsibilities very seriously.

Where Seán McLoughlin was concerned, there was an awful lot of moulding to do. This recent incident was just the latest in a litany of misdemeanours. He was neither a troublemaker nor a disruptive student, but he was burdened with an apathy and a general intractableness which made him almost impossible to teach. He'd discussed Seán's progress or lack thereof with the boy's mother on several occasions, but his behaviour had remained the same. So when his secretary told him that it was Seán's grandmother, a Mrs. Patricia McLoughlin, who was waiting in his office when he arrived at 8.15 this morning, he had hoped for a more constructive meeting. Perhaps this woman could talk some sense into the boy? Instead, what he got was a dressing-down, a talking-to, the likes of which he hadn't experienced since his own distant schooldays. He'd tried to reason with her but it had proved impossible. She was immovable, irrepressible; an absolute nightmare, in all honesty. In the end he had been happy just to get her out of her office, agreeing to meet her again later, on the proviso that she leave so he could have his morning cup of coffee.

Seán briefly looked at Sheehan as he took his seat, receiving a deathly stare for his trouble. The teacher was not happy and, regardless of the outcome of this meeting, it seemed unlikely that he and Seán would ever reconcile their shaky teacher/student relationship. They were seated in the same kind of chair that Seán used in class, and he had to resist the temptation to lean back and rest his feet on the table. Instead he sat upright as advised, and waited for Mr. Aylesbury to begin.

"Now then, now then, yes, yes," the headmaster muttered, looking down at the table. There were a couple of sheets of paper and an official *Dooncurra Vocational School* stamp in front of him. Seán twisted his neck to try to read what was written on the paper, but it was upside down and too small for him to decipher. He had an idea of what was there, though: the details of his crime and quite possibly that of his punishment too.

"So," continued Mr. Aylesbury, "we all know why we're here so let us proceed, eh? Yes."

"Indeed," nodded Patricia firmly.

Sheehan sat back in his chair, his jaw jutting outwards, brow furrowed in annoyance.

"Now I've taken a statement from Maurice – Mr. Sheehan – about the events of yesterday afternoon. I believe the best thing would be to compare his version of events with Seán's, so that we have some common ground."

He looked at Seán expectantly. Seán in turn looked at his grandmother who nodded her assent, and so he began.

"Well, I was in maths yesterday, double class like every Tuesday, and it was about twenty minutes into the class. We were doing Pythagoras, I think, weren't we, sir?"

He looked at Mr. Sheehan, eager to involve him in the conversation: *We're all friends here, boy, don't be shy.*

"Yes," grunted Mr. Sheehan reluctantly.

"Okay, so we were doing Pythagoras and I don't know what happened but I must have been daydreaming, 'cos next thing I know Mr. Sheehan is in front of me asking a question, and to be honest, sir, I hadn't a clue what the answer was."

He looked at the headmaster, hoping to find some sympathy there.

"Go on, Seán," said Mr. Aylesbury quietly.

"So yeah, I didn't know the answer to the question. I could have made a guess at it, but what was the point? I was caught rotten. I hadn't a clue, and that was that."

"And then what happened, Seán?" asked Mr. Aylesbury.

"Well, I suppose we had a bit of a run-in, meself and Mr. Sheehan, that is."

"And what was the nature of the run-in, Seán? Yes."

"Well, Mr. Sheehan said something about me fancying one of the young wans in the class and I don't fancy her, sir; I don't. And it made me wicked embarrassed 'cos everyone was laughing, and I thought of the slagging I was going to get after class and I suppose I just flipped a little bit."

Maurice Sheehan suddenly sprang to life. "A little bit? *A little bit?* You told me to fuck off! Three times!!"

He pointed his finger accusingly at Seán. It was the worst possible thing he could have done. Patricia reared up like a dragon leaving its cave after years of hibernation.

"Excuse me. *Excuse me!* Who do you think you are, pointing your finger at my grandson like that? Who do you think you are? Sit down and put your slimy finger away, you horrible little man!"

Mr. Sheehan looked at her in astonishment, clearly he hadn't been warned beforehand. He had thought he was attending a routine meeting about a misbehaving student, which would involve said student being dragged across the coals and begging forgiveness for his sins. How wrong he had been; he was being faced down by a woman who ate men like him for lunch.

"But, but – " he spluttered, looking to his colleague for reassurance. Mr. Aylesbury was busy, however, reading the documents in front of him; a wise decision on his part.

Satisfied that she had seen off the threat to her kin, Patricia turned to Seán and requested him to continue.

"Anyway, as I was saying, we had a disagreement and I said some things I shouldn't have, and I'd like to extend my apologies to you, Mr. Sheehan." Seán stood up and put out his hand for the teacher to shake. Still reeling from his encounter with the dragon, Mr. Sheehan shakily got to his feet and sourly clasped Seán's hand. Seán smiled at him, a 'fuck you' smile, a smile that said, 'I've beaten you, and there's nothing you can do about it.'

They sat back into their chairs and Mr. Aylesbury resumed command.

"Now, I have some forms I need you both to sign: here and here. Just for our records, you understand, yes."

He slid the sheets of paper over to the McLoughlins and indicated where they were to sign. Patricia carefully read each page and then deliberately etched her signature where requested, passing the pen to Seán who signed with a flourish. The headmaster gathered up the sheets and stood up, offering his hand to them both and thanking them for their time. As they left by the main entrance, he called after them: "So we'll see you in school tomorrow then, Seán, yes?"

"Sure thing, sir," Seán called back as he skipped down the steps and away out the gate.

10.

AND HE WAS BACK THE next day. He felt slightly aggrieved at having to return so soon, but at least this way the memory of his heroic encounter with Mr. Sheehan would be fresh in the minds of his classmates. His social standing within the school hierarchy was ordinarily somewhere in the middle; not cool enough to hang with the really cool kids, but some way above the nerds, swots and acne-ridden B.O sufferers. He was comfortable with that. He and his small circle of friends went about their business with a minimum of fuss. They drank occasionally, smoked hash infrequently and copped off with girls every now and then. They were known but not well-known. Was that about to change? Was Seán McLoughlin, an unremarkable student from humble beginnings, about to be rocketed into the stratosphere? Was he ready to sit alongside the beautiful, the gifted and the rich at the very summit of Dooncurra Vocational School's most-influential list? It was a possibility. How many students had told a teacher to fuck off like that? Not many. And how many had sauntered off the school premises in the aftermath, only to return a couple of days later as if nothing had happened? Even fewer. In his view he was a warrior returning from battle, a soldier coming into port, the blood of his enemy still staining his fatigues. He had faced down the enemy, their common enemy, and sent it scuttling for cover. He was a legend, a king. No, not a king; that wasn't enough. He was a god, and as soon as he walked through those school gates he would take his place on the throne. His subjects would line up at either side of him, throngs of them, four-deep as they strained to catch a glimpse of their hero.

"McLoughlin, ya nutter, wanna hang out with us after school – go for a few joints?"

"Hiya, Seán. I heard what you said to Sheehan and it made me so wet. Would you like a blowjob?""Can I do your homework for you, Seán? Honestly, it's no bother."

"Seán, we need a new captain for our football team; can you do it?"

"Here, Seán, take this money and my new jacket; fuck it, here's my runners too."

And he would just smile in deference, eager to please his subjects. But not too eager, seeing as he was a god and all.

Seán usually walked to school with a couple of friends who lived nearby, Murt and Pegs. Because he was going from his grandmother's house, however, he would have to travel alone this morning. That suited him fine; he didn't want those two gobshites messing up his grand entrance. It didn't take as long to reach the school when walking from Ard Aulinn, so he set out a bit later than usual. His plan was to arrive at about five to nine, when the majority of kids were still skulking around the main gates. He wanted his audience as large as it could possibly be. If all went well he would be enveloped by his adoring public, hoisted onto the shoulders of some of the sturdier lads and carried onto the premises to rapturous applause. He strutted down the road whistling a nameless tune, saluting cars, merrily kicking cans, stones and whatever else crossed his path. Rarely had he looked forward so much to a day at school. He passed a few groups of students as he neared the school but they were only little lads, first years who probably already thought he was a god. It was the big dogs he was looking out for; the tough lads from his year, the hot young wans from his year and, most importantly, the fifth and sixth years. As the school's main building loomed into view he spotted a few lads he knew from his year, not friends, mere acquaintances, walking on the opposite side of the road.

"Hey, McLoughlin, what are you doing back? I thought you were being expelled."

"Nah, man. I'm back today, I was only suspended," he said cheerily.

The boy guffawed, as did his mates.

"Suspended? After ya told Sheehan to fuck off? Jaysus, they're going soft around here, I reckon."

"Must be," Seán called back.

And that was that; the boys continued on their way and Seán on his. Not one mention of the word 'legend', not one 'fair play to ya, boy'. But they were quiet lads; telling a teacher to fuck off wouldn't impress the likes of them. It was the hard cases that'd be doing the back-slapping, giving the friendly punches on the arm and looking at him with new-found respect.

He hurried onwards. The gates were just around the corner; this would be his big moment. As he rounded the path and gazed upon the old grey school, however, his heart sank. Only a handful of people hovered around the entrance: kids being dropped off by their parents, a couple of lads chugging on the end of a cigarette. He looked at his watch and realised he'd mistimed his arrival. It was nine on the dot, everyone was already in class. *Fuck it.* The one morning he hadn't wanted to be late. That was his big chance gone, now; the impact of his return would be lessened once word spread. People would still come up to him in the hallway to congratulate him, but that wasn't the same as receiving the acclamation of an adoring mob.

There was nothing for it now but to get into class and salvage what he could. If he was lucky he'd get there before the teacher, and claim at least a moment or two of glory before lessons began. He jogged through the quiet hallways to the back of the school and room G14, where his English class was due to begin. There was no one outside the door, and he couldn't hear the usual hubbub coming from inside; Ms. Enright was probably already here. What a disaster; now he would have to wait until break. But his lateness did allow him to make a grand entrance of sorts. He took a deep breath and opened the door. Ms. Enright – slim, mid-twenties, with mousy-brown hair and a penchant for long flowing dresses – turned to see who was interrupting her class.

"Hurry up, Seán, come on now. Sit there at the front beside Mary."

He did as he was told and took his seat beside Mary, boring Mary who never said a word outside of the class but couldn't shut her fuckin' hole inside it. There would be no congratulatory words from her. He didn't even get a chance to look back and gauge the reception. Were they shocked? In awe? Horrified? He would have to wait until this class was over to find out. It was a shame he was so distracted, because he liked English. They were studying *Lorna Doone* for the Junior Cert and, although he didn't care to admit it, he had read the book from cover to cover in just a couple of nights. He was destined to fail miserably in most of his subjects, but not English. He thought he could get an A in English. *Take that, Daryl.* But today he wasn't really interested in discussing the merits of R. D. Blackmore's work; he just wanted the class to be over so he could be showered with praise, and blowjobs, if there were any going. In the seat beside him, Mary was rattling on about the conflicting desires of John Ridd or some other such guff, while Ms. Enright sat propped on the edge of her desk, listening intently. She was one of the younger teachers in the school, not particularly attractive but young and a teacher, which made her desirable in most of the boys' eyes. Rumour had it that she was a lesbian, although that was based on nothing more than a lack of make-up and her resistance to the charms of the older lads.

It'd be great if she was a lesbian, thought Seán. Maybe that was why she liked Mary so much. The two of them were at it every evening after school. Ms. Enright provided grinds, and Mary was probably only too happy to receive them. They waited until the school was empty and then found a quiet room somewhere in the depths of the building, where they could do all the 'grinding' they wanted. Of course it wouldn't start like that; they'd keep up the pretence for a few minutes of a teacher guiding a pupil through her work, both of them sticking to the 'curriculum', while all the time their loins became increasingly inflamed. Eventually, when she couldn't resist any longer, Ms. Enright would put down her books, take off her glasses and approach Mary. The young student would look at her quizzically, but she knew well enough what was happening; she'd been waiting for this for a long time. She wouldn't complain when her teacher began to carefully undress her, maintaining eye contact as she slowly removed each item of clothing until Mary stood there, naked and exposed, but more exhilarated, more alive than she'd felt in her entire life. She'd allowed herself to be pushed to the floor, groaning with desire as Ms. Enright peppered her with kisses, brushing her lips all over Mary's naked body as she flitted in and out of her erogenous zones. Lost in the moment, Mary would pull Ms. Enright to her, whispering 'I want you' as she nuzzled and nibbled at her neck. The teacher would back away and for one horrible moment Mary would think she'd said the wrong thing, but when she saw Ms. Enright release her hair from its bun, shaking it free so that it spilled over her shoulders, her fears would be assuaged. The older woman would unzip herself and casually step out of her dress. She wasn't wearing underwear, she never did, and so Mary would see it all, that which she'd dreamed of for so many nights. Ms. Enright's figure was much fuller than she'd expected. Her breasts, plump and fat, hung free, their nipples erect in anticipation. But it was her pubic region that astonished her most; it was wild and unkempt, like a jungle just waited to be explored. And explore it she would.

"BRRING!"

The bell rang, rousing Seán from his reverie. For fuck's sake, he'd done it again. What was wrong with him? Another class lost to the dark corners of his mind. At least no one had pulled him up on it this time; Ms. Enright had probably been warned about the danger of interrupting the fantasies of young Seán McLoughlin. He carefully placed his books back in his bag, stalling for as long as he could, so that the protuberance in his trousers might recede. When he thought it safe he rose from his seat, looking back to see where his mates were. They were all there, Ginty, Pegs, Murt: the lads. They stood, expectant, waiting for him to look their way. Now that he had the attention he'd craved, however, he suddenly became bashful; sheepishly dipping his head, he walked back to where they stood.

"Well, Lockie, didn't expect to see you back so soon. Whatcha do, give oul' Sheehan a blowie?"

If there was any praise coming Seán's way, it wouldn't be coming from Alan Pegg.

"Nah, it was just a quick hand job in the end. He's easily pleased," Seán shot back.

Students for the next class were coming into the room, so Seán and his friends gathered their belongings and continued the conversation on their way to history class in 3F.

"What really happened, Seán?" asked Ginty. "I was expecting you to be expelled for sure."

"Begged me to come back didn't they," he replied casually.

"They didn't bloody beg you," Ginty asked in disbelief, "did they?"

"Well, I wouldn't call it begging, Ginty. Let's just say they were *very eager* for me to return."

"Why were they so eager, Seán? Did your mam threaten 'em? I bet she did, didn't she? My mam said she would!"

"Had nothin' to do with my mam, nothin' at all. I'm staying at my nan's now."

"Were you thrown out?" Ginty's eyes widened even more as he struggled to come to terms with this new revelation.

"Ah no, I'm just staying at my nan's till things calm down a bit."

"Oh, right," nodded Ginty knowingly.

They reached 3F. If it was going to happen, it would be now. All the class were in there and the teacher hadn't arrived yet. He suddenly felt incredibly nervous and somewhat exposed. Part of him wished he could just enter the room, take a seat near the back and carry on as normal; but another bigger, part yearned for recognition, for someone to acknowledge his achievements and allow him his moment.

He entered, pretending to be deep in conversation with Ginty.

"Look who's fuckin' back, lads! Look at this fucker!"

Thank you, Paul Muldoon. Thank you.

Conversation ended abruptly as all eyes turned to Seán. He took his seat and was immediately encircled by his classmates, all of them clamouring, bombarding him with questions; he was the centre of attention. He felt his face redden as Becky Forde and Sally Kinsella – 3A's most unattainable females – came to his side, so close that he could smell their perfume and see the liberally-applied foundation on their faces. His throat went dry, his tongue became tied and his body prickled with sweat.

"How come you're back so soon, Seán? What happened?"

"Did Aylesbury call the guards?"

"I told Becky you'd be back, I did."

"Are you okay?"

"Are you being sent to 3B?"

"I heard Sheehan wants you expelled."

"What did your mother say?"

"Will you still be allowed do your Junior Cert?"

They were like savages gathering round him, desperate for information. They didn't really care about him or what had happened to him, and they certainly didn't think he was cool. He was just a temporary source of fascination, something to gossip about for a couple of days.

"They just said I could come back, that's all," he said meekly.

Another volley of questions, mouths opening and closing mechanically, vacant eyes; vultures.

"Sit down please, everyone."

The focus of attention switched from Seán to Mr. Cunningham, their history teacher, as he entered the room. A few of the students continued whispering questions as they faded back to their seats. Sally Kinsella gave him one final sympathetic look as she joined Becky at the front of the class; then they were gone and he was alone again. Away from the harsh glare of the spotlight, he could finally relax. It wasn't how he'd imagined it would be. All the attention had unnerved him; he hadn't enjoyed it, and being in the presence of goddesses like Becky and Sally had been terrifying. He had fantasised about them both on countless occasions, but actually being near them, breathing the same air? He wasn't ready for that. He wasn't ready for any of it. There was a reason he didn't hang around with the cool kids; he didn't belong there.

The lesson began and for the first time he saw Rosie, or, more accurately, the back of her head. She was in front of him again, with her mad head of straw. Could she not have sat somewhere else? As if to underline the point, Paul Muldoon shouted from a couple of rows back, "Keep yer eyes off Rosie's head, Lockie, you'll only get yourself in trouble, boy." The laughter was more at him than with him, but he didn't mind.

And he did keep his eyes away from Rosie's head. He stared directly at his teacher for the duration of the lesson, even managed to listen to him too. When the bell rang to signal the end of another class, the questions resumed in earnest. He answered as best he could, with short and succinct replies that seemed to satisfy his inquisitors. There were more questions at break-time; kids from other classes and other years approached him, asking him to verify rumours they'd heard. He confirmed their stories, even the embellished ones which had him shoving, and in one case, punching Mr. Sheehan. By lunchtime, interest was dying down; a few remarks as he passed kids in the schoolyard, one or two catcalls from lads who still doubted the veracity of the story. And by the end of the day it had all been completely forgotten about. Seán filed out the school gates with his friends, pushing and shoving his way through the throng, just another student heading home for the evening. His brief flirtation with fame was over, and he felt nothing but relief.

11.

AFTER SPENDING A COUPLE OF nights at his nan's Seán usually returned home like a fattened calf, ready to be slaughtered. Those visits were pre-arranged, however; agreed on by all parties. This was different. It had been an emergency stopover, an unexpected midweek arrival which had subsequently stretched into the weekend. He didn't want to go home. He wanted to stay where he was, to make this his home; but he was afraid to mention the subject of his living arrangements, terrified that bringing it up would remind his grandparents that he wasn't supposed to be here. If he stayed quiet and said nothing, maybe they'd forget about it and a few weeks down the line it would just be accepted. Oh yeah, Seán lives here now; has done for a while, actually. There was every chance it could work out like that. Neither of them seemed overly concerned about his returning home. His mother, however, was another matter; it was only a question of time before she came knocking, asking him what the fuck he was playing at. Seán knew he had to face up to things at some point, it couldn't be allowed to drift along like this. He needed to discuss it with his grandparents to see what they thought, and then go to see his mother.

"Nan?" he began, muting the TV.

Eyes on her knitting, Patricia murmured, "Mmm?"

He watched her fingers dexterously move hither and thither as she carefully crafted another scarf that would never be worn.

"I suppose I ought to go home."

She put down her knitting and stared at him intently.

"You're welcome to stay here for as long as you like. You know that, Seán, don't you?"

She seemed to be willing him to ask her. *Go on, ask can you live here; I'll say yes, I promise.*

"I know, Nan. It's just – I need clean clothes and that."

"Clean clothes? Sure, your uncle Patrick has drawers of stuff up there you could wear. Drawers of it!"

"Um, thanks, Nan, but my style is a bit different to what Pat's was."

She threw back her head and laughed like an ass.

"Ho, ho, ho. Style? Ah, Seány, trying to look good for the girls, are we?"

He blushed; he loved his nan but she hadn't a clue what it was like being a teenager. At least his mother acknowledged that he needed to look his very best at all times, and gave him money to buy his own clothes at birthdays and Christmas.

"Well, y'know," he mumbled, waiting for this excruciating conversation to conclude.

"Not to worry. Why don't we go shopping in town right now?"

He looked at her, aghast. It was Saturday afternoon, and there was every chance of seeing someone he knew in town. It'd be bad enough being spotted out and about with his 'Mammy'. But his 'Nanny'?!

"Ah, no thanks, Nan. Maybe I'll just go home and get some stuff."

He paused; now was the time to drop the question.

"And maybe I could come back then and stay for another few nights?"

She nodded so forcefully he thought her head was going to come off.

"That'd be lovely, Seány. I'll come with you. We'll get a taxi."

"No, Nan, it's okay. I think I'm better off going on my own. I'll be back soon, I promise."

She looked at him doubtfully. "Okay, Seán, but don't let *him* make you stay. He has no right to tell you anything, remember that."

"I will, Nan."

A few minutes later he set off down the hill. The jacket he had brought as a precaution wasn't needed, so he pulled it off and slung it over his shoulder. A lawnmower sounded in the distance, getting its first airing of the year. Summer wasn't far off now, just a couple of months away. He allowed himself to dream of lazy days lying by the river, drying off after being dunked in the water by that bastard Pegs. But before any lazy days could be enjoyed there were exams to be sat, a Junior Cert to obtain. He felt its weight on his shoulders wherever he went. Of course, he could lessen his load by simply studying for his exams, but he never seemed to get round to it. Next week, he'd tell himself, next week is when it all begins. He'd lay out his plans in advance: an hour's study every night, increasing to an hour and a half and then two hours, so that by the time his exams started he'd be doing three hours study every night. When Monday came, though, he always found an excuse. *Ah I'm tired after the weekend; I'll start tomorrow night.* It had been like that all year, and he could count on one hand the number of hours he'd spent studying. He was running out of time, with just six weeks to go. More than anything he wanted it to be over, but in order for it to be over it had to first arrive. It was all very depressing.

*

He hoped to catch his mother on her own. Daryl usually spent Saturday afternoons at the bookies, and Kevin would most likely be out playing with his mates. If it were just the two of them they might be able to have a civil conversation, discuss what had happened and how they might proceed, without it descending into a shitstorm. He eased his key into the front door and stepped inside the hallway. The living-room was empty and the television off. Could it be that there was no one here? Perhaps he could creep in like a thief in the night, gather his belongings and leave without a trace. But, as he closed the door behind him, he heard music coming from the kitchen; insipid country-and-western stuff, his mother's favourite. He followed the sound. Sinéad was down on all fours, cramming clothes into the washing-machine. It looked like her entire wardrobe was already in there, but she still endeavoured to add a couple more items. Despite the effort involved in her task, she was still able to sing along to the charming ditty about love and betrayal which blared out of the stereo on the worktop. Seán looked at her – his poor mother, going about her day, getting on with things as best she could – and he wished it didn't have to be like this. If only he could just walk in the door and be welcomed with open arms, not just today but every day. He wished this felt like home and he could be at ease here. Most of all, he wished it were just the two of them, just him and his mam. No Daryl, no Kevin; just the two of them, like it used to be.

"Well, Mam."

No response. Of course not, how could she hear anything over that din? He walked to the worktop and switched off the radio. Sinéad swivelled round, her voice dying in the air. For a moment there was a flicker of warmth in her eyes, but then her features hardened; it was almost as if she'd been practising how to respond when she saw him again.

"You frightened me," she said, getting to her feet.

"Sorry."

She stuffed the rest of the clothes in the machine and fetched the washing powder from under the sink; just another busy mammy going about her day.

He didn't need to ask how she felt about seeing him; it was abundantly clear. His mother forgave almost everything, but when she decided he had crossed the line she made sure he knew it. She became cold, unapproachable and unrecognisable from the woman he had adored all his life. He had only seen her like this on a handful of occasions, but as soon as she'd turned around he'd understood the gravity of the situation.

"I'm just back to collect some of my stuff."

She slammed the washing machine shut and cranked it into life.

"Well, go ahead, then; don't let me stop you."

He felt the temper rise in his stomach. He had come here in peace, ready to admit he was wrong and ask forgiveness for his sins, but if she was going to be like this about it she could fuck off for herself. He went to his room, eyes brimming with tears, and quickly stuffed some clothes into his sports bag. *Fuck her.* He was angry now, not only at her but at himself too. He didn't want to get upset, to cry like a little baby. For a brief moment he considered going back to the kitchen and standing there before her, a picture of contrition, tears rolling down his cheeks. She would see how sorry he was, how upset he was, and respond in kind. They'd embrace and all would be forgiven. But he couldn't remember the last time he'd hugged his mother. It would be awkward and uncomfortable. He forced the thought out of his mind. There would be no reconciliation, he had tried his best and she'd thrown it back at him. *Fuck her.* He slung the bag over his shoulder, grabbed a few personal effects and stepped into the hallway. He listened out for any last words from his mother. But there were none. She didn't want him here. He opened the front door and without so much as a goodbye, began the walk back to his grandparents'.

Sinéad heard the door close and felt her stomach turn; he was gone. She'd let him go. It wasn't too late, though; if she hurried she could catch him. No, the moment had passed; their combined stubbornness had seen to that. He had gone and left her, and she'd let him. She slumped onto a chair and put her hands to her head. Would it have killed her to have been civil? They could have talked it out, just the two of them. She could have warned about him about his future behaviour and he would have promised to improve. That's what parents did: they disciplined their children, guided them through the tricky stages of life until they came out the other side, all shiny and perfect. Then, when they were old enough to understand, those same sullen kids began to appreciate all that had been done for them. What had she done for her boy? Had she given him the life he deserved, sacrificed her own happiness for his? That's what you were supposed to do. That's what being a parent was all about, but she hadn't done any of that. She had failed him, let him down and now he was gone. A sob caught in her throat. She didn't fight it, nor did she fight the tears that followed. And as she sat there weeping for her son, she wondered if things would ever be the same again.

12

"ARE YOU GOING TO STUDY this evening, Seán? Exams are only a couple of weeks away now, my boy."

Seán sat spread-eagled on the couch. He'd just obliterated a roast dinner and was allowing it to settle while he watched TV.

"I will, Nan, yeah," he mumbled.

One of the benefits of living here was the freedom he was afforded, but if she was going to carry on like this, maybe he'd move in with his uncle Patrick.

Patricia looked at him disapprovingly. However, she had planned this particular conversation well in advance.

"Do you know Mrs. Tiernan that lives in number twenty-three?"

Seán checked to see if she was talking to him. Why on earth would he know or care who lived in number twenty-three, or any other number for that matter?

"I don't, Nan," he said, wondering where all this was going.

"Well, she has a daughter, Alice, a lovely girl, who's also doing her Junior Cert. She goes to the convent school in Killynaveagh."

That got his attention; those convent girls were right dirty bitches by all accounts.

"Anyway, I was talking to Mrs. Tiernan about you, and she was saying that her Alice is a nightmare for the studying. They practically have to force her up the stairs."

Mmm, me and Alice upstairs, with no one around; keep talking.

"Are you listening to me, Seán?"

"I am, Nan."

"So we thought it might be a good idea to get the two of ye together. Studying partners, I think that's what they call it."

"Hmm, I don't know, Nan." He had to play it cool, he didn't want her thinking she could win him round that easily. But already he could feel a stirring in his trousers at the thought of biology lessons with Alice Tiernan from number twenty-three.

"Why don't you know, Seán? She's a lovely girl, and it'd beat sitting there on your own."

He sighed deeply, ensuring that she realised how big an undertaking this would be for him.

"Well, I suppose I could try it for a couple of nights and see how we get on."

"Oh, brilliant," Patricia squealed, getting up from her seat.

A couple of seconds later, Seán heard her on the phone.

"Hello, Irene. Yes, I did. He said he'd love to. I know. Is she? Ah, that's great. Okay, I'll tell him. Goodbye, Irene. I will. Bye now."

She returned to the living-room wearing a triumphant smile.

"You're to go up there in an hour. She'll be expecting you."

Fuck. An hour? He hadn't expected that. He was struck by a sudden bout of nerves. What if she was really hot, like Becky Forde hot? *Jesus.* Would he be able to cope? He could never control himself around girls he fancied, always sweating and blushing, mumbling and being a fucking idiot. He didn't want to go, now. He was scared. Why hadn't he just studied when he'd said he would? He could have avoided all this crap; clandestine dates with mysterious studying partners at number twenty-three, palpitations at the thought of her being as hot as Becky Forde. Fuck's sake. There was no getting out of it now, though. It was all arranged. She was waiting up there for him. Well, fuck it, if she was waiting for him the least he could do was make himself presentable. He got up from the couch, turned off the TV and headed upstairs for a shower. With any luck his grandfather's cologne would be in the bathroom.

13

SHE WAS ALL RIGHT, BUT only alright. Small and slim, with porcelain-white skin and eager, inquisitive eyes. She reminded him of a small prairie animal, a shrew of some sort. It was a real shame. He'd hoped for something in between, not as hot as Becky Forde but not a minger either. Someone attainable, who might fancy him and he might fancy back. What he'd got was Pippi fuckin' Longstocking.

At least she wasn't shy, though; that was something.

"So what will we start with?" she asked, all business-like.

"I don't care," Seán said, shrugging his shoulders.

"C'mon, you must have a preference?"

She sat across from him, nibbling on the end of a pen and gazing at him expectantly. Wasn't she supposed to be as much of a slacker as he was? Why all the sudden enthusiasm? He knew why: she fancied him. As soon as he'd walked into the door he'd seen it; overt friendliness and big, beaming smiles. Mrs. Tiernan, clearly dubious about allowing a sexually-charged fifteen-year-old boy into the house, had escorted them to a well-lit room at the back where a makeshift study centre had been set up. Seán had instantly decided he didn't fancy this girl, but he was still disappointed they weren't going to be working in her room — at least then he might have had a chance to rummage through her knicker drawer when she went to the jacks. Instead, here they were in their 'study centre' with nothing but books, pens, and paper to entertain them. Fantastic.

"Well, maths is my worst subject so – "

"Let's start with that, then!" She was off like a shot, fishing her book out of the bag and leafing through the pages like a lunatic.

If she had let him finish his sentence she would have heard " – let's leave that till last."

But she had her book out now, and he did need some help with his maths, so he followed suit and took out his own. The difference in the two textbooks was stark. Hers was as pristine as the day it was bound, carefully covered in transparent laminate and with barely a dog-ear in sight; his resembled something an archaeologist might find on a dig in ancient Egypt.

"How are you on algebra? I hate it. I got a C2 in my mocks. Mammy nearly kilt me!"

Seán had failed maths in his mocks; he'd got an NG, same as his Christmas exams.

"Ah, I'm not great at it, to be honest."

There was a knock at the door, followed by Mrs. Tiernan with a tray of refreshments. She was really here to check up on them though, that was obvious.

"How are the students getting on?"

She was grinning from ear to ear. Seán thought she looked a little bit demented. He reckoned she was in her mid – to late forties, a lot older than his mother. He was used to this when calling to his friend's houses; their parents were usually older than his and had more in common with his grandparents than his mother.

"Fine, Mrs. Tiernan."

"Great. That's grand, now." She set down the tray on the table; on it were two large glasses of orange cordial and a plate of chocolate digestives. Seán glanced at Alice. She stared daggers at her mother. *Ah, bless, she's trying to impress me and silly oul' Mammy is cramping her style.* Mrs. Tiernan lingered for a few seconds more, continuing to grin manically, then patted Seán on the back before departing with a wave. Seán exchanged glances with his educational partner. "Mothers, eh?"

Alice had flushed slightly. "God, she's so embarrassing," she said, glancing ruefully at the glasses of orange.

"It could be worse, girl, believe me," said Seán, grabbing a couple of biscuits. He tried to imagine how their study sessions might go in his grandparents' house, and shuddered; but that would still be preferable to bringing her to his mother's. At least they were guaranteed a warm welcome at his nanny's. At home, with Daryl around, anything was possible. A couple of glasses of orange and a cheesy welcome was small fare compared to the kind of shit Seán had to put up with. It had reached the point where he no longer invited his friends round. It was bad enough that Daryl spent each and every evening lying on the couch in the sitting-room, the remote control balanced on his chest. The fact he did so in a pair of tatty old tracksuit bottoms and a dressing-gown, could also just about be tolerated. What made it impossible to invite people over was his stepfather's outright hostility. He remembered when Ginty had come to stay over one Saturday night; poor Ginty, the most harmless fucker you could ever meet. He came in, all buck-toothed politeness, and was met by a pig.

"Hello, Mr. Cassidy," he'd said, offering Daryl his hand.

Daryl lay on the couch, looked at Ginty's little paw and grunted in derision. Unsure how to proceed, Ginty looked at Seán, who had turned bright red; he managed to nod towards his room and mumble, "Come on, let's have a game on the Mega Drive."

That was how Daryl greeted his friends on a good day. On a bad day, he'd make it clear he didn't want them there without actually coming out and saying it. This involved waging loud arguments with Sinéad within earshot of Seán's guests, or, if she wasn't there, slamming doors and banging pots while muttering expletives under his breath, again ensuring that everything he did and said could be heard by all in the vicinity.

No, poor innocent Alice had it better than she could ever imagine.

After he'd polished off all the biscuits and slaked his thirst, they set about doing some actual work. To his surprise, they made some progress. She explained some of the things he was too embarrassed to ask about in class, and in the space of an hour he'd learned more about algebra than he had in the last year of school. He wasn't sure what she was getting from it, though. Her maths was fine, way ahead of his. It only seemed fair that they switch to a subject in which he was her superior – if there was one.

"So what did you get in English in your mocks?" he asked, casually.

"B2, in honours," she replied with a grin.

He said nothing, waiting for the question.

"And you?"

He paused before answering. This would be the only time he could pose as her intellectual superior, so he might as well make the most of it.

"An A1 in honours."

"Wow! An A1! Janey mac!"

"Yeah, I like English," he replied bashfully.

"I bet you do. An A1!!"

He felt a warm glow in his chest. This girl whom he barely knew had just given him more recognition for his achievements than most members of his family.

"So maybe I can help you with yours, seeing as you did loads for me with the maths and that."

"Okay," she said, maintaining eye contact for longer than was comfortable. Seán darted his eyes away, looking anywhere but at her. He didn't think he'd led her on. Had he? No, he'd just been himself, and that was all it had taken for her to fall for him. Because it was clear to him that this young girl, with her pale skin and her inferior English grade, was smitten. Try as he might, though, he couldn't muster even a semi at the thought of seeing her naked, and he could generally muster a semi at the thought of almost anything. She dressed like a pre-teen, for a start, and she didn't wear any make-up. Seán liked make-up on his women. It showed they had a bit of class. What really put him off, though, was the way her light brown hair was pulled back into a ponytail, exposing a smattering of freckles on her forehead. He hated freckles, hated them. Pale, Irish skin with freckles all over it; there was nothing worse as far as he was concerned. However, this studying session had been very beneficial in terms of his schoolwork, so if and when she tried to take things further, he would calmly explain that he didn't feel that way about her and hope it didn't sully this mutually beneficial relationship.

In order for it to become mutually beneficial, of course, he had to repay the favour. So he ignored her increasingly suggestive stares and took her through the finer points of Dylan Thomas, Oscar Wilde, Tennyson, Shakespeare, O'Casey and Fitzgerald. All the while doing his utmost to keep things strictly professional; he was friendly yet mildly aloof, attentive but strangely distant. There could be no crossing of wires here. At one point his hand brushed against hers as he pointed to the opening line of a stanza and he could have sworn she emitted a moan of pleasure. The best course of action now was to bring this night to a satisfactory conclusion before someone got their heart broken.

"Look at the time, it's nearly ten!" he said, staring at his watch in amazement as though he hadn't been counting down the minutes since twenty to the hour.

"It is getting late, I suppose," Alice replied grudgingly, like a child being told it was bedtime.

Seán quickly began putting his things away, perhaps too hastily, but he didn't care.

"We got loads done," he said. "Turned out to be a pretty good idea, after all."

"Yeah, it was great," she said perking up a little.

"We can do it at my nan's next time, if you like?" He was aware of his double-entendre but doubted that she would notice it.

"That'd be brilliant. When? Tomorrow night?"

Steady on love. "I'm busy tomorrow night," he lied. "How about Thursday?"

"Grand."

"Well, that's that then," he announced, zipping up his bag and hesitantly moving to the door.

"Yes. Thank you, Seán. It was really helpful."

They stood staring at each other, Sean grateful there was a desk separating them, and Alice waiting for something, what, he didn't know. Whatever it was, he didn't intend to give it to her. He couldn't reach the door without brushing up against her, though, and she hadn't made any attempt to move. He was trapped, trapped by this sexual predator.

She sighed deeply as if admitting defeat, and led the way out. "You'd better say goodbye to my parents."

"I will," he replied, feeling strangely guilty for letting her down.

When they returned to the sitting-room there were two people present who hadn't been there when he'd arrived, a boy and a girl. The boy was clearly Alice's brother, he shared the pale skin and rusty-coloured hair handed down by Mr. Tiernan. He was older, though, in his early twenties perhaps. The girl didn't look like Alice or the brother, or Mr. Tiernan, or anyone in Dooncurra for that matter. She was beautiful. Her blonde hair was wet through as if she'd just emerged from the sea, like a surfer or a mermaid, and she glowed with radiance and good health. Her face also was bereft of make-up, but unlike Alice, this creature didn't need make-up. She was tanned, almost dusky, her skin that vibrant bronze colour that you saw on models in holiday brochures. But it was her eyes that held him, drew him to her and threatened to turn him to stone. A deep shade of green, they shimmered. They were commanding, mysterious. And yet there was something cold about them; the dead eyes of a predator as it silently observed its prey. It was like staring at the sun; he knew it was dangerous, but he couldn't help it. Only when you'd feasted upon these main attractions did you begin to notice the delicacy of her features: the small, dainty nose, the gently curved jawline and shallow cheeks. Her mouth was set in a slight pout, ready to break into a smile or a sneer at any moment, depending on her mood, conveying a thousand emotions without the need for speech.

Yet, despite her aching beauty, her remarkable, other-worldly refinement, there was something crude about her. Beneath all that elegance and allure lay something else, wanton and lewd. It was this that drew him, more than anything else. If he was to hazard a guess he'd say she was eighteen, but such was her calm self-assuredness she could easily have been in her twenties. She was curled up in an armchair wearing a T-shirt and tracksuit, eyeing him lazily like a cat deciding if and when to strike. Nervously he met her stare, looked away and then looked back, scared but invigorated. She scrutinised him unblinkingly, never taking her eyes off him. Seán felt a tingle in his groin. Rather than the beginning of an unwelcome erection, it felt as if his genitals were shrivelling up inside him. She was toying with him, and despite his confused anxiety he was quite enjoying it. He desperately wanted to be introduced to her, to see if she were real and make sure he wasn't just imagining her.

"Where are your manners, Alice?" asked Mrs. Tiernan as her daughter dragged Seán towards the front door.

"What?" she replied, irritably. But she knew what she was doing. Alice Tiernan had seen the effect her older sister had on boys before. And she was determined to get this boy, her boy, out of the room before he fell under the spell.

"Introduce your friend to your brother and sister, and don't be so rude!"

"Okay," Alice muttered, now very much a stroppy teenager.

"This is my brother, Gerard," she said, indicating the mass of arms and legs on the chair furthest from the door. Gerard waved a greeting and returned to the TV.

"And this is my sister, Leanne,"

The vision in the other armchair rose to greet him, taking his hand in hers before he could proffer it.

"Hi, Seán. I hope you've been looking after my little sister in there."

It was a fairly innocuous remark, the kind of thing any big sister might say, but coming from her mouth it acquired added meaning. The glance that accompanied it added to the intrigue. She looked into his eyes, a small smirk playing over her lips. Was she suggesting they'd been up to something in that little room? Perish the thought. He wanted to let her know that they hadn't done anything, that he would never do anything in any room unless it were with her.

"I – yeah, we got some great work done."

"Glad to hear it," she said, releasing his hand and returning to her chair. He looked to see if she was still watching him but, like her brother, she had returned to the TV, apparently finished with him. The disappointment was crushing. He would gladly have sold his soul to have her attention for a few moments longer.

Introductions over, he was finally propelled towards the door by Alice, who had ceased to exist in his mind, and after a terse goodbye, he was outside alone. Instead of walking the short distance to his grandparents' house, he decided to take a little stroll. He needed some time to digest what had just happened.

14

HE DREAMT ABOUT HER THAT night. They were in the Tiernans' study room: Seán, Leanne, Alice, Mr. and Mrs. Tiernan, Rosie Power, and his uncle Patrick. Mrs. Tiernan had just served up a plate of roast beef for everyone except Seán, who had his maths textbook in front of him.

"No dinner for you until you've finished studying," said Rosie mockingly, as she skewered a roast potato and planted it in her mouth.

Seán looked at Patrick for support, but he couldn't see his uncle's face behind the biker's helmet he wore. There was nothing for it, he would have to study. He flipped open the book in the hope of getting his work done before his dinner got cold, but all the pages were blank.

"Mrs. Tiernan, my book – "

"No dinner for you until you've finished studying," said Mrs. Tiernan, as Rosie nodded approvingly.

He looked at Alice, showing her the blank pages of his book, but she was too busy cosying up to Patrick to notice. She was stroking his thigh and whispering in his ear, or to be more precise, the side of his helmet. She occasionally glanced back at Seán, making sure he was watching before redoubling her efforts. Seán wondered if Patrick liked it.

Leanne sat directly across from him, but whenever he tried to look at her his sight became blurred. He squinted in desperation but it made no difference; all he could see was a shimmering outline, a blue-green hue where she should be. It was her, though, it had to be. His heart was beating fast and his palms were clammy with sweat. He moved his eyes in her direction once more, slowly now, hoping his sight would adjust if he made no sudden movements, and little by little she came into view. It was incredible. Her bee-stung lips pouted at him coquettishly, and her eyes, thick with mascara, spoke of things he dared not imagine even in his dreams.

"You came," she said.

"Yes, I was always going to come," he replied.

"For me?"

"Yes, for you. Who else is there?"

She smiled at him. His words pleased her. This made him happy. He would do anything to please her.

"What about my sister?" she asked.

He gazed at her indulgently. "Forget about her."

She stood up from her chair. Now everyone else was a blur and Leanne was the only one he could see. She wore a checked shirt, the kind often worn by lumberjacks and fishermen, and beneath it he could see the swell of her breasts. He tried to stand up to go to her, but he couldn't move. A whinny of frustration rose in his chest. He needed her so badly, but no matter how hard he tried he couldn't move. Mrs. Tiernan came back into view. She sat beside him now, looking at his groin.

"Seán, what on earth is this?" she asked, pointing to his erection. He couldn't recall stripping off, but he was naked now.

"I'm sorry, Mrs. Tiernan. This is for Leanne."

"Well, no dessert for you!"

Leanne shot back into view. She was on the table now, sitting cross-legged among all the cutlery and food. She was only a matter of inches away but still beyond his reach. His penis was throbbing so much he wondered if his bell-end might explode. He didn't want that to happen.

She began unbuttoning the shirt. She was bare underneath but, try as he might, Seán couldn't see what he wanted to see. He had to see them, had to see those breasts. By focusing hard he could see how they gently curved at the teat, pointing upwards and then back upon themselves. It wasn't enough; he had to see them properly. She reached the last button and popped it open, her mouth opening in faux surprise as she did so.

"Are you here for me?"

"I am," he grunted, on the verge of tears.

"Okay then, Seán."

She opened the shirt and gave him what he wanted.

He awoke. For the first few seconds he retained that beautiful post-dream feeling, where everything that had just happened was still real and life was perfect. Then he returned to reality. He was in his uncle's old room in his grandparents' house. And judging by the dampness in his boxers, he had some cleaning up to do.

15

"YOU GOT OFF WITH HER, Lockie, didn't ya? Ya dirty little fucker!"

Pegs stood before him, his eyes fixed intently on Seán. He wanted answers; they all did. Their friend had been quiet all morning, moping around like a lovesick puppy, wistfully gazing out the window, lost in thought. It was obvious what had happened; he'd copped off with his little studying partner and was now in love. What other explanation could there be?

"I didn't, Pegs, honest."

"Ya fuckin' did, Lockie. Don't give me that shit."

Alan Pegg shook his head, a knowing smile on his lips. He had to hand it to his pal, he'd got the jump on them all. A studying partner – it was genius, really. Some sex-starved convent girl; not allowed out at weekends, never so much as kissed a boy. And here comes young McLoughlin to corrupt her poor innocent soul. He playfully punched Seán on the arm, his way of displaying the deep admiration he had for his friend's cunning plan.

"Ow! For fuck's sake, Pegs!"

Pegs grinned at him and threw him a wink.

"Details, Lockie, now," he demanded.

"There aren't any details," Seán protested in exasperation.

What was he supposed to do? Nothing had happened; well, *something* had happened, but not what they thought. There was no way he was telling them about Leanne. She was his, not to be shared with the likes of them. Pegs wouldn't let up, though; he claimed to have a sixth sense for stuff like this, said he knew just by looking at Seán that he'd got off with Alice the night before. All he wanted to do was to help his friend through this exciting stage in his life, give him a few pointers, show him how it was done. He considered himself an expert in this field, affairs of the heart, as he liked to call it, although the heart had very little to do with it where Pegs was concerned. He viewed the opposite sex in the same way a lion might view a zeal of zebras, something to be hunted, chased down and then devoured. That was his approach and, to be fair, it had served him well. He attributed his success to his innate charm and good looks; his friends put it down to his hulking frame and the fact he was one of the few third years who could grow real stubble. Because, at sixteen, Alan Pegg was already essentially a man. In fact, he was bigger than most men. He was certainly taller than all their teachers, and broader than most of them too. He was a man-child. And, although he liked to portray himself as a gentle giant, that really wasn't the case. Pegs wasn't a violent kid and never used his mass to bully or intimidate, but he did like to put himself about; not so much a gentle giant as a wild, slavering bull in a china shop. Seán and his friends were just glad to have him on their side. On days like today, though, when Pegs wished to extract information from him,

Seán wished that all his friends could be as meek and unassuming as the harmless, defenceless Ginty.

"There's nothing to tell, Pegs, honest," he said, looking at Murt and Ginty for support.

Murt shook his head, not buying it. Ginty was trying his best to believe his friend, but his face was masked with doubt. Something was going on here, and it was about time Seán spilled the beans.

"You little fuckin' liar," Pegs said, taking a deep breath in the manner of a parent about to spank their child. He grabbed Seán in a headlock and led him towards the bench where they spent their breaks.

"Lemme go, Pegs, for fuck's sake."

"No. Not until you tell us what happened, ya dirty little cunt."

"For fuck's sake!" Seán was getting annoyed now; hot, sweaty and annoyed.

Pegs perched himself on the table, still holding Seán in his bearlike grip. Murt and Ginty joined him, while Seán was forced to stand at the side, bent uncomfortably as his tormentor held him captive.

"Let me go, Pegs, ya fuckin' wanker!"

Pegs knew his friend was getting pissed off, but he cared not.

"Details, Seány, details," he sang, as the three of them laughed in unison.

"All right, all right. I'll tell ye, now fuckin' let me go."

"Promise, Seán."

"I promise."

"What do ye reckon, lads?"

"I dunno," said Ginty.

"Ah, leave him go, Pegs; he'll tell us," urged Murt. *Good old Murt, always the voice of reason.*

Pegs released Seán from his grasp, and they stared at him while he rubbed at his neck and straightened himself out. Satisfied that he'd had enough time to compose himself, Pegs offered Seán a seat beside him.

"Well?" he asked.

Seán didn't fancy being taken to task again, so he began to talk. There was no way he was telling them about Leanne; it was bad enough coming to terms with the hold she had over him without having his mates tease him as well. And what if they wanted to see her for themselves? He didn't fancy sharing his obsession with that deviant, Pegs. No, he would tell the truth about what happened with Alice, with maybe a little embellishment to keep them sweet.

"Okay, okay," he said, bowing his head and indicating that they should do the same.

They did as they were told; this wasn't the kind of stuff you could discuss openly in the school playground. Seán lowered his voice and began recounting the previous night's events to his rapt audience.

"Right so, are ye listening?"

They nodded, solemn now. Grave.

"So anyway, I get there and Mrs. Tiernan answers the door. 'Hello Seán, glad you could make it. This is Alice.' A young wan comes out of the sitting-room, a small, skinny yoke. She's all right, nothing special; a bit childish, if I'm being honest."

"Bet you turned her into a woman, didn't ya, Lockie? Ya dirty little bastard!"

"Fuck's sake, Pegs, will you let him finish!" said Murt, irritated by the interruption. "Go on, Seán."

Seán ensured he had the floor once more and resumed his tale.

"So the mother brings us to this room, like a dining-room or something in the back of the house. And she has it all laid out like a proper study room, table cleared off, pens and markers in little cups, desk lamps, the whole fuckin' lot. I'm thinking to meself, 'Fuck this, I was only coming to see if there was a chance of a ride.'"

Pegs hooted in delight and held up his hand for a high-five. Seán complied before returning to his story.

"She's not shy, I'll give her that; mightn't be the best looking young wan you'll ever see but not shy, definitely not. She's all 'What'll we do first?' and that kinda shit, and I'm wondering if she's talking about study or something else entirely. I knew straight away I didn't fancy her, but I figured there was no harm in letting things play out and see where it ended up. Anyway, the books come out and we're going through algebra and trigonometry and, would you credit it, I'm actually learning a few things."

"A proper little swot," said Ginty, rolling his eyes to heaven.

"Yeah, she's a swot alright. But then she starts going on about how it's too difficult to work together when we're at opposite sides of the table, and would I not come around and sit beside her."

Pegs began hopping up and down on his seat in excitement.

"I look at her doubtfully but take it at face value. I mean, what can we do with her parents in the next room, right?"

They all nod in affirmation, eager to find out what you could do with her parents in the next room.

"I sit beside her and she's actually right, it's much easier to work when you're side by side. I must try it in class sometime!"

They ignored his joke; this wasn't the time for jokes.

Seán hadn't intended for the lie to go any further than this, but he looked at their faces, the way they hung on his every word, and knew he couldn't let them down. He'd got their hopes up now, he had to give them something decent. So he kept talking.

"We're sitting there going over the maths, and next thing she puts her hand on my leg."

Ginty's eyes widened, Pegs suddenly became very serious. Even Murt looked taken aback.

"I look at her and go, 'Eh what are you doing?' And she says: 'C'mon, my parents won't hear anything.' Then she grabs my hand and moves it up inside her top; she's not wearing a bra, so I get a proper handful. There's not a whole lot to grab but I'm tweaking her nipples and mauling the tits off her. I've a proper stalk on by this stage, and she moves her hand from my thigh slowly up my leg until she's got my cock. She starts wanking me through me pants while I'm feeling the tits off her, and all the while she's just staring at me with a dirty smirk on her face. Then, just when I thought I was going to blow me load, we hear someone in the hallway. I yank me hand out from under her top, she takes back her own hand, and we sit there full of concentration waiting for the door to open. In comes the mother with a tray of fuckin' digestives!"

The bell resounded around the schoolyard, bringing Seán's story to an abrupt end. His three friends appeared shell-shocked. Pegs in particular, was in a daze. As they trooped back into class, probing for more details, he cursed himself for not finding a study partner of his own. He was going to get one soon, though; no doubt about it.

16

BACK IN CLASS, SEÁN CURSED himself for being so stupid. Why couldn't he just have told the truth? He wouldn't have needed to mention Leanne. But no, he had succumbed to his machismo and sullied Alice's reputation in the process. He doubted she even knew what to do with a cock, never mind forcefully grab one without invitation. He had sworn his friends to secrecy, but it wasn't enough; there was no chance they would keep this to themselves. As they sat in geography, Pegs winking over at him every couple of minutes, he resolved to come clean at lunchtime. Whatever about clearing Alice's name, he wanted to be rid of the guilt.

When lunchtime came, however, he couldn't bring himself to do it. They were in awe of him, and he liked it. Between this and the set-to with Sheehan, his stock had never been higher. He was now a challenger of authority, with a side-line in boob-fondling. What next? Turning up for school on a motorbike? Anything was possible in the life of the new, improved Seán McLoughlin. So what if only half the legend was true? They didn't need to know that, not right now anyway. Maybe later, when the topic of conversation had moved onto something else, he'd reveal the truth; that Alice Tierney was a good Catholic girl and would never dream of behaving like such a strumpet. But for now she was a filthy little whore., and he the grateful recipient of her advances. Pegs was the only one of them to have popped his cherry, and as far as Seán was concerned it was a race between himself and Murt to see who'd be next; Ginty didn't count, as to the best of their knowledge he'd never so much as kissed a girl. Although his fictional account of last night's events hadn't included any actual coitus, Seán had gained crucial ground over Murt, at least in Pegs' eyes. The big man viewed him differently now, there was no mistaking it. He looked on him with new-found respect, a look that said: *We're men, you and I, not like those other limp-wristed losers.* So he kept quiet, revelling in his status as the current stud of the group, taking great pleasure in Murt's defeated demeanour. And, after a while, it began to feel like he had felt Alice Tiernan's tits while she wanked him off through his pants.

*

"When you seeing her again, Lockie? I bet you can hardly wait," said Ginty. While Pegs and Murt's admiration was tinged with jealousy, Ginty appeared genuinely thrilled by Seán's good fortune, like a proud father basking in his son's heroics.

They lay on the grass at the back of the school grounds, near the wall where Seán had made his great getaway. It was warm enough to dispense with their jumpers, but not quite warm enough to go topless like Pegs had. He never needed much of an excuse; as soon as the temperature hit double figures he was stripping off, parading his chest-hair and flexing his muscles like a weightlifter from the eastern bloc. His complaint now was that they were too far away from the main yard for any girls to see his nakedness.

Seán sighed deeply, as if the prospect of seeing this sex-crazed harlot was the least of his worries, which in a sense was true.

"I don't know, Ginty, to be honest. We're supposed to be meeting in my grandparents' house tomorrow night, but if she starts up that shit again I'll have to put a halt to it."

"WHAT?" Pegs propped himself up on his elbows. "Put a halt to it? What are ya, a faggot?"

His words stung Seán.

"I can't risk it, Pegs," he said, almost pleadingly. "If my nan catches us up to anything she'll send me back to my mother's, and I don't want that."

Pegs considered this.

"Fair enough, Seány. But when you're back in her house you're to go for it, do ya hear me!

"I'll try, Pegs."

"Do or do not," said Ginty sagely, "there is no try."

They all burst out laughing, even Murt. Ginty's *Star Wars* references usually went right over their heads, but on this occasion Yoda's words seemed entirely apt.

When the day was over and he'd said goodbye to his friends, Seán reassessed the situation. There was no turning back now. If he told the truth now, the respect he'd gained would be replaced by ridicule; firstly for being such a liar, and secondly for being sad enough to make up a story to impress them. No, he was tied to his lie now, and he'd have to live with it and its consequences. The extent of those consequences depended entirely on his friends' ability to keep a secret. Ordinarily this would have been an exercise in futility; Alan Pegg couldn't keep a secret to save his life. And one of a sexual nature? You'd have to stitch his mouth shut. Left to his own devices he'd have the whole class told within the hour and would then begin working his way through the entire year, before moving on to the years above and below. By the end of the week the word would be out: Seán McLoughlin called round to Alice Tiernan's house to study and ended up riding her up the arse, before giving the mother one too while the father watched on in his Y-fronts.

Realising the gravity of the situation, Seán had been quick to add a caveat to his story, something to ensure that bigmouth Pegs would have to keep it to himself. It was genius really, and it ensured that the story he'd made up would go no further than his three best mates. He'd told them she had a boyfriend in sixth year. That was enough. Sixth years held no fear for Alan Pegg, he was happy to take on all comers. For Seán, though, it was different, and the last thing Pegs wanted was his womanising little buddy being on the wrong end of a hiding from a lad two years his senior. They pressed him for details, begged to know the identity of the poor fool whose girlfriend had been felt up by a lad still in third year. but Sean wouldn't budge. He had gained a measure of control. His lie had been contained – at least for the time being.

17

ALL THIS PLOTTING AND SCHEMING had at least distracted his thoughts away from the other member of the Tiernan family, the one who made his stomach churn every time he thought about her. As soon as he got home he disappeared to his room, needing time alone with his thoughts. He couldn't think straight; all he could do was say her name over and over again. Leanne. Leanne. Leanne. Leanne Tiernan. Leanne. He tried their names together. Leanne and Seán. Seán and Leanne. Leanne McLoughlin. Mr. and Mrs. Seán McLoughlin. Leanne. He considered writing them down so he could see how they looked in print, but if he started doing that he might not be able to stop. He'd fill entire copybooks with her name until, having run out of paper, he'd begin daubing their names on the walls of his room, and beyond. It hadn't even been twenty-four hours but she had consumed him; he felt listless and empty, forlorn and detached, yet simultaneously more alive than he'd ever felt. Was this what being in love felt like? It had to be. This was no crush – only girls had them.

All that evening he moped around the house. He poked and prodded at his dinner, causing Patricia to query his health. It was a Champions League night: Manchester United and Juventus in the semi-final. He and his grandfather had been awaiting this one for weeks. They were both United fans and believed that this would be the year the club finally captured the European Cup, a full thirty-one years after their last success in the competition. They watched every game together, just the two of them. Patricia had learned to make herself scarce for those two hours, deciding it was better to stay out of the way. Once the game kicked off, the two men of the house were free to indulge their passion. So animated did they become during these games that on more than one occasion the neighbours had called round to see if 'everything was all right'.

On this night, however, one of the biggest in the club's history, Noel couldn't get a word out of his grandson. He lambasted Giggs, cursed Conte and declared Davids the dirtiest player ever to lace up a pair of boots. Meanwhile Seán sat in complete silence, barely taking in the game. At half-time, United were one down and lucky to be still in the tie. Noel muted the telly and turned to the boy.

"Is everything all right, Seán? You're awful quiet."

"Yeah, I'm fine, Granddad, thanks," he replied glumly.

"They could still come back. Fergie will give 'em a right tellin' off at half-time, wait and see," Noel reasoned.

"Hopefully, Granddad." In all honesty he couldn't give a shit about the match, and that scared him. He loved United, lived for them and wanted them to win the Champions League more than anything in the world, but he would gladly have seen them relegated to Division Four if it meant seeing her again. The only way he could see her, though, was by continuing his studying sessions with her sister Alice, the girl he'd lied about to impress his friends. She thought he was a nice, innocent boy who needed help with his maths; she had no idea what he was really like. If she ever found out... well, it didn't bear thinking about. She would hate him. They all would: Mrs. Tiernan, Alice's brother and even Leanne. He would be that weird, twisted kid who'd come to study at their house and spread vicious rumours about their daughter; a sicko, a sociopath.

The sensible thing would be to cancel their study sessions, all of them; that way the whole thing would eventually die down. But he needed her. Without her there was no Leanne. He needed to see Alice and for their study sessions to continue. He needed to swallow his guilt and act as if nothing had happened. Their next session was due tomorrow night, but it was to take place at his grandparents' house, not the Tiernans'. Could he suggest switching the study session back to her place? No, it was too late for that; his nan had been frantically preparing for their visitor since he'd come back the previous night. He couldn't disappoint her like that. What then? Suggest another session in the Tiernan's house on Friday night? He couldn't do that either. He didn't want Alice or indeed Leanne thinking he was a sad loser with nothing to do on a Friday evening. That ruled out Saturday, too. Sunday? It was worth the risk; imagine how impressed the Tiernans would be when they saw him arrive with a bag-load of books on a Sunday evening. He'd tell them he came straight from Mass. Before he could arrange anything, though, he would have to find out a bit more about Leanne and whether she would be there on Sunday evening. It wouldn't do to turn up on an evening that she wasn't there. The idea of being under the same roof as her for an entire evening lifted his spirits considerably. He didn't know what he'd do when he saw her again, but that would sort itself out when the time came.

The teams were coming back out for the second half. As Noel turned the volume back up, Seán let out a cry of: "Come on, United!"

Noel looked over at him with a grin. "That's the spirit, Seán. We'll win this yet."

18

"YOUR BROTHER AND SISTER SEEM pretty cool."

He delivered the line as nonchalantly as he could; just making conversation, that's all. All day he had agonised over how to broach the subject. He didn't want to make it too obvious, sensing that Alice was paranoid about her sister's ability to enchant every boy she met. The paranoia was justified; he for one had never been more enchanted.

"Ugh, they're awful. Well, my brother's not too bad, I suppose."

"Awful? In what way?"

"Leanne strolls around like she's royalty. They do *everything* for her. 'I can't pick you up right now, love, I've got to bring Leanne to swimming.' 'Turn that music down, Leanne is studying for her Leaving Cert.' 'Did you eat Leanne's yogurt? You know they're the only ones she can have,' and so on. I swear the rest of us are invisible to them half the time."

Seán nodded, doing his best to appear sympathetic, but his mind was elsewhere. She was studying for her Leaving Cert; this meant she was probably seventeen or eighteen. And she swam. He pictured her in a swimming costume, but quickly forced the thought out of his head. There was a time and a place for thoughts like that – maths class, maybe. She had dietary needs which involved special yogurts; he really had no opinion on that.

"Couldn't someone else bring her to swimming? Gerard, or her boy-friend, perhaps?"

"Ha, boyfriend, her? None of the poor fellas she brings home lasts five minutes before they're out the door. There was one guy, Rónan, she was seeing for a few months. He was lovely; got on with everyone, even Daddy, who thinks no one is good enough for his princess. Then out of nowhere he was gone; no explanation, nothing. Too nice, that was his problem."

"Sounds like she's a bit of a handful, your sister?"

"Oh, you've no idea."

He decided that he'd garnered enough information for one night and allowed the conversation to move away from Leanne and back to their schoolwork. Further questions about her older sister would arouse Alice's suspicions, and he needed to keep her on side. The books were opened and they quickly got back into the swing of things. He couldn't help but marvel at how much he was learning.

"I have to say, Alice, I'd be lost without you." He meant it, too. Until a couple of days ago he was a dead cert to fail his maths exam, but now he had a fighting chance.

She smiled bashfully, flushing slightly.

"Ah, you're a great pupil."

"I'm serious, though," he continued. "I literally hadn't a fuckin' clue until we started doing this, and now I'm beginning to think I might even pass the bastard!"

"Pass?" she jibed. "I'm expecting a B at the very least, Mr. McLoughlin."

Seán chuckled at her joke, immediately feeling guilty. Why did she have to have such a hot sister? Why did she have to be so nice? And why was he such a stupid cunt? His lies reverberated around his head once more. He had betrayed this sweet, considerate girl, and in return she was helping him pass his exams. What a charmer.

"What do you want to with yourself when you finish school?" he asked her. "A teacher? You're a natural, y'know."

"Really? Thanks." This time her embarrassment had a forced air to it. "I've never thought of becoming a teacher, to be honest. I love science, especially biology, so I was thinking I might be a biochemist. The points are pretty high for the courses I'd like to do, so I'll have to wait and see."

Points? Courses? Seán looked at her as if she were mad. How could anyone be thinking that far ahead when they hadn't even negotiated the Junior Cert? This girl might only live a few doors away, but academically they were worlds apart.

"And you?" she asked.

"I plan to finish my Junior Cert, get pissed, and spend the whole summer sleeping in till midday," he replied, grinning widely.

She looked at him uncertainly, realised he was serious and matched his grin.

"Do you get drunk often? My parents would go mad if I drank!"

"Ah, no, not that often, just every now and again. Once our exams are over, though, we're all gonna get hammered."

"Where will ye go? Do the pubs serve ye?"

"No," he said, laughing at the thought. "We'll just get drink from the off-license and go up the woods."

"Oh, cool," she said longingly.

There was a brief silence, during which Seán considering asking her to join them; then he regained his senses. He had to keep things as formal as possible.

"What will you do when you've finished your exams?"

She sighed in the manner of someone who had hoped this question wouldn't arise but knew that it was inevitable.

"Do I have to tell you?" she asked, scrunching her face up in embarrassment.

"Go on, it can't be that bad."

"Oh, it's bad."

He said nothing and waited for her to continue.

"We're supposed to have a double celebration, me and Leanne. The whole family are going to go out for dinner; aunties, uncles, cousins, grandparents – the whole lot. I'm dreading it; they're all so serious. It'll be 'Now, Alice, what are your plans for the future?' 'Our Mary got nine As in her Junior Cert, do you think you'll get the same?' They're unbearable!"

Seán had to laugh, firstly at Alice's impressions of her relations, which reminded him of something from *Monty Python*, and secondly at how ludicrous the whole thing sounded.

"Jaysus, that's fuckin' mad. Does everyone in your family go to college?"

"Pretty much."

"I don't think *anyone* in our family has ever gone to college."

"Really? How come?"

"Dunno, it's not like we're thick or anything; we just can't be arsed, I suppose."

"Well, *you're* definitely not thick, Seán."

"Try telling that to my teachers and my stepfather."

It came out more bitterly than he'd intended and she picked up on it immediately.

"You don't get on with your stepdad, then?" she asked softly.

"Not really."

"Sorry, Seán. If you don't want to talk about it, that's fine."

"Nah, it's just there's nothing to talk about when it comes to him."

"Okay, I'll drop it so, yeah?"

"Whatever you like."

They continued studying, Seán markedly quieter. Who was he kidding, sitting here with an honours student, trying to pretend he gave a fuck? This wasn't him. He was the kid who sat in the back of the class whiling away the time until the bell rang. He wouldn't be going to college in a few years, chances were he wouldn't even do his Leaving, so what was the point? He might as well just give in now and save himself the effort.

Alice tried to cajole a smile out of him but it was no use. She should never have asked about his stepfather. They'd been getting on so well until she'd put her foot in it. Their blossoming friendship had been damaged beyond repair, and it was all her fault. This time it was she who clock-watched, and when Patricia came to put a halt to proceedings she was packed and ready to leave within seconds. They weren't finished with each other yet, though.

"You're to walk Alice home now, Seán, do you hear me? Can't have a young girl roaming the streets at this hour," Patricia instructed with a sly wink in Alice's direction.

The two-minute walk from one front door to the other could hardly be described as 'roaming the streets', but Seán knew better than to argue.

It wasn't quite dark outside but a gloomy pall had descended on the estate. Curtains had been drawn, lights turned on and families settled in for the night; except the Connollys, of course, who never shut their curtains. Whenever you walked past their house you could look right in at them; Mr. Connolly marooned in his armchair, laughing away at the television, Mrs. Connolly sitting across from him reading her book. Had it never occurred to them to close their curtains? Did they have any? Maybe they wanted people to watch? Exhibitionists. Seán glanced in at their house as they walked past, but the living-room was empty, the lights were off and no one was home. Maybe they were having an 'early night'. *Christ, imagine Mr. and Mrs. Connolly going at it? Fucking hell.* He thought about saying this to Alice but she wouldn't get the joke, would probably think he was a pervert. They walked in silence along the footpath. An owl hooted in the distance, a car misfired, and neither of them spoke.

"I'd better see you in safe, I suppose," he said when they reached Alice's house.

He could have left her at the gate, but a sense of duty compelled him to see out his task to the bitter end.

"Thank you," Alice whispered as she eased open the gate and closed it shut behind them.

She walked to the front door and gently tapped on the glass partition. "You don't have a key?"

"No. Dad says it would only encourage us to stay out late."

"Right."

It was only when he saw the outline of a lithe figure approach the door that he realised what was happening. He'd been so caught up in his thoughts about Alice and what she must have made of him that he had temporarily forgotten about her sister. Even when his grandmother had told him to escort Alice home, he hadn't thought of the possibilities it presented.

"Oh hello, little studiers. All done for the night, then?"

There she was, fresh-faced and angelic, all ready for bed. She wore a green T-shirt, faded and slightly tattered, and a pair of pink pyjama bottoms. In spite of her attire, she didn't seem in the least bit embarrassed. Alice brushed past her without a word, then checked herself and turned to Seán. "Thanks, Seán."

"No bother, Alice," he said warmly. The previous hour was now forgotten; this was the suave, smooth-talking chick-magnet she had met on their first encounter. Alice gave him an odd look and once more turned to go.

"Wait!" Seán called after her. "When can we study again, do you think? Sunday night, perhaps?"

"Well – okay. Here at seven?"

"Perfect," he replied. "See you then."

"Okay. Bye, then."

"Bye, Alice."

She scurried upstairs, leaving Seán alone with Leanne.

"Well, I'd better be off then, I suppose," he said, not moving a muscle.

"Okay, Seán. See you on Sunday," she replied, smiling.

"See you, Leanne."

"Bye, bye," she said, fixing him with that gaze again.

He turned to leave, heart pounding in his chest; his legs felt as if someone else was controlling them. Reaching the gate, he unlocked it with shaking hands and left the premises. He started to close it after him, glancing in the direction of the house once more; there she was, standing in her nightclothes, staring at him.

"Night, now," she said softly.

"Night, Leanne," he replied.

He fumbled awkwardly with the gate, looking away for a moment as he struggled with the clasp. When his eyes returned to the door she was gone. He stared at where she'd been, willing her to return. The gate finally clanked shut. Sean checked it once more and headed for home. He needed a lie-down.

19

"SOMEONE GOT OUT OF BED on the right side this morning!"

Patricia stood and watched as her grandson shimmied round the kitchen, munching on a slice of toast, while straightening his tie with his free hand. Bland pop music crackled out from his grandparents' old radio, a teenage heart-throb insisting that there was no other girl for him in the whole wide world. Seán swayed and sashayed in time to the beat as the song reached a predictable crescendo before fading out in a sea of impossibly high falsettos. One song segued into another, an old Motown number, an up-tempo one. He seamlessly changed pace, humming and whistling, bopping and grooving; he was John Travolta and this was Friday Morning Fever.

Even Noel, who rarely communicated before midday, was moved to comment.

"Feck it, Seány, what's got into you at all?"

"Jeez lads, can't a fella be in good form round here without getting the Spanish inquisition?" Seán protested as he drank the last of his tea.

Patricia looked at her husband knowingly before addressing the boy. "Who or what might be responsible for this improvement in mood, I wonder?"

"No idea what you're talking about, Nan," he grinned.

Let her think what she wanted; he was finished telling stories. She'd be delighted with herself now; not only had she paired him up with a suitable study partner, she'd also helped him find a new girlfriend. It had never been her intention, but her grandson could do a lot worse. The Tiernans were a lovely family, she'd always thought so. That little Alice, what a sweetheart. And poor Seán was so quiet, a real introvert – why shouldn't his gran help him out? By the look of things, Seán was smitten. How long had it taken? Two or three nights? Made for each other, they were. Perhaps in years to come, when they were wed, she'd regale family members with the story of how she'd brought them together over their schoolbooks.

"I'd better be off. Thanks for the breakfast, Nan," Seán said, kissing his grandmother on the cheek. "See ye later."

"Bye, my love," cooed Patricia, already planning the wedding.

He left her to her fantasies, he had some thinking of his own to do. The previous night, when he'd gone to bed, he'd been sure that Leanne fancied him. The way she'd looked at him and said 'Night, now' had seemed coy and suggestive. But now, in the cold light of day he wasn't so sure. Was it really possible that such a goddess might be interested in him? What could that angel from heaven possibly want with a boy like him? A fifteen-year old, doing his Junior Cert? She could have been going out with lads that had their own cars, lads at college, lads who worked and got served in pubs. Maybe she had gone out with all those lads and grown sick of them? It was possible. Maybe she wanted something different, a younger man? Well, here he was, ready and waiting. And fuck it, he wasn't without his charm. His nan and his aunties constantly told him how good-looking he was. 'A little heart-breaker', that's what they called him. So what if they were related to him? They wouldn't have said if it weren't true. Anyway, loads of girls fancied him; there was always young wans giving him the eye. It wasn't his fault he was too shy to approach them. He preferred it when they came right up and asked, 'Want to go off with me?' 'Sure, why not?' he'd reply, even if he didn't fancy them – it was all experience at the end of the day.

He'd only ever approached one girl himself, Emma Ryan, in second year. He'd fancied her for ages, and when Pegs had convinced him that she fancied him back, Seán finally plucked up the courage to ask her out. He knew she got to school early every morning, arriving on a bus from some village far away in the hilltops, and she always went to one of the empty classrooms to go over her homework. So one morning he set his alarm for 7.30 instead of 8.00, and on arrival went straight to the room where he knew she'd be. There she was, head down, working away, his studious little paramour.

"Hi, Seán," she'd said when she'd seen him approach. "Don't usually see you in this early."

"Ah, I just woke up early today," he'd replied, his throat dry.

"How's things?" she'd asked.

"Grand. Listen, Emma, I was just wondering – "

He'd replayed that moment in his head time and time again. The look of surprise on her face, the bemusement mixed with false humility as she'd hummed and hawed her way through his rejection. Thanks, but no thanks; now be on your way, there's a good boy. He'd flushed bright red, lingered long enough to make them both uncomfortable, and then inexplicably apologised to her. *Sorry I bothered you, sorry for ever thinking you'd go out with me; sorry, sorry, sorry.* She'd waved him away with a dismissive movement of her hand and he'd slithered out of the room like the pathetic loser he was, vowing never again to ask a girl out.

It was different where Leanne was concerned. He was compelled to act; he had no choice in the matter. She needed to know how much he loved her. He wasn't afraid of rejection, even expected it. It didn't matter how she responded; she could never deter him or weaken his resolve. He would have to be careful, though. This was no ordinary situation, no ordinary girl. He needed some advice. He couldn't ask Pegs, Murt or Ginty, who were still digesting the news of his tryst with Alice. He had other mates, but none with whom he could discuss such issues. His mother? They still weren't really talking, and anyway this was far too personal to discuss with her. The same went for his aunts and his grandmother. This was a man's problem, and could only be solved by another man.

Not for the first time, he yearned for his uncle Patrick's presence. Pat would have been all over this, glad to recapture a bit of his youth via his nephew's love-life; but he was so busy nowadays, Seán hardly ever saw him. That left his granddad. His fuckin' granddad. Imagine asking your granddad for advice about girls? It was ridiculous. Sure the man was ancient, in his fifties. He wouldn't have a clue what to do. Chances were he'd sigh deeply and tell him he didn't like to interfere in such issues, to go ask his mother instead. But that wasn't good enough. Seán needed the wisdom of a man who'd seen all it before, someone who'd kissed but never told, a man who knew a thing or two about a thing or two; but his grandfather would just have to do.

20

HE DIDN'T GO TO THE Tiernans' on Sunday night as planned. Alice called to reschedule for the Tuesday night; she didn't explain why, just said that it suited her better. Seán was happy to go along with it, he needed more time to mull over his latest encounter with Leanne anyway. He hadn't managed to corner his grandfather yet, either. All weekend he'd waited for the moment, but the old fella was working all day Saturday, and as soon as he got home and ate he went straight to the pub. Sunday was no better; Adele and her kids came round and the place was a madhouse. By the time they'd gone, it was too late. He drew a blank on Monday too; his grandmother was there all night. But, Tuesday was Bingo night, and she always left the house at 7.30 sharp. Seán's study session with Alice was due to begin at the same time. However, his grandmother usually spent at least an hour getting ready for her weekly outing. This was his window of opportunity.

He waited until she'd gone upstairs, listening out for her footsteps as she flitted from bedroom to bathroom in the pursuit of elegant magnificence.

"Granddad?"

"Yes, Seán?"

"Can I talk to you about something?"

"Of course," he replied, laying down his newspaper.

"It's kind of embarrassing."

"Well, I promise not to get embarrassed if you don't," said Noel with a chuckle.

Seán looked around the living-room before continuing in a hushed tone.

"There's this girl – "

Noel smiled. "The young Tiernan girl."

"Um, yeah, but not the one you're thinking of."

"Irene, is it? Jesus, lad, I think she's a bit old for you!"

"Who the hell is Irene?"

Noel shook his head. He should have known better than to make jokes, his grandson was coming to him with woman problems after all.

"Sorry, Seán; just pulling your leg."

"It's the sister," Seán continued. "Alice's older sister, Leanne."

"Oh, yes, I know the girl. Works in the florists, doesn't she?"

This was news to Seán, valuable information that had somehow passed him by.

"I didn't know that."

"Oh, yes, she has for years, every Saturday. Lovely girl."

"She is, Granddad, but – she's two years older than me."

Noel mused on this while Seán stared at him, waiting for inspiration. After what seemed an eternity, he took his fags from the pocket of his work pants and lit up. This wasn't a good sign; he hardly ever smoked in the house, it was always out on the front step or in the back garden. He'd obviously lost the run of himself and would be of no use from this point forth. He took a long drag on his cigarette, exhaled and beckoned for Seán to come close. Seán did as he was told, ignoring the toxic fumes circling around his grandfather's head.

"The problem with women, Seány, is that they're very unpredictable. One minute they're mad about you, then they can't stand the sight of you. They want you to be nice to them, but they complain if you're too nice. They say everything is fine when it isn't. You can't feckin' win."

"That's all well and good, Granddad, but how does it help me?"

Noel ignored him, took another pull of his cigarette and continued at his leisure.

"At the end of the day, there's no point trying to impress them. There's no point acting cool or tough 'cos nothing you do will make a bit of difference. If you're lucky, one of the nice ones might like you, and if she does she'll let you know in her own special way."

"But what if I don't notice her letting me know?"

"She'll probably be subtle about it at first; the way she looks at you, the way she smiles when she talks to you, the way she plays with her hair. If you don't pick up on that she'll let her feelings be known another way, a more obvious way, if you get what I mean?"

This was becoming uncomfortable. Had his nan let her feelings be known in a more obvious way? He shuddered at the thought.

"So you're saying I should let her come to me, then?"

"Well, not quite that, Seán; they don't *ever* do that. But she will make her feelings known, at which point it is up to you to behave like a man of the world."

"And how do I do that?"

"Well, you wait for your moment and just do what comes naturally, my boy."

He made it sound so quaint, but the things Seán had been dreaming about these past few nights were far from quaint.

Noel checked himself for a second. Was it possible the young lad didn't know how to do what came naturally? He'd thought these youngsters were well up on that sort of thing nowadays.

"You do know how to do what comes naturally, don't you?" he ventured.

"Of course I do, Granddad!" Seán retorted crossly.

"Fine, fine, I was just checking," Noel replied defensively. "What about protection and all that kind of thing? I mean, we didn't use it in our day but – "

"Please, Granddad! I didn't come for a discussion about safe sex. I just wanted some advice about women in general."

"Okay, Seán. Did I ever tell you about the time I met that girl up in Mayo?"

Before he could regale Seán with his tales of seduction, the toot of a horn brought the conversation to an end. Patricia came clattering down the stairs in a cloud of scents and potions, almost choking them both. "That's for me, lads. It's Maura, bringing me to bingo."

"All right, Nan. See ya later."

"See you, Seán. Enjoy your studying," she said with a smirk which Sean, if he hadn't known better, would have described as smutty.

"I'd better head now too, Granddad," Seán said when she'd departed. He had no desire to learn about the girl from Mayo, and feared if he did so it would put him off sex for life.

"Okay, lad, and remember what I said," Noel replied, tapping the side of his head as if the great secrets of the world resided there. The problem was he hadn't said anything of any use to Seán; if anything, he'd just made him more confused.

"I will, Granddad," he said wearily.

He scooped his schoolbag off the floor and headed out the door, leaving Noel to his cigarettes and the memory of minxes from Mayo.

21

"You have a free house?" asked Seán as he was escorted to the living-room instead of their usual den.

"Mam and Dad are out. There's just Leanne, and she's upstairs in her room."

"Oh, right. Are we going to study in here, then?"

"God, it's all work with you, Seán, isn't it?" Alice teased, taking a seat on the couch and motioning for him to join her.

This was ominous. She'd obviously planned their session for when her parents were out, and now that he looked at her he could see she was done-up a bit more than usual. Gone were the baggy jumpers and ill-fitting jeans, the ponytail and the face devoid of make-up. Tonight she wore a low-cut top, revealing the top of her modest breasts, and a pair of figure-hugging black trousers with some sort of shiny design running up the leg. Her hair was flowing over her shoulders in long, unhindered tresses, and she'd gone to the trouble of applying some make-up, a subtle amount, but make-up nonetheless. It was certainly an improvement, and if the love of his life hadn't been upstairs he might have been tempted.

He sat on the opposite end of the couch and began searching through his bag. "Maths first?" he asked hopefully.

"Let's leave the studying for a while, will we?" she said with an air of impatience.

He put his book away and gently dropped his bag to the floor, terrified of what might happen next. Somehow she had inched closer without him noticing, and now they were separated by a matter of inches. Any second now and she'd pounce. He looked around the room in desperation, hoping for a way out, perhaps a hole in the wall he could jump through. But as he moved his hand away from the leg which had begun to snake its way towards him, he found salvation: the remote control. Quickly he swiped it up and pointed it at the TV, urgently jabbing the 'On' button.

"What's on tonight, then? Bet you love the soaps, don't ya?"

"Hmm," she replied flatly, drawing her leg away and turning to face him. He could feel her eyes boring into him as he frantically tried to turn on the TV.

"You need to press the button on the TV itself, Seán."

"Oh, right," he said, rising to do just that.

"Wait," she said, putting her hand out to stop him.

He looked at her hand, waiting for it to be removed from his person.

"Sit down here," she patted the sofa, "beside me."

"Alice – "

"It's okay, Seán. They won't be back for ages and Leanne is stuck in her books upstairs."

"It's not that."

She smiled reassuringly and repeated her gesture for him to sit down. He joined her reluctantly, bracing himself for the onslaught.

"You're a funny one, Seán McLoughlin," she went on. "It took me a while to figure it out, but I know what you're up to now."

"You do?"

"Yes. At first, I thought you weren't interested. Then you invited me down to your nan's house, and I thought maybe you were. Then you went all quiet on me and I didn't know what to think! But here you are again and now I finally get it."

Get what? he thought, looking at her blankly.

"Still playing dumb. Such a cool customer," Alice murmured in admiration.

"Listen, Alice, I'm not sure what you're thinking but..."

"Not sure what *I'm* thinking? You should try it from my side."

"Like I said," she continued, "I've finally figured you out."

She had been edging closer and closer to him throughout this discussion, and now her face was just inches away from his. He had no escape as she leant in and closed her eyes in anticipation of their long-awaited first kiss. He allowed her lips to brush against his but he didn't respond, just let her mouth rest on his and waited for her to stop. She drew back, a puzzled expression on her face.

"What's wrong?"

"That's what I've been trying to tell you, Alice. I don't really fancy you."

She looked at him uncomprehendingly. He *did* fancy her; what was he talking about?

"I'm really sorry you got the wrong idea," he said. "I like you, but I don't like you in that way."

Alice waited to see if this was another of his games. She stared at him, hoping he would break into a grin and tell her it was all just a big joke and he was actually mad about her.

But he said nothing, just sat there holding her gaze, almost afraid to breathe.

Her mouth opened and closed, her eyes flitted back and forth. He could see her mind working overtime, trying desperately to process the information it had just been fed. A flicker of rage passed across her face and he tensed, readying himself for a swift exit. But anger was quickly replaced by abject despair, her shoulders sagging as she seemed to finally accept the news. Eyes glossy with tears, she looked at him in disbelief. "But you said – "

He shook his head. "I never said anything, Alice. I just want us to be friends and study partners, that's all."

He saw the anger return and flinched as she rose from her seat.

"Friends? FRIENDS! You were just leading me on, weren't you? You thought it would be funny!"

"No, Alice, honestly."

"SHUT UP!"

He did as he was told, his main objective now was getting out of here in one piece.

"I can't believe it. I just can't – " She began to hyperventilate, waving her hands in front of her face as she struggled to control her breathing.

Seán looked on anxiously, concerned for her well-being.

"Alice, are you okay?" he asked, gently moving towards her.

"GET AWAY FROM ME!!" she screeched. "Go away!"

She'd gone from damsel in distress to possessed demon in a matter of seconds.

He shrank back to the sanctity of the couch, relieved that she appeared to be in rude health but now concerned for his own safety.

"You're pathetic, do you know that? And to think I actually liked you. Pffft!"

With one last dramatic movement she stamped out of the room and up the stairs – presumably to begin construction of a voodoo doll bearing a striking resemblance to Seán.

He sat alone in silence, afraid to move. Only when he heard the slam of a door did he allow himself to take a deep breath.

"Jesus Christ," he said out loud. His back was slick with sweat and his T-shirt clung uncomfortably to his skin. He'd never seen a girl behave like that, not up close anyway. It had been captivating. Amid his terror he felt a twinge of admiration for Alice. He didn't think she'd had it in her, thought she was just a little dormouse. Tiger, more like; with claws and everything. If he'd known she was going to react like that, he would have kissed her; a little snog, nothing major. It would have made everyone's life easier; but then she might have looked for more kisses and God knows what else. And what about Leanne? He couldn't be going around kissing Alice if he had designs on her older sister. No, he'd definitely done the right thing. He'd miss all the maths help, though.

He stood up to go, dusted himself down and mopped his brow. Before leaving, he peered dubiously up the stairs for signs of life. Perhaps if he could talk to her one more time, they could end things in a more amicable way. He couldn't see anything or anyone, but by remaining perfectly still he could just about make out two muffled voices coming from one of the bedrooms: Alice's; high-pitched and frantic, Leanne's; soothing and steady. Clearly Alice's assessment of her older sibling hadn't been entirely accurate, because here she was, big sister to the rescue, consoling her in her time of need. He tried to make out what they were saying, but could only hear angry sobs and the occasional expletive. Had he really led her on like she'd said? He didn't think so. But this girl was upset, very upset, and all because of him. The crying died down and the muffled voices quietened. A flash of panic ran through him. What was it they said about a woman scorned? He couldn't remember the exact words, but he knew it meant trouble for fifteen-year-old boys caught loitering at the bottom of staircases. It was time to go. As he made to leave, he heard a door open upstairs and footsteps on the landing. He froze. He was caught now; they had him. He listened for the sharpening of knives or the crack of a whip, afraid to look behind him.

"Seán," a voice said softly.

He slowly turned round.

It was Leanne. She descended the stairs quietly, holding her fingers to her lips as she guided him into the living-room. Shutting the door, she sat on the edge of one of the armchairs.

"Sit down, Seán."

He did as he was told, sitting on the sofa to face her.

"She's very upset, Seán," Leanne said, delivering the news as a doctor would the unwelcome results of a long-awaited test.

"I know. I'm really sorry; I never intended this to happen."

"That's okay, Seán. She really had a thing for you, though, you know?"

"I do now."

"Come on, Seán. You knew all along, didn't you?"

"I suppose I did," he admitted.

Leanne nodded solemnly. "It's not easy when someone has the hots for you and you just want to be friends, is it?"

Seán looked up at her in surprise. Was she sympathising with him?

"No, I suppose not."

She allowed herself a little smile, but it was the smile of someone remembering a joke, a joke which Seán wasn't privy to.

"Will you tell her I'm really sorry, and that I'm grateful for the help she gave me with my maths?"

Leanne nodded distractedly.

"I suppose I'd better go, then?" he said, rising once more to leave.

She shot him a bemused look, as if the thought of him leaving was the most curious thing in the world. Unsure how to proceed, anxiety rising by the minute, Seán made one final dash for the door. He wanted to be away from this house and its crazy women. But she got there before him, blocking his path, affixing him with that same bemused stare. He couldn't take any more of this. He felt like throwing himself to the floor, at their mercy. That was probably what they wanted, what they had planned. They lured innocent boys to their lair and then tortured them for their own sick pleasures. Well, at this stage he didn't care, they could do what they wanted. They could tie him up, flay him, burn him with candles; anything. He just wanted it to be over.

He stood staring at the floor, waiting for – what? He didn't know.

"I'm sorry," he mumbled, whimpered almost. It was the best he had.

And she giggled. Giggled? Here he was trying to repent his sins, to give himself up, and she was laughing at him.

"What's so funny?" he asked, slightly aggrieved.

"You," she said, touching him on the nose with her index finger, lightly bouncing it off him as if it were a magic wand.

Her touch seemed to revitalise him, to bring him to his senses. The love of his life was right here, standing in front of him; if he wasn't very much mistaken, she appeared to be flirting with him.

He moved a little closer until they were almost face-to-face. She was smaller than he'd thought, a full head shorter than he. He looked her up and down; bare feet, toenails painted bright pink, red jeans which swelled pleasantly at the hips, a striped top, her breasts free and unencumbered beneath, the gentle curves and inclines of her body. He inhaled her scent; strawberries, soap, mint and other womanly smells he did not yet understand. Then he brought his eyes to hers. This was it; he had to have her. He moved his head towards hers, her expression didn't change in the slightest; she looked both content and imperious. When she didn't move away, he closed his eyes and pressed his lips to hers. She kissed him back, casually, without a hint of desire. He pushed his body against hers, his lightning-rod erection rubbing against her lower abdomen. An animal desire consumed him as his lips began frantically to explore her mouth, his tongue sliding in and out, searching for hers, finding it, restful and compliant. Then when he thought he might explode he felt a hand on his chest, pushing him away, removing his mouth and body from hers. His lust denied, the warmth of her body replaced by the cold reality of rejection.

"Leanne," he gasped, close to tears.

"We can't, Seán. We can't."

For the first time there was genuine emotion in her words; remorse, regret, even a tinge of frustration.

"We have to, Leanne," he said, moving towards her once more.

"No, Seán," she said, pushing him back. "Not here, not now."

She wasn't rejecting him, not outright anyway. There was a chance.

"Okay, Leanne," he said calmly. "I understand."

He hoped he did understand, that if it weren't for Alice lying on her bed upstairs, gently weeping, they would right now be making sweet, hot love on the living-room floor.

He backed away, took a seat once more and waited for her to speak. She sat down beside him, saying nothing, staring ahead. He needed to know, he would rather die than live with this uncertainty.

"You do want to?" he asked, turning to face her.

She nodded sadly, as if admitting a sin. In a way it was; she was about to betray her sister, her little sister who'd never even fancied a boy before Seán. Alice's first crush, and along came big sis to wreck everything.

"Can we meet?" he asked.

She sighed. "I don't know, Seán. I just don't know."

He wasn't going to beg. In a way, it was enough to know she wanted him. They could be star-crossed lovers, kept apart by circumstance. It would be incredibly romantic.

Footsteps sounded upstairs. Seán instinctively got to his feet; this time he really had to go. Leanne went with him to the door, guiding him off the premises as if that would absolve her wrongdoings. He opened the door, the fresh evening breeze soothing his jangling nerves, and turned to look at her one more time.

"The Well at ten o'clock tomorrow night," she whispered closing the door gently in his face.

A date! A real date. She'd said it, he'd heard her. He hurried down the driveway, not bothering to look back, there was no need. On the street again, he looked towards the heavens. The sky was inky blue, the first stars of the night shining brightly in the distance. For a moment he was completely free of all thoughts, his mind deliciously empty, devoid of feeling or emotion. He slowly began to walk home, his head turned to the skies as if praising the Almighty.

22

IT HAD BEEN A LONG time since The Well had been used for its original purpose. Built in the late eighteenth century, it had become the primary source of water for the families who settled in the area. It had lasted for over a hundred years, continuing to serve the residents of the newly-formed township of Dooncurra until the advent of running water in the 1930s. Almost immediately The Well and its surrounding area fell into disrepair, becoming overgrown with weeds and wild, rugged greenery. By the 1960s it was hard to believe that it had once been the hub of the community. It was now just an eyesore at the bottom of a deserted laneway. Then Barry O'Flaherty came along. Barry was born and bred in Dooncurra, as his father had been before him, and his before that. He was proud of his little town and wished to restore it to its former glory. So he ran for mayor, centring his campaign on the restoration of several heritage sites dotted around the town, among them The Well. Barry wanted to revive the local well and make it a centrepiece, a place where people could gather. It would no longer be used to draw water, but it could be a local attraction, a place of interest. The project was completed in 1972, a full five years after Barry had been removed from office, and The Well was once more a hive of activity. No longer just a hole in the ground, it was a fully-operational tourist attraction with a grotto, a plaque detailing its history, and the obligatory metal pump for newcomers to yank. And yank it they did, over and over again. Tourists came, got their pictures taken, read the plaque's inscription and left, feeling they knew a little more about the people of Ireland and their history. Locals took advantage of the new amenity too, using it as a picnic area, a place to bring the kids during the school holidays. The older kids took an interest too; but these youngsters weren't there to learn more about the history of their town. They enjoyed visiting The Well because its secluded location and spacious seating area offered a perfect hang-out spot, a place to drink and smoke without falling under the prying eyes of their parents. By the early nineties, The Well had once more succumbed to the ravages of time. No longer was it a tourist attraction, it was now solely the refuge of the young and disaffected. The Well was where you went to drink your first can, smoke your first joint, to meet girls, to meet boys and to do things with and to those girls and boys when you'd met them.

Seán had visited The Well on many occasions, but in his case it had only been to drink and hang out. That looked like changing, though. He sat in his grandparents' living-room, watching the clock crawl its way toward ten and wondered what the night held in store for him. He'd been trying to stay positive, but paranoia had taken hold. He'd started to doubt himself. Had she really said to be at The Well at ten? It was possible he'd imagined it, that she'd closed the door in disgust without as much as a goodbye. Or maybe she had said it, but it was a trap. Seán would arrive at The Well, stinking of his grandfather's aftershave, a hopeful condom in his pocket, to be met by Mr. Tiernan and his son Gerard. They'd have hurleys, big ones, and not a sliotar between them. Because he was the sliotar, he would be the one getting pucked from one Tiernan to the other. Even worse, it might be Alice, Leanne and their mother, a trio of Tiernans, a coven of them. They'd do unthinkable things to him, things which at first would feel quite pleasurable but would gradually become more painful until he screamed for mercy and then death.

Even in his state of frenzied neurosis, however, he knew these outcomes were unlikely, figments of an over-active imagination. It was the all-too-real threat of being stood up which haunted him most. All day he'd been struggling to understand why a girl like Leanne would have any interest in him. It didn't make sense. She was two years older, achingly beautiful, and came from a well-to-do family. The more he thought about it, the more he was sure he was being set up. She'd concocted a plan with Alice, to get him back for what he'd done to her. He'd go to The Well, full of nervous anticipation, take a seat, and wait there quietly; an hour later he'd still be waiting, refusing to go home in case she was just running late. Meanwhile the two Tiernan girls would be at home, pissing themselves laughing. They might even keep an eye out for him as he returned home, heckling him from their window as he finally figured out what had happened.

There was still a slight chance that it was for real, however, that she really did want to see him. He had to turn up, just in case. Therefore, he had to devise a way of getting out of the house at such a late hour. His grandparents may have been loving and affectionate but they had rules, and being out after ten on a school-night would break more than one of them.

"Ah, feck!" Seán said suddenly, as the clock crept past a quarter to the hour.

"What's up with you, child?" asked Patricia, startled.

"I just remembered," replied Seán, scratching his head for effect, "I gave Murt my calculator earlier on and I need it back for the morning."

"Can you not get it off him before class tomorrow?"

"No, Nan. He's not in my maths class. I won't see him till after break."

This was all lies. He and Murt were in the same class for everything, and neither of them actually owned a calculator. It all seemed very plausible to Patricia McLoughlin, though; these youngsters today and their gadgets, they were forever losing them.

"Well, you'd better go and get it, I suppose."

"Yeah, I really should, Nan."

"Don't spend all night there. I'm sure his mother and father have beds to be going to as well."

"I won't, Nan, I promise."

Seconds later he was hurrying through the estate and on his way to The Well. He kept an eye out as he walked, hoping to bump into her on the way, but the streets were empty save for the odd group of drinkers and one or two late-night joggers. Arriving in good time, he scanned the area for copulating couples, dope-smoking stoners and cider-swilling scumbags, but there were none. If she came they would have the place to themselves. He took a seat on one of the benches, leaving his back to the entrance so that she might surprise him; then he waited, resisting the urge to pray. The sky hadn't completely darkened and the pale moon was doing its best to illuminate the scene, but it was still a murky, dispiriting evening. Come summer this place would be throbbing with activity, every kid under the age of eighteen making a nightly pilgrimage there. Now, though, it was just creepy and depressing. A fine drizzle began to fall, not enough to soak him but enough to send him running for cover inside the grotto. The grotto was small, with a cramped archway housing two stone seating areas, between which lay what had originally been the well-hole. It was now a closed-off shaft with a small opening where you could throw your coppers. As children, he and Murt had often discussed opening the shaft and climbing down the well to claim their fortune. Sadly, they had never got around to it.

Seán peered out from beneath the canopy, hoping to see a lone figure making her way towards him, but all he could see was empty benches, the dark laneway and a solitary streetlight in the distance. He glumly watched as the rain grew heavier, huddling inside the grotto, a chill running through him. Then he heard the scrabbling of feet outside the grotto, someone sliding down an embankment. He tensed, expecting to be joined by a couple of ruffians, romance the last thing on their mind. Instead he saw a small person in a hooded coat.

"Hi, Seán," said a voice from beneath the hood.

Leanne crept into the grotto and stood under the arch, shaking herself dry.

Seán looked at her in awe, scarcely able to believe she was there.

"Which way did you come?" he asked.

"The usual way, why? How did you come?" she replied.

"The usual way too, I think."

"Through the fields and round the back of the orchard?"

"Uh no, down Scanlon Street and in by the laneway."

Her smile was barely discernible in the darkness. "Oh, Seán, no one goes that way. I'll have to show you the usual way on the way back."

"Okay."

"Can I sit down?" she asked.

"Yes, of course," he replied, pushing over to make room for her. "Did you get wet?"

"A bit, but I'm grand now."

She pulled down her hood and sat beside him, close, so that their legs touched. He suddenly became very aware of his breathing, of his heartbeat, of the blood running through his veins. This was his moment to act. The time to put into practise all those things he'd dreamed of doing. But he was petrified, afraid to move. Now that she was here beside him, he didn't know how to proceed. Should he just pounce, or was subtlety the key? He wracked his brain, trying to think of films he'd seen and lines uttered by leading men well-versed in the arts of seduction. Nothing came. All he could do was sit there and try not to throw up.

"Well," she said, turning to him.

"Well," he croaked in response.

She stared at him curiously, a half-smile playing across her lips. Without thinking he moved his head towards hers, expecting her to pull away, to mock him and leave, but she stayed right where she was and allowed his lips to meet hers. All tension left his body. He felt serene. At home. At ease. Seán relaxed and began to enjoy himself. She took command, caressing his lips with her own, sliding her tongue slowly in and out of his mouth. He tried to force the pace, to wrestle back control, but was quickly forced back, subjugated and submissive. She was in charge here. The intensity, the outpouring of emotion was too much for Seán to bear. He wanted to envelop her, to hold her so tight they became merged into one, locked in an eternal embrace from which neither could ever escape.

She pulled away. He looked at her in a daze.

"Was that okay?" he asked.

She smiled contentedly. "It was, Seán."

"Good."

She moved closer still, wrapped her arms around his waist and then laid her head upon his shoulder. Seán automatically put an arm over her shoulder and laid his own head upon hers. They remained like this for some time, Seán once more uneasy, unsure of what to say. Eventually she broke the silence.

"This won't be easy, Seán."

"It won't?" he asked, panicked.

"Well, this is really not a good time for either of us. Don't you agree?"

He didn't agree; it was a great time, the best time.

"I mean, we've both got exams coming up. And then there's the thing with Alice."

Seán remained silent, resigning himself to the worst.

Don't you see where I'm coming from, Seán? Just a couple of days ago she was all set for a night of romance with you. Imagine how she'd feel if her older sister suddenly swoops in and takes you."

He liked the sound of that, being swooped upon, taken.

"Can you not just have a chat with her?" he asked.

"It's not that simple."

"Why not?"

"It just isn't, Seán."

"I don't mind sneaking around if you don't," he said mischievously, trying to appeal to her wicked side. But again he was rebuffed.

"No, Seán, we can't. I think we should wait until our exams are over and then talk about it again."

Fucking exams. Everything was about exams.

"Okay then, we'll wait," he said with exaggerated sadness. Maybe if he milked this she'd make it up to him in the future.

She squeezed him a little tighter. "We can wait, Seán."

It was only four weeks, and in fairness she had a point about Alice. There was no way he was going to be introduced to the Tiernan family as Leanne's new beau any time soon. There would have to be a cooling-off period, enough time so that their coupling seemed entirely unrelated to the time Seán had spent with Alice. They could make it seem like they'd met elsewhere, recognised one another from their brief meeting in the Tiernans' living-room and got talking; one thing had led to another and here they were. But there were other issues that also needed to be addressed.

"Leanne," he said, "you do know I'm only fifteen, don't you?"

"Yes, Seán, I do."

"And it doesn't bother you?"

"You're not that different to boys my age, Seán; if anything, you're more mature than them."

"Am I?"

"You are," she said, snuggling closer. "And you're such a little cutie!"

He felt his stomach curdle in a pleasant way. He was a mature cutie. It felt good.

"And does my age bother *you*, Seán?"

This seemed a bizarre question. Was she kidding?

"Not at all. Why would it?"

"I don't know; maybe we mightn't have much in common."

"Sure what do we need to have in common, only that we like each other?"

"So wise," she said in mock awe.

She looked at him once more, staring into his eyes for what seemed like forever. This time he needed no second invitation; he recognised the signs now, knew when it was his cue to act. Now he dictated the pace, more than holding his own, and were it not for the cramped conditions and the inclement weather there was no telling what the mature cutie might have done.

"It must be nearly eleven," she said as they came up for air.

"I suppose we should go," he replied, hoping to be contradicted.

"Come on," Leanne said, jumping from the seat and pulling him to his feet. "I'll show you the *usual* way to get here."

They walked hand in hand through sodden grass and muddy trails, happy to savour the moment, neither wanting to spoil it with words. When the time came to part they kissed again, more tenderly this time. Seán watched her go until she faded into the darkness, waving a final goodbye without knowing if she could see him. She had said it wouldn't be easy, that there were obstacles to overcome, but none of that seemed to matter right now.

23

"I HAVE TO GO AND see him before his exams start."

Daryl looked up from his plate. "Ah Jesus, Sinéad, not this again."

"What do you mean 'not this again'? He's my son!"

"He may well be, but he's made his decision. He clearly wants nothing to do with us."

"You could at least *try* and sound a little less smug about it."

"Oh, so it's my fault now?"

"For fuck's sake, Daryl," she spat out in frustration. "We're supposed to be the adults here!"

Daryl put down the cutlery with an air of resignation, his dinner would probably be cold by the time he got back to it.

"Go and see him if you like, but don't expect him to be grateful."

Sinéad chose not to dignify that with a response. She was well aware of Daryl's antipathy towards her son, but had hoped he would support her nevertheless. He'd got what he wanted, after all; it was just the three of them now. Although consumed by guilt, she had to admit that life had been a lot easier since Seán had moved out. It had been easier for her and her husband, and it had been easier for Seán. She'd been astounded to learn that her boy was taking study lessons with one of the neighbour's children. Maybe he was better off there – at least for the time being. A calm, stable environment, where the only arguments centred on which grandparent loved him the most. The fact her mother had been proved right, that Daryl 'could never be a father to that boy', rankled. But if putting up with her mother's self-righteousness ensured her son's happiness, she could live with it.

Sinéad put away the last of the plates, turned on the kettle and took her jacket off the hook.

"I'm going up to my mother's."

"What about the tea?"

"Kettle's boiling," she called back, opening the front door.

"Where're you going, Mam?" asked Kevin, miraculously emerging from the ether. He had an unerring ability to turn up whenever someone looked like they were going somewhere interesting.

"To Nanny's," sighed Sinéad, knowing there was no longer any possibility of escaping alone and unaccompanied.

"Can I come? I haven't seen Seán in ages!"

It was true. Between all the fussing and fighting there was one relationship that no one had given a moment's thought: that of her two boys, the brothers or half-brothers, depending on your viewpoint. Seán had never expressed much interest in his younger sibling, but Sinéad knew he cared about him. That was evident in the way he'd knocked seven shades of shit out of the kids who'd stolen Kevin's brand-new bicycle, and the way he painstakingly taught him how to trap a football during long training sessions in the back garden. All the same, she knew Kevin would always be tainted in Seán's eyes. He had some of Daryl in him, and that was enough for Seán. She still remembered his bitter words when they'd argued about Kevin accompanying him to a hurling match.

"He's your brother, Seán!"

"Anything that came from *him*," he'd said, jabbing his head in the direction of the living-room, "is no brother of mine."

And off he'd gone, leaving his wailing sibling behind, an innocent by-stander in the ongoing war.

Although Seán's feelings towards his brother were somewhat ambivalent, there was no mistaking Kevin's affection for him. He idolised Seán, worshipped the ground he walked on, which irked his father no end. Daryl had presumed he would be the one playing football with his son, settling scores with mean bullies and dragging Kevin up by his bootstraps until he became a fully-functioning man, a Cassidy. But it was Seán that Kevin sought to emulate. It was his older brother – the seed of another man – whom he looked to for guidance, and it was his older brother that he yearned to see now.

"Okay then, come on," said Sinéad, resigned to her fate. "Bring a coat."

"It's summer, Mam," he said nonchalantly, closing the door behind him and skipping out on to the road. She didn't have the heart to argue with him, to explain that it was still only April and summer wouldn't start for another three weeks.

24

SEÁN LAY ON HIS BED, his schoolbooks scattered around him. He'd tried to focus on study, but it wasn't easy; all he could think of was her. She'd be in her room now, only a matter of feet away, gazing at her own books, thinking of him – hopefully. It didn't have to be like this, they could easily be together. All it would take was a dash down the stairs, a gallop to her house and a knock on the door. He couldn't do that, though. He had to be patient. She'd said she'd make it worth his while. His mind spun with possibilities of how she might do so.

His first exam was English, at eleven the following morning. It wouldn't present too many problems. The best thing about English was the lack of studying. Sure, he had to read a novel and a play until his eyes bled, but he didn't mind that. It wasn't the same as poring over a science book, trying to come to terms with the musings of a mad German bloke with too much time on his hands. With English he could form his own ideas, make up his own answers and no one could tell him he was right or wrong. They probably would anyway, though, the bastards.

The knock at the door came as a welcome distraction. He lay there, silent and unmoving, listening to hear who it was.

"Oh, hello, Kevin!"

Kevin? What was he doing here? Their mother would never let him come here by himself.

"Come in, come in," Patricia continued. Amid the fussing and the shuffling of feet, he made out the lower tones of his mother. No sooner had he identified her presence when the call came up the stairs. "Seán! Visitors!"

He had hoped for a distraction, but not one like this. Of course he wanted to see his mother, but the thought of coming face to face with her made his throat go dry and his eyes well up. He didn't need this right now, and certainly not here, in front of everyone. He straightened himself up, took a cursory look in the mirror and slowly descended the stairs to greet his 'visitors'.

Kevin's excited voice filtered out from the living-room; he was probably already halfway through that packet of Bourbons Seán had earmarked for his tea later on. Seán didn't mind, though; there'd be other biscuits and other cakes. They preferred him; he was their favourite, no doubt about it. Let Kevin have his moment of glory, his day in the sun.

It was his brother who saw him first, his sensors detecting movement almost before Seán had walked into the room.

"Seán!" he cried through a mouthful of biscuits. "Sit here, sit here!"

He patted the couch upon which he and his mother sat, a Seán-sized space between them waiting to be filled.

He sat down obediently. "Well, Mam."

"Hiya, son. How's the studying going?"

"All right now, yeah."

"That's good."

"Well, you'll have to get back to it soon now, Seán, visitors or no visitors," advised Patricia. Sinéad elected to keep her counsel. What could she say? He lived with them now, and that meant their house, their rules.

"Leave it, Trish, for God's sake."

They all looked at Noel in surprise; he rarely contributed anything to these conversations, and he never spoke to his wife like that, or at least not in front of them. Patricia's head swivelled on its axis, her mouth primed ready to fire back. Her husband had returned to his paper. He wasn't looking for an argument; on the contrary, he just wanted the evening to pass without any simmering enmity between mother and daughter. Patricia turned her attention to Kevin, hoping that if she acted like nothing had happened everyone might think it hadn't.

"So how's school, Kevin?"

"Grand."

"Are you being a good boy?"

"I am."

"Do you like school, Kevin?"

"Not really."

"What class are you going into now?"

"First."

"Looking forward to the holidays?"

"Yep."

Sensing an opportunity, Sinéad nudged Seán. "Fancy a little walk in the garden?"

They slipped away. Kevin was too busy fielding questions and eating biscuits to query their absence. The McLoughlins' back garden was a modest affair, no more than thirty feet wide and a hundred feet long. It had grass, a small array of flowers, two large bushes and a stone path which wound its way from one to the other. Walking around it took all of a minute, but this was what mother and son did. They walked to the bottom of the garden, pausing to duck beneath the washing line, looped around the boxwood and then walked back up again. After two or three of these circuits it became clear that they could walk all night without either of them speaking. Seán took it upon himself to break the silence.

"I'm sorry, Mam."

Sinéad looked at him in surprise. "For what, love?"

"Ah, y'know, just for everything."

She took his hand. "It's not your fault, Seán. None of this is."

They continued to walk, now hand in hand, round and round Noel and Patricia's little garden.

"I can't come back, though, Mam," Seán said after a while.

"I wasn't expecting you to; that's not why I'm here."

"No, Mam, I don't think you understand. I can't come back *ever*, at least not while he's there."

His words stung Sinéad. She knew they had their problems, but she'd just presumed things would work out and that her boy would return home to her.

"Let's just wait and see, eh?" she said.

"No, Mam; waiting and seeing won't make any difference."

There was a hardness in his tone that she'd never heard before; he sounded resolute.

She stopped walking and turned to face him. "But I'm your mother; you belong at home with me."

He shook his head, as if pitying her for being so stupid.

"You just don't get it, do you, Mam?"

Her puzzled expression told him that he was right.

"I can't live under the same roof as that *cunt*." He spat that last word out in disdain as if it were a spoiled piece of meat in an otherwise sumptuous meal.

"Ah now, Seán, I know ye don't get on but – "

"*Don't get on?* How blind can you be, Mammy?"

"Ye've had yeer ups and downs and all that."

Seán placed his hands on her shoulders. He was a good six inches taller than her now, and his gesture made her feel like the child rather than the parent.

"Stop it, Mam, just stop."

He took a deep breath, as if preparing for a long public speech to an assembled audience.

"I hate him," he whispered quietly, "I fucking detest him. He's made my life a misery for as long as I've known him, and if things carry on as they are – " he allowed the sentence to trail off, leaving the rest to her imagination.

Sinéad felt numb. In a way she wasn't surprised; deep down she'd always known just how much Seán hated Daryl, but she'd managed to convince herself otherwise. They're just too alike, she'd say, two alpha males butting heads; they'll laugh about it when they're older. Then she'd see Seán stare at his stepfather, his beautiful little face consumed with loathing. She'd quickly look away, pretending she hadn't seen it; but she had and she knew what it meant. Then there was Daryl's obvious contempt for her son. He was a good husband in every single way, except for one: he behaved as if Seán didn't matter, as if he were an inconvenience, something to be put up with as part of the terms of their marriage. Who knew what went on when she wasn't there? On countless occasions she'd returned home from a late shift to a house thick with tension. She could feel it the minute she got in the door. She'd go to Seán's room to see if he was all right, and he'd be lying on his bed reading a book or listening to music, the same old Seán. "Everything okay, love?" she'd ask.

"Yeah, Mam," he'd reply, and she'd pause at the door, watching him and wondering if everything was really okay or ever had been. She'd ask her husband the same question. "Fine, love," Daryl would say, but she'd see the darkness in his eyes and know that they'd been fighting. He'd never hit her boy, she knew that; but Seán was a sensitive soul, always had been, and he was easily upset. All it took were a few well-placed comments and he was on the defensive, retreating to his room where he felt safe. But he'd never come to her, he'd never complain, he was far too proud, far too stubborn. He'd hold it all in and suffer in silence.

Her son stood rigidly in front of her, body tensed and fists clenched. She wanted to hug him, hold him, take his pain away; she wanted to lighten his burden.

"I'm sorry, love," she said.

Seán shook his head. "It's not your fault, Mam." The unspoken words hung in the air. *For marrying that bastard.*

"Your exams −" she said helplessly.

"I'll be fine. It's good that we've had this conversation."

"But I want to be there for you."

"You can be, Mam. You can come up any evening you want."

"It's not the same, Seán," she said, shaking her head.

"Well, that's just how it is," he replied.

That was it. He had spoken, and there was nothing to be done. He was gone and might never come back. It was nobody's fault, except her own. She had let him down, sacrificed his happiness for her own. She could admit it now, though for years she'd denied it and tried to convince herself otherwise, but it was the truth. She'd damaged the one thing she loved more than anything else, and now it was gone forever.

"Come on and we'll go inside, 'tis freezing out here," Seán said, shivering for effect. She allowed herself to be steered indoors, led through the door like a stricken child; her body rested against his for support, suddenly resembling a woman many years her senior.

25

HE LOOKED OVER HIS WORK for the umpteenth time. No, there was definitely nothing more to add. He'd been finished for some time now, at least half an hour, but he hadn't wanted to be the first to leave. That honour had gone to Alan Pegg, who'd winked slyly at him before handing his paper to the invigilator and strolling out the door. With his friend outside waiting for him, Seán was growing increasingly giddy. He knew it was stupid, this was an important exam, but he just wanted to be free. Had he done enough to get a pass? That was the big question. Science was second only to maths on his blacklist; anything above forty per cent would be a success. He reckoned he'd done enough; a few things on the paper had looked vaguely familiar and he'd reeled off some stuff about neutrons and electrons in response. Now he just wanted to get out of here. But the words of every teacher he'd ever had rung in his ears: Check and recheck your paper, read it over and then read it over again. He'd done that to the point where the words had begun to swim before his eyes and nothing made any sense – not that it had in the first place.

He looked around him at the half-empty room. The great and the good of 3A had departed, leaving only the tormented and masochistic behind. The invigilator caught his eye and he quickly looked back at his paper, terrified of being accused of something untoward. He'd never cheat; he'd rather fail miserably than do well by false means. One more look.

His name and ID number? Yes, both present and correct. A minimum of four questions answered? Try five. Diagrams and charts accompanying his work? For what they were worth, yes. There was nothing more to do, nothing to add. He got up from his desk, still feeling he'd forgotten something, handed his paper to the invigilator and carried on out the door to freedom.

True to his word, Pegs was there waiting for him. They grinned widely at each other and hurried away from the scene of the crime. At a safe distance, the merriment began.

"What a load of bollocks! I hadn't a clue, Lockie, not a clue!"

"Haha, me neither, boy. I'm definitely after failing."

"Fuck it, man, you can worry about that in September. We're free now. We're FUCKIN' FREE!"

Pegs charged out of the building with his hands in the air, screaming at the top of his voice:

"WE'RE FREE, WE'RE FREE. WE'RE FUCKIN' FREEEEEEEEEE!!"

"Fuck's sake, Pegs, keep quiet till we're away from the school."

But he was already gone; out through the school gates and down the road, arms aloft as he roared in triumph.

He was right though, they were free. There would be no more exams, no more studying, no more school and no more teachers; for the next three months they could do whatever the hell they wanted. Before all that, though, there was the end-of-exams party in the woods. It was to be the party to end all parties; there would be booze and drugs, there would be music and there would also be Leanne. She had finished her own exams the previous day and would be joining him to celebrate later tonight. Not only would this be the first time they'd seen each other in weeks, it would also be their official coming-out party, the night they announced to the world that they were a couple.

"Are we going to the off-licence, then?" Seán asked, catching up with Pegs.

"Yes," he declared, brandishing a crisp twenty-pound note. "What good is freedom without booze, after all?"

Seán had a twenty-pound note of his own to match Pegs', but he still couldn't decide what to spend it on. That was his biggest dilemma; choosing his poison. Unlike most boys his age, he didn't have to worry about the actual procurement of alcohol; he had Alan Pegg. They all had him; Ginty, Murt and half the third-year students at Dooncurra Vocational School. Pegs was a regular in all the local off-licences. He got so much drink for so many people that it was presumed he was a raging alcoholic.

"What about the lads?"

"Ah, I've their stuff got already. Poor Ginty didn't know what to get, so I bought him two flagons of cider. He'll be on his back after one."

"I can't believe he's actually coming."

"I know. Can't wait to see what he's like pissed."

"He told me he's always drinking at home, has a glass of whiskey with the father of a Sunday."

"Don't mind that fucker! The size of him, the smell of whiskey would have him in the horrors."

"What time we gonna head up there?"

"Soon as I buy this drink, get home, eat me dinner and wash me bollix, I'll be ready."

"Grand."

"There's probably people up there already. All the ones who finished their exams this morning were talking about heading up at twelve."

"Twelve? They'll be fuckin' hammered already!"

"I know, yeah; plenty of *disorientated* young wans for Alan Pegg to take advantage of," said Pegs, rubbing his hands together.

"Gonna be plenty there for you tonight, lad."

"Oh yes, but what about you, Lockie? Will Alice be there?" he said with a smirk.

"Nah."

Seán had intentionally avoided all talk of Alice since his raunchy, fabricated account of their first study night. His friends had asked about her time and time again, but no more information had been forthcoming. This had frustrated Pegs no end. He became convinced Seán was withholding valuable information and continued to pester him long after Ginty and Murt had lost interest.

"You're up to something, boy. I know you."

"I'm not, Pegs, honest. It just didn't work out with *her*."

He intentionally emphasised *her*, it was only fair to give the dog a bone.

"With *her*? What do you mean? Did it work out with someone else? You're full of mysteries, boy."

Seán grinned widely, the delicious grin of someone about to reveal a long-held secret.

"What the fuck are ya smiling for? Tell me or you'll get no drink!"

"It's her sister."

"What? Whose sister? What are ya on about?"

"Alice's sister, Leanne."

Pegs stopped dead in his tracks. "Yeah, right. Leanne Tiernan? Fuck off."

"It's the truth, man."

He stared at Seán, scanning his face for signs of a wind-up. He looked him up and down, this way and that, waiting for him to break into a smile and tell him he was only kidding. To his utter amazement it seemed that his friend was telling the truth.

"Fuck off," he repeated, trying to come to terms with this bombshell.

"Yeah, it happened a few weeks ago but we've been keeping it quiet 'cos of the circumstances," Seán confirmed.

Pegs raised his hands to the top of his head, left them there a moment and then pulled them over his face. He remained like that for some time, breathing heavily. After another lengthy pause he rubbed his face vigorously, as if trying to wake himself up, and grabbed Seán by the shoulders. "Tell me everything, you little shit, and don't leave anything out now, you hear me?"

Seán couldn't tell him everything, not just yet; he wasn't sure if he should even have told him this much.

"It just kind of happened," he said.

"What d'ya mean 'it just kind of happened'? Leanne Tiernan, for fuck's sake!"

"Ah, I can't say any more till later. It's awkward, y'know, with the sister and all."

"Oh, yeah! I bet she's fuckin' raging. No sooner has she her hands down your pants when her big sister swoops in and takes young McLoughlin for herself!"

"She doesn't know yet; that's why we've been keeping it quiet."

"Ah, I see," replied Pegs, tapping his nose. "Is this another one of your secrets I'm expected to keep, then?"

"For the time being, anyway."

They carried on towards the off-licence, Pegs shaking his head and muttering 'Leanne fuckin' Tiernan' under his breath.

"So what'll it be, young McLoughlin?" he asked once they'd reached their destination.

They stood in an alleyway a few doors down from the off-licence. Here Seán would remain until his friend returned with their beverages.

"I still can't make me mind up, Pegs."

"For fuck's sake man, you've had all week!"

"I know, but it's different this time. Leanne is going to be there. I want to be drunk, but not mouldy drunk."

"Gimme that money," said Pegs, grabbing the twenty out of Seán's hand. "I know the very thing for a chap in your situation."

He sauntered into the off-licence, to return with God knows what. Seán walked down to the end of the alley, away from prying eyes. He wondered if he'd done the right thing, telling Pegs about Leanne. It wouldn't have difficult to keep it quiet for just a few more hours, but fuck it, he was on a high. After all, how much damage could Pegs do between now and the party? He dared not answer his own question.

Minutes later Pegs came jogging down the alley, laden with bags.

"Whatcha get me?"

He handed Seán one of the bags.

"What the fuck is this shit?" said Seán pulling out a cloudy, rather effeminate bottle.

"Shit?! That, my dear boy, is peach schnapps."

"Peach schnapps? Sounds a bit gay."

"Try it, man, you'll love it."

Seán fingered the bottle dubiously before opening the cap and having a little sniff.

"Schnapps, eh?"

"Yep. Perfect for the horny young gent who wishes to get inebriated but not too inebriated."

"How much was that? Had you enough for a few cans as well?"

"We've loads of cans, boy, relax," Pegs said, lifting the bulging bags as proof.

"Jaysus, this stuff's not bad," said Seán, taking a sip of the schnapps.

"What did I tell you, boy? Aren't you lucky to have a connoisseur of fine spirits for a friend?"

"I am, boy," replied Seán, taking a longer slug of the schnapps and screwing the bottle shut. It didn't even taste like alcohol. Though he'd never admit it, Seán didn't really like the taste of booze. Cider was okay but most beers were vile, and spirits were best downed in one go so as not to taste them at all. But this schnapps was tasty, almost refreshing. He checked the front of the bottle for its alcohol content.

"Eighteen per cent, too. You wouldn't even taste the booze in it."

"And there's the danger," Pegs said sagely.

"How do you mean?"

"Well, if it doesn't taste like booze you're not going to give it the respect it deserves, are ya?"

"I don't get ya, Pegs."

"What I'm saying is here's young Seán, slugging away on his schnapps, having a great time and thinking to himself 'God, this stuff is lovely, not like booze at all.' Before he knows it, half the bottle is gone. He stands up to go for a slash and falls on his arse. He's fucked. Peach schnapps One, Seán McLoughlin Nil."

"Ah, I'll share it with Leanne; maybe we'll fall down together," replied Seán with a smirk.

Pegs returned the smile. He wasn't averse to plying young wans with drink when the occasion called for it; the two extra naggins of vodka in his bag were testament to that.

They parted ways at Pegs' house, arranging to meet outside the woods at six that evening. Seán continued up the hill by himself, a spring in his step at the prospect of the night ahead and the summer that would follow. Summers were great: stifling hot days spent lolling around in the park, playing football with his mates, summer drinks as they cooled off at half-time. Then the evening, drinking cans down the river bank, smoking a joint or two if they had it; getting stoned and deciding a dip in the water was a good idea, stripping down to their underwear and plunging in to the icy, murky water and then out, shivering and soaked, running around in their smalls to get warm again. All that stuff was great, but this year he had a girlfriend, a proper one. A girlfriend that would lie around in the park with him and watch him play football, watch him fly into tackles, try bicycle kicks and spectacular volleys in a desperate attempt to impress her, and plant a congratulatory kiss upon his cheek when he collapsed down beside her, sweaty and panting, to take a break from the action. A girlfriend that would jump into the river with him, both of them stripped down, their near-naked bodies touching under the water as they rose for a kiss. That he could huddle close to as they tried to dry off, and walk back home with as dusk finally fell. That he could kiss goodnight and lie in bed thinking of, unable to sleep, his stomach doing somersaults as he relived the day over and over again.

His mother and grandmother were waiting for him when he got home. Sinéad's presence came as something of a surprise; they hadn't made any concrete plans to meet up once his exams were over.

"Hi, Mam," he said, as he fended off Patricia's kisses. "Wasn't expecting to see you."

"And why not?" interjected his grandmother. "Sure, doesn't she want to congratulate the little scholar as well?"

"I'd hold off on them congratulations till I get my results if I were you, Nan."

"Nonsense, you'll do brilliantly, Seán. I'm sure of it."

"How was today's exam, love?" his mother asked.

"Ah, sure 'twas all right, I suppose."

"Science, wasn't it?"

"Yeah," he replied, rolling his eyes to heaven.

"Never your strong point."

"No, Mam."

He'd noticed her holding something the minute he'd walked in the door; an envelope. It was surely for him and it hopefully contained money, but he pretended not to have seen it and did his best to look surprised when she handed it to him.

"A little something for you, pet."

"Ah thanks, Mam," he said, stuffing it in his pocket.

"Well, open it, Seán, for goodness' sake!" said Patricia.

"Okay, okay," he said, pulling it out and opening the crumpled envelope. It was a 'congratulations' card which depicted a dog, or at least a caricature of a dog with a pencil in its paw, sitting at a desk with a big grin on its face and, in bright red letters, 'Congratulations on your exams'. He barely scanned that, going straight inside to see what lay within. A twenty; not bad.

"You'll get the rest when you've passed," said Sinéad.

"Thanks, Mam," he said, offering her a half-hearted hug.

She drew him to her and he stood, allowing himself to be hugged, until Patricia broke up the party with a gift of her own.

"Here, Seán," she said, solemnly handing him a large parcel. It was square and satisfyingly heavy. He wasted no time in opening it, but had only nicked the paper before he turned to Patricia in shock. "Nan! You didn't?"

"I did, Seán," she simpered.

He tore off the rest of the paper. A PlayStation! He couldn't believe it. He'd asked for one the previous Christmas, but had been told they were too expensive.

"Mammy! The price of them things!" Sinéad protested, her gift now meagre and insignificant.

"Hush now, Sinéad," Patricia said, revelling in her grandson's delight.

Seán studied the box excitedly, wondering if she'd managed to buy him a couple of games while she was at it. All thoughts of drinking in the woods and relations with seventeen-year-old girls now far from his mind.

"You can use Patrick's old TV for it. I have it set up for you and all."

"This is amazing, Nan. Thank you," he said as he pecked her on the cheek and bounded up the stairs to try out his new toy.

Sinéad stared at her mother, wondering how long it would take to strangle her to death.

26

"HERE HE COMES, BOYS," SHOUTED Pegs.

There in the distance was the unmistakable figure of Cathal Ginty, his sprightly gait immediately recognisable to his friends. Seán, Pegs and Murt sat on a wall by the side of the road, awaiting their friend. Once the final member of the gang had arrived, they could proceed to the woods and the party therein.

"Come on, ya little shit, there's drinking to be done!" roared Murt.

Ginty broke into a little jog and then a trot until he drew up beside his friends.

He stared disbelievingly at the four bulging bags of booze on the ground. "They can't all be for us, are they, lads?"

"Oh, they're for us, all right," said Pegs. "And there's a couple of lovely flagons in there for you, boy."

"Flagons? Is that what you got me?"

This pleased Ginty no end; he drank flagons now.

Pegs hopped down from the wall and gathered up the bags. "Gimme a hand, will ye? Wasn't enough I had to buy them all, I'm supposed to carry 'em as well?"

They each grabbed a bag and began the short walk across the fields and into the woods.

"Many up here already, d'ye reckon?" Ginty asked, hurrying along behind the rest of them, the bag of cans knocking against his legs as he struggled to keep up.

"The lads were saying there's been sessions going on since twelve this morning," Murt replied.

"Twelve! Wow, they're gonna be intoxicated!"

The other three looked at him in bemusement. "Intoxicated?" asked Seán. "Is that the scientific term for being langers?"

Ginty looked on in confusion as they all laughed at his expense.

"I reckon you'll be intoxicated yourself tonight, Ginty," remarked Pegs.

"I think I will, Pegs. Two flagons! Do you think I could just drink one and save the other one for another night?"

"For fuck's sake, Ginty, it's a party! There won't be any drink left!"

"Ah. I might give it to one of ye, so. I'll see how I'm feeling after the first one."

Pegs shook his head in disbelief but said nothing. As far as he was concerned, Ginty was getting shit-faced and there was nothing the little fella could do about it.

Approaching the edge of the woods, they saw the remnants of an earlier gathering. Empty drink cans littered the ground and someone appeared to have lost their jeans, a girl by the looks of things. Murt picked them up.

"Jaysus, lads, we should try looking for the owner of these."

"Fuckin' dirty bitch couldn't wait to get 'em off, I bet," said Pegs, taking the jeans from his friend and examining them. He sniffed the crotch. "Nah, can't say I recognise that scent to be honest."

"Come on, lads," said Seán, moving ahead. "I think I hear people over there."

"Wait!" said Pegs, holding his hand up to halt them. He tilted his head to one side, a picture of concentration. Listening to the sounds coming from afar, he quelled any interruptions with a forceful movement of his raised hand.

"Not our party, lads," he said finally.

"How d'ya know?" asked Seán.

"Fatboy fuckin' Slim, that's how I know."

They nodded in agreement, glad of their friend's keen ear.

"Fuck that shit," said Murt. "Probably them scumbags from 6B."

"Yeah, no taste whatsoever, them lads."

"What music are we listening out for?" asked Ginty, usually a year or two behind the trends when it came to music, and indeed everything else.

"Never you mind, Gintasaurus," said Pegs. "When we hear it, we'll know it."

Ginty screwed up his face in disappointment. A couple of band names would have been nice, keep him in the loop and that.

"Ciarán O'Donnell said he was bringing his stereo; if he has, then they'll be easy to find," Seán reminded them.

"Good man, Ciarán. He gave me a lend of that new *Roots* album the other day, unfuckingbelievable," enthused Murt. "He'd better have brought that with him."

Roots, thought Ginty, I must remember that.

Ciarán and his stereo weren't that hard to find. They guessed correctly that he would have set up camp as far away as possible from the 6B mob, but not so far away that no one would be able to find him. They skirted along the edge of the woods, occasionally interrupting heavy petting sessions and other, more serious copulations. Eventually Pegs halted them once more, his ear trained to the skies.

"Yep, this is them," he said happily. "Nas, *Illmatic*. I'd recognise it anywhere!"

They scooped up the bags once more and followed in his wake. Seconds later they heard the music themselves; it was Nas, he'd been right. Ginty was relieved; he'd heard of Nas, even had a couple of his albums. He didn't like them much, but that was beside the point.

"Ho, ho! Here they come," Ciarán proclaimed, as the new arrivals came rumbling through the undergrowth. "What took ye so long?"

"Ah, Pegs here had us off on a wild-goose chase; we'd never have got here if we'd listened to him," teased Murt, skilfully evading Pegs' retributive punch.

"Well, you're here now, so pull up a rock and join the party."

Ciarán O'Donnell considered himself the leader of 3A, and had been campaigning for the role with tenacity for the best part of a year. A combination of lavish house-parties, expensive material possessions and one of the loudest mouths in the school had enabled him to obtain this position with little or no opposition. He had won over his subjects with brute force and his name was now synonymous with fun-times and whimsy. While Seán and his friends admired Ciarán's taste in music and considered his parties second to none, they had little or no respect for the man himself. No one did; he was widely mocked and derided. But Ciarán ignored the barbs, charming his tormentors with drink, drugs, porn, whatever it took to win them over. He was the kid who could get them things, so they chose to ignore the fact that he was also a thundering idiot.

What Seán liked best about Ciarán was his CD collection. He had more albums than Seán, Pegs and Murt put together, and were it not for him they would never have heard of The Roots or Nas or any of their favourite rappers. As soon as he saw Ciarán's CD holder, Seán was on the ground looking through it.

"Where'd ya get this one, Ciarán?"

"Will we put on this one next, yeah?"

"Ah, ya have to give us a loan of this one, man."

Ciarán looked on deferentially. Seán could take the whole lot if he wanted, there was plenty more where they'd come from.

The newcomers took their place in the middle of the group, eager to enliven a rather tepid affair. The music was turned up, drink was doled out and idle hands were entrusted with rolling the first joints of the day. Less than half the class was present, mostly young lads sipping their first or second cans of the day. By nightfall, though, everyone would be here.

"Here ya go, Murt. Get them into ya quick now, ya hear?" Pegs instructed, handing a bottle of vodka and a six-pack of cider to his friend.

"And schnapps for the romancer," he continued, digging around in his bag and pulling out the bottle for Seán.

"What the fuck is that?" asked Murt, echoing Seán's earlier query.

"Schnapps."

"What's ssshhnaps?"

"I dunno, think it's Belgian or something. 'Tis twenty per cent, like."

"Did you get it 'cos it matched the grade you're gonna get for today's exam?" enquired Ginty, with a cheeky little wink to the others.

"Fuck you," Seán said, opening the bottle and taking a confident slug.

"And what's this about romancing?" asked Murt. "I thought 'twas all off with that Alice wan."

"Oh, Jesus," said Pegs. "Wait till ye hear this."

Seán took a deep breath. *Wait till ye hear this, indeed.*

"I'm meeting her sister, Leanne. She should be here in a while."

"That wan from the flower shop?" asked Murt.

Seán nodded in the affirmative, already knowing what was coming. At first he had loved the idea of telling everyone he was meeting Leanne, but right now he could do without all the fuss. He needed his friends to be cool, to not show him up. Although, by the looks of things, Murt would be far too depressed to embarrass him. He hardly tried to conceal his disappointment. You could be happy for your friends, but when it came to girls they were in constant competition with one another. Right now Seán was winning, by some distance. With Pegs sure to pull – he always did – that left Murt with the prospect of propping up the imaginary bar with Ginty.

"You're gonna have to up your game, young Michéal," declared Pegs, snapping open his first can of the day. "'Cos right now Lockie's knocking them outta the park!"

Murt lay back on the grass, still reeling from this revelation. Seán studied his friend and wondered if he would have been happy for him in the same circumstances; probably not, he decided. Murt had once been his closest friend, but things had never been the same between them since *the fight.*

*

When Seán was eight he'd been informed that they – his mother, Daryl and himself – were moving house. They were leaving behind the bungalow he'd called home for the past five years and moving into a brand new two-storey building in one of Dooncurra's recently-developed housing estates. This was disastrous news. It didn't matter that the new house was less than a mile away from the old one, he might as well have been moving to another planet. After all, his friends from the old estate were hardly going to come all that way to see him now, were they? And, try as he may, he couldn't convince his mother to allow him to cycle back there every day after school. So he would have to make new friends. He didn't want to make new friends, but new friends would be better than no friends at all.

On their first evening in their new house Sinéad had persuaded him to go outside and play, citing a lovely summer's evening and the hordes of kids out in the grass as reason enough. Reluctantly, Seán joined the masses, content to skulk on the side-lines, very much the outsider. He'd watched the girls play hopscotch, the boys hurl and the smaller kids run aimlessly round in circles, and known he could never fit in. The kids here were different, not like the ones in his old estate. One or two of them had come up and asked him questions which he'd answered politely, then they'd returned to their games. That was that; he was destined to be an outsider forever. But then he'd spotted a familiar face, someone he knew from school; Michael 'Murt' Walsh. He hadn't realised Murt lived here.

"Hey, Seán, what are you doing here?" Murt asked, skidding to a halt on his BMX.

"I live here now."

"Really? What number?"

"20."

"Wow! I'm in 26, that's only three doors away."

"Cool."

"Hey, me and some of the lads are playing Dinkies, wanna join us?"

"Okay."

By the evening's end, Seán's mother had to call for him four times before he'd come in. He'd waved his new friends goodbye and promised to meet Murt in the morning for the walk to school. They'd walked to school together the next morning, and then sat beside one another in class. A solid friendship had been formed, one that would last the rest of their childhood. They had sleepovers at one another's house, played up front together for the football team and even accompanied each other on family holidays. But from the moment they began secondary school things changed. Seán settled down much quicker than his friend. He made new friends and was generally liked by everyone in his class. Murt, on the other hand, struggled. He clung to Seán like a sailor lost at sea, tailing him everywhere he went, making no effort to widen his social circle. This wouldn't have been an issue if Murt hadn't been universally disliked. Seán was invited to things with strict instructions not to bring his 'weird' mate. He remained loyal to his pal however. If they didn't want Murt, then he wouldn't go either; it was as simple as that. But rather than appreciate the sacrifice he'd made for him Murt urged Seán to go, insisting that he was fine by himself.

In time a status quo was reached; Seán would hang out with his new friends whenever the mood took him, but always made sure to find time to spend with his best mate too. To his credit, Murt learned not to rely on him as much as before. He had befriended another outcast, Cathal Ginty, a bookish nerd whose appetite for learning made him perennially unpopular. As for Pegs, no one could pinpoint the moment he became part of the gang. They'd known him throughout primary school, and he lived just up the road from them, but he'd only ever flitted in and out of their company over the years. A week here, a week there and he'd be gone, hanging out with a different group. At some point during their first year in secondary school, however, he became a more regular fixture; joining them for lunch, walking home with them, calling to their houses after school and bruising their arms with his playful but manly punches. Seán realised he had no need for new friends because, almost by accident, he and Murt had acquired two good friends and formed a gang of their own. The four of them quickly became best friends, forming close bonds within their little group. Everything would have been perfect if not for the fight.

In truth, it had been brewing for a while. Within all groups of teenage boys there must be a hierarchy, consisting of a dominant figure, a subservient one and underlings with aspirations of reaching the top. Their group was no different: Pegs was at its helm, Ginty its base and Seán and Murt were in the middle, the two beta-males tussling for supremacy. Of course, neither of them fully understood this and neither could comprehend why they had begun to feel so much enmity toward the other. But to anyone looking in it was obvious they were on a collision course – from which there was no escape. Much of their resentment centred round their respective performances in school. Both were struggling, and both took perverse pleasure in the other's shortcomings. It was Murt who'd been having greater difficulty, and there had been repeated requests from his teachers that he drop down to the lower strand, the B class. Seán should have been upset by the potential loss of his pal, but instead he relished the prospect. Soon it would be just the three of them; no more Murt cramping his style, bringing up embarrassing childhood secrets. He'd be free from the past, free to be the person he wanted to be.

His antipathy towards his friend deepened. Their insults, once playful, became laced with hidden meaning. Hurtful retorts designed to scar the other, were thrown back and forth with abandon. Seán habitually referred to his friend's academic under-achievement, cutting him to the core and then laughing it off. *I'm only messing, boy, relax.* Pegs and Ginty looked on in dismay, wondering where it would all end.

The end, of sorts, came during lunch-hour on a bitter winter's day. So cold was it that most of the students had run for the sanctity of the radiators as soon as the bell had rung. A bit of frost wasn't going to keep Seán and Murt from their daily game of football, though. The numbers were down due to the inclement weather but they still managed to organise a decent kick-about, with fifteen players a side. The playing fields were off limits, so they turned to the basketball courts. That meant a hard concrete surface, with a generous helping of gravel to make falls even more painful, and there were plenty of falls; friends and foes charged into bone-shuddering tackles, with little concern for their own or anyone else's safety. If you got hurt, it was your own tough luck.

Seán and Murt lined up on opposing teams, nothing unusual about that, they were two of the better players and were invariably among the first picks once two captains had been nominated. Because they both liked to loiter around goal-mouths in search of easy pickings, they rarely came into contact with each other during a game. On this day, however, Seán took it upon himself to occupy a deep-lying midfield role, bringing him very much into contact with his friend. At first it appeared to be a coincidence; Murt received a pass in space and cocked back his leg for a shot at goal, only to be dispossessed with no little force by a determined Seán. The ball was cleared and both boys carried on with the game. No words were exchanged, no looks given; but then it happened again. This time Murt rose to nod in a far post cross but found himself thwarted by the suspiciously industrious

McLoughlin, who took ball and man in an effort to defend his goal. Murt stared after his friend, but Seán just trotted up the 'pitch' and threw himself back into the action. Some minutes passed before the ball came Murt's way again, and this time he was ready for Seán. He spotted him from the corner of his eye and, with a deft drop of his shoulder, sent his mate hurtling in the wrong direction before planting the ball past the hapless goalkeeper.

Pegs, playing on Seán's team, had picked up on their individual battle and shot Murt a questioning look as play resumed. Murt shrugged his shoulders and nodded in Seán's direction, intimating that he had no idea what was up with their friend. Something clearly was up. Seán hadn't enjoyed being made a fool of, and now stationed himself in the heart of his team's defence. His intentions were clear: thou shall not pass, and by 'thou' he meant Murt. He commanded things like a modern-day Beckenbauer: nipping attacks in the bud, striding out of defence with the ball at his feet and pinging precise passes to appreciative forwards. Murt left him to it. He wasn't in the mood for a serious game.

Eventually, though, Seán's demeanour began to irk him; the pleasure he was taking in his team winning, the way he barked out the scoreline every time his side scored. Murt decided that he was in the mood for a serious game, after all. He came in from his left-wing position to a more central role, a central striking role, and began demanding the ball from his team-mates. They did as they were told and the goals began to rain in, Murt either scoring or playing a part in all of them. Now Seán tersely announced the scoreline under his breath, annoyed by this unexpected fightback. With lunchtime almost at an end, there were only a couple of goals in it. This was the vital time; the remaining minutes and seconds would define the game and determine its victor. The rest of the players became mere extras, the game now essentially between Seán and Murt and no one else. Neither boy held back, straining every sinew in their efforts to best one another; cheeks red from their exertions, steam rising off them like a herd of cows in a dew-covered field. It was Murt who gained the upper hand, single-handedly pulling his team level and then going in search of a winner. The bell would ring any second, and there would be no injury time in this contest.

Sensing that victory was slipping away, Seán began to panic, charging up-field for a shot at goal only for it to sail harmlessly wide. A quick counterattack and Murt pilfered another, benefiting from Seán's absence, putting his team in the lead for the first time. As they crossed paths – Seán returning to his defensive station, Murt resuming his stance a few yards from goal – the goal-scorer couldn't resist a little dig at his friend's expense.

"You'd never make a defender, Seány."

Seán glared at him and shouted at his goalkeeper to clear the ball; time was running out but they could still draw level. The keeper's quick clearance seemed to do the job, the ball bypassing the opposing defenders and allowing Ginty, of all people, to bag the equaliser.

"Come on, lads," said Pegs, "let's call it a draw."

"Fuck that," replied Seán grimly. "Play to the bell."

A few players had drifted away, but enough remained to continue the game. As play resumed the bell sounded, and yet more boys left the fray. Murt looked at Seán, ready to call a truce, but his friend stared ahead in defiance. What choice did he have? He wasn't going to let Seán have the final say. Murt just knew that the minute he headed towards the main building, Seán would declare victory for his team. That wasn't going to happen, not today anyway.

"Come on, lads, just one more," he shouted, accepting the ball from his goalkeeper.

He looked forward; there was now only a handful of players left on either team. A quick one-two, and Murt was bearing down on goal with just one player to beat: Seán. They'd been in this situation thousands of times before and knew each other's game inside out. Murt ran at pace, he would do a step-over just as they came together; with any luck he'd leave his friend floundering and slot the ball past the keeper, putting an end to this tiresome charade. Seán, however, was wise to him. He'd watched Murt do that little trick for years and expected nothing less. As Murt drew closer, Seán waited for the predictable shift in movement. When Murt obliged, he simply plucked the ball from his possession and strode away with it at his feet; a clean tackle, probably his first of the game. But he wasn't done there; what better way to win the game than to dispossess his friend, run up-field and score? And that was precisely what he did, slamming the ball past an uninterested keeper, letting out a triumphant roar as he did so.

That should have been that, game over; but Seán couldn't let it lie. He marched down the court, arms aloft, reciting the winner's mantra.

"Champions! Champions! Champions!"

Murt knew it was directed at him, knew he was being goaded, but he wasn't going to rise to the bait. He put his head down and began the walk back to class, vanquished but taking his medicine like a man. That was until he felt someone's hands on his head.

"Unlucky Murt!" Seán called out as he ruffled his friend's hair.

He knew how particular Murt was about his hair. That was Murt's thing, his hair. He spent ages styling and perfecting it every morning, and hated anyone going near it. He had almost maimed Tanya Horgan when she'd playfully patted his head in class one day, swivelling round in his chair, ready to bear arms. You didn't touch Michael Walsh's hair, not if you valued your life.

"What the fuck ya doing, Lockie?" he shouted, frantically moulding his tresses back into their proper state.

"What's up with ya, boy?"

"You fuckin' know."

"G'way, boy, it's only a game. Get over it."

Something in his tone riled Murt. *Get over it.* It was dismissive, mocking. It made light of him.

"Go fuck yourself, boy."

At this juncture, Seán could have been the one to take the moral high ground. He could have walked away, refused to stoop to name-calling; but he didn't. Because, in a way, this was what he had wanted all along.

"The fuck you say?" he said, in that threatening tone so common in bucking young males.

"You heard me," Murt replied, defensive now, not wishing for it to escalate any further.

Seán stood in front of him, as if deciding whether he was worth it. His friend wouldn't look him in the eye, staring downwards in a slightly submissive posture. Satisfied he'd made his point, Seán chose to back away, but not before firing a parting shot.

"Ah g'way, ya fuckin' thick cunt."

To those watching, this might have seemed like a throwaway comment, but Murt knew exactly what Seán was getting at. He was referring to Murt's recent academic struggles, making light of something very serious. Murt didn't want to be demoted to 3B, he wanted to stay in 3A with his mates.

Suddenly he didn't feel so submissive, he felt aggrieved. He'd been struck, and he wanted to strike back.

"At least I know who my fuckin' father is," he spat out, regretting the words almost as soon as they'd left his mouth.

Murt was the only person Seán had ever confided in when it came to his father. He had never discussed it with anyone else; not his mother, his grandparents, Patrick, even Pegs; no one. He had told Murt because he was his best friend and he trusted him. It hadn't been easy, he was ashamed, but he'd felt better afterwards. And Murt had been great: sympathising, offering to help him find his real father and, most importantly, keeping it to himself; until now.

Seán lost control. He *allowed* himself to lose control, allowed all that pent-up rage and aggression to come tumbling out. Instead of directing it at those who had wronged him, however, he brought it to bear upon a long-standing ally. The first blow sent Murt staggering backwards, a look of surprise on his face as blood began to seep from his nose. He raised his hands to defend himself, but it was a half-hearted gesture. The second punch sent him spiralling to the ground, his attacker pouncing upon his prone figure. Seán continued his assault, raining blows down on his friend, his muffled cries drowning out the sound of his fists.

"YOU FUCKIN' CUNT! I'LL KILL YOU, YA BASTARD."

Murt fought back. He threw Seán off him, knocking him sideways, and dived on him, driving an elbow into his ribs. They tussled for supremacy, scrabbling around on the ground like a pair of upturned beetles, until the door to the school was flung open and a panicked figure emerged. It was Pegs, alerted to the hostilities by another student. He forced his way through the baying crowd and peeled his friends apart.

"What the fuck are ye doing?" he pleaded, close to tears. "Ye're supposed to be friends, for fuck's sake!"

Seán rose to his feet, cleaning dirt from a uniform which had been ripped asunder. "Tell it to that cunt," he said bitterly.

"What the fuck is going on, Murt?" asked Pegs.

Murt shook himself free from Pegs' grasp and made for the school gates. "I'm going home. Tell Sheehan I have the flu."

And that was that. The fight had happened, and now it was over. Seán returned to class, telling the teacher he'd fallen, and Murt went home. The next day Pegs, playing the role of peacemaker, brought the two of them together, made them say 'sorry' and forced them to shake on it. But things were never the same. They fell into an uneasy truce, always civil with one another but making sure they never spent time alone together. What Murt had said about Seán's father was never discussed but it was always there, hanging in the air between them.

*

Seán watched Murt digest the news of his latest love affair. He knew he was hurting, knew he was insanely jealous, and it felt good. Seán McLoughlin might not have known who his father was but he knew how to get off with young wans, and seventeen-year old ones at that. But as good as it was to have one-up on his friend, he was now starting to feel nervous. Basking in the glory of his new coupling was one thing, acting it out in front of a living, breathing audience was quite another. She was coming to the party and she was going to be with him. It was a date. They were going public. He had got by on his wits so far, improvising as he went along, but more would be expected of him tonight. He'd have to talk to her properly, not like the snatched snippets of conversation they'd shared so far. What had he to say that would be of any interest to a seventeen-year-old girl, who was probably going off to college at the end of the summer? He still collected football stickers, for fuck's sake! He took another long, hard drink of the peach schnapps, and wished he had something a little stronger.

27

THE PARTY WAS IN FULL swing. The music had been cranked up as loud as it would go; Dr. Dre and Biggie, Outkast and Cypress Hill. Heavy bass lines reverberated around their private idyll. Joints were passed around, half a dozen on the go at any given time; heavy-eyed smokers already skinning up another to add to the conveyor belt. Some of the girls had started dancing, swiftly followed by eager, uninhibited boys. Even at this early hour couples were pairing off, mate chosen for the night. Seán was on the outside looking in. He was drinking and smoking just like everyone else, but he wasn't enjoying himself. He couldn't get into the party spirit, not until he knew his fate. Was he going to spend the night in the arms of the first girl he'd ever loved or was he going to spend it here, checking and rechecking his watch, until he finally accepted that she wasn't coming? At first he'd been worried about how he and Leanne would get along, but now his fear was that she wouldn't show up at all. Whenever a new group of people emerged from the trees he looked over expectantly, his heart sinking as another mob of third years arrived to join their classmates. What if she couldn't find his party? He'd told her they'd be in this part of the woods, but there were two other parties going on nearby. What if she found the 3D mob and their shitty techno music? She'd take one look at that lot and decide third-year boys were no longer for her. He couldn't take it anymore; he was going to look for her. Taking another gulp from the half-empty bottle, he rose unsteadily to his feet.

"Just going for a walk, lads."

"Whoa," said Pegs. "Where are you going? Your girl will be here any minute."

"I don't think she'll be able to find us, Pegs. I'm going to look for her."

Pegs placed his hands on Seán's shoulders. "What time did she say she'd be here, Seán?"

"Seven."

"And what time is it now?"

Seán looked at his watch, although the gesture was unnecessary; he knew exactly what time it was.

"Quarter past."

"She's fifteen minutes late, Lockie; that's normal for women. If she said she'd be here at seven, then you should expect her at eight."

Seán looked at him uncertainly, but his friend's unflinching stare reassured him. Pegs knew the score.

"Okay, Pegs, you're probably right," he conceded, sitting down again.

"Of course I'm right, Lockie," Pegs said, joining him on the grass and starting another spliff.

Seán accepted the joint when it came his way, but his heart really wasn't in it. He took a couple of cursory drags and held it out to Ginty, then remembered that the wee man didn't partake in the consumption of illegal substances.

"Oh, sorry, Ginty," he said, reaching past him towards Murt.

"Hold on there, Lockie," Ginty protested, grabbing the joint from Murt's outstretched hand. "I think I'll have a go of this and see what all the fuss is about."

His three friends looked at one another in amazement. They'd been trying for months to get Ginty to have a smoke, to give them a laugh if nothing else. Time and time again he'd steadfastly refused, saying it wasn't for him but thanks all the same. And they'd respected his decision, stopped pestering him, left him to it; now here he was, fat joint between his fingers, ready to get high with the rest of them.

Ginty held the joint in his hand and examined it, looking as if he might swallow it whole. Just as Pegs was about to offer some advice, Ginty brought it to his lips and took a clumsy yet effective drag of the cheap Moroccan Black. The resulting convulsions were expected, but no less funny for it. He bent forward on his hands and knees, spluttering and coughing like an ailing asthmatic, red in the face, drool hanging from his lips. Murt belted his back until eventually Ginty regained himself and took a drink of cider to settle his throat.

"Where's that joint gone?" he asked, his eyes watering as he drained the flagon and threw it into the bushes behind him. "Give it back to me, Murt; come on, man!"

"Hold your horses, Ginty, you'll get it in a minute."

Unable to wait a moment more, he moved on to another group and within seconds they saw him with a new joint in his hands, puffing away like an old pro.

"Look at him," said Pegs, wiping away an imaginary tear. "What have we done?"

"We've unleashed the beast, lads," said Murt, looking over at Ginty in admiration. "Proper little pothead now."

Seán had been so caught up in his friend's first drug experience that he hadn't noticed the new arrivals, a group of girls. They came in from the opposite side of the clearing, the side he wasn't watching. These girls were a couple of years older than the rest of people here. And there were four of them. The boys who'd been dancing around the middle of the copse stopped to stare at them, suddenly self-conscious. Music still thumped out from Ciarán O'Donnell's stereo, but the accompanying whoops and yells had died down. These girls weren't supposed to be here. They were up to something, probably checking things out on behalf of those scummy bastards from 6B.

"Keep an eye on that drink," a voice said as the girls made their way through the crowd. They appeared to be looking for someone; one girl in particular was peering around the group as if expecting to find someone she knew; then she smiled and beckoned the others to follow her. Her unsuspecting target was too busy laughing at the antics of Cathal Ginty to even notice her. She crept up behind him, crouched down and placed her hands over his eyes.

"Guess who!" she whispered into his ear.

He didn't need to guess. The sound of her voice and the heat of her breath made his stomach flip and his chest lift. But he played it cool.

"No idea," he said. "Give me a clue."

The voice returned to his ear, closer this time. "Someone who's been waiting to get her hands on you for a very long time."

"No, still no idea," he said, his grin widening. He really hoped the others were seeing this.

She leaned her head over his shoulder and removed her hands.

"Surprise!"

Leanne brought her face around to meet his and planted a kiss on his forehead. Now Seán McLoughlin was no longer the morose drunk dampening everyone's spirits. For him the party had just begun.

28

"Where are we going, Seán?"

"You'll see in a minute."

He was taking her to his favourite place in the woods, his secret place. He called it his secret, but other people may have known about it too. He'd just never seen anyone else there.

"I hope it's not far."

"It's not."

Leanne held his bottle of schnapps and he was drinking a can of cider. Their free hands were clasped together, allowing him to guide her through some of the rougher terrain as they made their way. The schnapps had been a great idea; it had allowed him to get royally pissed without ever descending into the kind of drunken messiness he'd been fearful of. He was in control, confident without being cocky, merry but not rowdy. Leanne, surprisingly, had turned out to be a total lightweight. She'd barely finished her second can before she was slurring her words, and a third had seen her overtly groping and mauling Seán in an altogether unbecoming fashion. Not that he'd minded. But if they were to get up close and personal he wanted it to be somewhere private, away from prying eyes.

"Are you drunk, Miss Tiernan?" he asked, teasing.

"I am not," she giggled, trying for the umpteenth time to pull him to the ground.

"Come on, Leanne," he said, wrestling her upright. "It's not far now."

Much as he wanted to be dragged to the ground, he was more anxious to reach the secret place. Soon it would be dark and much of the effect would be lost without daylight.

"Come on," he said, ushering her forward, "nearly there."

"Ah, Seán," she whined. "Where are ya taking me?"

"You'll love it, I promise."

"Okay," she sighed, taking a swig of the schnapps and blundering on.

Five minutes later, they were there. To Leanne it appeared to be just another part of the forest; all trees, branches and briars. But Seán knew better.

"We're gonna have to squeeze in through this bit here, Leanne," he said, moving towards what appeared to be an impenetrable wall of leaves and bushes.

Leanne stood truculently, arms crossed. "Ah, Seán, give over. I'm not going in there."

He chuckled. "Come on, ya big pisshead. I'll look after you. Just follow me."

Haughtily she did as instructed, plunging through the bushes and flailing along behind him. It was horrific. Branches sprang back against her face, causing her to shriek in pain; prickly twigs clawed her clothes and scratched at her eyes. This wasn't what she'd had in mind when she'd suggested they find somewhere romantic to be together. Seán sent encouragement and reassurance from up ahead to keep her moving, but she couldn't help but wonder if this was what dating a fifteen-year old boy would always be like. Would they build a fort upon reaching their destination?

Gradually the foliage became less dense. No longer did she have to claw her way through. They were now in a tunnel of sorts, a hollowed-out section of vegetation which allowed for easier passage than before. She had to stoop to move forward, but now there was a definite sense of emerging from the undergrowth and heading to somewhere in particular. Through the gloom she saw Seán racing ahead; he had reached the end of the tunnel and was waving at her to catch up. She hurried forward, spilling some of her drink as she went.

"Look, Leanne," he said. "Look at it; isn't it amazing?"

They were standing by the edge of a pond which opened out into a small clearing. The woods closed in on all four sides, thick and uniform, but here in this private paradise there was room to breathe, to look around you and savour the sense of pure isolation. Several misshapen trees criss-crossed the pond's murky black water, like a network of roads at a busy junction. The pond brimmed with life: dragonflies darted around the surface, tadpoles shot back and forth beneath the lilies and a number of indeterminate insects dithered this way and that, content to be a part of it all. Several of these insects latched on to the newcomers; Leanne had to bat them away as she took in her surroundings. It was amazing, she had to admit; a real treasure. The kind of place she'd have loved to have found – when she was fifteen.

"Will we go back now?" she asked.

"Wait, I haven't even shown you the best part yet."

Seán walked along the edge of the pond and she trudged after him, noting with displeasure that the ground was now decidedly sticky; one false move and she'd lose a shoe, or maybe even a foot. Cute and all as Seán was, he was starting to push his luck.

He waited for her at the base of a tree, one which had grown horizontally outwards and over the pond, serving as a bridge to the other side. The tree's trunk was sturdy and wide, strong enough to walk upon. As it reached across the water, the branches at the top straining upwards for sunlight, it interrupted the path of a tree coming in the other direction. The two converged above the water, melded together by nature, creating a vantage point which Leanne correctly assumed to be their final destination.

"Come on, let's go," Seán said, taking her hand. "Don't worry, it's perfectly safe."

Too tired to argue, she allowed herself to be led across the gangplank, expecting to meet her watery death at any moment; but they safely traversed the overpass and moments later reached their very own watchtower. He escorted her into the crook, affording her the best seat and squeezing in beside her. The pond was only ten feet below but they were immune to its dangers, safe in their lofty perch. Above them; brightness, a break in the forest canopy enabling them to peer upwards at the velvety blue sky and the stars glittering in its midst.

"It's lovely, Seán," Leanne murmured.

She felt for his hand and took it in hers.

"Lovely," she repeated.

There was nothing more that needed to be said. It had turned out just as he'd dreamed. This moment, which he'd played over and over in his head, was now a reality, and even as it was happening he knew he'd remember it for the rest of his life.

Leanne snuggled up close to him, wrapping her arms around his waist and laying her head on his chest. He looked down at her and smiled. She met his gaze and lifted her face to his. The kiss had none of the raw passion which had characterised their first, but it had something else: tenderness, affection. It filled him with hope and a burgeoning belief that maybe life didn't have to be so difficult, that someday he might be happy, just like everyone else. That one simple gesture, the touch of her lips upon his, transformed him, infused his soul with something approaching fulfilment. She pulled away from him and smiled contentedly. Burrowing her head in his chest, she giggled self-consciously at a thought she wasn't willing to share. Seán took a deep, satisfied breath and pressed her as close as he dared.

They stayed like that for some time, the only sound an occasional hiccup from Leanne as she slowly sobered up and the splash of water as the pond-life went about their business. It was getting dark now. Night was falling and they would soon have to go. He'd never been here so late and, although he was pretty confident of finding his way back, he didn't like the idea of stumbling around the forest like a couple of extras from *The Blair Witch Project.*

"Leanne," he whispered.

"Yeah?"

"We should go back. It's getting dark."

"Aw, can we not stay a while longer?"

"I'd love to," he said, "but if it gets any darker we won't be able to find our way back."

"Oh, Seán," she sighed, "you're so sensible."

"One of us has to be," he replied as they untangled their legs and arms and set off down the bridge. When they reached the pond's edge Leanne daintily hopped off, scooping up the bottle of Schnapps she'd left there for safekeeping.

"Come on, let's polish off the rest of this right now!"

There was at least a third left, but it didn't matter now how drunk he got. The pressure was off.

"Okay," he said, snapping the bottle from her and taking a healthy glug of its contents. "Your turn."

They went back and forth for the next five minutes until, with one dramatic tilt of her head, Leanne tipped the last few droplets into her mouth and declared the game at an end.

"Happy now?" Seán asked, eager to make their way back.

"Not yet," she replied, taking his hand and pulling him away from the pond towards a dryer patch of land. She laid her jacket on the ground and sat on it.

"Come on," she said, with a look of serious intent.

Seán instantly knew what she meant, but he hesitated. He hadn't been expecting this and he wasn't sure if he was ready, but there was no time to think, or to consider how ready he might be. He joined her on the forest floor and allowed himself to be pushed onto his back. She kissed him, more lustily this time, and her hands began working on the fly of his jeans.

"Wait, wait," she said.

Had she changed her mind, and would he be relieved or disappointed if she had? No, it was still happening. She'd merely shifted the focus of her attention, moving away from his face, down, down. He felt his flies being opened and then a moment's hesitation. What was she doing down there? He dared not ask. He felt her hands on his belt. She unbuckled him, undid his button and with some difficulty yanked down his trousers and boxers. His throbbing cock sprang out, happy to be free, ready for whatever might come its way.

"Ooh, Seány. Look. At. You."

It was the first time he had ever been exposed in front of a girl. He felt helpless and empowered all at once.

"Well?" he asked, wondering what came next.

"Well indeed," she replied and began nuzzling his crotch, taking care not to engage his penis just yet. Instead teasing him with kisses and caresses around his lower stomach and upper thighs.

Seán lay back, waiting. Was he getting a blow-job, then? It looked like it. He had been wanked off by girls in the past but he had never been given a blow-job. Being a fifteen-year-old boy, he worried about losing his virginity, but as Leanne wrapped her lips around his quivering member he declared himself happy – first blow-job at fifteen, that wasn't bad, right?

Pegs had told him about them, and how magnificent they were, but nothing could have prepared him for what followed. It was as if his penis was being bathed in golden nectar. Every nerve-ending tingled with pleasure as his phallus was showered with more care and affection than even he had ever given it. He had no idea what was going on down there, but it felt like she was equipped with more than just a tongue and a pair of lips. She'd clearly done this before. This thought filled him with anguish, but he quickly pushed it away; she was with him now and that was all that mattered. She began massaging his balls, gently squeezing them and cupping them in her hands as she worked her mouth up and down his cock. This was too much; it was sensory overload. An orgasm began to build in his pelvis, uncontrollable, unstoppable. His moans of pleasure, growing louder by the second, and the involuntary bucking of his hips should have warned Leanne, but she spluttered in protest as he released his load with a feral cry, sending several birds fluttering into the night sky.

"For fuck's sake, Seán," she said, allowing the rest of his seed to squirt harmlessly onto the forest floor. "You could have warned me!"

Seán pumped his cock with his hand a couple of times, making sure it was completely drained, and then exhaled dramatically.

"Was I supposed to?" he asked.

"Yes, you were supposed to!" Leanne replied, rinsing her mouth out with the dregs of his can of cider.

"Sorry, I didn't realise," he said, putting an arm around her. "That was brilliant, though."

Leanne's pout disappeared. "Glad you enjoyed it," she said primly.

There was a brief silence. Seán wondered if he should repay the favour. He didn't know how these things worked.

"Should I do you now?" he asked.

Leanne smiled at him, a sympathetic smile. "Aw, Seán, you're so cute."

"So will I, then?"

"No, you're okay. Maybe next time."

"Okay."

He hastily pulled up his boxers, not wanting Leanne to see his once-proud penis reduced to its dormant state, and wiped the dirt off her jacket before handing it to her. He watched her put it on, smiling to himself as she patted away the dirt from its sleeves. She was so beautiful it almost hurt him to look at her. And she had just sucked him off.

"What?" she asked as he stood there staring at her.

"Nothing," he replied, taking her in his arms.

He held her tight. There was nothing sexual or sensual about this embrace; he just wanted to be close to her, to feel the warmth of her body upon his.

He released her, stared into her deep green eyes and kissed her softly on the cheek. He was in love, of that there was no doubt. He would have to tell her, but not tonight. Maybe tomorrow, or the day after.

"Come on, we'd best get back," he said, taking her hand and leading her through the bushes.

29

A FIRE HAD BEEN LIT; a vast, all-consuming wall of heat and energy. Bolstered with tyres, it burned high and wide, its warmth so intense that no one could stand within ten feet of it. The dynamic of the party had changed now. Everyone was gathered around the fire, staring solemnly at the crackling wood as they ruminated on the future, the past, anything but the present. Occasionally someone rose to throw another carefully-sourced bushel onto the inferno; this fire would burn long into the night. Music still played but it was a background noise, a means of maintaining the ambience. They still drank, they still partied. But it was more restrained now; the wildness had left them. Ginty had succumbed to his excesses and was asleep in Roisín Prendergast's lap. One of the larger girls in their class, she stroked his hair sweetly like a nurse tending to a soldier's wounds. Pegs had made his acquaintance with one of Leanne's companions and was busily undressing her from the inside out – or at least that was how it appeared. Murt sat alone by the edge of the fire, can in his hand, staring blankly into the embers.

"Where will we sit?" Seán asked Leanne as they returned to the fray.

"Let's not sit," she said. "Let's dance."

She opened her arms in invitation.

"It's not really dancing music, Leanne," he said as Biggie Smalls re-counted his days in the New York State Penitentiary.

"It doesn't matter, come on," she said, grabbing him. "We'll do our own little dance, a nice, slow romantic one."

Seán looked around. All sorts of erotic behaviour was taking place, no one would notice a pair of slow-dancing romancers. He put his hands around her waist as she draped hers around his neck. She rested her head on his shoulder and they began to sway slowly from side to side. Leanne's hands clung to his back, holding him tight, pulling him to her. Only half an hour ago she had serviced his needs; but he was a young man in his sexual prime and his loins awoke once more; ready to answer their master's call. He pushed himself against her, hoping that this simple gesture would inform her of his condition, but she scarcely noticed, humming happily, oblivious to his needs. He peered over her head, scanning the area for somewhere quiet but still within range of the fire. Perhaps if he casually moved them to a more secluded spot, his desires could be sated once more? He surveyed the scene, calculating distances and estimating privacy. There were youngsters strewn everywhere, like a battlefield the morning after a bloody skirmish. Lots of faces were familiar to him; friends, acquaintances, kids starting out in life, just like himself, innocence everywhere he looked, and Alice. Alice Tiernan. Alice?!! What the fuck was she doing here? She stood in the shadows, flanked by a couple of girls he didn't know, all sipping nervously on indeterminate alcopops. They appeared to have just arrived, looking fresh-faced, unsullied and entirely out of keeping with the realm of decay and devastation which lay before them. Seán hastily looked away, hoping they hadn't been spotted, and tried to guide Leanne further from the fire where they wouldn't be seen.

"No, Seán," she moaned, resisting. "Stay near the fire where it's warm."

"Your sister is here," he said flatly.

"Don't be silly."

"She is; she's over there with a couple of her friends."

Leanne jolted into life, peering round Seán's back for affirmation.

"Where? I can't see her. You'd better not be joking."

"It's not a joke. I saw her over there a second ago."

"What's she doing here? She doesn't even drink!"

"How the fuck would I know?"

"Oh, God, you're right," Leanne said with horror. "I can see her. Come on, quick, we have to hide!"

She bent double and scuttled towards the dark edges of the woods. Seán allowed himself to be dragged to a safe distance before stopping her. "I thought you'd told her," he said.

"I haven't! I was waiting for the exams to be over. I didn't want to upset her during them. Do you think she saw us?"

Seán looked back to where Alice was stood. A couple of boys had joined her group and she was enjoying their attentions.

"You have to tell her now," he said, turning back to Leanne.

Her shoulders sagged in despair. "I'll go talk to her," she sighed, "but you stay out of sight, okay?"

"Don't worry, I won't be coming anywhere near ye."

"Okay," she said taking a deep breath and collecting herself. "Am I very drunk?"

"You'll be all right. Go on."

She paused one more time, turned to kiss him and then tottered off in the direction of her sister. He watched her go, fearful; not for Alice, but for himself. She might try to talk Leanne round, tell her what a bad person he was. It was possible that he had just spent his last moment with the love of his life. He searched her out in the crowd but couldn't see her. For a second he wondered if she'd run away rather than divulge her shameful secret, but no; there she was, striding through the empty beer cans and the unconscious teens to where her younger sister stood. He could just make out Alice's face as she saw Leanne approach, a mixture of surprise and fear: *Don't tell Mammy.* The last thing Leanne would do was tell Mammy.

It was out of his hands now. Sitting here trying to lip-read or decipher body language would do him no good. Keeping a close eye on them, he walked over to Murt and joined him in silent contemplation. Murt grunted a greeting, wordlessly offering him a can. Seán popped it open, continuing to watch the Tiernan girls from the corner of his eye. As far as he could tell, things appeared to be going well so far. Alice chatted away enthusiastically to her older sister, probably about her exams and how easy they'd been. They'd moved away from Alice's friends to a quieter spot, somewhere more suitable for breaking earth-shattering news, but he could still see them. Alice now saw him too. Their eyes met, hers harsh and unblinking, his passive and slightly pitying. Leanne had her back to Seán, but he could tell from the movements of her shoulders, of her arms, that she was attempting to impart sensitive information. Alice didn't seem interested. Her gaze was fixed on Seán, the slow steady stare of a woman scorned. He hastily looked away, feeling that the less he antagonised her, the better at this stage.

"Having fun, Murt?" he asked.

"Yeah," Murt sneered. "A right laugh."

From his exalted position on top of the pecking order, Seán felt a smidgen of sympathy for his erstwhile best friend. It couldn't be much fun sitting here on your own while, all around you, bodies writhed and contorted in unison. Had he even tried to get off with someone? There were plenty of girls he could easily have bagged. But no, he'd just sat here drinking like a miserable shit until everyone was either spoken for, out cold or gone home. That was his problem, though, not Seán's. He wasn't going to be dragged down with him. As soon as Leanne had sorted things out with her little sister, he'd leave him to his soul-searching. They sat in silence, Seán staring straight ahead and Murt looking down at the ground, further apart than ever before.

"Have fun with yer wan, then?" Murt asked sourly.

"Yeah, man, a great time."

"Well for some."

Seán was hardly listening to him now, though; there'd been some movement where the Tiernan sisters had been conversing. He'd been afraid to stare but now, unable to resist, he stole a quick glance. They sat cross-legged in the grass, chatting and laughing away like, well like sisters really. It was all settled. Everyone was happy. There'd be more blow-jobs and who knew what else for Seán. He tried to catch Leanne's eye, waiting for a sign, but a curt shake of her head told him that, although the two sisters were now on excellent terms, it wasn't quite time for a group hug. Warning heeded, he left Murt to his misery and went to check on the rest of his friends. Ginty was still asleep, curled up in Roisín's arms with a happy smile on his face.

"Aw, look at the happy couple."

"Oh, hiya, Seán," she replied, cradling Ginty in her arms.

"A few too many shandies, eh?"

"Yeah."

"Well, you look after him, Roisín, ya hear me?"

"Oh, I will, Seán; don't you worry about that."

And she would, too. Poor Ginty. He left them to it and went to see if he could locate Pegs, but he was nowhere to be found. The last reported sighting placed him at the edge of the woods, trying to coerce his new friend into the darkness. Seán was sure he'd succeeded; Pegs could be very persuasive when he needed to be. He'd almost certainly offer a blow-by-blow account of his exploits the following day and expect the same in turn from Seán. This time, even little Ginty might have a story to tell. All things considered, it had been a fine night indeed for the lads – with the exception of Murt, who continued to sit by the fire scowling at anyone who crossed his path.

Seán continued to wander, occasionally stopping for a chat or a drink but never taking his eyes off the two sisters in the shadows. As ridiculous as it sounded, he missed her. She'd only been gone an hour, but he couldn't wait for her to come back just so he could be around her once more, holding her and feeling her body pressed against his. Without her he felt incomplete, as miserable and alone as Murt sitting by the fire. He would have to remain patient, though. This was the final obstacle they had to overcome, and once it had been cleared they were free to do whatever they liked for the rest of the summer and beyond. The thought comforted him. He sat down with a couple of his classmates and joined in a sing-song. He didn't like the song, some awful cheese-fest from an American punk band, but it felt good to sing. One of the boys had a guitar, and someone else had fashioned a set of drums from some empty boxes. Seán was content to be a backing singer, mumbling along during the verses and then blasting out the chorus with everyone else. They were good people, his classmates; he didn't get along with all of them but he didn't hate any of them. He was lucky really, to be here with them having a sing-song, everyone drunk and stoned. Really, his life wasn't that bad. He was happy living with his grandparents, and went to bed every night feeling safe, secure and loved. That sick, nervous feeling in his stomach had disappeared as soon as he'd moved out of home. With life on an even keel, who knew what was possible? Maybe he'd try harder in school, even get into college, the first in his family to achieve the feat. Why not? There was nothing stopping him. The kid playing the guitar switched chords. Seán recognised this one; he loved that band as a kid. He put an arm around Joey Costello and sang as if his life depended on it.

"There you are!"

It was Leanne. She stood over him, smiling expectantly. As much as he'd enjoyed polluting the air with his caterwauling he knew where his priorities lay.

"Well, how did it go?"

She shrugged her shoulders. "Okay, I suppose."

"You're still alive, anyway."

"I am, but it'll take a lot of fixing."

"Well, I'm willing to make peace with her if she is with me."

"Oh, that's not going to happen; there's no chance of her ever forgiving *you*."

"Oh well," sighed Seán, "we'll just have to find someone else to be bridesmaid."

"Ha ha, very sure of yourself, aren't you?" she said, digging him in the ribs.

He poked her back but then stopped, unsure of how to proceed. "Can we act like a couple while she's here?"

"Of course," she said, leaning in to kiss him then thinking better of it. "But let's not flaunt it, eh?"

They found a place at the edge of the campfire on the opposite side to Alice, and made themselves as comfortable as circumstances permitted. It wasn't easy, though; every time he looked at her he wanted to kiss her, touch her. They settled for holding hands, their fingers interlaced in the grass as they kept their distance. He couldn't relax. Maybe she'd find someone herself, and disappear into the woods with them; that would be a favourable outcome for all parties. He furtively searched the crowd for her, his hopes rising the longer it took. There she was, still very much here, and still very much in their line of sight. She looked as if she were enjoying herself, though. He could barely keep track of her movements. One minute she was encircled by 'Fat' Eddie Donovan and his mates, shrieking with laughter, scolding their brazenness. The next she was lying down in the grass with Terry O'Toole, playing with her hair and listening attentively as he regaled her with stories about whatever insufferable Japanese anime he was currently obsessed with. She was revelling in the attention, even if it was only from those drunk, unwanted souls who had reached this ungodly hour without getting the shift. It was a new experience for her, being fancied by boys. Living in the long shadow cast by her older sister had led her to believe that she was unattractive, undesirable, and Seán hadn't done much to debunk this theory. He was happy for her, though. She could hate him all she wanted, he still wished her well and it cheered his heart to see her coolly work her way through his classmates, leading them on and then denying them their goal at the last. Wherever had she learned that?

He sought her out once more. By now she'd reached the end of the line: Skid Row, aka Michael 'Murt' Walsh. This would not end well. He watched her hunker down and strike up a conversation with his brooding friend. Remarkably, they appeared to hit it off. Within seconds she'd managed to raise a smile from the previously morose Murt, and he was now more animated than he had been all night. Seán watched on in wonder as polite introductions gave way to gentle flirting, then to rather saucy play-fighting with hands and legs everywhere, laughter and eye contact. And then the inevitable. They kissed. The whole business had taken less than three minutes. He had to hand it to Murt, he'd underestimated him; the cold and distant outsider thing had obviously been a ploy, a way to pique the interest of the few remaining young wans. *Who's that guy over there? He looks so dark and mysterious. Whatever could be going through his mind? I have to know.*

Now all four of them had pulled, which was a first; a momentous night. Murt and Alice, though? Wasn't that dangerous? In his happy, drunken haze Seán decided it could only be a positive thing. A happy, paired-off Alice would benefit his relationship with Leanne. She'd be too wrapped up in her own affairs to give them any grief. And with Murt. One of his friends. It was perfect, really; he could get Murt to tell her what a great guy he was, and in turn he'd tell Leanne that Murt was a fantastic match for her little sister. The two of them would charm the pants off the whole Tiernan family and before long they'd be over for dinner, sitting down with Mr. Tiernan and Gerard, watching the football while the women did the washing-up. It might even help repair his friendship with Murt; they'd have something in common now, a Tiernan woman on their respective arms.

As he pondered this idyllic future, imagining double weddings and holidays together in the Caribbean, his hopes and dreams were dashed. Murt, having decided he wanted more than just a kiss, had begun what could only be described as a sexual assault on Alice. *How many pairs of hands does he have?* thought Seán as he looked on in horror. One hand disappeared up her top and was shoved away, only to reappear at her arse, grabbing and mauling, before again being rebuffed. And his other hand, his free one, diligently worked away at the button of her jeans, completely oblivious to the slaps it was receiving from their demure occupant. Eventually Alice, fed up of being manhandled, held up her hands in warning and delivered a stern lecture to the over-eager Murt. Point taken, they returned to kissing; within seconds, though, Murt had resumed his onslaught. He pawed, groped and did everything in his power to compromise her integrity. She shoved him away and stood up to leave. However, Murt had clearly left his chivalrous hat at home and wasn't ready to give up just yet. He rose to face her and an argument ensued. Seán couldn't hear what they were saying, but he tensed as they became more and more heated, hoping and praying that the matter could be ended amicably and he wouldn't have to step in.

"Let it go, Murt, for fuck's sake let it go," he muttered under his breath. What had started out as a minor incident was beginning to escalate into an episode. It was only a matter of time before it became a scene. Mercifully, no one besides Seán had noticed what was happening. If he got there in time, the whole thing could be sorted out with a minimum of fuss. He moved quickly, leaving Leanne dozing by the fire and making a beeline for the quarrelling duo. They were shouting at one another now, gesticulating and accusing. Alice's face was contorted with indignation but Murt shrugged his shoulders, as if above reproach. It was only then that Seán realised what was happening. He began to sprint toward them, praying he wasn't too late. He ran harder than he'd ever run, hurdling bodies, knocking over bottles of booze. As he approached them he saw that his efforts had been in vain. He was too late. Alice's anger was no longer directed at Murt; her gaze was now fixed upon him, Seán McLoughlin, the boy who'd been making up stories about her.

30

HE SLOWED TO A JOG and then to a stop. Alice was coming towards him, fists balled up at her sides. There was no escape.

"What the FUCK have you been saying about me?"

He raised his hands in submission, ready to plead innocence; but he was wasting his time, she had heard it all. His defence, if he even had any, was paper-thin.

"What the fuck have you been saying, Seán? Tell me!"

"I... what?" Seán stammered, looking around for assistance, for inspiration.

"You know exactly what I'm talking about! Your friend Murt over there told me all about it," she said, jabbing her thumb towards Murt who had returned to his drink, oblivious to what he'd set in motion.

"Hey, Alice," said Leanne, strolling up to join them. "You two back chatting again? Aw, that's great."

Seán stared at her in horror. "I thought you were asleep!"

"I was, Seán, but I'm awake now," she replied. "So what are we chatting about?"

"We're chatting about *him* and what he's been saying about me," Alice hissed.

"Oh, Alice, we've been over this already," said Leanne, rolling her eyes. "It was just a misunderstanding, that's all."

"A *misunderstanding*? Is that what you'd call it?"

She was now breathless with rage; apoplectic.

"Yes," replied Leanne, offering her a placating smile. "Seán liked you, but not in the way you thought."

She delivered the line with the utmost condescension, like a parent trying to explain the intricacies of the adult world to a confused child.

"That didn't stop him spreading lies about me," Alice retorted.

"What lies, Alice?"

She hesitated, unable to repeat the words such were their awfulness.

"What lies, Alice?"

"He said ..."

Her voice faltered, and for a fleeting moment it appeared that she might tell them to forget about it, that it *was* all just a misunderstanding. Then she took a deep breath, composed herself and went on.

"He told his pals that he and I did stuff in the spare room, that I came on to him and let him feel me up and ..."

"And what, Alice? Tell me!"

She hesitated, unsure of how to phrase it, ashamed by the mere notion of it. "And he said that I wanked him off." Her voice dropped on the last words as she dipped her head in embarrassment.

Leanne studied her sister closely. "Are you sure, Alice?"

She nodded solemnly, tears welling in her eyes.

Seán had stood aside during this exchange, but he knew that very soon he would be returning to centre stage. He was fucked, and he had no one to blame but himself. The girl of his dreams turned to face him. She looked different now; gone was the winsome smile, the mischievous glint in her eyes. In their stead was something else; not quite hatred, more disgust, or maybe even pity.

"Seán?" she said grimly.

"It's not what you think. If you'd just let me explain ..."

Even now amid this unfolding tragedy he still thought she might forgive him, that they could salvage their relationship. He hadn't meant to hurt anyone, he'd just wanted to get his friends off his back. *Pegs? You know what he's like! I had to tell him something!* But they didn't know; all they knew was that he was a snivelling little creep who had spread shameful lies about an innocent girl. And, once he'd done that, he'd taken up with her sister, probably hoping to drive a wedge between them.

Leanne shook her head ruefully, unable to credit how stupid she'd been. Once more she'd picked the wrong guy, and this one had seemed so nice; a bit young, yes, but really sweet, kind and good-natured. As it turned out, he was none of those things; he was evil. He was scum and he was disgusting.

"Come on, pet," she said, putting a consoling arm around her sister.

"Leanne, please," begged Seán, in tears himself now.

She looked at him witheringly. "Go away, Seán, and leave us alone from now on, eh?"

He watched them go, the older sister escorting the younger, upset girl away from the scene of the crime. They didn't look back, just kept on going, away from the party; away from him. He sank to his knees, crying like a child, softly repeating her name over and over again. He had never known what true pain was like until this moment.

31

HE WAS WALKING DOWN A road, that was all he knew. The trees and the darkness had been replaced by neon lights and the occasional whoosh of a car. There was a bottle in his hand, its contents swilling around as he stumbled blindly forwards. He raised it to his lips and took a long swig, ignoring the burning in his throat which carried on into his stomach, causing him to retch. Then it settled, warming, soothing and strengthening him. He stopped. A moment of clarity. Where was he? He looked around, squinting like an old man trying to read without his glasses. There were fields and houses and then more fields, but nothing familiar. He sat by the roadside, plonking down heavily in some grass, and began to cry. Maybe if he cried loudly enough someone would come to rescue him; maybe she would come. He wailed and called out her name in a long, tortured lament, but he might as well have been the last person on earth. He was all alone; neither she nor anyone else was coming to save him. At least it was comfortable here in this grass, a fine place to die. He curled up in a ball, shivering but tired enough for it not to matter. Just a little rest and he'd be on his way. He closed his eyes and felt sleep's gentle embrace beckon him forth. All he had to do was to nestle into its arms and everything would be okay.

Then he remembered what he'd been doing: he'd been going to her. That was it; he'd been on his way and had somehow got side-tracked. What a silly thing to do. He rose to his feet, full of renewed hope, and came crashing back down to earth. Did that hurt? He couldn't tell; alcohol had cocooned him, made him impervious to pain. Good old alcohol. He sat in the middle of the road for a while. It was nice there; comfortable, for a road. Wasn't this absurd? Wasn't it all absurd: life, his circumstances, everything? He cackled loudly. Absurd. He got up again, but this time he was more careful and found solid ground. The bottle was still in the grass, so he picked it up and continued on his way. He had a purpose now, and to think he'd almost given up, accepted defeat and lain on the side of the road like a pauper. No, not he, not Seán McLoughlin; he was no quitter.

He went on, sticking to the verge, following the lights. He took another tumble, a bad one this time; there was blood. He was okay, though. Up he got, not forgetting the bottle, and moved forward once more. There was a wall by his side now. He used it for leverage, bouncing off it, scratching his cheek against its gritty surface. More cuts, no doubt, but a small price to pay. Pausing for breath, he noticed something familiar in the distance; a building. He'd been in there once, but he couldn't remember why. He was on the right track. Not far now. It was getting bright and there were more cars on the road, their back-draft whipping around his legs as they zipped by. He would have to be careful; it wouldn't do to drunkenly meander into the path of an oncoming truck, not when he was so close. He forced his eyes open, tried to channel his thoughts, but it wasn't easy. A couple of times he jolted awake in mid-stride to find himself in the middle of an empty motorway. Scolding himself, he returned to the hard shoulder and redoubled his efforts. He overcompensated, trying too hard to stay off the road; he veered inwards and tumbled into ditches, over walls and fences and down soft grassy inclines. With each landing, every fall, it felt as if he'd just flopped into bed. Rocks were as comfy as pillows, briars and branches like a warm inviting mattress. Seán refused to give in, hauling himself up each time and stolidly marching on. The bottle was gone. He didn't know what had happened to it. He missed it. The rest of the journey would have to be tackled alone. Finally, the hard shoulder turned into a path and the motorway into a normal, regular street. So close! He began to jog, excited now. A car beeped at him and he waved, not breaking his stride. *No time to stop and chat. Things to do, people to see.* He knew where he was now, could have run the rest of the way blindfolded. There was the hill, the hill to Ard Aulinn. One more push and it'd be over. She was up there. As soon as she saw him, her heart would melt. She'd bring him inside, tend to his wounds, bathe him and tuck him into bed; her bed, where he belonged. Her parents would come in to see him, awed by his bravery, by the lengths he'd gone to in order to reach her. *It must be love*, they'd say.

He reached the top, the morning sun coming to greet him as he crested the summit; it felt lovely and warm on his face. Now it was simply a matter of making sure he went to the right house. Green gate, brown door, red Volvo in the drive: the Tiernans. He opened the gate, wincing as it creaked, and crept round the side of the building. In the back garden, he paused and looked at the house. Her bedroom was upstairs on the left, she'd told him so. The curtains were drawn. Asleep? Not for long. He grabbed a handful of pebbles from the ground and gently lobbed one at her window. It fell short, landing back in front of him. Steadying himself he threw another, this time with more force, but it sailed over the roof of the house and into the front garden. *For fuck's sake!* He'd come all this way, and now he couldn't even throw a pebble a few feet in front of him. Taking a few steps back, he lined up his shot with as much precision as he could muster, and this time his aim was true. He had thrown it harder than he'd intended, but the outcome was more than satisfactory; it bounced off the window with a satisfying crack. He waited for the curtains to open and her head to appear, but nothing happened. Not to worry, he had his range now. A handful of carefully-aimed projectiles later, he finally saw the pink curtains twitch. It was her; she had answered his call.

Leanne looked down at the drunken, dishevelled young man in her garden. It was him; the boy she had, up until a few hours ago, harboured deep feelings for. The boy she had fancied, pursued and ensnared, and with whom she had intended to 'go all the way' before the summer's end. She opened the window with a jolt.

Seán looked up at her, gratitude in his eyes. "Leanne!"

"What do you want?" she asked him in a hushed tone.

"Leanne," he repeated, "can we talk?"

"We have nothing to talk about," she said, slamming the window shut.

He stared up at where she'd just been, confused and dismayed. There was no need to be like that. What was her problem? He picked up some more pebbles, larger ones this time, and threw them towards her window. They all found their target – maybe he'd take up darts after this. But she didn't reappear. He wanted to tell her he loved her; if he could do that, then she would finally understand. They'd laugh about it in years to come, and tell their grandchildren about the time Granddad threw stones at Nanny's window and told her he loved her. *Aw, Granddad, you big softie.* He bounced stone after stone against her window without any response. Still no Leanne. Was she fucking deaf? He glared up at her window, annoyed now, not noticing the curtains move in the bedroom opposite.

"Well, fuck ya so, girl," he said bitterly, as he picked up what could only be classed as a rock; the time for pebbles had passed. Cocking back his hand, he readied himself for the sound of breaking glass when the back door sprang open.

"Put that rock down, you little shit!" roared Pascal Tiernan.

Seán spun round in surprise, the rock dropping harmlessly to the ground. Mr. Tiernan, the very man. A quick chat with the father and all this would be resolved.

"Ah, Mr. Tiernan," he smiled. "I was hoping for a quick word with your daughter."

"You're to stay well away from my daughters, and I'll be having a word with your grandparents about you too."

Seán had no idea what his grandparents had to do with anything, but he played along; best to humour him given the circumstances.

"Okay, Mr. Tiernan, I won't be a second," he said, weaving past him towards the open back door.

"Where the hell do you think you're going?" Pascal Tiernan demanded, outraged.

"I'll only be a second, boy, relax," replied Seán blithely.

Seán felt the ground come towards him. He was on the grass; Mr. Tiernan had put him there, the fucker. As he lay flat on his back in the middle of the Tiernans' back garden, he looked at Leanne's window once more. They were both there, the two sisters, staring down at him. *The fuckin' bitches.* He scrambled to his feet and picked up the rock he'd had earlier. How dare they do this to him, make such a fool of him? He flung the rock at the kitchen window and it sailed right through, leaving a perfect, rock-shaped, hole in its wake. *How about that, Tiernans? Not so funny now, is it?* And he wasn't finished yet. By the time he was done, the Tiernan house would be draughtier than the local bus-shelter on a cold winter's night. He searched around for another rock, but before he could find a decent-sized one he felt arms going around his shoulders. Ah, a hug, that was more like it. But these weren't friendly arms, they were rough arms, hostile arms. He struggled to shake them off, becoming increasingly irate, flailing and windmilling defiantly. But these arms were stronger than his and once more he met the ground. Not again! Why couldn't they just leave him alone? They wouldn't be happy until they'd broken every bone in his body. He lay still for a moment, feigning surrender, and then shoved upwards with all his might. It worked, and he stood victoriously back on both feet. Mr. Tiernan was spread-eagled in the grass, his shrivelled manhood peeping out of his pyjama bottoms. This was Seán's chance. The back door was open and unguarded. He bolted towards it, but Mrs. Tiernan (who'd obviously been loitering in the kitchen) got there before him and slammed it in his face. He pounded on the door in frustration.

"Open up, ya bitch! Open up!"

He turned around just in time to see Pascal Tiernan hurtling in his direction. This time it really hurt, and when he hit the ground he had no desire to get up.

He stayed like that for some time, buried face-first in the grass with Mr. Tiernan on top of him. If he'd been able to speak, he would have told Mr. Tiernan that he'd learned his lesson and was ready to go home now. All he could manage were a series of muffled grunts, each of which saw him pinned harder to the ground, so he stayed quiet and waited for his ordeal to be over. He heard footsteps and voices, deep manly voices. This didn't sound good. There was a blue flashing light too. What was the significance of that? He knew it meant something, but it was hard to think straight with thirteen stone of Tiernan on his back. He wriggled around, trying to get a look at the light, and Mr. Tiernan released him, just like that. The blue lights were obviously a good thing, some sort of rescue team probably. He got to his knees, eager to thank his liberators. But then more arms came, and these ones were very unfriendly; they belonged to the owners of those deep voices. He felt cold, clinical metal on his wrists and wondered what kind of rescue team this was. He was lifted off his feet and carried down the drive. It was nice not to have to walk any more. He'd done enough walking for one night. The car was nice and cosy and he was more than happy to lie down on the back seat. Hopefully they were going somewhere nice. A nice, long drive; that would be great. The sooner he got away from all this madness, the better.

32

His throat was dry, so dry he could barely swallow. There was a glass of water nearby, he was sure he'd seen one, but in order to get to it he would have to wake up. He didn't want to wake up. He liked it where he was. If he could stay asleep, everything would be okay.

"How are you feeling this morning, young man?"

It was one of those deep, manly voices again. He didn't want to talk to its owner, so he sank deep into his dreams, away from the voice, away, away.

But the voice persisted.

"Wake up, you little shit. You've got some cleaning up to do."

He felt a foot on his arse, kicking him gently, almost playfully. Still he resisted, desperately hanging on, forcing himself back down to his dreams, away from manly voices and playful feet. But the foot returned, shaking him forcibly until he had no choice but to respond. He opened his eyes, back to reality, and the first thing he felt was pain.

"Ha, I'm not surprised you have a sore head, the state you were in."

Seán closed his eyes; the light intensified the agony. He curled into a ball, searching for sleep once more, but there was no escape.

"I want you out at the front desk pronto, sunshine. There's some paperwork to be done. But first ..." Seán heard the sound of sloshing water "... you have to clean up that puke."

The voice departed. Relief. He could go back to sleep now.

"GET UP!"

Another voice, a different one, but no less manly than the last. And then banging, the clank of metal upon metal. There was no more sleep to be had here. He rose gingerly from the bunk and looked around him. He was in a prison cell, a stark, dimly lit prison cell. There was puke on the floor, presumably his, and what looked like piss on the walls, owner unknown. Alcohol had been at work here. He'd been drinking and landed himself in a bit of mischief. Why had he been drinking, though? And what kind of mischief had he landed himself in? It hurt his head to think, but he had to try to unravel the mystery. They'd been in the woods, lots of them; Pegs, Murt, Ginty, the whole class. Exams, that was it. But there was more; it wasn't just the exams he was celebrating. Someone was coming, someone special: *her*. She was coming. The pain intensified, but this time it was different. It was more than a headache or an upset stomach. It came from deep within his soul and threatened to tear him apart.

She had come. Leanne had come. The most beautiful girl he'd ever seen, and she had come to see him and be with him. They had been together, finally, after all that waiting. He'd been so sure it would go wrong, but it hadn't. It had been amazing. They'd gone to the secret place, walked across the bridge, sat in the look-out and gazed up at the stars. It had been ro-mantic, just as he'd planned. It was love. He'd been in love. And then she'd done something amazing to him: his first ever blowjob. A momentous oc-casion, and what then? They'd returned to the party and danced by the fire. He'd held her close, not wanting to ever let her go. Then Alice, and Murt. He was running toward them, stopping, realising what was happening. He tried to push the memory away, but to no avail. It came roaring back vividly, mocking him. The shame, the sorrow and the guilt. He'd watched them go, his heart disappearing with her, and knew life would never be the same again. That was when the pain had started, but it was also where his recollection of the night ended.

How had he ended up in here? He clearly hadn't returned home to lick his wounds and ruminate on the strangeness of love. Maybe he'd been fighting, taking out his anguish on another drunken reveller? That sounded like something he might do. He remembered faces, angry, sneering faces, and then walking to what he thought was salvation. Had the guards picked him up on the side of the road, asleep? Roaring at traffic in the time-hon-oured fashion of a seasoned drunk? No, there was more. Something so terrible, so unspeakably bad that his brain was doing its best to prevent him recalling it. He looked at his hands, which were cut to shreds. His face hurt, too. He rose to his feet, head spinning and body aching. There was a mirror above the sink. He went over to it, resting his hands on the basin, head bowed. He knew he wasn't going to like what he saw, but he had to do it. He lifted his head. It was far worse than he'd imagined. Both eyes were heavily swollen with ugly, angry bruises, flaring purple and blue, ready to pop at any moment. His lips were caked in blood. Cuts and scrapes of various shapes and sizes adorned his cheeks and forehead. His left ear was swollen in the manner of a prop forward after a day of hard scrummaging, and his nose! Oh, Christ, his nose. Could you even describe it as a nose anymore? It pulsed and throbbed, blood oozing out of the nostrils, forming a crusty discharge on his upper lip. Fuck! He tried to cry but no tears would come.

No matter how bad this was, he knew the worst was yet to come. The guards hadn't picked him up on the side of the road; that was wishful thinking. He'd done something awful, and it involved Leanne. He searched his mind, afraid of what he might find, but there was nothing coherent there, just a mass of images, sounds and feelings – all of them bad. It didn't matter, though; they'd tell him what he'd done. That was what they did here.

A voice called out from the corridor. "Have you cleaned that up, young man?"

He tried to reply with something witty, something that would show them he wasn't afraid, but all he could manage was a pitiful croak. He picked up the mop and stared at the mess at the floor. This was something he could fix. He'd fucked up everything else beyond repair but this puke, which came from his body, could be cleaned up. He tackled it with as much gusto as he could manage until it was all gone, each movement sending a spasm of pain shuddering through his body. As he squeezed the mop and propped the bucket against the wall he noted, for the first time, that he was being held here against his will. The door of the cell was firmly shut, its iron vastness making escape impossible. There was a window high on the wall opposite, but it had bars in front of it. Sunlight poured in, forming a small rectangle in the middle of the floor, his only connection to the outside world. The fresh air and open skies that he'd always taken for granted were now out of reach. It was just him and this tiny room; he was a prisoner. Panic set in.

"Hey," he shouted, finding his voice. "I'm finished. Let me out!"

He went to the door and began pounding on it frantically, his bruised hands no longer a concern. "Hey! I'm finished. LET ME OUT!"

By now his hangover, deformed features and lost love were of secondary concern; his desire for freedom outweighed everything else. He had to get out of here.

A panel shot open in the middle of the door and a face appeared at the other side.

"What's up with ya, boy?"

Seán stepped back sheepishly, suddenly ashamed of the fuss he was making.

"I've cleaned that up, like you asked."

The guard peered in through the hole. "So you have."

"Can I come out now?"

The guard looked at him blankly, as if he'd never been asked such a question before. Seán knew exactly what he was doing, it was always the same with these types; they loved the power, lived for it. He probably wanted Seán to beg, get down on his knees and plead for mercy. Well, he'd be waiting a long time. Seán stared back at the guard, almost willing him to leave him there but secretly praying he wouldn't. Realising there was no more fun to be had, the guard paused a moment longer before unlocking the door and swinging it open. Seán casually stepped out into the hallway.

"You said something about paperwork?"

33

IT WAS HIS GRANDPARENTS THAT came, both of them. He didn't remember giving the Garda any contact details, but they probably knew who he was and that meant they knew who his grandmother was. Everyone knew who she was. At least it wasn't his mother and Daryl that came; that would have been much worse. His grandfather didn't even bother coming in, opting to stay in the car while his wife dealt with the nasty business inside. Seán was waiting outside the sergeant's office when he heard her voice. She was a few rooms away; they were separated by at least four layers of brick and mortar, but he could hear her. He couldn't make out what she was saying, but he could decipher the tone. It wasn't what he'd hoped for. There was no sense of outrage, no ill-advised threats; she sounded contrite and apologetic, like someone eager to atone for sins they might have committed. He knew then that he was alone. If his greatest backer, his one true ally, didn't have his back, then no one had. The voice came closer and suddenly she appeared, flanked by an officer with whom she was deep in conversation. He looked at her and their eyes met briefly before she looked away, but he'd seen enough to know that he was no longer her favourite grandson. She went to the front desk, signed a few forms and continued into the sergeant's office, leaving Seán to wait outside. After a couple of minutes, he was called in to join them.

"Sit down there, Seán," said the sergeant.

He did as he was told, taking the chair beside his grandmother, and waited for his penance to be passed down.

"Now, Seán," said the sergeant, "what have you got to say for yourself?"

Great, one of those open-ended questions designed to capture the victim in their own web of lies. Well, he wasn't going to fall for it. He would play it safe.

"Well, Sergeant, I'd been drinking and I had too much and ... things just got out of hand."

Patricia snorted in derision. Seán turned to look at her, scarcely able to believe how quickly she'd jumped ship, but she refused to meet his gaze and stared ahead impassively.

"You left quite a trail of destruction, so you did," said the sergeant. "Let's see: common assault, criminal damage, trespassing, breach of the peace, under-age drinking, abusing a police officer ..."

He trailed off, letting the words hang in the air. Seán could feel the sergeant's eyes boring into him, this was serious now. He'd thought it would be a rap across the knuckles and 'on your way, you little scamp'. With this list of offences, however, there was no telling the outcome. He could end up in one of those juvenile detention centres near Dublin. There were proper hard lads in those places; he wouldn't last a day.

"Luckily," the sergeant continued, "Mr. Tiernan has decided not to press charges. You will be expected to pay for the window you broke, of course."

Mr. Tiernan? A broken window? Jesus, it was worse than he'd thought. There were no charges being pressed, though, the sergeant had just said so. There was a chance yet that he'd end the day a free man.

"The damage to his daughter's reputation isn't going to be so easily fixed, unfortunately."

Ah yes, his greatest crime of all: slander. Assault and criminal damage they were used to, just young lads acting the maggot; but a fella spreading lies about a poor innocent young wan? He was the lowest of the low, the kind of person they put in a separate wing alongside the nonces and the rapists.

"Listen, Seán," the sergeant said, revealing an unexpected compassionate side. "I know what it's like being a teenager. It's not that long since I was chasing girls, breaking hearts and getting into fights with fathers."

Seán looked at him doubtfully.

"But one thing I never did was spread lies about a girl, and especially not one as nice and innocent as Alice Tiernan."

That was his cue. He needed to show them both how deeply sorry he was.

"It was a horrible thing to do, and I regret it immensely."

"Yes, you do, I can see that."

"If Mr. Tiernan would permit it I would like to formally apologise to Alice, and Leanne too if possible."

Anything to see her.

"Oh, no, Seán, that won't be happening," the sergeant chuckled. "Mrs. McLoughlin, over to you."

Patricia cleared her throat and glanced briefly at Seán before she spoke.

"You can't live with us any longer, Seán. I've spoken to the Tiernans, and we all agree that it would be best for everyone if you returned to your mother's. And I don't want you in and around our avenue either, at least not until Leanne has gone to college. What those girls have been through ..."

Seán sat in stunned silence; she was washing her hands of him, just like that. It was her manner that hurt the most, cold and clinical. He had become a problem that had to be dealt with, and her way of dealing with that problem was to send him back like a broken toy; send him back to the place he hated more than any other, back to live with Daryl.

34

HE LAY ON HIS OLD bed in his old room in his mother's house. The tightness in his chest was back, the anxiety too, and now they were accompanied by a deep mourning, a sense of loss. Not only was he right back where he had started, but now he had to live with the thought of what might have been. If he hadn't told that stupid story about Alice, who was nice and innocent and didn't deserve any of this, he wouldn't be here now. He'd been weak and stupid and had got precisely what he'd deserved. Of course, the irony was that he had ended up with the older, hotter sister and had got far more than an imaginary hand-job, but nobody cared about that now. The whole affair was shrouded in shame. He couldn't even revel in the glory of having a seventeen-year-old girlfriend, not that he would have revelled. It wasn't like that, Leanne wasn't some slut he'd coerced into sex, she was his first love. And now she hated him, detested him, probably regretted going anywhere near him. He wasn't the nice boy she'd imagined; he was a sick pervert who went around telling lies about innocent young girls. He was disgusting and the thought of his cock in her mouth made her sick. Sick.

When he awoke, it was dark. He was still in yesterday's clothes, but someone had put the covers over him and taken off his shoes. Light filtered in from the hallway; someone was still up. He was thirsty and he hadn't eaten all day. Was it safe to go to the kitchen? Had Daryl gone to bed? He went out into the hall. The living-room door was shut, but he could see the light of the television filtering through the transom window. The kitchen door was shut too but there was a light on inside. His mother must be in there. She often went to the kitchen at night to read a book and smoke a fag. Once he had got up for a drink of water at half four in the morning and there she'd been, engrossed in a crime novel, chugging away on her cigarettes. He edged the door open and tentatively peered into the room. She was there at the table, smoking a fag, but there wasn't a book in sight.

"Hi, Mam."

She looked at him sadly. There was no anger there, just deep sadness, and it killed him. He didn't mind if she got mad, he deserved it, but he never wanted to disappoint her. Now, not only had he disappointed her, he'd failed her too.

"Are you hungry?" she asked.

He recognised her tone; it was the same one his grandmother had used at the station.

He couldn't handle any more of this coldness. *Get angry. Scream at me. Do something, for fuck's sake.*

"Say something, Mam, please."

Sinéad rose from her chair, propped her cigarette in the ashtray and went to her son, her broken little boy. The force of his embrace surprised her; he hadn't hugged her like that since he was a child. Now he held on for dear life, relief pouring over him. Finally, there was someone who didn't hate him. It had felt like the whole world was against him, but now here was his mother accepting him, not judging his actions. When the tears came, he didn't fight them. He let it all out, sobs racking his body as he buried himself deeper into her arms. Her new sweater would be ruined, the blood from his, still tender, wounds seeping deep into its fabric. She'd get the stains out, though; she was great at stuff like that. Eventually his crying faltered, the sobs died down, but he didn't want to let go. Because he knew that once he prised himself free he would have to return to life in this house, this place which housed so much fear and anxiety. As soon as this hug was over and his mother had made him something to eat, he would go to bed, and as soon as he woke up in the morning, battle would resume. Daryl would have been told everything and he'd be champing at the bit. Restrictions would be put in place: curfews, household tasks, the banning of friends – anything which might help make his life a misery. Then, when it was just the two of them, the abuse would resume in earnest. It would probably start off slowly, a few comments here and there: *sleazeball*, *sicko*, that kind of thing. Then he'd ratchet it up a level, goad Seán until he got a response. That would be his aim, and Seán wouldn't be able to resist. He'd fight his corner and Daryl would get his argument, what he'd been waiting for. Then he could let loose and get it all out, all those insults and put-downs he'd been saving up. He could sermonise, lecture and admonish to his heart's content, and Seán would just have to sit there and take it because it was Daryl's house and Daryl's rules. He was just a lodger, and a perverted, creepy one at that.

Jonathan

1

JONATHAN AWOKE WITH A RAGING thirst. He tried to ignore it, to roll over and go back to sleep, but it was no use; he was parched. These summer nights were far too hot for his liking. He got up and tiptoed out into the hall, cursing himself for not bringing a glass of water to bed. It would have been much easier to drink from the tap in the bathroom, but his mother always said that the water that came out of there wasn't hygienic, so he carried on downstairs. The clock on the hall table glowed brightly: 3.36. He hoped he'd get back to sleep; tomorrow was a big day. He'd made it to the County finals, and a top two finish would see him qualify for the regionals. In the kitchen, he went to the sink without even bothering to turn on the light and took a glass from the draining board. He filled it to the brim and gulped down the water in one go. He filled it again, drank it off and placed it in the sink. He felt much better. Those poor saps had no idea what they were in for; he was the next Seb Coe.

"Everything all right, son?"

The voice startled him. He spun round to locate its owner and for the first time saw the figure hunched at the kitchen table.

"Dad, is that you?"

"Yes, son."

"Christ, Dad, you frightened the living daylights out of me. What are you doing, sitting there in the dark?"

He went to turn on the light but his father stopped him.

"Don't, Jonathan, you'll disturb the others."

Jonathan stood there, puzzled. As his eyes adjusted to the darkness, he saw why his father was sitting here on his own in the middle of the night. He had a little plastic tumbler in front of him, and beside it a bottle of dark liquid.

"Everything all right, Dad?" he asked, knowing that everything couldn't possibly be all right.

"Yes, son, don't you worry. Go back to bed now, you've a big day ahead of you tomorrow."

"Are you going to bed too, Dad?"

"Yes, I'm going up after this," he said, shaking the contents of the tumbler.

Jonathan hesitated. It was clear that something was up, but what he was supposed to do? He had a big day ahead of him tomorrow, his dad had said so, and he needed his rest.

"Okay, Dad," he said. "See you in the morning."

"Yes, Jonathan," replied Malcolm, knocking back his drink and reaching for the bottle once more.

*

"Are you nervous, Jonathan?"

"A little bit, Mum."

"Well, make sure you eat all that, now. You're going to need your energy."

"I know, Mum."

Since becoming serious about athletics he had been forced to adhere to a strict diet, and his mother had been on board from the start. If he needed a carb-heavy breakfast full of proteins and iron, then that was precisely what he got. A light lunch, designed to tide him over until after his training, likewise. He appreciated the effort she made, but although he'd woken to find another immaculately prepared meal waiting at the breakfast table, he didn't feel like eating. He was feeling tense about the race, but something else gnawed away at him. What he'd seen last night. At the time his main concern had been getting back to bed, but now with a clear head he was worried about his father's well-being. Maybe he'd just been down the pub and fancied a quick nightcap before bed? That was probably it. It wasn't so much the drinking that concerned him as his demeanour. His dad was a warm, loving man, always smiling, always happy; a great dad. The man at the kitchen table last night had been a cold, distant figure. It had looked like his father and sounded like him, but it wasn't the father that Jonathan knew.

His father never displayed weakness; he wasn't a man prone to emotion. He went to work every day with a smile on his face and came back hours later, as if he'd just been down to the shops for the newspaper. On a Friday evening he might relax by the telly with a glass of whiskey but, as far as Jonathan knew, that was the extent of his vices. His life revolved around his job and his family. If he wasn't working, he was with them. If Jonathan or Sophie needed to be somewhere, then he drove them; if they needed to be collected afterwards he would be there again, waiting outside at the assigned hour. Jonathan knew he was lucky. He might have been adopted, but it was unlikely that any biological father could have bestowed as much love on him as his dad did.

His parent's marriage was good, wasn't it? He could hardly recall an argument. Perhaps they were having issues and had been keeping it from Sophie and himself? He watched his mother as she cleared away the plates, humming as she worked. She looked the same as always, a woman content with her lot in life, determined to help her son on his big day. He instinctively knew that whatever was troubling his father was as yet unknown to his mother.

"That was great, Mum," he said, pecking her on the cheek and going upstairs to gather his gear.

They got to the track in plenty of time. Because it was the summer holidays, the sports complex was milling with kids and flustered, out-of-breath parents as they dropped them off, collected and corralled them.

"It's just up here, Mum."

"Okay, Jonathan," she said, coming to a halt in the designated area.

He undid his seatbelt and fished his ID card from the glove compartment. "You know where to go from here, Mum, don't you?"

"Yes, Jonathan. Be sure and look out for me before it starts."

"I will, Mum."

He was disappointed his dad couldn't make it but understood that he was busy. Sophie had half-heartedly offered to come, but he knew she had no real interest so he'd politely declined and let her off the hook. If he could finish in the top two and qualify for the regionals, he would expect them all to be there, but today it was just his mother and that was good enough.

He accepted her hug and the numerous kisses that accompanied it before fetching his bag from the boot. Waving a final goodbye he headed for the check-in zone, where his coach and team-mates would already be assembling.

2

He waved to her just as he'd said he would, and cringed when she stood up from her seat and called his name. There wasn't time to be embarrassed by an overly-enthusiastic parent, though; he had to focus. He had to go to that faraway place where the only things that mattered were the track beneath his feet and the steady cadence of his legs as they pulled him further and further away from the rest of the field. He knew that if his mind was right and his body was right, none of the other runners could compete with him. His biggest enemy, the main obstacle to his success, was himself.

He heard his name being called out over the public address system and took his place in lane five. Not long now. They were called to their marks. He bent down, waiting for the gun. It always seemed to take an age, as if they were teasing him; he felt like standing up and telling them to get a move on, but that wouldn't help anyone. *BANG!* He was off. All the tension, all the nerves immediately left his body. No more thinking was required, now he could finally race. His coach had told him to forget about his competitors and focus on his own race; everything else would take care of itself. That was what he did. He positioned himself in the middle of the pack, right by the kerb, maintaining a steady pace, concentrating on not getting bumped and jostled by the other athletes. The 800 metres was a dirty business, and even at this age level the runners weren't above unscrupulous tactics.

It was a fast pace, so fast that the field was already being stretched out. By the 300-metre mark, a couple of runners had been dropped. Those at the front had gained a lead of twenty metres on Jonathan, but he wasn't concerned. *Just stick to your pace and you'll be fine. Don't get drawn into a dogfight.* His coach's words echoed in his head; to disobey them now would be folly. He waited until the end of the first lap, when the bell rang to signify the last lap, before upping his tempo. Gradually moving through the gears, he moved from fifth place to fourth and then to third as he cruised down the back straight. This was where he excelled; this was his zone. When they hit the 600-metre mark he would crank it up a little more; draw alongside the leaders, perhaps pause for a little chat and then kick for home, leaving them in his wake.

He bypassed the runner in second place with nary a second's thought, which just left the leader, an old foe of his: Paul Whitworth, tall and fair-haired with incredibly pointy elbows. They'd competed against one another on three previous occasions. The first time Whitworth had pipped him on the line after Jonathan eased off in the home straight. The defeat had crushed him; he wasn't used to losing, and his coach had flogged him in training for weeks afterwards. It did the trick, though, because the next time they faced off Jonathan had beaten his adversary comfortably. In their most recent encounter it had been a little tighter; Whitworth had stayed with him all the way around the final lap, and as they came down the home straight they were neck and neck. Then Jonathan found something extra, summoned fresh energy from within and gained the advantage. He'd been pushed harder than ever before; his reward was a new personal best.

Personal bests were the last thing on his mind right now; he just wanted first place. It didn't matter that the top two went through to the regionals; winning was everything, anything else was failure. As on their previous encounter, Whitworth matched him stride for stride as they entered the home straight, but Jonathan had left plenty in the tank and still had another few gears to go to. He sneaked a glance at his rival; Whitworth was blow-ing out of his arse. This was in the bag. All that extra training was about to bear fruit; all those evenings working on his speed endurance with his coach, Ernie, bawling at him from the edge of the track were about to pay off. He lengthened his stride, opening up fully, and powered ahead, now in full-flight. He poured it on, leaving nothing to chance. He dared not look back but knew he was clear. Whitworth was receding into the distance, a tiny speck on the horizon. The finishing line loomed large, but rather than stumble towards it as he'd done in previous races he sailed through, savouring the moment, relishing the victory. He crossed unopposed with Paul Whitworth at least fifty metres behind. He had not only won, he had decimated the field. He looked for his mother. It wasn't difficult to find her; she was the deranged lunatic in an otherwise sane crowd. Jonathan raised a victorious fist in her direction. He couldn't wait to see her and be lavished with praise. But even more than that, he couldn't wait to see his dad.

Once the formalities had been completed and he'd received another trophy to add to his collection, Jonathan went to the mix zone where he knew his mother would be waiting. As soon as she saw him Margaret came running through the throng, easing children out of the way as she rushed to her little hero. The force of her hug almost bowled him over. He still had the trophy in his hands, and it jabbed into his ribs as she smothered him with kisses.

"I'm so proud of you, love."

Jonathan offered a sheepish grin to a couple of teammates who had come over for a look at the cup.

"Ta, Mum," he said, as she finally let go and looked at the trophy for the first time.

"Oh, my God, it's huge," she said, grabbing it from him and reading the engraving aloud.

"First place, North-west Under-Fifteen's 800 metres," she called out, ensuring that everyone in the vicinity was fully aware that her son had won his race.

Jonathan's teammates walked away with knowing smiles, by now familiar with his mother.

"Did you phone dad?" Jonathan asked.

"I tried, Jonathan, but his secretary said he'd been out of the office all day. We'll try again when we get home, shall we?"

"Sure, Mum," he said, disappointed. He'd hoped his father would be nervously waiting by the phone for news of his son's endeavours, but that didn't appear to be the case.

They walked back to the car, Jonathan's bag slung awkwardly over his mother's shoulders so that he could carry the trophy unhindered, and set off on the short journey home. As soon as they got in Jonathan went straight to the phone and dialled the direct line to his father's office, which he'd been told to use only for emergencies. It rang out. He called the standard number and got through to his father's secretary.

"Oh, hello, Jonathan. How are you?"

"Fine, Mrs. Walker. Is my dad about?"

"He left about twenty minutes ago, said he was taking a half-day. Didn't you know?"

"No, I didn't. Thanks, Mrs. Walker."

"Okay, Jonathan."

He hung up the phone. A half-day. If he could take a half-day, just like that, then surely he could have made time to see his son's race? There had to be a logical explanation, his dad was always there for him. Chances were he'd received word of his son's exploits and was now rushing home to congratulate him. Any second now he'd burst in the door, probably with a cake, and they'd dance around the living-room in a celebratory jig. Yeah, that was it.

But he didn't arrive. There was no cake, no jig. Jonathan sat in the living-room, staring out the window, waiting for the car to appear, but he gave up after an hour. As much as it hurt him he had to accept that his father simply didn't care about his race, or that he had obliterated one of the strongest fields he had ever raced against. For reasons known only to himself, he had been too busy to bother with his son's big day.

"I'm making your favourite tea," his mother said, as he went into the kitchen to mope around there for a while.

"But Coach Tur-"

"I've rung your coach, and he said you can have whatever you want after a performance like that."

Jonathan smiled; good old Mum, she thought of everything. Lasagne and chips it was, then, but it wasn't the same without some ice-cold Coke to wash it down. He checked the fridge; nothing. Sophie, the little guzzler, had drank the lot.

"We haven't any Coke, Mum."

Margaret pulled out a fiver from her purse and pressed it into his hand before returning to the oven.

"Get some nice ice cream, too," she called as he closed the front door behind him.

3

"ANOTHER ONE THERE, MATE," SAID the man in the expensive suit, raising his empty glass.

The barman studied him closely. There were only two other people in the pub, both regulars. This bloke was new.

"No problem, pal," he said, taking the glass and refilling it with a measure of vodka. "You from the area?"

"Aye," said the man in the suit.

"Whereabouts?"

"Not far from here."

He didn't seem the conversational type, so the barman let him be. As long as he paid for his drinks and didn't cause any trouble, he could sit there in silence for as long as he liked.

Malcolm knocked back the drink in one go. He didn't even like vodka, but it left less smell on his breath. It would soon be time to go home, and he didn't want to walk in the front door reeking of booze. The thought of returning there made him feel sick – no mean feat considering the amount of alcohol he'd consumed without once feeling even remotely nauseous. How could he face them? They hadn't a clue. As far as they were concerned, everything was fine; Daddy was at work, earning the money on which they would all live from here to eternity. They had no idea what was going on or what he had done. They didn't realise that he was a fraud – worse, a pervert; a dirty old man who couldn't control his urges. He couldn't tell them what he'd done. But he couldn't live with the guilt either. So here he was drinking his cares away, drowning in a sea of alcohol; the coward's way out.

Life had been so good. Two beautiful kids, a wife he wanted to grow old with and a well-paid job that he loved. The small business he'd started with his best friend almost ten years ago was continuing to grow. They now employed more than fifty people, and Malcolm was in charge of them all. He let Dennis take care of the business side of things; Malcolm had always been more of a 'people person'. They each knew their role: Dennis was the executive, spending his days in the office brokering deals with new clients, thinking up ways to move the company forward and lure new investors; Malcolm was the shop-steward, keeping the workers happy, dealing with office politics and monitoring productivity.

It worked perfectly. They were a great team. Malcolm enjoyed liaising with the staff. He demanded their respect, but also encouraged the kind of banter necessary to keep morale high in an office environment. When the time came to charm new partners, he was always on hand to show them round, present the business at its best and, if required, wine and dine them at a local restaurant. He called it 'HR mixed with PR'. Business wasn't quite booming, but it was certainly flourishing. Best of all, he actually enjoyed his work. Most of the time it didn't even feel like work.

He and Dennis often joked about how things would go if they swapped roles for a week or two. They both agreed it would go only one way: right down the pan. Malcolm did his utmost to ensure he spent the bare minimum of time behind his desk. He didn't even like staying in his own office for more than a few minutes at a time. No, he preferred to be on the move, where he was at his best. Dennis, for his part, would happily have remained ensconced in his quarters from the moment he arrived in the morning until his departure in the evening. He often admitted to Malcolm that the workers terrified him. He'd never imagined himself as a manager or a boss-man, and on the rare occasion that someone came to him with a query, he hastily passed them on to Malcolm. The women scared Dennis most because their office, like most offices, was a matriarchal society. Not that this bothered Malcolm; he knew how to deal with female staff. He was naturally flirtatious, and although he wasn't particularly attracted to any of the staff, he still enjoyed the back and forth between them. It enlivened his working day.

So, when he got a call from the employment centre, offering him the services of a young hopeful on two months' work experience, he was more than happy to add her to the team. She'd work for nothing, and it'd be good to have some young blood about the place. It might even put a few noses out of joint, which would be amusing. According to her CV she had some accountancy skills and although they already had three people in their accounts department, he agreed to add her to the team – he was generous like that. He made sure he was there to meet her at the main entrance on her first morning; their office could be a scary place for even the most hard-nosed newcomer. Her name was Katie Pendleton. She was twenty-four, slim, brunette and attractive. And, although he didn't like to admit it, she beguiled Malcolm right from the start.

4

HE GOT HER SETTLED IN, introduced her to her new colleagues and made sure she had enough work to keep her busy, promising to check in with her later that day. And he did. He checked in with her just before morning break, twice before lunch, three more times in the afternoon and again as they were finishing up, in case she needed someone to walk her out. The next morning he went to her desk before he'd even had his morning cuppa and they exchanged some harmless chit-chat, again just to help her settle in. They had lunch together on her third day. That was no big deal. Yes, he almost always had his lunch with Dennis at a separate table. But this girl was new, and he had to make sure she was okay.

By the end of her third week he was directing all accounting queries through her. By the start of her fourth he'd arranged a weekly meeting, just the two of them, so they could discuss privately any issues that might have arisen. She was the work experience girl, this was what you did; it would have reflected badly on them if he hadn't looked after her. Perhaps, with his help, she could get a full-time accountancy job when she'd finished with them. It was a noble gesture on his part and on behalf of the company. When the office gossips started to talk he told her to ignore them, they were jealous because she was doing such a great job. Anyway, he was married and she had a boyfriend; nothing was going to happen. They were just friends who liked spending time together, as all friends did. He was happily married, for Christ's sake. He hadn't always been married, though. In fact, in his younger days, he had been quite the lad; out on the town every Saturday night with his mates, chasing skirt, living the life of a single man, ending most nights with a kiss, a phone number and sometimes even more. Oh, he'd sowed his wild oats, all right, but everything had changed when he met that delicate young woman with the shy little smile which brought to mind a small child reluctantly accepting a fifty-pence piece from an elderly neighbour. She had a naive innocence about her, a sense of wonder rare among women her age. He was instantly attracted to her, and even more so when he glimpsed the no-nonsense attitude so at odds with the rest of her personality. *Yes, you can buy me a drink, but don't think it means anything.* He'd loved that, the way she'd sternly accepted the rum and coke and gestured to him to keep talking. This was a girl who believed in being courted, and he was just the man to do it.

By the end of the night, he found himself accompanying her home – only to her door, not a step further. They briefly kissed and she disappeared inside. That was that, as far as Malcolm was concerned. He had met the love of his life. She was the one for him. More dates followed, and a year later Margaret Moore became Margaret Philliskirk. They bought their first house and settled down for a life of wedded bliss. And now, twenty years later, he loved her more than he ever had. Not that he needed to remind himself of that; after all, he was only flirting.

*

As Katie's two-month stay drew to a close, Malcolm began to panic. They needed her; their accounts department was far too small. He told Dennis as much. Dennis, in his usual way, just waved submissively and told him to do whatever he thought best. So he did. He chose to ignore the young graduate who'd recently applied for a position within the company, who had a degree in accountancy from Manchester University and had so impressed at his interview the previous week. Katie would be offered a permanent position as a junior accountant. It was settled. He could hardly wait to tell her, but he'd wait until she was alone before doing so. No need to make a big scene. It would just be the two of them. He'd break the news and officially welcome her to Philliskirk & Barnes. She'd be thrilled; it wasn't easy finding work in the current climate.

One afternoon when most of the workers were away at lunch, he seized his opportunity.

"Hi, Katie," he said, sitting on the desk.

"Oh, hi, Malcolm," she smiled, all doe-eyed, like Bambi.

"Aren't you taking lunch today?"

"I had it at my desk," she said, indicating a half-eaten sandwich.

"Our Katie, such a hard worker," he teased.

She smiled demurely.

"I've got some good news," he said, hardly able to contain himself.

"Yes?"

"It's about your role here."

"Oh?"

"I've discussed it with Dennis, and we'd like to offer you a full-time position as a junior accountant."

The squeals of delight and words of gratitude were music to Malcolm's ears. She was happy, and he liked to see her happy. More than that, they needed her. A terrific acquisition, that's what she was.

5

ONE MORNING, A COUPLE OF months after Katie had been made permanent, Malcolm set out for work an hour earlier than usual. He'd told Margaret he had some important calls to make, vital stuff that needed to be sorted as soon as possible. It was only half the truth; he did have some calls to make, but they weren't that important. He was really going in early because he knew Katie would be there early too. Not that he'd admit this, even to himself. If she did happen to be there, and there was no guarantee she would be (even though she was always first in), then maybe they could go to the canteen, just the two of them. That'd be nice; they could catch up. They hardly ever spoke these days.

Making his way through the early-morning traffic, Malcolm hummed along to the music on the radio. He was in a good mood. There was nothing untoward in what he was doing. They were just friends who got on well; he was her mentor. Deep down, though, he knew why he was coming to work early. He couldn't ignore the butterflies in his stomach or the sordid fantasies he conjured up as he lay in bed at night. He wanted this girl, and despite his love for his wife he was willing to risk everything to have her. Those were the cold, hard facts. Even now, as he got closer and closer to the office, he could have prevented it. He could have stopped the car, gone into a café and waited until he was sure she wouldn't be alone. That would have been the sensible thing to do, the thing that a happily-married man would have done; but he didn't do it. Instead he turned up the radio, leaned on the accelerator and thought of topics they could discuss over coffee.

He drove into the car park at a little after eight. Sure enough, the blue Micra was there in its usual spot. She'd probably been here since cockcrow: so dedicated, so assiduous, they were really blessed to have her. He bounded up the stairs and into the main office space, looking over to the little cubbyhole which housed their accountancy team. It was empty, as was the entire office. He flicked on the lights and strolled around their little enterprise, poking his head inside each cubicle in case she was in there. But there was no-one here. Malcolm frowned in annoyance. Where could she be? He couldn't wait to tell her about what had happened on the way in, about the van driver flicking him the V-sign; she'd love that one. The canteen!

That had to be it. He hurried back down the stairs and into the canteen, which served their company as well as two others in the industrial park. Apart from a couple of sleepy factory workers and a lone member of the kitchen staff, it was deserted. Now he was really flummoxed and more than a little disappointed. The rest of the staff would be in soon, and then there would be no chance of a chat with her. He sloped back up the stairs and into the office again; her seat remained empty. He stood there, pondering her whereabouts. *She must be in the ladies' room.* The sensible thing would have been to wait; she wouldn't be gone long, and there'd still be plenty of time for a chat. He wasn't thinking sensibly, though.

Once more he left the office, but this time he went straight on until he reached the end of the corridor. The ladies' room was the first door on the right. He looked around to make sure no one was watching and then gently put his head to the door, but he couldn't hear anything. She had to be in there. He was vaguely aware that what he was doing was a gross invasion of privacy, but he pushed those thoughts away and continued to listen. And then he heard it, faintly at first, but growing more pronounced, a gentle mewling, coming from inside. It was Katie, and by the sound of things she was rather upset. He listened a moment longer, oblivious now to the danger of being caught outside the women's toilets with his head at the door. The sobbing was constant and plaintive. It broke his heart to think of poor Katie in there all alone, sad and in need of comfort. He tapped the door gently.

"Katie, is that you? Is everything okay?"

The crying stopped abruptly.

He remained still, listening intently. What if he'd frightened her and made things worse?

"Malcolm?" a voice said hesitantly.

"Yes, Katie, it's me. Are you all right?"

He heard footsteps as she walked towards the door and he rapidly pulled away from it. She appeared before him, a picture of vulnerability, all smeared make-up and tears.

"Oh, Katie, whatever's the matter?" he said, taking her by the arm.

She tried to speak but nothing came out, nothing decipherable at least. The tears resumed in earnest, accompanied by sobs and ragged, helpless breathing.

"You poor thing," he said, leading her back to the office. They went through the main doors and into Malcolm's private office. He closed the door behind them.

"Sit down, love," he instructed, steering her into a chair. "Will you have a cuppa?"

He picked up the pot of tea left by the catering staff.

"Two sugars, isn't it?"

She nodded glumly, a tissue pressed to her nose.

Tea poured, Malcolm pulled over a chair and sat beside his stricken colleague.

"Now, Katie," he said, pressing the cup of tea into her hands. "You just take your time, and when you're ready to speak, I'll listen. Okay?"

She nodded and took a small sip of the tea. Malcolm waited patiently, ready to assist in whatever way he could. When she'd finished, he took the mug and placed it on the desk.

"Do you think you're ready to talk about it now, dear?" he asked softly.

She nodded, but as soon as she opened her mouth the tears returned. She fell into Malcolm's arms, burying her head in his chest. He flinched, but this was his duty; he had to help his staff in whatever way he could. Then she began to wail loudly, like a police siren. The force and volume of her cries took him by surprise. Briefly he thought about bringing her downstairs and letting someone else deal with the problem, but then he composed himself.

"Hush, now," he urged, worried that someone would hear and interrupt them. "Hush, Katie."

She carried on bawling, hysterical now. He held her tightly, coddling her as if she were a child who'd fallen over and grazed her knee. After a spell, she calmed down and the crying subsided, replaced by the occasional sob and small, sad gasps of despair. Crisis averted, Malcolm began to savour the moment – he hadn't held anyone like this since he'd met his wife, twenty years ago. He put an arm around Katie's neck and another around her waist. He would protect her. She was safe now. They remained like this for several minutes, the tops of their bodies intertwined but each still in their own chair. It was a bit awkward. It'd be so much easier if she joined him on his chair, or if they at least stood up. What he really wanted to do was scoop her up in his arms and place her on his lap; of course he couldn't do that, it would be entirely inappropriate. However, if she wanted to join him on his chair, then he would allow her to. But they remained as they were. That was fine, too; he was enjoying it. This was enough. He looked down at the top of her head and sighed contentedly. This was nice.

The more he looked at her head, the more he wanted to stroke her hair; tell her everything was going to be all right, that he was here for her. He was a married man, though; he already had someone's hair to stroke, someone to be there for. Katie shifted her position slightly, quiet now. Was it time to disengage? Had he done his job? If anything, though, she'd moved closer to him. He could feel the swell of her breasts on his chest. It set his heart racing and his senses into overdrive. He breathed the scent of her perfume, felt her warm breath on his neck, the rise and fall of her body as the sobs died down. His body responded in the only way it knew how; an erection ripped against his trousers. And all the while this poor distressed girl sought refuge, solace, in his arms. But she was coming round now, the crying had subsided. Yet still she remained in his arms. What was going on here? The tumescence in his trousers told him one thing but his brain told him quite another; Malcolm chose to listen to his trousers. Her skirt had ridden up when she'd leaned towards him, revealing firm, supple thighs beneath a pair of tan-coloured tights. He looked down at her again. Her head was still buried in his chest, her bosom on his abdomen. *What is she thinking? I'm a married man.* He laid a hand on her knee and waited for a reaction. A second passed, maybe two; no complaint was made, so he moved his hand further up her leg. Still nothing. It was happening, it was about to happen. Desire consumed him. His hand went straight between her legs and up her skirt. He pulled her towards him, with force, because that what was she wanted. He felt resistance, but chose to ignore it; pulling harder, hurting her now.

She protested, her voice somewhere in the distance as he worked his way inside her underwear.

"MALCOLM!" she screeched.

He sprang away, ready to deny everything. "I wasn't – I didn't – " he stammered.

She looked at him, aghast, unable to comprehend what had just happened. Was this what it was all about, all those friendly chats, the glowing reference, the job offer? This nice man, her boss; he was just like all the rest.

"I can't fucking believe this!" she said, storming past him out of the office. Malcolm stood there, stunned, his erection rapidly diminishing. All he could think was: *That's the first time I've heard her swear.*

He collapsed into a chair, head spinning. What had he done? What would happen now? He slammed his fist down on the desk in frustration. What an idiot. He'd fucked it all up. Everything was ruined. He sat there in a daze, desperately trying to arrange his thoughts into something approaching a plan. But nothing would come. He started to panic. There was only thing for it. He locked the door, pulled down the blinds and opened the locker he liked to refer to as his drinks cabinet. There wasn't much in there, he didn't keep much alcohol on the premises given his previous transgressions. This was an emergency, however. He spied a bottle of spirits at the back of the cupboard and pulled it out for further inspection: ouzo, sent to him the previous year by a grateful Greek customer. It would do. His hand shook as he poured himself the first glass, but it wouldn't shake for long.

*

He'd have stayed in there all day if he could. He would have taken the phone off the hook, and informed the receptionist he was not to be disturbed under any circumstances. Polishing off the best part of a bottle of Mediterranean spirits had left him with a very full bladder, however, and by early afternoon he could ignore it no longer. He told himself he'd wait until everyone went for their lunch. As soon as the clock struck one they would all file out of the office, leaving him with a clear run to the toilet. He could sneak out, relieve himself and sneak back before anyone noticed. Sure enough, at one o'clock on the dot the mass exodus began. He listened as they streamed past his office, but there was no mention of his name. If they knew what had happened, they weren't talking about it. He'd already imagined how they'd react; the looks of disgust, the women all ganging up on him like a flock of hens. *That dirty bastard. Afraid to come out of his office. Fuckin' typical.* He waited another couple of minutes to be certain they'd all gone, then carefully unlocked the door and dashed to the lavatory. In his haste he didn't see the solitary figure in the cubbyhole in the corner of the room, but she saw him.

As Malcolm splashed urine against the wall, he went over things in his head. It wasn't that bad, just a simple misunderstanding. These things happened in office environments. Hadn't Barry from sales been caught having a fumble with one of the temps at last year's Christmas party? He himself was married, though, and he was the boss; he'd also taken advantage of a vulnerable young woman. That wasn't the same as a drunken tryst at a work do, not the same at all. He decided that he'd emerge from his office sometime after lunch and assess the mood among the staff. If there were little or no reaction to his resurfacing, then everything would probably be okay. She'd have decided to keep quiet. Their friendship was almost certainly over, and it would be awkward between them from now on; but when her contract was up in a year's time, they could let her go. She'd be glad to leave and he'd ensure she got a glowing reference. That would be the least he could do.

He zipped up, washed his hands and looked at himself in the mirror; he was fine, everything was going to be fine. He returned to the office feeling refreshed, almost invigorated. Striding through the door, he glanced cursorily towards the cubbyhole where the accountants worked; there wouldn't be anyone there now, it was lunchtime. Force of habit made him look, anyway. There was someone there, and she was staring right at him. Katie had stayed behind to work on an important account. She met his gaze without flinching; she'd been waiting for him to return. What he saw in her eyes made his blood run cold. It was a look of pure hatred, utter malevolence. Things were far from fine, that was clear. He rushed back to the sanctuary of his office, locking the door behind him. This time he didn't even bother refilling his glass but drank straight from the bottle.

6

A WEEK HAD PASSED, DURING which he'd spent less and less time in the office. He had gone to work the following morning determined to put the whole thing behind him; it was a simple misunderstanding, and if she complained about him that would be his response. But he found the tension unbearable. Every time he saw her talking to someone he wondered if she was telling them about the incident. It was agonising waiting for the guillotine to drop, for his dirty secret to be revealed. He did everything he could to avoid her, but that set the rumour mill into action. The gossips who had once speculated about the nature of their relationship now wondered why the two hardly ever spoke.

"Had a falling out, have yer?" asked one, nodding in Katie's direction.

"No, no, nothing like that. Just very busy at the moment, that's all."

But they weren't buying it; they knew something was up. This added to his anxiety. It was surely only a matter of time before someone figured out what had happened, that the lecherous old boss had made a pass at the naive young worker and been told where to go. *How pathetic. What must his wife think? Does she know? Someone should tell her.* Scenarios spun around his head, each more disastrous than the last: court cases, divorce papers, visitation rights, a broken man living in a hovel – all because he couldn't control his urges.

He spent two days hiding in his office until the weekend came around. It offered him a brief respite. Instead of using it as an opportunity to regroup, to figure out what to do next, however, Malcolm spent it in a drunken stupor. He told Margaret he was working, that they were trying to get a new client and he needed to be at the office all day. Instead he went to a bar; a dark, dingy little place which opened early and asked no questions. He sat there, steadily drinking, plunging further into despair. There was no way out of this. Monday loomed large. Katie would have mulled things over, confided in a friend; maybe even taken legal advice. His life was over; she would see to that.

Somehow he dragged himself in on Monday morning, fully expecting to see the police waiting for him outside the front entrance; but it was business as usual. Katie was in her usual spot, head bowed, industrious as ever. And the rest of the office was carrying on as normal. He went to his office, palpitating, desperate for a drink. The cabinet had been fully replenished by this point. He poured himself a large one and sat there, listening. Try as he might, he couldn't decipher the garbled chatter made by forty-odd people in a cramped environment. They might have been talking about him, but he had no way of knowing.

In the afternoon, he told Dennis he wasn't feeling well and left, driving straight to the pub. The following day he was outside that same pub at nine a.m., waiting for the doors to open. Wednesday was the same. He rang Dennis. *Must be a bug or something; I should be back in tomorrow.* But he wasn't back in tomorrow, or the next day. He stayed in his new drinking den which opened early and didn't ask questions. He didn't know its name; it probably didn't have one. And he stayed there all day, every day until today. At a quarter to five, after another hard day's graft, he downed his last drink, thanked the barman and left. He'd had enough; it was time to go home.

He opened the door and stepped outside, the brightness of the early evening sun momentarily blinding him. It wasn't safe out here, not for a guy like him. He got in his car. Was he okay to drive? It didn't matter. His thoughts turned to home and what he could expect when he got there. They'd be pleased to see him, they always were. He hadn't been home this early all week; usually arriving back at nine or ten o'clock and going straight to bed, citing tiredness and the need for an early night. He'd been avoiding them, of course, afraid they'd see the guilt on his face. He couldn't bear to look at them; those wonderful children, and his wife, who had done so much for him. They didn't need someone like him in their lives; a pitiful, pathetic drunk who preyed on the weak and then hid from his problems. He would sell his half of the business to Dennis and disappear, send them the money from the safety of a far-flung watering hole somewhere in eastern Europe. Margaret was still young and attractive, she'd find someone else, and the kids were getting to the age where they'd begin to grow curious about their biological parents. He'd done his job with them. They could move on; no harm done. He'd sit on his stool in a strange little bar in Moldova or Latvia, one of those ex-Soviet states, and he'd drink until he could drink no more, and eventually the pain would cease. Eventually it would all be over.

Eastern Europe would have to wait, however. Right now he was tired, dog-tired. He couldn't remember the last time he'd slept, or eaten for that matter. If he hurried, he could get home in time for tea; a nice family meal with his loved ones, the last supper. He pulled out of the car park and made for home. He was drunk and most certainly over the limit, but it wasn't far. And anyway he'd done this loads of times. If the police pulled him over, then so what? He had nothing more to lose. But he drove carefully, no one pulled him over and he made it home unscathed. He eased into the driveway, killed the engine and waited a moment. Any second now they'd be out to greet him: *Hi, honey, I'm home! Drunk? Don't be silly, a couple of pints after work, that's all.* He studied his features in the rear-view mirror: unshaven, bloodshot eyes, unkempt hair – not bad. The smell of his wife's cooking wafted out from the house. Food, a proper dinner; God, that sounded like the greatest thing on earth. He couldn't remember ever being so hungry. Malcolm stepped out of the car and walked up the drive. No one had come out to greet him. He turned his key in the door, expecting a torrent of abuse, certain that they'd found out. Peeking into the living-room, his worst fears were confirmed: Jonathan stared back at him with a face like thunder. Panic set in; they knew. Katie had called here and told Jonathan, and now they were going to blackmail him in return for their silence. Whatever it takes, he told himself, I'm willing to do it.

"Hi, Jon," he said hesitantly.

His son continued to glare at him. Had she really called here?

He made his way into the kitchen, genuinely fearful now. But he was greeted warmly by his wife, his beautiful, smiling, faithful wife.

"Malcolm! You should have said you'd be home early. I'd have put more chips on!"

She stood before him, studying him. This was the acid test.

"You look exhausted, love. Tough day at work?"

"Yeah, we're up the walls. I thought I'd get home early for a change."

She nodded fervently. "And rightly so. As soon as you've finished this it's upstairs for a bath, and then an early night. Okay?"

He nodded in agreement and took a chair at the table. "That's a good idea, Marge. I think I will."

"Before you do," she said, her voice dropping to a whisper, "I think you should apologise to that lad in there."

Malcolm had no idea what she was talking about, but he knew he was supposed to know so he played along as best as he could.

"I'll do it now," he said, leaving her to set the table.

"All right, mate?" he said hopefully, as he walked into the living-room.

Jonathan was thrown across the sofa, the remote control in his hand, absent-mindedly hopping from one channel to the next.

"Anything good on?"

No response. He looked at his son. Did he really know about Katie? He couldn't have. No one knew. It had to be something else. Had he done something stupid while he was drunk and completely forgotten about it? He didn't think so; he did his best to avoid the children when he'd been drinking. He looked around the room for inspiration, a sign from God, but everything seemed to be in place. He'd clearly fucked up, that was bad enough, but not remembering how he'd fucked up was far worse. His eyes rested on the glass display case which housed his son's ever expanding collection of medals and trophies, a source of so much pride for both mother and father. Something was off. He could list the contents of that cabinet in his sleep, had spent hours gazing in awe at all the awards. Through his drunken haze he scrutinised the various gold, silver and bronze cups, prizes and medals. Right there, in the middle of the centre shelf, was a newcomer. He squinted to see. It was for first place, and by the looks of things from an important race. Malcolm racked his brain. What was the date? Fuck. Never mind the date, what day was it? All concept of time had disappeared since he'd opened that bottle of ouzo. His world had stood still, but everyone else's had continued as normal. From somewhere in the dusty corners of his mind, it finally came to him: A big race, Jonathan's big day. But that had been ages ago, and he'd been there in the stands, cheering his boy on. Hadn't he? He was sure he had. He had been there, at the county finals. Jonathan had won and qualified for the regionals, which had been – today. His big day.

He cleared his throat. "Listen, Jon, I tried to make it today, but we've been up the walls recently."

"You didn't even ring to see how I'd got on."

"I know, I know. I meant to, but by the time I got the chance it was too late. Anyway, I thought it'd be better to have you tell me in the flesh."

Malcolm had only recently realised how creative a liar he was.

His son looked at him, measuring him up. Malcolm's mouth went dry. A double brandy would have gone down well right now.

"You should have been there, Dad."

Malcolm breathed deeply. He'd passed. This was easy.

"I know, son, I know. I'll make it up to you, I promise."

"How, Dad?"

He hadn't thought this far ahead. He hesitated, reached for his wallet; money was always a good option in such circumstances, but a quick glance at the boy told him that forgiveness couldn't be bought, not this time. He would have to draw on more of his newly-discovered creativity.

"You tell me, son."

"A couple of days away in a hotel, for the finals, just like we discussed."

The *finals*. Where did it all end?

"It's in August, so me and Sophie will both be off school. We could head down on the Friday morning, check into the hotel, see the sights, go shopping – whatever we want, really."

Which finals were these? What came after regional, national? The national finals; was his boy on the brink of becoming the best 800-metre runner in the country? He had no idea.

"Your tea's ready, boys!" Margaret shouted from the kitchen.

Malcolm got up, expecting his son to do the same, but Jonathan didn't budge. He stayed where he was, staring intently at his father like a guard dog waiting for the postman to come through the gate.

"Let's discuss it over tea, will we, son?"

*

By the time he'd filled his belly and crawled up to bed, Malcolm had agreed to it all. They'd be staying in a hotel called the 'Mercurial' which, he was reliably informed, was just a twenty-minute drive from the race venue. They'd travel down on the Friday and check in around noon, then the female contingent would head to Oxford Street for some shopping while father and son toured the museums in the centre of London. Then on finals day – and yes they *were* the nationals – they'd all head to the track to cheer on their boy. Afterwards, win or lose, it was off to a posh restaurant for a slap-up meal (Margaret's words, not his) and maybe a show or a movie to wrap up the evening. Sunday offered no respite, a trip to the Westfield shopping centre, before the long drive home – they'd probably play eye-spy on the way.

Ordinarily he would have been counting down the days in anticipation, but not now, not with all this hanging over him. He could just about stomach the thought of betraying his wife. She'd be devastated, hurt and upset beyond all reason, but she'd get over it; she was resilient. The kids, though. If they saw him for what he was, if they saw the real him, it would crush him. A better man would have confessed everything by now, thrown himself at their mercy and accepted his punishment. But that wasn't him, he had chosen to hide under a rock and hope it would all go away. It was still there though, in the office, staring at him every day. Katie knew what he was, and every time he looked at her he saw himself reflected in her eyes: a pitiful, wretched creature. She had his number. She knew exactly what he was, and it was only a matter of time before everyone else did too.

7

JONATHAN FELT GUILTY EVEN THINKING about it. He knew it was natural to wonder, but even so it felt like a betrayal. They'd taken him in and given him a life most kids could only dream of, and here he was, throwing it all back at them. Was this to be their reward? Feed him, clothe him, look after him for fifteen years and then be dispensed with like an old rag? It wasn't like that, though. They were his parents, and they would always be his parents. But the fact remained that someone else had brought him into this world. Somewhere out there were two people, a man and a woman, who had come together and created him. They may not have wanted to do so but they had, and here he was, in the flesh, living proof of their coupling. Did they think about him? Did they regret giving him away? He remembered that when he was younger he'd asked his mother those very same questions, and to her credit, his mum had answered them as well as she could. He'd been just a kid then, unable to fully grasp the situation. He vaguely recalled promising his mum that he'd never, ever leave her and that she'd always be his mum, no matter what. He still believed that, he still loved her with all his heart, but he wanted to know. He wanted to know where he came from. Although his parents had always been open and had told him that when the time came they would assist him in his search, he wanted to do this by himself. He knew it would hurt them. They'd try to brush it off, tell him how happy they were, but deep down it would kill them. They'd wonder what they'd done wrong and why he no longer trusted them. It wasn't like that, though; they'd done nothing wrong. He just needed to do this by himself.

Therein lay the problem; he had no idea where to start. He was just a kid; you needed an adult for something like this. He wasn't even sure if he was allowed to look for them; didn't you have to be eighteen? You had to be eighteen for almost everything else, so it made sense that you'd have to be eighteen for this too. He considered going to his aunt Ellie and asking her about it. She was his favourite aunt and he knew he could rely on her to keep quiet. It would be unfair to weigh her down with such a burden, though. No, this would have to be done completely and entirely on his own.

One day when he was home alone, he decided to take the first step. He fished out the Yellow Pages and began leafing through the book. He didn't really know what he was looking for, but he decided he'd search under A for Adoption and see where it took him. There was something called 'Adoption Search Reunion'. That would do. Without thinking he dialled the number, but as soon as he heard a voice at the other end he hung up. He rang twice more, but on each occasion he put down the receiver when his call had been answered. What was he supposed to say? *Hello, my name is Jonathan. Can you find my real mother, please?* They'd probably ask him where his mum and dad were and tell him not to call again until he had their consent. At the very least they'd need official documentation and the like, and he had no idea where any of that stuff was. There was no point in him phoning anyone; it would just lead to questions that he couldn't answer.

What he needed was information, pamphlets and the like. He'd read up on it, find out what he could and couldn't do and take it from there. But where would he get pamphlets? The library? He checked his watch; it was after four now. By the time he got there, it would be almost closing time and it'd be really busy now, anyway. He'd be better off going in the morning, early, when they'd just opened. He could casually browse the bulletin board, where they kept the pamphlets, and if anyone asked what he was doing he could say he was looking for part-time work. They put jobs on that bulletin board; he'd seen them.

That night he lay in bed imagining what it would be like, finding them, meeting them. She was a shop assistant, Heather, one of those friendly ladies who called you 'love' when handing you your change. Younger than his mum – still in her thirties – she lived not far away. They arranged to meet for a cup of tea in a café near where she worked. He got there first and ordered a Coke. As soon as she walked in he knew it was her, and vice versa. She sat down at the table and they just stared at each other, unable to get over how alike they were. Heather grew tearful and apologised for giving him up. He reassured her, said he understood.

"Are you married?" he asked.

"Yes, with two children."

Two children, his siblings.

"Can I meet them?"

"Of course you can," she said with a smile. "Not today, though. It's all a bit sudden, I'm sure you'll agree".

He nodded. "It's incredibly sudden, Heather, you're right. What are their names?"

"Well, Kirk is nine and Daniel's just had his fifth birthday."

"Two boys, eh? My little brothers."

"Yes, Jonathan, your little brothers."

"I really can't wait to see them. Do they like football?"

"Yes, they love football. They're both big City fans."

"City? You've got to be joking!"

"Afraid not, Jonathan."

"Well, it's probably too late to save Kirk, but if I can get to Daniel quickly I might be able to avert disaster."

Heather laughed and he laughed too. They shared the same sense of humour, that much was obvious.

"What about your mum and dad? What are they like, Jonathan?"

"They're the most amazing people in the world."

"I bet they are. I can see they've raised you well. Maybe I could meet them some day."

"Certainly. You could bring the boys; we'll make a day of it."

"That sounds great, Jonathan."

She looked at her watch. "I really should be getting back now, love. I only get half an hour for lunch."

"Okay, Heather."

"It was lovely to meet you and I can't wait to see you again."

"Me too."

She took his hands in hers, looked at him intently and left the café. He watched her go, thinking how great it was that he now had two lovely mums.

Wait, they hadn't made any plans to meet again, and she hadn't given him her number; probably just an oversight on her part. His gut told him differently, though. She didn't want to see him again; she already had a family, she didn't need him coming along complicating matters. He'd never meet Kirk and Daniel, his two little brothers. Heather would return home and her husband would ask how her day had been. "Oh, fine," she'd say. "Went to Robson's for my lunch; they do a terrific cup of tea in there." There would be no mention of Jonathan, the boy she'd given away and had no intention of taking back.

The next morning, as soon as he'd finished breakfast, he went to the library. School had only just broken up for the summer so it was unlikely he'd meet anyone he knew. All his friends and classmates would still be in bed, enjoying the first of many lie-ins. When he got there, the library was almost completely deserted. An elderly couple were sitting at the large table reading the morning papers, and two members of staff were on duty, one behind the desk and another replenishing the shelves with returned books. Neither were anywhere near the bulletin board. He sidled over to the board, trying to look as if he were just browsing but all the while focused on the tall display unit which housed the pamphlets. He spied them from the corner of his eye: *Information for School Leavers, Getting back to work, Guide to entitlements for people over sixty*. None of those was what he was looking for. He moved a bit closer, forgetting the bulletin board, now actively scanning the array of pamphlets and booklets: *Volunteering in the local community, Review of Sign Language Interpretation Services, Rights and Entitlements for young people*. Maybe that one would be helpful.

"Can I help you, love?"

He hadn't heard the woman approach.

"I'm all right, thanks," he said, not turning to face her.

"Are you looking for something in particular?"

He couldn't even look for information without being pestered. He wanted to do this by himself.

"No, just browsing," he said impatiently.

"A part-time job for the summer, maybe?"

He ignored her, hoping she'd go away.

"We're looking for staff here, if you fancy it?"

Jonathan turned around.

"I'm just browsing. Why can't you leave me alone?"

The woman, older than he'd realised, – small and fragile – recoiled, her face of mixture of indignation and dismay.

"Well!" she said. "This is what I get for trying to help. Never have I – "

Jonathan didn't wait to hear the rest. He grabbed a handful of the pamphlets, ensuring he'd got the one about young people's rights, and rushed out the door. He didn't stop there; as soon as he got outside he started to run, far away from the library and the nosy old woman. He came to a halt a couple of streets away, near a playground to which his parents had brought him as a child. Like the library, it was deserted. The younger kids were still at school. He sat on one of the benches overlooking the play area and pulled out the pamphlets. Most of them were of no use; information for school leavers, the elderly, unemployed and infirm, those sections of society that frequented public libraries on a daily basis. But there was that one about young people's rights. Well, he was a young person and he needed to know his rights. He opened the pamphlet and checked the list of contents: *How to Claim Benefits, Looking for Work, Paying your Council Tax, Are You a Parent?* Nothing about adoption there. He flicked through the pamphlet, finding a list of numbers at the back; various helplines for young people seeking information. Some looked promising: there was one for the Citizens Advice Bureau, which was probably where he should have gone in the first place. He didn't know where the nearest one was, though, and when he got there he'd have to deal with more nosey parkers, people doing their utmost to thwart him. He screwed up the pamphlet and put it, along with all the others, into a nearby bin. He'd sit here a while and think things over, then later on he'd go home and try to find out where this bloody Citizens Advice Bureau was.

8

"What's going on, Malcolm?"

Dennis had entered his office uninvited and was standing in front of him. He looked exasperated, annoyed even. It took quite a lot to ruffle Dennis' feathers, so there could be no doubting the gravity of the situation.

Malcolm looked up from his imaginary worksheets and hastily shoved the bottle of Smirnoff into the drawer. "What's up, mate?"

"Don't give me that," Dennis said, pulling up a chair. "Something's going on, and I'm not leaving here till I find out what it is."

"I have no idea what you're talking about," Malcolm replied weakly.

He yearned to tell someone, to spill his guts, but he couldn't bring himself to do it.

"I've hardly seen you for the last two weeks; you're either off sick or meeting a client. On the rare occasions that you actually come in, you're holed up in here like a hermit," Dennis said.

"We're busy, mate. You know that as well as I do."

"*I'm* busy," Dennis said, pointing to himself. "You're doing fuck all. I'm not supposed to deal with Mary's maternity leave, the health and safety report, potential customers enquiring about our yearly expenditure and the lack of fuckin' teabags in the canteen! But I have been."

Malcolm's shoulders sagged. Another person he'd been letting down; *join the queue, pal.*

"I'm sorry," he said quietly.

Dennis remained seated, awaiting an explanation that was long overdue, but all Malcolm could muster was a few rueful glances and a despondent shake of the head.

They could have sat like that for hours, Dennis eyeballing Malcolm while he moaned and groaned in despair. Sensing that his colleague was in need of a friend right now, however, Dennis opted for a softer approach.

"Look, Malc, whatever it is, I'm here for you. If you don't feel like talking to me, maybe I could give Margaret a call?"

Malcolm emerged from his malaise all at once. "No! Don't call Margaret!"

"Okay, so whatever's going on, your wife doesn't know about it. Would I be correct in saying that?" enquired Dennis.

Malcolm nodded glumly.

"Gambling? Alcohol? Has your bit on the side given you the heave-ho? Which is it?"

"I'm not like you," Malcolm said firmly.

"Eh?"

"I don't spend all my money in the bookies and have 'bits on the side' as a matter of course. I'm not like you."

"Well, excuse me; I didn't realise I was in the presence of Saint Francis of bloody Assisi! So, oh holy one, if you've not given in to one of the deadly sins, whatever's got you in such a state?"

He was mocking him now, but it was true; he wasn't like Dennis. That is, he hadn't been until recently. Now he was just like him, he and all those other husbands who constantly complained about their wives and found any excuse not to go home. He'd always pitied those men, how sad their lives must be, he thought. He usually couldn't wait to get home. He still got excited about the prospect of seeing his wife and kids on the drive home every evening. Now he was another man lumbered with a ball and chain, another sinner keeping secrets from those he loved.

It made sense to tell Dennis, and not just because he was staring him down like a pitbull. He was his business partner for a start, so he was duty-bound to tell him. He had to keep him informed of everything that went on in their office, no matter who was involved. Legal issues aside, Dennis was the perfect person to confide in. He was one of life's problem-solvers, a fixer, blessed with the ability to make the biggest of crises seem miniscule, trifling affairs. Once Malcolm had poured out his heart, Dennis would spring into action. He'd find a way out, offer a solution. Best of all, he wouldn't judge him; if anything, he'd congratulate him for trying his luck and curse himself for not getting there first. Malcolm usually found that side of Dennis' character rather unsavoury, but right now he was all for being one of the lads.

"Something happened," he said.

Dennis gave him a look that conveyed 'You don't say?' but allowed him to continue.

"It happened here in this office, in this very room. I should have told you before, but I couldn't."

The pressure bubbled up in Malcolm's chest. Every ounce of his being wanted to blurt it all out, but still he held it in. His conscience told him that telling someone was the right thing to do, but his heart thought it folly. He continued to wrestle with his emotions, wavering, until Dennis threw up his hands in despair and rose to leave.

"Katie from accounts," Malcolm blurted out with a pleading look.

Dennis nodded; he understood now. He sat down again, took some loose sheets of paper from the desk and removed the pen from behind his ear. "Okay, what are we dealing with?"

FINDING WORK HADN'T BEEN EASY for Katie Pendleton. She'd been signing on for almost a year when she'd been offered two months' work experience at a local web-design company. It would be unpaid and there was no guarantee of anything at the end of it, but it was better than sitting at home doing nothing. Even though it wasn't like starting a real job, she was still excited and wanted to make a good impression. You never knew what could happen, after all; one minute she'd be a junior temp, the next she'd be on the board of directors! She was up early on her first morning, perhaps a bit too early; six a.m. seemed excessive, even to her. But she had to make sure she looked her best, first impressions were everything in these situations. Her mother had bought her a rather severe trouser suit, bless her. Katie tried it on and nodded amenably as Mrs. Pendleton told her how sophisticated it made her look, but there was no way she was wearing it, at least not on her first day. It made her look like a power-hungry feminist, and that wasn't what she was aiming for. She wanted to look smart and professional but with a touch of glamour. That didn't mean exposed cleavage and a skirt up to her arse, but it did mean an air of elegance and at least a hint of femininity. After an hour of preparation, including three changes of outfit and a last-minute panic with her hair-straightener, she declared herself content. She headed out the door, giving herself an hour for the fifteen-minute drive.

Her first day was made a whole lot easier by her new boss. He was friendly and helpful, a really nice, genuine guy. Her new colleagues in accounts weren't so welcoming. They were all older than her, in their thirties and forties, their best years well behind them. It was clear they were jealous of her and of the attention she was getting from the men in the office. Katie chose to ignore the snide comments and remarks. She would dress as she liked, and if it gave the men in the office something to look at, so be it. There was no harm in it, after all. The work itself was easy; she'd done all this stuff during her course a couple of years ago. Even when the most jealous, gone-to-seed member of accounts, Nadine, had tried tripping her up with a difficult spreadsheet, she'd calmly assessed the document and had it processed within the hour. By the end of her first week she felt like she'd worked there all her life, which was thanks, in no small part, to Malcolm, her boss. He really was a gentleman; constantly checking to make sure she was all right, answering all her queries, even accompanying her to lunch so she wouldn't have to sit on her own. What did it matter if no one else in the office really spoke to her? She was friends with the boss.

The notion that his interest in her might not be purely work-related did cross her mind, but he was married with two kids and she had a boyfriend. They flirted a bit, true, but he was probably like that with all the temps. She couldn't blame him, considering the state of some of the women here. And, if some playful office innuendo helped her get a step up the ladder, that was okay too. When he assigned special duties to her, including directly liaising with him on a weekly basis, she just assumed he was pleased with her work. Nadine and the others grumbled and made pithy remarks, but she laughed it off. They'd been here for years, sitting in those same chairs since the day they'd got here, and they'd probably be sitting in them for another twenty years until the day they retired, old and bitter. She was the bright young thing of Philliskirk & Barnes. She was moving up in the world, and they were just going to have to deal with it. But no sooner had she settled in and begun to enjoy herself when her finish date loomed large. She was only here for two months, after all. Soon it'd be back to the dole queue and sleeping till midday. The others couldn't wait for her to fuck off, she could tell. They visibly relaxed at the start of her last week, stretching out their legs shooting smug smiles in her direction. Pretty soon things would be back to normal, no more ambitious wannabees making them look bad. She still held out hope that Malcolm (or the other guy, whose name she couldn't remember) would call her to the office and announce they were extending her work experience for another couple of months. She would have given anything to see the look on Nadine's face as she returned to her seat with a smug smile of her own. Then, on the Wednesday of her last week, something extraordinary happened; something even better than having her work experience extended.

At lunchtime she'd gone to the canteen as usual, but there was no sign of Malcolm and she didn't want to sit at a table by herself. So she returned to her desk, choosing to eat alone in the office rather than risk contact with her colleagues. Having finished her sandwiches there was little else for her to do, so she decided to get a head start on the work she'd planned for that afternoon. She hardly noticed the grinning middle-aged man approach her desk.

"Hi, Katie," her boss said, casually sitting on her desk.

She jumped at the sound of his voice. "Oh hi, Malcolm."

"Aren't you taking lunch today?" he asked.

"I had it at my desk," she replied.

"Our Katie, such a hard worker," he teased.

She smiled shyly. He often made fun of her dedication to the job, but it was always good-natured.

He took a deep breath. Something was clearly on his mind. She hoped she hadn't done anything wrong; maybe that was why he hadn't joined her for lunch today.

"I've got some good news," he said.

"Yes?" she replied, trying not to get her hopes up, but failing.

"It's about your role here."

"Oh?"

"I've discussed it with Dennis, and we'd like to offer you a full-time position as a junior accountant." Had she heard him right? Had he just said what she thought he'd said?

"Really?" she asked.

He nodded and smiled.

"Oh, Malcolm, that's unbelievable! I mean, of course, yes – I accept gladly."

"Great. I'll bring over the forms and we can go through the details. It should be official by the end of the day."

As he walked back to his cubicle she allowed herself a little fist-pump: a full-time job as an accountant, a career girl. This would be just the beginning for Katie Pendleton. Now that she had a full-time job with a steady income, she could finally afford to move out of her mum's. She could get a place with Ian, her boyfriend. They'd been together for six years; it was about time they took the next step. They'd have to rent somewhere at first, but eventually they could look at getting a mortgage, which would probably mean getting married. Well, that wouldn't be a problem now, either; she'd be able to afford a proper wedding. Her car would have to go too; she'd been driving that crappy Micra since she'd got her licence, four years ago. A business woman couldn't be seen in such a vehicle. It was time for an upgrade, but to what? A Polo? Yes, that sounded nice.

With her place in the company secure, Katie set about making an even bigger impact. She didn't care whose toes she stepped on; sod those miserable gits, she'd have passed them all out within a year anyway. If she could land a full-time position on the back of two months' work experience, there was no telling what she could achieve with a bit more hard graft. And, true to form, she was gradually given more and more responsibility. It might have said 'junior accountant' on her payslip, but she was practically running the place. She whizzed round the office, attending to her duties with maximum efficiency and smiling as she went. What an asset she'd become – was it any wonder they'd kept her on? She started doing over-time three or four evenings a week, even came in on a couple of Saturdays when Malcolm suggested it. At the rate she was going, she'd have enough for a down-payment on a house by the end of the year. She was still in her Micra, though. The new car would have to wait.

But her devotion to her job began to affect other areas of her life. She didn't have as much time for Ian as she'd had before. What did he expect, though? She was saving for *their* future. She was working all these extra hours for their new house, and if that meant fewer nights out and occasionally being too tired for sex, then he'd just have to put up with it. He ought to see the bigger picture, as she did. It'd all be worth it in the future, she told herself, as she cancelled dinner plans for the fourth time in as many weeks. They'd been together since she was eighteen, six years now, and they were strong enough to endure anything. Eventually they would be married, have children and live happily ever after. That was a given, they'd discussed it on countless occasions. So even when his complaints became more vociferous, she didn't think much of it. *He's just letting off steam. I'll make it up to him at the weekend.*

She didn't make it up to him; instead she worked all day Saturday, and when she got home she was too tired to go out for a drink. He came round to see her, even though she'd told him not to. He had a go at her, saying that her job was destroying their relationship. 'But if you loved me you'd understand', she told him. 'I'm a working girl now; I'm doing this for us.' She couldn't believe how pig-headed he was being, how selfish. He left in a huff and they didn't speak for the next couple of days. He'd get over it, though; he'd understand eventually. They'd survived worse than this. Then came the text.

She'd just arrived at work and was parking her car when the phone bleeped. Noting the time, 8:04, she opened the message. It was from Ian.

This isn't working, Katie. I think we should split up.

Her first emotion was anger. *Six years together, and he breaks up with me by text?* That was quickly replaced by anguish and remorse. What had she done? He was the love of her life, *the one*, and now he was gone. She sat in her car, looking blankly at the phone. What was she supposed to do now? She tried calling him, but it went straight to voicemail. She needed to talk to him, to see him, to find out if their relationship could be salvaged; but she couldn't take a day off work, not for showdown talks with her boyfriend. Imagine what Nadine would say if she heard that? She'd have a field day.

Katie tried the number again. Once more it went to voicemail. She could go to his workplace; it wasn't far. It would be the ultimate romantic gesture. She'd stride through the factory, ignoring the looks from grimy men in boiler suits until she found her man. Then, not caring who was watching, she'd throw her arms around him, dirtying her blouse, smudging her make-up, and proclaim her eternal love. All the men would coo, and she and Ian would share one of those Hollywood kisses where the woman leans back and is almost swept off her feet. That would show him how much he meant to her. But she couldn't take a day off work; she couldn't even take a few hours off. They were really busy at the moment and she had to keep on top of things. So she rang him once more and left a message.

"Ian, when you get this, please call me back. We need to talk. I love you."

That would have to do. She went inside and upstairs to the office. She was first in, as always. As she sat down in her chair and clicked on the computer, she suddenly crumbled. The enormity of the situation hit home, and with it came the tears. She still had enough about her to vacate the office and make a dash for the toilets; if anyone saw her crying her eyes out, she'd never live it down. Inside the stall she let it all out, weeping ceaselessly and with abandon. She rang him again and again, a dozen times or more, leaving incoherent voicemails, each one more hysterical than the last. It was no use; he hated her. It was over.

There was a knock at the door; not the door of the cubicle but the main door. Christ, had she really been that loud? A voice called out to her; it was

Malcolm. Hearing him calmed her. His was the only friendly face in the entire office, and she needed a friend right now. She left the cubicle, taking deep breaths, trying to compose herself. She knew she must look a mess but she didn't care. Gingerly opening the door, she peered around and there he was, a picture of concern. As he took her by the arm she broke down again. Fresh floods of tears, talking gibberish as she tried to explain what had happened. When he suggested they go to his office she went willingly; a cup of tea and a shoulder to cry on, just what she needed. And boy did she cry; she hadn't thought it possible to shed so many tears. All the while, her boss was the gentleman she knew him to be. He held her softly in his arms and told her everything was going to be all right, and eventually she began to calm down. When she felt his hand on her knee, she thought it was a sign for her to stop snivelling into his shirt and pull herself together. Just a couple of moments more, she thought, as she laid her head on his chest; then she felt his hand move up her leg, slowly but unmistakably towards her crotch.

His face! His disgusting, pathetic little face, mouth opening and closing like a fish. It was pitiable. Did he really think he had a chance with her? Was this what it was all about? Clearly it was. As she scurried away from his office, she felt the tears return. She'd been such a fool. As if anyone would hire her based on her work; no, he'd just wanted to get into her knickers. There she was, telling herself she was this up-and-coming career girl, some-one with a bright future, when all along she'd been just a piece of meat, a fantasy shag for a middle-aged has-been. She wouldn't let him defeat her, or any of them for that matter. So she made another trip to the bathroom, gave herself a little pep talk and reapplied her make-up, then returned to her desk. She was going to sit there and do her work, and if any of them so much as looked at her there would be hell to pay.

It was the other one who approached her, Dennis; that was his name, apparently. He'd never formally introduced himself, but from what she could gather he was the other half of the dynamic management duo. He never seemed to stray far from his private quarters, so when she saw him making a beeline for the accounts department she knew something was up. He looked ill at ease and out of his depth. She could see why he spent most of his time in his office.

"All right, Dennis, to what do we owe the pleasure?" asked Nadine.

"Oh, y'know, just checking on the troops," he replied.

"Well, someone has to, now that Malcolm doesn't come to see us anymore," said Nadine, shooting Katie an accusing look.

"Malc's been busy of late. Things'll get back to normal around here soon enough."

"I should hope so," harrumphed Nadine, as if her fate depended on it.

"It's actually Katie I've come to see," said Dennis, turning his attention to her.

Katie didn't need to ask about the nature of his query; she already knew what he was here for. He'd been sent to do his mate's dirty work.

"What is it?" she asked.

"I wondered if you could come see us after work, in my office?"

"Am I in trouble?" she enquired, knowing she wasn't.

"No, no, nothing like that. Just need to discuss a few things with you, that's all."

"Okay, I'll be there," she said, flashing him her most winning smile.

"That's the lass," he winked, ambling away back to his office.

The time had come; he'd finally plucked up the courage to have it out with her. It had taken two weeks. She had no qualms about facing him; she'd done nothing wrong, after all, but she was glad Dennis would be there too. He'd probably back up his mate but that didn't concern her, she just didn't want to be alone in a room with *him* again. If they tried to gang up on her and make out that it was no big deal, she'd bloody well show them. This was not going to be swept under the carpet and forgotten about.

10

MALCOLM WRUNG HIS HANDS NERVOUSLY. He looked at the clock: 4.55, almost time. He needed a drink, just a wee dram to settle him down; but Dennis had cleaned out the cupboard, taken it all. He'd even found the back-up stash, the emergency bottles that he'd thought no one knew about. Malcolm could hear a low murmur circling around the office outside, the uneasy air of people waiting to down tools. They officially finished at five every evening, but not one of them worked beyond ten to. Coats were being pulled on, computers shut down and chairs pushed under desks.

Occasionally he would emerge during this early evacuation and ask what time it was, to be met with looks of derision. It annoyed him that they did this, but he didn't want to become the kind of boss that went around tapping his watch, asking for more productivity. He had a healthy relationship with his staff and he wanted to keep it like that. Well, he had a healthy relationship with most of them.

He listened to them shuffle out the door, full of plans for the evening, eager to enjoy their time away from the old nine-to-five – how lucky they were. He peeped out through the blinds, looking over towards the cubby-hole. There she was, quietly playing with her phone, waving half-hearted goodbyes to the others. Had she told them she had a meeting with the bosses? They'd surely be gossiping about it, speculating as to what she could have possibly done to get an audience with not one but both commanders-in-chief. Malcolm crept out the door and made his way to Dennis' office, not daring to look behind him in case she was on her way. Dennis had set out three chairs in the middle of his office, none of them behind a desk, in an attempt to create a neutral environment. He nodded to Malcolm as he entered the room.

"You sit there, mate," he said, pointing to one of the chairs.

It mattered little which one, they were all equidistant. Malcolm wondered if his colleague had used a measuring tape during the process.

"Had to make sure the girl didn't feel threatened, Malc," he said, by way of explanation.

"Of course," said Malcolm.

He had been so caught up in his own wretchedness that he hadn't stopped to think how difficult this was going to be for Katie. A crime had been committed against her, and it was important she should be made to feel relaxed.

There was a light tap at the door. Malcolm felt his knees go weak. He quickly sat on the nearest chair.

"Come in," said Dennis.

Katie popped her head round the door, surveyed the room and entered with a smile, briefly acknowledging Dennis and taking a seat without looking at Malcolm.

"Now then," said Dennis, looking from one to the other. "Who'd like to begin?"

Katie stared ahead silently. She wasn't going to make this easy for them. Malcolm looked down at the floor, at his feet, anywhere but at Katie.

This wasn't what Dennis had expected. He'd done his part; he'd brought them together and organised a favourable environment. They were now supposed to resolve their issues.

"Well," he said, attempting to seize the initiative. "We should start by – "

Katie looked at him in bemusement. She was almost enjoying herself watching these two, all hot and bothered. *Let them squirm*, she thought, *I'll just sit here and watch them sweat.*

"Look, we've got a situation here and we need to bloody well sort it out," said Dennis, shedding any last smidgen of formality.

Katie raised her eyebrows in surprise. It looked as if one of them had some balls, after all.

"Malcolm, I believe you owe this girl an apology."

Malcolm lifted his head slowly. If there was any chance of him getting his life back, it all rested on these next few minutes. He turned to look at her, ensuring that he didn't stare or allow his eyes to linger on any part of her person.

"Katie," he started. "I understand if you hate me, because I hate myself after what I did to you."

Dennis shifted in his chair; he hadn't been expecting this.

"I took advantage of the trust you placed in me," Malcolm continued. "You came to us in good faith in the hope of beginning your career, and I ruined it all. I was foolish, so foolish. I thought that maybe you liked me and that if I was nice to you there was a chance ... a chance that something might happen between us."

Malcolm gulped twice, wordlessly accepting a glass of water from Dennis. Katie watched him drink, wondering if it was her turn to speak, but as soon as he set down the glass he continued.

"I was kidding myself, I know that. A young girl like you? How could you ever be interested in someone like me? But I allowed myself to think otherwise. I told myself I was doing nothing wrong, we were just friends; that's what I said to myself. But every morning when I woke up the first thing I thought of was you, and how I couldn't wait to see you again."

Katie flushed a little. If he weren't such a creep, this would have been slightly romantic.

"I suppose I was just infatuated with you," he continued. "You made me feel young again and I was willing to risk everything to be with you. My wife, my kids, my job ..."

He coughed back tears, wiping his eyes with the sleeve of his shirt.

"I know now how very stupid I was, how ridiculous it was of me to think in such a way. What I did to you, taking advantage of you when you were upset – I'll never forgive myself for that, never."

Malcolm stopped, realising he had forgotten himself. He looked sheepishly at Katie and put his head down, as if waiting for sentencing.

Dennis once again took the reins.

"Okay, Malc. Well done, mate, that can't have been easy. Katie, what do you want to say to Malcolm in response?"

Katie cleared her throat. Malcolm's words meant little to her; it was easy to be sorry after the event. He was right, she did hate him but as she looked at him, head bowed and shoulders slumped, she felt some pity also.

"You manipulated me," she said, "used me for your own titillation. You made me think you believed in me and that I could make a difference here. But all you wanted was to cop a feel, get your end away, whatever you want to call it. But more than that, you betrayed me. I actually liked you, Malcolm. I thought you were a nice guy. I went home and told my mum all about you, my friends too. 'My colleagues are all wankers but the boss is great', that was my running joke."

She had thought she was in control of her emotions, that she could come in here, ice-cold, and make him suffer. But it was affecting her too, dealing with this, the feelings it brought up.

"... and the way you did it ..." she said, the words choking in her throat.

She cursed herself for being so weak and tried to fight it, but that only made it worse. She was crying now, angry shameful tears, brought about by this whole sordid episode. All she wanted to do was to get out of here and never return, but she had to see it through to the end.

She didn't want him thinking his behaviour had had so much impact on her, that someone so despicable could affect her life.

"All I wanted was a good job, and you destroyed it," she blurted out, this final effort sending her into fresh floods of tears.

Dennis looked to Malcolm for guidance, but Malcolm had been here before and he wasn't about to compound his errors. He shrugged his shoulders and sat there dejectedly.

"There, there, love," said Dennis, standing over her, terrified to lay even a finger on her. He filled another glass of water and held it hopefully in her direction.

"For fuck's sake," said Katie bitterly, fishing out a tissue from her handbag.

Dennis took a step back, fearful of further recriminations.

She was angry at herself now, not just for crying when she'd planned on keeping her cool, but for the whole sorry affair; for being stupid enough to get excited about some poxy work experience and for believing that she was actually good at her job, that her boss had faith in her and that she could make something of herself. There was no chance of that. There never had been. She was just something nice to look at, an object of desire, a fantasy.

"Fuck you Malcolm," she spat out suddenly. "You're a devious little weasel. How dare you? I should bring the company to court and destroy you. How would your wife feel then? I know you haven't told her. Have you?"

Malcolm had lapsed into a fugue state, but under the face of this assault he regained his focus, albeit shakily.

"No, not yet," he mumbled.

"Not yet," she mimicked sarcastically. "So you're going to tell her, then?"

"Eventually," he replied, knowing that, despite the depth of his guilt, he had no immediate plans to tell his wife anything.

"Why not now?" asked Katie.

She was in full flow now. Enraged. It felt fantastic.

"Let's deal with this first, shall we?" Malcolm replied hopefully.

"But this is dealing with it, Malcolm. In order for us to resolve this situation, I think it's necessary for your wife to be informed. Dennis, could you ring her, please?"

Malcolm shot up from his seat, grabbing the phone from Dennis' desk. "No!" he cried. "Please don't."

He pressed the phone against his chest, terrified they would wrestle it from him.

"Oh, sit down, you idiot," said Katie with disdain. "I'm not going to ring your wife."

He looked at her, his face clouded in doubt, still cradling the phone protectively.

"Sit down, mate," said Dennis, gently relieving him of the apparatus and guiding him back to his seat.

Dennis' concerns now went far deeper than the state of his friend's marriage. He had heard her use the word 'court'. This had to be nipped in the bud.

"Katie, love," he said, "I know you're very upset right now and you're not thinking straight."

She had started to calm down and was ready to find some middle ground, but Dennis' condescending voice telling *her* how *she* was feeling got her hackles up again.

"Am I not, really? Well, how would you like me to think?"

She waited for his response but he just stood there, dumbfounded.

"Go on, Dennis, tell me. How should I think?"

"I don't think there's any need to mention 'court', Katie."

Ah, that was it; that's what had him so worried.

"Why not, Dennis? Hasn't a crime been committed, or is sexual assault considered legal where you come from?"

Malcolm flinched in his seat. It had started; he was going to jail. It was only a matter of time now.

"No, of course not," replied Dennis. "What Malcolm did was downright wrong, but I fully believe we can sort it out without the need for court cases or the police."

"How do you suggest we do that, Dennis?"

Malcolm looked at him curiously, wondering exactly how Dennis could do that.

"What do you want?" Dennis asked her flatly.

"No, Dennis, you tell me."

All sorts of legal permutations ran through Dennis' head. If he offered her money for her silence, was that akin to bribery? Should he absolve himself of all blame and let Malcolm deal with this on his own? He really should have brought a lawyer.

Much to the surprise of both Katie and Dennis, it was Malcolm who spoke next.

"A formal apology, written and signed by myself, and an extension to your contract with a rise in salary. Alternatively, a handsome redundancy package with glowing references from both of us. Choose whichever you prefer. If you decide to stay, I promise never to bother you again. We would have to maintain a working relationship and be civil to one another, but that will be it. You won't be treated any differently than any of the other employees, I'll make sure of that. If you do decide to take us – me – to court, then I fully understand your decision and am willing to accept whatever punishment comes my way."

Dennis nodded his head in fervent agreement, looking at Katie, trying to gauge her mood. For Katie it felt like the first time they'd treated her with anything approaching respect. She'd been a bothersome child up to now, an irritation which had needed to be dealt with. However, it seemed that following her threats (none of which she had any intention of carrying out), they were willing to take her seriously.

"I'm not going to take you to court," she said quietly. "Even though I really liked my job, I don't think I can stay here either."

Her tone was reflective, almost melancholy.

"They don't like me," she said nodding her head towards the empty office, "and the one friend I had here – well, we all know what happened there."

She sighed deeply, glad that things were coming to a close but sad that it had to be like this. "How much notice do you need?"

Dennis rose from his chair, seeking out the P60 he'd kept handy just in case. He moved his chair back behind the desk and began leafing through the pages in a business-like manner.

"Now, love," he said. "If you'd really like to get out of here as soon as possible, you can finish at the end of the week. As for your severance package, we can ..."

Malcolm sat to one side, no longer involved in the exchange. He should have been relieved, he had dodged a bullet after all. His wife and children weren't going to find out. As good as that was, though, it wasn't enough. He had damaged this girl, and, as he watched her, sitting there, listening to Dennis offerings, he knew she would never forget what he had done to her.

11

IT WOULD HAVE BEEN OVERLY dramatic to say Jonathan was born to run, but ever since taking part in his first proper race he knew it was something he wanted to do. He wasn't much of a footballer, cricketer or rugby player, but he could run. He'd always been a fast runner – leading the pack during any schoolyard activity involving fleeing or chasing – and he had the stamina to go with it. At first it seemed as if he were the same as any other kid; running here and there, constantly on the go, a bundle of energy. But as he got older it became clear he had a talent, a talent which needed to be honed. At the age of eleven he joined the local track and field team. In his first competitive race he obliterated the field, racing away and leaving bigger, stronger boys in his wake. It felt natural, normal, and winning quickly became a habit, one he maintained into his teens.

As a sport, running rewarded hard work and dedication, two things at which he excelled. Its main appeal, however, lay in the fact it was much less capricious than other sports. If something went wrong, then it was invariably your own fault. You couldn't blame the referee, the weather or the bounce of a ball. It was one man on a track racing against seven others. All he had to do was get out of the blocks, avoid contact with his competitors, and the rest would take care of itself. Although winning came easy, it didn't make it any less satisfying. Suddenly he was good at something, more than good, the best. This provided him with something he hadn't experienced before: personal pride.

On some level he'd always believed he was damaged goods, an unwanted entity discarded without a second's thought. His parents told him otherwise and insisted they wouldn't change him for anything. The fact remained, however, that he was an accident, a disaster in someone's life. The person who had borne him didn't want him inside her. She had carried him for nine months with only one thought in her mind: I wish he wasn't there. His entrance into this world wasn't greeted with joy or excitement. Instead he was wordlessly taken away, his mother glad to be rid of him. There he lay with all the other unwanted children until Malcolm and Margaret Philliskirk took a chance on him. They could just have easily chosen a different baby, and right now they would be telling him that they wouldn't change *him* for anything or anyone. It was pure luck that he'd ended up with them.

He looked at his friends and their parents and wondered how their lives differed. Did they have a shared connection, a bond that he could never have with his? There was no way of knowing. What he did know was that his parents loved him unconditionally, and he loved them in return with all his heart; but he always sought their approval. He yearned to show them that they'd been right to take a chance on him, that he was worthy of their love, and just as good as any child they could have had by natural means. He ran for them, really. Each victory, each medal, was his way of showing them that they'd chosen well. It was his way of repaying them, and the better he became and the more they praised him, the more he wanted to excel.

That devotion didn't stop him wondering, though, and as he entered his teenage years he continually thought about those who'd discarded him. While his friends grew up and followed in their fathers'/brothers'/uncles' footsteps, he ploughed a lone furrow. Why did he like the things he liked? Was it because his friends did, or was there a deeper meaning behind it? And what of his personality traits? His mum often teased him for being such a solemn young man: *so thoughtful and contemplative, mature beyond his years.* Where had that come from? Had they said the same things about his birth father when he was young? If they were ever to meet, would they both sit there in silence, thinking and contemplating? He had no clear identity. He didn't laugh like his dad or scowl like his mum. He was just an odd young man; origins unknown.

In athletics it didn't matter who he was or where he came from, he was just Jonathan, the kid who was great at running. Those watching him race didn't care about his birth parents or that he didn't know where his mannerisms came from; all they saw was a fifteen-year-old boy powering round the track, a master at work. When he crossed the finishing line, they rose to acclaim his talent. That's what he was, talented. His birth parents might not have wanted him, but if they could see him now, graciously accepting all this applause, they'd wish they had kept him.

12

HE FOCUSED ON HIS BREATHING, on his stride pattern, on the asphalt beneath his feet. He was weightless now, floating through the air, poetry in motion, in complete control; a running machine. His coach stood at the side of the track, barking encouragement.

"That's it, lad, keep going. Yes, Jonathan, yes, my boy. Incredible, absolutely incredible!"

But Jonathan didn't hear him, chose not to, only tuning in at the finish of each lap when his time was bellowed out by the excitable man in the red tracksuit.

"One minute, four point six-two seconds."

Good; not his best, but consistent. Consistency was key.

The motivational messages resumed, and Jonathan returned to his own world. He didn't need coaching when he was out there. Coach Turner knew that; he yelled and screamed for his own benefit, to make him feel like he was doing something, contributing to the master-class taking place before him. They had devised a plan which involved Jonathan running longer distances than he was used to; three kilometres, five kilometres or maybe more, depending on which training manual Ernie Turner had read the night before.

He'd said they needed to work on Jonathan's stamina, run further, strengthen his legs and expand his lung capacity. Some runners might have complained about the extra workload, but not Jonathan. Running was what he did, and if Ernie wanted him to run all night then that was what he would do. These longer distances weren't an issue; he actually enjoyed them. Maybe he'd found his true calling as a marathon runner. The way he felt right now, he could easily complete the 26.2 mile distance and still be fresh enough to run an 800-metre race at the finish. He was enjoying himself so much that he didn't notice the tall, burly man with the thatch of black hair take a seat in the grandstand. Ernie Turner didn't notice either, he was far too busy coaching his protégé to pay heed to curious onlookers. Even when the man came closer for a proper look, he didn't register on Ernie's radar.

"That's it, Jonathan. Keep going, son. Nearly there now," he enthused, hopping up and down. "Just two more laps to go".

The interested bystander came closer, crossing the track and joining Ernie in the grassy centre.

"Things are going well then, Ernie?" asked the man.

He might as well have been talking to himself. There was just one lap to go, and young Philliskirk needed all the assistance he could get.

"One minute, four point nine eight!" Ernie cried, eyes ablaze with excitement.

Then he was gone, in hot pursuit of Jonathan, stopwatch in his hand. The tall man smiled, wondering how Jonathan put up with a coach who was clearly demented. Jonathan didn't show any sign of distraction; on the contrary, he made his way round the track with ruthless efficiency. It was quite a sight.

"Fourteen minutes, fifty-eight point two-four seconds!" Ernie yelled, breathless now. "You beauty!!"

Jonathan slowed to a halt, resting his hands on his knees as he caught his own breath. His coach repeated the numbers over and over again but Jonathan didn't need to be told his time, he already knew it was good. As he rose and turned to bask in his acclaim, he saw the tall man for the first time.

"DAD!" he yelled, jogging over to his father and almost knocking over Coach Turner in the process. The tubby man in the red tracksuit was completely overlooked as the boy ran to the man he sought to impress more than any other.

"Did you see it, Dad? A PB in the five kay!"

Malcolm smiled and nodded; of course he'd seen it.

"Only the last few laps, Jonathan, but wow, that was incredible."

Jonathan beamed with delight. "Really, Dad?"

"Really, son. Amazing."

"Great. Just give me a second to shower and dress and I'll be right back, okay?"

"No hurry, Jon. I'm not going anywhere."

"Okay, Dad," he said, scampering off to the changing-rooms.

Ernie sidled up to the boy's father, clearly put out by his presence.

"He's still got a lot of work to do, Mr. Philliskirk."

Malcolm raised his eyebrows in exaggerated surprise. "Didn't he just get a PB, Ernie?"

"Yes, but all the boys competing in the nationals will be getting PBs right now. It means nothing."

Malcolm's dealings with his son's trainer were as infrequent as they were brief, but he had learned enough to know that he was one of the world's most miserable men. Maybe that was a good thing, though, because Jonathan excelled under his tutelage and Malcolm had never once heard him complain that Ernie was too hard on him.

"Only four weeks to go now, Ernie. How do you think he'll do?"

"Hmph," Ernie replied, shuffling off to the changing-rooms.

Malcolm sat down and waited for Jonathan to return. He had left Dennis and Katie to thrash out the finer points of her redundancy, offering one final apology as he went. She'd barely acknowledged it, but at least it was over now and had reached a satisfactory conclusion. He had got away with it, learned a valuable lesson and would never be so stupid again. He still felt like shit, though. He'd done something terrible and avoided any real punishment. The jury had voted in his favour and exonerated him. But, leaving the courthouse as a free man, he knew he'd bucked the system. He should have been cuffed and escorted away by two surly policemen to a future of uncertainty, a place where he would recant his sins and serve his penance.

"Ready, Dad!" chirped Jonathan, reappearing with his hair sopping wet.

"Good lad. We'd best hurry, your mum's got our tea in the oven."

"Brill, what is it?"

"Steak and chips; plenty of sustenance for our young athlete."

"How was work, Dad?" Jonathan asked as they began the short drive home.

Well, lad, if you must know, it was a pretty tumultuous day. The girl I tried to get off with decided not to press charges, and instead accepted a generous redundancy package in exchange for her silence. In addition to this, I am currently suffering alcohol withdrawal symptoms which, if you look closely, cause occasional shakes and tremors throughout my entire body. Other than that, though, everything is just fine.

"Ah, same old, same old."

"You've been working late a lot recently, Dad."

"I have, son," Malcolm replied, recalling those afternoons spent drowning his sorrows in that depressing little bar.

"We miss you at home."

"I know, lad. But things are more settled now. I should be home earlier from now on."

"Great."

They travelled in silence for a few minutes, comfortable in each other's company.

"Dad?"

"Yes, Jon?"

"Remember that night, when I got up for a drink of water?"

Malcolm didn't remember, but decided to play it by ear.

"Yes?"

"What were you doing?"

Fuck. What had he been doing? Had the boy heard his parents having some 'Mummy and Daddy time' in the wee hours? No, it couldn't be that; he was fifteen now, no longer a child. Besides, Malcolm couldn't remember the last time he and Margaret had done *that*.

"Which night was it again, Jon?"

"Remember, Dad, a few weeks ago; I got up for a drink, and you were sitting there in the dark, drinking from a bottle."

Malcolm shuddered, a vague recollection of the incident in question coming to him from the depths of his memory.

"Oh, that. I was just having a couple of drinks and must have lost track of the time."

"It was half past three in the morning, Dad."

Malcolm looked at his son and sighed deeply.

"I've been under a lot of pressure at work recently, son, and sometimes I need a couple of drinks at night to unwind."

"At half past three, Dad?" Jonathan repeated.

"I know, it was a bit late. Don't tell your mother about it, okay?"

"I won't."

He thought that was the end of it, but a minute or two later Jonathan spoke again.

"If something was wrong you'd tell me, Dad, wouldn't you?"

Malcolm looked again at that expression of innocent sincerity. How could he lie to him?

"Course I would, son. Don't you worry about your old dad."

"Okay, Dad," said Jonathan, lapsing into a silence that lasted all the way home.

13

"YOU SEEM MORE LIKE YOUR old self tonight, love."

Margaret and Malcolm lay in bed, reading. She was halfway through the latest Robert Pattinson, and Malcolm was half-heartedly shuffling his way through the *Manchester Evening News*. It was just after ten, but the Philliskirks were an early-to-bed, early-to-rise family.

"Do I?" asked Malcolm, realising that for the first time in ages he actually *felt* like his old self.

"Yes. You've been so distant lately. And you've looked terrible, really dishevelled and untidy."

Malcolm turned to his wife, smiling. "Oh, really? Tell it like it is, why don't you?"

Margaret smiled back. "I didn't want to say anything, dear. I know you get very busy at work."

"I do, love. The last few weeks have been a bit mad, but hopefully things have settled down now."

"Good," she said, gently stroking his cheek and returning to her book.

He was thinking about calling it a night when his wife piped up once more.

"Got the phone bill today," she said flatly.

"Oh, yes," Malcolm murmured, waiting to hear about the lengthy calls made by their daughter and how he would have to talk to her about it the next day.

"Mmm. There was a strange number on it."

"Oh."

Margaret closed her book and turned to her husband. "Malcolm, are you listening to me?"

"Of course I am. Strange number. Go on."

Satisfied that he was alert and attentive, she continued.

"Usually I wouldn't notice such things, but it came up at least half a dozen times."

Malcolm shuffled his paper impatiently, wishing she'd get to the point but knowing any attempt to hurry her would result in an even lengthier story.

"I knew I hadn't called that number, and you hardly ever use the home phone for outgoing calls. It didn't look like one of Sophie's friends' numbers, either, so I thought I should check it just in case."

Now Malcolm was listening. His first thought was sex lines; maybe Jonathan had been ringing those numbers you saw advertised on TV late at night? He had been tempted to ring them himself a few times.

"So I rang the number."

She paused for dramatic effect. Malcolm knew she was waiting for him to ask what had happened when she rang the number, but he didn't feel like indulging her tonight. He remained silent while she stared at him, waiting for her prompt.

"So, anyway, I *rang it*," she repeated.

For fuck's sake. It was easier to just play the game; if he didn't, they'd be sitting here all night.

"And?" he asked.

"A lady answered, and she said, 'Good afternoon, North-West Adoption Search Reunion, how can I help you?'"

It felt like he'd been punched in the chest. *Adoption Search Reunion.* Their kids wanted to leave them. That's what he got for being such a terrible father.

"Jonathan?" he asked.

She nodded sadly.

"How do you know?"

"I just know, Malc. I can tell it's been on his mind."

He shook his head in disbelief. "How many times did you say the number appeared on the bill?"

"Half a dozen or more."

"And when did the calls start?"

"About a month ago."

"Why couldn't he come to us with this, Marge? He knows he can ask us anything."

"I don't know, Malc. I've asked myself the same question a thousand times."

"Maybe we could bring it up discreetly?"

"Well, we can't let him know we've been tracing his calls, that's for certain."

"But we have to talk to him about it. He's only fifteen, for God's sake!"

He realised he'd raised his voice and mumbled an apology. She leant her head on his shoulder and felt for his hand, gripping it in hers. Her gesture said it all; they had to stick together, because pretty soon their kids, or the kids they thought of as theirs, would be leaving them. In a few years they would be right back to square one, back to where they were the day they left the doctor's office, childless and lonely. Malcolm couldn't blame the children for leaving. They had such a terrible father, after all; tawdry office shenanigans, days spent drinking in dingy bars, missing important events in their lives, and lying, lying all the time. Was it any wonder they couldn't wait to get away?

He'd failed them. And he'd failed his wife too. She didn't deserve this. But now, because of his shortcomings, she would be made to suffer too. He stifled a sob, his self-loathing complete.

"Oh, Malcolm," Margaret said, stroking his hair tenderly, "it's just curiosity. They told us this might happen."

"We've brought them up well, haven't we, Marge?"

"We have, Malcolm. We should be proud of them."

"I am proud of them, and proud of you too, love."

"Ah, thanks," she said, wrapping her arms around his neck.

They remained like that for a few minutes, Malcolm gently weeping, but feeling nothing. He was numb now, almost immune to the sadness which permeated his life. Maybe if he told her now it could all be resolved; he would confess his sins, say goodbye and be gone by the morning. Jonathan would never ring that number again and Margaret would have her children, the two best things that had ever happened to her. He lay there in her arms, mulling this over, figuring that he had almost nothing left to lose, when he felt her hand reach inside his pyjamas. What the fuck? He couldn't remember the last time they'd been intimate. It had been several months. He didn't want this; he couldn't bear to do it, not now, after everything that had happened. But she knew what buttons to press, she always had. Within seconds he was moaning in pleasure, succumbing to his desires.

"Oh, Margey," he said as he nuzzled her neck.

"Ssh, the kids," she whispered, clicking off her bedside lamp and indicating that he do the same.

He did as instructed; offering no further complaint as his wife climbed on top of him.

14

JONATHAN SAT ON THE SOFA, pretending to be engrossed in some awful daytime TV show. They'd been getting ready to go now for what seemed like hours. It was always the same. Ordinarily he wouldn't have cared, but today he wanted them out of the house as soon as possible. He was going to call that number again, and this time he planned to speak.

"Soph, have you seen my keys anywhere?"

"No, Mum."

"Will you help me look for them?"

"Yes, Mum."

Jonathan knew she wouldn't be helping. She was most likely still in her room, strutting in front of the mirror, pouting like a femme fatale.

"Jonathan, will you help me look too?"

He half-heartedly flipped over the cushions on the couch and ran his hand through the pile of magazines on the coffee table.

"Not in here, Mum," he called out.

But the quicker those keys were found, the quicker he'd have the place to himself. So he trotted out to the kitchen where his mother was emptying the linen basket, scattering dirty clothes all over the floor.

"I'll look in the hallway, Mum; they might have fallen out of your coat."

He left her to the job of piling all the clothes back into the basket, and began searching under the table in the hallway. The sound of Britney Spears asking a baby to hit her one more time could be heard drifting down from Sophie's room. *Bingo.* There they were; he'd hardly had to look.

"Found them, Mum," he called out triumphantly.

"Where were they?" she asked, appearing in the hall.

"Just under there, must have fallen out of your coat."

"Oh, for God's sake," she said accepting the keys and ruffling his hair in gratitude. "SOPHIE! COME ON!"

"Coming, Mum."

His mother went out the front door, closely followed by the whirling dervish that was his sister, and then they were gone; he was finally alone. He watched them drive off and waited another five minutes in case they'd forgotten something. Then he waited another five to be extra sure.

"Right," he said to himself. "Here goes."

He picked up the phone and began dialling the number, he knew it off by heart now. He wondered who would answer. Would it be Elizabeth? Gregory? Or Rachel? She was his favourite, she sounded fit.

At the sound of the first ring, he slammed down the phone.

"Shit," he muttered.

He hadn't meant to hang up. This was meant to be the call where he'd finally speak. He returned to the living-room and sat down again on the couch. He couldn't do it. It would have been much easier if his dad was still being an idiot, but he'd collected him from running yesterday and they'd all had a lovely dinner together afterwards. It had been great, just like old times. But Jonathan had already earmarked today as the day he'd make the call. He couldn't chop and change based on how well things were going at home. That didn't come into it. Not really anyway. This was his own personal crusade, and no matter how many times he hung up the phone that wasn't going to change. His thirst for information was still there; he needed to know. The thoughts and fears which had been circling around his head for months weren't going to go away by themselves.

He went out to the hallway again, picked up the phone and pressed 'redial'. With gritted teeth he listened to it ring, fighting the urge to slam down the receiver and smash the whole thing off the wall.

"Hello, Adoption Search Reunion, Rachel speaking. How can I help you?"

Rachel. His favourite. If anyone would understand, it'd be Rachel.

"Hello? How can I help you?"

Any second now and she'd hang up; it'd be another failure, another wasted opportunity.

"Hello? Is there anyone there?"

"H – hi – "

"Hello? How can I help you?"

He put down the phone and bashed it against the table a couple of times. Tears of frustration rolled down his cheeks, but at least he'd spoken to her this time.

*

That evening, after the girls had come back, he watched on as Sophie paraded around the house in her new clothes. They'd spent the day shopping, and most of what they'd bought was now draped around the tiny figure of his nine-year-old sister. He found her insufferable at the best of times, but right now she was especially annoying. Didn't she ever wonder? She must do. It couldn't just be him who was dealing with this torment. Maybe they'd lied to him and she wasn't adopted at all? No, that was ridiculous; she looked even less like them than he did.

"You look a right state, Sophie"

She stuck her tongue out at him and continued to gyrate in front of the mirror. Yes, she was adopted, probably from another fucking planet.

"Leave your sister alone," chimed his mother as she came in to see how the fashion show was progressing. "She's absolutely beautiful," Margaret continued, planting a kiss on her daughter's forehead. Jonathan exhaled dramatically and resumed his idle channel-surfing.

"Oh, my programme's coming on soon," Sophie said excitedly.

"What programme?" Jonathan replied defensively.

"MTV Select. I'm allowed watch it aren't I, mum?"

"Yes, Sophie, of course you are."

"But mum, I'm watching this," Jonathan said, gesturing to a tacky chat-show he'd never seen before.

"Jonathan, we agreed that your sister could watch her programme every day at four, it's the only time she gets the television to herself."

He remembered them discussing this and he remembered agreeing to it, but it still felt like an injustice.

"Give it here," his sister said, sticking out her hand and waiting for him to pass her the remote.

Jonathan considered resisting, but decided it wasn't worth it. Like a man handing over the keys to his lost treasure he placed the device in Sophie's hands and got up to leave. The programme had already started and the first song of the day was playing. Predictably, it was one of Sophie's favourites. She turned up the volume and began miming the lyrics into an imaginary microphone.

"Ooh, that's a catchy one, isn't it Soph," said Margaret, joining her daughter on the makeshift dancefloor.

Jonathan watched the two of them prancing around in front of the television, and sighed deeply.

"You two are unbelievable, do you know that?" he said witheringly.

"Aren't we just," Margaret replied as mother and daughter broke into peals of laughter.

He left them to it, traipsing up the stairs and slamming the door of his bedroom for effect. Jonathan doubted they'd even noticed. That was the problem with this house; no one noticed anything.

15

IF JONATHAN WERE TO RING the number again, and speak to someone, he needed to have some details. That was probably why he'd been so hesitant before; he'd been unprepared. No wonder he'd clammed up. But if he armed himself with the relevant paperwork he would be able to answer whatever questions came his way. The most obvious piece of paperwork was his birth-certificate; that would have stuff on it, official things that he could chorus back to Rachel when she asked why he was calling. He didn't know where his birth-certificate was, but he could hazard a guess. His mother kept a small wooden box in her room, it was full of important items; his first tooth, a lock of Sophie's hair, a picture of her grandmother. Jonathan's birth-cert was bound to be in there.

In order to check the contents of the box however, he needed to have the house to himself once more. All this sneaking around and acting behind his parents' back only deepened his guilt, but it was for their own good. Again it was a mother daughter shopping trip which presented him with his opportunity, their thirst for the latest fashions seemingly not sated by the previous splurge.

"Are you sure you don't want to come, Jonathan?" his mother asked for the hundredth time as they made to leave.

"Positive, mum."

"Okay then, we shouldn't be too long."

He watched the car pull out, waited five minutes, waited another five and then ascended the stairs. Just entering his parents' room made him feel uneasy, he never went in there unless they were there too. It felt wrong, almost illicit, as if he were entering a restricted area. It was still the same room, though, just an ordinary mum and dad bedroom. There were his dad's trainers, the ones he'd worn yesterday, neatly tucked under the bed, and the necklace Sophie had bought Margaret for her birthday. The bed itself, immaculately made, and the built-in wardrobe where Jonathan hung his school shirts. It was there that he'd find the box, behind the third door; at the bottom, beside all the old shoes. But when he opened the door there weren't any shoes at the bottom, nor was there a box containing vital paperwork. Instead it was all tidy, his dad's suits hung from the rack, his shirts and ties accompanying them. There weren't any shoes, old or otherwise. It appeared that his mother had taken it upon herself to do some spring cleaning since Jonathan had last been in here. She could have had the decency to inform him.

He tried the other doors, dragging clothes this way and that as he scanned the wardrobe's depths for that all-important box. Instead he found some other items of interest; old books with his name pencilled in on the first page, an electric car-racing game, an unopened parcel with the label torn off and what suspiciously looked like Sophie's birthday present. On another day these finds might have stolen his attention, but he hadn't time for frivolities right now. However, after a lengthy, concerted search he had to admit defeat. The box wasn't in there. She had moved it. But to where? He looked around the rest of the room; her bedside locker was a possibility, as was underneath the bed. Both options however felt a step too far, a peek into potentially upsetting parts of his parents' life. Who knew what they kept hidden in those places? What if he came across something *sexual*? God, it didn't bear thinking about. But he had to look. He quickly opened his mother's locker, promising himself that if he saw anything questionable he would close the door and purge the memory from his mind. There was nothing of note in there, just books and pens and bits of jewellery; no weird stuff and no wooden box. Buoyed he got down on his knees and peered under the bed. Absolutely nothing, not even an old sock.

How did they live like this? The last time Jonathan had checked under his bed he'd found over four quid in loose coins and a packet of crisps only two months out of date.

Having ensured that he'd removed all trace of his being there, he exited his parents' room and went downstairs. If she'd moved the box then chances were it was in the kitchen, in that cupboard above the cutlery. He knew she kept important stuff in there, usually bills and old Christmas cards. There was a chance she'd got rid of the box and just put all its content in the cupboard. But after checking that cupboard, and two others like it, he came up blank. Jonathan stood in the middle of the kitchen growing increasingly frustrated; he had to find his birth-certificate today, he was sick of waiting around and there was no telling when he'd have the house to himself again. He moved the search to the living-room, emptying the large cabinet behind the television, not even bothering to cover his tracks anymore. But it wasn't in there either, just loads of old photos and newspaper clippings of his races. The dining-room proved similarly fruitless, as did the garden shed. By now he was chucking things out of his way, more blundering burglar than private investigator.

"Where the hell is it?" he said out loud, "this is ridiculous."

Then it struck him; the one place where everything eventually went, the end of the line, the attic. Hurrying up the stairs he came to a halt on the landing and stared up at his goal. He'd never actually been in the attic, had only caught glimpses of it as his dad ferried stuff up there – usually in the second week of January. But what better reason to become acquainted with a previously unexplored part of the house. Realising he'd need the step-ladder he thundered back down the stairs and outside into the shed. The ladder was jammed beneath the lawnmower and some half-empty buckets of paint. Carefully positioning himself, he managed to extricate the ladder without making too much of a mess, only knocking over two tool-boxes and tearing open a bag of compost in pursuit of his goal.

Returning to the top of the stairs he placed the ladder in the middle of the floor and clambered up into the attic. Isn't there supposed to be a light, he thought as his eyes struggled to readjust to the darkness. Jonathan moved his hands around, hoping they might alight on something helpful, and felt a ceiling switch swing against his fingers. He pulled it and suddenly the dark, pokey attic was illuminated. He was surrounded by yet more boxes, big cardboard ones with writing on them. There weren't any small wooden boxes, but that didn't mean there wasn't one inside one of the cardboard boxes. He opened up the nearest box, it was full of old junk, stuff that really should have just been thrown out. Shoving it to one side he tried the next box: old clothes, fashion faux-pas that their wearers were determined to forget. He found an old Christmas tree, the plastic one they'd bought a couple of years ago that Sophie had hated, the rowing machine that was supposed to get his dad in shape, Jonathan's punch-bag and the gloves, he'd have to get back into boxing...

"JONATHAN, WHAT THE HELL ARE YOU DOING?!

He froze. He'd completely forgotten about the time. How long had they been gone and what state was the house in?

"Erm, just looking for my old tennis racket, mum."

"Tennis racket? Come down from there this minute."

"Okay, mum."

He shoved everything back into its box, switched off the light and guiltily stepped out onto the step-ladder. Margaret stood at its foot, Sophie beside her slurping on an ice-cream. "What are you doing up there, Jonathan?" his sister asked, genuinely intrigued.

"I told you, my tennis racket," he replied, attempting to brush past them.

"Whoa, hold on there," his mother said. "What about the mess you made downstairs. Were you looking for your tennis racket in the kitchen, dining-room and living-room too?"

"I'll tidy it now," he said sheepishly.

"Honestly, Jonathan, if you can't be trusted to be in the house on your own we'll have to get you a babysitter."

"Haha, Jonathan's getting a babysitter," said Sophie gleefully.

He was flustered now, annoyed at being caught in the middle of his search and irritated at being treated like a child.

"Look, just let me tidy it up," he said tugging at the step-ladder which Sophie was now sitting on. She got up, allowing him to clamp it shut and carry it down the stairs.

"That boy," Margaret said, shaking her head as she watched him go.

"Do we have tennis rackets, mum?" Sophie asked. "I quite fancy a game."

*

Later on, after everything had been tidied away and Sophie was in the living-room watching her 'programme', Margaret went looking for her son. He was in the back-garden on the bench enjoying the late summer heat. She sat down beside him.

"So did you find the racket then?"

Jonathan smiled in spite of himself. "No, I don't know where it's got to."

The only tennis racket Margaret could remember her son owning was a tiny wooden little thing when he was four-years old, but she chose not to labour the point.

"Is everything all right with you, Jonathan, in general I mean."

She didn't know exactly what he'd been doing or what he'd be looking for earlier on, but she sensed that it had something to do with the phone number for the adoption agency they'd seen on their bill. "Yeah, why wouldn't it be?"

"I don't know, you've just not been yourself lately."

"It's the nationals," he said. "I think the pressure is getting to me."

"Is that all, there's nothing else?"

He wavered, on the brink of pouring out his heart. But then he checked himself and the barriers were put back up.

"That's all, mum, honest."

Margaret could have asked him about the number, this was her opportunity, but something stopped her. It didn't feel right; there was no way of bringing it up without making it sound like an accusation.

"You know if there's anything else you can always talk to me about it, don't you?"

"Of course, mum."

"Anything," she repeated.

"I know, mum."

She placed her hands in hers and laid them in her lap. They remained like this for a few moments, gently rocking back and forth on the bench.

"You'll smash it at the nationals, Jonathan."

"Hope so, mum."

16

It had been a poor session, the second one in a row, and there had been three bad ones last week as well. Normally he would use whatever ailed him to his advantage, fuel for his fire, to drive himself on. But this was different. It gnawed away at him, ebbing into his psyche, distracting him and making everything else seem irrelevant. The runner who'd been clocking up personal bests as a matter of course had all but disappeared, he was sluggish and lacklustre, a pale shadow of the boy hotly tipped to win this year's national final. Coach Turner had stopped barking out his times after the first lap, and from that point Jonathan was just going through the motions. He wondered what would happen if he just kept running round and round for hours on end. Would Ernie stand there and wait for him, even at two in the morning? Probably. He was champing at the bit, ready to offer the sternest of lectures. Even if Jonathan stayed out there for the next month, the miserable bastard would be there waiting for him when he finally stepped off the track.

As soon as he came to a halt it began.

"What was all that about, lad? Perform like that down in London and you can forget about any medals!"

Jonathan glared at him sullenly, unable to muster a worthwhile response. He wasn't even scared. Time was when he'd have run through brick walls just to avoid Ernie's wrath, but what could his coach possibly say or do to make things worse?

"Well?" Ernie beseeched, his eyes glinting menacingly.

Jonathan sized him up a moment, as if weighing up the possibility of giving him a good hiding, and then simply walked past him towards the changing rooms. Ernie watched him go, utterly perplexed. He'd been such a good pupil, doing whatever he told him to and improving on a weekly basis. Now look at him, with just a few days until the national finals! It beggared belief. Ernie's first instinct was to chase after him, grab him by the shoulders and give him a proper rollicking, but something in the boy's eyes told him that would be of little use. Ernie had a reputation as a drill sergeant, one who used brute force to get the best out of his students, but there was much more to him than that.

In an ideal world his relationship with Jonathan, and all the others he'd trained, would have been based on athletics and nothing more. Over the years, however, he had become well-versed in the travails of the average teenager's life, and he knew that sometimes these delicate little flowers needed nurturing. He watched Jonathan – arguably the best talent he had seen in his thirty years of coaching – walk away and decided that it was time for a new approach. If he was lucky it'd be something straightforward: girl trouble, a falling-out with a mate, something he could relate to. Whatever it was, though, needed to be resolved quickly; he couldn't have his star athlete seizing up days before the big race.

When Jonathan came out of the changing-rooms, his coach was waiting for him at the bottom of the grandstand.

"Sit down, lad," he said, patting the bench beside him.

"Look, Coach, I just – " Jonathan began, but Ernie stopped him short.

"Forget about it, son. We all have our off-days."

Jonathan looked at him in amazement. Had the old fucker gone soft? In the two years they'd been working together he'd never given him an easy ride, not once. A training session such as the one he'd just stumbled through was punishable by death in Ernie Turner's world. He sat down as instructed, on edge, waiting for his coach to revert to type. This was probably just a trick; he was going to play 'nice cop', lure him into a false sense of security and then, as soon as Jonathan had relaxed, it'd be back to frothing at the mouth, steam coming out of his ears as Jonathan cowered under the seats for protection.

"How's things at home, kid?"

"Um, all right, I suppose."

"What about your girlfriend?"

"I don't have one."

The old man made a weird phlegmy noise in his throat, a legacy of a recently discontinued forty-a-day habit.

"Well, something's up, Jonathan."

Jonathan nodded in agreement.

"Don't just nod, son. I don't care what you do in your time away from here as long as you eat right and sleep right, but when it starts affecting your performances out there," he jabbed a finger in the direction of the track, "then it becomes a problem."

"It's just an off-day, Coach."

"Hmph."

"It is, really."

"It's not just today though, is it? You've been up and down for the past week, and anytime I ask you if everything's okay you just shrug your shoulders and mumble."

Jonathan shrugged his shoulders and mumbled.

Ernie turned to face him, fixing him with what he hoped was a caring look.

"It's all going to shit, son. A week to the finals, and you've suddenly turned into a lame duck. What's happening, Jonathan? Tell me."

He was almost begging him now; and he was willing to beg, if that's what it took, because he couldn't bear to see it all go to waste. All that hard work, all that talent, down the drain for no good reason. It broke his heart.

Seeing his coach like this made Jonathan feel guilty. He knew Ernie had a job away from his coaching duties and didn't need to be here. But he was here, every day, setting up the training sessions; clipboard in hand, sheet after sheet of paper full of stats that Jonathan didn't know the first meaning of. What did he get in return? A brooding protégé who'd suddenly decided to stop trying a week before the biggest race of his life.

"It's complicated, Coach."

Ernie sighed; he needed a fag, or at the very least, a cuppa. He tried to imagine what could possibly be complicated about this young man's life.

"Part of being a successful athlete is dealing with complications, son."

"I know, Coach."

"All the greats: Coe, Snell, Cruz. They all went through difficult times in their lives, but they came out the other side stronger, and that was what made them who they were."

He just doesn't get it, thought Jonathan, what was the point in even *trying* to discuss it with him? Talk would inevitably turn to the greats 'back in my day', of men without feelings who could perform like robots no matter what life threw at them.

Jonathan rose from his seat and put his kitbag over his shoulder.

"See you tomorrow, Coach."

With that he was away, slowly trudging to the bike rack, the weight of the world seemingly on his shoulders. Ernie watched him go, shaking his head in remorse. "With great talent comes great responsibility," he said softly to himself.

18

ON THE FRIDAY BEFORE THE race, the Philliskirk family set out early for the drive down to London. Margaret had organised this first leg of their journey with military precision. Their route had been planned in advance, and Malcolm had been informed of the various speed limits he was to adhere to over the course of their journey. There would be two designated toilet stops, zero diversions and they were to arrive in London no later than 11am. Sandwiches and snacks were on hand, ready to be dished out at the first mention of hunger; games, music and even topics of conversation had been arranged beforehand. It would be incredible fun.

Jonathan sat back and allowed himself to relax. This was what he'd been waiting for. He could forget about everything else for the next couple of days. This was about spending time with his family, a fun-filled jaunt to the capital — oh, and the small matter of taking home the national championship, of course. Thinking about the race made him nervous, but it was an excited nervousness. He knew that if he performed to his best, he would win. Although his last few training sessions hadn't gone well, he knew he had such a performance in him. He had worked hard all summer. He was in great condition, at peak fitness, ready and primed for whatever came his way.

It helped that he'd finally spoken to Rachel. After all that fretting and frustration he'd done it without thinking, on a whim really. Returning home from training to an empty house he'd simply picked up the phone, dialled the number and started talking when she answered. He'd explained his situation, outlined that he didn't want to involve his parents and asked all the questions which had been rattling around in his brain. Rachel had confirmed what he'd already suspected; that he did need to be eighteen and that he would have to talk to his parents about it, but despite that it still felt like progress. He had taken the first step. It may not have been much of a step but it would make the following ones all that easier. And now he knew that the only thing preventing him from beginning his search was the system, he had done all he could for the time being.

Not only had Rachel answered his queries and done so in the strictest confidence, she had also told him that he could call back whenever he needed, that there were people on hand for him to speak to whenever he felt down or had a problem he couldn't discuss with his parents. That in itself was a comfort, he didn't know if he would ever call them again or avail of the services Rachel suggested, but just knowing they were there gave him solace. It eradicated the sense of loneliness, the feeling that he had to shoulder this burden entirely by himself; Rachel and the other people at the agency would support him, and no one other than himself would ever have to know about it. He would still have to wait three years before any real progress could be made but in truth he probably wasn't ready to meet his birth-parents yet anyway. By the time he was eighteen everything would be so much easier; he'd be at university and living away from home, with more privacy and the freedom to do whatever he wanted. He could arrange meetings with Rachel without anyone asking him where he was going. Talk on the phone without fear of anyone overhearing. And receive important letters to his own address that he could open at his own leisure.

It was an adult issue that would be resolved when he became an adult. In the meantime he would just get on with his life. He would work hard in school, be nice to his sister and tell his mum and dad that he loved them. He would ask that girl he fancied whether she wanted to go to the pictures with him and he would play football with his mates. He would finally learn how to play the guitar and suggest to his mates that they start a band. And he would win every single race he took part in so that hopefully, one day, Coach Turner might eventually crack a smile.

*

After checking in at the hotel and freshening up they all met up in the lobby, but from there they would part ways. It had been decided in advance that Margaret and Sophie would go to Oxford Street to do whatever it was they did, while father and son took in some culture.

"Where to first, son?"

"The Imperial War Museum!"

"Okay, the Imperial War Museum," Malcolm said, pulling out a huge, unwieldy map from his back pocket.

"No need, Dad. I know where it is. We have to get the Tube to Lambeth North."

Malcolm smiled, clearly impressed. "Okay, then. Lead the way, young traveller."

Jonathan did just that, following the signs until they reached the nearest station, Waterloo. Their next challenge was purchasing a ticket, a task which might have proved beyond them were it not for the help of a friendly Brazilian tourist. Tickets bought, they boarded the train to Lambeth North and the war museum. Being a Friday afternoon, the carriage was quite busy but Jonathan managed to find a seat between two businessmen reading their broadsheets. Malcolm, meanwhile, was content to stand. He might have been somewhere in the murky depths of England's capital, surrounded by sweaty, clammy strangers, but he couldn't have been happier. He caught his son's eye, saw the wonder and excitement contained therein and grinned widely, a sudden, unexpected burst of love filling his chest. On the cusp of manhood and yet still so innocent, Jonathan represented everything that was good in Malcolm's world.

Unlike other boys his age, he had never defied his parents or rebelled against them in any way. If anything, he had become even more loving and considerate with age. Oh, he had his sullen teenager moments, but he could always be cajoled out of them with offers of movie nights or new running equipment. Malcolm listened in shock whenever work colleagues detailed the troubles they were having with their teenage children, resisting the urge to say, "Not my boy. No, not Jonathan; good as gold he is." They would never have believed him, and anyway he didn't like to gloat.

But amid all this pride, the joy he gleaned from watching his boy enjoy himself, there was a tinge of sadness. He knew about the phone calls; Margaret's information had checked out. Pretty soon *his* boy would have to be shared with someone else, returned to his rightful owner like a puppy found in the park. Who knew what the future held? Maybe Jonathan was only marking time until he found his real parents and began calling *them* Mum and Dad, relegating Malcolm and Margaret to a place on the sidelines. They'd raised him well, loved him as he if were their own, but how could they match that bond? Because that's what he would have with these people: a bond, forged by blood. They'd created him and brought him into this world. He and Margaret couldn't compete with that.

For all Malcolm knew, this could be the last time they would ever have a proper 'father and son' day together. Soon he would want to go out with his friends instead of having a movie-night with his family. He'd finish school, go to university and make new friends, a girlfriend. He'd become a pro athlete. There wouldn't be much time for Mum and Dad then. And all the while he'd be seeking *them* out, making more phone calls, filling out forms, talking to those who knew, until one day he dropped it on them. *Mum, Dad, I've found my parents.* Then nothing would ever be the same again.

"It's Lambeth North, Dad," said Jonathan, breaking Malcolm's train of thought.

"So it is. We'd best get off, then."

The War Museum wasn't far from the station, so they walked the rest of the way. Malcolm had always been careful to let his son choose his own path in terms of hobbies and activities, but he couldn't hide his delight when Jonathan began showing an interest in military history. He preferred football to rugby league, had no interest in punk music, and cared not for the works of Alfred Hitchcock, but here was something they could share.

Jonathan spotted the building first, his eyesight keener than his father's.

"There it is, Dad, look," he said, pointing as they approached Harmsworth Park. The distinctive structure seemed a mere speck on the horizon to Malcolm, but even from a distance Jonathan could make out its defining features.

"There's the cannon, Dad. It looks just like the pictures."

Malcolm squinted. He might have seen something resembling a cannon, but it could just as easily have been a tree.

"Well, come on, lad," he said. "Let's get us some culture!"

He broke into a sprint, taking Jonathan by surprise as he dashed across the grass. Jonathan gave chase, grinning as he caught up with him and then passed him within seconds. Some tourists sat on a nearby bench tut-tutted as the boisterous pair legged it through the park and up to the museum entrance. The two Philliskirks didn't even see them.

19

"How was your day, boys?" asked Margaret, flopping into the booth, laden with shopping bags.

"Brilliant, Mum," smiled Jonathan, returning to the menu.

Malcolm had hoped for gourmet cuisine at one of London's finest eateries: exotic seafood, the finest fillets of steak, expensive wine from the finest vineyards in Chile. With the choice of venue left to his fifteen-year old son, that was never going to happen.

"I need carbs, Dad, and protein," Jonathan had explained as he'd led them into a cosy little Italian restaurant.

It might not have looked much from the outside, or the inside for that matter, but Malcolm was pleasantly surprised by the range of food on offer. It wasn't the same as that fancy French place he'd spotted down the road, but it would do the job.

"Ready to order, kids?" he asked, flipping the pages of the menu impatiently.

"Give them a chance, love," protested Margaret. "It's not often they get to eat out."

"This place closes in five hours," he replied, only half-joking.

"I'm ready," announced Sophie, immediately staring at her brother to see what was holding him up. "Can't you find anything, son?" asked Malcolm.

"Mmm."

Sophie fixed her mother with a forlorn look, but was quickly shushed.

Finally, Jonathan put down his menu and, without missing a beat, hailed a waitress and told her exactly what he fancied. Malcolm glanced at his wife, rolling his eyes in faux annoyance. She replicated the gesture, smiling quietly to herself.

Service was prompt, and within ten minutes of ordering the booth containing the Philliskirks was silent, save for the sound of frenzied chewing and occasional, appreciative grunts.

"Slow down, Soph," her mother pleaded. "You'll make yourself sick."

"I can't, Mum," she replied between mouthfuls. "It's too delicious."

Jonathan looked over at his sister. Her cheeks bulged as her tiny mouth struggled to deal with the volume of food being shoved into it. She looked like a squirrel. He began to giggle. But he must have looked the same, because when she saw him she began to giggle too. Soon they were both bent double, silently chortling away as they fought to keep their mouths closed. It was no use though, every few seconds a piece of chewed-up food flew into the air, unwittingly released by a mouth full to overflowing.

"Kids!" scolded Margaret, scanning the room to see if anyone had noticed. "Stop that!"

This finished them completely. Sophie abandoned all decorum, laying her head flat on the table with her mouth wide open, exposing what food was left, cackling like a witch. Tears were streaming from Jonathan's eyes, and they looked as if they were about to pop out of his head as he choked down the rest of his food, tried to drink his water and slapped the table in mirth all at the same time. Malcolm chuckled quietly to himself in the corner.

"You two," he laughed. "Can't bloody bring you anywhere!"

Even Margaret was smiling now. She stopped caring who was watching them. *Let them watch*, she thought, *we're allowed to go mad every now and then.*

After dessert they cleaned up the table as much as they could, paid and headed out into the warm summer evening.

"What now, kids?" asked Malcolm warily. He wanted nothing more than to return to the hotel, find a seat at the bar and relax for the rest of the night.

"Can we go to see *Star Wars*, Dad? There's a cinema just down there," Jonathan asked, pointing to a multiplex in the distance.

Malcolm sighed. He knew little about the *Star Wars* movies, but he knew they ran for at least two hours, if not more.

"What do you think?" he asked the women.

Sophie screwed up her nose in doubt. "Would I like it, Jonathan?"

"You'd love it, Soph. It's got cool aliens and light-sabre battles, and there's this bloke called Darth Maul whose face is red with black dots ..."

He stopped short; his description wasn't exactly winning her over.

"... but yeah there's that. And then there's this love story between a princess and a handsome knight. And Ewan McGregor – you like him, don't you?"

Sophie's eyes lit up at the mention of the actor's name. "I *do* like Ewan McGregor. Can we go, Mum, please?"

"I think that's settled, then," declared Margaret, linking arms with her two children and heading in the direction of the multiplex. Malcolm trailed behind, calculating the cost of four cinema tickets, four large popcorns and four large Cokes.

20

BY THE TIME DARTH MAUL had been laid to rest and the galaxy had been saved, Malcolm was fifty quid out of pocket and had a numb backside.

"Bloody hell, how long was that?" he asked, stretching his aching joints.

"Not long enough," smiled Sophie who, against all odds, had loved every minute.

She was the only one; even Jonathan was mildly disappointed. "Not as good as the old ones," he muttered, when asked what he thought.

Malcolm looked at his watch; it was almost 10 p.m. Dare he ask: "where to next"? All this quality time with the kids was great, but he didn't half fancy a drink.

They stood outside the cinema, watching the London nightlife pass them by. Malcolm waited for the next suggestion, the next wallet-crunching adventure, but none was forthcoming.

"Can we go back to the hotel now, Mum? I'm wrecked," said Sophie.

Malcolm had hailed a taxi and ushered them all in before the words had left her mouth.

"Ah, that feels good," Malcolm said, sinking into the comfy armchair.

"Straight onto the whiskies, eh?" Margaret asked, a hint of disapproval in her voice.

"It's too late to drink pints now, Marge. I'd be going to the toilet all night."

"I see. Well, just make sure you don't overdo it. We're both going to need a clear head in the morning."

"Of course not, love. Just a couple to round off the day, that's all."

He hadn't had a drop since the whole Katie thing, hadn't felt the need to; but they were away on a break, so he could surely indulge himself a little.

"Well, if you're having one of those, then I'm getting something too," his wife announced, making for the bar. She returned seconds later with a hearty-looking glass of white wine and settled back into her seat.

"Clear head for the morning, Marge, remember?"

"Hmph," she said, sipping on her Pinot Grigio.

They allowed themselves to relax. Just a little nightcap before bed, that was all. In no time at all, however, Malcolm was on his fourth whisky, greedily taking advantage of the hotel bar's late licence. Margaret was in no position to condemn him; in the same amount of time she'd worked her way through the equivalent of a bottle of wine. They conveniently forgot about their early start – they'd earned this, let the morning look after itself. After all, how often did they get time together like this, with no kids, no work and no distractions? Rarely, if ever.

They sat and talked, talked properly, for the first time in months. Yes, they spoke every day but brief discourses over dinner and hurried exchanges in the morning didn't really count; but now, with none of life's stresses to occupy their minds, they were like a pair of old friends reunited. They told each other what was happening in their lives; the boring stuff, the minutiae, the details which there wasn't usually time for.

Margaret told him about the trouble she'd been having with the neighbour's cat, who kept shitting in her garden. Instead of just nodding agreeably, he actually listened. When that story came to an end she started another, and another and then another. None of them would ever make the front page, but this was his wife's life and it was important that he took an interest. She became quite animated in the telling of these stories. Her eyebrows danced across her forehead, the eyes beneath darkening with rage, then lighting up during a humorous passage before finally narrowing with murderous intent as she threatened to string up that cat by its unmentionables. Her voice pitched all the way up to falsetto as she railed against the injustice of it all, and plunged back down to baritone when she sheepishly admitting to misdemeanours on her part. She could make the contents of a DIY catalogue seem interesting when she was in this kind of form.

"I love you, Margie."

She stared at him in surprise, the tale of the missing wheelie-bin cut short.

"Oh, Malcolm Philliskirk! Getting all romantic, are we?"

Her teasing spoiled the moment somewhat, but she quickly redeemed herself.

"I love you too, Malcolm," she said, leaning over and taking his hand in hers.

She had a twinkle in her eye, a look of devilment which Malcolm hadn't seen in quite some time. He knew precisely what it meant; the tingling in his groin confirmed it. They sat there, holding hands and gazing into each other's eyes like a pair of love-struck teenagers. She was his world, all he had ever wanted; so why had he done what he'd done? Why had he been so stupid? He'd almost forgotten about his betrayal, had pushed it to the back of his mind. But now, sitting here, cosying-up to his wife, all he felt was guilt: sickening, stomach-churning guilt. Luckily for him, she didn't seem to notice. She went on staring into his eyes, utterly devoted to her one-and-only. He needed another drink, something to take the edge off.

He broke the silence, hastily removing his hand from hers. "Another drink, love?"

"All right," she said passively.

He stood at the bar watching the barman pour his drink, silently urging him to hurry up. As soon as it was presented to him he drained it and asked for another, making sure his wife still had her back to them. He took his drink, the second one, back to their table, along with her wine. Marge was resting in her chair, observing him.

"Twenty years, Malc, and still as strong as ever."

He sipped nervously from his drink, afraid to meet her eye.

"And we'll get through this too, Malc."

Get through what? How had she figured it out?

No, she was referring to Jonathan and his calls to the adoption agency, of course. Paranoia had taken hold now. He just wanted to finish his drink and get to bed before things got any worse.

But Margaret had no intention of hitting the hay just yet. She had passed the frisky phase and was now ready to party.

"Is there any music in here?" she asked loudly, turning her head this way and that as if searching for a big red sign with the word MUSIC emblazoned across it.

Malcolm remembered the last time they'd had a weekend away, and how she'd commandeered the jukebox at the little country pub they'd found themselves in. She'd pleaded with the owner to crank it up as loud as it would go, and then played 'Madonna's Greatest Hits' on a loop for the rest of the evening. Rather than being offended, the locals seemed content to play up to the newcomers, many of them joining her on the dance floor she'd created by rearranging a few tables and chairs. She didn't let her hair down very often, but when she did she really went for it.

"Come on Malc, drink up," she instructed.

He dutifully did as he was told. "Want another?" he asked.

"I certainly do," she replied, scanning the room once more. "And Malc?"

"Yeah?"

"Ask the barman to put on some music, will you? It's dead in here."

He returned less than a minute later with a double whisky for himself and another glass of wine for his wife. She looked at him accusingly. Where was her music?

"Oh," he replied dully. "The barman said they can't play music this late 'cos most of the patrons are in bed."

"Do you think we could sneak out to a disco?" she inquired hopefully.

"Don't be silly, Marge, we're too old for discos. I don't even think they call them discos anymore."

"Oh, well," she sighed, taking a large gulp from her drink. "We'll just have to make our own entertainment."

The sparkle in her eye had returned. "How about finishing these drinks upstairs?" she asked suggestively.

"I think I'll stay on a while here, Marge."

"Malcolm! How about FINISHING THESE DRINKS UPSTAIRS?"

"I'd rather not, love."

His words stung Margaret. She turned away from him, her ardour dampened.

"Oh, Marge, I didn't mean it like that."

"Hmph."

"Come on, Margie, let's go up," he said, far too resignedly.

"I'm fine here, thank you very much."

He withdrew, fearing that to continue would be to make things worse. He returned to his drink, allowing it to numb his senses and dull his emotions. He suddenly felt very drunk. It wasn't an unpleasant feeling. He resolved to continue his drinking first thing in the morning.

When she turned to face him he was shocked to see tears in her eyes.

"Am I not attractive any more, Malc? Is that it?"

"It's not that at all, Marge, not at all," he replied, vigorously shaking his head.

"I know I'm not what I once was, but I keep my weight down and dress nicely. Don't I? Don't I?"

"You do, Marge, you do. It's not that. It's got nothing to do with that."

"Well, what is it, then?"

He wavered, on the brink now.

"What is it, Malcolm?"

This moment could define the rest of his life, for good or bad.

"Malcolm?

He looked at his wife and made his decision. He chose liberation, to unload his burden and to face up to a future of uncertainty. "I've got something to tell you, Marge."

She leaned forward in her seat.

"It's bad, Marge, really bad."

All at once dozens of possibilities flashed through her mind, each one worse than the last.

"How bad?"

"Bad," he repeated, putting his head into his hands.

Now she was worried, scared even. He was dying, that was it; he had cancer, an incurable disease, mere months to live. This would be their last weekend together.

"What is it, Malcolm?"

He laughed bitterly. "I'm such a piece of shit."

"Malcolm, you're not making any sense. Please tell me what's the matter."

He looked at her, humbled by her concern, knowing that she would never look at him like that again. When he told her what he'd done, there would be no more kindness, no more looks of concern.

"It happened at work," he said calmly. "There was a new girl, a young girl. We became friendly; I was helping her to settle in." He paused.

If he was going to own up, he should do it properly.

"No, it was more than that. I fancied her and took an interest because I wanted to be near her. I knew what I was doing was wrong but I couldn't help myself. I don't know what I expected to happen, but the possibility that something might, excited me..."

Margaret looked at him, dumbstruck. This man she'd loved and given her life to had become a complete stranger.

"And then what?" she asked.

Malcolm continued, barely pausing for breath, on autopilot.

"I made a pass at her. No, it was more than a pass. One morning, I came in early and found her crying in the ladies'. I brought her into my office for a cup of tea to calm her down. While I was consoling her I put my hand on her knee, on her thigh, and then between her legs. She screamed in protest and stormed out of my office, even more upset than she'd been to start with."

He gazed at his wife, acutely aware that he was looking at someone whose entire world had fallen apart.

"I wish there were an answer, Marge, a simple explanation, but there's not. I thought of everything I was risking and went ahead and did it anyway."

She recoiled in horror. "Who are you? What kind of person are you? Who would do such a thing?" Lost for words, she rose from her seat, backing away from him as if he were a leper.

"Please don't take the kids away from me, Marge."

She didn't hear his words, couldn't have heard them even if she'd wanted to. It was all she could do to pick up her handbag and make her way to the lift. She didn't look back; she didn't want to see him, not ever again. The door to the lift opened and she got in. There was no one else inside. She waited for it to move, but nothing happened; the doors remained open. She froze. What if he came after her? What if that man tried to join her in the lift? She looked at the doors, willing them to close but they weren't budging. She had to press a button, it didn't matter which one. There was a round one with a number on it, she jabbed at it furiously; the door closed and she began to move upwards. A wave of relief rushed over her. She was safe now. She was away from that man; away from that sick, twisted man.

Malcolm stayed in his chair, watching her go. Relief poured over him; the pressure was off, he couldn't sink any lower. He finished his drink and looked at the bar. They were still serving.

21

How long had he stayed at the bar? He couldn't be sure, but he was definitely the last to leave. They'd been turning off the lights and putting chairs on tables when he'd finished his last drink. Had he told the barman about his marital difficulties? He thought he had told someone. His request to sleep on one of the couches in the bar had been flatly refused. And the night porter was similarly unmoved by his pleas to bed down in the lobby. With no other rooms available in the hotel, he faced quite a predicament. Did he skulk around the lobby until sunrise, head out into the unfamiliar streets of London to see what he could find, or go upstairs to his room? It was still his room; he'd paid for it. He understood that she might not want him sharing her bed, but surely she'd allow him to sleep on the floor? She wouldn't have him wandering the streets like a dog.

He entered the lift, the same one his wife had made her escape in a few hours previously. There was a mirror across one whole wall, a means for party-goers to check their appearance one last time before hitting the town. Malcolm had no desire to check himself out, the thought of what might be staring back terrified him. He put his back to his reflection, haphazardly pressing at the control panel until the lift jolted into life. The porter had told him his room was on the fifth floor. He would keep going until he saw the number five. It could be a fun game, a little late-night entertainment. The lift stopped and the doors opened. Someone came in, a man; a fat man. Maybe he'd know what floor they were on.

"What floor are we on, mate?"

"Second."

"Where're you going?"

"Fourth."

"Can you bring me to the fifth?"

Silence. He thought about asking another question but didn't want to impose. The doors opened again and the man started to leave.

"Hey, mate! Can you press 'five' on that?" he asked, pointing in the general direction of the control panel, which was now at head height; he was sitting on the floor. He guffawed loudly as the man walked away and the doors closed again. *Maybe I'll just sleep here*, he thought, resting his head against the wall, *it's really comfy*. Then the doors jarred open again. Five; it had to be.

He struggled to his feet, plunged out of the lift and slammed into the wall opposite. Lights blinkered on.

"Hello?" he shouted. "Is anyone there?"

He'd just triggered the lights in the hallway, the ones to help guests find their rooms. He clambered to his feet once more, grunting in annoyance, and surveyed the scene. It was just like any other hotel corridor: beige walls, closed doors and soft, spongy carpet.

"Is this the fifth floor?" he enquired of no one in particular.

There would be fives on the walls, wouldn't there? Fives everywhere. Fifth-floor fives, quite a tongue-twister. He turned back towards the elevator. It was shut now. That was okay; he wasn't getting back in.

"Five?" he asked, staring at the wall beside the elevator.

This part of the wall was a different colour, not beige, darker. Brown? There was a number on it, in a lighter shade, beige, and it looked like a five. It was a five.

"Five," he declared contentedly. "Five."

Their room was on the fifth floor, and so was he. The room – but wait, the room number, what was it? He had memorised it earlier, but that was hours ago. It began with a five, he knew that. Five one six, five hundred and sixteen. That sounded very familiar. Too familiar for it not to mean something.

He stumbled onwards, repeating the digits over and over in his head; but having what he thought was the room number and locating the door with that number were two different things entirely. He stopped at the first door he came to and stood, swaying, in front of it. Why did they have to make the numbers so small? He couldn't see a thing, not from back here anyway. He needed to get closer, but not too close; he didn't want to wake anyone up. Five-two – what was that, an X? A sudden, unexpected collision sent him reeling; he bounced around, crashing against a couple of walls, before coming to rest in the middle of the floor, cross-legged with his head in his hands. What had happened there? He looked back up at the door accusingly. It remained in place, looming over him, its number still a mystery. Why did everything had to be so bloody complicated?

Amazingly, no one had come out to see what all the ruckus was about. So, once his world had stopped spinning, Malcolm set about dragging himself upright once again. He managed it but it didn't feel right, it was too precarious. Instead, he took to his knees.

"There, that's better," he mumbled as he shuffled back towards the door. At least now if he hit traffic, he wouldn't have so far to fall.

He made it to the door without incident, resting both hands upon it while he pondered his next move. Looking upwards, he could see the outline of the valuable digits, but he'd need to be face-to-face if he wished to ascertain their identity. Sighing deeply, he rose to his feet once more, using the door for balance until he stood at full height, his hands planted on either side of the door frame. He tried to focus on what was in front of him, but his head lolled from side to side like a ship in a storm, making the numbers moving targets. He closed his eyes and rested his head against the door, reasoning that the occupants must have already resigned themselves to death at the hands of the bogeyman. Taking a deep breath, he opened his eyes and gazed forward, hoping for answers.

But it was like looking at ancient hieroglyphics in a lost Egyptian tomb; nothing made sense. His eyes were sending the relevant information to his brain, but it wasn't being computed correctly. Finally, though, his senses awoke and familiarity swept over him. The first number was a five. He already knew that, but still there was a sense of mild elation; he was on the right track. The second had notions of being an eight but eventually became a big fat zero, and the third was a two. Five oh two. He had to sit down again, the strain of it all was too much. Once settled, he crunched the numbers. Five one six, five oh two. Hotels always had the even numbers on one side, the odd on the other. So if he was at 502, where was 516? If only Dennis were here, he was the maths ace.

He tried counting on his fingers, but discovered to his horror that he only had three of them on his right hand. Not to worry, that could be dealt with in the morning. Lacking the necessary digits, it was left to his overworked brain to figure things out all by itself. He subtracted 502 from 516 and got 504, which meant there were over two hundred and fifty doors to go; that surely wasn't right. So instead he subtracted 516 from 502, and ended up with minus twenty-four. Did that mean he had to go back twelve doors? He looked down the other end of the hallway, which came to a halt at the elevator; there were no doors that way. This was hopeless. He would have to knock on every single door until he found the right one.

People would be upset, and he might get told off, but there was no other way round this. He prepared to knock on the door in front of him, bracing himself for the sight of an irate, semi-clad man, when it came to him, his 'Eureka!' moment: eliminate the five hundred. Now, instead of having 516 and 502, he had sixteen and two. That was easy. Sixteen minus two equals fourteen, divided by two is seven. Seven doors to go. Now he just had to count them.

He stayed on his knees, it would have been impossible to count and walk at the same time, and began crawling along the corridor like an unruly infant. One, two, three, on he went, knees burning from the carpet, brain unable to process the pain. Four, five, six, seven. He stopped and looked up at the door. Even from down here he could see that this was Room 516. Now for the hard part. He got to his feet, cleared his throat, and did his level best to regain some composure. Tapping the door gently, he called out his wife's name. "Margie, it's me. Let me in."

"Marge," he continued. "It's Malcolm. Let me in."

He put his ear to the door; nothing.

"Marge," he said, louder this time. "Let me in, please."

Still no response. He knocked a little louder, a proper knock this time, and put his ear to the door once more. He fancied he heard something so, encouraged, he knocked again.

"Margie, it's me."

The door opened, but only wide enough to show half of his wife's furious face.

"What do you want?" she hissed. "Go away!"

"Margie, let me in, please."

"Malcolm, if you don't get away from this door right now, I'm going to call security."

"Oh, Marge, don't be so silly. Come on, let me in."

He put his hand through the small gap and tried to push his way into the room. She resisted, pushing back, her tiny little frame doing its best to repel the intruder.

"Margie, come on!!" he moaned, throwing his full weight against the door. "I just want to sleep!"

Margaret valiantly held on, at one point almost gaining the upper hand, but with one final surge he propelled himself into the room, taking them both to the floor in an unceremonious heap.

"MALCOLM!"

They lay there in a tangle of arms and legs, Malcolm already on his way to the land of nod, his wife about as far from it as she could possibly be.

The commotion had alerted Sophie, who had been sleeping in the adjoining room.

"Mum, what's happening?" she asked, standing by the door.

"Nothing, love, go back to bed. It's just your father being silly."

"What's wrong with Dad?"

"Just a bit too much to drink, that's all. Go back to bed."

"Is he okay, Mum? I don't think he is."

Malcolm lay flat on the floor, face down, gurgling and groaning like a sick pig.

"He's fine, Sophie, I assure you. Now go back to bed, please!"

Far from convinced, Sophie backed away towards the door separating the two rooms.

"Go on, love. I'll come in to you in a minute, okay?"

"Okay, Mum."

Margaret took a deep breath. Her next task was to get her husband out of the room. It appeared unlikely she would be able to manage this feat by herself. She was just about to call reception when a member of staff appeared at the door.

"Is everything all right, madam?" he asked, looking at the snoring mass of flesh on the floor.

"I don't want this man in my room; can you arrange to have him removed?"

The staff member, small in stature and young in years, looked at Malcolm and then back to Margaret.

"I may need to ask for some assistance, madam."

"That's fine, as long as he's taken out of here."

He took out a walkie-talkie and went into the hall, presumably to recruit a team of weightlifters.

A couple of minutes later he returned with two other men, both of whom looked far more equipped for the job.

One of them sized up the situation. "Friend of yours, love?" he asked.

"My husband," she said quietly.

"Ah, I see," he replied, taking one of Malcolm's arms and nodding to his colleague to grab the other. "He'll be spending the night in the doghouse, then?"

"He will."

Malcolm woke up, looking around in confusion as he was lifted from the floor. It had taken a lot of time and effort to get here. And now, after finally making himself comfortable, he was being manhandled against his will.

"Oi! Put me down!" he growled. "Let go of me!"

"Now, now, sir," the first man said. "Your wife has decided she doesn't want you in here, so we're taking you somewhere else."

"PUT ME DOWN!" roared Malcolm, now fully coming to his senses.

He began to struggle, flailing his arms wildly as the men attempted to get him out of the room. The young staff member who had been watching from a distance suddenly sprang into action, grabbing Malcolm by the legs and holding on for all he was worth.

"LET ME GO, YOU BASTARDS!"

A kerfuffle ensued, with the four men jostling for position by the doorway: Malcolm screaming blue murder, while the other three fought to get him into the hallway. A lampshade was sent spinning to the floor, Margaret's jewellery box came toppling down from the dresser and Malcolm lost both of his shoes. Finally, after much consternation and no little drama, they got him out of the room and away from his wife. Now all she wanted to do was to close the door behind them and cry herself to sleep, but she couldn't do that — because someone else had been alerted by the goings on in room 516.

22

JONATHAN HAD BEEN WORRIED THAT he might not sleep. As soon as he'd returned to his room, the nerves had begun to kick in. And as he lay down in the unfamiliar bed, he willed the powers-that-be to bring him a good night's rest. He needn't have worried; within minutes he was out for the count. The day's activities had worn out the seemingly indefatigable fifteen-year-old.

But then, from somewhere deep in his dreams, he heard voices, voices he knew. They were raised in anger. He tried to ignore them, to drift back to oblivion, but it was no use. Those voices weren't any old voices, they belonged to the people most important to him. He awoke and looked groggily around the room. He knew he'd woken up for a reason, but couldn't remember what it was. Then he heard the voices once more. They were coming from the room across the hall, his parents' room. He jumped out of bed and went to the door. What he saw next would haunt him for years to come.

His father – the same man who he had toured the Imperial War Museum with only hours earlier – was suspended in mid-air, his arms and legs corralled by three panting, red-faced hotel workers. He couldn't see his father's face, but he knew it was him, or at least a version of him, by his voice. That voice was unloading expletives at a dizzying rate, words Jonathan had never heard come from that mouth before. His initial reaction was to run to his father's side, to protect him from these thugs by any means necessary; but when he saw his mother looking on in anguish, he realised that the only person his father needed protecting from was himself.

"Mum!" he shouted across the hallway. It was neither a cry for help nor an offering of assistance, it was the voice of a frightened child unnerved by the sight of his parents at war.

Margaret's face crumpled in despair at the sight of her elder child. If only he could have been spared, everything might have been all right.

"Jonathan," she called out above the din, "your father's just had a bit too much to drink. Go back to bed."

But she knew it was pointless. How could he possibly go back to bed without seeing the last act of this dreadful charade?

Jonathan crossed the hallway and watched aghast as the men grappled with his father. They had pinned him to the floor, the two bigger ones taking out their frustrations with unnecessary force. Malcolm cried out in pain, the fight now completely knocked out of him.

"Hey, leave him alone!" Jonathan cried, unwilling to renounce his father just yet.

"It's his own fault, mate," one of the men replied ruefully, tightening his grip.

Another yelp of agony spurred Jonathan into action. He shoved his father's assailant, sending him clattering against the wall. The man reared up, fists raised, before being calmed down by his colleague. With only two men holding him down, Malcolm strained to see who had come to his rescue.

"Jonathan, is that you?" he asked, twisting his neck upwards.

"Yes, Dad," Jonathan replied, keeping a watchful eye on the man he'd just assaulted.

"Good lad, Jonathan. These bastards just attacked me for no reason."

Jonathan looked at his mother for affirmation; had they just attacked his dad for no reason? If so, why was she standing there silently, doing nothing to help him?

"Jonathan, I don't want him here," she said, choosing her words carefully. "He's very drunk, and I can't have him near me when he's like this."

"Talk some sense into her, lad," Malcolm slurred as the men eased their grip and allowed him to get to his feet. "Just a few beers, no need for all this."

His father looked like a complete stranger, wild-eyed and cantankerous. Jonathan didn't know this man.

"I think you should go, Dad," he said assertively.

"Eh?"

This was too much for Malcolm. His son, the one he could always depend on, was turning against him too. "Come on, Jon, not you as well?"

Jonathan cast his eyes downward.

"Please take him away," said Margaret, standing by Jonathan's side in a gesture of unity. It was as though Jonathan had risen in rank; he was the man of the house now.

"Jonathan," Malcolm pleaded as the men led him away. "JONATHAN!"

His cries grew louder as they escorted him down the hall and into the elevator, until he disappeared and there was nothing but silence.

They returned to the room to find Sophie standing there, in floods of tears.

"What's happened, Mum? Is Dad going to prison?"

Jonathan set about tidying up the mess while his mother attempted to soothe her daughter. He also wanted to know what had happened, how their lovely evening had descended into chaos, but he was afraid to ask.

"Jonathan, leave that, love," Margaret said, sitting on the edge of the bed and beckoning her children to either side of her.

"Now I don't want either of you two worrying, do you hear? Your dad just had a little too much to drink and things got out of hand."

Jonathan knew there was more to it than that. He'd seen his parents argue before, but not like this. Why was his father so angry, and what had he done that had made his mother want him removed from their room? He looked at his mother's face, tear-streaked and drawn, and knew there was nothing to be gained by pressing her further. It would only add further upset, and there was Sophie to consider too; she had seen and heard enough for one night.

"Are you okay, Mum?" he asked.

"Yes, dear, I'll be fine," she sniffed, cuddling them to her. "Go back to bed, you need your sleep."

The race: he'd totally forgotten about it. What time was it now? The clock on the bedside table told him it was after three; he was due at the starting line in eight hours' time.

"Are you sure you're all right, Mum?" he asked again as she ushered him out the door.

"I'll be fine, Jonathan. Your sister and I are going to have a sleepover, aren't we, Soph?"

Sophie smiled faintly from her place in the king-size bed.

"Okay then, see you in a few hours. If you need me, just knock on the door."

She smiled softly, touched by the offer. "We'll be fine, love."

Back in his own bed, Jonathan tried to find sleep, but to no avail. He replayed the last few minutes in his mind, over and over again. What had they been fighting about? Was it about him? Were they going to break up now? And where had those men taken his father? Malcolm's transformation into an alcohol-fuelled lunatic had repelled Jonathan at the time, but now that the dust had settled he was worried about him. If those men had hurt him, they'd be sorry. It was awful, the way they'd dragged him off like that as if he were a common thug. That was his dad; they couldn't do that to him.

Then there was his mother; seeing her like that had upset him more than anything. His poor, gentle mother, the most caring person he had ever known; she didn't deserve that. His father was at the root of the problem, that much was clear, but whose side should he take? He was going to be like Gary Richards now; his parents were divorced and constantly made him choose between them. Jonathan didn't want to have to pick just one, he loved them both. It was probably all his fault anyway. If he hadn't been trying to find his birth parents, none of this would have happened. He was being punished for his selfishness. This was God's way of telling him he should be grateful for what he had. It was too late now, though; he'd ruined everything.

23

THE PHONE RANG AT 8.30, his wake-up call. They needn't have bothered; he was already wide awake. He'd hardly slept a wink; how could he, after what had happened? Jonathan answered the phone, thanked the recep-tionist and got out of bed. He was exhausted and in no fit state to race. All night long he'd lain in bed, going over and over what he'd seen, wondering what had caused it. He just wanted to sit down with his mum and dad and make sure everything was okay. After a quick shower, he gathered his running gear and went across to his mother's room. They were already up, Margaret drying Sophie's hair by the dresser. One look at her son confirmed her worst fears.

"How are you feeling?" she asked hopefully.

"I'm okay, Mum," he lied.

There and then she would gladly have killed her husband. All this build-up, all Jonathan's hard work ruined by his stupidity. If he'd simply confessed his mucky secret and left it at that, it wouldn't have been so bad. She would have absorbed the blow and dealt with it when they got home. But he'd compounded things by making a scene and upsetting their son on the eve of the biggest day of his life, and that was simply unforgivable. She looked at her boy, so sluggish and lethargic. What chance did he have of winning now?

"We're ready now, love, if you want to head down for breakfast."

"Okay, Mum."

He was like a zombie.

Over breakfast, Sophie chatted giddily about their plans for the day. She appeared to have completely forgotten about the events of the night before. Usually Jonathan would have been infuriated by her incessant chattering but he just stared into space, dully chewing on his food, swallowing it without tasting a bite. No one mentioned Malcolm; it was as if he had ceased to exist. When they'd finished their breakfast, they booked a taxi and waited in the lobby for it to arrive. Margaret looked at the staff milling around, wondering if they knew that she was the one with a lousy drunk for a husband.

The drive to the arena was conducted in the same fashion; Sophie gabbling away while Jonathan stared out the window like a man condemned. He knew that the outcome of this race was of huge importance but, try as he might, he couldn't muster up any enthusiasm for it. He should have been bouncing around the inside of the cab, barely able to contain himself. Instead he sat there, wishing it was time to go home. Margaret watched him, wondering what she could do to lift his spirits. If someone didn't do something his chance was gone, and opportunities like this didn't come around very often. Sophie had switched her attention to the taxi driver, and was quizzing him on the workings of inner-city London. Margaret turned to her son.

"How are you feeling, Jon? Nervous, I bet."

"Mmm."

"Did you sleep okay? You know, afterwards?"

Jonathan looked at her sadly. "What's going on, Mum? Where is he?"

"I don't know, Jon."

"I can't concentrate on the race until I know he's all right."

"I'm sure he's fine, Jonathan."

"But where is he, Mum?"

Margaret couldn't give him an answer. She had no idea where her husband was, but, unlike her son, she didn't care.

"Look, Jonathan," she said, adopting a more forthright approach. "Your dad is big enough to look after himself, wherever he is, and you'll see him soon. Right now you've got a race to win, an important race – the biggest race of your life. So forget about your dad and focus that head of yours, do you hear?"

She tapped the side of his head for extra emphasis, hoping to almost literally knock some sense into him.

Jonathan looked at her doubtfully. "What were you two fighting about? Are you splitting up?"

Another question she couldn't answer.

"I don't know, Jon. We'll discuss it later, okay?"

"So you might be splitting up, then?"

"I didn't say that."

"Is it something to do with me?"

"No, of course not. What makes you think that?"

"I don't know."

"Listen Jonathan," she said, taking his hands in hers. "Whatever happens between me and your dad has nothing whatsoever to do with you. We –"

He stopped her short with a dismissive shake of his head and pulled his hands away. Whatever it was she was about to say, he wasn't interested in hearing it. They were splitting up and things would never be the same again. He was going to be the exact same as Gary Richards: weekdays with Mum, pretending everything was normal, and then off to Dad's crummy flat every Saturday for stilted conversations and awkward attempts at bonding. It was going to be shit.

24

ERNIE WAITED ANXIOUSLY AT THE entrance to the arena, craning his neck every time he saw a car approach in the hope that it would be the one containing his prized asset. When Jonathan finally alighted from his steed, his coach was there to greet him or, more precisely, to assess his state of mind. The sight of the pallid athlete with dark circles around his eyes sent Ernie Turner into a frenzy.

"What's up with you?" he asked in a panic. "Are you poorly?"

"No, Coach, I'm fine."

"You don't look fine."

He ushered him to the registration desk, probing him for information as they went.

"Did you sleep all right?"

"What did you eat yesterday?"

"Have you been getting fluids down you?"

It was no use. The boy was gone. He was in the same place he'd been for the past couple of weeks, somewhere he couldn't be reached. They signed in and Jonathan went to the dressing-rooms, promising to join Ernie in the warm-up area when he was ready. Ernie wasn't having that, though. He was going to wait outside for him, just in case; the way things were going, the kid was capable of doing anything. But Jonathan emerged a moment later in full attire, ready to go; he looked the part if nothing else.

They reached the warm-up area and joined the other athletes. Everyone was going through their pre-race routines, stretching, focusing their minds. Jonathan just dropped his belongings on the floor and sat on top of them. This was too much for Ernie. He wasn't having this, not by a long shot.

"What the hell do you think you're playing at?" he asked, dropping to his haunches.

"Nothing, Coach," Jonathan replied in that same, maddening monotone.

"Nothing? Exactly!"

Jonathan stared right past him as if he weren't there.

Ernie got right up in his face, inches away from him.

"Now listen here, Jonathan," he said, feeling his blood pressure rise. "If you think we're going to throw away all our hard work, all those hours spent on that fucking track, because you don't feel like trying today, then you can think again."

Jonathan tried to turn his head away, to escape the reality of the situation, but Ernie wouldn't let up. He placed his hands on the boy's shoulders, forcing him to meet his eyes.

"Do you realise what's at stake here? Win today and you go on to represent your country in the World Championships, the Commonwealths, maybe the Olympics, for fuck's sake! Can you not push aside whatever's going on in that head of yours for just five minutes and give it your all?"

A light flickered on. Something registered. At first Ernie thought he'd imagined it, but there it was again; a hint of aggression, a touch of menace; the elements that made this kid worth all the effort.

"Well?" he said encouragingly, as Jonathan got to his feet. "Can you?"

"Okay, Coach," said Jonathan, and this time he seemed to mean it.

He rose from the floor like a butterfly emerging from its chrysalis and began limbering up, half-heartedly at first but then with more intent until it became a proper, no-holds-barred, pre-race exercise routine.

"I don't fucking believe it," Ernie muttered in astonishment. "It lives and breathes."

Five minutes later the order came for the coaches to leave the holding area. After ensuring Jonathan wasn't just putting on a show to convince him, Ernie left with a spring in his step. Maybe, just maybe, everything would be okay.

Jonathan hadn't been putting on a show; something in his coach's words had hit home. Whatever happened between his parents was going to happen, regardless, but whether he experienced it as a national champion or not was entirely up to him. It still felt as if his world was falling apart, but here was something he had control over. He'd always felt in control on the track; it was the one place where he knew no one could touch him. And he was fucked if he was letting Paul Whitworth steal all the glory; he didn't deserve it, none of them did. Jonathan was the real talent here, the one destined for stardom. He'd show them how it was done, even without a proper night's sleep. What was it Ernie had said about the greats overcoming adversity? Coe, Snell, Cruz *et al*. Well, here he was, facing some adversity of his own, and if he could win despite all that had happened, maybe the name Philliskirk would someday be added to that list.

They filed out onto the track. It was perfect weather for eight-hundred-metre running, warm but overcast, a slight breeze refreshing them as they went to their lanes. There were a lot of people here, by far the biggest audience any of them had yet experienced. Usually Jonathan would be able to pick out his mother, but that wasn't possible today. He knew she'd be up there though, roaring him on. The thought gave him extra impetus and strengthened his resolve. Forget about the Olympics or Ernie or personal glory, he wanted to win this for her. They lined up and were told to wait for the stadium announcer to call their name. This was the big time; they would be introduced to the crowd individually, but the real fanfare would be reserved for the winner. Jonathan measured up his opponents as he waited for his name to be called. He'd never been easily intimidated, but standing here among the cream of British talent he suddenly felt quite insignificant. He felt small in stature, too. When had everyone grown so big? He knew most of these runners, had raced and beaten all but two of them, but they all seemed to have grown substantially. Many had grown upwards, which was natural enough, but some had also grown outwards; a couple looked like real powerhouses and could be mistaken for grown men. Then he remembered where he stood in the order: fifth. Lane five, the best lane, the lane awarded to the runner with the best qualifying time. That meant one thing: he was the best one here. These boys might be taller or stronger than him, but none of them had his natural ability, his God-given talent. They had used their physical attributes to get here, beating the opposition with size and strength, but as soon as these lads reached the senior stage where everyone was tall and everyone was a powerhouse, they would falter. Jonathan still had growing to do, both upwards and outwards. If he could beat this lot without being fully developed, then who knew what he'd do in years to come. This was the first step; succeed here and everything else would fall into place. He felt no pressure. He was at ease. This was what he was born to do.

Jonathan's name was announced; he waved deferentially and readied himself for the starter's gun. His mind focused, his world narrowed and everything else ceased to exist. The other runners, the spectators, his father's whereabouts, the identity of his birth parents – all that became secondary. Now it was just himself and the track. The gun sounded. He leapt into action; head down, driving forward, all thoughts of tiredness pushed to the back of his mind. But he didn't come out hard enough, and as soon as the athletes broke from their lanes he found himself boxed in, trapped behind one runner with another on his outside. Almost immediately the pace dropped; it was slow, dangerously slow. What were they playing at? It was as if they were conspiring against him. Whitworth had probably had a word with some of the others and planned all this: *bunch up and block off Philliskirk while I race ahead to glory.* He needed to get away from the kerb, to find some free air, but the runner on his outside was an immovable barrier. Jonathan gently brushed against him, testing the waters. The runner pushed back, forcefully. *So this is how it's going to be.*

He hadn't time to sit here in the middle of the pack; he needed to be near the front, keeping an eye on things. He had runners on either side of him now, and one behind him who was growing increasingly impatient too. Jonathan felt a leg come into contact with his, knocking him off balance, forcing him to place his hands on the back of the athlete in front of him.

"Fuck off!" A Brummie accent; the midlands champion.

"Not my fault," Jonathan called back. "Someone's pushing behind."

As they approached the end of the first lap the pace began to quicken, but he was still stuck in this cluster of runners. He could see ahead now: Whitworth was at the front with another runner, one he hadn't raced before. This just wouldn't do. He stepped off the kerb, moving directly into the path of the runner behind. Once more their legs tangled but Jonathan held his ground, using the athlete on his outside for leverage. That runner, incensed by this show of aggression, pushed back, trying to force Jonathan back onto the kerb. But Jonathan wasn't having it. He nudged him with his shoulders, daring him to engage, knowing that any more contact could see them all tumble to the ground. The runner on his outside yielded, happy to survive to fight another day. Finally, Jonathan was out. He was now at the head of the chasing pack, a full twenty metres behind the two leaders.

The bell sounded. One lap to go. All thoughts of pacing himself and running his normal race were out the window now; it hadn't been that kind of race, things hadn't gone to plan. From here on in it would be a matter of fitness and who wanted it the most. Slowly but steadily he ate into the front runners' lead, cutting it from twenty metres, to ten, to five, until he joined them on the back straight. *Hello, lads; weren't expecting to see me today, were you?* Whitworth turned to see who had joined them. The look of surprise on his face was a sight to behold. His partner in crime, a lanky, awkward kid with a prep-school haircut, continued on unabated, clearly not realising he was obstructing a personal battle. But catching up had taken its toll on Jonathan, he needed a breather, a moment to regain himself. The other two weren't in a charitable mood, and almost as soon as Jonathan had joined them the pace was upped once more. With a little over two hundred metres to go, the lanky kid made his move. He stepped to one side and thrust himself forwards, instantly gaining a few metres on Jonathan and Paul Whitworth; but it was a move born out of panic. Within seconds he began to falter, his bolt shot and his race finished. They gobbled him up as they rounded the last bend. Jonathan Philliskirk and Paul Whitworth were alone once more, ready to write another chapter in their storied rivalry.

Jonathan was struggling now; he was barely hanging on to Whitworth's coat-tails and his opponent wasn't even going at full pelt. The two of them made their way down the home straight, Whitworth, the taller, more graceful athlete, seemingly in complete control. While behind him,

Jonathan flailed and flapped in desperation, his form completely gone, nothing working as it should have been. Yet despite all this, despite Jonathan's poor preparation and his battle to get back into contention, it looked like he might just do it. With fifty metres to go he drew up alongside his contemporary, and for a moment or two he drew ahead. In the stands his mother jumped up and down on her seat, grabbing the shoulders of the spectator in the seat in front. She was screaming and swearing, repeating Jonathan's name, the Lord's name, urging the gods to favour her boy; but then, almost without trying, the other boy began to pull clear, the tall blond boy whom he'd beaten so many times before.

Jonathan panicked, redoubling his efforts, digging deeper than he'd ever dug before, but it just wasn't there. He was running on empty; he had nothing more to give. The world around him became a blur, a sickening blend of colours and sounds. He was vaguely aware he'd crossed the line and that it was time to stop running, but no more than that. Paul came towards him, patting him on the back, offering consolation. Jonathan stared at him as if he were a ghost. Second place. He sank to his knees and buried his head in his hands. He wished he could stay like this forever, or at least until everyone had left the arena; but a pat on the back and pair of hands under his armpits forced him upwards into the glare of the public; the third-placed runner, happy to have won a medal, eager to share the moment with somebody. Jonathan shrugged him off, every inch the sore loser. He wanted to get out of here. Now they were all crowding around, checking the electronic scoreboard, seeing what times they'd run. Through the haze Jonathan looked at his own time and then at the winning time; the latter was over half a second slower than the time he'd set in qualifying. Whitworth hadn't beaten him, he'd beaten himself. What had happened? Why had his body failed him at the crucial moment? He knew precisely why. The disturbance from the night before had put paid to his hopes and dreams.

Everything he had worked for, all that effort, all that toil ruined by the actions of others. His father, pissed drunk, roaring and shouting in the dead of night, so consumed by his own demons that he hadn't stopped to consider the needs of others. Any ounce of concern Jonathan had for him evaporated as he gathered his stuff and made for the changing-rooms. He knew that if he looked up at the crowd he would see his mother, standing on her own, offering her support, but he couldn't bear to look at her, couldn't bear to see the pity in her eyes. Perhaps later, when the true enormity of his failure hit home, he would need her consolation, but right now he needed to be alone. He kept his head down, hoping to make it to the sanctuary of the changing-rooms without having to speak to anyone. Going underneath the stands, straight by team-mates preparing for their own races, past his coach, whose disappointment would be on a par with his own, he hurried to the sanctuary of the dressing-room, walking past them all without a word. One person tracked him all the way, forging a path through the throng until only a barrier separated him from the second-placed athlete in the 800 metres. He ran to greet him, to congratulate him on his marvellous performance.

"Jonathan!" Malcolm shouted, hanging over the railings.

The voice dragged Jonathan from his stupor. He looked towards its source: it was his father, looking none the worse for wear after his night of destruction. Jonathan went on walking.

"Jonathan!" Malcolm shouted once more, certain that the boy hadn't heard him.

Jonathan walked on, head down, until he reached the changing-rooms. For the second time in a matter of hours, he ignored the plaintive cries of his father. He had no desire to answer them, not now, not ever.

2003

Seán

1.

THE ALARM SOUNDED, ROUSING SEÁN from his slumber. He groaned involuntarily and groped for the clock. Half seven. Time for work. How much sleep had he had? Not enough, four hours at best. This was going to be a long day.

He hadn't intended to stay out all night. The plan had been to go to Forde's for a couple and be home before midnight. But that was the problem with Thursdays; it felt like the weekend had already arrived. You'd just got paid, there was only one more day of work to go, it was all too easy to lose the run of yourself. They'd had their couple and were ready to call it a night when Pegs suggested they finish up with a few large whiskies. Never one to turn up his nose at whiskey, Seán had thought this a splendid idea, and from that point forth the night had took on an altogether different character. Naturally enough, they'd stayed until closing. It wouldn't have been too bad if they'd left it at that. He could have been in bed by one; six and a half hours' sleep, hangover gone by lunchtime; but as they were on their way out the door they met Paudie O'Brien, who suggested they go back to his for a session. Usually they wouldn't have gone near Paudie or set foot inside his house, but you didn't get many sessions in Dooncurra of a Thursday night and Paudie said he had loads of drink. That was enough for them.

Even the fact that Paudie wasn't long out of prison didn't deter them. He'd just got himself into a spot of bother, that was all. Two years for actual bodily harm? Sure, that could mean anything. Paudie was a decent sort, a bit reckless but sound really. So what if he'd fallen right back into his old life upon release? Round-the-clock drinking, late-night brawls in the middle of town, dealing drugs with flagrant disregard for the authorities, stealing anything that wasn't nailed down – he had to make a living too, didn't he?

If you were to meet him in the pub, you'd think him one of the friendliest fellows on the face of the earth. He'd buy you a drink, join you at your table and instantly become the life and soul of the party, regaling all present with his roguish tales of high jinks and tomfoolery. Then he'd take over, getting louder and louder, shouting at you, shouting at everyone, thumping you on the back, almost shattering your spine with his fist. His stories would become more sinister, the glint in his eye telling you that a new story, with a similarly macabre finale, could be created at a moment's notice. He'd order a round of double brandies for the table, watching you as you drank, making sure you didn't waste a drop. That charming man you'd met less than an hour ago was now a liability. You and your friends made eyes at one another, trying to think of ways to ditch him, because you knew he was nearing his tipping point. Things would soon turn nasty, and you didn't want to be around when they did. If you were lucky, he'd accept your excuses and allow you to leave without too much fuss. But if you weren't, and he took offence to your premature departure, well, you'd be drinking your next double brandy through a straw.

On the face of it, then, heading back to Paudie's for a Thursday night session wasn't the brightest idea, but it was somewhere to go, a place where they could keep on drinking. Seán had never been to Paudie's house, but he'd heard stories about it. Inherited from his grandmother, it had once been a cute little cottage, with a well-tended garden and a homely interior full of kitsch trinkets and photos of happy, smiling grandchildren; a lovely Nanny's house. Then Paudie assumed ownership and within weeks it became a den of iniquity, the go-to venue for every drunkard within a five-mile radius. The garden, once Mrs. O'Brien's pride and joy, became a dumping ground with empty bottles and cans strewn all over it. Bike parts, rusty engines and old washing machines took the place of hydrangeas, lilies and forget-me-nots, the few remaining flowers wilting under a nightly dousing of urine from disorientated winos. That was just the outside; what lay beyond was anyone's guess, but a front door hanging off its hinges, broken windows and crumbling brickwork hinted at something far from cosy. This situation had worsened during Paudie's spell in jail, the local winos all but moving in and claiming it as their own. That arrangement had come to a premature end upon his release, however, his unexpected return home and the ensuing fracas leaving two of Dooncurra's more loveable souses hospitalised for an unspecified length of time. After that, people were reluctant to call to the house uninvited. The open-door policy was no more. Paudie still entertained, still had guests over, but there was some indication that he was trying to make the place a home once more, to return it to its former glory.

He hadn't done a great job, though. It was still a shithole. Once he'd managed to get the door open – 'just a second lads, there's a knack to this' – and led them inside they gawped at their surroundings; it was as if someone had gone to the local dump and built a house right in the middle of all the waste. You had to wade through the rubbish to get from one room to the next, and when you got there you wished you'd stayed where you'd been. There were signs of better days: patches of carpet here and there, pink and thick, no doubt chosen by his nanny; a three-piece suite, again pink but in a lighter shade; and wallpaper, ornately patterned, matching the colour scheme perfectly. The mantelpiece bore one lone picture, a smiling Paudie, maybe twelve years old with his beloved nan, the glass cracked across the front. These were gentle reminders of a happier past, of a time when people lived here rather than existed, but they were ultimately overwhelmed by the carnage, the stacks of rubbish, the brown stains all over the walls and the indefinable odour which caught in your throat if you breathed in too deeply.

Remarkably, the house had electricity, although it wasn't much use without heating or appliances. It did afford them some light, though, via the naked bulb which hung miserably from the living-room ceiling. Predictably there was no television, but Paudie did have a battered little radio with a tape deck. As soon as they saw it they knew what was coming: traditional Irish music, and lots of it. True to form, Paudie procured a tape from the inside pocket of his denim jacket, and within seconds the Chieftains were singing loud and proud through the radio's tinny speakers.

"What the fuck are we doing here, lads?" Seán whispered, careful not to upset their host who had disappeared to find the drink he had promised them.

"Ah, relax, Seán, will ya. This is great craic," Pegs replied, his knees hopping up and down, mimicking the playing of an imaginary bodhrán.

"For fuck's sake, Pegs, don't encourage him. He'll have us all on our feet singing the national anthem at this rate."

That was Hooch, a workmate of Pegs' who had been hanging around with them a lot lately. After some initial misgivings, Seán had warmed to the friend of his friend and now considered him a friend in his own right. They shared the same hobbies; football, music, drinking and drugs. Were of the same age and social status, and had a similar outlook on life; here for a good time, not a long time. Their friendship, while a surprise to them both, was, in many ways, written in the stars.

"Comfy, lads, are we?" queried Paudie as he returned to join them.

"Grand now, Paudie, thanks," replied Pegs, not looking up from the joint he was busily rolling.

"Ah yeah, a few tunes and a few drinks; sure that's all you need, isn't it, lads?"

"'Tis, Paudie," said Hooch solemnly.

They sat in silence for a moment, Seán wondering whether to compliment their host on his home and thinking better of it; Hooch sipping from his can, pausing, and then sipping from it again. Only Pegs seemed entirely unperturbed by the situation, amiably nodding his head to the music and burning the hash into the joint, as if he spent most nights hanging out with the local sociopath.

Finally, he sparked it up, took a couple of drags and passed it to Paudie.

"I don't smoke that shit," their host retorted, aggressively downing another can, his third since they'd arrived half an hour earlier.

He stood up, wiped the beer from his long, straggly beard and announced that he'd be back with some 'real booze' in a couple of minutes.

"Fuckin' hell, lads, why did we come back here?" asked Hooch, stifling a giggle.

"He's not right in the head, lads, I'm tellin' ye," said Seán, nervously looking over his shoulder. "If he starts on any of us, we all jump on him at the same time, agreed?"

He looked to his friends for reassurance, but all he got was a big stoned smile from Pegs and an 'I'm a lover, not a fighter' look from Hooch. Neither of them seemed to understand the gravity of the situation, that a word out of place could see them buried in the garden with the rest of Paudie's victims. He could be heard clattering away in the kitchen, pots and pans crashing against the walls, the occasional 'fuck' as he struggled to find his 'real booze'.

"That's probably where he keeps his tools, lads," Seán whispered. "C'mon to fuck, let's go."

"Relax, Seán, for fuck's sake," said Pegs. "He's just gone off to get more drink. With any luck, he'll have some vodka or something."

"FOUND YA, YA BASTARD!!"

Paudie's voice sounded out triumphantly from the kitchen; whether it was alcohol or a murder weapon he'd located they couldn't be sure. He returned, kicking cans and rubbish as he went.

"Look at this, lads," he said proudly, holding up a bottle full of clear liquid.

"What is it, Paudie?"

"Poitín, lads. Poitín."

"Jesus," muttered Seán.

"This is the kinda tack we need, lads, fuck that hash shite!" said Paudie, scouring the room for glasses. "This'll fuckin' sort ye. Men from the fuckin' boys now, I tell ye."

They watched his shaved head bob up and down as he ducked and dived through all the junk in search of some drinking glasses – Sean saying a silent prayer that he wouldn't find any.

But he was not to be denied, and after a long, dramatic salvage operation he emerged with a chipped pint glass, a child's beaker and two mugs, their handles long since departed.

"Now, lads, we're set."

"Erm, can we give these a wash, Paudie?" asked Hooch hesitantly.

"Ha, ha," Paudie cackled, uncorking the bottle. "Can we give them a wash? Ha, ha."

Hooch took that as a 'no' and remained in his seat, trying to ignore the ring of dirt around the rim of the mug. Paudie poured a healthy measure of the poitín into his glass and signalled to his companions to hold out their various drinking vessels.

"Now, lads," he said when he'd served everyone, "this is the *real* shit, SO FUCKING DRINK UP!"

Seán jumped at the sound of his voice. He'd been lost in thought, wondering how they could extricate themselves from this grave situation, but now, under Paudie's fierce instructions, he did precisely as he'd been told. He knocked the drink back in one, its acrid fumes attacking his nose before the liquid had passed his lips. He waited for it to hit him. But there was nothing. Maybe he'd got away with it? This poitín stuff was fuck all. Then it came. A fiery blast; beginning in his throat, rolling down into his chest, burning his lungs, carrying on into his stomach, poisoning it, and ending by cutting off the oxygen supply to his brain.

"Fuck," he gasped, struggling for breath. "Jesus!"

He looked around at the others to see if they were experiencing the same, but he couldn't see anything except a whirl of colours and misshapen objects. He was blind now; thanks a lot, Paudie. He bowed his head, covered his face with his hands and took some deep breaths. Gradually he felt his senses return; he could hear the Chieftains, he could smell the dirt of Paudie's house and, if he focused, he could just about see.

"What the fuck is that shit?" he asked, bewildered.

"Good man, young McLoughlin," Paudie laughed. "That's the real shit; I told ya!"

Seán looked at his friends, neither of whom had finished their drink. Hooch had taken a sip of his before putting it to one side and Pegs having sniffed the contents of his mug, had cried off completely.

"Only man among ye, lads, young McLoughlin here! Fair play to ya, boy." Paudie rose from his seat, offering Seán his hand. He gripped it firmly, pulling Seán to his feet.

"Fair fuckin' play to ya, boy!" Paudie growled, shoving his face right into Seán's. Pegs and Hooch looked on in concern, but there was no aggression in his actions, only admiration.

"Only fuckin' man among ye," repeated Paudie, holding Seán's arm aloft. He poured them another measure of the drink, just himself and Seán, the two men of the house.

That was where Seán's memory ended. He recalled singing and shouting, a little dancing and then more shouting, but that was all. He couldn't remember getting home or going to bed, but he had got there, so it wasn't all bad. Now all he had to do was get up. He made to move, but stopped abruptly; the slightest movement of his head had caused the room to spin violently, and only by remaining completely still did it come to a halt. This was never a good sign. Given the choice he would have rolled over and gone back to sleep, but he wouldn't give Daryl the satisfaction. His stepfather would absolutely love this; Seán crying off work with a hangover. He'd bleat on about it for weeks, citing it as further proof of Seán's weakness and his inability to behave like a real man. Seán felt sick though, really sick. This was no ordinary hangover. He wrestled with his emotions, weighing up the cost of taking the day off, measuring the grief he'd get from his stepfather against the pain he felt now. He'd almost decided to go back to sleep when the decision was made for him.

"Come on, Seán, get up. It's quarter to eight."

He hadn't heard Daryl get up but he was out there, readying himself for his own day of work. He obviously knew Seán had been out the night before and was taking great delight in his condition.

Seán tried again to move and this time the spinning wasn't as bad, but now his stomach turned and twisted in a way it had never done before. He lay there motionless, waiting to see if he was going to get sick, but nothing came. His stomach felt empty. Chances were he'd already been sick. He hoped it hadn't been in the house.

"You getting up, Seán?" came Daryl's voice from the hallway.

If he didn't rise now the fucker would be in here asking questions, and he didn't need that.

"Yeah," he croaked back, the sound hurting his head.

Lying there moaning and groaning wasn't going to get him anywhere. It was like taking off a plaster, you had to do it quickly and without hesitation. He took a deep breath and sat up in one swift motion, swinging his legs out of bed at the same time. The pain in his head intensified to such a level that for a second he thought it might explode. It was too much to bear; all he could do was concentrate on not dying. He'd never had to do such a thing before but he thought he made a good fist of it, and it must have worked because after a minute or so the pain eased, leaving him dizzy and light-headed but alive. Getting to his feet was the next challenge. He did so unsteadily, fighting the urge to sit back down, and stood in the middle of the room trying to get his bearings. Only now did he realise he was still fully dressed in his work clothes; a 'uniform' which consisted of a black pair of trousers, black shirt and grey tie. He'd at least managed to kick his shoes off at some point during the night, or at least he hoped so; they'd cost him fifty euro and he was fucked if he was buying another pair solely for work. But there they were, at the end of the bed, safe and sound. Better still, there, on the floor, was his jacket, a bit dirty but present and accounted for. It seemed that he'd made it back relatively unscathed. True, he had a hangover quite unlike anything he'd ever experienced and he had to go to work, but all things considered, it wasn't a bad result.

"Seán, who the fuck is that in the sitting-room?" hissed Daryl, his head appearing in the doorway.

Please be Pegs or Hooch or Saddam Hussein; be anyone but Paudie O'Brien.

"What?"

"Get him out. Now," Daryl whispered, doing his best to convey annoyance without disturbing the sleeping interloper.

"Okay, okay," replied Seán irritably, brushing past him to see whom he'd brought home. Maybe he'd got lucky and brought home a girl, given her a good seeing-to and then banished her to the sofa, like a true gent? If only. It was Paudie; psychotic, poitín-drinking Paudie, curled up on their couch like butter wouldn't melt. And it turned out that Paudie was a snorer, only it wasn't like the normal snoring of normal people, more like the feral cries of a wild boar as it rutted its mate to near-death. Seán had to cover his ears to stop the angry grunts from worming their way inside his throbbing head. You could get used to the snoring, though, but the smell was something else entirely. It was like the smell in Paudie's house but somehow worse, the kind of smell you'd expect to find on exhuming a graveyard full of recently-buried corpses. It filled Seán's nostrils, stung his eyes and caused his stomach to lurch dangerously.

Paudie sighed and shifted his position. A shawl, which had been draped over him, slipped, revealing two stockinged feet. The culprits. It was they who were responsible for this crime against humanity. They were clad in a pair of thick grey socks, but that was just the outer layer; at least three other pairs lay beneath those, each of varying degrees of thickness and each smellier than the last. Why he wore four pair of socks was anyone's guess. Perhaps he added or removed a pair depending on the weather, the bottom pair remaining in situ all year round. Smelly feet or not, though, Seán had to wake him up and get him out of here as soon as possible. He gently shook Paudie's shoulder, trying to wake him without waking him, as it were.

"Paudie," he whispered. "Paudie!"

The guest snuffled testily, wrapping the shawl tightly around him.

Seán shook him a little harder, readying himself for flight at the first sign of an adverse reaction.

"Paudie, come on. You have to go home now."

"Blurgh," Paudie replied loudly, turning his back on Seán and emitting a surprisingly dainty fart.

Seán was getting annoyed now. He didn't need this shit. He had a hangover of his own to deal with, he had to go to work and he was in the shit with his stepfather. Paudie O'Brien could just fuck off for himself. He grabbed the shawl firmly and pulled it from Paudie's grasp.

"Up," he demanded. "Now!"

"Wha? Fuck off," Paudie responded, opening his eyes for the first time.

"You've to go now, Paudie," Seán said coldly.

Paudie looked at him, blinking, confused.

"Where am I?"

"You're in my parent's house and you need to go."

"McLoughlin, isn't it?" he asked.

"Yeah. Seán."

"Ah yeah, Seán McLoughlin. Any fags, Seán?"

"No, sorry, I've nothing."

"Drink?" he asked hopefully.

"Come on, Paudie. You have to go."

"All right, boy, relax," he said, sitting up and rubbing his head. "Where's me shoes?"

Seán pointed to them on the floor, unwilling to step any closer for fear of catching whatever it was that lingered within.

Paudie put them on, stood up and grabbed his jacket from the chair. "Nice place ye have here."

It was, thought Seán, *until you came in with your disgusting feet.*

"Anyway, I'd best be off," Paudie said, making his way out. "Sure I might see ya for a few after."

"Yeah," replied Seán, the mere thought enough to send his stomach on another merry jaunt.

Visitor departed, Seán tried to assess the situation. He opened a window and sprayed a bit of air-freshener where Paudie's feet had been, all he could manage in his current state.

"What the fuck's going on, Seán?" asked Daryl, reappearing.

"What?" replied Seán defensively.

"You can't just invite any Tom, Dick or Harry into our house."

"I didn't invite him."

"How the fuck did he get in, so?"

"I dunno."

"And the smell! Jesus Christ, is he a tinker or something?"

Seán sighed heavily.

"Oh, this is an ordeal for you, is it? Are you the one that's going to clean up after him? I doubt that very much."

"I will clean up after him."

"Well, go on then," Daryl beckoned, spreading his arms theatrically.

Seán hesitated, how did you clean up something you couldn't see? This was all very abstract.

"I'll do it later," he offered.

"Oh, yeah," Daryl said, raising his eyes. "I'd say you will, all right. Nah, it'll be fuckin' me that has to do it, clean up after some knacker that you brought in off the street. Who the fuck do you think you are, boy, really?"

Seán tutted irritably; this shit again.

"God, you really have it bad, don't ya, boy?" Daryl continued. "What a terrible life you have, out drinking till all hours, coming home drunk out of your mind with some scumbag in tow; just another night in the life of Seán fuckin' McLoughlin."

"Give it a rest, will ya?"

"I won't give it a rest, no. Why should I?"

More rhetorical questions. If only he had the answers.

"Look, do what you like, clean it or don't, but I've to go to work," he said, attempting to push past Daryl but finding his path blocked.

"Excuse me," he said, as politely as he could manage.

"You're skating on very thin ice, boy, do you know that?"

Now idioms to go with the rhetorical questions.

"Am I, yeah?"

"Yeah, you fuckin' are."

"What'll I do at all?" Seán asked, trying out some rhetoric of his own.

"You'll fucking watch yourself, that's what."

"And what if I don't?"

"I'll break your fuckin' jaw."

Ah yes, there it was, the threat of violence; his stepfather's favourite method of intimidation.

"Well, hurry on if you're doing it. Like I said, I've a job to go to."

There was a brief stand-off, Seán the picture of compliance as he waited for his jaw to be detached from the rest of his face, and Daryl sizing up his foe, wondering whether this was the time to take hostilities to the next level.

"Fuck off for yourself," Daryl said finally, deciding against some early-morning fisticuffs and moving over to the couch for a closer look at the damage.

That was Seán's signal to leave and he did so, slouching to the bathroom for a shower which he hoped would pour some life into him.

When he emerged, feeling marginally better, the house was ripe with the smell of air-freshener. In addition, Daryl had opened every window and both the front and back doors. The chill of the fresh, spring morning snaked its way through the house and into every room. As Seán grabbed his coat his mother appeared in the hallway, fuzzy-haired, eyes thick with sleep.

"What's going on? Why are all the doors open?"

"Nothing Mam. Go back to bed."

He left her there, in her pyjamas, scratching her head in confusion. As usual, she didn't have a clue.

2.

"WHAT THE HELL?" LAUGHED GINTY. "You had that headcase in your house?"

"I know," said Seán. "We're lucky he didn't rob us blind or kill us."

"Jesus Christ, Lockie," Pegs muttered, shaking his head in disbelief.

They were settling into their first pints of the weekend, having hit the pub early to mark Ginty's return from Dublin. That is to say, Ginty and Pegs were settling into their first pints; Seán had opted for an orange juice, his stomach too dodgy to even countenance alcohol.

"You seemed grand when we left you," said Pegs.

"What time was that at?"

"'Bout half two."

"And why didn't ye bring me with ye?"

"You wouldn't come, boy. Yourself and Paudie were stood to attention, singing rebel songs to beat the band. There was no talking to ya."

"Fuckin' hell, I don't even like trad music."

"You did last night."

They thought the whole thing was hysterical. Seán, however, was struggling to see the funny side. He was still nursing the hangover from hell and there was a shit-storm brewing at home. His headache had receded as the day progressed, but his stomach showed no signs of recovery. There was a chance he'd done irreparable damage to it. For all he knew, he'd burned the lining of his gut or poisoned his lower intestine, you heard about stuff like that happening to young lads after too much drinking. Fucking Paudie O'Brien and his poitín, and on a Thursday night, too. That was the end of Thursday night drinking. It just wasn't worth it.

"Daryl must have been bulling, was he?" asked Ginty.

Seán rolled his eyes and shrugged his shoulders. "Ah yeah, the usual story."

Ginty smiled apologetically, he knew what Daryl could be like. When they were younger, Seán had invited his friend to stay over one Saturday night. They'd stayed up late, watching movies and eating rubbish, until Sinéad and Daryl had returned home from the pub. Rather than leave the boys to it, Daryl had decided to gatecrash the sleepover, ordering them to 'turn off that racket and get the fuck to bed'. Seán had tried to protest, but his mother's pleading look convinced him to stay quiet. So they'd gone to bed at 11.30, with over half of *Jurassic Park* still to watch and Seán more embarrassed than he'd ever been in his young life. In the morning Ginty hadn't been able to get out of the house quick enough, and there'd never been any question of him coming to stay again. In fact, Paudie was probably the first person Seán had had over since.

"Well, if he gives you any grief he'll have me to answer to," proclaimed Ginty, puffing out his pigeon-chest and flexing his non-existent biceps.

"Ha, thanks, Ginty."

Seán appreciated the gesture even though that was all it was, a gesture. They always tried to offer their support when he was going through a difficult spell at home, but they were teenage lads and expressing themselves didn't come naturally. Once or twice while under the influence he'd opened up to them and told them about the bullying, the verbal abuse and how he hated Daryl more than anyone in the world. They'd consoled him, told him they'd help in whatever way they could and joked about helping him 'kill the bastard', ending with uncomfortable but well-meant hugs. Then it was forgotten about until a few months down the line, when someone else felt like sharing his feelings and the process was repeated again. It drew them closer and strengthened their friendships, but they hadn't reached the point where they could discuss their innermost anguish without chemical assistance.

As the night progressed Hooch and a few other friends joined them and Seán, frustrated at missing out on the fun, even tried a pint of cider. After a couple of sips, however, he admitted defeat and gave it to Pegs. His major concern now was being well enough to drink the following night. He certainly couldn't face another night like this, being the only sober person in a pub full of riotous drunks. It was utterly depressing.

"I'm gonna fuck off home, lads," he announced sadly.

"Ah, come on, Lockie, for fuck's sake, get a few drinks into you!" roared Hooch, to the agreement of everyone else at the table.

But Seán's mind was made up; he'd cut his losses and hope to fight another day. He waved goodbye to the clamour of the pub and made his way home.

He returned to an empty house. Kevin was spending the night at his grandparents', his mother was working in the pub and Daryl was there with her, staring daggers at any man foolish enough to engage her in conversation. He had the place to himself, for now at least. The smell hadn't gone away, he noticed it as soon as he opened the door. Whatever Daryl had done; it hadn't been enough. That stink was here to stay. It caused his keeling stomach to take another unhappy turn; it wasn't enough for Paudie to almost kill him with his fuckin' poitín, he was still tormenting him long after he'd departed. Ignoring the odour, Seán went out to the kitchen. Perhaps some food would settle his insides? He hadn't eaten all day, hadn't been able to. Today was Friday, shopping day; chances were there'd be some decent grub in the fridge.

A quick search brought up a good score: microwave pies, frozen chips and crispy pancakes, exactly what he'd been hoping for. His stomach growled in anticipation. This would be just the job; a nice feed and then an early night. He tore open the chips and scattered a generous helping onto an oven tray, setting aside the pies and pancakes for the time being. When the chips began to brown he chucked a few pancakes on top of them and put two of the pies in the microwave. He filled a pint glass with chilled Coke from the bottle in the fridge, and made a place for himself in front of the TV. Friday night telly was always decent, with the distinct possibility of tits throughout. With any luck, they wouldn't be home for a few hours yet. The ping of the microwave signalled dinner-time, and with an overflowing plate he returned to the TV just in time for *The Jonathan Ross Show*.

He took a couple of hesitant mouthfuls, but everything seemed fine. There was no sign of it coming back up, so he attacked his plate in earnest. He slathered ketchup over everything – he loved ketchup – and began cramming pie and chips into his mouth. He pierced the crispy pancakes and let their red-hot innards ooze all over the chips, the beautiful, beefy sauce perfectly complementing the ketchup, and then added them to the party inside his mouth. It was sublime. He couldn't be sure, but this may have been the greatest meal he'd ever had. And then he heard the key in the door.

He stopped chewing, listening to see if she was with him. Hearing the scuffing of boots on the mat, his heart sank. Then he heard his mother's voice, soft and cajoling. Relief. Pure relief. He would be spared the worst of it. Sure, Daryl would probably still have a go, still have a few things to say, but the presence of his mother would ensure things didn't go beyond name-calling and insults.

"Hi, Seán," said his mother as she came in.

She'd had a couple of drinks, he could tell straight away. It only took one or two to make her tipsy, and it looked like she'd had at least three. He couldn't abide her when she was drunk. She fawned all over him, pestered him for hugs and got irate when he didn't reciprocate her displays of affection. If she were as tactile when sober, he wouldn't have minded dishing out the odd hug here and there; but what irritated him was the fact that because she was drunk and felt like connecting with her son, she thought he should comply.

"Well, Mam."

"What have you there?" she said, peering into his plate.

"Ah, a few pies and that."

"Good man. I got them for you. Are they nice?"

"Lovely, Mam, thanks."

Daryl had made his way out to the kitchen and already Seán could hear him slamming press doors, rattling cutlery, snarling, swearing, sighing and ensuring that everyone realised just how unhappy he was. The cause of his unhappiness was in the sitting-room eating his food, Daryl's food, the food Daryl had paid for, and the food Seán had no right to be eating.

"Nades!" he called out.

"What?" Sinéad replied irritably, having just sat down with the bottle she'd brought back from the pub.

"C'mere!"

She shook her head dramatically and went out to see what ailed her husband. Seán continued eating, hoping he'd be finished before Daryl's grand entrance. True, there was no point in disposing of the evidence, he'd been caught red-handed, but it'd be better if he didn't have to eat it in front of him. As he ate he listened intently, trying to gauge the mood out in the kitchen. But there was nothing, just the sound of the microwave humming away. He heard the bathroom door close. Who had gone in there? If it was his mother, then Daryl would surely avail of the opportunity. The footsteps in the hallway confirmed that he would.

"Enjoying that, Seán, yeah?"

"It's all right."

"Ever think that some of the rest of us might like some pies?"

"I only had two."

"Yeah, and there were four in the pack; one for you, one for me, one for Kevin and one for your mother."

This was complete bollocks. Seán had never seen his mother eat a pie in his life, and Kevin just took whatever he was given. In fact, Seán had often seen his stepfather polish off entire packets of pies, four of them or more in one sitting. There was no fixed allocation, it was a case of first come, first served. Daryl should have been grateful he'd left him a couple.

"And what about the crispy pancakes, how many of them have you had?"

Seán looked at his plate, where two pancakes remained. He'd eaten at least three, maybe more. So in answer to Daryl's question: 'a lot'.

He shrugged in response.

"You're some boy, huh," Daryl said, shaking his head. "Inviting your druggie mates back one night, and eating us out of house and home the next; some boy."

He whispered the last words, as if in awe at how much of a 'boy' Seán was.

The ping of the microwave interrupted his diatribe and sent him lumbering back to the kitchen. At that same moment, Seán heard his mother emerge from the bathroom. He prayed for her return, hoped that she wouldn't decide to have an early night. Thankfully she rejoined him moments later, plopping down into her chair with a contented hiccup. Somehow she had managed to become more drunk in the time it had taken to go to the toilet and return to her seat.

She sat across from Seán, smiling to herself, content to be at home with her boys.

"Any plans for the weekend, pet?"

"Might go out tomorrow night."

"Oh, lovely; with Alan, is it?"

"Yeah, and Ginty."

"Ah, is Cathal home? Why didn't you tell me?"

Like all mothers, Seán's mother loved Ginty. He had a certain quality which made him adorable to any woman over the age of thirty.

"He only got back today."

"Be sure to tell him I said hello."

"I will."

Sinéad returned to her drink, her smile growing ever wider as she thought about the loveliness of Cathal Ginty.

By now Seán had eaten himself to a standstill. There was no more than a handful of chips and the shattered remains of a pancake left on his plate, he couldn't eat another morsel. He left the plate on the coffee table and drained the last of his Coke. It was time for bed now, time to leave them to it. As he rose from his seat, Daryl returned.

"Whoa, where are you going? You're not getting off that easy, boy."

"Leave it, Daryl, will you?" Sinéad said wearily.

"No, we need to have a word with him about last night."

"Can it not wait until the morning?"

"Sit down there," Daryl instructed, pointing Seán in the direction of the chair he'd just vacated.

Seán remained where he was, looking at his mother for guidance. It was only when she nodded her agreement that he took his seat.

"Do you want to start or will I?" asked Daryl, relishing the opportunity for a certified browbeating of his stepson.

"Relax, love, relax," said Sinéad, sitting up. "You're like an antichrist there."

"And why wouldn't I be? This fella," he said, jabbing his thumb toward Seán, "bringing all kinds of scum into this house. The fucking smell of him and all!"

Sinéad turned to her son. "You really need to tell us beforehand if you're having any of your friends over to stay, Seány."

"He's not my friend."

"Not your friend?" Daryl interjected. "Then why the hell did you bring him back?"

Seán ignored him. This was a conversation between himself and his mother.

"Well, whoever he was, Seán, unless it's someone we know, like Alan or Cathal, then we'd prefer it if you ran it by us beforehand."

"Okay, Mam, sorry. I will."

"Good man."

"Is that it?" Daryl asked. "Is that it?! If you'd seen this fella, Nades; a proper scumbag! Inside our house!"

"I know, Daryl, I know. But sure, look, the poor chap probably hadn't the price of a taxi home. Was that it, Seán?"

"Yeah, Mam, I think that was it."

"See, Daryl? Seán was only doing the lad a favour. How many couches have you slept on in your day?"

"That was different. I didn't stink out someone's house with me mouldy feet."

Sinéad nodded sagely. "You should really tell your friend that his feet stink, Seán. There's all sorts of things you can get nowadays."

"He's not my friend, Mam."

"But still, Seán, if you see him, say it to him."

While Daryl sat on the couch, frothing at the mouth, ready to consign Seán to the depths of hell, his mother was more concerned about the state of Paudie O'Brien's feet. If it had been she and not Daryl who had discovered him this morning, he'd probably still be here, with brand-new shoes on his feet, a belly full of soup and a clip round the ear for being such a little scamp.

"If I see him, I'll say it to him, Mam."

"Good man. And Seán, in future a phone call or even a text, okay?"

"Okay, Mam."

"Good lad."

She rose from her seat, signalling an end to proceedings.

"Now, lads, I'm off to bed. No fighting, d'ya hear me?"

"I'm going myself anyway, Mam," said Seán, stealing a quick glance at Daryl.

It was a delicious sight. He was crestfallen; his kangaroo court had failed spectacularly. The McLoughlins had sorted it out among themselves like civilised folk, and were now retiring for the night. There'd been so much Daryl had wanted to say, so much he'd wanted to get off his chest, but somehow they'd diffused the situation and made light of his concerns. He watched them go, mother and son, and felt a familiar sense of isolation. No matter what he did or how hard he tried, he could never be part of what they had – and it killed him.

3.

As SOON AS HE WOKE up the next morning, Seán's thoughts turned to his stomach. It felt a bit better. He got up and drank a glass of water. It felt a lot better; *he* felt a lot better. It seemed as if the poitín had worked its way through his system and now, thirty-six hours later, he had finally recovered; which was just as well because it was Saturday, and no one stayed in on a Saturday night.

His mother and Daryl were still in bed, but Kevin was back from his nanny's and was watching the early kick-off on TV. It was Spurs and some-one, one of the lower teams, Bolton maybe. At one point Seán could have named all ninety-two clubs in the English Football League, and most of the players too, but as he'd grown older he'd lost interest. He still followed

United and watched them whenever they were on, but it was no longer the all-consuming passion it had once been.

"All right, Kev?"

"Grand."

"Who scored?"

"Keane."

"Who else?"

"He got both."

Kevin didn't like to talk when there was football on. Unlike Seán he was still very much obsessed with the game, and if there was a match on, any match, he would be watching it. He supported Arsenal passionately. This had led to some interesting evenings as they and United annually battled for the top prizes in the English game. Seán fondly recalled reducing his brother to tears during one encounter in which the Old Trafford club rattled six goals past his beloved Gunners.

"Arsenal playing today, Kev?"

"Tomorrow."

"Against who?"

"Charlton."

"Home or away?"

"Home."

"Reckon they'll win?"

"Yeah, *easily*."

That was as much as he was going to get from his little brother, so he left him to his Spurs match and went out to see what there was for breakfast. He really fancied a few rasher sandwiches, but his mother wasn't up yet. He could have made them himself, but they were never as nice. The rashers always turned out too greasy, melding with the butter, soaking up the bread and turning the whole thing into a doughy, congealed mess. No, he'd wait until she got up. Perhaps if he pottered around in the kitchen for a while, she'd hear him and get up to make them for him. There was no fear of waking Daryl, he wouldn't stir until lunchtime; hungover and spoiling for an argument. Seán would be long gone by then.

He poked around the fridge, and checked to see how much bread there was. These were just precautionary measures, however; he knew there was a fresh sliced pan and two packets of rashers; sausages too, if he wanted them. Maybe he'd have a sausage sandwich and two rasher sandwiches. That'd keep him going. There was still no sign of her getting up, though. He went out to the back garden and sat down, drying the damp off the bench and making himself comfortable. It was warm out, the weather finally turning after a seemingly endless winter. There was a sense of spring in the air, of life resuming; summer was only around the corner. He was definitely going on holidays somewhere this year. They'd talked about Ibiza, but the prices were crazy.

"If you want the best, you have to pay the price," Pegs had said.

But Seán had heard stories about having to pay fifty quid to get into nightclubs and another twenty for a drink; all that on top of whatever it cost for flights and accommodation. Ginty had suggested a city break, Rome or Barcelona; see the Coliseum, the Sagrada Familia. They'd laughed. All they wanted was a beach, some birds and some drugs; you didn't get those inside the fucking Coliseum.

"What are you doing out here, Seán?"

She was up. Time for sambos.

"Ah, just getting some sun. It's lovely out."

His mother peered outside, shading her eyes from the sun's weak light. "I dunno, Seán."

"It is, Mam. Have a seat," he said, patting the chair beside him.

"Ah, I won't now, maybe later. Would you like something to eat?"

"Yeah, please, only if you're making it, like."

"What d'you want?"

"What is there?"

"There's rashers there. Rasher sandwiches?"

"Please, and a sausage one?"

"Okay. One of each?"

"Two rasher and one sausage, that okay?"

"Yeah, of course. Hold on till I see if Kevin is hungry."

Job done. As soon as he'd finished his sandwiches, he'd call over to Pegs' house. There'd surely be some stories to tell about last night and plans to make for tonight. Hopefully he'd got some pills for them. Saturday nights were great, but if they didn't have Es they weren't worth a fuck.

4.

PEGS HAD GOT SOME PILLS, good ones too by all accounts.

"Speckled Doves, Seán. They're supposed to be immense."

He handed him two of the tablets. Seán looked at them closely, like a jeweller inspecting some expensive diamonds.

"They've got little brown bits all over them."

"Hence the name, you fool."

"Oh yeah, speckled. Supposed to be good then, yeah?"

"The best."

"The *best*? Better than the Rolexes?"

Pegs nodded gravely.

"Fuckin' hell," said Seán, looking at the strange brown pills in an entirely different light. "We're in for some night, so."

They sat in Pegs' bedroom, outlining their plans for the night ahead. They regularly went to clubs in Cork, Waterford, Limerick and sometimes Dublin, but tonight they were staying in Dooncurra. There was nothing wrong with Dooncurra, though; Moody Blues was one of the best night-clubs around. Later on they would meet up in Pegs' house, have a few cans and head into town at around nine to Forde's, their local, where they would stay until sometime between eleven and midnight. The pills would be kicking in by that point and it'd be time to go elsewhere, somewhere with banging tunes: Moody Blues.

They had taken Ecstasy for the first time three months previously, and had both immediately declared it the single greatest thing on earth. This was the life for them, they'd found their calling. The drug opened up a whole new world to them, a world where life's stresses and worries faded into obscurity. On Ecstasy all that mattered was the here and now, living in the moment – and what a moment it was. For Seán it felt like the music existed within him, this house music from the streets of Chicago, flowing through his veins, infusing him with life, with joy, bringing him to another dimension, a wonderful place where all was well and love and happiness were the norm. Previously too shy to dance, he had joined the throngs on the dance floor, at one with them and yet in a beautiful universe of his own creation. The beat belonged to him, the floor belonged to him, Moody Blues, the world – it all belonged to him. Each groove, chord and vocal was assimilated, taken on board and sent forth in the form of perfectly projected movements. He could dance now, dance like he'd never danced before. Perhaps it wasn't really dancing; dancing was something you thought about it, practised and choreographed. He was just moving unconsciously, allowing himself to be controlled by something else, something intangible. It wasn't just about the dancing, though, it was the people too. He was a part of something; everyone who took it was. You only had to look at them to know that they knew, they understood. Nothing needed to be said, it was right there in your face. People from all walks of life were brought together by this wonderful drug. There was nothing to be afraid of, no reason to be self-conscious, you could be yourself here and no one would judge you. It was peace and love, and if you couldn't buy into that then more fool you. Speaking to girls was easier too, there was none of the messiness that came with alcohol. His head was clear, his thoughts lucid. He approached women with confidence and if they knocked him back, so what? He was just chancing his arm, living in the moment, going from girl to girl until he found one that liked the cut of his jib. He wasn't after anything serious, just someone to spend the night with if he was lucky. There would be no second dates, not here, not in this world.

The only shame was that the night eventually had to come to an end, but even when the lights came up and the music stopped, it wasn't over. They spilled out onto the street like children entering a theme park and went off in search of sessions, house parties, anywhere that would have them. And, thanks to Pegs' ubiquity, they invariably found them, gaining access to all but the most exclusive soirées. In this new environment, in the living-rooms, bedrooms and kitchens of Dooncurra, where the music was that little bit lower and the conversations more meaningful, Seán came into his own. He loved how the drug allowed him to open up, to speak freely about things he'd never mention under normal circumstances. He shared his deepest, innermost thoughts with these people, these strangers, these new friends. He opened up about his situation at home, how he hated his stepfather and didn't know who his real father was. He told them about his low self-esteem and his feelings of worthlessness Those he spoke to understood; they nodded attentively, sympathising, not judging, because they had shit of their own, shit they wanted to share when they'd finished listening to his shit. And he listened, glad to do so, only too happy to offer what advice he could. There was nothing to be ashamed of; everyone had their own shit to deal with, and talking about it made it better.

Eventually, with the sun peeping out over the horizon, they'd slink home, the living dead returning to their graves. They'd crawl into their beds, heads still ringing with the sounds of the night they'd left behind, and lapse into a fitful sleep. When they woke, it was to the same old world they'd left behind the day before, back to reality. The next day would be torture, and the one after that and the whole week, for that matter; but it was worth it, it was always worth it. Those few hours made everything else in their lives seem insignificant, and at the same time made it all worthwhile. They would shuffle through their nine-to-five, through their low-skilled, minimum-wage jobs from Monday to Friday, because they knew that at the end of the week there was a prize waiting for them, a prize like no other. Saturday night was when it all came together. That was when they came alive.

5

A FEW HOURS LATER SEÁN and Ginty arrived at Pegs' door in their finest threads, smelling like a pair of fifty-dollar whores.

"Howya, Mrs. Pegg. Is Alan in?"

"Yes, lads, of course he is. Go on up."

There was an open-door policy in the Pegg household. Usually they would just have walked in through the front door and straight up to Pegs' room, but Ginty had insisted they knock and announce their arrival.

"How are you, Cathal?" asked Mrs. Pegg, as Seán waved a greeting to Mr. Pegg and thundered up the stairs.

"I'm grand, Mrs. Pegg, thanks."

"And college? Up in Dublin, isn't it?"

"Yes. It's going really well so far, fingers crossed!"

"Oh, you won't need to cross any fingers, a chap like you!"

"Thanks, Mrs. Pegg. I'd better head up," he said, nodding in the direction of Pegs' room.

"Of course, Cathal. Have a good night now and take care."

"I will, Mrs. Pegg."

Ginty followed Seán upstairs and into Pegs' domain. It hadn't changed much over the years; the posters of Ryan Giggs and the Gallagher brothers had been replaced by ones of Che Guevara and Marvin Gaye, but it was essentially the same. There were still CD cases scattered on every available surface, piles of clothes kicked into all four corners, and dirty plates, cups and spoons lying in wait, ready to soil someone's polished shoes. Ginty took a seat on the edge of the bed and listened in on Seán and Hooch's conversation. They were talking about Es again; they were obsessed with Es. He was happy enough with his pints, and maybe a brandy at last orders if he was feeling adventurous. He'd smoked hash with them a few times and enjoyed it, but Ecstasy was something else entirely. It had long-term effects, he'd read up on it. People died after taking it too. But his friends knew what they were doing and they seemed to enjoy it, so he didn't try to stop them.

"Putting the moves on my mother again, Gints?" Pegs asked.

"Feck off, Pegs," Ginty replied, smiling. "We were just chatting, that's all."

"G'way, boy, I'm wise to you. Acting all innocent, sweeping my poor mother off her feet."

"Ah, I've enough women up in Dublin, lad."

"Eew!" Pegs retorted in exaggerated shock. "D'ye hear this fella, lads? Studying economics by day, riding half of Trinity by night! And I remember ya when you were nothin' but a little squirt from the mountains."

"He'll always be a little squirt from the mountains to me," Seán said.

Ginty threw a playful dig at his friend and a friendly bout of rough-and-tumble ensued, only coming to an end when Pegs found the CD he'd been looking for and commanded them to be silent. The album was *Discovery* by Daft Punk, the same one he played every night before they went out.

"Would you not put on *Homework* for a change, man?"

"Yeah, Pegs, haven't listened to *Homework* in ages."

"Fuck off, nothing beats *Discovery*."

"I think *Homework* is better," said Seán.

"Yep, I agree," said Hooch.

"Would ye g'way out of it?! *Homework* better than *Discovery*? Fuck off! Ginty, tell 'em!"

Ginty didn't know his Daft Punk from his punk-funk and had long since grown tired of keeping up with his friends' musical preferences. His new friends in Dublin liked local bands, singer/songwriters: The Frames, Damien Rice, Paddy Casey, that kind of stuff, and he liked them too. All these years he'd pretended to like what his friends liked, when all this great music was out there just waiting to be explored. But because he knew it'd annoy Pegs and he enjoyed it when Pegs got annoyed, he decided to side with Seán and Hooch.

"Nah, Pegs, *Homework* is a far superior body of work, and I think you know it."

Pegs shook his head defiantly.

"Fuck off! Ye don't know what ye're talking about. Wait till we're in Forde's, I'll ask the lads in there and I bet ya every one of 'em will say *Discovery* is better."

"Ah, they won't, Pegs; don't be stupid, now," Ginty continued, a glint in his eye.

"Yeah, Pegs, don't be so stupid," added Seán, laughing.

Alan Pegg turned his back on them. They didn't know what they were talking about. *Discovery* was one of the great albums of their time, a musical masterclass incorporating everything from jazz-fusion to disco and synth-pop. It was without peer. Granted, *Homework* was a fine piece of work, and at the time of its release he'd enthused about it as much as the next man, but better than *Discovery?* They were off their fucking heads.

6

AFTER LISTENING TO *DISCOVERY* IN its entirety and once more for good measure, they made their way into town. There was no real debate about where they were going; they always went to Forde's. On the face of things, the pub didn't appear to be anything special; a medium-sized dwelling with low ceilings and a long bar stretching from one end to the other, it was much like any other drinking establishment. Like all the best bars, though, there was something about the place, something undefinable which made it more than the sum of its parts. By day it could almost be described as quaint; a homely little hideaway inhabited by coffee drinkers, old-timers and the occasional hard-core alcoholic. When you entered its environs after dark, however, it became an entirely different animal. Whether by a trick of light or some subtle atmospheric alteration, it underwent a dramatic transformation. The snug, by day a drab enclave filled with sour-faced gamblers, seemed to grow outwards, its capacity growing as the night went on until there appeared to be hundreds, if not thousands, of people crammed into its tiny dimensions. The laughs of those lucky enough to be inside could be heard all around the pub, drawing other patrons to its boundaries in the hope of gaining access.

The main part of the pub, the top-end bar, became standing-room only. Those who drank there considered themselves Forde's more sophisticated clientele. Not for them the bear-pit that was the pub's lower end; no, they would stay up here, drinks in hand, ready to move on to somewhere better when the time was right. Their presence gave the bar a mildly cosmopolitan feel. They were the first people you saw when you came into the pub, which encouraged more of their kind to enter while simultaneously dissuading the hooligan element from crossing the threshold. For Seán and his friends, these people didn't matter; they were mere obstacles to be bypassed as they made their way to the back bar at the end of the pub. This was where the action was, where the music played and the drink flowed in equal measure. The bar itself ended here, allowing for more floor space and seating areas for Forde's 18-30s. This was their haunt, the place where, not everybody, but most of the people knew their name. They would find a nice dark corner and set up camp for the night. If you were lucky you got one of the booths, everyone piling inside before a drink had even been bought. Inevitably one or two had to make do with a stool, dragging it over and trying to make themselves a part of things. But it wasn't the same; you needed to be in the booth. With so many smokers present, however, opportunities would arise. As soon as they disappeared to the smoking area you slid into their vacated spot and, on their return, acted like you'd been there for days.

Over time Seán and his friends had claimed a booth of their own, one dug so deep into the pub's brickwork as to be almost invisible. It was their hideout, their little corner. Getting it hadn't been easy, but thanks to repeated trips, sometimes three or four nights a week, they had marked it as theirs. Others didn't so much as shy away from their corner as find themselves outnumbered and overwhelmed should they be stupid enough to sit there. It reached the point where people always knew how to find them and where they'd be; no one ever had to ring ahead or even send a text. If Pegs and the lads were out, then they were in that dark little corner down the back of Forde's.

That was where they were tonight, or at least where they'd intended to be. They'd arrived later than usual and found, to their horror, that their booth had already been taken. Older lads, three of them, were in their spot, in their seats. Nothing was said, just a few curious looks thrown in their direction. They hovered nearby, ignoring another vacant booth a few feet away. They wanted their own booth, and were willing to wait all night to claim it. The three intruders were nearing the end of their drinks; one of them had an empty glass. Were they going to get another round? Could Seán and his friends move in while they were at the bar? There was movement; the one with the empty glass was leaving. He said goodbye to his friends and departed. This was their sign to move in. The two remaining drinkers suddenly had their numbers swelled to six, Pegs and company piling into the booth beside them; but there was no hint of aggression, they were friendly if anything. Message received, the two interlopers drank up and left for pastures new. Job done; the boys had their booth back. Seán scooted into the best seat, on the inside nearest the wall, the corner-most location in the entire pub. No one fought him for it, certainly not Pegs; he preferred to be on his feet, keeping an eye out for anything or anyone of note. Meanwhile Ginty, in a further sign of his personal development, wandered off, announcing he'd be back in a while. He'd spotted some college friends, people he knew from journeying up and down to Dublin on the bus. The others watched him go, their little Ginty all grown up.

Some girls joined them, friends of Pegs, wans they'd been seeing on and off. Greetings were exchanged, admiring glances cast and flirtatious comments shared, no one willing to commit to anything at such an early hour. More friends came, people they knew from school, from work and from nights gone by. By eleven o'clock, their corner was teeming with life.

"Pegs! Pegs!"

Seán beckoned to his friend above the din, calling him close.

"What's up with ya, boy?"

"Did you take yours yet?"

"No. You?"

"Yeah, about fifteen minutes ago."

"Getting anything off it?"

"Not yet, no. He is, though."

Seán pointed to Hooch. He was hunched forward in his seat, looking agitated and ill at ease.

Pegs smiled and waved over to his friend. "All right, man?"

"Grand, yeah, Pegs." Hooch nodded enthusiastically.

"Any good?"

Hooch widened his eyes and took a deep intake of breath.

"That good, eh?"

"Unreal, man," he replied, his jaw twitching involuntarily. "What time is it?"

"Just after eleven."

"Will we go in?" he asked, nodding in the general direction of Moody Blues.

"'Tis too early, boy. Sit back down for yourself."

"Ah, come on, we'll go in," he persisted.

Pegs came closer, shielding Hooch from anyone who might be watching. "Look, boy, if you go in there now in that state, you'll be fucked out by the bouncers. Better to wait until there's a crowd, more discreet, like."

Hooch nodded dumbly, not really hearing the words but getting the general message.

"Sound, Pegs," he said, slumping back into his chair. "We'll go in in a while, so."

Pegs smiled at Seán, shaking his head as if to suggest he would never get into that state from a few pills. But the drug was starting to have an effect on Seán too. His head felt prickly, as if ants were crawling all over his scalp. Rushes of feverish energy snaked their way along the length of his back, stopping at his neck before joining the ants on his head. His shoulders were tight, tensed, he was tense.

"Come on, Pegs, we'll head in," he said, rising from his own seat.

"Fuck's sake, not you as well? Sit down ta fuck."

"G'way, boy," Seán said dismissively, taking his coat and wandering off.

"Where are you going?"

Seán wasn't listening. He needed to be outside; a bit of fresh air, that'd set him straight. Pegs watched him go, making sure he wasn't going into the nightclub. He watched him amble out to the beer garden and relaxed; Seán always liked a bit of fresh air when he was coming up on a pill. Seeing the state his friends were in, Pegs thought it high time he took a pill himself. He liked to leave it late to take his. He didn't want to be out of it while still in the pub; he had a reputation to keep up, after all. Glancing furtively around him, he fished one of the pills out of his pocket and popped it in his mouth, washing it down with a slug of cider. He looked over at Hooch, who grinned back, eyes half-closed, gurning quite violently now. Best to avoid him for the time being. Everyone else was locked in their own conversations, bunched in twos and threes, laughing and joking at stuff he probably wouldn't get. Pegs stood there by himself for a while, listening to the music and scanning the bar for any fresh talent. The place was busy tonight, with a few faces he didn't recognise; female faces, young nubile female faces. They'd probably be in Moody Blues later. He'd have to keep an eye out for them.

"Where's that fuckin' Ginty lad gone?" he asked after a spell.

"Don't know, man. What time is it?" replied Hooch.

"Jesus Christ, it's quarter past, all right?"

Hooch sat back in his chair once more, sipping his pint nervously. "Where's Lockie?"

Pegs looked around; was Seán still in the beer garden? His pint was there on the table, untouched. Pegs knew what Seán was like; he was likely to go anywhere, do anything. Pegs couldn't go off looking for him in case Seán came back here and wondered where he had got to. If these pills were as mad as everyone said, it was vital that they all stuck together. Ginty had seen the signs early on and abandoned them. Now Seán was gone too, maybe for good. These other people were sound, the lads from work and those young wans, nice people and all, but they couldn't be trusted, not in a situation like this. He was gonna be left here with Hooch, the gurning fuckwit. It was all gone to shit.

Pegs stopped himself, laughing at his own stupidity. This was just the paranoia that came during the early stages of an Ecstasy rush. He had to calm down; everything would be fine. Fucking hell, though, he'd only taken it ten minutes ago and already he was feeling the effects. He took a long slug from his pint. It tasted of nothing. He needed something stronger, a vodka or a rum and coke. But the place was mobbed; a visit to the bar would be filled with danger, strangers pushing up against him, strait-laced types looking at him, wondering what was wrong with him. Then he'd have to talk to the barman, pretending that everything was okay, ordering a drink, avoiding eye contact and giving him the money. No, it was too dangerous, anything could happen. He was better off staying put.

If only Ginty were here, he'd keep him sane. Ginty always knew what to do, that was what a college education got you. Pegs didn't even mind if he ran off with his mother. He'd only been joking earlier on, but if Ginty wanted to elope with Mrs. Pegg then he wouldn't stand in their way; just so long as he'd sit here and chat to him for a few minutes before they went. If he'd do that much for him, he'd be more than happy for him to move into their house and take up with his mother. His father could move into his room; they'd go tops and tails. It'd be like being a kid and going camping, a right laugh, and if they heard Ginty and Mrs. Pegg going at it like the clappers, they'd tell ghost stories and make up jokes to distract them from the noises. In the morning they'd all shuffle down for breakfast; his mother all airy and light-hearted after getting a good seeing-to, his father defeated and sombre, cuckolded by a man twenty-five years his junior. It might get a bit weird but fuck it, Ginty was his friend, and if he loved Pegs' mother then so be it.

Pegs went to take another sup from his pint, but it was empty. Was that his pint? He could have sworn he'd had a full one not two minutes ago. There was a half-full pint of something on their table; he raised it to his lips without hesitation. *Ugh, Heineken.* But it was liquid, and that was all that mattered. Hooch had sparked up a conversation with some lads from another table. Pegs knew their faces, might have been at a session with one of them, but no way was he getting involved. He didn't like the look of them; they were too enthusiastic about everything, far too cheery for his taste. Now Hooch was talking to them and he was totally alone. Hooch had been his last remaining hope, and he was gone too.

Some friends they were, running off and leaving him at the first sign of trouble. They'd probably known all along that he wouldn't be able for these pills. *Rather him than me,* that's what they'd said as they made their escape plan; *I'm not gonna be the one going with him in the ambulance.* Bastards.

They'd been clever about it, too; Ginty had slipped off quietly without anyone really noticing, then Seán had sauntered away like he always did, the Judas cunt. And now Hooch; but for Pegs he wouldn't even know Seán and Ginty, and now he was colluding with them against him! What a prick. He drained the last of the Heineken and scooped up another glass from the table. It looked like Smithwicks or some other murky shite, but it didn't matter at this stage. Whatever it was, it was quite tasty, kinda fruity, he'd have to find out what it was later on. He was watching the cheery lads now, the enthusiastic boys with their toothy grins and their crew-cuts. Fuckin' eejits. They were having a right laugh with Hooch, probably talking about Pegs and how he was going to die after taking a Speckled Dove. Laughing their heads off, they were. He tried to make out what they were saying, staring at their mouths, but he couldn't figure it out. Something about Hula Hoops or Pot Noodle Poodles, he couldn't tell.

"Hey, Pegs, you alright man?" shouted Hooch.

Pegs looked at him dumbly. What did that mean? Did he not look alright? That's what they'd been discussing: how fucked-up he looked! Well, he wasn't going to let them have any more laughs at his expense. He decided to play it cool, nodding slowly, trying not to give too much away. But Hooch didn't take the hint, leaving his new friends to join him.

"Hey, Pegs, man, you're freaking the lads out. They think you wanna box the heads off 'em or something."

"What?"

"You're staring at the boys. They're all right, I know them from school. So, y'know, chill out and stuff."

Pegs nodded again and averted his gaze. What were they so paranoid about, the cheerful bastards? He'd only been trying to lip-read what they were saying in case they were plotting against him, what was wrong with that? He'd had enough of this shit, bunch of wankers in this place, he was going home. Alan Pegg knocked back the last of the fruity, murky pint, grabbed his jacket from the back of a chair and rose to his feet. Home to bed, that's where he was off to, away from these cunts. As he got up, though, he hesitated. Instead of storming out the door in a fit of pique, he stood still. How had he not noticed this before? Forde's, this pub that they visited every weekend without fail, was home to some of the most beautiful people he'd ever seen. He looked at them in amazement.

Their faces shimmered in the light, their eyes twinkled and their mouths danced as they regaled each other with tales of mischief and tomfoolery. He looked from one person to the next, hearing every syllable, smelling their perfume and their stale cigarette breath. He wanted to join them, to laugh at their jokes, to slap them on the back and tell them what good people they were, but he didn't need to because he was there with them all. They were his kin, they were the good people of Dooncurra; salt-of-the-earth folk, just like him. They might never understand the significance of this moment, but it didn't matter, because he did. This was what it was all about, life and living, being at one with your fellow man, sharing experiences, unity and togetherness. If they could harness the power in this room, who knew what they might achieve? Anything was possible. He wanted to climb on a table and call for silence, tell them all that by cherishing one another and staying true to themselves they could conquer the world.

"Pegs, you ready?"

He heard the voice but ignored it; it could wait, everything could wait.

"Pegs, man, are you alright?"

He forced himself away from this magical vista. It was Ginty, lovely little Ginty with his innocent face and his secret romance with his mother.

"Ginty," he said softly, taking his friend's hand and nursing it gently.

"You okay, man?" Ginty asked, mildly perturbed.

"Yeah, Ginty. What's happening with you?"

"I'm grand. We're heading to the nightclub now, come on."

"Okay, Gints," said Pegs, putting an arm around his friend. "Where's Seán?"

"He's right here," Seán said, appearing out of the ether.

"Seán, man, where were ya?"

"Ah, just here and there," he replied with a smile.

The two friends looked at one another, each checking to see if the other was feeling it. They didn't need to say anything, it was all there in their eyes, and it said: *Best yokes ever.*

7

As soon as they entered Moody Blues, everything fell into place. The fidgeting anxiety of the pub disappeared, to be replaced by a sense of rapture, of freedom. The dance floor was already full of faces just like theirs; happy-eyed, contented souls, high on love, high on life. Thumping bass-lines reverberated throughout the club, the music seeming to rise up from the floor and pulse through their bodies, compelling them forward in a series of contained, controlled movements. The song changed key, the bass softened and an ear-piercing falsetto instructed the crowd to 'reach up'. They did as they were told, roaring their approval as the lights went down and the music slowed to a halt. For a few seconds there was complete silence, only the whistles of the revellers breaking the spell. The DJ had them in the palm of his hand, the only decision being when to release them. Just when it seemed he'd left it too long and the crowd were about to revolt, he set them free, spinning the record back into action. Moody Blues exploded into life, born again, the cheers and whoops of euphoria audible even over the crashing house music.

They quickly ordered some drinks and left them with Ginty as they made their way onto the dance-floor. Cathal looked on with a tinge of sadness as they joined the party, went off to another dimension, or whatever it was they did. He wasn't jealous; he could have had a Speckled Dove if he so desired, he could have been right there with them, wild-eyed and joyous. But his life was different to theirs now. He was at college, Trinity College, and he had worked hard to get there; he wasn't going to waste his opportunity. He was going to get an economics degree and then a decent job. What would become of his friends, though? Where would they end up when the party was over? Seán worked in a department store and, while Ginty didn't look down on his vocation, it didn't strike him as the kind of job with good career prospects. Pegs accompanied his father on painting and decorating jobs a few days a week, and spent the rest of his days in bed. Their attitude to life was different to his; they thought only of the here and now. As long as they had enough money to go out every weekend, they were content. Ginty was already thinking of his future; he had it all mapped out. Once he'd graduated, he planned to travel for a few years; America, Australia, mainland Europe, get some life experience. Once he'd got that out of his system, he'd return to Ireland, Dublin probably. He'd take a well-paid job, start saving and eventually return to Dooncurra, with a wife in tow, to start a family. He hoped they'd all still be friends by that point, thought they would be. Chances were, even then, that they would still be doing the same thing, living in the moment, not thinking about the bigger picture. Well, fuck it, if they were still in shitty jobs and spending all their money on booze and drugs when they were forty, they'd still be his best friends. Who cared what you did for a living? Good friends were for life and these would always be his. Ginty sank the last of his Guinness, slammed the empty glass on the table and went to join his friends on the dance floor.

"Hon Ginty!" Seán called out, as the little man busted moves that could only have been learned from some weirdos in Dublin.

Seán moved over beside him, trying out some moves of his own. If they could only see him now, Daryl, his grandmother, Leanne, they'd realise how wrong they were about him. He wasn't a sicko or a loser or anything like that; he was cool, a good guy, a nice lad and by fuck could he dance. Pegs and Hooch joined them, brothers in arms, dancing in sync like extras from *Saturday Night Fever*. If you'd told them a few months ago that they'd be in Moody Blues behaving in such a manner, they'd have laughed at how *gay* it sounded. They were blokes, and if they danced it was only ever in an ironic way. But the pills had changed all that. They'd liberated them, made them realise that expressing affection for your fellow man didn't have to be gay. They might have been stuck in crappy Dooncurra but their minds were being broadened, albeit thanks to synthetic drugs made in some dodgy factory in Poland.

"I'm gonna go up there, Pegs, up on the stage."

Seán nodded in the direction of the upper level of the dance-floor, an area of the club everyone called 'the stage'. It was only ever populated by impossibly hot women and the occasional lothario who never lasted long in such esteemed company.

"G'way, boy, don't go up there."

"I'm going, Pegs. I'm going up."

Pegs shrugged his shoulders; if that was where Seán wanted to go he wouldn't stop him, but he'd keep an eye on him. He knew what those women were like, leading on young lads like Seán and then acting all innocent when their headcase of a boyfriend came up and beat seven shades of shit out of the hapless paramour. That wouldn't happen tonight, not to his friend. Seán wasn't concerned about any of that though, the thought of a jealous boyfriend watching while he bumped and ground with their beloved meant nothing to him. He was going to join the glitterati; this was his moment. He could do anything tonight, and the presence of a dozen long-legged, large-breasted babes wasn't going to overawe him. If anything it would be the opposite: they'd be overawed by him. He stood by the side of the stage savouring the moment, waiting until the time was right. A couple of lads were already out there trying their luck, fuelled by the same substance as Seán; let them try, he'd show them how it was done. He strode confidently into the middle of the floor, the lights beaming down and exhibiting him to the peasants below. It was brighter here than in the rest of the club, and just walking across the floor made you feel the centre of attention. One or two of the women looked at him curiously, their faces betraying their thoughts. *What the fuck is he doing up here? This isn't the place for any old punter.* Seán took no notice of them; who were they to judge him?

He found a spot away from all the others and began doing his thing. He shimmied his way across the floor, languid and insouciant, arms, legs, hands and feet in perfect harmony. He wondered if anyone below was watching; he wouldn't blame them if they were. The thought of being watched spurred him on. He didn't even care about the women; this was just about being up here unafraid. He wouldn't stay for much longer. It was fine for a few minutes, but eventually people would start to wonder who the fuck he was and what he was doing up there. All he wanted was a taste of the glory.

"Well, boy, you're some little dancer, do you know that?"

His nostrils filled with cheap scent, chewing-gum and cigarettes. One of the girls was talking to him. It was a distraction he could do without; this was just about him and the music.

"Cheers," he said, looking at her for the first time.

She was familiar. He thought he'd seen her walking round town pushing a buggy, or in the passenger seat of a souped-up Mitsubishi. She was the kind of woman who usually terrified him: dominant and aggressive, world-weary and jaded. But up here, right now, she was just another soul seduced by the power of those magical pills. She was attractive; not a natural beauty, not classically pretty but attractive. The first thing he saw was a shock of long, dark hair which cascaded over her shoulders, loose and untamed; it had a life all of its own, its movements independent of the head to which it was attached. Beneath that was a face so full of contradictions that he didn't know what to make of it. Harsh eyebrows, dark and mystical, cut a swathe across her forehead, giving her the appearance of a mildly irate witch on the hunt for ingredients to add to her cauldron. Her wide, flaming nostrils seemed to pulsate before his eyes, opening and closing with mechanical regularity as they hungrily sucked in air. Amidst all this severity lay something endearing, a softness which hadn't yet been eradicated by life's travails. She was vulnerable, he could see that, like someone wishing to be saved but determined not to cry for help lest there be no response. He imagined that away from here, on a regular night at home, away from all this madness, she might be considered wholesome.

Tonight there was nothing wholesome about her. She wore a small furry top, or was it a bra? He couldn't tell, but it just about covered her cleavage, while exposing her midriff and revealing a couple of tattoos on her belly. Further down, a pair of shorts, gold like the ones Kylie Minogue wore in that video, and boots, fluffy like her top, which looked incredibly difficult to dance in. It made for a quite thrilling package, one he would definitely have liked to unwrap. It had been just himself and the music up to now, but he was willing to allow her into the inner sanctum if she so wished. It was clear to Seán that she was there too though, in the same place that he was; the Speckled Doves. Her eyes seethed out from her skull, their pupils so large he couldn't make out the colour of the irises, and her mouth jerked up and down as she pummelled a piece of gum to death. Oh, she was there all right.

"Some yokes, aren't they?" he said.

"Unreal, boy," she replied, taking a spot beside him and resuming her own peculiar style of dancing.

She wasn't the best mover, but as he looked her up and down he knew, that although not really his type, he wanted, no needed, to devour this woman. Sex was usually the last thing on his mind when he was on Ecstasy, but she screamed sex, hollered it from the rooftops for all to hear. Chances were she was a bit of a slapper, like all the girls up here, but he had no problem going where dozens had gone before. They continued dancing together for a while longer, exchanging the occasional smile. As time passed and she stayed right there beside him, he began to consider his prospects. She'd approached him, talked to him and was dancing beside him; these were positive signs. He found it difficult to read women at the best of times, never mind when his thoughts were chemically altered, but this looked promising. For whatever reason, this woman appeared to be into him. He was having such a good time that it didn't matter either way; if he got off with her, great, and if not, no harm done. Maybe that was what she liked about him? His cool exterior. That and his sensational moves obviously.

"I'm Danielle," she said, holding out her hand.

"Seán," he replied, taking and kissing it.

She moved in front of him, blocking his view as she strutted her stuff to the crowd below. But she was giving him a different view, something that no one down there could see. Right before him, just inches away, were a pair of long, tanned legs, and an arse which explained why she wore those little gold shorts. This was her money-maker, her tour-de-force, her show-stopper. It was mesmeric. A proper arse, just the way he liked them, plump but firm, round, but not overly so. He had to touch it, he couldn't resist, but what about playing it cool? Leave her sweat it out for a bit, he thought; then she moved closer, her buttocks now only millimetres from his midriff. Cool or not, he couldn't wait any longer. He cupped her cheeks gently with both of his hands and waited for her to protest, but she danced on undeterred. She moved even closer and began grinding against him. *Jesus Christ.* He looked over her shoulder at the rest of the dance-floor. They were looking now all right; Seán McLoughlin getting his freak on with Danielle in the gold shorts. Take that, Dooncurra! He could see Pegs waving up at him, grinning widely, two thumbs up. That was what he loved about his friend; there was never any bitterness or jealously, he was always happy for his friends, wanting to share in their successes. Seán smiled back almost shyly and returned to the matter at hand. Now she was arched against him, her shoulders on his chest, sliding up and down the length of his body with her arms around him. He bent down to kiss her but it was too awkward, the angle was all wrong, so he grabbed her by the waist and spun her round. They shared a brief, druggy smile and then kissed, not a full-on, 'I must have you' kiss, but a more refined, circumspect, brushing of the lips.

"Not here," she said, taking him by the hand.

They stepped off the floor, away from the limelight, into a quieter, more secluded area where you could have a conversation if you so wished. There wasn't a whole lot to say. He kissed her again, this time with everything he had and she responded in kind, her jaw grateful to have a new outlet on which to work. It was all he could do to stop himself from yanking down her shorts and taking her there and then. If he played things right, maybe that would come later.

"Mmm," she purred as they parted. "I knew you'd be a good kisser."

He smiled, saying nothing; to talk would be to jeopardise this.

"Come and meet my friends," she said, dragging him over to a corner of Blues he'd never been in before; an exclusive area, populated by people beyond his reach.

Seán enjoyed the moment; walking through the club with this half-naked, leggy brunette. Lonely single men gazed on enviously. It was all he could do to prevent himself from patting them on the head and saying "There, there," as he passed.

"This is Seán, everyone," she said, guiding him to a seat and sitting down beside him.

There were eight people in the booth, all older than him, in their middle to late twenties. They nodded and waved in greeting, a couple of them going so far as to stand up and shake his hand. It was all peace and love here too; the Speckled Doves had reached every corner of Moody Blues tonight.

Danielle put her hand on his knee and fixed him with a meaningful stare. He wasn't sure what it meant, but took it as an invitation to devour her once more. There had to be a chance of a ride here, surely, and if so it would be unlike any ride he'd had before. This was a woman, not a girl. She was certainly older than him by a few years, and no doubt infinitely more experienced also. He had to get her into bed; failing that, down an alley or up against a tree in the park.

"Will we go back out dancing?" he asked when they came up for air.

She smiled indulgently. "You love your dancing, Seán, don't you?"

"I do," he said, rising from his seat. "Want something to drink?"

"Vodka Red Bull," she replied automatically.

"Back in a sec," he said, planting another kiss on her lips. "Don't go anywhere now."

He floated off towards the bar. She was his now; buying a drink signalled ownership. All he had to do was get the drink, bring it back and place it beside her, then there'd be no doubt. But when he returned a few minutes later, she was nowhere to be seen. He looked at where she'd been sitting and wondered if he'd blown it somehow. Maybe she'd had a chat with one of her friends and been talked out of it. It was his own fault for leaving her there on her own; what had he been thinking! Well, he wasn't going looking for her; he wasn't desperate, but more than that, he didn't want to find her in someone else's arms.

"She's just gone to the toilet, love; she'll be back in a sec."

A woman was talking to him, one of Danielle's friends.

"What?" he said.

"Danielle said to tell you she's gone to the toilet, and she'll be back in a sec."

He smiled at this kind woman, this bearer of great news.

"Cool," he said, nodding his head. "No problem."

Panic over, he took a couple of gulps from his bottle of cider and went to the side of the dance-floor, ready to return to the fray. All he needed was his companion. She returned moments later, still his, and together they rejoined the sweating throng. Seán searched out Pegs and Hooch and introduced them to his new squeeze. Both were only too happy to accept the hugs and kisses which accompanied the greeting.

"We're having a session back in my mate's house," she said. "Ye're all invited."

Pegs and Hooch nodded enthusiastically; a session sounded good to them. To Seán, though, it was more than good; it was exactly what he'd wanted to hear. *Yes!* he thought, *fucking yes.* A session meant a house, which meant a bed, which meant...well, he could only imagine what that meant.

They spent the rest of the night dancing together, occasionally breaking off for beverages and bouts of passion. He allowed himself to relax; she wasn't going anywhere now. When the lights came up, they returned to their seats, to her friends.

"Who's your new fella, Dani?" one of the girls asked with a smile.

Something about her tone unsettled Seán but he chose to ignore it.

"This is Seán," Danielle said, throwing her arms around him dramatically, "and he's a sexy little bastard!"

Her friend grinned suggestively, and there and then Seán knew he would get what he wanted. Those legs, that arse: he would be exploring them all. Now it was just a matter of getting to this session and finding an empty bedroom.

8

"Who lives here?" Seán asked incredulously.

"Maggie and her fella."

"Jesus."

They were the first to arrive, Danielle acquiring a set of keys, presumably from Maggie or her fella, and shoving Seán into the first available taxi.

"It's some place," Seán said, walking through the open-plan living room and into the kitchen. "They must be minted."

"Ah, they have a big mortgage to pay off. It'll take them years."

"Still, though."

"What do you want to drink?" she asked, opening the fridge.

It was an Aladdin's cave of alcohol, full to the brim with something to suit all needs.

"Jesus," he repeated, eyeing the array of cans and bottles. "I don't suppose they have spirits as well, do they?"

"Course they do," she answered, crossing the kitchen and opening up a press. "That enough for you?"

More booze: whiskey, wine, vodka, schnapps and other stuff he didn't recognise.

"Oh, they have schnapps," he said matter-of-factly. It was a drink he still enjoyed, despite its unpleasant associations.

"Want some?"

"Yeah, go on."

She poured him a glassful and opened a bottle of wine for herself.

"Now," she said. "Why don't we take these drinks somewhere more comfortable?"

He followed her up the stairs, taking in the view as he went. They passed a kid's bedroom and a bathroom bigger than his entire house before reaching the guest bedroom. It had an en-suite, which was a relief; he didn't want to be walking around an unfamiliar house in a state of semi-undress.

"Look what I have," Danielle grinned, holding out her hand.

It was a pill; a Speckled Dove.

"Halfies?" he enquired hopefully.

"Of course," she said, biting it in half and handing him his share.

He wolfed it down with the schnapps and looked at her expectantly. What next? Was it too early to strip off?

"Let me just freshen up and I'll be with you in a sec," she said and disappeared into the bathroom, leaving him alone with the schnapps and his thoughts.

Those thoughts immediately turned to his groin and whether the potency of these pills would prevent him from performing. Pegs had told him stories of struggling to get it up while on Ecstasy, how he'd wept in frustration as his flaccid member stubbornly refused to co-operate despite the presence of a ready and willing partner. Seán prayed that he wouldn't suffer the same fate.

He peered down into his boxer shorts. It didn't look promising. His penis had never been smaller; it rested upon his testicles like a tiny worm bedding down for the night, curling up into itself for extra warmth. Well, it had better wake up soon; this was no time for sleeping. She was in there now, *freshening herself up* for him and his penis. He was about to get full, unfettered access to that arse and those legs, but he couldn't focus. He knew what was in there and what it meant, but his penis wasn't listening; it just carried on snoozing away, glad of a night off. He put his hand down his boxers and played with it a bit, attempting to rouse it into life; it barely stirred, however, flopping about limply like a fish out of water. His only hope now was that the sight of Danielle in her naked glory would spur the fucker into life.

At least he had a condom; he wasn't going to make that mistake again. A few months back, after a prolonged drinking session in Forde's, he'd found himself walking a girl home; someone he'd fancied for months. He'd hoped for a kiss and maybe a sneaky feel before she disappeared into her parents' house, but to his amazement he was invited in and led upstairs.

Everything was going fantastically and he was just about to seal the deal when she stopped him in his tracks.

"Have you got – y'know?"

He didn't know, so he ignored her and carried on with what he was doing.

She persisted.

"Have you got any protection?"

He'd had sex on three previous occasions with three different partners, and not one of the girls had been bothered about 'protection', but this one was, and she wasn't letting him go an inch further without it. He cajoled and coerced, begged and beseeched, but the lady wasn't for turning. In the end he'd sullenly accepted a hand-job and made his way home immediately after.

A valuable lesson had been learned, though, and from that night on he'd always carried a condom on his person. Because you never knew, did you? And when he pulled a girl at a festival up the country a few weeks later he merrily brought her back to the tent, safe in the knowledge that he was prepared for all outcomes. The next day he replaced the departed prophylactic with a fresh one. He was a modern man now, a carrier of contraception, a participant in safe sex.

Despite that, a condom wouldn't be much use to him if he had nothing to put it on. He decided to strip down to his boxers and see if that helped. Perhaps it would send a message to his brain. *Hey, we're having sex here, would you tell your man below?* As he undressed, he caught a glimpse of himself in the mirror. He didn't look like a man about to have sex; he looked like a child. There was a tuft of hair on his chest and a thin, narrow strip from his bellybutton to his midriff, but those were the only signs of masculinity. He stood there looking at himself, at his thin, pale frame with its skinny legs and puny arms, and wondered whether he should turn off the light and hop into bed. Wasn't it usually the woman who insisted that the lights were kept off? Leaning in close, he took a proper look at himself, at his face, at his eyes, with their huge dilated pupils. He stared at himself and told himself everything was going to be all right. Danielle was going to emerge from that bathroom and they were going to have a night of amazing sex, and that's all there was to it.

"What are ya doing, ya mad yoke?"

He hadn't heard her come out.

"Ah, just looking at meself," he said, distracted by what stood before him.

She'd freshened up, all right. She hadn't been wearing much to begin with, but now her sole item of clothing was the little red thong he'd been clawing at all night.

"Well, you can look at me now," she said, coming over and kissing him gently on the cheek.

He responded by nuzzling her breasts – breasts he had initially written off as insubstantial but was now quite taken with. They might have been small, but they were delightful in their own little way. She moaned with pleasure and began stroking his chest, slipping a hand inside his boxers as they moved towards the bed. He flinched. But as he looked downwards, following her hand as it moved toward his groin, he saw that somewhere along the line his penis had got the message. Maybe it had been the sight of her in that thong, or the feel of her breasts against his lips, but something had awoken it. It had never been so awake. He'd been foolish to think it would do anything else in these circumstances. As she gently massaged it it became harder still, jutting out from his child's body like a proud soldier ready to go to war. She yanked down his boxers and began wanking him off with a dexterity and skill which reinforced his belief that her experience far outweighed his.

"Lie down," he said, suddenly infused with confidence.

He'd read something in a men's magazine the other day, something about letters of the alphabet while going down on a woman. He was going to put into action, right here and now. It would be impress the shit out of her. She did as she was told, arching her back so he could relieve her of her underwear. Bald. Completely shaved. Or waxed. Who knew? He'd never seen anything like it, not in the flesh. All he wanted to do was plunge right in, bury his head there, press his mouth up against it, smear her juices all over his face. He held off, however. He had to savour it; stuff like this didn't happen every day of the week. Slowly placing his head between her legs, he positioned his lips over her labia. Moving his tongue to where he hoped her clit was located, he began 'writing out' the alphabet. He flicked the tip up and down, over and back, finishing each letter with an artistic flourish: A, B, C, D. He got a bit stuck with G and had to start again from scratch. But, judging by the groans of pleasure coming from up top, it seemed to be having the desired effect.

Growing in confidence he continued, imagining himself a modern-day Casanova, the Don Juan of Dooncurra. M was an absolute nightmare; he kept running out of space but eventually he nailed it, and before long he'd made it all the way to Z. Somewhere around T she'd begun bucking her hips, forcing herself against him, and now her movements became more urgent and needy. Was she really about to reach orgasm as a result of his alphabetic skills? It appeared so. If he could pull this off, it would rank as one of the greatest achievements of his life. Having reached the end of the alphabet he was loth to start all over again, so he started spelling out words, just random stuff, anything to take his mind off the enormity of what was about to happen. He spelled out D-A-N-I-E-L-L-E and S-E-A-N M-C-L-O-U-G-H-L-I-N and still she bucked and moaned. His mouth was getting dry; he couldn't keep this up much longer, but he daren't stop now.

He decided to do a complete sentence, and if she hadn't come by then maybe it wasn't to be. On he went: T-H-E-S-E S-P-E-C-K-L-E-D D-O-V-E-S A-R-E-A-M-A-Z-I-N-G. The letter A seemed to be a particular favourite, and the proliferation of these at the end of his sentence sent her over the edge. The bucking became more forceful, the moans loader. She grabbed him by the head, clenching her thighs around his ears as he spelled out his sentence.

"Mmm. MMM. AAH, OOH, YEAH. FUCK, FUCK, FUCKIN YEAH. YEAH, YEAH, YEAH, YEAH, FUCKIN HELL, YEAH, AAH, OOH, YEAH. Yeah, yeah, yeah, yeah, fuck yeah, yeah."

He'd done it, he'd fucking done it! He'd made her come. He'd made a woman come with his tongue and the alphabet, of all things.

He lifted his head, a smug smile playing over his lips. She smiled back contentedly.

"Full of surprises, aren't you?"

"Sometimes I even surprise myself," he said sincerely.

She took hold of his penis again. "I think it's time we gave this fella what he wants, don't you?"

"I do," he said, reaching for his jeans, pulling out his wallet and plucking out the condom. He opened the packet and slid it on where it was supposed to go. A pro, that's what he was.

"Let me get on top," she said, pushing him back on the bed.

He was more than happy to accede to her wishes, and happier still when he saw that she meant on top with her back to him; reverse cowgirl style, with him as the bull. The view was bound to be incredible. He watched as she lowered herself onto him, shuddering with pleasure as he went up, and inside, her. She began slowly moving up and down, sliding along the length of his penis until it almost popped out and then driving it deep back inside. He grabbed, mauled and smacked her buttocks, kneading the cheeks with his hands, spreading them so he could take a look at her arsehole. He wondered if he should stick a thumb inside it. That'd be kinky, right? But you couldn't just go around sticking thumbs in people's arseholes without asking them first, so he left it. Removing his hands completely, he just enjoyed the show. Under normal circumstances, he wouldn't have lasted more than a couple of minutes in this situation; the sight of that arse, coupled with the velvety warmth of her pussy would have had him blowing his load after a couple of thrusts. The Ecstasy, though, was acting as a deterrent. In the same way he'd been unable to get an erection at will, he was now incapable of reaching orgasm. The lines of communication between his brain and penis no longer worked; she could have ridden him until flames erupted from his balls and still there'd be nothing. This, of course, was great; not only had he made her come with his magnificent feats of cunnilingus, he was now displaying the staying power of a stallion. He'd love to be a fly on the wall when she recounted their fun and games to her friends.

"Do me from behind," she said, dismounting.

She moved to the edge of the bed and got on all fours, looking back at him impatiently. Seán wasted no time, bending his knees and guiding his throbbing cock inside her.

After pounding away for a few minutes she began to moan loudly again, backing into him and meeting every thrust with one of her own. How easy is this, he thought; get up on the stage, pull a stunner, quick snog, back to her mate's and multiple orgasms all round. Not a bother.

"Harder," she instructed. "Harder, Seán."

He redoubled his efforts, really giving it his all, determined not to disappoint her. She began playing with herself as he assaulted her with increasing force, his balls smacking rhythmically against her, the sound spurring him on. And once more she came, with more ferocity this time.

Instead of the dainty groans and moans that had accompanied her first orgasm there were screeches, feral grunts, guttural emissions and throaty, quite frightening, growls. It was all very unbecoming, he thought, and yet so very, very enchanting. He slowed down and then pulled out altogether, needing a break. These marathon sex sessions were hard work.

*

"Tell me about yourself, Seán."

They lay on the bed, naked and drenched in sweat. He'd serviced her for another hour, until she'd complained of saddle-soreness and they'd called a halt to affairs.

"What do you want to know?"

"Anything," she said. "Tell me about your family; your mam and dad, brothers and sisters, whatever."

"I don't really have a family."

"What, are you an orphan or something?" she joked, then seeing his solemn expression, she panicked. "God, you're not an orphan, are you?"

"No," he smiled. "Not quite."

"Phew, thank fuck for that. So what, then? Why don't you have a family?"

"Well I have a mother and she's great, I love her; but I also have a stepfather."

His expression changed; his face clouded over. There was an edge to his words. Danielle, feeling like she'd said something she shouldn't, laid her hand on his arm in concern. "I'm sorry, Seán. I didn't mean to be nosy."

"No, no," he said dismissively. "I was just thinking about how to phrase it, my relationship with him."

"We can talk about something else if you like."

"No, I'm happy to talk about this."

"Okay, then, if you're sure."

She waited for him to continue, fearing the worst.

"He bullies me," Seán said finally. "He always has, ever since I was a child."

"Does he..." she paused. "Beat you up?"

"Nah, nothing like that; there's never been any physical abuse."

Danielle couldn't understand how someone could be bullied without a finger being laid on them.

"I don't get it, Seán," she said. "What does he do?"

"He picks on me, verbally abuses me, I suppose. Constantly puts me down, belittles me, tells me I'm nothing, that I'm not wanted there with *them*."

"With who? With your mam and him?"

"Yeah, and my brother. They've a child together."

"And he makes you feel like you're not a part of the family?"

"He doesn't just make me feel like that; I'm *not* a part of the family."

"But what about your mam? Doesn't she stick up for you?"

"She doesn't really know about it, to be honest. She obviously knows we don't get on, but I don't think she's aware of the extent of it."

"Well, tell her, Seán. Tell her!" Danielle urged, sitting up and looking at him earnestly.

"I'm not a rat," he replied, meeting her gaze. "Anyway, I can fight my own battles."

"But if he's treating you like this, she needs to know."

"Maybe," he conceded, "but she chose to marry him and bring him into my life."

She took his hand and held it tightly. He saw pity in her eyes; he didn't like it.

"I'm not telling you this so you'll feel sorry for me, y'know."

"I know that, Seán."

"I just think it's good to talk about stuff like this, get it out of your system."

"I agree."

"But there's people much worse off than me. I should be glad I have at least one parent who loves me."

"Yes," she said, holding his hand tighter. "And what about your real dad? Do you see him?"

"No. I don't even know who he is."

"Does your mother know who he is?"

Seán laughed suddenly. "I flippin' hope so!"

She flushed with embarrassment, realising what she'd insinuated. "I didn't mean it like that!"

But he didn't seem to notice, and showed no sign of being offended by the suggestion that his mother had had so many lovers that she couldn't tell which was his father.

"I've never asked her about him, and she's never brought up the subject, so I suppose we've both kind of avoided the issue."

"Do you not know *anything* about him?"

He shook his head.

"Is he from around here?"

"I haven't a clue. All I know is that my mother went to England to have me adopted but then decided to keep me at the last minute. Then a few years later she came back here, took up with Daryl and my life has been a misery pretty much ever since."

"Oh, Seán," she said wrapping her arms around him and holding him close.

She began kissing him on the top of his head, whispering words of consolation in his ear. He wasn't in the slightest bit upset, but he accepted her comfort nonetheless; it was the least he could do.

"I'm all right, Danielle," he said, "honestly."

She let go of him and scanned his face for signs of emotion, certain he was hiding his true feelings.

"I bet your mam's glad she didn't give you away, anyway. Look at how lovely you are."

"I am, yeah," he said in self-deprecation.

"You *are*," she insisted. "You are!"

He looked at her, with her pupils still dilated, her jaw still jerking involuntarily, and smiled. She was off her head, out of her mind on Speckled Doves, but her heart was in the right place.

"Thanks, Dani. You're not bad either."

"Aw," she simpered in exaggeration.

They lay back down and snuggled up together. He thought that was the end of the deep and meaningful conversation, but she sat up again abruptly a fresh thought coming into her head.

Her perfect little breasts jiggled as she shifted her weight to face him.

"You should try to find your real dad. I'll help you!"

"Grand, we'll start tomorrow."

"I'm serious, Seán," she said, and for all the world she looked it too.

In a few hours' time, however, the drugs would have left her system and the long, painful comedown would have begun; then she'd be too apathetic even to talk to him, never mind accompany him on a search for his long-lost father.

"You're mad, girl."

"Why am I mad? Why, Seán?"

"Look, we're both off our heads on yokes right now, so I wouldn't be taking anything we say too seriously."

"Seán, I might be off my head, but I know that this is something you *have* to do. It makes perfect sense. What have you got to lose?"

He had nothing to lose. That wasn't the point, though.

"I wouldn't know where to start or who to ask."

"Your mother, of course!"

"Ah, you don't understand; we have a weird kind of relationship. We don't really discuss things like that."

"So you're going to go through life wondering who he is, until one day you find out he's dead. Is that it?"

The thought had never occurred to him that his father might someday die before he got to meet him. Seán had always presumed he'd be out there waiting for him until the day he decided to go looking.

"He could be dead already."

Danielle shook her head at him, scolding him. "Don't talk like that, Seán. He's not dead."

"He could be."

"Stop it," she said, taking him by the arm again and forcing him to look at her. "He's out there right now, probably wondering about you and thinking about the day you'll finally meet."

"I doubt it, Dani."

"Why, Seán? Why?"

"I just don't think he's interested."

"But you've no way of knowing that."

Seán shrugged his shoulders. He'd been happy to open up and talk about his feelings, but now they were just going round in circles.

"Promise me something, Seán," she continued.

"What?"

"You'll ask your mother about him."

"I will," he said, planning to do no such thing.

She shook her head. "Promise me, Seán; *promise* me."

He was genuinely surprised by the force in her words. She'd become quite emotional, almost upset on his behalf. Underneath that perfect little body and all that make-up was a kind-hearted soul, someone who cared about him and his life, at least temporarily. It touched him, made him feel that they had a connection, that it wasn't just the drugs.

He cupped her face in his hands. "I will, Dani, I promise, and thank you."

"It's okay, Seán," she whispered.

And for a second it was perfect. He looked into her eyes, which now brimmed with tears, and saw how honest she was, how caring. He saw the purity of her heart and the goodness inside her. Right there and then, in that instant, he loved her. He thought they could have been a couple, a real couple, two people who loved one another and would always love one another. They could wake up in the morning in each other's arms, and nothing would have changed. There would be no awkwardness, no embarrassment; it would be just like this, and it would stay like this for as long as they wanted.

He kissed her softly on the lips, pushing away a lock of hair that had spilled into her eyes. "Thanks, Dani," he repeated. "Thanks."

*

When he awoke a few hours later she was utterly comatose, silent and still for the first time since he'd met her. He lay gazing at her, wondering what would become of her and how her life would play out. A girl like that, so naive and carefree, he couldn't help but fear the worst. But she wasn't his concern any more. He knew how it went; they hadn't exchanged numbers or made plans to meet again. This was just a one-time thing. Next weekend some other fella would be here looking at that face, wondering whether to wake her or just creep out quietly. It was for the best though; they'd spent the perfect night together and nothing would ever come close to it. Further dates would only sully its memory.

He gently stroked her hair and brushed his lips against her cheek. "See ya, Dani," he said softly and left her to her dreams.

As he made his way downstairs he heard voices coming from the living-room. Had Pegs and Hooch made it back here? He'd forgotten all about them. He didn't really want to talk to anyone right now; didn't want to field any questions or tell any tales. So he silently slipped out into the mid-morning sun and left them to it, whoever they were. Now he just had to figure out where he was. By the look of things, he was on the outskirts of town; the walk home would be a long one.

9

"HI, MAM," HE SAID, SAUNTERING into the kitchen.

The walk home hadn't been too bad; half an hour, if even that. Enough time to allow him to clear his head, but not enough to tire him out.

"Oh, hello, pet. A good night?"

"Yeah, wasn't bad now."

"Good, glad to hear it."

The dinner was already on; a Sunday roast, which he'd have to force down, his mouth as dry as sandpaper, his stomach full after one bite. Another side-effect of Ecstasy, suppressed appetite; great for supermodels, not so good for nineteen-year-old lads. He started to go to his room but wavered at the door.

"Mam?"

"Yes, love," she replied, not looking up from the carrots.

"I want to have a chat with you about something later."

She turned round, a bemused look on her face. "About what, Seán?"

"Tell you later, okay?"

"Okay, Seán."

*

He thought sleeping on it might change his mind, but it hadn't. He'd gone to bed after his dinner; switched off his phone, pulled the curtains and drifted into an uneasy, dreamless slumber. It was dark when he woke, but not 'middle of the night' dark. He checked his watch: nine o'clock. The weekend wasn't over yet. He got up, dressed and went to see what everyone was up to. Kevin was in his room, on the PlayStation. Seán could hear him from the hallway, huffing and puffing in frustration. Daryl was in the sitting-room, telly blaring but probably asleep, and his mother was in her bedroom, the shuffle of the Sunday papers audible as she worked her way through the week's events.

He gently tapped on the door. "Mam? You busy?"

"No, not at all," she replied, looking up from the *Sunday World*.

She was already dressed for bed and actually in bed, under the covers. But with the guts of four newspapers to read, it'd be a while before she slept. Seán came in and sat on the end of the bed. He hadn't really prepared what he was going to say, but he knew he had to say it now before the weekend ended. Once Monday morning came, reality would kick in; he'd be back in work and the moment would have passed. It had to be now.

"Mam, I want to know about my father."

There it was. How she dealt with it was up to her.

She remained impassive, not moving and betraying no emotion.

"What do you want to know?"

"A name would be a good start."

Something about his manner riled her; it was as if he were accusing her of something.

"You could have asked me about him any time, you know. It was never a closed subject."

"But why should I have to ask?" he enquired. "Surely it was your job to tell me?"

"I didn't think you were bothered. You never so much as mentioned it."

"I'm mentioning it now."

A silence fell as wounds were licked. The first round had been contested and declared a draw.

"His name is James Fitzgerald."

A tremor ran through him. A name. His father had a name; he was real now, not just a mysterious entity. He took on a personality of sorts. James Fitzgerald. Seán Fitzgerald. James and Seán Fitzgerald. The Fitzgeralds. Fitzy. He quite liked it.

"What else?"

She shrugged her shoulders. "We went out for a while, a few months, but when he found out I was pregnant he wanted nothing more to do with me."

She expected a reaction, condemnation, anger, but Seán barely flinched.

"How old was he? Same age as you?"

"A year or two older."

"Why wasn't he interested?"

"He said he was too young to be a father, had plans to go to college, get out of Dooncurra."

That sounded reasonable enough to Seán. He would probably have reacted the same in similar circumstances; like father, like son.

"So where is he now, then?"

"I have no idea."

This came as a surprise. He had presumed she'd know everything about him.

"So he could be anywhere?"

"I suppose so. His family still live in Belkee, as far as I know."

"What family?"

"His parents, maybe one of his brothers. I'm really not sure, Seán."

She was being so casual and offhand, as if it had nothing to do with her. He had expected to be given a full description of his father: what he looked like, his personality, how they'd met, what had forced them apart. Most of all, he'd hoped for a phone number or a postal address. Instead he'd got a few glib responses and a haughty shrug of the shoulders.

"Is that it, then?" he asked.

"Well, what more do you want to know?"

She sounded exasperated, as if this whole thing was a wretched inconvenience.

Seán glared at her, angry now. She met his gaze, inviting him to continue, but he just shook his head and got up to leave.

"Never fuckin' mind," he said and walked out of the room, leaving her with the newspapers.

He went back to his own room, waiting to see if she'd follow him. Five minutes passed and no one came. He'd been told everything he was going to be told; there was nothing more to be said. Well, that suited him fine. He didn't need her help. He had a name now, he could do the rest by himself. All he had to do was get a phone number; how hard could that be?

He crept out into the hallway, determined now. Fuck her, he thought, I'll fucking show her. The phone book was usually under the table in the hall. In the dark of the night he rummaged through old catalogues, magazines and schoolbooks until he'd found what he was looking for. Quietly pulling it out, he stole back to his room and shut the door behind him. He hesitated, wondering whether to lock it and decided against it; this wouldn't take long. The Fitzgeralds from Belkee; they would surely be in here. He opened the book at F and swept past Fagans, Fenlons and Finnans before landing on the first page of Fitzgeralds. There were a lot of them, eight pages' worth, and they were spread far and wide: Mr. A. Fitzgerald, 54 O'Cullen Road, Urlingford, Mr. and Mrs. Seán Fitzgerald, 11 Aherloe Heights, Castlecomer, Mrs. N. Fitzgerald, Knocktopher, but no sign of any from Belkee. As he ran his finger down each page, working his way through family after family of irrelevant Fitzgeralds, he began to lose hope. The fuckin' bastards were probably all dead; just his luck. Maybe they were alive and not in the book, purposely delisting themselves so he wouldn't be able to find them. If they weren't in here, he'd have no way of getting in touch with them. He'd wake up in the morning and just fall back into the old routine. His mother wouldn't mention it again, and after a while he'd forget about it too.

"There!" he said out loud. "There they are." He jabbed the page excitedly, wishing he had someone to show it to: Mr. and Mrs. W. Fitzgerald, Turlow, Belkee.

W. Fitzgerald, that's why it had taken so long; fuckin' Willie and his stupid initial. He was there though, himself and the missus, in the phone book, in Belkee. They were the only Fitzgeralds from Belkee in the book. They were his family, his father's family, and they had been there all the time just waiting for him to find them. Well, he'd found them now, and this was only the start of it. His whole life was about to change. There was no need to hurry, though; he'd done enough for one day. It was late on a Sunday evening, not the time to be making that kind of phone call. Maybe tomorrow he'd ring them. *Yeah, it's me, Seán, your long-lost grandson. Round for tea, Friday evening? Why, that'd be delightful.*

While her son sat in his room dreaming of his new family, Sinéad lit up another fag and stared dumbly at the pile of newspapers. Where had that come from, so suddenly, with no warning? She'd always presumed he wasn't interested; he'd never given her reason to think otherwise. Of course, she should have told him about his father, she knew that, but the more years that had passed, the easier it became to say nothing. Anyway, she was protecting him, preventing him from having his heart broken, because that's what would happen. As soon as his father heard he was looking for him he'd run a mile, the same way he'd done when he found out about the pregnancy. He'd have his own life now, a wife and kids; he wouldn't want Seán coming along and ruining all that. How could she explain that to Seán? How could she stop him from searching for his father? She couldn't. There was nothing she could do. It was like watching a road accident from a distance and being helpless to prevent it. All she could do was wait until it was over. Then when her boy came back crestfallen, his hopes and dreams shattered into a thousand pieces, she would mend him, fix him. Just like she always did.

10

SEÁN ARRIVED FOR WORK ON Monday morning bright-eyed and bushy-tailed. The weekend's excesses had taken their toll, but just recalling the events of Saturday night brought a smile to his face. And not only did he have a notch on his bedpost to be proud of, he had also taken the first step towards finding his father, the man who had helped bring him into this world. Yes, it had been quite a weekend, one he certainly wouldn't forget in a hurry.

It didn't take long for his good mood to be tested. Lorcan, the manager of the department store where he worked, had been singling him out for special attention of late. As Seán approached the staff entrance, he saw his boss standing there waiting for someone. That person was him.

"Morning, Seán," Lorcan said, with deceptive warmth.

"Morning, Lorcan," Seán replied cautiously. He didn't like the look of this.

The manager, a pasty-faced individual with pockmarked skin and a permanent film of sweat on his brow, held out a black sack to Seán.

"Take this and pick up all the litter from the car park."

"But I haven't clocked in yet!"

"That doesn't matter. This will make up for all those extended lunch breaks you've taken."

Seán stared at him balefully, snatching the sack from his hands and stamping off. He'd let him have his fun, allow him to think he was getting the better of him, but Lorcan wouldn't break his spirit, not today. Seán whizzed around the car park, scooping litter into the sack until, satisfied he'd done enough, he returned to empty it and begin his work-day proper. Lorcan was waiting for him again. He was smiling, smugly; it accentuated his thin, moist lips and his beady rodent eyes. Seán emptied the sack and paused, waiting for affirmation that he had satisfactorily completed his task. He didn't get it.

"Seán, I thought I asked you to pick up all the litter in the car-park?"

"You did," Seán replied, his good mood receding into the distance.

"Well, how come I can still see litter from here?"

Seán followed his gaze. He was right, there was still some litter in the car park; miniscule bits of paper, but litter nonetheless.

"Now go back out there and pick up all that litter, and don't come in until you've got it all."

"Can I at least clock in now?"

"No. I told you, this is only making up for all the time you owe this company."

His pompous little smirk made Seán want to grab him by the ears and smash his face repeatedly off the floor. Instead he smiled, a toothy Hollywood grin, and went back out to the car park.

It started to rain, a light drizzle drifting in from the river and hanging limply in the air. Seán didn't even have a jacket; it had been such a nice morning, he'd thought he wouldn't need one. He considered going inside and asking one of the lads for a loan of a coat, but that would be sure to thrill Lorcan. So he continued on, picking up litter, in the rain. All that kept him going were his memories of Saturday night. What had Lorcan been doing on Saturday night? Not much, probably. Maybe a microwave meal for one, a quick pull of his sad little todger and an early night with a cup of cocoa. Seán, on the other hand, had been living it up till the wee hours, off his head on Speckled Doves and balls deep in a hairless pussy. How could he do anything but pity his boss? Let Lorcan come in to work on a Monday morning and order him around; they both knew who the real winner was here. Lorcan may have been manager of one of the largest department stores in the southeast and have climbed to the top of his profession by the age of thirty, but he was miserable. He had to be. He had no social life, no friends and spent the majority of his waking hours running after apathetic types like Seán. In a few years all the current staff would be gone, Seán included, and Lorcan would still be there, rallying the troops, haranguing the newcomers and trying to break the spirit of the ones he didn't like. What kind of life was that? Thinking about this made Seán feel much better. What did it matter if he had to pick up a bit of rubbish on a rainy day? In the grand scheme of things, his time here was of little importance. It was a mere stepping-stone in his life, a stopover while he planned for something better.

He circled the car park a dozen times more, leaving nothing to chance, going over the ground like a forensic scientist at a crime scene. He even picked up a dirty nappy, using a misshapen coat-hanger to ensnare it and carefully dropping it into the fresh sack Lorcan had given him. He crossed the road to pick up rubbish from nearby pathways, lest a gust of wind send it spiralling onto his territory. When he returned there was no doubt in his mind: the car park was spotless, cleaner than it had ever been. That didn't stop Lorcan from scrutinising it once more, staring outwards like a seaman searching for land, desperately seeking a reason to send Seán back for another go. He couldn't find one.

"Go on," Lorcan said, beckoning Seán inside.

It was half nine; he'd worked off the clock for an entire half-hour. He clocked in with great gusto, already thinking about how he might recoup the time he'd just wasted. He worked in the men's department. A manly job. For a man. It was the only position in the store that held any gravitas. And he worked there. Okay, it wasn't Savile Row, but working there afforded Seán the kind of status that the plebs in the supermarket could only dream of. He spent his days advising middle-aged men which slacks suited them best, fitting executives into suits and chatting up single mothers while junior tried on his new school shoes. It was a sophisticated role, not the kind of thing everyone could pull off; but he was a sophisticated guy, everyone said so. The customers loved him.

"Where do you think you're going, Seán?"

Lorcan again. What did he want now?

"Upstairs. Why?"

"What's upstairs?"

"Erm, that's where I work," he said, slowly.

"Not today it's not," said Lorcan, waving Seán to follow him as he headed in the general direction of the storeroom.

What was this shit? He didn't work down here and never had. He'd been at Abbot's for almost a year now and had never set foot inside the storeroom, but what could he do only follow his superior? He trudged after Lorcan, dread enshrouding him.

"Here you go," said Lorcan. "I need you to sweep the floors for me."

He held an industrial-sized sweeping-brush in his hands, and appeared to be waiting for Seán to take it from him.

"Sweep what floors?" Seán asked helplessly.

"The ones outside, of course."

"But I work upstairs, in Men's."

"I've decided to move you. I want to try Brian up there for a spell."

Brian? Fucking Brian! Brian had only been here a month. He hadn't earned the right to work in the men's department.

Lorcan held out the sweeping-brush again, jabbing it impatiently in Seán's direction. He sullenly accepted the brush and turned to go outside. Sweeping floors? He'd never swept a floor in his life, not even at home. What the fuck was going on?

While Seán might have thought he was merely the victim of a staff shake-up, the truth was far more sinister. Lorcan Murphy, staff manager of Abbot's Stores, had been keeping an eye on Seán for some time now. He remembered his first day, and how impressed he'd been by the smart-ly-dressed, punctual, polite and assiduous young man. He looked like being a real asset. Within a month, Lorcan had moved him from his position in the hardware department to the men's clothing section. Someone like Seán needed to be pushed to the front of the store, to a section which traditionally attracted some of their more affluent customers. They would surely be impressed by his gentle manner, his softly-spoken voice and his willingness to go the extra mile. Hopefully, while those men tried on the finest cheap Italian clothing money could buy, their wives would be shopping downstairs, filling their trolleys and vowing to come back next week.

The move worked perfectly, better than Lorcan had imagined. Seán was a hit; there was no other way to describe it. The customers couldn't get enough of him. The men's department rang with the sound of happy, contented voices and, more importantly, the ring of the cash register. Takings were up, almost at an all-time high. They brought in new stock, tried out new lines, and it all flew off the shelves. That boy could sell snow to an Eskimo. Then, to Lorcan's dismay, something changed.

Seán began to relax, to get comfortable and take his role for granted. No longer was he a mild-mannered sales assistant, always on hand to help a customer in need; now he was a Jack the Lad, engaging in witty banter with the store's patrons, laughing and joking, not taking things seriously at all. He sauntered around the store as if he owned the place, a real strut in his stride. His appearance began to change, too. When he'd started he'd been doe-eyed and dewy, a fresh-faced cherub; now he wore a slightly vacant look, an empty stare. He looked spaced out. He was either in love or there was something more sinister at play.

Lorcan had seen it all before, of course; youngsters like Seán were ten-a-penny in his line of work. Before he could take further action, he would need to do some detective work. In order to decide what to do with Seán, he had to ascertain the cause of the young man's malaise. For all he knew, it could be something entirely harmless, but he had to find out nonetheless. He liked to keep tabs on all his staff, find out as much about them as he could. The only problem was that they couldn't stand him. Any attempts to engage them in conversation were met with terse, cautious replies. So Lorcan improvised, using the kind of cunning needed if you were ever to get ahead in this life. He became a master at eavesdropping, always finding a reason to linger in the background whenever a couple of the lads had a good old chat in the stockroom, hovering nearby when the women gathered for their hourly gossip sessions and generally keeping his ear to the ground. Gradually he began to learn more about his underlings. He learned that Daphne, the middle-aged woman from the homeware section, had caught her husband in bed with another man. He learned that Mike, a part-timer studying for his sociology degree, had failed all his exams and would have to resit them in the summer. And that Chloe, the dim-witted checkout girl with the lazy eye, had failed her driving test for the ninth time in a row. He also learned far more than he needed to know about the love lives, drinking habits and musical tastes of the store's many twenty-somethings.

Seán, however, remained an enigma. He couldn't find out anything about him. Occasionally he'd see him locked in conversation with Mike or one of the other young lads and he'd swoop in, ears pricked, ready to gather valuable intel; but they were just talking about football or work or what they had for their lunch. None of that was any use to him. It was as if Seán had sensors; whenever Lorcan got within hearing distance, the conversation immediately switched to mundane matters.

Lorcan didn't give up, though. He bided his time, stayed alert and waited for something, anything, which might shed some light on the lifestyle of the mysterious Seán McLoughlin. And one day in the canteen he made a breakthrough. He finally got what he was looking for. Lorcan always sat by himself in a quiet little corner during his breaks, his newspaper in front of him and a cup of tea in his hand. People thought he did this because he enjoyed being alone, because he needed to rest his overworked brain before returning to the fray. None of that was true. He took himself away from the crowds so that he could listen. The paper was just a prop; he never even read it. Instead he listened. Whether there were twenty people in the canteen or two, he always listened, and during one of these surreptitious paper-shuffling sessions he struck gold. The canteen was quiet that day, as it generally was at ten o'clock on a Tuesday morning, but a couple of girls from the deli counter were sitting at a table across from him.

As usual he was listening, but after ten minutes of 'this lad got off with this wan,' and 'that fucker didn't even text me,' Lorcan had started to tune out. Then he heard them mention Seán, or 'that nice-looking lad in Men's' as they called him. Lorcan didn't think Seán was particularly nice-looking, certainly not nicer looking than him. He wondered if they discussed him when he wasn't around. What terms did they use to describe him? But he'd think about that later. He continued to listen, turning the pages of his paper ever so quietly as the girls discussed the nice-looking lad in Men's. They said he was funny and a right flirt, and that he'd kissed such-and-such a girl; nothing of note. And then, the bombshell.

"Mad into drugs, that fella."

Those were their exact words: "mad into drugs."

He should have known. Lorcan continued 'reading' his paper and sipping his tea, rapt by this casual conversation. They continued talking, on and on, digging an increasingly deeper hole for Seán.

"Yeah, he do be fucked on a Monday, worn out after taking yokes all weekend."

"Always off his face, sure."

"He told me he smokes a couple of joints at lunchtime, most days."

"Ha, wouldn't surprise me. Sure he's off his head, that fella."

Eventually the conversation drifted back to more mundane matters; their favourite type of foundation, a nice handbag they'd seen in town, things Lorcan had no interest in. He'd heard enough. He drained his mug and left them to their chitchat. So that was it: Seán was a druggie. It was no surprise, really; a youngster like that, from an underprivileged background, with no prospects, no skills. Why wouldn't he turn to drugs? That didn't mean Lorcan had to tolerate it though. Certainly not; he didn't want him working in his store, giving the company a bad name. However, without any proof he couldn't sack Seán; he couldn't just call him to the office and give him his marching orders. He couldn't breathalyse him or test him for drugs, either. Unless he caught him on the premises doing something he shouldn't, Lorcan's hands were tied.

He had a plan, though; he'd just do what he'd done last time and the time before that: he would hound Seán out. He'd make his life unbearable, pick on him for no good reason, change his shifts without any notice, assign him mundane, soul-destroying work and act as if nothing had happened. He could do what he liked. He was the manager, this was his domain, and something, *someone*, unsavoury had infiltrated it. Someone who had to be dispensed of. Yes, in time he would break the young man's spirit, he would send the 'nice-looking lad in Men's' packing. It was as inevitable as night following day.

11

SEÁN BEGAN THE LONG WALK around the store, sweeping-brush in tow. It felt as if all eyes were on him, not just the customers but the other members of staff too. They'd be looking at him, wondering why the lad with the strut in his step was down here sweeping the floors. Sweeping the floors! It was the kind of work usually assigned to lads on their first day, idiots who couldn't be trusted to do anything else, not someone like Seán; someone who'd helped the local councillor chose a new tie for his nephew's wedding a couple of days previously. Here he was, a lowly floor-sweeper; this was his life now. A couple of the lads stopped him to ask what he was doing down there. Like a disgraced star having fallen from grace, he made up an excuse, told them it was just a temporary thing and he'd be back upstairs before the end of the day. He fucking would be, too. He wasn't staying down here doing this shit.

After completing one lonely circuit he returned to the storeroom, and hung out there for a bit, wondering what to do next. As if by magic, Lorcan appeared. The rubbish compacter needed clearing: could Seán possibly do it? Seán wanted to take the sweeping-brush, break it in half and jam its splintered end up Lorcan's hole. Instead he grimly accepted his assignment, heading outside into the mist to the rubbish compacter. He sometimes came out here for a joint, sneaking round the back of the prehistoric machine where he knew he couldn't be spotted, blowing the smoke into the slot from which he now had to wrestle rubbish. There were no joints today though, no feckless displays of insubordination. He stuck to his task, ignoring the rain and the damp shirt on his back. When he was finished he headed back inside, took the sweeping-brush and went out for another circuit. He understood how this worked; Lorcan was testing him, seeing what he was made of. Well, he wasn't going to break. He was made of stern stuff.

The only advantage of such mundane work was that it allowed him to take his mind elsewhere, to the future and his father, this strange, otherworldly being he'd built up in his mind almost subconsciously, never imagining that they might one day meet. It had taken Danielle, with all her innocence and forthrightness, to point out how simple it was: look for him, find him and meet him. Coming from her it sounded straightforward, the easiest thing in the world. She had cut through the nonsense, made his reservations seem trifling and ultimately given him the courage to do it. And now he was on the cusp of finding him. He already had the number; all he had to do was ring it and take things from there. How would they react to hearing from him? With surprise certainly, but perhaps excitement as well. The long-lost relative, the prodigal son, the one they dare not mention. They'd tell him where his father was, but not before insisting they meet him first. The whole lot of them, the entire Fitzgerald clan, gathering around the sitting-room awaiting his arrival. He'd get a taxi out to Belkee, arrive in style and bashfully make his way up to the door, knowing they were all clustering around the window for a look at him. *Come in, come in,* they'd say. *Look at you there now, only the head off him; a proper Fitzgerald to be sure.* He'd sit there with a cup of tea and biscuits, on his best behaviour, fielding questions, being a charming bastard, until they said: *We have a surprise for you, wait there.* A figure at the door, tall, formidable and instantly familiar, the man himself: James. Dad. His father. He'd rise to his feet and there'd be manly handshakes and some awkwardness, then all of a sudden his father would grab him in a great big hug and hold him tight with tears in his eyes, and all the woman would go:'Aw, isn't that lovely.' He was getting ahead of himself, though; he hadn't even rung the number yet. Maybe he'd do it tonight after work when he got home.

By the day's end he'd completed innumerable circuits of the shop-floor, cleared the rubbish compacter at least a dozen times, and cleaned up four spillages – one of them so bad it had threatened to submerge the entire township of Dooncurra in Coca-Cola. It had been a hard day, no doubt. But tomorrow he'd be back upstairs, he was sure of it. However, the evening ahead threatened to be as difficult as the day which had preceded it. He'd be returning home to an atmosphere even more fraught than usual. He was nervous. It was bad enough living with someone who bullied him, who did his utmost to make his life as miserable as possible, but he couldn't abide being on bad terms with his mother. He hated fighting with her. It served only to deepen his sense of isolation and made him feel that he hadn't a friend in the world. She was the only person he spoke to in the house these days. Kevin, who had once idolised him, had become a distant figure, preferring to hang out with his own mates or be left alone entirely. Seán put this down to his getting older, but he also wondered whether his half-brother was following in his father's footsteps; now more Cassidy than McLoughlin, a fully-fledged member of the opposing forces. Obviously Seán didn't speak to Daryl unless he had to, and would never speak to him again if given the choice. That just left his mother, and even then it was difficult to get her on her own, to have a conversation that was just theirs. Someone was always butting in: Daryl emerging from the sitting-room in search of a biscuit to go with his tea, Kevin hassling her for money she never had. Now it wouldn't matter if they butted in, because he and his mother probably weren't talking. Maybe he would live in total isolation from this point forth, live in his room, mute and alone. They wouldn't bother him and he wouldn't bother them. His exclusion from the family would be complete.

As he turned the key and entered the house, his mood instantly lifted. Something smelled good, amazing, in fact; lasagne, his favourite. A peace-offering or just a coincidence? He stuck his head in the kitchen door to see how soon dinner would be ready.

"Hi," he said, cautiously.

"Hiya, pet."

Her tone told him all he needed to know. They were friends again; last night had been forgotten. He should have been relieved and he was, but this wasn't something that could just be swept under the carpet. They had to deal with it.

"Lasagne, eh?" he asked.

"Yeah, we haven't had it in ages."

"Chips?" he asked. "Homemade?"

She nodded.

"Listen, Mam, about last night."

"It's okay, Seán. I understand."

"No, Mam, I should have been more considerate."

"Seán," she said, stepping away from the oven and moving towards him, "it's my fault for not saying anything. It was selfish."

Seán winced, unused to such candid speech from his mother.

"I should I have said something to you before now," she continued. "I owed you that, but the longer it went without you mentioning it the less I thought about it, and it got to the stage where I just thought you weren't interested. Or at least, I hoped you weren't interested."

"Why, Mam? Why did you hope I wasn't interested?"

"Oh, I don't know, Seán," she said sadly. "I suppose I don't have very fond memories of your father."

"But that shouldn't mean you don't want me to meet him."

"That's true, but I'm worried about you too. I'm worried that he won't want anything to do with you."

"Well, I can handle that if it happens, but to be honest, I haven't even decided yet if I want to look for him."

That wasn't entirely true but it felt like the right thing to say, something she needed to hear.

"Well, if you do, Seán, you don't have to make a secret of it. Okay?"

"Okay, Mam, thanks."

She looked at him tenderly, raising a hand to his cheek. "You're a good lad, Seán, y'know that?"

"Ah Mam," he said, pushing her away.

"And I love you."

He tried to reply, to tell her that he loved her too and that, no matter what happened, he would always love her; that she was the most important person in the world to him and no one would ever replace her. But the words wouldn't come, they caught in his throat and, before he could get them out, Daryl joined them in the kitchen.

"That nearly ready, Nades? I'm fucking starving."

The moment was lost. She returned to her cooking, moving out of the way to allow her husband a look inside the oven. Seán slipped away, grabbing a knife and fork as he made his way to his room. He always ate his dinner in his room, preferring it there. When it was ready and his mother brought it up to him, it was sensational; not so much a dinner as a culinary experience, a taste sensation handed down from the gods. When he'd finished he brought the plate out to the kitchen, left it in the sink and returned to his room. How could he ever have doubted her?

12

He arrived to work the next day, tense and on edge. All he wanted was to return to his rightful place, to be allowed to go back to the men's department; none of this sweeping floors shit. Was that too much to ask? Life was hard enough without being routinely humiliated in his place of work. At least Lorcan wasn't waiting for him at the entrance today, that was something. In fact, he was nowhere to be seen. Maybe he was off today. Seán didn't wait around to find out, scurrying upstairs to the men's department, back to his old job. As he mounted the stairs, his heart sank. In the middle of the men's department, locked in deep conversation, were Lorcan and Brian. The manager appeared to be giving his new charge a pep talk, briefing him on what it took to successfully run such an important section of the shop. Seán could have done that. He could have told Brian what it took, or, better still, he could have just told him to fuck off downstairs for himself.

"Ah, Seán, the very man," said Lorcan as Seán approached.

There seemed genuine warmth in his voice, not the forced geniality with which he usually addressed his staff. Perhaps Seán had passed his challenge and was now being viewed in a different light.

"Job for you," Lorcan said, leaving Seán to follow as he scuttled back down the stairs.

Seán gritted his teeth, shot Brian a vengeful look and went back from whence he had come.

He followed Lorcan down the stairs, past the check-out tills and once more into the storeroom.

"This yard," Lorcan said, pointing outside, "it's filthy out there. I need it tidied up, properly cleaned and scrubbed and all that clutter taken away. Can you do that for me?"

He phrased it as a question, as if Seán had a choice in the matter. Well, he did have a choice: he could tell him where to stick his poxy job. But no. Not yet.

"I suppose I could," he replied.

"Good man."

Then he was gone, leaving Seán to face a yard full of trolleys and containers, pallets and boxes; old junk that had nowhere else to go. He'd been working in the store for almost a year and he could never remember the yard being cleaned. There was no need to clean it; no one saw it apart from the staff and the delivery lads. However, he accepted his chore with grace, reasoning that when Lorcan realised he couldn't break him he would move on to someone else. It was raining again, though, and heavier than yesterday; within minutes he was soaked. He hurried back inside, assuming even Lorcan wouldn't have him work in those conditions. His boss was there waiting for him with a set of oilskins in his hand, as if he'd planned the whole thing, weather and all.

"Get them onto you, now," Lorcan said, his tone almost fatherly.

They were a bright yellow set, like those worn by fishermen. Lorcan watched him put them on, offering the occasional word of encouragement, and then sent him back out into the rain to complete his duties.

Seán toiled away, lifting and pushing, shoving and grunting, every movement made more difficult by the oilskins. So this was what physical labour was like. This was how real men spent their days. Well, they were welcome to it. He'd already got three splinters in his hands from the pallets, he'd bumped his head trying to prise apart two inexplicably entangled combi-trolleys and he was sweating like a dog. Seán wasn't cut out for this kind of work. He was a delicate sort, more suited to life indoors, using his brain rather than his limited brawn.

When the time came for mid-morning break he climbed out of the oilskins, flung them on the floor and traipsed upstairs to the canteen. Mercifully it was quiet; only Pete from the butcher counter was there, sipping his tea and reading one of those in-house brochures that were always lying around.

"Ah, Seán. How're you getting on, boy?"

Seán lifted his eyes to heaven in a theatrical fashion.

Pete knew the score; he'd been there long enough.

"That good, eh?"

"Yeah, that fuckin' prick," Seán said, nodding his head in the direction of Lorcan's office.

"Giving you a going-over, is he?"

"Yeah."

Pete took another sip of his tea, contemplating Seán's situation. He'd been here since the store had opened fifteen years ago, starting out as the youngest staff member on the meat counter and working his way up to head butcher. His attitude to management contrasted sharply with Lorcan's: he was firm but fair, never afraid to give someone a bollocking but man enough to admit his own mistakes when he made them. Starting out at the bottom had given him perspective, allowed him to see things from both ends of the spectrum. And he never forgot where he came from. He afforded everyone the same level of respect, from young lads on their first day to colleagues who had been there almost as long as himself. Seán would have applied for a job with him if he hadn't been so squeamish around blood.

"You know what he's doing, don't you?" Pete said.

"Acting the cunt?" Seán suggested.

"Apart from that, I mean."

Seán shrugged his shoulders, not knowing what Pete was getting at.

"He can't sack you, so he's trying to make you quit," the older man said sagely.

"But why does he want to sack me? I'm good at my job."

"Ssh," Pete said, pressing his finger to his lips. "These walls have ears."

He motioned Seán close, lowering his voice. "You want to be careful what you're telling people around here, boy."

Seán nodded, but still didn't understand.

"Think about it, Seán. The stories you do be telling the lads, the craic with the young wans."

Seán remained nonplussed, at a complete loss.

"Y'know, about the yokes and that," Pete whispered, moving his hand towards his mouth in a pill-popping motion.

"But what business is that of his?"

"Oh, Seán," Pete laughed. "You've a lot to learn about this place, boy."

"Why should he give a fuck what I get up to when I'm not here?"

"Doesn't matter where you're doing it, Seán; as far as he's concerned, you're a druggie and he doesn't want you here. And he won't stop until you're gone."

Pete rose from his seat and emptied the remains of his tea down the sink.

"Here's the thing," he said, leaning in for a final piece of advice. "He can't sack you unless you give him a reason to. So don't give in, you hear me?"

"Okay, Pete," Seán whispered. "Thanks."

"No bother," he replied, winking at Seán and heading back downstairs.

Seán sat back in his chair, digesting this latest revelation. He had to laugh at the absurdity of it all. He, a humble department store worker, was the subject of secret, clandestine plotting. 'Operation McLoughlin,' that was probably what he called it; speaking in code, issuing directives, planning Seán's demise, the ultimate goal to rid the store of his repugnant presence. Well, fuck him; he definitely wasn't quitting now. He'd actually been considering it earlier that morning, but now there was no way he was leaving. He went for a quick piss and headed back down to the yard, not even flinching as he climbed into the soaking wet oilskins. He shook off whatever rain still clung to them and headed outside, whistling as he went.

Sometime later, he couldn't be sure exactly how long, he heard a voice calling him. He pretended not to hear. He was too busy, whoever it was.

With his hood up and the rain drumming down, he had become lost in his own little world; seeing only what lay in front of him, hearing nothing but his own grunts and groans as he toiled away. He'd even begun to sing to himself, a nameless tune with bouts of humming and whistling thrown in at various interludes. It wasn't so bad, this physical labour. The voice continued to call his name, insistently now. He knew it was Lorcan but still pretended not to hear. The little fucker could come out in the rain if he wanted him. Eventually though, after the cries grew louder, almost desperate, Seán relented; he'd made his point. He pulled down his hood and looked towards the storeroom.

"I think you've done enough out there now, Seán," Lorcan called out.

Seán heard him loud and clear but nevertheless put a hand to his ear, mouthing the words 'Can't hear you,' before resuming his duties. As the rain continued to tumble down, he afforded himself a little chuckle under his hood. This Lorcan fella didn't know who he was messing with.

"Seán!" shouted Lorcan, exasperated. "Come in out of it. You've enough done."

Seán shot him a glance, apparently irritated by this distraction. "Yeah, just a minute now, Lorcan. I've a few more things to do and I'll be with you then."

"Come in out of it," Lorcan repeated firmly.

Seán carefully placed a trolley into the corner of the yard and came inside out of the pouring rain, away from his lovingly tended yard. He'd done an incredible job. The yard, once home to every rodent within a five-mile radius, was now pristine. The rain enhanced the effect. Even Lorcan, a stickler for details and a neat-freak obsessive, was taken aback by Seán's efforts.

"That looks well now, Seán," he said quietly.

"I'm not quite finished, Lorcan. I might go back out after lunch."

"It's grand, Seán," Lorcan muttered.

He'd spent all night coming up with ideas, dirty jobs designed to test Seán's will, and been certain that this would be the one to finish him off. They'd even promised rain on the weather forecast. Instead it seemed to have brought out the best in Seán, revealing a side of him Lorcan hadn't realised existed. He might have been a drug-addled wastrel, but he couldn't half work when the mood took him.

"What do you want me to do now, Lorcan? I'd say the floor out there needs a good sweeping at this stage?"

"Yes, Seán, it does," said Lorcan distractedly.

"Grand so," he said, stepping out of the oilskins. "I'll get right onto it."

He grabbed the nearest sweeping-brush and went out to the shop floor, resisting the temptation to click his heels as he went. Lorcan watched him go, a puzzled expression on his face. He was going to have to rethink this one.

13

With so much going on at his place of work, Seán thought it best to wait until the weekend to make his important phone call. He was far too stressed to deal with it right now; better to wait until there were no distractions, to do it with a clear head. But the coming weekend promised to be a busy one in its own right: they were going to Wexford, a big bus-load of them, to a new club: Ambience. The jaunt had been planned for months in advance. When the club had first opened, they'd been sceptical. It may have had four different rooms, been flying in some of the best DJs from all over the world and had revellers travelling from every part of the country to sample its unique experience, but it was in Wexford. *Wexford, for fuck's sake!* All that place was good for was strawberries. As the weeks passed, however, the legend grew. Friends returned speaking of a mecca for dance-music enthusiasts, a multi-storied arena where anything went, a place unlike any other. They had to see it for themselves. They set a date, Friday the twelfth of April, and left it to Pegs to organise everything. Not that he objected, he wouldn't have it any other way. In his mind, no one else could be trusted to look after the finer details. He would hire the bus, take the names, collect the money, and tell everyone where to be and when to be there.

In this instance, it was Forde's at half seven on Friday evening. You were to bring your own alcohol for the journey, and smoking was prohibited on the bus. A whip-round would be arranged for the driver on the way home. That was all you had to remember. He would take care of everything else, including the procurement of drugs. According to Pegs the Speckled Doves were inbound once more, and their regular dealer would be taking delivery of a large shipment on Wednesday evening. Ever the facilitator, he had even agreed to collect pills for many of those travelling on the bus. It was all part of the 'Alan Pegg Fun Bus to Wexford' experience.

It was likely to be a night of great debauchery and decadence, one which would take most of the following day to recover from; but as long as he could speak in a clear and coherent manner, Seán was going to call his long-lost family on Saturday. He was going to take the next step and ring the number he'd found in the phone book for the Fitzgeralds of Belkee. Friday night would be all about getting off his head and enjoying himself, forgetting about the week he'd just had. On Saturday, he would set about meeting his maker, tracking down the man who'd sired him. Sunday – who knew?

Before any of that, he had to make it to the end of the working week in one piece. His task was made a whole lot easier when he arrived on Wednesday morning to discover that Lorcan was off for the next two days. Apparently he'd booked the leave to visit a sick relative on the other side of the country. Seán knew better, though; he'd obviously been so crushed by Seán's show of strength that he'd had to take time off to recover, the poor craythur. While Lorcan sat at home licking his wounds, Seán would grow stronger. He would use the two days to reassert himself, to show everyone that despite locking horns with the big bad boss-man, he wasn't at all downtrodden. And he would start by regaining his spot in the men's department.

It wouldn't be difficult. Lorcan's second-in-command, the store's assistant manager, was quite pally with Seán. Much like Pete from the butcher's, Niall Molloy had come up through the ranks at Abbot's and was therefore far more approachable than his superior officer. You could have a laugh with Niall, even mess about a bit, as long as you didn't take it too far. Seán had instantly warmed to him. He enjoyed his company but respected his authority. Niall was his boss and Seán obeyed his orders, but theirs was a harmonious working relationship, built on trust and camaraderie rather than fear and intimidation.

"Well, Seán, are you down here again today?"

"I was hoping to talk to you about that, Niall."

"Oh, yes?" Niall replied, raising an eyebrow.

He already had an idea where this was going.

"Listen, Niall," Seán continued. "You know I'm not supposed to be down here as well as I do. That men's department is nothing without me. Brian's a nice enough fella and all, but he doesn't know the job like I do."

Niall was silent, weighing up his options. He knew that Brian hadn't earned the right to be up there, and that Seán had a way with the customers which reflected well on the store and on all of them; but he also knew that his boss, Lorcan, was conducting some sort of crusade against Seán. Niall didn't want to get involved, and he certainly didn't want his boss giving him grief when he returned in a couple of days' time. But he was in charge now. When Lorcan wasn't there, it was up to him to run the store as he saw fit.

"Leave it with me, Seán," he said, patting him on the shoulder.

"Great, Niall, thanks."

"Don't thank me yet, boy. And give that floor an oul' sweep, will you?" he said, laughing.

Niall disappeared, presumably to break the bad news to Brian. Seán picked up a brush, certain that it'd be the last floor he'd be sweeping for a couple of days at least.

True to his word, Niall delivered the goods. Seán had barely reached the third aisle when he saw Brian slowly making his way towards him. Seán carried on sweeping, pretending not to see him.

"Niall says you're go upstairs to Men's."

Seán stopped in his tracks, feigning surprise. "Oh, really?"

"Yeah," Brian said, holding his hands out for the brush. "I guess I'm back on sweeping duties."

Seán handed him the brush with a sympathetic shrug and made a beeline for the stairs. It paid to have friends in high places.

14

A FEW REGULARS CAME IN, looking thrilled to see him. They'd wondered where he'd got to. That other fella had been no help at all; they had queries only Seán could answer.

"When will those cufflinks be back in stock?"

"Is it worth my while buying these now, or should I wait for the sale?"

"How much would it cost to take these in? I'm after losing a few pounds."

Seán answered them all, because he had all the answers. This was his beat, these were his people. He was back. The day flew; it was the best day he'd ever had in work. He was actually enjoying himself. You never appreciated what you had until it was taken away. By five o'clock he had everything back in order, the way he liked it, all traces of Brian washed away.

The next morning he didn't even bother to ask, he just went straight upstairs and continued where he'd left off. Brian knew his place now; he wouldn't be coming back, not while Seán was around. How would Brian have dealt with the elderly couple that came in just after midday? Not as deftly as Seán did, that was for certain.

They were old, older than his grandparents. Seán loved these situations. The elderly generally didn't know what they wanted, and were always open to whatever suggestions he had for them. These two were off to Australia to see their new grandson for the first time, and needed to purchase suitable attire for the trip.

"We need to get him shorts and some new shirts, because of the heat," the lady explained.

"Don't worry," said Seán. "I've got just the thing."

He returned moments later with an array of bright floral shirts and some army-style combat shorts. The man looked at him doubtfully, but the wife loved them.

"Oh, these are fantastic. Look, Séamus," she said, fingering an orange shirt. "This would be lovely on you."

Séamus gave Seán a look that said, 'Are you fucking kidding me, boy?' but allowed himself to be led to the changing-rooms with the garish outfits.

While Séamus was getting decked out in the latest high-street fashions, Seán selected more items for him to try on. He found some old Bermuda shorts that had been gathering dust in the back for months, a selection of baseball caps and some fetching flip-flops, and brought them all over to the woman.

"How about these?" he enquired.

"Oh, you're very good," she said, taking the clothes off him and disappearing inside the cubicle.

Eventually Séamus emerged like a shy bride, all coy and demure, doing his utmost to appear uncomfortable but secretly loving his new gear.

"Turn around, turn around," Seán said, encouraging him to do a twirl.

Séamus shot him a deathly stare, but not before he'd finished eyeing himself up from every possible angle.

In the end they went with some of Seán's suggestions, but mostly with what Séamus chose for himself. However, one final proposal turned out to be a huge success. They needed a hat, Seán advised; that Australian sun could be fierce hot, and the last thing Séamus needed was sunburn on his exposed dome. The baseball caps were dismissed out of hand, but how about a fedora, or even two. Séamus' eyes fairly lit up when he saw the hats. "I'll be just like Sinatra," he said, placing one on his head and adjusting it for effect. He ended up buying both, so happy with his purchases that he even wore one leaving the shop. To be fair, the old bugger did look kind of suave in it.

Pegs rang him that night. A few of the lads were heading out for a couple, just to get warmed up for the weekend ahead and go over the details of the trip to Wexford. Seán's first impulse was to drop everything and join them, but then he thought: *No, things are going well in work now. I'll go in with a clear head tomorrow.* Pegs was mildly shocked but didn't pester him. He'd see him tomorrow night at half seven in Forde's. Seán went to bed early in preparation for what lay ahead, with a lovely, excited feeling in his stomach. It was like being a kid at Christmas, but instead of toy cars and selection boxes, he'd be getting his kicks from mind-bending drugs and scantily-clad women.

He awoke the next morning with a spring in his step. In twelve hours' time he'd be on that bus. 'Pegs' Fun Bus to Wexford'. It was going to be the night to end all nights; he'd finally get to see this Ambience place for himself. Then tomorrow, after he'd spent the afternoon recuperating, he'd ring his new family. Everything was moving in the right direction now, his life was changing for the better. Before all that, though, he had to navigate one final day in work. Lorcan would be back, but that battle had probably run its course. Seán would just carry on up the stairs to Men's and no one would say a word. Friday was always the busiest day of the week, and the time flew. It'd be six o'clock before he knew it.

As chance would have it, Lorcan's was the first face he saw when he arrived at the store, but he wasn't waiting for him this time; at least Seán didn't think so.

"Will you go back up to Men's today, Seán?"

Seán nodded, barely able to conceal his delight.

"Yeah, no problem, Lorcan," he replied, fairly bolting up the stairs.

The first hurdle overcome, the rest of the day stretched out before him like a soft meadow, its grass swaying in the warm summer breeze.

Niall had probably told Lorcan what had happened, and explained that having Seán anywhere but upstairs in the men's department was folly. Lorcan, to his credit, had seen the error of his ways. He'd realised that what happened outside the confines of the store didn't really matter, that Seán was a valuable asset, and one to be treated with due care. Seán had to hand it to him, he'd got him all wrong. He'd thought Lorcan was a conniving shit, incapable of goodwill or kindness of spirit; but here he was, admitting his wrongs, bowing to Seán's superiority. He'd had a go, fair play to him, but once he'd seen how worthy his competitor was, he'd backed off. Well, there was no shame in that, many a man had come up against a McLoughlin over the years and left with his tail between his legs. Lorcan Murphy was just the latest in a long line of fallen foes.

Lorcan, of course, hadn't fallen; he had merely made a tactical retreat. He was a master of psychological warfare, an expert in his field, and his next course of action was to back off and allow his adversary to believe that victory was his. It was a tried and trusted tactic, used by many generals to great effect; Stalin, Montgomery and his beloved Churchill had all duped unsuspecting enemies by similar means, lulling them into a false sense of security and then striking when they least expected it.

Lorcan's chance to strike presented itself earlier than he had anticipated. He went for his coffee break at a little after ten on this fateful Friday morning. The canteen was busy, a group of the store's younger element presiding over three tables. He didn't need to go undercover today, knowing enough about Seán by now, but these girls were so loud it was almost impossible not to listen. The topic of conversation was a trip to Wexford. They were going that night, apparently, a busload of them, leaving Forde's at half seven sharp. The girls would barely have enough time to shower, dress and doll themselves up before the scheduled departure. They'll be cutting it fine, thought Lorcan, it wouldn't do to make them stay behind for a stock-take or some other time-consuming chore. But no, Lorcan knew enough to realise that you didn't mess with groups of girls, young or otherwise; they had a way of crowding together and making life very difficult for men like him. No, these girls would finish at six, just as they were supposed to. Then Lorcan got to thinking. *A big night out and a bus to Wexford; was Seán planning to be on that bus?* Lorcan knew how much Seán enjoyed his nights out, taking drugs with his friends. He'd be loath to miss a night like this. Come six o'clock he'd be hankering to get away, eager to have a shower of his own, get dressed, and make that all-important bus. What would happen if he was told he couldn't leave at six, that he had to stay awhile longer, until, say, seven? What then? Lorcan couldn't be sure, but he had a fair idea.

15

"SEÁN, COULD YOU COME HERE a moment?"

Lorcan had waited until the time was right, until Seán could see the finishing-line right there in front of him. It was five o'clock, just an hour to go.

"Yes?" Seán said, skipping over to his boss, thinking nothing of it.

"We're very busy downstairs. Could you come and help out for a while?"

"Sure, no problem."

This sometimes happened on Fridays. With the supermarket extremely busy, and custom in the store's upper levels winding down, Seán and some of the others were called on to help out downstairs. It would only be for an hour, packing bags at the check-outs, helping old ladies with their trollies and even stacking the occasional shelf. It was usually a welcome distraction, a chance to sample the mayhem of an average Friday afternoon in the supermarket; it was also the last hour of the day, of the week, and being busy made the time go faster.

"Where do you want me, Lorcan? Sweeping, is it?"

"No, no. Brian is sweeping. I want you at the check-outs, helping the customers. And if any of them want a hand with their trollies, you're to bring them out for them. Okay?"

"Yeah, no problem."

This was easy work, somewhat demeaning but easy nonetheless, and he loved pushing trollies for the women. Sometimes there were sexy MILFS who needed help, flirtatious sorts who'd make suggestive remarks as he accompanied them to their car. Some of them were definitely up for it, he could tell; frustrated housewives with husbands too tired or too busy to service them in the bedroom. Seán would happily have stepped into the breach, hopping into the boot of their SUV and lying there silently as the dirty bitch drove to a remote spot somewhere in the countryside. Then, when the coast was clear, he'd jump out and show the old mare what he was capable of. Yeah, sometimes there were sexy MILFS, right dirty fuckers, but mostly it was just little old ladies who hadn't the strength to push their trolleys out of the shop; like Mrs. Delahunty.

Mrs. Delahunty was a regular in Abbott's Stores. She'd most likely been doing her shopping there since the day it opened. Everyone knew her, and everyone knew that her old legs didn't work so well these days. They knew that she was too mean to get a taxi to her house a couple of streets away, and preferred to get one of the store's 'fine young men' to push her trolley all the way home. This was a much sought-after gig. It meant at least twenty minutes away from the confines of the store, and a nice little stroll through town into the bargain. Today, on this beautiful spring evening, it was Seán who landed the coveted job.

"Ah, you're very good. Seán, is it?"

"Yes, Mrs. Delahunty."

"Have you helped me home before, Seán?"

"Just the once, Mrs. Delahunty."

"I don't remember you at all, Seán."

"Ah, but I remember you, Mrs. Delahunty."

The old woman laughed. "You're a funny one, aren't you?"

"I am, Mrs. Delahunty."

On they went, Seán leading the way, dextrously moving the trolley through the crowds, while Mrs. Delahunty trailed along behind. Across one road, down another, up a little laneway, and then all the way along the main street. A few drivers beeped their annoyance as Seán wheeled the old woman's shopping in and out of traffic, but he waved dismissively at them, pointing to his companion by way of explanation. They came off the main street, down one more laneway and finally circled into a small housing estate.

"Down the back, isn't it, Mrs. Delahunty?"

"Yes, Seán. Lead the way."

He did as instructed, disappointed that his jaunt was coming to an end. Abbot's needed more customers like Mrs. Delahunty, in his opinion.

As he rolled the trolley up to her front door, he checked the time on his phone: it was almost half past five. He could feel the butterflies in his stomach now, could see Pegs and Hooch, smiling at him, gurning at him: *Best yokes ever, boy.* Too right, lads; too fucking right.

To make things even better, Mrs. Delahunty was having trouble locating her keys. With any luck it'd take her until six to find them and his day would be done.

"Just a second now, Seán. I have them here somewhere."

"Take your time, Mrs. Delahunty. There's no hurry."

"Oh, where did I leave them? I'm such a fool."

"Ah you're not. Sure I lose me keys all the time."

"Did I give them to you, Seán?"

"No, Mrs. Delahunty, you didn't."

"Are you sure?"

"Positive."

"What are we going to do, Seán?"

Seán had no idea what she was going to do, but he was going to stand here debating the whereabouts of her keys until six o'clock and then fuck off home for himself.

Seeing the look of dismay on her little old lady face, however, he found some compassion in a heart that dreamed only of the weekend ahead.

"You didn't leave it under the mat or anything like that, did you, Mrs. Delahunty?"

"Oh, Jesus!" she exclaimed. "I think I know what I did!"

She went to the window-sill and lifted up the flower pot; underneath lay the key.

"There you go now, Mrs. Delahunty."

"Thanks, Seán," she said, fumbling with the lock until finally the door opened and he was ushered inside her modest abode.

She offered him a cup of tea, and for a split second he thought about taking her up on it. That would be taking liberties, though. It was enough to land this cushy gig last thing on a Friday evening without taking the piss by staying for tea and bourbon creams as well.

He waved her goodbye and made his way back to the store. Twenty to six; just twenty minutes to go. It was still busy inside, but the frenzy had died down a little. Seán took his place at the end of the check-outs and carried on packing bags with zest. Each bag, each customer represented another minute and each minute helped him towards his goal. He dared not look at the clock behind him; it would only make the time pass more slowly. His cheerfulness was replaced by anxiety and a deep sense of frustration. *Come on to fuck, six o'clock, where are you?* His heart was racing, his palms sweaty; it was almost as if he'd taken his pills already. Seán couldn't resist any longer. He spun round to stare at the clock: ten to six. How had that happened? He'd been sure it was at least five to. Back to packing bags. He was flinging stuff in now, milk on top of eggs, bleach in with bread; he didn't give a shit any more, let them all die of poisoning.

Then Lorcan appeared in front of him; Lorcan, whom he'd vanquished earlier in the week. He was here again, and he had that horrific obsequious grin on his pathetic little face.

"Seán, come here a sec, will you?"

It had better only be a sec. He was dealing in seconds now and he hadn't many of them to spare.

"You know how to face-off, don't you, Seán?"

He made it sound like the most innocuous question in the world, as if he were asking: "Do you like cars?" or "Isn't green a lovely colour?"

"I do, yeah," he replied warily.

"Good man," Lorcan said, swanning off towards the back of the shop.

Seán watched him go, hoping that he would magically disappear, fall down a black hole or get spirited away by angry demons, but after a few paces Lorcan stopped, turned his head towards Seán and waved him onwards. This didn't look good.

"I want the entire shop faced-off, every single aisle, starting here and finishing at the freezers," Lorcan instructed.

Facing-off involved pulling all the stock to the front of the shelves in order to make them look full. It was a tedious job, usually done by the women when the shop was about to close. Even when they were hurrying the job still took them at least an hour, and that was with half-dozen or more of them doing it. Seán looked at him incredulously, scarcely believing that someone could be so cruel and so sly. It was his own fault for thinking he'd got the better of his boss. He'd assumed that a truce had been agreed and the war was over, but Lorcan had just been reassembling his troops for another assault. Now Seán had no way of responding, no way of repelling the superior forces.

"What about the women? They're all still on the check-outs."

"Never mind the women, just focus on facing-off."

"On my own?"

"Yes, on your own, and you're not going anywhere till it's done."

"But I finish at six."

"Well, you'd better hurry on then, hadn't you?"

With that he was gone. Seán watched him go, staring daggers into his back. The prick knew exactly what he was doing; he wanted to keep him here, forcing him to miss his bus. Someone had told him about the night out in Wexford and now he was using it against Seán, daring him to kick up a fuss and see where it got him. Well, Seán wasn't going to let him win, no chance. He'd face off Lorcan's poxy shop *and* make the bus to Wexford; see how he liked that!

Grabbing the bread loaves, Seán began facing-off like a man possessed, his hands moving at a blurring speed. If he was fast he'd get out by 6.45, or maybe seven. He would have to break the world facing-off record in the process, but it'd be worth it just to see the look on Lorcan's face. Focusing intently, he managed to get the first aisle done by six. He should have been out the door by then, on his way home, but there was no time to feel sorry for himself. Facing-off, that's what mattered right now. He saw Brian and a couple of the other lads clock out and felt his ire rise once more. Off they went laughing and joking into the Friday evening sunshine and all it entailed, while he, the most senior of them all, was stuck here facing-off.

His phone rang. Pegs. Did he have time to answer it? He'd have to. Pegs would keep ringing otherwise.

"Seány wawney!"

"Pegs, I'm still in work," he whispered, continuing to face-off with his free hand.

"What! It's five past six, Seán."

"I fuckin' know what time is it. The little bastard has me facing-off."

"Who? What's facing-off?"

"Lorcan. Never mind."

"When will you be finished?"

"Whenever I have this done."

"How long will it take?"

"Not too long. I'll call you when I'm out of here."

"Fucking hurry on, boy."

He hung up the phone. They were all getting ready now, every one of them; wolfing down dinners, hopping into showers, getting a good lather on and scrubbing those hard-to-reach areas. Whacking on some tunes while they dressed, doing a little dance as they buttoned up their favourite shirts and added a little spray of cologne. Jogging down the stairs, slinging jackets on; wallet, phone, keys, yokes and then out the door. "See you, Mam," "See you, love," then into Forde's, with time for a pint or two before the bus came. And where was Seán? Stuck in work, doing the job of six people all on his own. He redoubled his efforts; tins of beans, cartons of orange juice, nappies and cornflakes all fell under his spell as he worked his way steadily round the shop. He was sweating, he'd be wrecked by the time this was done but he'd do it, no doubt about it. By 6.45 he'd done all but the last aisle. He dared not relax; he was still up against it, complacency was his biggest enemy. Zooming down the aisle, he faced-off with hands, arms, legs, ears and anything else he could use. Ten minutes later he was finished.

"There!" he said triumphantly. "All done."

Everything had been faced off, in a little over an hour, by just one man: Seán McLoughlin. In years to come they'd speak of this night, the night one man faced-off the entire shop on his own. Children would listen, rapt, as their parents spoke of Seán's exploits, their little mouths opening in awe as the story reached its climax. But reverential story-telling could wait, right now he had a bus to catch.

On cue, Lorcan came trotting around the corner. He'd been looking for him. Seán tried to read his face for a trace of sympathy, of generosity, but he couldn't see any, he couldn't see anything at all.

"Finished, Seán?"

"Yes, Lorcan."

"My, you were very fast."

"I was."

"Come on, we'll take a look at your work," said Lorcan, clip-clopping ahead like a show-pony on parade.

Seán looked at the clock: it was seven. If he didn't get out of here now, he could forget about it.

"Come on, Seán," Lorcan shouted. "Let's take a look."

Seán breathed in deeply and followed his boss. Five more minutes and he was leaving, by hook or by crook.

"You call this faced-off, Seán?"

Lorcan was pointing to some cans of deodorant.

"Yes," he replied, defensively.

"Who taught you to face-off?"

"One of the trainee managers, I think."

"Which one?"

"I can't remember."

"Well, whoever it was, they didn't teach you properly."

Lorcan thrust his arm to the back of the shelf and pulled three of the deodorant cans to the front.

"When you're facing-off you don't just bring one item to the front like you did, you bring three forward. That way, when someone buys something, there's still two more behind."

He looked at Seán, waiting for a response. He didn't get one.

"Do you understand what I'm saying to you, Seán?"

He was treating him like an idiot, a moron for whom even the simplest task was difficult.

"Yeah, I do," he replied, through gritted teeth.

"Good," said Lorcan with a smile. "Now that you understand, you can start again. Do it properly this time."

He'd been keeping his emotions under wraps, controlling himself in the face of severe provocation, but this was too much. He didn't care about winning anymore, or about besting his boss.

"Fuck off!"

"What was that, Seán?" asked Lorcan.

"You fucking heard me," Seán said, as he made for the exit. "Shove your crappy job up your hole, you little cunt!"

He spat the last word out with as much spite as he could muster, and walked out the door without even bothering to collect his belongings from upstairs.

Lorcan stood in the middle of the shop, watching Seán go. He had quite enjoyed that performance.

"Gone," he announced to no one in particular before taking a deep breath and heading upstairs. He would have to phone the HR rep and notify her of a staff departure. There would be lots of paperwork, but all that could wait until Monday.

16

SEÁN RARELY LOST HIS TEMPER, but when he did, the results were never less than spectacular: the first time he'd met Daryl, the incident with Mr. Sheehan, his drunken assault on the Tiernan household. When he flipped his lid, he liked to do it properly. His encounter with Lorcan had been no different; he'd been pushed to his limits and reacted accordingly, but, unlike previous occasions, he didn't feel sorry for what he'd done. His only regret was that he hadn't smashed his fist right into the middle of Lorcan's smug little face. He had almost turned back; the thought of Lorcan, cowering on the floor, begging for forgiveness, proving almost impossible to resist. He could have run in, landed a few haymakers and departed again before anyone noticed. It might have seen him returning to the guard's barracks for another chat, but it would have been worth it.

He still had a bus to catch, though. Standing up to his boss and quitting his job would all be for nothing if he didn't make it to Wexford. It was ten past now; if he was lucky the driver might wait an extra five or ten minutes, but Seán would still have to get home, have a shower, change and make it back into town. His phone rang for the umpteenth time. He'd been ignoring it up to now, but maybe Pegs could ask the driver to wait.

"Yeah?"

"Where are you, man?"

"On me way home now, Pegs. Can you get him to wait?"

"Jesus, Lockie, how long will you be?"

"Half an hour. I'll be there for twenty to."

"Fuckin' hell, boy. He won't be happy about waiting."

"I know, Pegs, but ask him, will you?"

"I will, I will."

"Legend. I'll see you there."

"Twenty to, Lockie, he won't wait any longer. I know him."

"No bother."

Seán hung up, filled with fresh hope. He wasn't done yet. Breaking into a jog, he worked out the arithmetic in his head: ten minutes to get home, ten minutes to shower and change, ten minutes to get back into town. He could fucking do this! He'd have to get something to eat in Wexford or on the way, but he was going to be on that bus. He hadn't quit his job for nothing; the night was still alive.

He navigated the streets of Dooncurra like an Olympic athlete going for gold in several events at the same time. Hurdling walls, jumping over fences, sprinting through startled onlookers, all he lacked was a pole to vault some of the more difficult obstacles. He was a man on a mission, and that mission was within touching distance. He'd have to take the world's quickest shower and run all the way back into town at an equally frantic pace, but he was going to do it, despite everything. He rounded the last corner into his avenue, a few metres from home, and his heart sank.

Outside their house in its usual spot was Daryl's car. What was he doing here? He was never home on a Friday. He usually went straight to the pub after work. Perhaps he'd just dropped his car here and walked to the pub. He did that sometimes, didn't he? But as Seán turned the key and entered the house, he discovered that no, that wasn't something Daryl did. And, not only was Daryl home but he was in the bathroom, taking a shower in preparation for a night out of his own. Tears welled in Seán's eyes, desperation rose in his chest. The bus was probably already waiting outside Forde's, welcoming its first occupants as they cheerily stepped on board.

"Will you be long in there, Daryl?" he shouted, not bothering with any forced familiarities.

No answer.

"Will you be long, Daryl?"

"I'll be as long as I want."

The fucker, the complete and utter cunt. He knew what he was doing. He knew exactly what he was doing.

"I've a bus to catch."

"Not my problem, Seán."

He'd been drinking. They must have got off early; that's why he was home, freshening up before returning to continue the session. Seán went to his room, flinging his jacket on the bed in annoyance. He bet none of the others had to go through this kind of shit. They'd gain access to their respective bathrooms with a minimum of fuss, be sent out the door with a kiss, and maybe an extra twenty in their pockets. As for him, he had to live on his wits and hope that his malignant stepfather was in a good mood. And he was never in a good mood. At best he was indifferent, at worst he was hateful and vindictive.

It was nearly quarter past now. If he was going to make it, he had to get into that bathroom now. He poked his head into the hallway to hear what Daryl was doing. The hum of the shower had been replaced by the occasional splash of water, probably from the sink. He was shaving, and taking his time by the sound of things. Seán's temper, which had been gradually dying down, stirred anew. Why did he have to put up with this crap? Why couldn't he just have a normal life, live in a normal house with people who weren't constantly out to get him? He didn't ask for much, just enough time to have a quick shower before a night out. They'd been planning the fuckin' thing for weeks, talked of nothing else, and now because of Daryl and that little cunt in work, Seán was left wondering whether he'd even make it to the new superclub of the southeast.

He was just about to head out to the kitchen to wash himself in the sink, 1930s style, when the bathroom door opened. He darted out into the hallway, ready to throw himself fully-clothed into the shower.

"I told you, Seán, I'm not finished in there."

Daryl's jaw jutted out in defiance, almost asking Seán to protest. Seán stared at him, seeing a wild-eyed man full of cider and hate, telling him what he could and couldn't do. He'd been looking at that baleful stare all his life, those maniacal eyes boring holes into him, that coiled mouth waiting to fire another salvo.

"Well, I'm going in there now. I've a bus to catch."

He stepped inside the bathroom, its sink still full of Daryl's shaving water, and locked the door behind him.

"Seán! I told you I'm not finished in there!"

"I won't be a minute."

"Get the fuck out!"

He began hammering on the door as if his life depended on it. Seán ignored him, quickly stripping off and stepping into the shower; he needed to be spick and span for all them sexy bitches up in Wexford. Five minutes later he was done. He'd washed his hair, lathered himself in Daryl's shower gel and scrubbed himself all over; fixed his hair, sprayed his pits and scrambled into his clothes. Now all he needed were his shoes. Once he had those he'd be out the door, and Daryl could move into the bathroom and live there if he wanted. The hammering on the door had stopped. He'd probably got bored, either that or spent the time constructing an explosive device to flush him out. Seán eased it open, hoping to get in and out of his room without being noticed, but Daryl was waiting for him, enraged by this show of insubordination.

"Who the fuck do you think you are?" he asked, stepping in front of Seán.

Seán sighed wearily. "Get out of me way."

Daryl stepped closer to him, his face inches from Seán's. This wasn't someone content to pepper him with insults, this was someone looking for a fight. He stood in the universal pose of a street brawler, face forward, chest out, arms back. *Bring it on.*

"What'll ya do if I don't?" Daryl asked.

"Oh, fuck off boy, will you!"

"I won't fuck off," he continued, moving even closer.

Seán could smell the sickly sweetness of the cider on his breath. Daryl nudged him gently with his chest, his opening gambit, but Seán resisted. He had a night out ahead, a big one. He didn't want any part of this.

"Look, just get out of me way, will you?" he asked in his most placatory tone.

"Why? So you can head off to Wexford with all your druggie mates, is that it?"

"What difference is it to you where I go?"

"Well, you're living under my roof so it makes all the difference."

Seán really didn't have time for this. He stepped to one side to get around Daryl, but his stepfather moved to block his path.

"What's wrong, boy?" he asked. "No smart comments for me today?"

"Look, just get out of my way," said Seán, trying to hide the tremor in his voice.

"I won't, no."

"Fine, I'll go in my fuckin' socks, then," he replied, heading for the front door.

This threw Daryl momentarily. He watched Seán go, intrigued by the notion of someone heading out for the night in their socks. Seán hoped this dramatic gesture would bring an end to hostilities and allow him access to his room. As desperate as he was to make the bus, he had no intention of going in his stockinged feet. It almost didn't come off; he had turned the latch on the door and stepped outside when Daryl finally spoke.

"Go up and get your fuckin' shoes, you eejit," he said sourly.

Seán spun on a sixpence and made his way back up the hall, ignoring his stepfather's glare as he went into his room. Where were his shoes? The space where his tan loafers always stood was empty. They should have been on the floor at the end of his bed. Where the fuck were they? He'd left them out this morning. He turned to Daryl, still standing in the hallway.

"Where's me shoes?"

"How the fuck would I know?"

In his frantic state of mind a thought occurred to Seán, one that seemed wholly reasonable given the circumstances.

"What the fuck have you done with 'em, you prick?"

"What?"

"What have you done with me shoes?"

"I didn't fuckin' touch your shoes."

For once, Daryl's outrage was genuine; he hadn't touched Seán's shoes. Remembering that her son had a big night out in Wexford, Sinéad had taken his shoes, buffed them, scrubbed them and polished them before leaving them in the hallway so that he'd see them. They lay there now, neatly positioned by the table. But neither man had seen them; they only had eyes for one another.

"You fucking must have," said Seán, desperately.

"The fuck you saying boy, eh?"

"You sad fuckin' bastard."

Anger reignited, Daryl entered Seán's room and stood over his stepson, daring him to continue the accusations.

"I didn't touch your fuckin' shoes, ya little cunt."

Seán sat on the edge of the bed, angry, frustrated and upset, no longer sure he believed it himself.

"You did!" he shrieked, getting to his feet and shoving Daryl in the chest.

Physical contact; Daryl could scarcely comprehend it. All those years of toing and froing, being painted as the villain, and now it was Seán who was starting on him. He needed no second invitation.

Stepping toward Seán he shoved him back, causing him to lose his balance and flop harmlessly onto the bed.

"COME ON!" he shouted, standing over Seán.

"Fuck off," Seán retorted, sitting up but remaining on the bed, the fight seemingly knocked out of him already.

This wouldn't do. You couldn't wind someone up and expect them to back off at a moment's notice. Daryl shoved him again, pushing him onto his back but not hurting him. Seán propped himself up once more, head bowed deferentially.

It was hopeless. There was no fight to be had here; one little push, that's all he'd mustered. Daryl snorted in derision.

"Fuck's sake, boy, is that all you've got?"

Seán remained silent, casting his eyes down and waiting for it to be over.

"Fucking useless! What a fucking loser," Daryl laughed, leaving the room with a swagger, his place at the top of the food-chain restored.

Seán, choking back tears, half-heartedly resumed the search for his shoes. He wasn't even sure he wanted to go to Wexford any more. He didn't want to go anywhere, do anything anymore, not really. Tossing runners this way and that, he searched in vain, even upending the linen basket in case they'd somehow found their way in there. He was practically inside his wardrobe, throwing clothes recklessly over his shoulder, when his phone rang.

"Seán?" a hopeful voice inquired.

"Pegs," began Seán, trying to come up with something, anything, which might see him on that bus.

"Where are ya, man?"

"Still at home," Seán said sadly.

"I can't ask him to wait any longer, Seán. He's losing the rag already."

"I know, Pegs. Thanks all the same, man."

"Fuck's sake, Lockie, isn't there a late bus? Or a train?"

"Nah, man. I checked already, there's nothing."

"What about a taxi?"

"It'd cost me about a hundred quid, and I'm unemployed now."

"Eh?"

"It's a long story. Look, enjoy the night out; I'll talk to you tomorrow."

There was a long pause on the other end of the phone, Pegs still reluctant to accept the inevitable. Seán loved him for it, but all hope was lost now.

"Fuck," said his friend. "Not gonna be the same without you, man."

"Definitely won't be for me, anyway," Seán said with forced humour.

"We'll get wrecked tomorrow night, eh?"

"Yeah, sounds good. Talk to you later."

"Sound, Lockie."

Seán lay down on the bed, disconsolate. He didn't care about missing the night out in Wexford or even about being unemployed; it was bigger than that. His life was shit, and he was shit too. His only purpose was to make others feel better about themselves, a punch-bag for weak individuals to take out their frustrations. Lorcan, a feeble shadow of a man, ordering him around as if he was nothing. And Daryl, a bitter, dejected bastard who lived to make Seán unhappy. What was it about him that aroused such hate? Was he really so vile and contemptible? Looking back at his life suggested so. He had been unwanted since the very first moment of his being. A disaster, causing dismay to all concerned. His father had taken to the hills as soon as he'd learned of his existence. His mother had gone to a different country to get rid of him, only to be told she was stuck with him. And he'd been a burden ever since. He had burdened his mother, his grandparents, Daryl and everyone he came into contact with. The Tiernan girls, Leanne and Alice: look what he had done to them; a sad, craven weirdo acting out his sordid fantasies at their expense. That was who he really was; a dark, miserable entity, a parasite. Everything that had happened to him he had deserved. He was pathetic. It had been coming his way.

He began to sob; heavy, violent convulsions which shook his whole body. It felt good to submit to it, to let go. No longer did he have to pretend he cared. He had no pride, no self-respect. This was the real Seán McLoughlin, a wretched loser curled up in a ball, crying his eyes out. He didn't ask for pity or concern, just to be left alone to wallow in the abject despair of his existence. He remained like that for some time, whimpering like a child, shivering and helpless. Then inexplicably he began to laugh. What an idiot he was, lying here on his bed bawling like a baby and over what? Lorcan, that little fucker? Jesus Christ. Daryl? The world's most pitiful man! *Get a grip, Seán, for fuck's sake.* He sat up and rubbed his eyes, embarrassed at the way he'd let himself go. He still had a lot to live for, despite the many obstacles placed in front of him. He was better than this, anyway, that was for sure. He didn't have to hide away in his room like a terrified slave. He had as much right to be here as anyone. Why was he taking shit from Daryl? Who did he think he was, talking to him like that? Something in Seán snapped. He'd had enough. Now he felt like making a statement.

17

IT WOULD BE JUST LIKE his childhood fantasies, where he'd plunged the knife right into Daryl's chest and watched with glee as the blood spurted out in high fountains, almost touching the ceiling. Except he wouldn't actually stab him. He wasn't that stupid. He'd just scare him a bit, make him understand that things were changing around here and that Seán McLoughlin was nobody's whipping boy. Oh, he'd bring the knife all right, wave it about a bit and pretend he was serious, but he wasn't going to kill him; he had more sense than that. He'd wait until Daryl begged for mercy, grovelled a bit, and then he'd back off. He would walk away, return the knife to its rightful place and head out for a couple of drinks. And when he returned later that night it would be to a different house, where he no longer had to live in fear. Daryl would understand then. He would see what happened when you pushed someone to their limits, and think twice before doing it again.

Seán crept out of his room, making sure not to disturb Daryl. He was in the living-room now, eating by the sound of it. Seán plucked a knife from the block, wielded it and replaced it; too small. He needed a bigger one, the biggest. He went through them all, finally settling on a blade more suited to jungle warfare than household disputes. It was at least a foot in length and thick with it, thick enough to pierce a chest cavity and carry on through to the internal organs. As he held it, feeling the power, the strength it gave him, he wondered whether he might go through with it after all. Maybe he would fulfil his fantasy right through to the end: murder in the first degree. Or was it the second? He couldn't remember which, but either would carry a long prison sentence and he didn't like the idea of that. He could claim self-defence, but these cases were never straightforward. No, just a little fright for Daryl, that was all.

He walked to the sitting-room, calm and in control, no longer afraid. Daryl was crouched forward, shovelling food into his mouth; lots of gravy, mashed spuds, meat, probably beef. It looked nice.

"Enjoying that, yeah?"

Daryl turned to look at him, mouth full, ready to skewer another sliver of meat. He grunted a response and returned to his dinner, not noticing the knife in Seán's hand.

"I asked you a question, Daryl."

He looked at Seán once more, irritated now. Hadn't the festivities ended for the night? Hadn't he already bested him? What was this nonsense?

"G'way, boy."

Seán sprang into action, grabbing the plate and smashing it off the wall in one fluid movement. Then he shoved Daryl back into his chair and stood facing him, the knife pointed at his chest.

"What the fuck!"

"You can only push people so far, Daryl."

"For fuck's sake, Seán."

It felt amazing, sensational, in fact. This was the defining moment in his life. Everything had been leading up to this moment, and from here on in nothing would be the same. He was no longer scared, he was in control. He was the master, and his demeanour said as much. He stood in front of his stepfather, feeling taller, bigger, and stronger, than he'd ever done before. Even his voice, usually a soft, well-mannered instrument, sounded different, its tone now one of authority.

"For years I've had to listen to your shit, Daryl, every day of my fucking life. I've been put down and mocked, bullied and abused. Well, no more. No fucking more!"

He made a swipe at his stepfather, intending just to frighten him a little, but his aim was off. A thin streak of blood appeared on Daryl's cheek.

"Oops, sorry about that, Daz."

Daryl raised a hand to his cheek, felt the blood and looked at Seán. His expression was pleading, that of a man desperately trying to appeal to his tormentor's sensitive side. It was one Seán had worn himself on numerous occasions.

"So what do you have to say for yourself?"

Daryl looked at Seán with wide eyes, mouth opening and closing but no words coming forth. It was just as Seán had imagined it, only better.

"ANSWER ME!"

Daryl started in surprise. "What – I – "

"The fucking tough guy, huh? The hard-man of Dooncurra; look at you now!"

Cocky now, Seán juggled the knife from one hand to the other, as if pondering how the fatal blow was to be applied.

"Fuckin' tough guy," he repeated as he juggled.

The knife danced from one hand to the other and then back, and back once more. Seán wasn't paying attention, indeed had almost forgotten about his weapon. Daryl hadn't, though. Sensing his opportunity, he leapt forward, driving his fist into Seán's midriff and knocking them both backwards. As they fell to the floor, Seán's head collided with the solid oak coffee table, clipping its edge. His right temple hit it with a sickening jolt, knocking him unconscious. By the time he reached the ground he was out cold, his head lolling on his shoulders as it flopped to the carpeted floor. Daryl, his focus on being first to rise, pinned Seán to the floor, ready to continue his assault.

"Now, ya little prick!" he said triumphantly.

He launched a volley of heavy blows to Seán's unprotected head, but the thick, clubbing shots were met with no resistance; his adversary was out for the count. Daryl had won, he was triumphant. He rose hesitantly from the floor, worried now that he might have gone too far. Seán was still breathing, as far as he could tell. He'd leave him for a few minutes and come back then.

18

SEÁN'S HEAD HURT AND HE couldn't see; worse, he couldn't breathe. His mouth was blocked, and his nose too. He tried to suck in air but nothing came. Maybe if he moved his head, things would improve. He cranked it to the side and his passageways unblocked instantly. Oxygen gushed into his lungs. He could breathe again. He lay on his side in the middle of the floor, gasping for air, wondering how he'd got there. He focused on breathing, that was his main priority right now. His brain wasn't working properly. He couldn't think of anything but air and his need of it. Slowly, though, his sight began to return. Everything was fuzzy and brown, but it was an improvement on the nothingness that had preceded it.

After some time, he couldn't tell how long, his breathing settled down and he took stock of the situation. He remembered that he had arms and legs; it would be a good idea to try to move them. He stretched his legs; they worked. Then his arms; they worked too. Now it was just a matter of using them both at the same time. Slowly he hauled himself off the floor and took in his surroundings. He was in the living-room of his house. He should go to the kitchen and get some water. Moving towards the door, he was stopped in his tracks by a sharp pain in his right temple. He raised his hand to his head, to the source of the pain. It was tender to the touch but there was no blood. His whole head hurt, but the pain centred on that spot. It pulsed and throbbed under his skin, accompanied by a piercing ringing noise which was almost too much to bear. He shook his head, trying to rouse himself, but that just made it worse. He tried to pull his thoughts together. What had happened? Why was his head so sore, and where were his shoes? Then he remembered the fight. He and Daryl had been fighting; over what? It hardly mattered. He'd been winning because he'd had a knife. That was where the memory ended.

But if he'd woken up on the floor with a sore head it seemed unlikely he'd won the fight. Where was Daryl now? Was the fight over? He didn't want to hang around to find out, he was in no mood for fighting. He went to his room, ignoring the pain in his head and the dizziness. He had to get out of here. It was only when he saw the bag of cans that he remembered what he'd been doing. He'd been getting ready for a night out, a big night in Wexford, in Ambience. There was a bus at 7.30. He had to be on that. His shoes were nowhere to be seen so he pulled on a pair of trainers, hoping the bouncers at Ambience would look kindly upon them, grabbed the cans, his phone and his wallet and went back out to the hallway. He felt fine now. It was going to take a lot more than a bump on the head to keep him away from that bus.

He stepped outside. It was dark now, too dark; darker than it should have been. He pulled out his phone and turned it on. The luminous green background came to life, the time displayed in stark black numbers in the foreground: 7.55. He was too late, he'd missed the bus. He wouldn't be going to Wexford. But maybe it hadn't gone, maybe Pegs had made the driver wait. He called his friend.

"Pegs?"

"Yeah?"

"Are ye gone?"

"We are, man. I told you we were."

"Oh, did you?"

"Yeah. Is everything all right, Seán? You sound a bit weird."

"I'm okay, Pegs. I was just fighting, that's all."

"With who?"

"Daryl."

"That fucking prick."

"I was winning, though. I had a knife."

"What the fuck, a knife?"

"Yeah, no one was stabbed, though."

"Fuck's sake, Lockie. Where are you now?"

"Just walking, might head down by the river."

"Take it easy, okay?"

"Of course I will, Pegs."

"Might ring you later."

"Grand."

He hung up. The river, that was a good idea.

19

IN ORDER TO GET THERE, he first had to walk along the main street. There were other ways of getting there, but that was the quickest. Once he reached the end of the street, he could duck down a laneway and carry onto the river. The town was already busy, as another Friday night swung into action and the crowds flocked to the numerous pubs dotted along Dooncurra's prime thoroughfare. People hurried past him as he walked, all clacking heels and expensive scents, making arrangements over the phone, planning the night ahead. Seán kept his head down, hoping he wouldn't meet anyone he knew. His headache was getting worse and now he felt faint as well. He could still walk well enough, but his footsteps were light, almost floaty. *Just focus, just focus, Seán.* He still had his cans, but if he were to spend the night by the riverbank he would need something stronger; some spirits and maybe a few more cans, just in case. There was an off-licence at the end of the street. He'd go in there, get the booze and disappear into the darkness, away from prying eyes.

As soon as he walked into the shop he felt worse, much worse. The lights dazzled him, causing his head to spin and his legs to turn to jelly. *Just focus, just focus.* There were people around him, loud voices shouting at one another from opposite ends of the store. He ignored them, keeping his head down, focusing on his task.

"Howya, Seán," said a voice.

"Fine," he croaked in response, not looking up.

"Jaysus, boy, you must have been on the booze all day, were ya?"

Seán tried to laugh but it came out wrong, a strange, strangled utterance.

"Fuckin' hell, boy, you'd want to go home for yourself," the voice continued.

He walked down to the fridges, his sight blurring round the edges. Two more cans would do. He opened one of the doors and pulled out the first cans he touched; it didn't matter what they were. Now he just needed a bottle of something. There were bottles on the wall to his left. He took one down from the shelf. It was brown, it would have to do. With his purchases in one hand and his existing bag of cans in the other, he headed for the counter.

Reaching into his pocket for some money, he put what he found on the counter, hoping it was enough. The cash register rang and he felt his change being pushed into his hand.

"Want a bag, Seán?"

"Nah," he managed and headed for the exit, for the sanctity of darkness.

Once he was back outside, he felt better. It had just been the lights and the noise in there that had sent him into a daze. He was fine now, he really was. It still felt like someone else was propelling him forward, like he wasn't really walking; aside from that, though, everything was okay. Even his headache had improved, his head just felt numb now. The only real pain came from his temple, which continued to pulse away like a second heartbeat. He reached the riverbank and stepped onto the track which ran alongside it. He was safe. No one would bother him here. He'd walk further than he'd ever gone before and settle down for the evening. It'd be great. He'd get pissed, take some pills and meet up with the lads later.

He walked for a few minutes, feeling happier the further he went. Along the way he passed a group of kids, younger than himself. One or two nodded in recognition, another might have asked for a cigarette, but he wasn't in a talking mood. He continued on his way, determined to find perfect isolation, and after twenty minutes of walking he found it. No one came up this far, except maybe the fishermen.

Satisfied that he'd gone far enough, he looked for a nice spot to while away the evening, somewhere he could set up camp until he returned to civilisation in the small hours. A few minutes later, he found precisely what he was looking for. The path broadened out to reveal a small picnic area with a couple of benches. It wasn't so dark here; the moon shone down, bathing the area in a gloomy pall. This was the spot. It was perfect.

Sitting on one of the benches, he popped open a can and set about rolling a joint to accompany it. The headache had returned and he felt dizzy, slightly woozy too; that wouldn't last long, though. Once he got them Doves down him, he wouldn't feel a thing. He gazed out at the river, at the water shimmering under the moon's milky light. It was so peaceful here, the only sound that of faraway traffic as it brought people to and from the public houses of Dooncurra. Cars full of happy people dressed in their finest garments, excited to be going out on the town. Once they reached their destination, they'd spill out of taxis, giggling, then head inside to be greeted by smiling, welcoming faces. Their night would begin with merriment and warmth and end in dishevelled confusion a few hours later. That was how his nights ended, anyway. These folk were probably different. Normal people didn't overdo things, content just to have a few jars. They got tipsy, maybe even a little drunk, but no more than that, and when the taxi pulled up at the prearranged spot, they were ready and waiting to go home. They clambered inside and were ferried back to loved ones, to mothers and fathers who'd been lying awake in bed listening for their return. These sensible drinkers with loving parents would wake early the next morning, around the time Seán was usually weaving his way home, and stumble out of bed to join the rest of the family at the breakfast table.

"Oh, here she comes," they'd tease, as Carol, the mad wan, gingerly tiptoed into the kitchen.

Talk would turn to the events of the night before, Mammy and Daddy captivated as Carol told them all about the fella she'd kissed, a fine cut of a lad from out the country somewhere.

"Are you meeting him again tonight?" they'd ask.

"Jaysus, I'm not," she'd say with forced embarrassment, and they'd all laugh.

That was Carol for you, kissing blokes right, left and centre; never anything more than that, though. Right now she was just enjoying herself, playing the field, not looking for anything serious. Her studies were her main focus. She hoped to become a barrister, but that wouldn't happen unless she got her degree. She worked hard all week, harder than most of her peers, so she was entitled to enjoy herself once the weekend came. And after she'd qualified there wouldn't be much time for nights on the town. There wouldn't much time for anything by then, and the weekends home would become less frequent too.

When she did come home she'd bring Fergal, her new boyfriend, and he was a gas lad altogether, a real charmer. He'd immediately hit it off with Carol's father, the two men taking up residence in the living-room, watching the rugby, setting the world to rights while the women did whatever it was they did. He'd quickly become part of the family and everyone, especially Carol's father, would be overjoyed when the wedding was announced. First, though, they'd have to build a house, you couldn't forget that; there was a certain way of doing things, after all. House built, wedding over, Carol would set about starting a family of her own, and soon the weekend visits home would include a husband and child; her parents' first grandchild, and boy, would they spoil him. He'd be the star of the show, entertaining them all with his funny little ways, his granddad's nose and his nanny's smile. Then Thomas, Carol's younger brother, would emerge from his slumber. He was an adult now and had recently started going out on the town with his friends, following in his sister's footsteps. Now he was the one being ribbed about his Friday night shenanigans, getting teased as the love-bite he thought he'd concealed was spotted by his observant sister.

Seán wondered if he could have a family like that one day. He could, y'know. Just because the adults in his life had failed him didn't mean he had to follow in their footsteps. When he had kids, he'd make sure he did it the right way. They would be born into a loving, caring home where Mammy and Daddy loved them as much as they loved each other. His kids would never have to retreat to their room for safety, or creep around the kitchen looking for something to eat. What was his would be theirs. They would be happy children who would grow into happy, well-adjusted adults. They'd start families of their own and produce grandchildren for him, further evidence of the good he'd done in his life. And, as he looked at them, gazed into their innocent little faces, he would realise he'd finally done it. He'd escaped his past, not quite erased it but done enough to ensure it couldn't hurt anyone else. These children would be untainted by his badness; they would know nothing of his youth. He would just be a sweet old man who liked going for walks in the woods, their granddad.

20

THE DRINK HADN'T HAD THE desired effect. His headache was still very much *in situ*; if anything, it was getting worse. He was starting to feel nauseous, too. In a situation like this, there was only one thing for it: out came the pills. He downed one and immediately felt better. In another half an hour or so there'd be no more headaches, no more bellyaches, just pure, unadulterated bliss. He took out his phone to text Pegs.

"Hey man, how's Wexford? I'm up the bank having a few cans and just took a yoke! Session when ye come back?"

Pegs was probably too off his head to even find his phone, never mind read a text, but he'd see it eventually, possibly on the bus on the way back. Now that Seán had a pill down him, he began to reassess his plans for the night. He'd never taken one on his own before and thought it might get boring all alone, miles from town, without so much as a Walkman with him. Could be interesting too though, a fascinating sociological experiment or something like that. Right now it was best to wait until the drug took hold and take things from there. He might end up going into town; if he was off his head, it would hardly matter that he was on his own. Maybe he'd bump into Danielle? They hadn't exchanged numbers, and there'd been no indication of it being anything more than a one-night stand, but they were good together and she knew it. It could be awkward, though, seeing her again, all dressed up, on the pull again. What if she was with someone else? That would hurt. No, he wouldn't approach her if he saw her, she could come to him. But he'd probably stay here anyway, so it didn't matter. *Maybe tomorrow night, Dani, if you're lucky.*

He stood up to piss, but before he could take a step he swayed violently to one side. Fumbling his way back to the bench, he contented himself with pissing from a seated position; it wasn't easy, but he managed it. He'd only had three or four cans and a couple of joints, and the pill, of course, but none of that could explain the dizziness; he had been almost literally legless. He stood up again to test his limbs and once more the ground gave way beneath his feet, forcing him to sit down. His nausea was returning, too. A sudden retch almost brought up the entire contents of his stomach. It must have been the pills, those fucking Doves. He'd felt a bit iffy while coming up on them last week, but nothing like this. Just as well he'd bought that bottle of spirits, that would settle his nerves. He shakily unscrewed the cap and took a slug, but it didn't have the desired effect. It just slithered down his gullet and sat in his stomach, acrid and burning. For fuck's sake! It had to be the Es. They were getting him in a right state, but that just meant that the buzz would be even better when he finally came up. There wouldn't be any stumbling and staggering then, just smooth, slick moves as he sauntered back to town and into Moody Blues.

His phone went off: a text from Pegs. Seán fumbled in his pocket for the device and, feeling its familiar cold bulk, pulled it out of his pocket to see what his friend was up to. But, try as he might, he couldn't read the text. He could barely make out the screen, which was just a green blur in front of his eyes. After a considerable period of time he managed to unlock the phone, but none of the icons were where they were supposed to be. Usually he could have navigated its interface blindfolded, but the more he focused the harder it became.

"Fuck," he said quietly.

The voice no longer sounded like his own. Was it his own? Was there someone else here? He looked around for signs of life. But it was just him. Just him and the bench, and the river. He didn't want to be here anymore; he was afraid. He just wanted to be at home in bed, but not in Daryl's house, at his grandparents' house. That was his real home, the only place he'd ever felt safe. He remembered staying over on Friday nights as a child, the fun he and his nanny had had. They'd sit by the fire, playing games and eating chocolate until it was time for him to go to bed. She'd carry him up, tucking him in so tight he could barely breathe and his feet were in danger of bursting into flames from the hot-water bottle. After kissing him goodnight she'd leave the light on in the hall, promising to come back in a few minutes to look in on him.

"Okay, Nanny," he'd say as he snuggled under the covers, tired but too excited to sleep.

When sleep did come he went with it willingly, because he knew there were no strange men here, no one trying to take his mother away from him. In this house, everyone loved him.

Downstairs, Noel had returned from the pub, and was cursing his wife for putting the boy to bed before he'd got the chance to see him. Ignoring her protestations, he'd march upstairs for a look, secretly hoping the little fella was still awake. He wasn't, but Noel would tiptoe into the room and while Seán slept and dreamt of togging out for Fergie's boys, his grandfather would bend down and kiss him gently on the forehead.

"Love you, Seány," he'd whisper, all sentimental from the whiskey. "Goodnight, lad."

Then he'd creep back downstairs, wondering if the oul' wan might let him have a leg over given the night that was in it.

21

How long had he been sleeping? He couldn't tell, but he wished he were still asleep. He felt terrible. The pain in his head was worse now, much worse, and the ringing in his ears had reached fever-pitch, shattering the peace and quiet of his secluded location. Putting his hands over his ears didn't help; the noise continued, unabated. Movement of any kind made everything worse. Seán lay there, moaning softly, as the world closed in around him. His thoughts became scrambled as he tried to piece together the last few hours of his life. How had he got here? Why was he lying on a bench in the middle of nowhere? Was that the river over there? It looked like it. Had he come here after work, with Pegs, maybe? Where was Pegs now?

If ever he needed his friend, it was now. Pegs would sort things out, he always did. Seán tried to call out for him but the sound was lost, drowned out by the ringing in his ears. He was scared now, scared beyond belief. He began to pray, unable to hear the words but hoping that they'd reach their intended target.

"Dear God, I'm sorry for all the bad things I've done.

Please let me get through this and I'll never sin again.

I know I've said stuff like this before, but this time I mean it.

And I know I haven't been very holy up to now, but that will change too. I'm sorry, God, really I am, but I'm not a bad lad, am I?

There's worse than me out there, we both know that.

Just let me see the morning and I promise that I'll never take drugs again.

I'll tell my mother I love her and be nicer to Kevin

I'll even try and get on with Daryl.

Please God, just this one time and I'll never ask for anything again.

Please, please, please. I'm sorry, God."

As his lament to the almighty died out, he lapsed into sleep once more. It was better than being awake, he embraced it with open arms.

He dreamt of Leanne. They were holding hands and walking on the beach. It was night-time, and they had the entire seafront to themselves. The ocean lapped gently against their bare feet, tickling them. Leanne giggled as she kicked some water at Seán and ran away, laughing, hoping he would give chase. He did, catching her easily, grabbing her by the waist and dragging her down into the soft, warm sand. He lay on top of her, looking down at her face, so beautiful, so vulnerable. He wanted to fuck her to death and cradle her in his arms, all at the same time.

"Seány," she whispered.

He knew what she wanted and he gave it to her, wordlessly, without effort. She sighed contentedly. They were as one, their bodies connected, both wishing they could stay like this forever. Neither of them pushed or thrust against the other, they were content simply to be. Their mouths met in the darkness, again with no pressure. To do so would have been to push the other away. They breathed in each other's air, connected in every way possible. This was where he would remain for eternity, where he'd always wanted to be.

"Seány," she murmured again, her voice echoing inside his head.

Once more he understood. He understood her every need and desire. It was his duty to fulfil them. He forced himself deeper inside, straining but remaining as gentle and as still as he possibly could. All he wanted was to crawl inside her skin, to become a part of her, have her heart beating over his, her lungs inhaling the same air. She tugged at his hair, encouraging him, letting him know that it was time and she was ready. He let himself go, relieved to have given her what she wanted; he never wanted to disappoint her or let her down. Leanne sighed appreciatively. Taking it as a sign, he came up for air. The cold wind immediately blasted him, chilling him to the bone. He tried to envelop himself in her arms once more, to return to the warmth and comfort of her touch, but she no longer wanted him. Her eyes were vacant and uninterested, even contemptuous. He reached out and pawed at her, pleading with her to take him in her arms once more. She looked away, waiting for him to depart. She had no use for him anymore. He felt sick, disgusted by her betrayal. She had used him for her own sordid needs and now wished to dispense with him as if he were nothing.

Bile rose in his stomach, forced upwards by his rage and sorrow. Leanne raised her hands to protect herself, apologetic now, trying to reason with him; but he would never harm her, not intentionally. She was his life's blood, without her he was nothing. No matter what she did, no matter how badly she hurt him, he would always nurture and protect her. He couldn't control this though, something bad was about to happen; it was flowing through him, the badness, ready to come to the surface. He tried to speak, to tell Leanne to run, to get away from him, but the only sound was a muffled burbling, a suffocated plea. He tried to move his arms to push her away, but they flapped around aimlessly like a fish fighting for its life on dry land.

"LEANNE!" he screamed, the word almost causing his head to explode.

She turned her head away, fighting with him now, wanting to escape but unable to do so. He stared into her face, hoping to convey his message through sight alone, and there staring back at him was Alice, the young Alice, the one he'd betrayed. She shook her head in silent recrimination. It tore his heart asunder.

"I'm sorry," he mouthed, but to no avail. She was gone too.

"Why are you sorry, Seán?"

Danielle was there now, her pupils dilated, the size of saucers. She was chewing a piece of gum.

"Dani," he said with a frightened whimper, "I'm sorry."

"Why are you sorry, Seán?" she asked, still chewing.

"I'm sorry, Dani," he said and fell into her arms.

She took him and consoled him. There was nothing sexual in her gesture, she wanted only to mother him, to protect him against evil.

"Don't worry, Seán," she said. "I've got you now."

When he awoke it was almost dawn. Was it over? Not quite. Soon though. He could no longer see; he was completely blind, but he could still hear. Birds sang nearby, the dawn chorus. It was pleasing at first, all these little creatures coming to life, introducing themselves to the world. *Hello, little birdies, how are you this morning?* Then the pain returned, the maddening, inescapable throbbing in his head. The noise of the cheerful birds bore into his skull, each separate note drilling a hole in his tender, aching temples. There was nothing he could do to stop it or them, they were a part of nature, part of God's beautiful kingdom. The noise continued unabated, reaching a pitch so high that it became white noise. That felt better, he could tune out it now. The last thing he wanted to do was stop the birds singing, to interfere with God's plan for the world.

His other senses stirred momentarily. He sensed dampness on his head, around his ears. Had it been raining? Perhaps, but the rest of him didn't feel damp, just cold, incredibly cold. Wait, there was dampness elsewhere too, around his groin, he'd soiled himself. And around his face on the bench where he lay. He'd been sick. The stench was overpowering, his face pressed right into it so that it covered his mouth and nose. It was the smell of death and decay, the final expulsion of a body about to breathe its last. Soon he would join that filthy, useless matter, unless someone came to help him. No one would come, though; he'd made sure of that by walking so far out of town. He made one last effort, tried to rouse himself, but there was no response, nothing was working as it should. It was over. All hope was lost, the fight knocked out of him. It had all been for nothing, all that railing and raging. This was where it had got him, on a bench listening to the birds, lying in his own waste. He crawled back inside his head to the white noise and waited for it to stop.

Now that he'd accepted his fate, he began to feel better about it all. It wasn't so bad here. He had his own little spot where no one could get him. Soon the pain would disappear and he would go somewhere else. It would be nice there, he could feel it. But his mother! Oh, his poor mother, what about her? He panicked for a moment and thought about resisting, thought about holding on, just in case. But it was too late for that now, far too late. She'd just have to manage. Sorry, Mammy; sorry for everything. Sorry for being such a burden and messing up your life. Be good now and don't get upset, don't cry, because I'm going somewhere good, a place where people like me. I'll be happy there; they'll look after me, they've promised they will. Maybe one day we'll see each other again, wouldn't that be grand? There'll be no Daryl there, no Kevin; it'll be like old times, just me and you. We'll chat and joke, tell each other that we love one another and go for walks in the woods, and it'll last forever. So see you soon, Mammy. I'm off now. I'm just going to stay on this bench a little while longer and wait for the birds to stop singing.

22

SERGEANT GERARD TOOMEY DROVE SLOWLY through the housing estate.

"Do you see it yet, Dymphna?"

"No," she replied, staring intently through the window.

The sergeant sighed. He hated this. He'd only just started his shift when they'd got the phone call: a body had been found up by the river. A young fella, drugs probably. They'd gone out there in the shivering cold to meet the ambulance crew; all of them sipping coffee and talking in low voices. The body had lain on top of a bench. He'd barely looked old enough to drink, but he had been drinking, and quite heavily by the looks of it;

there were cans scattered all around him and an empty whiskey bottle too. A couple of greedy crows had been perched beside him, pecking at the vomit, grateful for the unexpected meal. He hadn't choked on his own bile, though; the blood seeping from his left ear pointed to another cause of death. Well, that would be a job for the pathologist. Gerard was just a lowly sergeant; what did he know?

It was his job to find out who the kid was and then inform his next-of-kin. Not for him the dissection of organs in a laboratory, oh no; he only did the important stuff, the good stuff. The Social Services card in the kid's wallet revealed that he was a Mr. Seán McLoughlin. Gerard knew a few McLoughlins around town; Patrick McLoughlin often drank in the same pub as him. Maybe this kid was related to him. God, he hoped not. Further inspection revealed drugs: a small amount of hash and two Ecstasy pills. That explained things. He'd seen kids die from these tablets before; heart-attacks, strokes, all sorts. This lad had probably taken dozens of them, fried his brain and died a horrible, lonely death.

The sergeant thanked the ambulance crew and told them to take the body to the mortuary. He'd be in touch later, but first someone had to tell the parents. He'd never understood why it had to be the guard's job to tell them. Could it not be the doctor's job, or the priest's? Far better for someone with a gentle heart to break the news, and Gerard's heart was far from gentle; he'd seen too much in his life to possess one of those. All he could do was deliver the news with as much sympathy as he could muster.

He was in luck this morning, though; the new girl, Dymphna, was on shift with him. She was a frumpy kind of thing, not what the lads had been hoping for but keen, very keen. They were all like that at the start.

"Have you ever seen a dead body before?" he'd asked her.

"Only my granddad's," she'd replied, unable to avert her gaze as the medical staff bundled Seán's corpse into the body-bag.

"Such a feckin' waste, huh?" the sergeant said, as they rolled the trolley into the back of the ambulance and slammed the doors shut.

"Yes," she replied numbly.

She'd better liven up, thought Gerard, *she's got some talking to do.*

23

"THERE IT IS," SHE SAID. "Number nineteen."

"That's the one," he said, pulling up the squad car outside the house.

"Are you ready?" he asked. "Last thing we need is you getting all hysterical."

"I'll be fine," she replied haughtily.

He'd played it perfectly. She'd be so eager to prove herself that he wouldn't have to do a thing; he could just stand in the background and look sad. Dymphna would take care of the rest.

"Hello?"

A young boy answered the door, tousled hair, puffy eyes.

"Hello, son. Are your parents in?"

"Yes."

"Could you wake them up for me, like a good lad?"

"Okay."

He shuffled off down the hall, then turned. "Who will I say it is?"

"The Guards, son," Gerard replied.

"Mam," Kevin whispered, "the Guards are at the door."

No reply, just the steady rhythm of their breathing as they enjoyed a Saturday morning lie-in.

"Mammy," he whispered once more, slightly louder this time.

"What is it, Kevin?" growled his father.

"The Guards, Dad. They're at the door."

"What the fuck?" Daryl muttered harshly. "That fucking young fella!"

Daryl shook his wife and, after a sustained period of resistance, she finally woke up.

"What? WHAT?" Sinéad moaned, already in a bad mood.

"The Guards are at the door."

"Oh, shut up, Daryl," she said, turning to go back to sleep.

"Sinéad," he urged, "they're outside."

"They are, Mam, honest," Kevin added. "A man and a woman Guard."

Sinéad looked first at her husband and then at her son; their earnest faces indicated that the Guards were indeed at the door. She rose from the bed, not daring to imagine what they might want with her. Throwing on a dressing-gown, she went to the front door.

Sergeant Toomey nudged his young companion as Sinéad approached. It was her show now.

"Mrs. McLoughlin?" asked Dymphna.

"No, Mrs. Cassidy. What's this about?"

"Can we come in, Mrs. Cassidy?"

Sinéad opened the door wide and ushered them into the living-room, guiltily picking up an empty wine bottle from the coffee table which had a small crack near one edge.

"Take that out to the kitchen, love," she said, handing the bottle to Kevin. "Do ye want some tea, Guards?"

The sergeant shook his head silently as he attempted to recede into the background.

"We're fine, thanks, Mrs. Cassidy," replied Dymphna.

"Is this something to do with Seán?" she asked, cutting to the chase.

He'd had that incident with the Guards a few years back, but nothing since. Her son wasn't the type to get into trouble with the law, at least not as far as she knew. Anyway, he'd been in Wexford for the night; how things could have got from there to here was a mystery.

"It is, Mrs. Cassidy," Dymphna said, swallowing hard. "I'm afraid there's been an accident."

Gerard studied the pictures on the wall, thanking his lucky stars he'd been paired with the new girl today.

"What kind of accident?" Sinéad asked, her blood running cold.

"I'm afraid your son's dead, Mrs. Cassidy. His body was found by the riverbank earlier this morning. We'll know more after the post-mortem."

Sinéad smiled hesitantly; what sort of joke was this? Seán never went up the riverbank, had no reason to. Who did these Guards think they were? She stood up from her seat.

"I think you'd better leave now."

"Mrs. Cassidy, I know this is a big shock, but please try to remain calm."

Dymphna tried to put a consoling arm around her, but it was swatted away.

"Get your hands off me! How dare you come in here, saying such things!"

Dymphna persisted. "Your son's body was found this morning about two miles outside of town, up by the riverbank. Here's his wallet, see."

She handed her the wallet and Sinéad took it hesitantly. "Where did you get this?"

"We found it in your son's pocket. He's dead, Mrs. Cassidy. I'm very sorry."

Sinéad stared at the young officer for what seemed like an age.

"I want to see him," she said firmly. "I want to see him now."

She returned some moments later, dressed and ready to leave.

"Isn't your husband going to accompany you, Mrs. Cassidy? This is not the kind of thing you should face alone."

She'd heard that before, some time long ago in her past, and just as before she wished to tackle this very much alone. This was between herself and her boy. If he'd been up to no good or got himself into trouble, then she, and she alone, would deal with it.

"No, he's not coming with me," she replied, referring to Daryl.

He'd offered, but the last thing she needed was him and Seán staring daggers at each other while she tried to smooth things over with the Guards.

"Very well, Mrs. Cassidy. We'd best be off, then."

The sergeant led the way, suggesting that both women sit in the back. Dymphna could offer support that way, he explained. The truth was that he didn't want Sinéad up in the front beside him, in case she started crying.

"Are ye right?" he asked, looking back at the two of them.

The mother was in denial; he'd seen it countless times before. It was almost as if they knew before you even told them, but when you did tell them they chose not to hear it. They tuned out, nodding along silently while you offered your condolences; then, as you neared the hospital, they began to unravel. Hospitals did that to people. Some broke down at the sight of the building, the ambulances, and the patients outside having a fag; it drove the message home. Others lasted a little longer, holding out until the doctor arrived, but they all caved at the sight of the body. There was nowhere left to hide by then, nothing left to deny.

This wan here was completely oblivious, one of the worst cases he'd ever seen. She was like a zombie, sitting in the back of the car like a kid being taken to the beach; gawping out the window, lost to the world, completely shut down. Even a cold-hearted bastard like Gerard Toomey could see that she shouldn't have been facing this on her own, that they should have insisted she bring someone along for moral support; but it was early in the morning and he just wanted this to be over. Maybe Dymphna would go down to the morgue with her; she'd been doing a great job so far.

24

THE HOSPITAL WHERE THEY'D TAKEN Seán was in a neighbouring town, Dooncurra's being too small to deal with anything beyond a sprained ankle. It took about twenty minutes to get there, time enough for Sergeant Toomey to start thinking about what he might have for breakfast. All he'd had so far today were two cups of tea and a slice of dry toast. He fancied getting something in that little café near Plunkett Street; they did great baps in there, bacon, eggs, sausages, whatever you wanted. The ladies behind the counter always gave him a little extra, fuel to help him fight crime they said. Yes, that's where he'd go. A couple of baps and a big pot of tea, maybe a Twix as well; it was Saturday, after all.

"Nearly there now," he said, as they passed the sign for Stoneyford.

Just a few more minutes till they offloaded their passenger and he could turn his attention to his stomach.

"How are you feeling, Mrs. Cassidy?" he heard Dymphna ask.

"Fine," came the airy response.

She was holding out longer than he'd expected, but the sight of the hospital would probably do the job.

The mortuary was at the rear of the building, hidden away so as not to offend those who intended leaving at some point. The car park was deserted except for the '02 Nissan right by the door; the mortician's he presumed. Gerard glanced at Sinéad through his rearview mirror as he parked. She was still gazing silently out the window.

"Here we are now," he said, staying in his seat.

The message was clear: *Ye two fuck out of the car and leave me here with me paper.*

He caught Dymphna's eye and nodded in the direction of the building.

"Come on, Mrs. Cassidy," she said softly. "Let's go inside."

"Okay," Sinéad replied.

They got out and headed for the mortuary entrance. Gerard watched them until they'd disappeared inside and then breathed a sigh of relief. "Well, thank God for that."

25

DYMPHNA WAS UNSURE OF THE protocol, of where to go and whom to ask for. But at this point she had ceased being a member of the police force, now she was just one woman helping out another.

"Here we are, Mrs. Cassidy," she said, escorting Sinéad to the seating area. "You sit there and I'll just have a quick chat with the receptionist."

She went to the front desk and peered over the counter. There didn't appear to be anyone on duty. There wasn't even a bell to ring. She looked back at Sinéad, and then at the doors leading to the mortuary's inner sanctum.

"I'll be back in a sec, Mrs. Cassidy. You just wait there."

Sinéad nodded dumbly, watching Dymphna go through the heavy wooden doors. She was still only vaguely aware of her surroundings. Everything had become fuzzy since she'd heard Kevin's voice: *They are, Mam, honest. A man and a woman Guard.* She wasn't stupid, she knew what that meant. At this hour of the morning? It could only mean one thing: something had happened to her boy. When had she last spoken to him? What had she said? She couldn't remember. Could she have prevented this? Probably. A few simple words on her part and maybe she wouldn't be here now. She'd be still in bed and so would he; a happy household, all silently sleeping with no Guards coming to disturb them.

But in they'd come, that prick of a sergeant and the young woman, polite but efficient. She dared not look them in the eye, was afraid to, because the truth was there, staring back at her. So she nodded compliantly, did as she was told, and asked them to bring her to her boy. And this was where they'd brought her, this cold, silent building. How had he got here? Why hadn't he told her he was coming here? But that was Seán for you, always going off somewhere, never thinking to tell anyone where he'd be.

She wouldn't be too hard on him, even though he'd ruined her lie-in. A quick telling-off and then they'd get out of here, back home, away from this grey, lifeless place.

Dymphna returned and beckoned to Sinéad to follow her. A man came to greet her, a solemn man, and together they walked, the three of them, down a deserted hallway, the only sound that of their footsteps as she was brought to her boy. This place seemed to be devoid of colour, its walls, its doors and its lights all a drab shade of nothing. Even the doctor who walked beside her was an empty shell, faceless, nameless, characterless.

"Just down here, Mrs. Cassidy," he said, as they turned yet another corner.

Dymphna was still there, Sinéad was vaguely aware of the young guard's hand upon her own.

"Okay," said the doctor, stopping at a pair of cast-iron doors. "He's just in here. Do you want to take a moment first?"

Sinéad shook her head. The mortician glanced at Dymphna and led the way into the morgue.

It was a small room, not much bigger than her bedroom, but with a very high ceiling. Two sets of long halogen lights ran across it, their bulbs giving off a weak, insipid light and casting shadows across the tiled floor. To the left was a cleaning area with large industrial sinks, disinfectant and rubber gloves, and to the right were four large metal containers. Everything was as grey and as grim as before, carefully crafted uniformity from beginning to end. Sinéad had seen what was in the middle of the room as soon as she'd entered. There were three slabs, metal and clinical, and upon the middle one lay a long black bag. The mortician walked towards it, gently encouraging her to follow. She tried to move, but nothing happened. She was stuck here in this horrible room, with two strangers and a long black bag. They would have to get someone to carry her out. To her surprise, she found the slab coming closer; suddenly it was beside her. The doctor was there, tight-lipped and stoical. The woman, the guard, still gripped her hand, tightly now. Sinéad wanted to go home. This was quite enough for one day; maybe she could come back tomorrow. But the black bag lay before them, its long, gloomy mass stretching into oblivion, and the doctor was getting ready to open it. She couldn't leave, not without seeing what was inside.

"Okay, Mrs. Cassidy?" the mortician asked.

She stared at him, her eyes glassy, and watched his hand move slowly to the top of the bag. He pulled down the zip, the sound reminding her of the big duffel coat she'd had as a child. She noticed the mortician's fingernails, impossibly well-manicured, and wondered whether he trimmed them himself or got someone to do it for him. Maybe he had a special guy, who did all the mortician's nails; he knew the exact length and shape they needed to be and gave them all a discount. The mortician carefully lifted the top of the body-bag and pulled it to one side. She saw a face there, a handsome face. A young man, popular with the girls no doubt. He seemed so much at peace, so content with life, that she almost tilted her head to admire him. But then she realised it was her boy, the boy she'd fought so hard for, who had always seemed to be slipping away from her since the day he'd been born. Her boy. Seán. He'd slipped again, only this time she couldn't save him. He was gone, and she knew she could never get him back. Her world collapsed.

Jonathan

1

SLEEP CAME QUICKLY, A DEEP, unnatural sleep from which she feared she might never wake. Her dreams were upsetting and inescapable, dreams of loss and emptiness, of a void that could never be filled. She was in a well, miles below the earth's surface, above her a small window of light. Reaching out, she strained her arms as far as they could go, but they disappeared into the void along with everything else. In desperation, she scrabbled for a way out, but only succeeded in falling further down. When she came to rest, she looked up for the light but it was gone; now there was only darkness. Something touched her shoulder, a hand, cold and unwelcome; another curled around her waist. There were dozens of them pulling at her, dragging her towards some unknown terror. She flailed at them but they were strong, far too strong for her. The light flickered on above, filling her with hope. She fought back, gaining ground, but they overwhelmed her, dragging and pulling until all the fight was drained out of her. She was tired of fighting now. It was easier to give in. They dragged her away and she was relieved. *No more fighting; take me away, I give in.*

They took her from the darkness into somewhere different, a new hell, a place beyond the limits of her imagination. Jeering, mocking faces lurked in the shadows. They struck out at her and then retreated, gorging on whatever it was they had taken. This was a place full of crashing noise and sickness, of malignance and horror. She would never be safe here; no one was. Here, you merely survived, but life could never get any worse — for this was the end.

Sinéad awoke gasping, soaked in sweat, still trying to fight them off. It took her a moment to realise she was safe, that they couldn't get her any more. Then a fresh horror revealed itself. The past nine months: Her burden. Was it still here or had they taken it? She looked at the cot. It was in there, sleeping soundly. She had refused to take it when they'd offered it to her, turning away, asking the nurse to look after it; but now it was just the two of them. Could she take a peep, just a little look? It shifted in its sleep, gurgling contentedly. No bad dreams for it. She felt her resolve weaken, felt a dangerous urge to take it in her arms. No, she mustn't do it. That had never been part of the deal. It was bound for a better life, a life she could never hope to provide. The worst thing to do would be to get attached to it.

So she settled back beneath the covers, back to that hateful place of sickness and terror. The dreams picked up where they'd left off, glad to reclaim her. Until finally, as if sensing she'd had enough, they released her and she lapsed into an empty slumber. And when she next awoke it was gone. The place where its cot had stood was empty. She started to sob, quietly at first, but rising in volume until someone came in to quiet her. They gave her something to help her sleep, and before she knew it she was back in the darkness, fighting off the hands and arms.

*

She left the hospital the following day, numb and still in shock but glad it was over. This chapter of her life had come to an end, and now it was time to move on. For her, moving on meant going back, returning home. There would be questions, but she wouldn't answer them. They'd just have to figure it out themselves; she really didn't care. She would simply arrive at the door as if she'd just spent the weekend away, and that would be that. If they didn't want her, she would go elsewhere. She could do that now; she'd been through a lot.

Her cousin dropped her off at the port and told her she was welcome any time, but they both knew she would never be back. Their relationship was tainted now, forever marred by this wretched affair. She went to the deck, watching her home of the past six months recede into the distance, glad to see the back of it. She was alone now, entirely alone. To her surprise, she found that she missed having it inside her. It had given her a sense of purpose, a reason to live. Without it, she felt worthless. What did she have to offer the world now? Nothing at all.

After a while she headed back inside, to the bar. She hadn't had a drink in months, not since she'd found about it. It may have been her burden, but she hadn't wanted to damage it in any way. Well, it was gone now, and she didn't have to worry about anyone but herself. So she went to the bar and got a drink and then another; it helped pass the time. People talked to her and she talked back, noticing that she was just another young woman to them now. No longer was she afforded the near royalty-like status that had come with her burden, and she missed that too. She missed the respect, the protection from concerned strangers; people helping her out of chairs, opening doors for her and carrying her bags. She had been precious; they had been precious, both of them. Now she was just a drunken young girl on a ferry.

She slept all the way down on the train, her mouth wide open, drool dribbling down her chin – most unladylike. When she awoke, the elderly man in the seat opposite smiled a greeting, and she felt embarrassed, embarrassed of what she'd become. She couldn't bear to speak to him, feigning sleep until it was time to get off. Then she took a taxi home, the driver mercifully taciturn, until she found herself walking up the path towards the front door. She still had her key, but it didn't feel right, just walking right in. So she knocked politely and waited. Her sister, the one who knew, came to the door and took her in her arms. "It's all right," she said, "everything is all right." And it was. They all took her in their arms, even her mother, and there weren't any questions. They were just happy to see her, happy to have her back.

2

WHEN THE NEWS CAME IT wasn't the life-affirming moment Jonathan had thought it would be. He'd just finished a lecture and was heading to one of the bars on campus with some friends. Then his phone rang; it was Rachel from the adoption agency.

"I'll catch up with you," he told the others, moving to a quiet spot.

"Hi, Rachel."

"Hi, Jonathan. How are you?"

"I'm fine, Rachel, thanks."

"Jonathan?"

"Yes?"

"We've found her."

"Oh."

And that was that. They'd found her; his journey was complete – or at least part of it anyway. Rachel wouldn't say much, only that she was Irish and lived in Ireland. His first question was a natural one: why was he in England then? How had this child of an Irish woman, who lived in Ireland, ended up in England? He had been born in England, hadn't he? Rachel assured him he had. So what had happened, then? Had this Irish woman, who lived in Ireland, been here on her holidays and decided to pop him out before scurrying back across the Irish Sea, or had she set up residence here, become pregnant and then returned home? Was his father Irish too? I can't say any more, Rachel told him, but you'll get the answers to all your questions in good time.

The next step was to reach out, to send a letter to this woman in Ireland. The letter would advise her that the son she'd given up eighteen years ago would very much like to meet her. If she was open to the idea she would have to contact Rachel, who in turn would contact Jonathan, and so on. He would have to continue to play the waiting game, but what was another few months? He thanked Rachel for her efforts, made her promise to call him as soon as she heard anything, then hung up.

Jonathan stood in the middle of the university campus, students milling around him, hurrying back and forth. He began to walk, aimlessly following the crowd.

So he was Irish, then, or half-Irish at least. He wasn't sure how he felt about that. He didn't feel Irish, he felt English. He spoke with an English accent, supported the English football team and had, at one point, very nearly ended up representing England in the 800 metres. How were Ireland fixed for runners, he wondered. Maybe if he put an 'O' before his surname, they'd let him compete. The standard over there probably wasn't as high, he could be national champion within a year, an Olympian within three. His mothers would be so proud, both of them. But he'd never even been to Ireland and didn't really know anything about the country apart from the usual; they all had red hair, spoke with funny accents and drank Guinness from morning till night. If he was to visit her he'd have to learn some useful facts, try and fit in, because they didn't like the English over there; that was another thing he knew.

When could he visit her? He was busy with college at the moment, in the second year of a business degree, and might not have time to go and see her. She might have to come to him. Would that be a problem? Maybe she hated it here, and that was why she'd left. No, he would definitely go to Ireland. He'd talk to his course director and explain the situation; Mr. Jenkins was a fair man, he'd understand. It'd be better if he went to Ireland anyway, he could meet the rest of his family, presuming they were all Irish too. He'd go over to Ireland, meet his mother and his family, drink some Guinness, wear green things and they'd all live happily ever after. How exciting. He was already looking forward to it.

3

Sinéad McLoughlin read the letter again, but the words hadn't changed. The past hadn't changed either, and hers had finally caught up with her. That shameful secret she'd hidden for so long was out in the open and lay there in front of her in clear black print. Her son wanted to meet her. Despite everything, he wanted to meet her. The cigarette she'd lit before opening the letter had burned down to the tip without ever passing her lips, its ashes toppling to the floor unnoticed. She was scared. What could he want with her? Didn't he know what he was letting himself in for? And how had they found her? The thought of people digging around in her past, unearthing things she'd rather forget about, unnerved her. It was an invasion of privacy. If she and her son wanted to meet, that was their business; why did these other people have to get involved?

The truth was that he would never have found her without assistance. She'd intended it to be that way. The hospital got in touch with her afterwards, but she'd refused to forward them any information. They had her name and that was it; they weren't getting anything else. In the intervening years they'd occasionally mailed her, asking for details in order to update their records. Those letters were destroyed until eventually they gave up.

No more letters had come. They would still have her name on file, but the hospital's records would all be computerised by now. With any luck, all trace of her would have been lost in the update. Yet they'd managed to find her, to track her down, despite her best efforts to prevent it. Her little boy was out there and he wanted to see her. If he only knew what her life was like: thirty-six years old and living in a grotty little flat with no job, no husband, no kids, no boyfriend and no money. On top of all that, there were her mental illnesses A recent severe bout of depression had left her bedbound for three months. Her social anxiety made any public outing a prolonged and painful affair. And a crippling, debilitating lack of self-esteem was threatening to destroy the few remaining relationships she had. It wasn't a rosy picture to present to her son.

Aside from all that, what could she possibly say to this boy, this young man? How could she explain her actions? Did he really want to hear the truth: that he was an accident and she had been determined to get rid of him? What did he expect to find? Whatever it was, he wouldn't find it here. She was bound to be a crushing disappointment, however low his expectations. All the same, that small part of her which had never stopped thinking of him felt a frisson of excitement. This was what she'd wanted all along, what she'd dreamed of: the storybook ending. They would be reunited, mother and son, after all these years and it would be magical. There would be no recriminations, no accusations or guilt, just relief that they'd found one another at last.

As quickly as these thoughts formed in her head Sinéad pushed them away again, scolding herself for being so foolish. She'd only just started to rebuild her life, and something like this could send her into a tailspin again. The doctors had told her to avoid stressful situations, to take it easy and not allow herself to get worked up unnecessarily. Meeting a child she'd given away eighteen years previously was probably something they'd consider a stressful situation. And they were right. It had taken a lot of hard work and effort to get where she was right now, and the last thing she needed was more upset.

She carefully folded the letter and put it back in its envelope, then rose and went into the living-room. The letter would go in the drawer where she kept all her important documents. She had no intention of ever replying to it, but she would keep it just in case.

4

JONATHAN'S ROUTINE WAS THE SAME every morning. As soon as he woke up he went straight to his phone, hoping for a missed call or a text. When that came up blank he bounded down the stairs to check the post. Finding only bills and junk mail bearing other people's names, he went to the kitchen to greet his mother. He was always careful to appear casual when he asked whether there had been any phone calls or messages left, but when she replied in the negative he found it hard to conceal his disappointment. Another morning had passed without any news, and a whole day of waiting lay ahead.

It had been two months; two months and not a word. She must have received the letter by now, so why hadn't she replied? Rachel had told him it could take some time, that cases like this often took months or even years to resolve. That was easy for her to say; her future wasn't on the line. Jonathan had always feared rejection, but he'd allowed himself to dream when they'd found her. Now that he'd got his hopes up, when he'd finally begun to believe they might meet, the whole thing was about to blow up in his face.

"Hello, Adoption Search Reunion, Rachel speaking. How can I help you?"

"Hello, Rachel."

"Oh, hello, Jonathan. How are you?"

"I'm okay. Rachel, I just wondered if there was any news."

"Nothing yet, Jonathan. But we only sent the letter a couple of weeks ago, so I wouldn't be too worried yet."

Wouldn't be too worried? What did that mean, that he should be a little bit worried?

"How long does it usually take, on average?"

"There is no average, Jonathan."

"I know, but how long might it take?" he persisted, desperate for something, anything, to raise his spirits.

"I've had cases where the recipient hasn't replied for over a year, and I've also had cases where they've responded within days. There's no way of telling how long it'll be, Jonathan, I'm afraid."

"Okay, Rachel," he said sadly. "You'll call me as soon as you hear anything?"

"I promise, Jonathan."

"Thanks, Rachel."

He hung up and lay down on his bed. These top-secret calls were always conducted from the privacy of his room.

There was a knock on the door.

"Yes?"

Margaret's head and torso appeared.

"Everything okay, love?"

"Yes."

"Who were you talking to?"

"No one."

"Have you got any lectures today?"

"Yes."

"When are they?"

"Later on."

"Okay, Jonathan."

She closed the door and left him to it.

All he wanted to do was call after her and ask if she was available for a chat. He wanted to tell her everything. But this was the one thing he could never talk to her about. It had been bad enough telling her that he'd begun searching for his birth-mother; the hurt in her eyes as she told him how happy she was, how she'd support him no matter what.

He'd felt awful afterwards, as if he'd done a terrible thing, played a dirty trick on her, thrown it all back at her after everything she'd done for him. It was the ultimate betrayal. Because it was she, his mum, who'd cared for him and nurtured him and who'd been with him every step of the way. And now he needed her advice, her reassurances, her ability to make everything seem that little bit better, no matter how bad it appeared. She was the only one who could make sense of it all and calm the storm-clouds gathering in his head. He couldn't do that to her, though; it wouldn't be fair.

There was little chance of him discussing it with his father, either; they barely spoke these days. In fact, no one in the house had much time for him, apart from Sophie. She was the only one who seemed unaffected by that fateful weekend in London. In her eyes the drunken squabble had just been one of those silly things that parents did late at night. It hadn't diminished her father's status or the high regard in which she held him. By the next morning she'd forgotten about it and seemed completely oblivious to the tension hanging in the air on the drive back, which lingered in the weeks that followed.

Eventually the tension dissipated, but in its stead came a chill, a cooling of relations. It was evident whenever their parents were in the same room together; they were distant with each other and overly polite. Jonathan saw this and knew that he was right to shun his father. Clearly his mother hadn't forgiven him, so why should he? He would join her in her stance against him. Sophie could have him all to herself; she was welcome. So they settled into a fully-functioning, dysfunctional routine. Margaret and Malcolm communicated with efficacy and brevity, and ensured that on the surface at least, their marriage appeared as strong as ever. Their roles in Sophie's life remained the same; they both showered her with love and attention. Her world was as proper and as just as it had ever been.

But the bond shared by father and son was at once severed. Jonathan shut out his father, refused to speak to him; barely acknowledged his existence. For a time, Malcolm put it down to teenage rebelliousness. He imagined his son growing out of it and returning to him, closer than ever. When he saw how Jonathan was with his mother, how loving he was, how he doted on her, he realised otherwise. He tried to bridge the gap, to sit him down, thrash things out. It was no use. Jonathan didn't want to know. Malcolm was *persona non grata* and there was no telling if or when he might be welcomed back into the fold.

He discussed it with his wife. Her answers were curt and unhelpful. It was as if she enjoyed seeing him suffer. But no, she wasn't that kind of person, never had been, bitterness simply wasn't in her nature. Her children were what mattered to her, and if her boy didn't wish to speak to his father, then he had her backing until he decided otherwise.

5

THE TRUTH WAS THAT JONATHAN didn't know why he was so angry with his father. Yes, he had ruined his chances of becoming national champion, and revealed a shocking, hitherto unseen, part of his character in the process. But was that what it was really all about? Was that worth four years of near-silence on his part? Probably not. Jonathan knew there was more to it; he saw it in his mother's eyes every time he looked at her. Occasionally he would bring it up, ask her what had happened and what was going to happen in the future. She'd wave him away, tell him everything was all right, and he would drop it. The longer he went without answers, though, the more insistent he became. He confronted her, demanding an explanation, and became increasingly irate when he didn't get one.

One afternoon, after another frustrating phone call with Rachel, he approached his mother with an all too familiar expression. He couldn't control what his birth-mother did, but he could attempt to rectify the problems in his own home. And today, that was what he intended to do.

"Mum, can we talk for a minute?"

He'd been sure to wait until Malcolm and Sophie were out. Dinner was at least an hour away.

"About what, Jonathan?"

"Things."

She put down her book, wondering if she was finally about to discover the cause of his dark moods, or the identity of the person on the other end of those mysterious phone calls.

"What kind of things, love?"

"About Dad."

She sighed, not this again.

"What about him, Jonathan?"

"What did he do in London, Mum?"

"Jonathan, we've been over this ..."

"No, Mum, I want the truth this time," he interrupted.

"I've told you everything, Jonathan."

"Tell me again, then."

She shook her head in frustration, but it was easier just to tell him and hope that it would suffice for now.

"We'd had a bit much to drink, and your dad and I had a row. I told him he wasn't welcome in our room that night. He came up to the room anyway, very drunk, and then I called security."

Jonathan looked at her dubiously. "And that's it?"

"Yes, Jonathan, that's it."

"What were you fighting about?"

"Oh, Jonathan, I can't remember."

"Well, it must have been something bad."

"It wasn't, Jonathan, it was something silly. We were drunk, that's all."

"Then how come you two hardly speak nowadays? You've never been the same since."

"What are you talking about, Jonathan?" she protested.

"Come on, Mum, don't treat me like an idiot. I see how you are with each other, you're not the same."

"Okay," she conceded. "We're not on great terms at the moment, but that shouldn't affect how you feel about your father."

"But it does, Mum."

"Why, Jonathan?"

"Because if you're still this cross with him, then he must have done something bad."

"He didn't do anything bad, Jonathan, nothing at all."

"What exactly did he do, Mum? It wasn't just any old argument, was it?"

"Your dad was very drunk and we had words. That's all it was."

She was faltering now, though, he could sense it.

"What did he do, Mum?" Jonathan persisted.

Margaret let out a little sob and immediately raised a hankie to her nose, as if to prevent her emotions from spilling forth.

"I'm sorry, Mum. I didn't mean to upset you."

"No, don't be silly, love. I'm just feeling a little under the weather, that's all."

Jonathan put a consoling arm around her.

"I wish you'd tell me, Mum. Maybe I could help."

She continued to shake her head, hiding behind the handkerchief.

"Did he hit you, Mum?"

"No, Jonathan. Don't be silly, for goodness' sake!"

"Because if he did, Mum ..."

He trailed off, allowing her to figure out the rest for herself.

"Your father would never lay a finger on me, or you and Sophie. Don't say things like that about him."

"Okay, Mum. I'm sorry."

He had been convinced. If it wasn't that, then what could it be?

Margaret, aware that her defences were down, sought to bring an end to the conversation.

"Look, Jonathan, you're right; your dad and I aren't getting on at the moment. And, to be honest, I don't know how long it will take for us to get back to normal. That doesn't change how either of us feels about you or your sister. We love you dearly and we are still a family, no matter what."

She stroked his cheek tenderly. "Okay, love?"

"Okay, Mum," he murmured in acquiescence.

He would drop it for her sake, he saw how much it upset her; but he knew his father had done something bad. He hadn't hit her as Jonathan had suspected, but he'd done something, and whatever it was it still upset his mother four years after the event.

6

A SECOND LETTER WAS SENT, and a third; neither elicited a response. There had to be a mistake, surely? He rang the agency over and over again. Were they sure they had the right address? Could they track the letters? How did they know she hadn't moved? He couldn't understand it. If she'd received the letters, why hadn't she responded? Despondency set in, he began to despair. It started to affect the rest of his life; his frustrations spilled over at home, in university, everywhere. He knew it was wrong to take it out on others, but he couldn't help it.

It was for his father that he reserved the most vicious of his outbursts. Their stilted relationship now became a simmering feud, likely to explode at any time. Jonathan eyed him like a hunter stalking its prey; baleful stares across the dinner table, noxious glances whenever he walked into the room. Malcolm did his best to ignore it, but he heard the embittered comments, the disdainful sniggers and snorts of derision, any time he spoke. Under normal circumstances the elder Philliskirk would have taken his son to task, but he still lived in fear. Had Margaret told him the cause of their argument in London? Did Jonathan know about his attempts to seduce a co-worker? He certainly seemed to have ratcheted up the hostility a notch. Malcolm dared not provoke him, in case everything came tumbling out, causing a conflict he'd been actively avoiding for years. So he took his punishment in silence, absorbed the malevolent stares and contemptuous words, hoping it was just a passing phase.

If Malcolm thought things were bad now, however, they were about to get a whole lot worse. With his studies over for the summer, Jonathan had requested a meeting with Rachel. He wanted to bring things to a head, send a final letter. One which stated there would be no more chances: an ultimatum. Rachel resisted, explained that wasn't how they did things, but he persisted, until finally, probably just to get him off her back, she arranged an appointment to discuss his case in greater detail.

The appointment wasn't till 11.30, but Jonathan was in the waiting room at a quarter past. He fidgeted nervously in his chair, scanning his surroundings, wondering which door would open. Even though Rachel had told him there'd been no fresh developments, he still held out hope. She might have a solution, a fresh course of action they could take; and if she didn't have any new ideas then he would simply break in here at night, steal his mother's details and go visit her himself. That would show her. *This is what happens when you don't reply to my letters, Mother. I arrive unannounced and pissed off, demanding answers.* She'd shuffle uncomfortably, shooing her children – his siblings – back inside, and tell him he'd made a huge mistake; she didn't know any Jonathan Philliskirk, and he must have the wrong address. *Au contraire, Mother dearest, this is very much the right address. Although you might not recognise me, you certainly know me. Don't you see the resemblance? There can be no denying that.* Then it would dawn on her. A sickening, slow realisation; this was the bastard child she'd given away all those years ago. He had come back to haunt her, and he wasn't leaving without answers.

"Jonathan?"

Rachel had emerged from one of the offices and was ushering him in.

"Now then, Jonathan, let's see where we're at."

There was no need to see where they were at. She knew exactly where they were at; his countless phone calls had made sure of that. Jonathan didn't want to annoy her at this juncture, so he kept his counsel while she faffed about with the paperwork.

She found what she was looking for and fixed Jonathan with the earnest, sympathetic smile he'd become accustomed to.

"So, the third letter was sent a fortnight ago."

"Yes."

"As of yet, we haven't received a response."

"I know."

"Don't lose heart, Jonathan. There could be any number of reasons for the lack of reply."

"Like what?"

"Well, fear, for one."

Fear? What did she have to be afraid of? He wasn't really going to turn up on her doorstep and start issuing threats. That was just an idle fantasy.

"I don't get it. What might she be afraid of?"

"Jonathan, a lot of women in her position feel very guilty about what they've done. They think that they've betrayed their children by putting them up for adoption. When they're faced with the possibility of finally meeting that child they have to deal with a whole range of emotions, fear being just one. They fear they won't match up to your expectations, or that their reasons for giving you away will seem inadequate. These are just examples, Jonathan; I'm not saying they apply to your situation."

Jonathan wasn't really listening; this sounded like an excuse to him. He was the one who'd been discarded. He was the one who'd reached out. Why should he feel sympathy for this woman?

"And not only is there a chance she's scared," Rachel continued, "but she might not have informed her family members of the adoption. I've had cases where mothers have been married with five or six children, and none of them have known about the child she'd put up for adoption. There are many factors to consider here, Jonathan."

"Okay," he replied, mulling over this new information. "What can we do now?"

Rachel sighed deeply. "Not a whole lot, I'm afraid."

"So that's it?"

She nodded glumly, that same sympathetic smile on her face.

"We've sent the letter, and now all we can do is wait. But like I said, don't lose heart; there's always the chance – "

"Just forget it," he said, pushing back his chair and getting to his feet. "What's the fucking point?"

Rachel didn't respond. She'd been expecting this; he'd got his hopes up, and now the rejection was too much to bear. She'd seen it many times and knew the anger wasn't directed at her, not really. And as she watched him storm out the door like countless others before him, she hoped she'd see him again and that this particular story hadn't reached its end.

7

JONATHAN DIDN'T WANT TO CRY in front of anyone, public displays of emotion were not his thing, but the car park was busy and he could no longer fight back the tears. He ran around the side of the building, hiding between some bushes as the first sob left his throat. People could probably see him, but it was an adoption agency; if you couldn't have a good cry here, where could you? When he'd let it all out, all the frustration, all the heartache, he looked around to see if he'd been spotted. No, his meltdown had gone unnoticed, his blushes were spared.

He regretted his actions, though; not the tears, they were unavoidable, but the way he'd spoken to Rachel. She was only doing her job and didn't need to put up with that kind of shit. He hadn't been brought up like that; abusing people, swearing at them. There was only one thing to do: go back in and apologise. He went around to the entrance at the front of the building. As he approached the door, he heard the sound of laughter followed by footsteps as a group of people came his way. He stepped back to allow them out, turning his head away, but they barely noticed him. There were three of them, two women and a boy. One of the women was around his mother's age, the other a little older than Jonathan. The boy was young, not yet a teenager. The sounds of their voices, carefree and full of joy, echoed around the car park as they went to their car. The older woman got in the driver's seat and, after a brief discussion, the boy was allowed to ride in the passenger seat. The other woman got in the back, still smiling and joking despite being outdone by the youngest member of the group. Jonathan watched as they all buckled up and the woman reversed out of their spot. His eyes never left them as the car pulled out, drove past him and continued onto the motorway.

They never stopped smiling, especially the young boy. Where were they going? Somewhere fun probably. Somewhere with more smiling, happy people. Aunties and uncles, grandparents, brothers and sisters, maybe even a father. Which of them was the new arrival? It was the younger woman, Jonathan reckoned. She looked young enough to be the other woman's daughter, but old enough to have been the result of her teenage pregnancy. The happy little boy was her brother, thrilled to have acquired an older sister who would lavish him with gifts. Yes, they were all heading back to the mother's house now, this new family, reunited and looking forward to a wonderful evening. All of them together at last.

He looked back inside the building. Rachel stood at reception with her back to him, locked in conversation with another young man. She'd already forgotten about him, moved on to her next case. The story of Jonathan Philliskirk and the Irishwoman who didn't want to see him now consigned to history. His file had already been pushed to the back, along with all the other tragic stories; kids just like him, who'd come here full of hope and left tearful and bitter. Eventually those files would be destroyed to make room for other, more important, files, those belonging to people who actually wanted to meet one another. He stood watching Rachel and the young man for a few moments longer, wondering how his case would turn out. Would it be one of the successes, or would he be like him, a sad, failed venture, which everyone would rather forget about? Jonathan couldn't help but hope it would be the latter; at least that way he would know he wasn't the only one. He took one final look inside the building, zipped up his coat and made for home.

8

WHEN HE GOT BACK THE house was deserted, but he could hear screams of delight coming from the back garden. Sophie had received a Swingball set for her thirteenth birthday and, after weeks of promising, it appeared that Malcolm had finally set it up for her. They were all out there, father and daughter engaging in epic horseplay, Margaret watching on from the decking. Jonathan bristled at the sight of his father, still in his shirt and tie, running around like an idiot, acting as if nothing had happened. It sickened him. He joined his mother, pulling up a chair to view the fun and games.

"Hello, love. How did the job interview go?"

He'd forgotten about the hastily created lie, the one he'd used to explain where he was going that morning.

"Erm, not bad, actually. Think I might have got it."

"Really? That's great! Your dad will be so proud."

"Yeah, I'd say he will," Jonathan muttered discontentedly.

"What's the score now, Mum?" Sophie yelled as she pounded another winner.

"Twenty-eighteen, to you!"

"Yes!"

"I can't beat her, Jonathan, she's too good," shouted Malcolm.

Jonathan didn't acknowledge him, staring into the distance as if he hadn't heard a thing. Malcolm, noting the rebuttal, made to say something, but instead shrugged his shoulders and returned to the game.

"What's wrong, Jonathan? Are you in a bad mood?"

"I'm just sick of this, Mum, sick of *him*," he said viciously, jutting his head in Malcolm's direction.

"Why, what's he done?"

"Well I don't know, do I?" he said haughtily.

"Oh, please, Jonathan, not this again," said Margaret, her heart sinking.

"No, Mum, enough is enough."

Jonathan rose from his chair, making a beeline for his father.

"You can play the winner, Jon," Sophie said when she saw him approach. But he brushed straight past her, eyes set on his target.

"What's up, son?" Malcolm asked, hands on his knees as he caught his breath. "If you want to play, then take the racket. I need a break, anyway."

"You need to go now," Jonathan told him.

"Go where, Jonathan?"

"I know what you did to Mum."

Malcolm looked to his wife in desperation, trying to catch her eye. She shook her head briefly and then averted her gaze. He was on his own now.

"Look, Jonathan," Malcolm said, putting his hands up in defence. "Whatever's gone on between me and your mum has nothing to do with you two. We're going to sort out our differences, I promise."

"Get out," Jonathan said, moving closer.

"Jonathan, what is this? Margaret!"

His wife joined them, but she wasn't coming to his aid. She stood to the side, just behind her son. Jonathan needed no assistance; he grabbed his father by the shoulders and began pushing him towards the side of the house, to the gate which led to the driveway.

"We don't want you here anymore, Dad," he said, harrying and hassling him away from the Swingball set. Reluctant to aggravate the situation any further, Malcolm went without complaint.

"Where are they going?" asked Sophie, perplexed.

"Jonathan, please…" Margaret whispered tearfully.

"It's okay, Mum."

He shoved his father through the gate and onto the driveway. When he briefly removed his hands from his shoulders, Malcolm took it as a gesture of goodwill, a chance for one last plea.

"Look, Jonathan, I don't know what your mother's told you but …"

"Get in the car."

"Eh?"

"Get in the car."

"Oh, Jonathan, come on."

His son stared at him resolutely, waiting him for to obey his command.

Margaret and Sophie watched from a distance, Sophie not entirely believing her mother's assertion that they were 'just playing around'.

"IN," Jonathan repeated, raising his voice.

He didn't want to fight with his father, but if he had to he would.

Malcolm reluctantly opened the door of his Audi and sidled into the seat.

"Now go."

"Go where?"

"I don't care where, just away from here. We don't want you anymore."

Malcolm shook his head in desperation, once more looking to his wife for assistance. Margaret continued to watch impassively, so he did as he was told. He put the key in the ignition and started up the car.

"Jonathan," he said, looking intently at his son, "I'll call you later, okay?"

Jonathan closed the door of the car. There was nothing left for Malcolm to do but leave. He reversed out of the driveway, waved at Sophie and was gone in a matter of seconds. Jonathan turned to his mother and sister.

"Want that game of Swingball, Sophie?"

9

WHEN THEY'D FINISHED THEIR GAME, they trooped inside to help with dinner. This entailed one of them setting the table while the other lingered in the background, asking how long till it would be ready. No one mentioned Malcolm, not even Sophie, and as they sat to eat his place at the head of the table remained empty. It would be just the three of them tonight. They ate in silence, neither child's appetite affected by the day's events. When they were finished Margaret shooed them away, refusing their token offers to help with the washing-up. She needed to call her husband and find out where he'd got to. Or did she? Did she care where he was? She felt bad about what had happened, and regretted not intervening. But watching him being taken to task had been strangely satisfying. She couldn't deny that she'd enjoyed seeing him squirm. Wasn't this what she'd wanted all along, to see the back of him? She'd told him that they were only staying together 'for the sake of the children', and now it appeared that at least one of them didn't want him here at all. However, this wasn't the way to go about it. She couldn't let her son make that kind of decision for the whole family; and although she would never forget what Malcolm had done, she still loved him and wanted to try to salvage their marriage.

She checked to make sure her teenagers were occupied and then rang Malcolm's mobile.

"Where are you?"

"I'm sitting in the park. What's got into him? What did you tell him?"

"I didn't tell him anything."

"Then where has all this come from?"

"Look, Malcolm, things haven't been right in this house for a long time, and what happened today has been brewing for ages."

"But I've been trying my best with him, Marge, I really have."

"I know you have, but it goes deeper than that."

"What do you mean, Margaret?"

"We need to talk, Malcolm; talk properly."

There was a pause at the other end; he appeared to be gathering his thoughts.

"Do you want a divorce, Marge?"

"No, Malcolm, don't be silly. We need to get together and talk, the four of us. We have to get things out in the open."

"Okay, Marge," said Malcolm, thankful for the reprieve. "Whatever you think is best."

"We need to talk about what you did, and then we need to tell them."

"Okay, Marge."

"But we'll give them a watered-down version, a sanitised version. You know what kids are like; they jump to conclusions."

"Yes, that's probably for the best...I'm sorry, Marge."

"That's okay, Malcolm, but we need to talk too, you and I. You have to do more than just apologise and promise it'll never happen again, and I need to listen to you and try to understand why you did what you did."

"Are you suggesting counselling, Marge? I'll pay for it, go as many days as you want. I can ring someone now and try to arrange an appointment, if you like."

"We'll see, Malcolm. I think it's good that we're at least talking about it, that's enough for now."

"Okay, Marge, but what about Jonathan? Will I come over now and try and talk to him?"

"No, I think it would be better if you don't come back tonight."

She could hear him sigh in disappointment, but knew he would do as she'd asked. His willingness to put things right made her think that maybe they could recover from this, that their family could be a fully-functioning unit once again.

"All right, I'll book into a hotel," he said.

"Yes, do that. I'll talk to Jonathan."

"Okay, Margie. Bye."

She hung up. With Malcolm out of the house for the night she could turn her attention to Jonathan, and take what she hoped would be the first steps towards reconciling her family. Before she could do that, however, she had to deal with the other member of the household.

"Soph?" she said quietly, tapping on her bedroom door.

"Come in, Mum."

She was sprawled on the bed, reading *Harry Potter*, her latest obsession.

"Is it good, love?" asked Margaret, nodding at the weighty tome.

"Brill," Sophie smiled happily.

"Is that film still on in the pictures, the one with Johnny Depp in it?"

"Yes," replied Sophie expectantly. She liked where this was going.

"Do you want to go and see it?"

"YES!" said Sophie, closing her book and immediately reaching for her trainers.

"Would one of your friends be able to go with you?"

"Why? Aren't you coming?"

"I want to talk to your brother about a few things."

"Ah, about today. I see," she said knowingly. "I'll ring Emily. She'll probably come. She always has money."

Twenty minutes later, Margaret had dropped two excited teenagers off at the local cinema and was making her way back home. Jonathan had been told to stay put, as she wished to discuss a few things with him on her return. True to his word, he was still in the living-room, exactly where she'd left him.

"Jonathan, will you turn that TV off? I want to talk to you about something."

"It's nearly over, Mum; five minutes."

"Now, Jonathan, please."

He knew better than to argue.

"Come sit beside me on the couch, love," she said, patting the seat beside her.

He duly obliged.

"I think you know what I want to talk about, don't you?" she asked.

Jonathan shrugged his shoulders. He'd turned off the telly and sat beside her, he wasn't going to start the conversation for her too.

"What happened today, what was that all about?" she asked, choosing her words carefully.

"You know."

"I'm afraid I don't, Jonathan."

"He shouldn't be here, acting like that, as if he's done nothing wrong."

"We've been over this, Jonathan. I understand you're still angry with him, but why today? Why this, sudden anger?"

"I don't know; just sick of it, that's all."

"Is there anything you want to tell me?"

"Like what?"

"Well, I don't know; is there anything going on in your life that you'd like to talk about? You've not been yourself lately."

Did she know? Had she figured it out, or was she just trying to coax some information out of him? She had a way of making him talk even when he didn't want to, *especially* when he didn't want to. In a past life, she'd probably been an interrogator for the KGB. That was why he never lied to her, it was pointless; she sussed it straight away. He wasn't lying to her now, though, he was simply withholding information.

"Ah, it's just Uni stuff, Mum."

"But Uni finished a month ago, Jonathan."

She wasn't going to be fobbed off so easily. He could say it was something to do with a girl; that'd stop her in her tracks. But what if it didn't? Then he'd have to talk to his mother about an imaginary girlfriend. No, thanks. The other option was to tell the truth. It didn't matter so much now. His birth-mother had rejected him, so he didn't have to feel guilty.

"She doesn't want to see me, Mum."

"Who doesn't want to see you, Jonathan?"

"My birth-mother."

It was the first time he'd said the words out loud. Hearing them made it all the more painful.

"Oh, Jonathan, what happened?" Margaret asked, genuinely distraught.

"She just doesn't want to see me, Mum. They sent letters, but there was no reply."

"But that could mean anything."

He raised a hand to stop her. "Please, Mum, don't. I've heard it all already."

"Okay, Jonathan."

It upset her to think of her little boy going through this wretched experience all by himself, with no support from any of them.

"I'm just going to have to get over it, that's all."

She drew him close. Maybe if she held him long enough, and squeezed hard enough she could compensate for the loss of this other, unknown woman; but he pulled away, cranky and unwilling to be cuddled.

"We'll help you, Jonathan, all of us," she said, carefully.

"*All* of us? I'm not sure I want Dad and Sophie knowing about this."

"It's up to you, love. Anyway, I want us all to sit down and talk about everything that's happened lately."

"What happened today, you mean?" he said sourly.

"Yes, that, but other things too; that weekend in London, for a start."

Jonathan raised his eyebrows quizzically.

"Your father wants to sit you both down and explain exactly what went on there, and then we'd like to talk to you both about some other things."

"Are you getting a divorce?"

"No, Jonathan, we're not getting a divorce; but we do need to work on some things, all of us, as a family."

He mused on this for a while. It certainly sounded like a good idea; he'd become tired of their charade, the pretence that everything was rosy in the Philliskirk garden. If they were willing to sit down and tell them what was going on, then he was willing to listen.

"Okay, Mum. That sounds good."

"And afterwards, if you like, you could talk about your search for your birth-mother, explain it to your father and sister."

"I'm not sure about that, Mum."

"That's okay, Jonathan. It's just a suggestion."

He nodded thoughtfully, enjoying the new phenomenon of being spoken to like an adult.

"Mum?"

"Yes, love?"

"I think this chat will do us all good."

"Me too, love."

She patted him on the knee and rose to leave.

"Oh, Mum?"

"Yes, love?"

"Tell Dad it's safe now, if he wants to come back," he said with a mischievous wink.

THE FOLLOWING NIGHT THE FOUR of them gathered around the kitchen table. Although Malcolm had been restored to the head of the table, no one was in any doubt as to who was chairing the meeting.

"Right, then," said Margaret. "Has everyone been to the toilet? Does anyone need a drink?"

"We're fine, Mum," said Sophie, eager to get things over with.

"Okay," Margaret said, taking her seat. "The purpose of this meeting is ..."

"Can't we just start, Mum? I think we all know why we're here," interrupted Jonathan.

"I don't!" said Sophie.

"Look, kids, just let your mum talk," said Malcolm.

Clearing her throat for effect, Margaret resumed. "The purpose of this meeting is to clear the air. There's been a lot of tension in this house lately, for various reasons, and it's about time we dealt with it. We're a family and we should be able to help one another with our problems and be there for one another, but most of all we should be able to talk freely, even if what we have to say might upset other members of the family. That's what we're here to do now."

"Oh, exciting!" said Sophie, putting her phone in her pocket.

"I believe your father would like to start. Malcolm?"

All eyes turned to Malcolm. He'd gone over his story with Margaret, but he was still nervous. There was a lot on the line.

"Okay, then," he started. "I want to talk about what happened in London a few years ago."

"London?" Sophie asked, confused. "What's that got to do with anything?"

"Sshh, Sophie, let your father continue."

"Firstly, I'd like to apologise to Jonathan."

He turned to his son. "I've never really apologised to you for what happened that night, not properly. That race was very important to you, and were it not for my stupidity you'd probably have won it. I wish I could turn back the clock, but I can't. All I can do is say how sorry I am and hope that one day you can forgive me."

Jonathan nodded indifferently; he was interested in confessions, not apologies.

"Do you accept your father's apology, Jonathan?" Margaret asked.

"I think I'll wait to see what else he has to say first, Mum."

"No, Jonathan, that's not fair. We're dealing with this issue first."

"Okay, then. I accept your apology," Jonathan said, holding out his hand. Malcolm duly shook it, but he knew he still had a long way to go.

"Now, that's one thing settled," Margaret said, pleased with herself.

"Is that it?" Sophie asked.

"No, love, there's more. Stay where you are," instructed her mother, nodding to her husband once more. "Go on, Malcolm."

"Okay, this may be difficult for you kids to hear, but your mother and I have discussed it and we feel it's best for you to know everything."

Jonathan moved forward in his seat. Finally, some answers.

"Before that night in London, the reason we were arguing ... no, wait, I'll start again. I made a pass at another woman, a woman I worked with."

"What's a pass?" asked Sophie indignantly.

"It means he tried to get off with someone," Jonathan answered. Sophie stared at her father, dumbfounded.

"Yes, in more modern terms that's what you'd call it. I don't know why I did it, it was in the heat of the moment and as soon as I'd done it, I regretted it. Then, to make matters worse, I kept it a secret until – "

"London", Jonathan said conclusively. It made sense now, but he still had some questions. "Why then? Why that weekend?"

"It just happened, Jon. It was the first time we'd had a proper night out together in ages. We were drinking and chatting, and the guilt overcame me. I told your mother what I'd done, then she told me she didn't want me staying with her that night, and after that ... well, you saw what happened."

"Are you getting a divorce?" asked Sophie, her eyes wide with fear. "Is that what this is all about?"

"We're not getting divorced, Sophie," replied Margaret.

"But Dad had an affair!"

"He didn't have an affair, Sophie; but he did betray my trust, and it may take some time before he can win it back."

Malcolm weighed in, eager to assuage his daughter's fears. "Your Mum and I still love each very much, Sophie."

Jonathan watched impassively. In truth he'd thought his father's misde-meanour would be something far worse. He'd made a pass at someone – was that really such a big deal? It happened all the time in the soaps. It seemed to be something that was just part of married life. It wasn't like he'd had an affair or anything; it was an isolated incident, if a regrettable one. He had realised his mistake and was trying to make up for it. Maybe he wouldn't give him such a hard time from now on, but there would have to be some conditions.

"What about your drinking, Dad?" he asked.

Malcolm was caught off guard, having assumed he'd done his bit.

"What about it, Jonathan?"

"You have to promise us that you'll never act like that again, get drunk and start fighting."

"I promise, Jonathan. I promise you all. I haven't had a drink, not a proper one anyway, in months. Your Mum will tell you." Margaret nodded in verification.

"Okay, Dad. As long as you promise never to drink like that again, then I can forgive you for what happened."

Malcolm sensed genuine warmth in his son's words. That chilly exterior had disappeared, and behind it lay the boy he adored.

"That's good, Jonathan," he said, trying not to sound too grateful. "I hope that someday we can get back to the way we were before."

"Hopefully, Dad," Jonathan replied warily, "but it'll take time."

"That's okay, son. We could go to that new history museum in town, though. Maybe next weekend?"

"Maybe, Dad. We'll see."

Malcolm knew when to leave it. He'd made a breakthrough, but it was best to quit while he was still ahead. But whereas he'd made progress with one child, he now found the other one eyeing him testily from the other end of the table. It appeared that Sophie looked dimly on those who made passes at work colleagues. He smiled hesitantly at her, and was rewarded with a scowl for his efforts. Maybe now would be a good time to get her the pony she'd always wanted.

"Now then," Margaret said. "Has anyone else got anything they'd like to share?"

At first Jonathan didn't realise what she meant, that she was prompting him to speak. He hadn't decided yet whether he was going to tell them all about it. With his father baring his soul, however, and his mother so keen to have everything out in the open, he felt obliged to talk.

"I've been searching for my birth-parents," he said, without prelude.

All eyes turned to him: Margaret's full of admiration, Malcolm's contemplative and Sophie's incredulous.

"What's going on, Mum?" she asked despairingly. "What the hell is going on?"

"Calm down, Sophie. Your brother is just ..."

But she'd gone, out the door and up the stairs. Margaret swiftly followed her, leaving father and son to continue the meeting by themselves.

Malcolm began drumming his fingers on the table and humming an unidentifiable tune, unsure of what to say, suddenly nervous in his son's presence. Should he try to talk to him about his birth-parents, or did Margaret need to be here for that? There hadn't been any mention of this beforehand, it hadn't featured on any memo he'd received; but if he were ever to rekindle their relationship, moments like this would decide it.

"So how's the search going?"

"Not great, Dad."

"Oh, no, how come?"

Jonathan found himself wanting to open up, to pour his heart out to his dad, maybe because he was a man, he'd grown tired of women fawning over him. His father would offer a different perspective, a less sugar-coated one perhaps.

"Well, they've found her; but they've sent letters and she hasn't replied."

"What does that mean?"

"According to the agency, it could mean any number of things. But to me, it seems like she doesn't want to see me."

"Well, that'll be her loss," Malcolm said indignantly. "She doesn't know what she's missing."

"Thanks, Dad."

Jonathan had missed this, chatting to his father, the two men of the house together. It felt good.

"Oh, and guess what, Dad?"

"Yes?"

"She's Irish, my birth-mother."

"What?" Malcolm said in faux-outrage. "My son, a Paddy?"

"I'm not a Paddy, Dad!"

"You bloody well are," he said, poking Jonathan in the ribs and ducking to avoid retaliation.

"Stop it, Dad!"

"I think we have a little leprechaun on our hands here, to be sure, to be sure."

Jonathan started to laugh, throwing good-natured punches at his father as their scrap continued.

"Oh, begorrah, he's a tough one this lad, a real son of Éire!" Malcolm cried as Jonathan grabbed him in a headlock.

"Argh, get him off me, us Brits are no match for the Paddies!"

Margaret returned to this scene and momentarily thought all her hard work had been for nothing. She'd only left them on their own for two minutes, and already they were kicking lumps out of one another.

"Stop that, you two! Stop it!"

She hurried across the floor, arms aloft, ready to wedge herself between them; then she saw Malcolm's smiling face peeping out from under Jonathan's arms.

"We're just mucking about, Marge. Relax, love."

By way of confirmation Jonathan loosened his grip, allowing his father to emerge relatively unscathed. "Just playing, Mum," he repeated, backing away from Malcolm as proof of their amiability.

Margaret shook her head in annoyance. "I can't keep up, honestly!"

Jonathan and Malcolm stared sheepishly at each other, still breathless from their wrestling match.

"Jonathan was just telling me that his birth-mother is Irish."

"Is she, Jonathan?" Margaret asked in surprise.

"Yes, Mum. I'm Irish now," he said, deadpan.

"No, you're not, Jonathan. Don't be silly."

"I am, Mum," he persisted, gloomy now.

"Is this your fault, Malcolm? Is that what you've been telling him?"

"Don't look at me, love. I just told him that we'll have no Irish children in this house!"

Malcolm punched his son on the arm and then scarpered to the living-room, chortling like a child. Jonathan vaulted the kitchen table in pursuit, almost knocking his mother over in the process.

"Come back, ya English buggah!" he bellowed in an implausible Irish brogue.

At that moment Sophie reappeared in the hallway, ready to resume chatting, and was instead dragged into the sitting-room by her brother.

"Oi've found one. Oi've found one," Jonathan hollered in his new accent. "A little English gurl, oi've found one!"

"Put me down, Jonathan," Sophie protested, but she was laughing too now.

She didn't know why her brother was talking in a funny voice or why her father was hiding behind the couch grinning like an idiot, but she liked it. She liked that they were all running around like fools, it was fun. So she joined in, mimicking Jonathan's accent and tackling her father with glee when he tried to come out from his hiding-place.

Margaret thought of following them to admonish them for being so ridiculous, but instead she stayed put in the kitchen, just listening. It had been a while since their house had reverberated to the sounds of laughter, and she wanted to savour it.

11

IT WAS THE THIRD LETTER which caused her to act. On the surface, it was much the same as the previous two, but with one small difference: this one stated that it was the last of its kind. There would be no more. This was her last chance, so she called Adele. She always called Adele in times of need.

"Hi, Nades. What's up?"

She was her usual airy self, probably up since cockcrow; organising lunches, sending kids to school, pecking her husband on the cheek, getting her house in order and generally being a domestic goddess. Sinéad, on the other hand, had crawled out of bed at midday and had used an unwashed cup for her tea.

"Adele, are you busy?"

"Not really, just watching *Loose Women*. They're some laugh, there's this wan ..."

"Could you come over? It's important."

"Okay, Sinéad," she said, suddenly serious. "Is everything all right?"

"I'm fine, just need to talk to you about something."

"Okay, I'll be over in ten minutes."

Sinéad set about tidying up a bit. This involved emptying ashtrays and throwing various items of cutlery into the sink. Her flat was in a constant state of disarray. It was too small; a poky little kitchen, a living-room not much bigger and a bedroom which had long since been swamped by her meagre belongings. She hated it, but it was all she could afford. The alternative was moving back in with her parents – and that didn't bear thinking about. They had tried to insist on her moving in with them during her latest bout of depression, but she had resisted, knowing that a night spent under their roof would send her over the edge completely. Her flat, bleak as it was, was preferable to a stay at that madhouse, with that woman.

The doorbell rang. Adele had been quick; she probably thought Sinéad was having another one of her 'spells' and had hurried over in a panic. She could rest easy on that front. Sinéad was relatively calm by her standards; if anyone was going to get into a frenzy today, it would be Adele. She alone knew about the child Sinéad had given away, but they rarely discussed it and hadn't done in years. She had been a rock, a little trouper; always there for her, helping in whatever way she could and guarding Sinéad's secret with her life. When everyone had wondered what had befallen Sinéad, how she'd gone from being the sparkiest McLoughlin girl to a morose young woman, Adele said nothing. She was her only confidante, the one person she could turn to when grief threatened to overwhelm her. Through it all: her failed marriage, the troubled relationships that followed, the guilt, sadness, anger and descent into depression, Adele had always been there by her side, aiding her as best she could. And now, with another potential crisis in the offing, it was Adele she turned to once more.

"What's up, sis?" she asked as Sinéad let her in.

The youngest McLoughlin sister was the success story of the family. While Sinéad stumbled from one disaster to the next, Adele had become the daughter her parents had always dreamed of. She'd married well to a trainee barrister called Marcus, who would eventually become a defence lawyer earning six figures per annum – Patricia loved him. They lived in a four-bedroom palace on the outskirts of town, a home so regal that their mother got dressed up just to visit. Three magnificent children were produced: two girls and a boy, each lovelier than the last. They owned separate cars – a people-carrier for her and a saloon for him – holidayed in the Caribbean and hosted dinner-parties on the last Friday of every month. They were part of Dooncurra's elite, if indeed such a thing existed. In a manner befitting the wife of a successful barrister, Adele was always immaculately turned out, sporting fashions her sisters wouldn't discover for another five years. Despite having three children under the age of six, she maintained the svelte frame of a woman ten years her junior. The others marvelled at how she managed it, but then again she was at Pilates, aerobics and yoga every other day, why wouldn't she be a yummy mummy?

"How are the kids?" Sinéad asked, not wanting to spring the news on her without some polite preliminaries.

"Oh, they're in great form. Dylan loves his hurling practice, he talks about nothing else all week. We got him a new helmet the other day and he wears it around the house."

Adele tailed off; she could see that her sister had little interest in Dylan's fledging hurling career.

"Sinéad, what is it?"

"I'll just put the kettle on," she replied, heading to the kitchen.

Adele stared after her, irritated. Why did she have to drag everything out? It drove her mad. *All this humming and hawing, this big build-up; just tell me, for Christ's sake!* If she tried to force Sinéad's hand, though, she might decide not to tell her at all. She'd get all sniffy and say it was nothing. *Don't worry, I'm grand.* So Adele had to sit there and wait until her highness felt ready to spill the beans.

With the tea poured, they settled in at the kitchen table. Adele saw that her sister was holding a letter. "Is that what you wanted to talk about, Nades?"

Sinéad looked at her, took a deep breath and handed her the letter. Adele took a quick slurp of her tea and opened the mysterious missive. As she read, Sinéad scanned her face for a reaction. She hoped Adele wouldn't get cross at her for ignoring the first two letters.

The letter was short, and it didn't take Adele long to get to the end. She put it down, and stared open-mouthed at her sister.

"Oh, my God, Sinéad," she whispered. "Oh, my God."

Sinéad nodded glumly.

"Aren't you delighted? He wants to see you! Imagine!"

"Ah, I don't know, Adele."

"What d'you mean?"

"It's just not a good time."

"Are you kidding me? 'Not a good time'? Don't be ridiculous."

"I'm not being ridiculous," Sinéad said defensively. If she'd known Adele would react like this, she wouldn't have told her.

"But he's your son, Sinéad; you *have* to see him."

"It's not that simple."

"It is from where I'm sitting."

Sinéad shook her head forcibly. "What's he going to think of me? Nearly forty, living on my own; no husband, no children, no job. I'm an embarrassment."

"Oh, Nades, you're not an embarrassment. Don't say things like that."

"But look at me, look at *this!*" Sinéad said gesturing around her. "He's probably from a well-off family; what's he going to think?"

"None of that matters, Sinéad. If he's anything like you, he'll be able to see beyond all that stuff and realise what a wonderful person you are."

Sinéad snorted her disagreement. "Then there's the fact that I gave him away; how do I explain that?"

"We've been over all this, Sinéad. We discussed what we'd do if this day ever came."

"It doesn't make it any easier, though."

"Well, look at it this way; would you rather risk meeting him now or ignore this letter and risk never seeing him, ever?"

Sinéad knew Adele was right. Her shoulders sagged in defeat. She'd been hoping her sister would offer her a way out, an excuse not to go through with it. She'd done quite the opposite. She'd confirmed what Sinéad had suspected, that she didn't have a choice. She had to do this, but at least now she had someone to blame when it all went wrong.

They spent the rest of the afternoon chatting about it all. Adele's imagination running wild:

"I bet he's really posh."

"I bet he's really handsome."

"I bet he's really tall."

Adele didn't have a very vivid imagination.

By the time her sister left to resume her wifely duties, Sinéad had allowed herself to get caught up in the excitement. Maybe it wouldn't be a disaster after all. She'd try and lose some weight, give her flat a big tidy-up, get herself in order. She could tell him she was between jobs, a career woman; that sounded better, more impressive. Before she could prepare for their meeting, though, she had another little job to do: telling her parents about their long-lost grandson.

12

SHE DECIDED THAT THE BEST course of action was to tell her father and let him look after the rest.

She just couldn't face telling her mother; the condemnation, the reprisals, the drama, it would be too much. Obviously she would have to discuss it with her at some point, but it would be best to let her father soften her up first. Breaking the news to him wouldn't be easy either, in spite of how close they were. She was his favourite, the one he'd doted on more than any of the others; the news would hurt him, just as he'd been hurt by her mysterious disappearance all those years ago when she'd vanished in the middle of the night without any warning and returned six months later, offering nothing in the way of an explanation. To his credit he'd welcomed her back with open arms, never questioning her or airing whatever suspicions he might have had, and within weeks things were back to normal, their bond as strong as ever. She and her father were different to the rest of them. They needed one another.

This was confirmed during her decline into an all-consuming depression which threatened to cut her off from society completely. She spent most of her days in bed, not leaving her flat for months on end. Over time, her visitors dried up. First her mother stopped calling, then Valerie, then Patrick and finally even Adele; but her father came every day without fail. He never stopped believing in her. He arrived at her door every evening, not leaving until she let him in, then busied himself with her dinner, heating up a stew or a casserole cooked by Patricia earlier that day. He put on the kettle, did the washing-up, the hoovering, and brought in the tea for his daughter. She asked to be left alone, complaining bitterly when he opened the curtains and let in the failing light, but he took no notice. Instead he pulled up the little hard-backed chair and sat by her side, all chatty and nice, and told her about his day. He told her how he was sick of work and couldn't wait to hit retirement age in a couple of years. How he was going to buy a camper van and bring her off up the country to see those places they'd always talked about: The Giant's Causeway, the Wicklow mountains, the Ring of Kerry; maybe they'd even look for the house from Father Ted, which was in County Clare somewhere. He told her stories about his own childhood, silly little anecdotes about how different life was back then. And he told her about his own mother and how she had suffered from depression. How he had had to look after her when his father died, and how she'd spent week after week laid up in bed, just like Sinéad was now. And how she had eventually got through it and resumed normal life again. Most of what he said washed over her, she just wanted to be left alone, but when he told her about his mother, her grandmother she listened intently. It was comforting to know she wasn't the only afflicted one in the family.

"How old was she when this started, Dad?"

"Oh, I couldn't tell you, Sinéad. I barely remember her being any other way."

"Was it before or after Granddad died?"

"I think she always suffered with it, but it definitely got worse after my father died."

"And what would she be like?"

"She wouldn't be able to function; she'd take to the bed and leave me and your uncle Mike to fend for ourselves."

"Like me," Sinéad said to herself.

"Yes, Sinéad. But she always pulled through, and you will too."

"Do you think that's where I get it from, Dad, the depression?"

Noel nodded sagely. "There's a touch of it in all the McLoughlins."

"Really? Who else, Dad?"

He looked at her coyly. "Your old dad has been consumed by the darkness from time to time."

"You, Dad? God, I would never have known."

"Ah, this is going way back, Sinéad. You were only a little thing at the time."

"What happened?"

He waved her away dismissively, less comfortable when talking about his own travails.

"The point is, Sinéad, I'm sitting here looking at you now, which means I came through it."

He took her by the hand and looked at her intently. "No matter how bad things seem right now, they will get better, I promise you. I promise you, Sinéad."

That was enough to set her off, but her tears weren't the empty, hopeless tears she'd shed night after night for the past month; they were tears of gratitude and love, tears of appreciation for her father, the man she'd always loved and who'd always loved her back unconditionally.

He was right, she did come through it. It was a slow process, but with his support she found the strength to rally against what ailed her. He encouraged her to go to the doctor, something neither he nor his mother had ever tried, and it turned out to be the best thing she'd ever done. There was so much help out there, services she'd never known existed: group sessions, cognitive behaviour therapy, one-on-one counselling. It was fantastic. And then there was the medication. She'd been reluctant at first, having heard bad things about the tablets, but they provided the boost she needed to overcome her daily struggles. It took time, and there were still mornings when all she wanted to do was turn over and go back to sleep for the rest of the day, but gradually her quality of life began to improve. There was always the threat of the depression returning, it loomed over her all the time, but if it was to come back she felt better equipped to deal with it. She'd achieved a level of control; her life had become worth living again. Then those bloody letters came and threatened to ruin everything.

*

Her plan was to break the news during one of their long walks in the woods. They still shared these walks, something they'd done since Sinéad was a child, and made a point of going at least once a week. She'd been invited to her parent's house for Sunday dinner, just her, none of the others – they had all families of their own – and this provided her with the perfect opportunity. Her father loved a long walk after his Sunday dinner. "Have to burn off all these spuds," he'd say, marching out the back door. This coming Sunday they could burn them off together. There'd be no chance of her mother accompanying them; her arthritis was so bad that she could barely walk down to the hill to the shop these days. It wasn't so much that she hated her mother, she loved her dearly, with all her heart – she just couldn't bear to be around her for too long. The sanctimonious statements, thinly-veiled insults and needling criticism which characterised her every word tore away at Sinéad until she had to go out to the back garden for a fag, lest she throttle her. That was just her way, Sinéad reasoned, she couldn't help it. None of the others came in for that sort of treatment, though, they were treated like royalty on the rare occasions they came to visit. Sinéad made an effort to go and see her most days; she helped out with anything that needed to be done around the house, went to the shop for her, and played the dutiful daughter, receiving barely a word of thanks. If, however, Adele chose to grace them with her presence, Patricia would bubble up in appreciation, moved to tears as she wondered what on earth she'd done to deserve such an amazing child. For the next few days, that was all she would talk about: how amazing Adele was, how her children were a credit to her and how she was everything Sinéad wasn't. Even Valerie, who lived fifty miles away in County Tipperary, was afforded heroine status if she so much as picked up the phone to ring her mother. Sinéad chose not to dwell on the injustice of it all. Thanks to her counselling, she was learning to adopt a more positive attitude. She was growing as a person, and even her mother couldn't halt her progress.

"Fancy a walk, Dad?" she asked as the last plate was dried and put away.

"Yes, I think so. Will you be all right on your own, Trish?"

"Oh, I will," Patricia replied sadly. She wasn't particularly bothered about being left on her own, but never missed an opportunity to play the victim.

"C'mon so, girly," Noel said to Sinéad, ignoring his wife's plea for martyrdom.

"The woods, Dad, yeah?"

"Yep".

Because of the damp weather, there weren't as many walkers around as usual. Sinéad preferred it that way. Bumping into other people only ruined the sense of isolation, reminding her that eventually they would have to return to normality. As soon as they entered the quiet serenity of the forest, she began planning her assault. She'd already figured out exactly what she was going to say, so all that was left was the when and the how. Would she casually drop it into the conversation as they strolled through the ferns, wait until they were taking a rest at one of the seated areas, or just spring it on him when he least expected it?

"Are you all right, Shin? You're not usually this quiet."

"Mmm," she replied, distracted.

They walked in silence for a little longer. Sinéad was losing her nerve. It would be much easier not to tell him, to walk around and chat about how nice the woods were looking. She could tell him later, tomorrow, or maybe not at all. She could ignore the letter and Adele and carry on as if nothing had happened. Yes, that would be much easier and probably better for everyone in the long run, but that was the coward's way out and she was sick of being a coward, sick of letting life pass her by. She could see out the rest of her days in relative peace if she so chose, safe and secure but alone and dissatisfied, or she could take a risk, put herself out there and see what happened.

"I've something I want to tell you, Dad," she said.

"What's that?"

"Do you remember when I went to England, over to Colleen?"

"Course I do".

"Well I wasn't just going to get away for a while."

That had been her excuse at the time, which sounded as flimsy now as it had then.

"Oh, right."

He didn't seem particularly interested in the topic of conversation or surprised by this revelation.

"I went there because I was pregnant, Dad."

"Ah, sure we knew that," he replied, neither changing his tone nor breaking his stride.

"What? How did you know? Did Colleen tell you? She promised she wouldn't!"

"No one told us anything, Sinéad. We're not eejits; we figured it out for ourselves."

"But how? I could have been going over there for any number of reasons."

"You could have, but you were completely different when you came back. Your mother and I knew straight away what had happened; you weren't the same girl at all."

"And you didn't think to ask me about it at all?"

"No, sure why would we?"

Sinéad was exasperated. So they had known all along! Not only that, they hadn't even been interested enough to ask her about it.

"Because I'm your daughter!"

"Ah sure, look, it was your business and we had to respect that."

"But why didn't you say something?" she shouted, finally losing her cool.

"Hey, you were the one keeping secrets, not us," he replied, his tone almost jovial.

"Ah, for fuck's sake!" she said bitterly.

Noel laughed genially, apparently finding the whole thing hilarious.

"All these years of hiding this big secret from you, and you knew all along," she said ruefully.

"It wasn't that we didn't care, love. We just reckoned you'd come to us in your own time."

"I bet you didn't think it'd be nineteen years later."

Her father chuckled. "No, we didn't."

"How the hell did Mammy keep herself from saying anything? It must have been killing her!"

"Oh, I dealt with your mother. You think she has the run of me, but she doesn't; not when it really matters."

Sinéad smiled. He was right, she did think her mother had the run of him; she had the run of everyone. But her father had an inner toughness that not many people saw, and when pushed he was a match for anyone, even Patricia McLoughlin.

"I'm thrown now, Daddy," she said with a sigh. "I thought it was going to be a lot harder than this."

"No, you have to get up early in the morning to pull the wool over your father's eyes."

She laughed, both at his mixed metaphors and his smugness; little did he know that she wasn't finished yet.

"There's more, Dad. And if you tell me you already know about this, I'll feckin' kill ya."

"Oh, I probably do, Sinéad, but sure tell me anyway."

"The child that I gave up for adoption. He – it, he's a boy – wants to meet me. I've received three letters so far."

That stopped Noel in his tracks. He turned to face her, suddenly serious.

"When did all this happen?"

"Fairly recently. I got the first letter about six months ago."

"Six months?"

"Yes, Dad."

This had been the kind of reaction she'd been expecting and secretly hoping for.

"How long does something like this take?"

"I don't know, Dad. I only decided the other day that I wanted to see him."

Noel scratched his head in bewilderment. "Why wouldn't you want to see him?"

"You know what I've been through recently, Dad; all the depression, low self-esteem, lack of confidence ... I just didn't feel ready."

"Ah, Sinéad," he said, all pretence gone out of him.

Tears welled in his eyes, and for a moment she thought he was going to hug her. Instead he placed a hand on her shoulder and left it there a while, removed it and resumed walking. It was his way of saying she had his support.

13

"WE'RE BACK, MAMMY!"

"So ye are. Did ye get drenched?"

"A bit. We were on the way home by the time it started."

Sinéad and her father stood in the hallway, relieving themselves of runners, coats and anything else that had got wet in the sudden shower.

"Ah, ye're drowned, lads; hold on till I get a towel."

Patricia hobbled off to the hot press to get towels, while the two walkers dried off by the fire.

Sinéad waited till the tea had been poured and they were all sitting comfortably, then she broke the news.

"So anyway, Mam, me and Dad were talking about things in the woods."

"I bet ye were," she said, not taking her eyes off the telly.

"No, Mam, important stuff. Stuff you need to hear."

"Sounds ominous."

"Not really. Well, maybe a little."

"Well, go on then," she said, turning off the TV and giving her daughter her full attention.

"According to Daddy, you already know why I went to England that time years ago."

"What time?" Patricia asked, playing dumb. It was true, her father did have the run of her.

"You know, Mammy, come on."

Patricia looked at her husband for assent. Noel nodded agreement.

"When you sneaked off in the middle of the night and didn't come back for six months, is that the time you mean?"

"Yes, Mam."

"Well, what about it?"

"Why do you think I went away?"

Patricia was uncomfortable in this role. She much preferred to be the one asking the questions. She liked to hold all the aces, and at the moment she had none.

"Oh, I don't know, Sinéad," she said irritably.

"Well, I went over to have a baby, Mammy."

Her mother looked flustered, unsettled. Sinéad continued, eager to get it all out before she could respond.

"I gave him up for adoption, and now he's contacted me to say he wants to meet me."

"Oh, Jesus," Patricia said. "We'll have to paint the front of the house. I told you to do that during the summer, Noel!"

Sinéad brayed with laughter, relief pouring over her.

"For feck's sake, Mam! I'm sure he won't be looking at the house."

"And why wouldn't he? You know what them English are like! We'll have to get the place done up especially for him. And you, young miss," she said, pointing to her daughter. "You'd better start dressing a bit more glamorous, too. We can't have this young fella thinking his mother is some kind of *frump!*"

Sinéad shook her head in disbelief. All that worrying for nothing! Her mother's primary concern didn't centre on how her daughter had become pregnant, left the country and returned empty-handed. No, all she was worried about was what that child might think of them if and when he came for a visit now, nineteen years later.

14

OF COURSE, IT WASN'T ENOUGH to decide to reply to the letter. Now she had to go through with it. After the initial excitement had worn off and everyone had been told, she was still left with the job of picking up a phone and ringing the agency. There was no escaping it, either; Adele badgered her every other day, her mother constantly enquired as to when the 'little English boy' was coming to visit, and the entire extended family bombarded her with various questions and queries. The pressure was coming from all sides, and it was relentless. It got so bad she had to stop visiting Adele, ignore the doorbell and screen her phone calls in case someone was ringing to see if her son had arrived yet. They wouldn't leave her alone. The only solution was to get it over with, but it had to be done on her own terms.

So one morning, after spending hours cleaning and tidying the flat, she went to the kitchen and got the letter. Tidying up always made her feel better, made her feel good about herself, almost confident. She unfolded the letter and carefully dialled the number. The phone was ringing before she had time to think about what she was doing.

"Hello, Northwest Adoption Agency, Rachel speaking. How can I help you today?"

"Oh, hello, Rachel," Sinéad began, realising she had no idea what to say.

"Hello, can I help you?"

"Well, I hope you can. I got a letter, three of them in fact. They're about a boy, my son."

"Oh, great! And what's your own name?"

"I'm Sinéad."

"Sinéad what?"

"Sinéad McLoughlin."

There was a pause at the other end, and for a moment she wondered if it had all been a mistake. They were going to check their records and come back and tell her they had no Sinéad McLoughlin on their files. All that upset for nothing.

"Yes, Sinéad McLoughlin of Dooncurra, County Kilkenny, in Ireland. Is that right?"

"That's right."

"Oh, I'm so pleased you've called, Sinéad."

"You are?"

"Yes, we have a young man who is very eager to contact you."

Sinéad felt her knees go weak and stumbled her way to a chair. "You do?"

"Yes. I'm so thrilled you've called, I really am!"

"Oh, thank you."

"Now, Sinéad," Rachel continued in a more official tone. "What we need to do now is to get the two of you in contact. Usually what we suggest is that you exchange phone numbers via the agency and take it from there. How would you feel about that?"

"Oh God, would we have to do that today?"

"No, no, whenever you feel comfortable, Sinéad. I know it's not easy, but you've taken the first step today and that's the important thing."

"Okay."

"What I could do is inform your son that you've made contact and ask him if he'd like to exchange numbers. That will give you some time to prepare."

"Yes, that sounds like a good idea."

"He's going to be so pleased, Sinéad."

"Is he?"

"Yes, he was beginning to wonder if you wanted to see him, but I told him these things take time."

"They do. You were right."

"Anyway, I've said too much. I'll contact him straight away and let him know you've been in touch, okay?"

"Okay, Rachel. What will happen then?"

"I'll ring you, Sinéad, probably tomorrow and we can take things from there. Remember, there's no pressure. Take things at your own speed."

"Okay, Rachel. Thank you."

"No problem, Sinéad. Bye now."

"Goodbye, Rachel."

She hung up the phone. Her palms were slick with sweat. Trembling, she raised a cigarette to her mouth and lit up.

15

IT HAD BEEN SIX MONTHS since Jonathan had received that phone call, the call he had thought would change his life. In some ways it had. Life at home was much better now, less fractious, less moody, and he and his father were rebuilding their relationship. His little sister had reacted negatively to his news at first, but had since come round. They had spoken at great length about adoption and about how much they loved their parents, about finding their birth-parents and what that would mean. In the end, they found they weren't so different after all, and shared the same outlook on many things. Sophie didn't want to find her birth-parents just yet, but she respected his decision to search for his. It was enlightening to have a discussion like that with her. He'd always just seen her as his ditzy little sister, thought her incapable of having a grown-up conversation on such a weighty issue, but she'd displayed an unexpected maturity during these chats. He was impressed, and he promised that if and when she began her own search he would support her in any way he could. He understood the process and the emotions involved; most importantly, he understood how painful it was when it didn't pan out like you'd hoped.

His own hurt was starting to subside. He'd given up on the idea of meeting his birth-mother. His father was right, it was her loss. He'd done all he could. If she didn't want to see him, then there was nothing more to be said. Life went on, and he intended to live his to the fullest.

Then Rachel called again.

"Oh hello, Rachel. Listen, I'd like to apologise for my behaviour last time."

"Never mind that, Jonathan. I've got some news, good news."

"Yes?"

"She's contacted us, Jonathan, your mother; she wants to see you."

He thought he'd misheard her. It didn't seem possible.

"Could you say that again?"

"She wants to see you, Jonathan, I've just got off the phone with her. You do still want to see her, don't you?"

"Um, yes, I suppose so."

"Are you sure, Jonathan?" Rachel asked jokingly.

"Yes. It's just a big surprise, that's all. I'd almost forgotten about it, to be honest."

"Well, I did tell you that these things take time, didn't I?"

"I suppose you did."

"Not that you were too keen on hearing it," she added.

"No. I thought you were just fobbing me off."

"Would I do that?"

He didn't feel like sharing in her jubilation. If this had happened six months ago he would have, but not now. Did he still want to see her? He'd already dealt with her rejection and moved on as best he could. Now this. A response completely out of the blue and once more on her terms.

"What happens now?"

"Well, with your permission I provide both of you with contact details, phone numbers and email addresses. From there on, it's all up to you."

How strange it felt to finally acquire something you'd dreamed of for years, just at the point when you'd given up on it.

"Okay, then, Rachel, you can give her my number."

"I must say, Jonathan, I thought you'd be more excited than this."

"Well, you caught me off guard; in all honesty I'd given up on her. Have you spoken to her? Did she explain why it took her so long to reply?"

"I have spoken to her, yes, but I think it should be up to her to explain things like that."

"Sure, that makes sense."

"Is there anything else you'd like to ask me, Jonathan? You're going to be on your own from here on in."

"Oh, really?"

"Yes. We generally step aside at this point unless either party requests some form of mediation."

"So this will be my last contact with you?"

"Not quite. I'll check in with you from time to time to see how things are going, but for the time being, this is it. Is there anything else you want to know?"

"I think I've asked all the questions I'm going to ask at this stage."

"Okay then, Jonathan, I'll forward her details to you. Oh, I almost forgot! Her name. It's Sinéad. Sinéad McLoughlin."

It couldn't have been more Irish. He'd definitely have to work on his pronunciation before any potential meeting.

"She's definitely Irish, then?"

"Yes, she lives in the southeast of the country, in a small town in County Kilkenny."

"Okay," he said, not sure what to do with this information.

"Well, if you've no more questions..."

"Yeah okay, Rachel. Thanks, thanks a lot for everything."

"You're welcome, Jonathan. I'll speak to you soon. Good luck!"

"Bye, Rachel, and thanks again."

"Goodbye, Jonathan."

A couple of minutes later he received a text with her number, his mother's number. He looked at it a while. By dialling that number he could speak to the women who gave birth to him. It was that simple. She was there, living her life, in her world, and he could reach out and touch it. He decided that he would much rather be the one calling than the one being called. Better still, he could just text her: *Howya Mammy, what's the craic?* That was how they talked. He'd have to discuss the meaning of the craic with the little Irish lady who worked in the newsagents. He hadn't seen her in a while, though; hopefully she hadn't died. Then there was the meeting itself: how would they go about arranging it? Would she come here, or would he have to go to Ireland? He couldn't go on his own. Obviously he was old enough to travel by himself, but going to a strange country to meet all those strange people? He would need someone with him, preferably his mother, but that could be awkward. There was so much to think of, so much to organise. It would have to keep until morning, though. He switched off his phone; if she called or texted him, she would have to wait. He had to clear his head, and he had to tell his parents.

16

HE WAITED UNTIL AFTER DINNER, until the washing-up was done and they were in the living-room drinking their tea. Sophie was out; she'd disappeared the minute her plate had been cleared. Maybe that was for the best; he could talk to her in private about it later.

"Mum? Dad?" he said breaking the silence.

His father was watching the six o'clock news.

"Yes, love?" Margaret answered, looking up from her magazine.

"Dad, can you turn off the telly? I've got something to talk to you about."

Malcolm looked over, saw the sincerity in his son's eyes and did as requested.

"What is it, love?" asked Margaret.

"It's about my birth-mother."

"Yes, what about her, love? You can talk to us about anything, you know that."

"I know, Mum. Well, here's the thing: she's replied."

Margaret looked at her husband in an attempt to gauge his reaction, but he was already up and across the room, grabbing his son in a bear-hug and slapping him heartily on the back. She rose to join them, hoping Jonathan hadn't seen the momentary flash of horror that had crossed her face. They stood in a group-hug for a few seconds, then dusted themselves down and returned to their seats.

"Where will it be, Jon? God, I haven't been to Ireland in years!"

"Steady on, Malc. Maybe he wants to go on his own."

"I don't know what's happening yet. I'm going to have to arrange it with her."

"With your birth-mum?" asked Margaret.

"Yes."

"Do you have her number, then?"

"Yes, and she's got mine too."

"What's her name, Jonathan? Do you know?"

"Yes, it's Sinéad."

"Very Irish," Margaret said gravely.

"I know, and her second name is just as Irish: McLoughlin."

"You're from very strong Gaelic stock, Jonathan," Malcolm mused.

"Any other information? Has she got a family, maybe some brothers and sisters for you?"

"I don't know, Mum. The agency wouldn't tell me any more."

"That's understandable. So what now? Are you going to ring her?"

"Not yet, not tonight anyway. I've turned my phone off; I don't want to think about it right now."

"Okay, son," said Malcolm, fixing his wife with a meaningful stare. This was their cue to back off and stop crowding him, to save their questions for later.

Malcolm turned the television back on, signalling that the topic was now closed. Jonathan sat back, relieved to have cleared another hurdle. Although not wanting to press things, Malcolm was already calculating how much time he could take off work for a trip to Ireland. Meanwhile, Margaret eyed her son nervously, worried about what he was getting himself into. She worried about herself too. Her boy was leaving her to return to his kin, and soon she would be forgotten. She could live with that, as long as he was happy; but if this woman, this Sinéad McLoughlin, upset her boy in any way, shape or form, there would be hell to pay.

17

"Go on, Sinéad, just press send, will you!"

"Are you sure, Adele?"

"Yes, I'm sure!"

"What if he thinks I'm an old fuddy-duddy trying to be cool?"

"He won't think that. Everyone texts nowadays."

"And it's not too formal?"

"No, it's just right."

"I don't know, Adele."

"Give me the phone," Adele said firmly, losing patience.

"No!" Sinéad replied, grasping it tightly.

"Well, send the flippin' text, then!"

"No."

"Why not?"

"Ah, I don't know, Adele. He's probably in college or something. I don't want to be disturbing him."

Her sister looked at her in exasperation. "No matter what time you text him, you're going to be disturbing him. Now just send it, before I take that phone off you and send it myself."

Sinéad looked at her warily. Adele was the strongest of them all, maybe even stronger than Patrick; if she wanted to take the phone then that's exactly what she would do, and Sinéad would probably suffer a few broken bones in the process.

"Okay, okay, I'll send it," she said. "Just let me read over it one more time."

Adele sighed but called off her threat for the time being. "Go on, then, read it out to me."

"Hello, Jonathan, this is Sinéad McLoughlin. I spoke to Rachel from the Adoption Agency and she gave me your number. I hope you don't mind me texting you, I just thought it would be easier than calling each other straight away. I hope you are well and look forward to hearing from you. Sinéad."

"Perfect. Now send it!"

Sinéad hesitated once more. It had taken them an hour to construct that text message, it was unlikely to get any better. She pressed 'send'.

"Hurray!" cried Adele. "Thank the lord for that!"

"I think I need a fag."

"What are you going to be like when he replies? Or when you've to talk to him on the phone?"

"Don't, Adele, please," Sinéad replied, her stomach sick at the thought.

Adele smiled warmly. "You did well, sis."

She knew how hard this was for her older sister, but she also knew how much she needed it. Even if she had to drag her to England kicking and screaming, she was going to make sure that Sinéad met that poor boy.

*

Jonathan felt the phone vibrate in his pocket. A text, probably from that girl he'd been seeing; he really liked her. Of course, it could be from

Sinéad, his birth-mother. It had been three days since he'd been given her number but, on principle, he hadn't contacted her. He'd done all the leg-work up to now, and it was about time she did her share. Even if weeks, months or years passed, he wasn't going to be the one to act first. What if he got his stubbornness from her, though? What if each was as bad as the other, neither willing to make the first move? They'd both be sitting by the phone twenty years from now, wondering what was keeping the other one from phoning.

He resisted the temptation to check his phone. He was in a lecture and was busy taking notes; the text could wait. The more he tried to focus on the lecture, however, the more he wondered about the identity of the texter. He asked himself which he would prefer, a text from Melanie (the girl he'd been seeing), suggesting they might up tonight, or a text from Sinéad to say hello. It was a toughie. On the one hand, he dearly wanted to meet Sinéad, the woman who had brought him into the world; on the other hand, there was Melanie, who was by far the fittest girl he'd ever been out with. Girls like Melanie didn't come around very often, and it was probably only a matter of time before she tired of him and moved on to someone else, so he was determined to enjoy every minute of their relationship while it lasted. Meeting Sinéad had been a long time coming, however, and even now there were no guarantees it would eventually happen.

He hadn't heard a word the lecturer had said for the last ten minutes and there were only ten more to go. There was hardly any point in tuning in for the remainder. He slipped the phone out of his pocket and glanced at the screen. It was from her; not Melanie, Sinéad. He felt sick, but happy sick; it was going to happen. She'd texted him. His birth-mother had texted him. She did want to see him, after all. He stuffed the phone back into his pocket and began speculating on the contents of the message and how he might respond.

*

Adele had only just left when the phone bleeped. Sinéad stared at it in terror. It had to be him; no one ever texted her. What was she supposed to do now? The logical answer, of course, was to pick up the phone, read the message and respond in kind. No way was she doing that; she'd only just sent a text, and now she was expected to send another! But what if he thought her rude for not replying? What if he'd taken time out of his busy schedule to send her a message, and was now wondering why he'd bothered? She couldn't have that, couldn't have him thinking she had no manners. It wasn't like the letters; that was different. They hadn't come directly from him, but this text had. It was a personal message sent directly from her son. She picked up the phone and opened the message. It was from him, all right; from her son. From Jonathan.

Hi, Sinéad, great to hear from you! Texting is fine, much easier than ringing right now. Less nerve-wracking, I'm sure you'll agree ;). I'm fine, hope you're well too. Just finished uni for the day, what are you up to? Jonathan.

She sank back into her chair, clasping the phone tightly to her chest. He was lovely. Her little boy was lovely. She began to cry; tears of joy and relief, years of tension and sorrow released by those few simple sentences. This was enough for her now, this text. She wouldn't ask for any more. It was perfect. He was perfect. Her little boy was texting her, telling her about his day and asking how she was. So considerate and conscientious. Sinéad felt a sudden, immense gratitude to his parents. She wanted to reach out and hug them and thank them for taking care of him. She read the text again, smiling at the little winking face he'd used. He was just as nervous as she was, he understood her feelings completely. And he was at university; that would make him the first McLoughlin ever to gain a third-level education. Wait till her mother heard this! None of Adele's children were in college, though admittedly that was because the eldest was only six, but her child was. Her little boy, her clever little boy with his English accent and his university degree.

But now she had to reply. Jesus Christ, what was she going to say? Adele wasn't here, she'd gone to the tanning place and couldn't be reached. Who else could she call? Her father? She could ask him to dictate an answer to her over the phone. No, he wasn't very good at stuff like this. Her mother? She'd have her asking how many bedrooms their house had and what kind of car his father drove. No, it would have to be done alone and if she fucked it up, so be it.

Hi, Jonathan. You're right about the nerves but it will get easier in time, I'm sure. I'm just having a quiet day at home today, every day is a quiet day where I live! :) What are you studying in uni if you don't mind me asking? Sinéad.

That was the best she could manage. How could she explain how she was living? How could she tell this young student, who probably had a bright future as a doctor or lawyer, that his mother was an unemployed divorcée who suffered from depression? There was no way of dressing it up. The best she could hope for was to paint a picture of an idyllic country life, and hope he saw her as some free-spirited artistic type who spent her days reading the classics in her back garden. She didn't even have a garden. Sinéad sent the message, feeling a sense of accomplishment. She hadn't needed her sister after all; this was easy. And if he asked her about work or family or anything personal, she'd just tell him the truth. If he was as nice as he sounded, then it probably wouldn't bother him at all.

18

"WHAT ARE YOU LAUGHING AT over there?" Patricia asked in bemusement.

Her daughter, the depressed one, was curled up on the couch giggling at her phone like a teenager.

"Oh, nothing, it's just Jonathan," Sinéad said, tapping away at the new Nokia she'd bought a couple of days previously.

"What's he saying? When are we going to meet him?"

"Shush, Mammy. I'm texting."

"Hmph," grumbled Patricia. "I suppose I'll have to do the washing-up meself, then?"

"I'm afraid so, Mammy."

Patricia made a big show of moaning and groaning as she cleared away the mugs and plates, but to no avail. She would have to do the washing-up and probably the drying too. Sinéad had ostensibly called to the house to help her mother with any jobs that needed doing, but she hadn't left the couch since getting here. She was far too busy texting Jonathan. They had quickly progressed beyond those first tentative texts and were now in constant communication, sending anything up to thirty texts on a daily basis.

Now that she had someone to text, Sinéad thought it only right to treat herself to a new phone, something befitting a busy little texter like herself. She'd traded in her ailing device and got a spanking new Nokia, with a flip screen and everything. It also had a distinctive message alert which was threatening to drive them all mad.

"Oh Jesus, Sinéad, can you not put it on silent or something?" her mother said as another message found its way across the Irish Sea.

"Sure how would I hear it then, Mammy?"

Patricia muttered something under her breath, incoherent but uncomplimentary.

"You know you can't keep texting him forever, Sinéad," she said, returning to the sitting-room. "You're going to have to talk to him eventually."

"Ah whisht, Mammy, will you?"

"I'm serious, Sinéad. *Texting*! It's ridiculous."

Sinéad dragged her eyes away from the phone. "*Mammy!* I'll ring him when I'm good and ready, okay?"

Patricia chose not to reply, instead returning to the washing-up, muttering as she went. Satisfied that she'd got her off her back, Sinéad returned to the phone and her conversation with Jonathan. He was telling her about his parents, Malcolm and Margaret. They sounded like lovely people. Malcolm ran his own business, some sort of internet company, and Margaret stayed at home; a lady of leisure, like herself. Even from his texts she could tell how much he adored them. She asked if she could meet them some day. *Why not?* he replied. *But you and I should probably meet first.* Her mother was right, they couldn't keep texting forever. No sooner had she grown used to texting and begun to enjoy it when another hurdle presented itself. Now they had to talk about meeting up, make travel arrangements, concrete plans which she couldn't back out of. Why couldn't they just continue to text about their favourite films or what they were having for tea that night?

She set about composing a text, one entirely out of keeping with how she was feeling but one she felt Jonathan needed to receive.

I'd be happy to go to England to see you, and that way I could meet your parents too. I have a cousin who lives in Manchester so I could stay with her, that wouldn't be a problem. When do you finish Uni? We should probably wait until then.

Lies, every bit of it. 'Happy to go to England'? Like fuck she was. She hadn't left Dooncurra in four years. She didn't go anywhere, ever. It was easier not to go anywhere, safer; there was less chance of bad things happening if she stayed where she was. Ideally, she'd like Jonathan to come to Ireland, but she couldn't ask him to do that; so she'd made the gesture of offering to go to England. If he took her up on it, she'd have no choice but to go through with it. How much Valium could her GP prescribe at any one time? Probably not enough. Then Jonathan replied and her mind was set at rest.

I was thinking of coming to Ireland tbh, I've never been and I'd really love to see it. You don't mind, do you? Maybe you could come to Manchester next time round. My parents might come with me. I suppose we can figure it out as we go along. I'm finished Uni in a month's time, so we could start making arrangements then.

Thank God. At least this way she only had to worry about the actual meeting, and not all the stresses which would accompany a jaunt across the water.

Okay, Jonathan, that sounds great. There's space at my mam and dad's if you want to stay there, but I'd understand if you'd rather book a hotel or whatever. I'm happy to wait until next time to go to Manchester. Hopefully there will be plenty of trips back and forth from now on anyway :)

More lies. No way did she want them staying at her mother's house. They'd probably leave after one night, pale and terrified, vowing never to return. She had to make the offer, though. Her instinct told her that Jonathan wouldn't want to stay with them. He was as nervous as she was, and staying at a hotel would make things easier. As for the trips back and forth – if, and it was a big if, she survived the first trip, then she might consider another.

Yeah I hope there's plenty of trips back and forth too ;) As for this visit, I think we'd be better off getting a hotel. There might be four of us and it'd be a lot to ask of your mother. Thanks for the offer, though. I've got to go to a lecture now but will text later.

More relief. They would get a hotel, somewhere out of the reach of Patricia McLoughlin. If the first meeting went well she would consider introducing him to her mother at a later date, but only under strict supervision.

Okay, Jonathan, talk later. Enjoy your lecture!

She put down the phone and went into the kitchen. Her mother was busy preparing the dinner.

"What are you doing, Mammy? I told you I'd make that."

"Are you sure you're not too busy *texting?*"

Sinéad didn't react, too happy to be bothered by her barbs.

"Oh, Mammy," she said witheringly. "Go in there and watch some telly, and I'll look after this."

Patricia looked at her daughter, started to say something and then did as she was told.

19

"JUST GOING UPSTAIRS TO TAKE a phone call, Mum," Jonathan announced, smiling enigmatically.

"Okay, love."

He lingered in the hallway, waiting for her to ask who was calling, but she returned to her book, seemingly uninterested.

"Aren't you going to ask who's ringing me?"

"I don't need to know who's ringing you, love; you have your own phone."

He sighed. She wasn't making it easy for him.

"Ask me who's ringing, Mum."

"Okay, who's ringing, Jonathan?"

"Sinéad."

"Oh, great, tell her I said hello."

"Mum, this will be our first ever phone call. We've only texted up to now."

"I didn't know that, love. That *is* exciting. What will you say?"

"I don't know. We're just doing it to hear each other's voices."

"I see. Well, speak nicely, Jonathan. None of that slang and no swearing."

"Of course not, Mum."

He hurried upstairs. They'd arranged for her to call at 7 p.m. and it was almost five to. He should have been nervous but he was entirely at ease. It might have only been a week since that first text, but they'd already built something; a connection, a bond; he didn't quite know what to call it. Of course, that was illogical; you couldn't foster a worthwhile relationship through a few text messages. But how else could you explain it? Within a couple of days their conversation had assumed an easy, natural flow, a relaxed manner which should have taken months to develop. Her sense of humour was so similar to his that he responded to her witticisms instantly without having to think, knowing instinctively that she'd understand what he meant. He'd never had that with anyone, not with his oldest friends, not with a girlfriend, not even with his mum. He could tell how Sinéad was going to reply before he'd even sent the message. That wasn't normal, was it? It pointed to a deep, innate understanding which you can only share with a blood relation. This woman, his mother, shared something with him that he couldn't explain, something he'd never experienced before. This was what it felt like to be someone's son.

The phone rang.

"Hello?"

"Hi. It's me, Sinéad."

"Hi, Sinéad," he said softly.

"Hi, Jonathan."

"Hi."

Silence reigned for a few seconds, longer than was comfortable but not long enough to be awkward.

"You don't sound like I thought you would," he mused, eventually.

"Don't I?"

"No."

"How did you think I'd sound?"

"I'm not sure. More Irish, I suppose."

"Well, I'm speaking in my very best phone voice at the moment. If I were to speak normally, you wouldn't understand a word I said."

"Really?"

"No. Well, not quite. Maybe a bit."

Jonathan laughed. "How do I sound?"

"Very British," Sinéad said decisively.

"Oh God, will that be a problem?"

"It might be."

"Should I cancel the trip?"

"I think you'd better."

They both laughed.

"Your exams start tomorrow, then?"

"Yes."

"Are you nervous?"

"No, I'll be fine."

"Such confidence."

"I know, and probably misplaced."

Another silence, longer than the first one; they were finding it difficult to replicate the easy back-and-forth of their text conversations. They both began to speak and then stopped.

"Sorry, after you."

"No, you first."

"Okay."

They both started to speak again, drowning the other out, interrupting one another. Now things were becoming awkward.

When she was sure he wasn't going to speak, Sinéad attempted to steer things toward more serious territory.

"There must be a lot of things you want to ask me, Jonathan."

"Yes, but I think we should wait until we meet before getting into the heavy stuff, don't you?"

"I agree," she replied, "but you must wonder why it took me so long to reply to the letters."

"Yes, I have wondered a little."

"Well, I just want you to know that it wasn't because I didn't want to meet you, nothing like that. The problem was with me and *my* issues. I suppose I was worried that I wouldn't match your expectations."

"Really?"

"Yes. I'm not exactly a success story, you know!"

"None of that stuff matters to me. I just wanted to find out about you and get to know you."

"Still, Jonathan, you must have been expecting something a little different."

"I didn't really know what to expect. You've not been a disappointment so far, anyway."

"Haha, you're too kind."

"Honestly, I really like you. We get on great, don't we?"

"Yeah, we do, don't we? I like you too, Jonathan. You're a credit to your mum and dad."

"I'm not having that! It's all me, they had nothing to do with it."

She laughed; he had a strange sense of humour, a bit like her father's.

"Seriously, though, they must be very proud of how you've turned out."

"I suppose they are, but I have my moments too."

"Oh, I'm sure you do. Have they decided yet whether they'll come to Ireland?"

"I'm still not sure about my mum. Dad is dead keen, he's booked time off work and everything, but she's been quiet about it."

"Oh God, do you think it would be too upsetting for her? Is that why she doesn't want to come?" Sinéad asked, panicked.

"She hasn't really said anything, but I suppose it's pretty tough on her."

"Do you think we should cancel it for the time being?"

"No, no. I should probably have a chat with her really and see how she feels."

"That'd be a good idea," Sinéad agreed. "Would it help if I spoke to her?"

"I'm not sure about that; not yet, anyway."

"Okay, Jonathan."

More silence.

"Any news?" Sinéad asked hopefully.

"Not really," Jonathan replied, wondering whether he should tell her about Melanie and what they'd done last night. "And you?"

"No, it's all quiet here too."

"Right."

"Will we say goodbye, so?" she asked.

"Okay, Sinéad. I'll call you next week when my exams are over, but we can text in the meantime."

"Great. Jonathan?"

"Yes?"

"Please tell your mother that she has no need to feel threatened in any way. I don't want to come between the two of you."

"Thanks, Sinéad. I'll try to speak to her about it over the next few days."

"Okay, Jonathan. Very best of luck with your exams. Talk soon."

"Bye, Sinéad."

He hung up. It seemed to have gone quite well. There'd been a few silences, but they'd talked quite a bit too. It'd be much easier the next time, and easier again the time after that; and once they'd met, they'd be chatting all the time. Chatting and texting.

He went back downstairs. Margaret was still at the breakfast bar.

"How did it go?"

"It was fine, Mum. I'm more interested in how you're feeling about the whole thing, to be honest."

"What do you mean?"

She really was a terrible actor.

"It's okay, Mum. I realise this is hard for you."

"Don't be silly, Jonathan. I'm thrilled for you, I really am."

"I know you are, but what about you? How are you feeling?"

"Don't you worry about me, love. This is a big deal for you."

"Please, Mum," he said. "I need to know you're okay with this, and I don't think you are."

Margaret sighed deeply. "It's just dredged up a lot of emotions for me, Jonathan; that's all."

"What kind of emotions, Mum?"

"Oh, I don't know, Jonathan."

"Tell me, Mum."

She looked at him helplessly, tears welling in her eyes. "I just don't want to lose you, Jonathan."

"Mum! You're not going to lose me."

He laid his hands on her shoulders and looked her squarely in the eyes.

"There's nothing to be afraid of, Mum, I promise. You're my mum and I love you more than anyone in the whole world. No one will ever take your place, *no one*. No matter what happens with myself and Sinéad, no matter how well we get on, *you'll* still be my mum. You'll always be my mum."

"Are you sure, Jonathan?" Margaret asked, no longer trying to hide her vulnerability.

"I promise you, Mum. Sinéad even said the same thing."

"Did she? She sounds nice, Jonathan."

"She is, Mum. You'll see that when you meet her."

"I don't think I can come with you, Jon. Is that okay?"

"Of course, Mum. Dad and I will go. It'll be a boys' holiday."

Margaret chuckled. "He's so looking forward to going."

"I know; he hasn't shut up about it since I told him."

"He's got so many things planned, you'll hardly have time to meet Sinéad!"

"I know," Jonathan laughed.

"Do you think you'll be okay, just the two of you? You won't fight or anything?"

"We'll be fine, Mum. All that stuff is forgotten now."

"Good, Jonathan."

"I'm glad we had this chat, Mum."

"Me too."

"Just remember," he said, fixing her with a steely gaze. "You're my mum, the best mum in the world, and I love you."

"I love you too, Jonathan."

They hugged. Margaret did feel better; she didn't have to pretend any more. Maybe there was room in his life for the two of them, an English mother and an Irish mother, a mum and a mammy. He was lucky, in a way, having two women who loved him. Some kids didn't have anyone.

20

WHEN THE DATE HAD BEEN decided she'd cheerily circled it on her calendar and set about telling the world her son was coming to visit. It was exciting having something to plan for, having a purpose in life. But even then, as Sinéad made all the necessary arrangements, chose which outfit to wear, rehearsed what she might say to him, the nerves were bubbling under the surface. She chose to ignore them; it was weeks away, there was nothing to get worked up about. As it drew ever closer, however, as the reality of the situation began to kick in, she began to dread the arrival of that fateful day. A sense of growing unease surrounded her, increasing on a daily basis, threatening to reach fever pitch and send her completely over the edge. At one point, with only a week to go, she decided to cancel, even going so far as to compose a text explaining her reasons. *I'm really very sorry, it's not your fault. Maybe we can try again in a few months?* She couldn't send it, though; she couldn't do that to him. That was the coward's way out, and she was sick of being a coward. She was going through with this no matter what. She would face her fears and stare them down. Dealing with those nerves wasn't easy, though, especially when her mother was on hand to voice her worst fears at any given moment.

"What if you have one of your fits?" she'd asked.

"I don't have *fits*, mammy."

"Ah, you know what I mean."

"They're called 'panic attacks'. They're not fits."

Patricia pouted at the distinction; they seemed like fits to her.

"But what if you have one, Sinéad, what will you do then?"

"I won't have one, Mammy."

"I hope not. The poor child won't know what to do with you."

Although she'd assured her mother she wouldn't be having any 'fits', Sinéad was less confident herself. It might have been more than a year since her last anxiety attack, but there was a reason for that. She led a regimented life, one suited to her needs. She didn't go anywhere or do anything. She didn't work, she lived alone and didn't answer to anyone but herself. Her life consisted of routine, safe and predictable routine. This allowed her to exist in relative harmony, and helped to keep her anxiety attacks at bay. However, once she'd replied to that letter her peace was disturbed. She was now hurtling towards something she couldn't escape, and it terrified her.

Her father and Adele did their best to reassure her. "What have you got to be anxious about?" they'd ask. "Sure, aren't ye getting on great?"

It was true; they were getting on great, but that meant she had something to lose. If she fucked it up from here she'd regret it for the rest of her life. It would be the latest in a long list of failures. *Poor oul' Sinéad, she can't do anything right.*

The day before Jonathan's arrival, and with her nerves shot to pieces, she went to see her counsellor, for what she hoped would be a morale-boosting chat. Unable to afford a private psychologist, she had had to make do with Phillip, a state-funded shrink, whose services came free of charge. He wasn't exactly Freud but he provided a soundboard, and he never judged her no matter how negative she was, or how much she moaned. A thin, middle-aged man with sandy hair and a piebald beard, he didn't seem like the kind of person in whom you'd confide your deepest, darkest secrets, but over time she had grown to trust him.

"What exactly is it that you're afraid of?" he asked, settling down in his chair.

"I'm afraid of fucking it up, Phillip."

"In what way, Sinéad?"

"I don't know exactly; by saying something stupid or upsetting him, I suppose."

"And what would happen then?"

"He'd run back to England and never contact me again."

Phillip leaned back, studying Sinéad thoughtfully. They sat in a pokey little room at the local community centre, the sound of the junior karate team being put through the motions could be heard from the adjacent sports hall.

"Do you honestly think that would happen, Sinéad, after the connection you've developed?"

"It could," she said gloomily.

"Do you think Jonathan would be willing to throw it all away after coming so far?"

"He doesn't even know me, Phillip. Once he realises what I'm really like, he won't be interested anymore."

"Hasn't he already said he's not bothered about things like that?"

"He has," she conceded, "but he doesn't know I'm a chronic depressive!"

"We've spoken about this before, Sinéad. There is no shame in suffering from depression or anxiety."

She shook her head dismissively. "It's not even that, I'm just worried that I won't be able to cope. I'll get myself into such a frenzy that I'll end up in the hospital, while he's waiting at the park wondering where the hell I am."

"That won't happen, Sinéad," Phillip said calmly. "You will feel tense, that's natural, but so will he."

"It's hardly the same thing, Phillip."

"How do you know?" he countered. "Maybe Jonathan suffers from anxiety, too?"

"No, he doesn't," she said, irritably.

"Look, forget about that. What you need to understand is that should the worst happen, should you suffer a panic attack, everything will still be okay. He won't run back to England or think any less of you, and it won't mess everything up."

She looked at him doubtfully. "And what if I end up in hospital?"

"You won't end up in hospital, Sinéad. Practise your breathing exercises, read those books I gave you about cognitive behaviour and maintain positive thoughts. You're strong, Sinéad, stronger that you realise, and you can do this. I know you can."

"Thanks, Phillip, you're very good."

He waved her words away. "Be sure to let me know how it goes, Sinéad."

"I will," she said, "if I survive it."

She decided to spend the night alone, rejecting Adele's offer of a few glasses of wine and a final pep-talk. The last thing she wanted was a hangover on the day she met her son. Instead she'd cooked herself a nice dinner, done some washing and spent a few hours tidying up her flat; it had never been tidier, not even on the day she'd moved in. She'd hoped that the housework would tire her out and send her to bed early, exhausted. Not a bit of it. At 10.30 she was upright and alert, staring at the television, one worst-case scenario after another racing through her mind. She rehearsed the answers that she had prepared for all the questions he was bound to ask.

Question One: Why did you give me away?

Answer: I was young, alone and afraid. Girls didn't bring up children on their own those days, it just wasn't the done thing. (This sounded hollow and insignificant, but then so did everything.)

Question Two: What about my father?

Answer: His name is James Fitzgerald. I haven't seen him in many years, he left as soon as he found out about you. I can help you find him if you like. (She really hoped he wouldn't ask about his father; this was to be their day and no one else's).

Question Three: How come you never had more children?

Answer: My husband brought it up constantly but I hadn't had the courage to tell him I was still haunted by the child I'd given away and couldn't face the thought of having another. He left me shortly after.

Question Four: Did you ever wonder about me, or try to find out about me?

Answer: There's not a day gone by when I haven't thought of you. From the moment I left the hospital until this very second, I've thought of you constantly; wondering what you were doing, what you looked like, how you talked, how you laughed. Every birthday, every Christmas, I've imagined you opening your presents, happy and smiling, and prayed that your life had turned out well (she would probably cry when delivering these lines, but it had to be said). I vowed that I wouldn't seek you out until you were older. I was afraid of unsettling you, disturbing your life and upsetting your parents. (Would she have sought him out, even when he was older? It would have been something she'd have planned on doing until the day she died).

Question Five: What have you been doing with your life?

Answer: Nothing, Jonathan. I'm an absolute failure, your mother is a failure; a washed-up, thirty-something woman with very little to offer you or anyone else. Happy now?

Those were the only questions she'd come up with answers for. If he asked anything else she'd have to improvise, think on the spot, and hope she didn't say anything ridiculous.

Sinéad switched off the television and sat in the darkness. It felt better, calmed her and allowed her to think more clearly. She'd ironed her clothes and left them hanging in the wardrobe, ready to be put on; nothing to worry about there. Her medication was on the dresser in her bedroom. She'd take a sleeping-pill tonight and maybe a Valium in the morning, depending on how bad she was. The alarm was set for half-eight in the morning, giving her a full five hours to get ready. That was everything, wasn't it? A camera? Was that too presumptuous? No, she wouldn't bring a camera; her mother was bound to have one handy if they decided to go up there. Was her phone charged? It wouldn't do if he rang her in the middle of the night and she didn't hear it. As if on cue, it bleeped into life. A message; from him.

Hi, Sinéad. We made it here in one piece! Just at the hotel now. Fairly tired after the day, so will probably have an early night. See you tomorrow!

Her little boy was here, in Dooncurra. It was amazing, incredible. It was really happening. She quickly replied, eager to help him settle in.

Brill. Glad you got here safely. I hope the hotel is okay. Yes, I will see you tomorrow. Very nervous but I'm sure you are too :)

He replied instantly.

I know, I can't believe it's really happening. Anyway, I'm gonna hit the hay now. Talk tomorrow. Night, Sinéad.

Night, Jonathan. See you tomorrow.

And that was it. He was gone, off to hit the hay in a bedroom in a hotel not far from here. When he awoke in the morning, it would be time to meet his mother. That was her, Sinéad McLoughlin; she was this boy's mother and he had come to see her. Suddenly it didn't seem so terrifying. This was something beautiful, something God had intended. Holding that thought, she went to the bathroom, brushed her teeth and readied herself for bed.

21

THE DAY AFTER HIS LAST exam, Jonathan sat in his father's car *en route* to Holyhead. They'd decided to take the ferry rather than fly; Malcolm wanted to bring his own car so they could see some of the countryside. Jonathan didn't mind, it made it more of an adventure, a road trip.

"Do you think Mum will be okay?" he asked as they drove along the M56.

"She'll be fine, son. She understands this is something you need to do."

"I don't know, Dad."

"Your mum's tougher than you think, Jonathan, believe me."

"Well, she's had to be, I suppose."

He hadn't intended it to sound like a dig at his father, but that was how it was received. It hung sourly in the air for a few moments, threatening to spoil their trip almost before it had begun.

"How do you think you'll feel if I decide to meet my birth-dad, Dad?" he asked, changing tack.

Malcolm exhaled theatrically. "It'd be strange, there's no doubt about that."

"Sinéad might not even know where he is."

"So you haven't spoken to her about him?"

"No, we thought it was best to wait until we meet before getting into all that."

"Probably right, son."

Deciding that he'd given his father enough to chew on for the time being, Jonathan tried to lighten the mood.

"I thought of a few games we could play to pass the time, Dad."

"Oh?"

"Have you ever heard of the 'Would you rather' game?"

"I can't say I have, Jon."

"It's brilliant, Dad; me and my mates play it all the time when we've had a few."

"Well, that doesn't fill me with hope."

"Really, Dad, it'll be fun."

"What do I do, then?"

"Okay, so it goes like this: I ask you a question, for instance, 'Would you rather have the power of flight or be invisible?' and then you have to answer it."

"Well, that's easy; flight."

"But why, Dad? Why flight?"

"So I could fly everywhere, would save a fortune on petrol."

"Think about it though, Dad. If you were invisible, you could get away with all sorts."

"Like what?"

"Well you wouldn't have to pay for your petrol for a start."

Malcolm looking at his son, a whisper of a smile playing on his lips. "You're serious?"

"Of course I'm serious, Dad. And that's only half of it."

"What else would you do?"

"Lots of stuff," Jonathan mumbled in response, suddenly uncomfortable. It was one thing discussing sneaking into women's changing rooms with his mates, quite another doing the same with his father.

"Let's try a different question, Dad. I don't think you quite got that one."

"Fair enough."

While Jonathan devised a more suitable teaser, Malcolm stared straight ahead, a broad grin spread across his face. Never could he have imagined this; he and his son on a trip, just the two of them, laughing and joking, as thick as thieves. He had thought their relationship sundered beyond repair at one point. Since that chat around the kitchen table, however, things had changed for the better. There was still the odd moment here and there, and he knew Jonathan's loyalty would always be to his mother, but for the most part it was just like old times. It was hard to believe really. He just hoped it would last. His son's behaviour suggested it would, he appeared to have moved on, and Malcolm felt he could do the same. He was getting to know his son again. Jonathan was a man now, nineteen years old, and hanging around with him was like being with one of his mates, only much better. They could laugh and joke like old pals, have a few beers and play games like 'Would you rather'.

"Have you thought of one yet?" he asked.

"Give me a minute," Jonathan replied, his eyes closed.

Malcolm was starting to worry about the nature of this question.

"Right, I'm ready!" Jonathan announced.

"Go on, then."

"Would you rather get sent to jail for a crime you didn't commit or accidentally kill someone and get away with it?"

"Eh? What kind of question is that?"

"It's a 'Would you rather' question, Dad."

"Yeah, but it's not much of a choice, is it?"

"That's what the game is like sometimes, Dad."

"I don't want to choose either."

"You have to, Dad. If you don't, you lose. And you have to be honest, too," he added with a glint in his eye.

Secretly, Malcolm had to concede that it was an excellent question, a real moral dilemma. He had to be careful with his answer; it was important he portrayed himself as a responsible adult.

"Do I get to choose whom I accidentally kill?"

"No," Jonathan replied, "it's just anyone, completely random."

"Okay, then," Malcolm said, giving it serious thought. "I think I'll have to go to prison."

"Are you sure, Dad? Even if it was life imprisonment in maximum security?"

"That's just something I'll have to accept. I don't think I could live with the guilt of taking someone's life."

"Very noble of you, Dad."

"Cheers, son. Would you come to visit me in prison?"

"No."

"Thanks a lot!"

"Will I tell you what I'd do?"

"Go on."

Jonathan liked to bend the rules a bit when playing 'Would you rather', which was a lot easier when playing with a rookie like his dad.

"I'd get sent to prison, too."

"Very good."

"But I'd befriend some gang members, make contacts on the inside and track down the person responsible for my crime."

"Hey, you never said anything about what I could do once I was in prison!"

"Hmph, it's not my fault if you chose to accept your fate, Dad. Anyway, once I'd tracked this bloke down, I'd hire someone to make him confess."

"But then wouldn't you be breaking the law?"

"How, Dad?"

"By using intimidation tactics."

Jonathan pondered this for a while. They were already halfway to Holyhead. Having left behind the satellite towns of greater Manchester, they were now surrounded by the picturesque landscape of north Wales. It had been a long time since he'd been to the port but there was little chance of getting lost, all you had to do was follow the lorries, all of which were going in that direction. Every now and then they passed a service station full of parked convoys and he felt his stomach rumble at the thought of a full English, but the plan had been to carry on all the way to the ferry and eat once they were on board.

"Okay, Dad, fair dues; you got me there."

"So you'd end up back in prison, then?"

"If you say so," Jonathan replied sourly.

"And probably alongside the guy you forced a confession from. You're making a lot of enemies, Jon. I think I fancy my chances in prison better than yours."

"Yeah, yeah, Dad, don't go on about it."

Malcolm drummed his fingers on the steering-wheel in satisfaction. He was getting the hang of this game now.

"Is it my turn now to ask a question?"

"Sure, Dad," said Jonathan, staring distractedly out of the window.

They both lapsed into silence, the only sound the mid-morning news bulletin on the radio and the swish of traffic as they were overtaken by impatient drivers.

"Okay, then, how about ..." Malcolm began.

"It's not 'how about', Dad, it's 'Would you rather.'"

"All right, all right. Would you rather work in a job you hate and earn loads of money or do something you love and earn very little?"

Jonathan tutted loudly. "Dad, that's a rubbish question. Everyone asks that."

"Well, I didn't know that, did I?" Malcolm was genuinely hurt, he'd put a lot of thought into his question.

His son resumed staring out the window, so dismissive of the question that he didn't deem it worth answering.

"Aren't you going to answer it then, Jon?"

"The second one."

"A job you love, and earn very little?"

"Yes."

"Is that all? No sneaky ways around it?"

"No. Will we play something else now?"

"Okay. What had you in mind?"

By the time they'd named every European Cup winner since 1955, England's starting line-ups in the World Cup final of 1966 and the rugby World Cup final of 2003, and agreed that a prime Muhammed Ali would probably beat a prime Mike Tyson on a split decision, they'd reached the dock. It looked like a fine day to sail; the Irish Sea shimmered under bright sunshine and there wasn't a breath of air in the sky. They passed through the toll and, after a slight delay, parked up inside the bowels of the *Seacat*.

"What'll we do first, Dad?"

"Food. I'm starving."

"Sounds good. Might have a few pints with mine."

Malcolm looked at his son curiously. "Might you now?"

"I might," he replied.

"Well for some, isn't it?"

"Do you mind, Dad, since you're driving?"

"No, enjoy yourself, son. We're on holidays!"

Jonathan's 'few pints' left him somewhat the worse for wear. His first sight of Ireland was a bleary, distorted one, and as soon as they left the noise and clamour of the dock, he fell into a dozy, alcohol-induced slumber. Malcolm tried to rouse him gently, but to no avail. He would have to entertain himself during this leg of the journey. Night was falling by the time they reached their hotel. Rather conveniently, Jonathan awoke just as his father pulled into the car park.

"Back in the land of the living, then?" asked Malcolm drily.

Jonathan yawned lazily.

"Where are we?" he asked.

"At the hotel."

"Already? Nice driving, Dad. Sorry I dozed off."

"Dozed off? You were comatose!"

Jonathan offered a guilty smile by way of apology.

"This is the place, then?"

"Yes. Get your bags and we'll check in."

They got their stuff from the boot and went around to the entrance. The Spring Peak, a three-star hotel, was situated on Dooncurra's main street, a fifteen-minute walk away from Sinéad McLoughlin's poky little flat.

"Looks all right, this," said Jonathan as they crossed the thickly-carpeted lobby to the check-in desk.

"Good evening, gentlemen. Checking in?" asked the young woman at reception.

Her accent was like Sinéad's, beautiful and lilting, much nicer than the ones he'd heard on the ferry.

"Yes, please. Philliskirk, two single rooms," said Malcolm.

While his father checked them in, Jonathan wandered into the hotel bar for a look. It was the same as any English bar he'd ever been in, all chrome fittings and plush seating, lonely drinkers and bored staff. He'd been expecting something more Irish, but you probably had to go further afield for that. A place like this was more likely to be used for events such as christenings and weddings. Had Sinéad ever been in here? She probably had. Maybe the McLoughlins held get-togethers here, perhaps this was where he'd have gone for his First Communion if he hadn't been adopted. A First Communion was something Catholic children had when they were about seven years old. It was all very holy, a big day out for the whole family; he'd read about it online. They had another one a few years later, a confirmation, like the Church of England one but at a different age. That was where the holy parties ended, though, until you got married.

He and Sinéad had discussed meeting in a pub, but they'd eventually decided on somewhere a little quieter, a nearby park. She'd given him directions: they would meet by a fountain tomorrow afternoon at one thirty. But he didn't know what she looked like. What if there were loads of people sitting by the fountain, all of them women around Sinéad's age? Potential birth-mothers, one and all. They'd briefly described themselves to each other – they had the same hair shade and eye colour – but it was all very vague. He'd suggesting exchanging pictures via email, but she didn't have an email address and didn't know how to set one up. Instead they agreed to text one another on the day, describing what they were wearing.

While he waited for his father, he texted Sinéad to inform her of their arrival. She replied almost instantly, telling him how nervous she was. He didn't feel like getting into a conversation about which of them was the more nervous, so he lied a little and said he was going to bed. She'd never know. Anyway, wasn't that what teenage boys did, lied to their mothers? There was nothing wrong with that, it was a sign of how well they were getting along. What chance was there of a proper dinner in this place, he wondered as he looked around for a menu. It was late, after ten; the kitchen was probably closed and the chef gone home. The best he could hope for was a sandwich.

"Jonathan, I have the key-cards," Malcolm said, appearing in the bar.

"Okay, Dad. Can we get something to eat first? I'm hanging."

"We won't get anything in here at this hour. We'll have to go somewhere else. Let's throw our bags upstairs and go out for a look around."

"Let's hurry, then," Jonathan said. "I'm really starving."

The rooms were in keeping with the rest of the hotel; nothing fancy but perfectly adequate for their needs. They each had their own television, which pleased Jonathan no end. He turned his on immediately to see what the local broadcasters had to offer and discovered the sum total of four channels, one of which was in a foreign language that he presumed was Irish. After changing his T-shirt and applying a fresh lining of deodorant, he crossed the hallway to his father's room.

"Does Ireland have its own language, Dad?" he asked, when Malcolm opened the door.

"Yes, of course. They speak Irish, don't they?"

"How come we haven't heard anyone speak it, then?"

"I don't think they use it much. If you hadn't slept all the way here you would have noticed the road signs. They're in English and Irish."

"Oh, right," said Jonathan, intrigued. "I think I might like to learn a bit of Irish while I'm here."

"Well, good luck with that," said Malcolm.

"There's an Irish channel on the television. If I watch enough of that, I might pick up something."

"Remind me again how you did at French in your GCSEs?"

"Good point," Jonathan admitted.

He sat on the bed while his father readied himself for a night on the town. It was Wednesday, so there was unlikely to be too much happening, which was probably just as well. Jonathan was still a little anxious about the idea of being an Englishman on Irish soil. His father had assured him they would be fine, and that speaking in an English accent wasn't any cause for concern. Jonathan wasn't convinced, though; he'd heard about the IRA and how much they hated the English. Hadn't they bombed Corporation Street in Manchester a few years back? What was to say they wouldn't come to Dooncurra and bomb himself and his father while they slept? He vowed to speak very quietly for the first few days, at least until he got a grip on things.

"What do you fancy, then?" asked Malcolm, emerging from the bathroom.

"Do you think they do Indian food over here?"

"Let's find out."

They did do Indian food, and it was as nice and as authentically Indian as the Indian food you got in England. The restaurant was almost entirely deserted except for a young couple by the window and an elderly foursome who seemed more interested in quaffing the cheap wine on offer than eating their food. Showing no ill-effect from his earlier drinking, Jonathan decided to have a pint with his Rogan Josh; to help him sleep, he told his father. They ate in silence and left as soon as their plates were cleared. It had been a long day, and they'd been travelling since nine that morning – both were content to be in bed before midnight.

"What time are you going to get up?" asked Malcolm, as they parted ways for the night.

"I'm going to set my alarm for half-ten," said Jonathan.

"Breakfast only lasts till eleven," his father warned.

"If I'm up, I'll get it. If I'm not, I won't."

"Fair enough, son. Sleep well."

"I will, Dad."

Jonathan went into his room, kicked off his shoes, wrestled his clothes to the floor and flopped onto the bed. He was asleep within seconds.

22

SINÉAD HAD BEEN AWAKE SINCE first light. She'd taken a sleeping tablet, hoping it would grant her a full night's rest and that she would waken feeling refreshed and energised. But it wasn't to be. Four hours' sleep; that's what she'd got. She'd lain there, listening to the day come to life, wondering what it had in store for her. This was *the* day, the day she'd thought would never come. She was about to meet her boy, the child she'd left behind in that English hospital. He was here in Dooncurra, and in a few hours' time they would come face to face.

At 9.30, she finally gave in. There was no chance of falling back to sleep, not now. Her heart was thumping, her mind racing. She just wanted it to be over, to be climbing back into bed, having survived the day. There were still another four hours to go, though, four hours until they were due to meet, plenty of time to have a nervous breakdown or worse. She got up, wrapped her dressing-gown around her and sloped into the kitchen. It looked like being a typical Irish summer's day, cloudy and drab, with just enough warmth to debate the merits of long or short sleeves; perfect weather for meeting up with your long-lost child.

She turned on the kettle and instinctively reached out for her fags, but they weren't there. She was off them and had been for a month now. Whose stupid idea had that been? More than anything right now, she needed a cigarette. This was an emergency, a situation of great peril. Why hadn't she planned for this? Bought a pack of ten, just in case? She should have known this would happen today, of all days.

All it would take was a quick trip to the corner shop. She could be back here in five minutes with a lovely cigarette dangling from her lips. That's how she could pass the time until the meeting, just smoking. She'd buy forty fags and smoke every one of them, turn up for the meeting smelling like an ashtray and sounding like a wheezy old bus. No, starting the day with a relapse was not a good idea. It would be a sign of weakness and a warning of bad things to come. She pushed thoughts of nicotine to the back of her mind. She was going to be strong today, a proper, grown-up woman.

It would have been nice to have some moral support, though. Jonathan had his dad, she had no one. It was the school holidays, so Adele was busy with her kids. Sinéad could have called over for a while, playing with the children always helped take her mind off things. She was operating on a high stress level today, however, her nerves so strained that one of Adele's offspring might end up being maimed if they stepped out of line. No, she wouldn't go there. The only other person she could turn to was her father, but she had no way of contacting him. He didn't have a mobile and ringing the landline would almost certainly bring her into contact with her mother. Because, in spite of her arthritis, Patricia McLoughlin had an unerring ability to get to the phone before anyone else, no matter where she was. If Linford Christie was over for tea and the phone went, she'd still get there before him. The last person Sinéad wanted to talk to right now was her mother; that would be like Superman eating a plateful of Kryptonite before he went into battle with Lex Luther. No, she was on her own for now, although she'd have some company in a few hours' time. *Oh, Christ.* She felt her stomach heave and ran to the bathroom, but it was a false alarm; nothing came up. She just dry-heaved for a while, spat and spluttered and flushed the toilet. Totally normal, all things considered.

That episode over, she returned to the kitchen and tried to map out her day, planning things in advance usually calmed her nerves. It was a thirty-minute walk to the park. It would take her an hour to get ready. She also had to try to eat something before she went. That would all take roughly two hours, which still left her with more than two hours to fill. What was she going to do for that amount of time? She couldn't stay here. She had to get out, it didn't matter where. She went to the bedroom, put on the clothes she'd been wearing the day before, fixed up her hair as best she could, and headed out into the early-morning greyness. A good walk, that's what she needed right now.

23

To Jonathan's surprise, he was up in time for breakfast the following morning. In fact, he made it with time to spare.

"Didn't think I'd see you for hours yet," said Malcolm, making room for his son's overflowing plate.

"I know. I slept really well, though. What time was it when we went to bed?"

"A little after midnight."

"Ten hours, then," said Jonathan, stretching contentedly. "That should set me up for the day."

"That breakfast should help, too," said Malcolm. "Are you sure you have enough?"

Jonathan looked at the array of sausages, rashers, beans, pudding, egg and tomatoes on his plate. "I forgot the toast. Could you get me some, Dad?"

Malcolm smiled wryly and went to the buffet to hunt down some toast, and perhaps a trough for his son to eat from.

Usually Jonathan wouldn't dream of starting a fry-up without some toast to hand, but he was starving so he decided to get stuck in and hope his father returned promptly with that most vital of ingredients. This is how all holidays should be, he thought as he speared a sausage and dipped it into the yolk of an egg. Just the lads. Eating and drinking whatever you want, sleeping it off and then starting all over again. There was no way he was going to the Canaries with his parents and sister later on in the summer, not a chance. He was going to ask his father if he fancied a trip to Scotland. Jonathan had already planned it out. He'd invite one of his mates, probably Stuart, and his dad could bring Dennis from work. They'd go to a remote part of Scotland, maybe the Outer Hebrides, and try their hand at fishing. Jonathan had never fished, but how hard could it be? You just sat on the bank, drinking cans and enjoying the fresh sea air. Then, when they'd finished for the day, they'd shack up in the village pub and sup real ale, that thick murky stuff you only got in the countryside. They'd get pissed, sing songs and then stumble back to their hotel, or better still, their camp-site.

"Is four slices enough?"

"Should be," said Jonathan, picking up a piece.

"We've got about three hours to kill before you meet Sinéad," said Malcolm. "Anything you fancy doing?"

Jonathan shrugged his shoulders.

"There's not much to do around here," Malcolm continued. "I spoke to the receptionist and she said there are some woods not far from here, with walkways and gift shops, the whole lot. Very popular with tourists."

"Okay," Jonathan nodded.

"Will we go there, then?"

"Mmm."

"If I go upstairs and change my shoes, do you think you'll be ready by the time I get back?"

Jonathan continued to nod, far too busy eating to respond in any depth. A walk in the woods did sound nice. It'd give him a chance to sample that fresh country air his father was always going on about. He could ask him about the trip to Scotland, too, catch him unawares while they were enjoying the great outdoors. When they'd finished their walk, he'd return to the hotel, take a shower and meet the woman who'd brought him into the world.

He finished the last of his breakfast, stifling a belch as he pushed the plate away. The sausages had been incredible, he made a mental note to enquire about them before they checked out. Sinéad had texted again that morning; just checking in, she'd said, making sure he hadn't changed his mind. He'd reassured her and told her he'd see her later on. He felt remarkably calm about the whole thing. All that build-up, all those years of wondering; he should have been in a frenzy by this point. But whether it was the buzz of being on holidays, the Guinness he'd consumed the night before or the steadying influence of his father, he was totally at ease with it all. It still meant everything to him, of course, but it held no fears. He and Sinéad had already clicked, and today would merely cement their relationship. If anything, he had to keep his excitement in check. This was going to be one of the best days of his life.

*

"Are you sure we've not gone past it, Dad?"

"No, no. She said it was just a little way out of town, up a hill."

"I don't know, Dad. I think we've gone past it."

Jonathan was glad now that they hadn't decided to walk. It appeared that 'just a little way out of town' meant a five-mile drive over increasingly bumpy roads to the outer reaches of human civilisation.

"There!" exclaimed Malcolm. "Dooncurra Woods, one kilometre. I told you."

Jonathan twisted in his seat to see the sign. It was battered and grimy, but legible. Malcolm triumphantly turned the steering wheel and reversed to the little byroad he'd just driven past.

"I had a feeling it was up here," he said.

Jonathan smirked to himself. Seconds before, his father had ridiculed his suggestion that the woods might be at the end of that narrow little laneway. "I don't think so, son," he'd said dismissively, his tone that of someone who was used to roughing it in the wilderness as opposed to Jonathan, a naive suburbanite who wouldn't last five minutes out here on his own.

They continued up the hill, keeping an eye out for the turn-off to the woods. Cows stared out at them from the adjoining fields, absentmindedly chewing the cud as they sized up the newcomers.

"There's the sign, Dad," said Jonathan, pointing.

"Yes, Jonathan," Malcolm replied, slightly miffed that he hadn't seen it first.

They turned off as instructed, heading into the woods and away from Ard Aulinn where, at that very moment, Jonathan's grandparents were discussing his whereabouts and when they might set eyes on him.

"God, this road is awful," said Malcolm, slowing to a crawl as he manoeuvred the Audi round the numerous potholes. Jonathan had lapsed into silence; he wasn't appreciating the bumpy ride and the way it made his breakfast slosh around his stomach. The whole lot, sausages, toast and even last night's Guinness, was in danger of making an unwelcome return.

"Take it easy, Dad!" he said irritably as the car hopped in and out of another crater.

"It's like summat from Blackpool Pleasure Beach, isn't it?" Malcolm replied cheerily as they rumbled through the minefield.

Jonathan said nothing. He was sweating now, his stomach growling in complaint. He was about to suggest that they get out and walk the rest of the way, when they swept around one last dramatic bend; there, in front of them, lay Dooncurra Woods.

"Are you all right?" Malcolm asked, watching his ashen-faced son step gingerly out of the car.

"Yes, but give me a minute," Jonathan replied, refusing to show signs of weakness.

He leant on the top of the car, took a few deep breaths, and followed his father who was already exploring.

"Is this the gift shop?" he asked, joining Malcolm outside a ramshackle hut which appeared devoid of life.

"Might have been once," his father mused.

It was more booth than hut. Signs on the outside pointed to better days, days when tourists had come and paid for walking maps, sunglasses and kitsch mementos to mark their visit.

"No one's here now anyway, Dad."

"Not to worry," said Malcolm. "We didn't come here for gifts. Let's head for the woods, eh? Looks lovely."

They set off down the path leading to the woods, Malcolm puffing out his chest and striding confidently ahead, Jonathan trailing behind, surveying his surroundings and marvelling at how peaceful it all was. Despite being the height of summer, it was a dank and dreary day. The sky appeared to have been consumed by one giant cloud, an infinite mass which stretched as far as the eye could see. This suited them. It was perfect walking weather. The air was thick with rain, cooling them as they trudged solemnly along the stone path which was more trail than path, and looked as if it had been beaten out by footfall until someone had scattered stones upon it. Malcolm continued onwards, determined to set a steady pace despite, or even because of, Jonathan's condition. He took great delight in sucking in the crisp, country air, making a great show of inhaling it deeply into his nostrils and letting it out with a contented sigh. Not for him the seedy sickness of the self-indulgent; he was alcohol-free, as pure as the earth around them.

Although feeling slightly ropey, Jonathan shared his father's appreciation of their surroundings, albeit not as openly. They had parks back home and the countryside was an hour's drive away, but this was different; this place felt untouched. Birds sang gaily, wildlife rustled in the undergrowth, this was their habitat, mankind was just a visitor here. What struck

Jonathan most was the smell. It was fetid, almost sickly, plant life in full bloom. It energised him, made him feel alive.

"Catch me if you can, Dad!" he shouted, breaking into a sprint.

He was fifty yards away before Malcolm realised what was happening. He watched him go, dumbstruck, hesitated a moment and then gave chase. At first nothing seemed to be happening; his head was down, his arms pumping and his legs a flurry of activity, but he was hardly moving. It was like being suspended in mid-air. Maybe this was what happened when you got old, your body just stopped working. He hadn't run in years, or taken any exercise for that matter. He'd grown soft without realising it. Gradually, however, he began to gain traction, the ground beneath him moving more quickly. He lifted his head and allowed himself to be propelled forward. It was magnificent. He let out a feral roar as he closed in on his son, who had long since slowed.

Seeing his father closing in on him, Jonathan popped up on his toes and sprung away into the distance once more. By now his own lack of fitness was becoming painfully apparent. He was already out of breath, his running days now but a distant memory. These days he was a beer-swilling student, his only exercise coming from frenzied, inebriated dancing at the campus nightclub. He was knackered, but a glance back at his advancing father spurred him on. Malcolm, flushed and labouring, was shortening the gap, and he couldn't have the old man thinking he had the measure of him. Jonathan concentrated on his running, maintaining his rhythm as Ernie had taught him years ago, and within seconds he'd left his father in the distance once more. That was it now, no more running; he was fucked. There was still time for a prank, though. Looking ahead, he saw a turn in the path. If he got there in time, he could keep out of sight long enough to hide. He'd take up residence behind some trees, and scare the shit out of his father when he came barrelling round the corner.

Sprinting forward, he circled the bend a good eighty metres in front of Malcolm, and went about finding somewhere to conceal himself. To his left were a cluster of thin, spindly trees, but they'd offer little in the way of protection. There were bigger trees on the right, with thick foliage and broad trunks, perfect for an ambush. He scurried towards them, laughing at the thought of his father rounding the corner, panting like a dog, only to be met by a long empty path and no sign of life. Hopefully he'd think

Jonathan had forged ahead and give further chase, effing and blinding as he went. Jonathan moved into the thicket of trees but stopped. There was someone up ahead, sitting in the picnic area. He'd been so intent in finding a hiding-place that he hadn't noticed at first, but there was a solitary figure sitting on one of the benches, smoking. She had her back to him, staring into the distance as she puffed on her cigarette. Although he couldn't see her face, he thought he recognised her. Something about her was instantly familiar, the way she hunched forward, shoulders raised for protection, legs crossed, as if trying to envelop herself, conceal herself from the world around her. She looked poised to take flight at a moment's notice, like a scavenging bird wary of larger, hungrier animals. He recognised her. He recognised himself. That was him sitting there or another version of him, an older female version. It was his kin, his family – his mother.

24

SHE'D RESISTED TEMPTATION TWICE, WALKING past Murphy's and McGettigan's without giving in. By the time she got to Bartley's, she couldn't take it anymore. This was her last chance before the woods; she had to get some. Sixty seconds later she stepped out of the shop, twenty cigarettes in her pocket. She felt at once excited and dejected. The thought of lighting up and smoking one was enough to make her go weak at the knees, but she knew she'd failed again; another attempt to kick her filthy habit had come to a predictable end. She hadn't smoked them yet, though. She could just leave them there in her pocket, unopened. They'd be there if she ever needed them, a constant reassuring presence, twenty friends ready to console her in times of trouble. Fuck that. As soon as she found a quiet spot, she was going to demolish the whole packet.

She set off towards the woods, up the little hill that she'd been walking up and down since she was a toddler. Once she got there, she'd have the peace and quiet she needed. She'd gather her thoughts, have a little smoke and return home. Her only fear was being spotted, either by her parents or someone else. It'd be just her luck to encounter a nosy neighbour, someone who might offer to accompany her up the road.

Sure, I'm going that way too.

Worse still, someone might stop and offer her a lift. She'd have to refuse.

I'm not going to my mother's, thanks.

Well, where are you going, then?

Just to the woods, that's all. Don't tell my Mammy you saw me.

But they would tell. They'd be straight on the phone to her.

I saw your Sinéad walking up the hill there, said she was going to the woods. Just thought you'd like to know, Patricia.

That was what they were like; you couldn't do a thing without someone reporting it. Small town mentality. There was another option: she could hop over the wall and take a short-cut through the fields, weaving her way past the bemused cows, doing her best not to step in their crusty droppings. That would ensure safe passage. She could be in the woods in a matter of minutes, unseen and unnoticed. What if one of the farmers saw her, though?

Oh hello, young McLoughlin, what brings you here?

Nothing, Micheal, just taking a short-cut through your field to avoid being seen by my parents. I'm 37 now, by the way.

No, that wouldn't do. She would just have to carry on up the hill and hope no one saw her. But, if she was to succeed, she would have to move quickly. She set off at something approaching a sprint, doing her best to retain an air of dignity, hoping to convince any onlookers that she did this all the time. Whenever she heard a car approach she slowed to a brisk trot, making sure to keep her head down until they'd passed by. Mercifully, only a couple of vehicles passed and the road was free of pedestrians. The pathway leading to the woods wasn't far now, less than fifty metres away. Dispensing with the last of her inhibitions she increased her pace, galloping like an unseated horse at the Grand National. A car approached from behind; its occupants could surely see her, but she couldn't stop now. The pathway was almost within reach. Let them stare, it wouldn't matter. They'd never know the identity of the mad sprinting woman. Maybe they'd think it was a ghost, a banshee that had stayed out too late and was looking for somewhere to hide until dark. She made it with a few seconds to spare, disappearing down the laneway as the car whizzed past, its driver gawping after her. But she was safe. They couldn't get her now. She carried on up the lane, through the car park, onto the footpath and into the woods. With any luck the first set of benches would be unoccupied. She could take a seat, light up a fag and relax.

*

That first drag; Christ it felt good, she would have climbed Mount Everest for that hit. Whether it was the nicotine, the runner's high or the joy of isolation, she now felt much better. Why had she been panicking? Everything was going to be fine. Phillip was right. Jonathan didn't care about her circumstances. He just wanted to see her and get to know her. What did he care if she was frumpy or depressed, or having a panic attack? He was a kid; kids didn't bother themselves with things like that. He'd probably just want money to buy CDs or a football or something. And she'd taken care of that already, buying him a little present to mark the occasion. She was good at buying presents, everyone said so, but it had been a real struggle buying for Jonathan. She'd fished for information, enquired about his hobbies, his interests, what he did in his spare time. There'd been nothing out of the ordinary; he liked football, music, girls, beer and cars, the usual. Normally, in a situation like this she would have turned to those close to him for ideas, but she couldn't do that this time. Just when she'd resigned herself to putting €50 in a card and being done with it, she had an idea. He said he liked sports, so why not introduce him to a new sport? The sport of his forebears, hurling. At first she thought it would be enough to get him a jersey; he could wear it with pride back in England. But then she decided to buy him the whole kit, and sure what good was the kit without a hurley and a sliotar? In the finish she'd got him the lot, helmet and all.

The idea of him returning home bedecked in the black-and-amber made her smile. What if his mother didn't like her buying him clothes, though? What if she disapproved of sportswear and thought it tacky? There was so much to consider. Even if she did like the jersey, she'd most likely be horrified when he produced a heavy wooden stick and a ball made of iron, and told her he was off out for a game of fuckin' hurling! She'd never let him go to Ireland again.

I'm not having you go over there so that they can arm you with more weapons, the crazy Irish bastards.

Well, it was done now; his presents were lying in her flat, all wrapped up and ready to go.

She checked her watch, it was half ten now. Twenty minutes of smoking and she'd head for home. She'd be there by eleven, giving her plenty of time to have some lunch, get ready and set off for the park. Her outfit had already been chosen: a brand new jacket and a dress she'd bought for 'good wear' two years ago, which had yet to see the light of day. Some judiciously applied make-up, a few squirts of Estée Lauder White Linen, and an hour spent straightening her hair would ensure she looked passable when her son laid eyes on her for the first time.

She must look a right state now, though. Had she looked in the mirror before leaving the flat? She probably looked like a vagrant and smelled like one, too. The frantic dash up the hill had caused her to sweat profusely. Her clothes were stuck to her skin and she felt itchy and grimy. If anyone saw her perched on a bench at this hour, puffing on a cigarette, her hair stuck to her head with sweat, they'd wonder where her flagon of cider was. All that could be fixed, though. By the time she'd finished doing herself up, she'd be restored to former glories. A MILF, that's what she'd be.

As she sat and smoked, she fantasised about how the day might go. In her dreams she saw them taking a little stroll together, idly chit-chatting, sharing the odd joke. They'd feed the ducks, skim stones and she'd point out some of the park's interesting features, like the tree planted in the memory of the recently deceased mayor or the stone monument bearing the names of local men who had fought in the Easter Rising. He'd like that; he'd said he was interested in history, especially military history. Once they'd exhausted what the park had to offer, she'd suggest they went for a drink somewhere, maybe with Malcolm; it would be easier with three of them, take some of the pressure off. From there, they could play it by ear. If they were really getting on, they might go for dinner. The restaurant in their hotel did a fine three-course on week nights.

Her mother, of course, had got it into her head that they'd all be having their dinner at her house that evening, despite being told no such thing. *What do they like to eat, Sinéad? Does the boy like lamb chops? How about mint sauce?* She would have to introduce Jonathan to his grandmother at some stage, but it wouldn't be tonight and certainly not over dinner. She liked the idea of showing him off, though, bringing him to Adele's house and Patrick's, maybe even to Valerie's. Even just walking down the main street with him would be lovely. Some oul' biddy would surely stop and ask who the handsome young man was: *Oh, this is my son; handsome chap, isn't he?* Of course, she couldn't do that, she couldn't refer to him as her son. Not yet, maybe not ever. Technically he was her son and she was his mother, but you had to earn the right to be someone's mother, and she hadn't done anything to deserve such an accolade. No, for the time being she would be Sinéad and he would be Jonathan. They were friends. They could figure out her title later on.

She'd smoked four cigarettes, each more delicious than the last, but she was growing hungry and a little thirsty, too. She hadn't really thought this out, storming out of the flat without so much as a slice of toast in her belly. If she hadn't been so preoccupied with getting fags, she might have thought to pick up something from the deli in the newsagents. A sandwich. A cup of tea. She could have had a picnic, but all she'd been able to think about were the fags. Now here she was in the middle of the woods, starving, dehydrated and too tired to walk back home. Here, in the middle of the woods, none of that stuff really mattered, however. She was in splendid isolation, away from the prying eyes of humanity, where no one could see her and no one could judge her. If only she could live up here, like a hermit, she would be happy.

What was that? Someone was behind her, watching. She could sense them, standing there, where the path bent, about a hundred metres away. A chill went down her spine. This was all she needed, a homicidal maniac out looking for fresh meat. Any second now she'd be bundled in the back of a van, driven to a secluded location and murdered in cold blood. And on today of all days. It hadn't occurred to her how vulnerable she was, up here on her own. But, as her mother constantly reminded her, times had changed; there were all sorts of loonies on the prowl nowadays. She thought of turning to face her tormentor, but that would have encouraged him, given him the stimulus he needed to come and grab her. So she stayed put, staring into the distance, pretending not to notice him. With any luck he'd turn on his heel and leave her be, deciding he could find someone better elsewhere, someone younger and prettier. That was how men thought, they always assumed they could find someone better. In this instance, her bedraggled appearance might work in her favour.

But ignoring him didn't appear to have worked. He was coming closer now; she could hear the gravel scrunching under his feet as he made his way towards her. He was slowly hunting her down, ready to strike once he came within touching distance. She remained rigid, not turning around to face him. He probably couldn't believe his luck. She wasn't even going to put up a fight; the perfect victim. He was very close now. She could hear him breathing, steadily and evenly, the calm cadence of the killer. His footsteps were light and uncertain, almost delicate. Maybe it was his first time? She would be his first, what a privilege! He'd go on to murder dozens of women but everyone remembered the first; she would go down in history as the first victim of the Dooncurra Butcher. She could see him now from the corner of her eye, he was tall and thin, quite young. Could she beat him in a fight? She'd soon find out. *Please walk past, please walk past.* But he didn't. He stopped a couple of feet away.

"Sinéad?" he asked. "Is that you?"

25

SHE SPUN TO LOOK AT him, ash flying from her cigarette. It wasn't a murderer or a rapist, or anyone planning to throw her into the back of a van. It was her son, her beautiful blue-eyed boy. He stood there staring at her with those same eyes, the ones she'd stared into before, briefly. They hadn't changed, he hadn't changed, not to her. It was as if they'd spent seconds apart instead of years. Her life had ended when he'd gone, but now it was ready to resume. She tried to speak but nothing came out; her mouth was dry, her throat empty. What did it matter? She could see him and he could see her. They could remain like this for the rest of eternity and she would be happy.

"Is it you, Sinéad?" he asked, wondering if he'd got it wrong and was talking to one of Dooncurra's most notorious tramps.

Still she stared, her eyes fixed unblinkingly on his.

"Oh, God," she said, rising to her feet.

Jonathan shifted uneasily. Was it her or not? He'd been so certain, but now he was doubting himself. She came towards him, tears welling in her eyes, rolling gently down her cheeks. Relief swept over him. It was her.

"Sinéad," he said, as she laid her head on his chest and wrapped her arms around his waist. She wept softly but contentedly, like a child rescued from a bad dream. He held her in his arms and, as he listened to her cry and felt the warmth of her body on his, he began to cry too. He held her tight, laid his head on hers and they cried together. There was no awkwardness or unease, just an overpowering sense of relief. It was over. They had found each other.

Malcolm came trotting round the corner, ready to admit defeat, wanting to wave the white flag and return to their gentle amble through the woods. He had expected to see Jonathan ahead in the distance, waving at him, goading him. Instead his son was standing at a picnic area, in the arms of a strange woman. Now that was impressive, he'd managed to acquire a new lady friend and reach the hugging stage in the time it had taken Malcolm to run less than a hundred metres. That was kids today for you. This mysterious female had her head burrowed into his chest, and all Malcolm could see was a shaggy mane poking out through his son's arms. Although he couldn't see their faces, he could tell they were both crying. They seemed to shudder and tremble as they held one another, their bodies heaving and lurching like a ship caught in a storm. Had they broken up already? Were they saying goodbye? He was mystified.

He walked towards them, wondering if it would be rude to interrupt. As he drew closer, he saw that the woman was older than he'd first thought. He could see some of her face now, a tear-streaked cheek, a partially closed eye. Her slight frame had led him to believe that she was a young girl, around Jonathan's age, but this woman was older. Then it clicked. It had to be her. Had to be. Why hadn't he spotted it? From here the resemblance was obvious, but even from a distance you could see the similarities. He cleared his throat, loud enough for them to hear but not so loud as to appear insistent.

Sinéad looked up and they locked eyes. It felt like he'd been struck by lightning. He'd seen that look a thousand times, stared into those eyes a million times. Seeing them now in the face of another chilled him to the bone.

"Hi," she said, shakily.

"Hello," said Malcolm.

They were still hugging; Jonathan didn't seem to realise they had company. It was only when Sinéad pulled away and nodded in Malcolm's direction that he acknowledged his presence.

"Dad," he said with a smile, "this is Sinéad."

"I guessed that much," Malcolm replied, holding out a hand for her to shake.

He was trying not to stare, but it was difficult. They were so alike; the bright, sparkling eyes, full of mischief and mirth, the pursed mouth ready to pout or smirk depending on their mood, and the peculiar little pixie nose. It went beyond their features, though. It was their manner, their demeanour, their stance as they stood side by side, waiting for someone to take control of the situation. Each was a mirror image of the other; one leg slightly bent, both hands fidgeting behind their backs, blinking in unison, like a comedy duo mimicking each other for the audience's titillation. He could have stood and watched them all day, and if it were left to them he probably would have. But he had been handed the reins now, he had to assume command. They had momentarily become embarrassed, sheepish in one another's company, and dared not look at one another, casting their gaze downwards, upwards, at Malcolm and anywhere else.

"Well, I see you've already met," Malcolm said with a smile.

"Yes," Sinéad replied. "Though not quite like I imagined it."

Jonathan smiled meekly, stealing a furtive glance at her.

"We just decided to come up here to kill some time," Malcolm explained.

"Me too," said Sinéad. "I didn't expect to see ye up here, as you can see." She held out her arms and looked down at her clothes. "The feckin' state of me."

Jonathan giggled and Sinéad shook her head mournfully. "Years of preparing for this day and I still get caught on the hop."

"It's okay," Jonathan said. "You look fine."

"No, I do not. Yesterday's clothes, last night's hair and reeking of cigarettes!"

They were all laughing now. Jonathan used the moment to edge closer to Sinéad, so close that their hands almost touched. Without thinking, Sinéad allowed her fingers to find his. Jonathan felt the touch of her hand and clasped it gratefully.

"Shall we head back into town, then?" Sinéad asked when the laughter had died down. "I've got an important meeting at half one."

It took Malcolm a second to catch on. "Oh, have you? We'd better go, then."

"Dad!" Jonathan said, rolling his eyes skyward.

"Oh, right," he replied, finally getting the joke.

They walked back down the path, Jonathan and Sinéad still holding hands, Malcolm doing his best to make the situation less awkward. But now it was only he who felt awkward. Mother and son could have walked like this forever, hand in hand, in perfect silence. Neither felt the need to speak, words couldn't convey what they were feeling. They continued all the way through the woods, occasionally stopping to point out a squirrel or marvel at the view.

It would be the first of many walks together. They would walk these paths again and again, through winter and summer, sunshine and rain. They would walk them just as they had on this first day; hand in hand, content and at one with the world. A time would come when she could walk no more and he would have to drive her there, grandchildren in tow, fighting for the right to wheel her along the path. Eventually she would become too sick to visit the woods at all, her days now few, their time together more precious than ever. But, even then, she never lost that feeling, that feeling which had visited her on that first day and never departed. It was the feeling of coming home, of entering a place where she knew she was loved and nothing bad could ever happen to her. It was the best feeling she had ever known.

Acknowledgements

THE AUTHOR WOULD LIKE TO thank the following people.

My mother, for her unflinching support, eternal belief and unconditional love. Jill Bourke, for instilling me with confidence and strength when it was most needed.

My editor, Elaine Kennedy, for opening my eyes and curtailing my excesses. Eddy Flynn, for his web-design skills and technological know-how. John Clancy, for telling it straight and providing invaluable feedback. Bill O'Meara, for his unexpected, but no less welcome, bouts of positivity. Derek Butler, for his inspirational words and encouragement. Cian Reinhardt, for taking time out of his busy schedule to take pictures of a reluctant, stroppy subject. And Robert Power, for his sage advice and rampant enthusiasm.

I would also like to thank each and every person who took even the slightest bit of interest during the lengthy, protracted process of writing this book.

About the author

HAVING SPENT THE MAJORITY OF his teens and twenties wondering just what would become of him, Simon chanced upon a hitherto unrealised ability to write. This ability, limited as it was, compelled him to enrol as a mature student of Journalism at the University of Limerick. His dreams of super-stardom were almost immediately curtailed by a punishing, unexplained illness which took away three years of his life but perversely, enabled him to write the book you've just read. Those were dark, depressing years but in spite of the toll they took on him, Simon understands were it not for that illness he would never have found the wherewithal to pen this, his first, novel. He has since returned to his studies and couples them with a weekly column for local paper, the Limerick Post. If you were to ask to tell you which career he'd prefer; journalist or novelist, he would smirk to himself and say that it's impossible to make it as a novelist these days. He would then smirk some more and say that journalism is a dying industry. For all his smirks and eternal pessimism, he is happiest when writing and is currently working on his second book.

Website: www.simonbourke.net
Email: bourke.simon79@gmail.com
Twitter: @Bionic_Simba

Made in the USA
Charleston, SC
14 January 2017